# THE AMERICAN
# TRANSCENDENTALISTS

# THE AMERICAN
# TRANSCENDENTALISTS

## ESSENTIAL WRITINGS

*Edited and with an Introduction*
*by Lawrence Buell*

THE MODERN LIBRARY

NEW YORK

2006 Modern Library Paperback Edition

Introduction copyright © 2006 by Lawrence Buell
Compilation and additional text copyright © 2006 by Random House, Inc.

Published in the United States by Modern Library,
an imprint of The Random House Publishing Group,
a division of Random House, Inc., New York.

MODERN LIBRARY and the TORCHBEARER Design are registered
trademarks of Random House, Inc.

Permission acknowledgments are located within the Acknowledgments section,
which begins on page 571.

LIBRARY OF CONGRESS CATALOGING-IN-PUBLICATION DATA

The American Transcendentalists: essential writings / edited and with an introduction by
Lawrence Buell.
p. cm.
Includes bibliographical references.
ISBN 0-8129-7509-X
1. American prose literature—New England. 2. New England—Intellectual life—
19th century—Sources. 3. United States—Intellectual life—1783–1865—Sources.
4. Transcendentalism (New England)—History—Sources. 5. American prose
literature—19th century. I. Buell, Lawrence.
PS541.A667 2005          818'.30809384—dc22          2005049580

Printed in the United States of America

www.modernlibrary.com

2  4  6  8  9  7  5  3

# CONTENTS

## III. SPIRITUAL FERMENT AND RELIGIOUS REFORM

## IV. SECULAR REFORM

### A. REFORM AS INDIVIDUAL TRANSFORMATION VERSUS REFORM AS SYSTEMIC SOCIAL CHANGE

## V. LITERATURE AND THE ARTS

### A. CRITICAL STATEMENTS

### B. "IMPROVISED" PROSE

### C. POETRY

# INTRODUCTION

New England Transcendentalism was the first intellectual movement in the history of the still-new nation to achieve a lasting impact on American thought and writing. Although its heyday was brief—a decade or so between the mid-1830s and the mid-1840s—it cast a long shadow stretching down to the present. American literature, religion, philosophy, and social thought were all strongly influenced by what the Transcendentalists did both through their own accomplishments and by inspiring others. This volume gathers a sizable collection of important work by a score of figures involved in the movement, as well as by some of the forerunners who made it possible, and by some of those whose lives it touched.

## THE TRANSCENDENTALISTS:
## A HISTORICAL AND GEOGRAPHICAL
## SNAPSHOT

The Transcendentalist nucleus consisted of some fifty to seventy-five men and women spanning several generations, though nearly all the central figures were born from the turn of the nineteenth century through the next two decades. They were linked not only by social exchange and correspondence but also by shared experiences and sometimes even blood relation. Although few Transcendentalists were truly affluent, most were from pedigreed families of greater Boston—

typically from ancient New England stock—and were very well educated for their day. Those of humbler social origins were acutely conscious of the fact. So Transcendentalism was a distinctly "elite"
movement so far as its demography was concerned, although it was
also staunchly opposed, on principle, to class distinctions and other
forms of social inequity.

Most of the men of the movement attended Harvard College
and/or its divinity school, the bastion and ministerial training ground
for Unitarianism. The liberal wing of Congregationalism, the church
of the Puritans, the Unitarians formally separated from the parent
body in 1815. The Transcendentalist nucleus also included a number
of strong-minded women. For a premodern movement, Transcendentalism was striking in its openness to the participation of women and to
feminist critiques of patriarchy. This is not to say that it was either free
of misogyny, or that most of the women in the movement were as radical politically as they were on philosophical or cultural issues. Significantly, the two daughters of Ralph Waldo Emerson (1803–82), the
movement's most prominent figure, led far more conventional lives
than he. Neither considered herself a feminist or even an intellectual.
Still, relative to the Puritan and Revolutionary intelligentsia, the
Transcendentalists were a remarkably gender-inclusive group.

Although Transcendentalism's geographical center was the regional
metropolis of Boston, its remote tentacles extended throughout the
New England diaspora, southward to New York and Philadelphia, and
across the Appalachians to the "old northwest," with Cincinnati,
Louisville, and St. Louis serving as outposts for different lengths of
time. Extension of Transcendentalist influence tended to follow along
the paths of the modest expansion of Unitarianism during the 1820s
and 1830s and of Emerson's widening circuits as a public lecturer, as
he became a household name first in New England and New York City
during the 1830s and 1840s, and afterward throughout the northern
states. Emerson was also responsible for making his hometown of Concord, Massachusetts, the movement's epicenter. During the mid- and
late-nineteenth century, as the fame of Emerson and then Thoreau
spread to England and elsewhere abroad, pilgrimages to Transcendental Concord became international affairs.

Transcendentalism's first stirrings occurred, significantly, during
the decade following the War of 1812, justly called the nation's "second war of independence," when the United States was both flexing its
economic muscles with a greater sense of national security and also

assessing with renewed confidence its sense of history and place in the wider world. Just as the cult of the Founding Fathers was reaching a kind of peak in the solemn commemoration of the simultaneous deaths of presidents John Adams and Thomas Jefferson fifty years to the day of the proclamation of American independence in 1776, the Transcendentalists were on the verge of becoming the first American youth movement, the nation's first counterculture. Transcendentalism was the first movement to argue vigorously for what mainstream popular culture today in the United States takes almost for granted: that youthful vision and vigor should count for more than the stodgy so-called wisdom of the elders.

This the Transcendentalists did in two disparate yet complementary ways. On the one hand, they stood for the principle of the fresh start. Each generation, each individual must take nothing for granted but refashion the world for him- or herself, starting from the premise that personal identity, moral values, and social arrangements are all up for grabs. Everything was to be put under question. "Why should not we also enjoy an original relation to the universe?" Emerson asks at the start of his first book, *Nature* (1836). On the other hand, no less crucial to this Transcendentalist critique was the proposition that the horizon of American thought was too provincial, too fixated on British models. Here the Transcendentalists aggressively argued for the significance of modern French and especially German thought, and for the need to engage the wisdom of Asian literature and spirituality—the classics of Hindu, Buddhist, Confucian, and Islamic culture—as seriously as the wisdom of the west.

So the Transcendentalists were both intensely now-centered *and* zealously cosmopolitan. This helps explain why their arguments for personal and social renewal are more often cast in universalizing terms rather than in nationalist terms. Not that they failed to comment on the state of the nation, too, particularly as the Civil War approached. For the Transcendentalists also rightly recognized that their cast of thinking made special sense in the context of the exceptionally unstable climate of the antebellum Yankee culture in which they lived. Even when they did not make direct reference to the fact, they remained acutely mindful that theirs was a moment of unprecedented territorial expansion, population increase and diversification, industrial transformation, inequalities between rich and poor, animosity between north and south over the slavery issue, and religious sectarianism. In order to understand the Transcendentalists' distinctive views in more detail, however, we need to take a closer look at who the movement's leaders were.

## A SHORT GUIDE TO MAJOR FIGURES AND THEIR ACCOMPLISHMENTS

Three Transcendentalists especially stand out from a twenty-first-century standpoint. First the renegade minister, essayist, and poet-philosopher Emerson, who by most accounts, then and now, was the movement's single most defining figure. Thanks in part to the popularity throughout the northern states during the middle third of the nineteenth century of the "lyceum" movement—town-based programs of public lectures and other performances that served as the quasi-equivalent of public television and radio—Emerson became, by the end of his career, a national celebrity, the country's first public intellectual. During the Civil War years, throughout New England and the New England diaspora westward, his fame as a spokesperson for the country's highest ideals was second only to Abraham Lincoln's.

No less widely influential in the long run, however, and far more widely read today, was Emerson's fellow Concordian Henry David Thoreau, (1817–62), essayist, naturalist, land surveyor, civil disobedient, and reform advocate. In his own time, Thoreau was pigeonholed as a cranky local character who aped his mentor Emerson. Even Emerson came to view his favorite disciple with mingled respect and disappointment, as Thoreau seemed increasingly to withdraw into a private world of daily nature walks and observations. But even more than Emerson's *Nature* (1836), "The American Scholar" (1837), and "Self-Reliance" (1841), Thoreau's *Walden* (1854) and his great political essay "Resistance to Civil Government" (1849) (better known as "Civil Disobedience") are the best known of all Transcendentalist writings.

The third figure most remembered today is Margaret Fuller (1810–50), pioneer educator, performance artist, feminist theorist, journalist, and—near the end of her life—political revolutionary. Emerson's close friend, and also his coadjutor in the editing of the leading Transcendentalist magazine, *The Dial*, Fuller was and remains best known for her *Woman in the Nineteenth Century* (1845), the nation's first significant feminist manifesto. This book reflects the ingenious and successful method of teaching through dialogue that she had previously developed in order to embolden women to express themselves more freely. Unlike Emerson and Thoreau, neither of whom ever felt at home outside the Boston area, Fuller eventually left the region in order to become a freelance writer for America's leading daily newspaper, the *New York Tribune,* witnessing the European revolutions of 1848 and becoming directly involved in the failed Italian Risorgimento.

It should come as no surprise, then, to find Emerson, Thoreau, and Fuller featured more prominently here than any other representatives of the movement. This book includes *Nature,* "The American Scholar," "Self-Reliance," and "Resistance to Civil Government" in their entirety. *Walden* and *Woman* are, unfortunately, far too long to print in a one-volume collection of this sort; but also included here are substantial portions of the long article that served Fuller as a trial run for her book, and Thoreau's on-the-spot journal account of the first weeks of the real-life homesteading experience that inspired *Walden,* much of which he cannibalized for the book itself.

Many of the other Transcendentalists were remarkable men and women in their own right. Among the movement's founders, the most significant were Amos Bronson Alcott (1799–1888), George Ripley (1802–80), Orestes Brownson (1803–76), Elizabeth Peabody (1804–94), and Frederic Henry Hedge (1805–90). Ripley, Hedge, and Brownson were Unitarian ministers. All three were crucial in calling their colleagues' attention to the significance of the new philosophic and social thought of Germany and France. Hedge later settled into a moderate conservatism and remained comfortably in the ministry throughout his life, serving for several years after the Civil War as president of the American Unitarian Association and, after that, as professor of German at Harvard for nearly a decade.

Ripley and Brownson, like Emerson, forsook the ministry in order to pursue very different paths. Ripley had been a key player in the theological and philosophical disputes that especially marked Transcendentalism's early stages, as the next section describes. But he left the ministry in order to found, together with his wife, Sophia, the commune at Brook Farm in suburban Boston that became the most ambitious and longest-lived of several Transcendentalist experiments in alternative living (1841–47). (Thoreau's twenty-six months of cabin living on the shores of Walden Pond during the mid-1840s was a solitary counterpart.) For a time Ripley even became a national leader in the "associationist" movement. After Brook Farm's financial collapse, the Ripleys opted for a more private and sedentary existence in New York, where George worked for the rest of his life as lead reviewer for the same newspaper that employed Margaret Fuller. Brownson was Transcendentalism's most outspoken early critic of economic and social injustice. His writings influenced his friend Ripley's turn toward social activism. Unlike Ripley and Hedge, Brownson was a self-taught genius who had to work his way up from a hardscrabble Vermont boyhood without benefit of a Harvard education. This background helps explain some of the vehemence and bitterness of his social criticism, which he increasingly turned against those who had been his colleagues in the movement. His Transcendentalist phase was brief and stormy. By the mid-1840s, Brownson had converted to Catholicism and was on the way to becoming one of the most prominent Catholic lay intellectuals of his day, using *Brownson's Quarterly Review* (a journal he edited and largely wrote himself) as a platform from which to berate Unitarianism and Transcendentalism as slippery slopes toward atheism.

Alcott, a self-taught Connecticut farmer's son, and Peabody, a physician's daughter whose sister married Nathaniel Hawthorne, were teachers and educational reformers who collaborated in a remarkable but disastrous venture in experimental education too audacious for proper Bostonians to stomach, described in Section IV-B below. Peabody went on to pursue a multifaceted career as educational theorist, reform advocate, student of historical linguistics, translator, publisher, bookseller, and memoirist. Alcott moved his family to Concord to be near his friend Emerson, who relished Alcott's intellectual companionship notwithstanding his chronic impracticality, which required periodic cash subsidies to keep his large family going. An ill-conceived, short-lived commune at Fruitlands, a dozen miles northwest of Concord, was another of his misadventures. Alcott's occasional "conversations," experiments in adult education through dialogue partially resembling Fuller's, were more successful albeit not particularly remunerative. Eventually the success of daughter Louisa May Alcott as a children's writer put the family on a secure financial footing, indirectly helping make possible her father's last and most durable venture, the so-called Concord School of Philosophy (1879–88), a Chautauqua-like medley of summer lectures, readings, and other events for which a younger admirer supplied the organizational energy but with Alcott serving as the host, patriarch, and icon.

A number of "second-generation" Transcendentalists also made important contributions to the shape of the movement, Thoreau most especially. Some were scarcely younger in age but all were influenced by the elder figures just mentioned. Among the ministerial group, Theodore Parker (1810–60) was especially crucial in carrying on the work of theological radicalism that Emerson and others had begun, and in helping ensure that the activist edge of Brownson and Ripley would be sustained. Indeed, Parker was a more important influence than any other Transcendentalist on the so-called Social Gospel movement within liberal Protestantism toward the end of the nine-teenth century. In the run-up to the Civil War, Parker became Tran-scendentalism's most fiery abolitionist preacher. The increased sense of impending crisis over slavery was also crucial in pushing Transcen-dentalists who had hitherto been standoffish about organized social activism, notably Emerson and Thoreau, into the public arena.

Meanwhile, Parker also helped lead the movement's religious thought toward a post-Protestant comparative spirituality, as did a younger Transcendentalist minister—and active abolitionist—Thomas Wentworth Higginson (1823–1911). Higginson's treatise "The Sympa-thy of Religions" (Section III) set the tone for the single most impor-tant focus of late-stage Transcendentalist religious thought during the decades after the Civil War. Later on, more ambitious comparatist work was undertaken by two other Transcendentalist ministers, James Freeman Clarke (1810–88) and Samuel Johnson (1822–82).

A larger fraction of the younger generation of Transcendentalists, however, became associated more especially with literature and the arts. These include Higginson, who today is better known as a man of letters than as a religious radical, remembered especially for his rather befuddled and sporadic attempts at mentoring Emily Dickinson and for eventually helping to publish a (doctored) version of her poems after her death. A number of the younger Transcendentalists turned to poetry, among them Ellen Sturgis Hooper (1812–48), Jones Very (1813–80), William Ellery Channing II (1817–1901), and Christopher Pearse Cranch (1823–92), the latter also a painter of modest accom-plishment. John Sullivan Dwight (1813–93), a ministerial dropout like Cranch and then a Brook Farm stalwart, became Boston's first signifi-cant music critic.

Like Dwight—and Emerson, Thoreau, and Fuller as well—most of these figures were more committed to the philosophy and criticism of art than to artistic production as such. Nearly all the Transcendental-ists wrote compellingly at their best. But the great majority, including most of the poets, were stronger in the medium of the essay or the oration than in those forms of more purely "creative" expression conventionally taken as definers of artistic accomplishment: poetry, fiction, painting, music. The most salient exceptions here were Emerson and Very, both of whom composed many striking poetic passages. Emerson in particular helped to ensure the persistence in American writing of a poetry of intellectually strenuous, epigrammatic, cerebral reflection. Emily Dickinson, Wallace Stevens, Robert Frost, A. R. Ammons, and many more were directly or indirectly touched by this influence. More important, however, the mastery of nonfictional prose that Emerson and Thoreau and (at their best) the other Transcendentalists achieved had immense significance for the course of U.S. literary history. It gave a more sophisticated direction to the rich body of meditation, moral reflection, and autobiography that had flourished in America, particularly in New England, for more than two centuries, in the form of sermons, orations, religious conversion narratives, and other forms of life writing. It wasn't only Emerson's *theory* of poetry that helped bring Walt Whitman "to a boil," as he himself once put it. Emerson's poetic prose was in itself a crucial model for Whitman's prophetic style of expression and free-verse form, which in turn became the nation's single most distinctive contribution to world poetry. Beyond this, the writings of Emerson and Thoreau in particular helped model and perpetuate the strong ethical and autobiographical emphases in American writing that persist to this day.

But the most broadly significant of all the aesthetic contributions made by Emerson, Thoreau, and their Transcendentalist colleagues was to help further a climate in the post-Puritan, post-pioneer, utilitarian United States more favorable to literature and the other arts—and in particular a climate of nondogmatic experimentalism in which proficiency in traditional forms of expression counted for less than artistic energy and innovation. Although Transcendentalist artistic accomplishment was finally less bold and innovative than its vision for art, both helped ignite those who read or listened to it.

But why does it make sense for a movement that began in the form of discussions of religious and philosophical issues among a group dominated by ministers to have metamorphosed within a few short years into a plethora of social reform initiatives on the one hand and an aesthetic movement on the other? In order to understand this better, we need to take a closer look at how Transcendentalism got started and what its somewhat nebulous core values were.

## TRANSCENDENTALISM'S ORIGINS

Transcendentalism began as a ferment within Unitarianism. Indeed, the Unitarians planted the seeds for a movement more radical than theirs in the very way they stated their differences from the Calvinist orthodoxy of mainstream Congregationalism. The Unitarians rejected the orthodox Calvinist doctrine that humankind is born depraved, contending that human nature is inherently improvable. Indeed, they also questioned the authority of doctrine itself, holding that the essence of spirituality lies in the formation of human character through life practice rather than in theology or assent to creeds. The Transcendentalist insurgents sought to carry such reforms further than Unitarianism was willing to go. William Ellery Channing, the most charismatic of all the Unitarian ministers, had come to hold that human nature was not to be defined primarily in terms of sin and need for redemption but in terms of "likeness to God" (see Section I), and a number of his peers were saying pretty much the same thing, though more guardedly. Why, then, should religious institutions have any claim to greater authority than the individual conscience or inner light? This question, or rather demand, seemed validated by the findings of cutting-edge German philosophy and theology, over and against what increasingly looked like Unitarian timidity.

Philosophically, the Unitarian view of the nature of the mind rested on the psychological theories of John Locke, the dominant eighteenth-century authority on the theory of knowledge throughout the Anglophone world. All thought and reflection, Locke maintained, is empirically derived from sense perception; the mind is incapable of direct apprehension of supersensible truth. The Transcendentalists objected to this view as rank materialism or "sensationalism." They reacted to Locke rather as many humanists today react to those forms of cognitive science that insist thought can be reduced to neurobiology. To the Transcendentalists, this was a lamentably diminished and also unspiritual view of humankind's higher capacities. They found support for their reaction in the philosophy of Immanuel Kant and his successors, as selectively filtered through to them by wishful British interpreters like Coleridge (see Section I). Through the magnifying lenses of German philosophy's Anglo-American middlemen, Kantianism seemed to give the imprimatur of avant-garde philosophy to the idea that the human mind possesses a higher "Reason," or divine intuition, distinct from mere "Understanding," or inductive reasoning, that is capable of direct intuitive perception of Truth with a capital *T*.

Theologically, the Unitarians had sought to establish that their brand of Christianity was both rational and supernatural by arguing that its supernatural warrant was validated by the record of the miracles performed by Jesus, to whom they accorded special authority despite their opposition to the traditional doctrine of a triune God (father, son, holy spirit). The Transcendentalists, by contrast, saw this fixation on empirical proof as symptomatic of the dead hand of Lockean materialism. It was a stumbling block in the way of an authentic, deeper spirituality. Here they were additionally helped by the momentum of German theology, culminating in David Friedrich Strauss's *Life of Jesus* (1835), toward reconceiving Christianity in terms of comparative mythology. From this standpoint, no religious system could be considered uniquely privileged, although in practice most Transcendentalists (and most nineteenth-century German theologians, too) remained more post-Christian than relativist in a strict sense. For example, Bronson Alcott's appeal to Jesus as the model for the ideal teacher (Section IV-B) both brings Jesus down to earth to take his place in the secular world and continues to grant him special authority as a standard of value.

In this shift from church-oriented religiosity to a nondogmatic, post-sectarian comparative spirituality lies Transcendentalism's single most coherent and distinctive long-range contribution to the philosophy of religion. The Transcendentalists were the first group of American intelligentsia to advocate that the great nonwestern faith traditions be taken seriously as possible paths to religious understanding. For the most part, they did so from a universalizing premise that seems naive today: the assumption of a fundamental unity of thought and values across cultures. "Can any one doubt," Emerson asks rhetorically, "that if the noblest saint among the Buddhists, the noblest Mahometan, the highest Stoic of Athens, the purest and wisest Christian, M[a]nu in India, Confucius in China, Spinoza in Holland, could somewhere meet and converse together, they would all find themselves of one religion?" Well, of course one can doubt it. Just look at the clash of religious fundamentalisms today. Yet if one thinks of the real heart of the Transcendentalist project as a desire to find moral and spiritual universals in the conviction that a greater degree of common ground can be reached, the project looks admirably cosmopolitan, even prophetic. Without a similar faith, for example, the United Nations' much-criticized but also justly treasured Universal Declaration of Human Rights would never have seen the light of day.

Transcendentalism's acute phase as *primarily* a religious movement was short-lived, however—an eruption during the late 1830s and early 1840s of which Emerson's Divinity School Address and the pamphlet war it provoked was the high point (Section III). Otherwise, what looks most noteworthy about Transcendentalism as a movement with a religious origin is that it mostly came to concentrate its energies elsewhere. As we began to see earlier, Transcendentalism was in the long run at least as important as an incentive for literature and the arts, for social reform, for a new conception and valuation of the human self. Through Emerson, Thoreau, Fuller, and other creative writers associated with the movement, Transcendentalism became a significant force behind the emergence of U.S. literature as an international presence during the mid-nineteenth century. Not only Whitman and Dickinson but also Hawthorne, Melville, Poe, and numerous other creative writers, major and minor, responded strongly to Transcendentalism (or what they took to be such). For Alcott and Peabody and Fuller, Transcendentalism pointed the way toward a much less authoritarian teaching ethic than the traditional drill-and-recitation pedagogy that then prevailed. For Fuller, Transcendentalism demonstrated that the relation between the sexes must be put on a new footing. For Emerson and Thoreau, Transcendentalism led to a new vision of the human self as defined in terms of its highest possibilities. For Brownson and Ripley, this new vision was social, a vision of a transformed society. For an increasing number of Transcendentalists during the 1840s and 1850s, including even the staunchly individualistic Emerson and Thoreau, Transcendentalism justified the appeal to a "higher law" above that of the U.S. Constitution, which countenanced slavery.

Only to a limited extent and for a short while, then, was the Transcendentalist movement confined to the venue of religion. The original nexus became a centrifuge, out of which spun a number of discrepant, sometimes antithetical initiatives. In the first instance, this centrifugal effect was simply a predictable outcome of the Unitarian starting point. Unitarianism was a movement originally sparked by liberal opposition to the whole idea of sectarianism as such. This in turn made it inevitable that its most liberal members would conclude that the original movement had lost its way when it tried, as it soon did, to consolidate itself into a sect. So it made sense for the Transcendentalist movement to take the form of a scattering process that would shift away from a specifically religiocentric focus in a variety of directions according to each participant's interest. But in order to understand why this scattering process took the form it did, we need to examine Transcendentalism's core values more directly.

## WHAT EXACTLY WAS TRANSCENDENTALISM?

The answer is trickier than it might seem. One might expect the very opposite, for the historical information that survives about the movement and its major figures is extensive, and scholars have been sifting through it for more than a century. The Transcendentalists were prolific writers, and many of them kept voluminous private journals as well as publishing freely. Moreover, they were positively addicted to summing up their perceptions in the form of penetrating epigrammatic, bottom-line statements. Emerson, Thoreau, Fuller, Peabody, Alcott—all were strongly drawn to the art of the aphorism. Surely, somewhere amid all those powerful, pithy pronouncements we ought to be able to find a comprehensive condensed statement of what the essence of Transcendentalism was. Yet the movement's sheer variety of interest, achievement, and percolation makes it far easier to itemize its initiatives, events, and dramatis personae than to define the concept of Transcendentalism per se. That most of the group disliked having their individualities lumped together, especially under such an abstruse label, aggravates the problem. "I suppose all of them were surprised at this rumor of a school or sect," the aging Emerson slyly recalled, "and certainly at the name of Transcendentalism, given nobody knows by whom." Many of the movement's leading figures issued such disclaimers. Emerson's was especially coy and disingenuous, for he knew perfectly well that movement insiders and outsiders alike considered him to be Transcendentalism's ringleader.

Yet it was not, after all, strange that Emerson should have backpedaled in this fashion. For one thing, "Transcendentalism" had in fact been slapped on the movement by its detractors as a synonym for "foreign" and especially "German" nonsense. For another, the Transcendentalists themselves, even when they made a show of defining their premises, preferred to state them in sweeping terms that mystified more than they clarified. A typical case (Section II) was Cranch's peremptory definition of Transcendentalism as simply "new thought" after a long harangue on how the movement had been misunderstood.

Nathaniel Hawthorne sized up the situation shrewdly in a tale written at the time he was most immersed in the social life of Transcendentalist Concord. In a satiric rerun of John Bunyan's *Pilgrim's Progress*, the industrial-era pilgrim train (which is, literally, a railroad train) whisks by the cave of one "Giant Transcendentalist." The giant, explains the narrator, is "a German by birth," "but as to his form, his features, his substance, and his nature generally, it is the chief peculiarity of this huge miscreant, that neither he for himself, nor anybody for him, has ever been able to describe them." Sure enough, the giant "shouted after us, but in so strange a phraseology that we knew not what he meant, nor whether to be encouraged or affrighted." This last sentence alludes to the Transcendentalists' common practice of deploying key terms in confusingly nontraditional ways (insisting, for example, on the polar opposition between "Reason" and "Understanding," which Lockean philosophy used synonymously), and, more broadly, to the Transcendentalists' preference for metaphorical and discontinuous discourse rather than for straightforward exposition.

What Hawthorne's satire doesn't quite grasp—or prefers to overlook—is that many if not most Transcendentalists tended on principle to look upon formal reasoning as profitless pedantry, even when they reluctantly engaged in it, just as their Unitarian predecessors tended to regard theological disputation as a waste of time. You did it if the situation demanded it, but it didn't strike at the heart of things. To inspire was worthier than to explain.

Why? Here we approach the heart of the Transcendentalist ethos: the idea of a divinity latent within each person, whose ordinarily underactivated potential is not to be reasoned into being so much as ignited. "I have only one doctrine," Emerson famously announced in his Journal: "the infinitude of the private man." His essay "Self-Reliance" (Section IV-A) unfolds his vision most pointedly. With a couple of significant complications we'll examine in a moment, Emerson's assertion not only sums up pretty well the core of his own thought, but the movement's as well. Thoreau's assertion in "Resistance to Civil Government" (Section IV-A) that the principled act of a single man might bring about the death of slavery in America expresses the same spirit. So too with Theodore Parker's insistence upon the authority of conscience to defy the authority of law when laws protect slavery. So too with Alcott's Wordsworthian faith in the intuitive insight of young children (as properly drawn out by him, of course).

This view of the potentiality of human nature at its best was not without precedent, as Emerson makes clear in his essay "The Transcendentalist" (Section II), which envisions the movement as the latest avatar of an "Idealism" dating back more than two thousand years. It is anticipated by the Quaker doctrine of the inner light and the Puritan doctrine of salvation as wrought by the solitary soul transfused by the Holy Spirit. It was anticipated even more closely by the first heresy that roiled New England Puritanism, the heresy of antinomianism, the view that the immediate dictates of the Holy Spirit to the individual soul must take precedence over law and doctrine. Long before that, Transcendentalism was anticipated by Jesus' insistence that "the kingdom of God is within you" and by the inner "daemon" that helped keep Socrates from going astray. Perhaps the Transcendentalists' most significant departure from these precedents was the democratization of the spiritual elect to include everybody, at least in principle. As one of the movement's early historians put it, American Transcendentalism was "the spirit awakened by the establishment of national independence on a basis of liberty and the rights of man, coming into contact with the deep religiousness of Puritanism, and its profound faith in God," in a process that was "helped" even if not "created" by the infusion of "European philosophy."

Now for the two complications. First, even as they pressed the gospel of the infinitude of the individual person, Emerson and his fellow Transcendentalists recognized the need to distinguish between a person's workaday self and the part of one's identity that justified the claim: between self with a small *s* and what Emerson called the "aboriginal Self" with a capital *S*, "on which a universal reliance may be grounded." Indeed, the dark or tragic aspect of Transcendentalism was that its definition of essential human nature set the bar so high as to produce intense frustration at the rarity and brevity of those moments of peak experience in which one's best self emerged and asserted itself. That largely accounts for the mood swings in much Transcendentalist writing between hope and anxiety, elation and disappointment.

The second and related complication arose from disagreements among Transcendentalists as to the relative importance of the elevation of single individuals versus the elevation of society as a whole. Virtually all of them cared about both, but they differed over the prioritization. Emerson and Thoreau staunchly believed that the key to social transformation lay through individual transformation. "Souls are not saved in bundles" was Emerson's terse summation. But for a number of other Transcendentalists, such as Orestes Brownson and George Ripley, social reform came to seem the top priority, to which end collective and institutional means were indispensable, however important it be to protect individual integrity and rights. In other words, the commune at Brook Farm and the solitary Walden experiment of Henry Thoreau are almost equally valid defining images of the Transcendentalist aspiration.

Given the ambiguities behind their pronouncements about the actual versus the ideal self, and given the internal disagreements about the priority of individual versus social transformation, it was small wonder that the lineaments of Giant Transcendentalist seemed a bit vague. But perhaps the single most significant reason for this was that the spirit of Transcendentalist perfectionism, of whatever stripe, led it to express itself in visionary rather than expository ways: as jeremiad, as prophecy, as poetry. This preference was partly a matter of individual temperaments. Many of the Transcendentalists, like Emerson, had a strong aesthetic bent from the start. But even more fundamental was that *as* visionaries, whether mainly focused on the individual or on the social, they were more excited by the vision and experience of the *process* of transformation than by the crystallization or codification of it. "To create,—to create,—is the proof of a divine presence," Emerson exclaims in "The American Scholar." "Whatever the talents are, if the man create not, the pure efflux of deity is not his." This reads at first glance like praise of the artistic vocation specifically, and up to a point it is. But what most deeply interested Emerson, here and elsewhere, was creativity in the extended sense: the spirit of inventive formation and reformation exercised in any worthy context.

## THE MOVEMENT'S PHASES

As might be expected from a group of visionaries, the *institutions* created by Transcendentalism were few and relatively short-lived. Among these, three stand out especially. First, a series of discussion groups, of which the first and most significant was the Transcendental Club, sometimes called simply "the club." It met periodically in Cambridge and Concord between 1836 and 1840. At one time or another, virtually all the individuals named above who were born before 1820 attended, usually more than once. It is symbolically if not causally significant that the club began during the year when by far the greatest single number of important Transcendentalist manifestos was published (see Section II for more details), and that it broke up just before the formation of Brook Farm, whose founding produced a cordial but also rather edgy split between individualists and collectivists (see sections II and IV-A). This split played itself out during the 1840s. This was the time of both Transcendentalist communes, Fruitlands as well as Brook Farm—a second form of institutionalized Transcendentalism. By 1850, both had long since failed, and several key members of the nucleus were dead (Fuller), or had either departed (Ripley) or defected (Brownson), while some others, including Emerson and Hedge, were qualifying their original idealism in degree if not in kind.

This waning of the original utopian vision of the possibilities of human and social transformation might be taken, and indeed often has been taken, as marking the effective end of the movement. It is common to speak of Thoreau's later years as an increasingly zealous empirical observer of the natural world as a "post-Transcendental" phase and to say the same of Emerson's "pragmatic turn," as it is often called, starting in the mid-1840s. As we see from Section VI, a number of the Transcendentalists themselves thought the same way. Sometimes I myself have fallen into this way of thinking and speaking. In my more considered judgment, though, it seems shortsighted to insist that the movement ended around 1850. For one thing, this fails to take fully into account the third and arguably most important kind of Transcendentalist institution, namely the series of intellectual magazines individual Transcendentalists or groups thereof maintained as forums for the "new thought." The most significant of these was another enterprise of the 1840s, *The Dial* (1840–44), edited first by Fuller and then by Emerson. But the whole sporadic series of ventures sponsored either by the original group or by younger intellectuals influenced by them stretched out over more than half a century, starting with the Transcendentalist takeover of Unitarianism's trans-Appalachian magazine *The Western Messenger* (1835–41), and continuing well past the Civil War years with *The Radical* (1865–72) and *The Index* (1870–86). *The Radical* always was and *The Index* eventually became the forum of a group of radical ministers and laypeople, the Free Religious Association, which included a number of second-generation Transcendentalists like Higginson and O. B. Frothingham, the movement's first bona fide historian (see Section VI). If we also count the senescent Alcott's Concord School of Philosophy, as surely we should, it's fair to claim that the movement, not to mention the output of writings by longer-lived individual Transcendentalists, persisted down to the end of the nineteenth century and even a little beyond.

But it is foolish to belabor the question of how long Transcendentalism remained vital simply by pointing to the existence of one or another institution or book, since as we have seen Transcendentalism is better understood as an outpouring of radiant energy than as an organized enterprise. This point is especially crucial to bear in mind when trying to come to terms with the later stages of the careers of those who shifted their intellectual ground significantly, as Emerson, Thoreau, and Fuller all did. When Fuller became a journalist for the *Tribune,* her writing became less abstract and more pointed, less focused on ideas and more on social issues. Do we think of these changes as a break or liberation from the confines of Transcendentalist idealism or as the ultimate payoff of that idealism? When Emerson shifted from his celebration of the freestanding individual in "Self-Reliance" to active collaboration with the very abolitionist radicals he had stigma-tized in that same essay as "angry bigots," did he abandon his Tran-scendentalist premises, or should his career as an antislavery advocate rather be considered a more pragmatic and sociocentric application of his lifetime commitment to the primacy of the individual person against the inertial restraints of the social order? When Thoreau turned to more systematic observation of the natural world, to what extent did he actually jettison his prior belief, strongly influenced by Emerson's *Nature,* in the spiritual coherence of the cosmos and the mystical correspondence between the realms of nature and of spirit?

There is no easy answer to such questions. Every conscientious reader needs to work out his or her own solution. In assembling this collection, I have operated from the principle of once a Transcenden-talist, always a Transcendentalist, barring strong evidence of an explicit repudiation. By this criterion, Emerson, Thoreau, and Fuller never ceased to belong, even if their final work looked somewhat unlike that of their earlier avatars. Brownson emphatically signed off Transcendentalism when he became a Catholic, Ripley implicitly so after Brook Farm, Very implicitly so after a short manic episode in the late 1830s (see Section V-C). But the broader point to make here is that they would not have become what they ultimately became if they had not been what they had been. The same holds for Transcendentalism's legacy to U.S. cultural history. No one can quantify precisely the Transcendentalist contribution to literature, religious comparatism, philosophical idealism and pragmatism, abolitionism, feminism, and educational theory. But one can say with confidence that had the Transcendentalist movement never taken place, in all of these arenas the course of history would have unfolded differently. I hope that the contents of this volume will help give twenty-first-century readers a better sense of why.

# A Note on the Texts

In rare cases, when it seems important for clarity's sake, I have modernized punctuation and spelling as they appear in the original source. Only for two selections, as explained in the introductory notes below, have I done so in more than scattered instances.

—Lawrence Buell

I

# ANTICIPATIONS

# MARY MOODY EMERSON
## LETTERS TO A FUTURE TRANSCENDENTALIST
### (1817–51)

Mary Moody Emerson (1774–1863) was Ralph Waldo Emerson's aunt and first mentor. She was a striking figure in her own right. She impressed all who came into contact with her—which included most of the Transcendentalist circle—with her unsystematic brilliance, her spiritual intensity, her biting wit, and her eccentric force. The younger sister of Emerson's father, she became the family matriarch after his early death. She had high hopes that Ralph Waldo would distinguish himself in the ministerial career that the men in his family had pursued for six unbroken generations back to colonial times. She wound up driving him toward Transcendentalism even as she tried to warn him away.

The many letters she sent him over more than forty years display her unique talents. They led Emerson, astonishingly, to praise her as one of the great prose stylists of her day, although she wrote almost nothing for publication. Both of them relished their correspondence. Many of Mary Emerson's turns of thought and even her turns of phrase resurface in his own later essays. They took a similar delight in the natural world, in ranging widely through Asian as well as western thought and literature, in moral and spiritual inquiry, and in a headlong free-associative style of thought and expression.

Here are a dozen passages from Mary's letters to her nephew, starting with a comically extravagant letter of congratulation upon the start of his freshman year at Harvard at the tender but then typical age of fourteen. Often she responds pointedly to his own letters and compositions, from a juvenile proposal for "reform" of drama through high-minded literary criticism (item 4) to major work like his 1838 Divinity School Address (item 11), which took her aback, as it did most of his elders. Mary's oblique reflection on the controversy, her fable of Urah, may have suggested Emerson's poem "Uriel" (see Section V-B).

Too conservative to approve of Waldo's Transcendental turn, Mary Emerson nonetheless helped set him—and the movement—on the way. But no matter how famous he became, she never ceased to admonish him when she thought he deserved it. Her charge that wealth was a topic unworthy of him (item 12) is a prime example.

SOURCE: *The Selected Letters of Mary Moody Emerson,* ed. Nancy Craig Simmons. Athens: University of Georgia Press, 1993. Spelling as well as punctuation of these letters have been partially normalized for the sake of readability.

## (1)

What dull Prosaic Muse would venture from the humble dell of an unlettered district, to address a son of Harvard? . . . In that great Assembly, where human nature is purified from its native dross & ignorance, may the name of my dear Waldo be inrolled.

[NOVEMBER 4, 1817]

## (2)

The spirits of inspiration are abroad tonight. I have rode only to go out & see the wonderous aspect of nature. . . . We love nature—to individuate ourselves in her wildest moods; to partake of her extension, & glow with her colors & fly on her winds; but we better love to cast her off and rely on that only which is imperishable. Shakespeare has admirably described the universal influence of the infinite Spirit by that of the sun, whose light & warmth brings to maturity the healthiest plant & the most poisonous—corrupts the corruptible, & nourishes the splendid tribe of flora with the same beam. What an illustration—and of what a truth! . . . *Right* and *wrong* have had claims prior to all rites—immutable & eternal in their nature . . . [JANUARY 18, 1821]

(3)

I have been fortunate this week to find a Visitor here from India, well versed in its literature & theology. He showed us some fine representations of the incarnation of Vishnoo. They are much akin to Grecian fable—and from his representation I believe the incarnations to be much like the doctrine of transmigration. At bottom of the histories of the incarnations is often the doctrine of the universal presence & agency of One God....

As to books, I've been only where you have, sometimes in Merlin's cave and Homer's shades, sometimes. Was delighted with the speech made by Ulysses to the shade of his mother. [Alexander] Pope's—*is it better* in original? Have been surprised to find in the 10th book of [the Roman poet] Juvenal some lines very like to the concluding ones of [Samuel] Johnson's "Vanity of Human Wishes." Could Johnson have borrowed from the heathen? [MAY 24, 1822]

(4)

... As to words & languages being so important—I will have nothing of it. The images, the sweet immortal images are within us—born there, our native right, and sometimes one kind of sounding word or syllable wakens the instrument of our souls and sometimes another. But we are not slaves to sense any more than to political usurpers, but by fashion & imbecility. Aye, if I understand you, so you think.

In the zeal of writing I began with the last sentence of your letter, & have just read backwards till I am now for the first time in cool possession of the whole letter—Glad to hear you complain of fine splendid expressions without proportionate fine thoughts. But not that in order to judge you must read all the pieces or rather that you intend a reform which will oblige you to go thro' such bogs & fens & sloughs of passion & crime.... And to me who am, if possible, more ignorant on the history & character of the Drama than any other subject, it seems a less usefull exercise as it respects the *reformer* than any scientific or literary pursuit. [JUNE 26, 1822]

( 5 )

... Would to God thou wert ambitious—respected thyself more & the world less. Thou wouldst not to Cambridge [to enroll at Harvard Divinity School.] ... It is but a garnished sepulchre where may be found some relics of the *body* of Jesus—some grosser parts which he took not at his ascent ... [NOVEMBER 7, 1824]

( 6 )

It is worse than idle to ridicule the fall—unless you can account for the origin of evil. ... The apple may be allegorical—but if it were real it answered for a sign, an arbitrary one, be sure, of a government disciplinary & perspective. The principle of obedience is the first in education—and the more trifling the object the more important the danger of defection. ... Evil must have a beginning. If it were eternal—! What should we infer—that eternal right was coeval with—& implied in its opposite? ... Well, one & all have the subject in the dark where God intended. And I never talk of the fall nor think of it—for the difficulties are too great. [JULY 8, 1827]

( 7 )

Would I could die today that this aching sense of immortality might be satisfied or cease to ache. The difficulty remains the same when I struggle with the extension of never never never—just as I repeated the exercise in childhood: cant form an idea, cant stretch myself to that which has no end. It may be owing to the limits of childhood repeating the idea & wishing to come at an end in vain. ... It is this impossibility of losing oneself, tho' ages pass over the change, that argues immortality. [SEPTEMBER 9, 1827]

( 8 )

My thanks for the sensibility you express at my being hurt to be thought by you distraught. But after *all* I *do appear so* to other folks, when under the influence of the indifference I feel to society (or something worse) with the extreme pleasure of wittnessing their fine things. The fears which I read in the countenance of my family lead me to act more independently than I should, if I were coaxed with their confidence.... You have borne with my outre manners and protected them better than any youth. Only forgive me greater & worser defects of character—and these which pass away with the discordant humours of the body are of no import.  [MAY 2, 1828]

## (9)

Let us not complain of calvinism—its most terrible points are better than nothing. If the bible is a fable I would cherish it now in age with undying zeal—It may have a truth of infinite weight like other fables which have a little. But it is not a fable I know. It answers to the living consciousness of God's impress on the soul. It develops the divinity within. Not the poetic *gospelless* divinity of German idealism—whose baseless fabrick will vanish into thin air.  [AUGUST (?) 1829]

## (10)

You most beloved of ministers, who seemed formed by face, manner & pen to copy & illustrate the noblest of all institutions, are you at war with that angelic office? ... And I may ask what you mean by speaking of "a great truth whose authority you would feel as its own"? In the letter of Dec 25 you [write] "whether the heart were not the Creator." Now if this withering Lucifer doctrine of pantheism be true, what moral truth can you preach or by what authority should you feel it? Without a personal God you are on an ocean mast unrigged for any port or object. Then why *not* continue to preach—& pray too? Where is the truth, so infinitely weighty with the true theist, injured? Some body must keep up these idle institutions & they may keep men from jail and gallows. What better scope for the intellectual reservoir? And such has been your integrity, whenever I have been indulged with hearing or reading, what St Paul, who had the fullest convictions of Jesus being the only medium of communication with the Incomprehensible, would not tax your sincerity, tho' he would regret the different character you assigned. Pardon me if I declaim with the garrulity of age.

[FEBRUARY 1832]

( 11 )

I love to gaze after the illuminati.... Yet believe with Burke that no improvement can be expected in the great truths & institutions of morality and religion. And I lost my inquiries in thinking of the fabled Urah, who belonging to the coterie of Plato, was sent down by that high person ... to reform a certain district and give it some utopian ornaments—so dully progressive so sober & stale that in his disgust he breathed a fire which consumed every old land mark—tore up the moss-covered mounds; and the very altars which had been the refuge of the poor & sinfull & decrepit instead of being bettered were almost demolished—and in the destruction it is said that the wings of the spiritual vehicle were so scorched that he was forced to ask aid of a disciple of the old reforming Patriarch who was buried on some old loved spot, and he, tho' looked on as a very plodder, constructed a chariot of clouds which conveyed the messenger home to new fledge his wings. And the story goes, that when they were in action again he visited the same place & found it overrun with barbarism & governed by an ugly Radicale.   [SEPTEMBER 1838?]

( 12 )

*Wealth* my dear Waldo: how could *you*—you gifted to rouse the interior to make even Christians think & feel at certain high sentiments—how, under what illusion, could you lecture to Concord of its advantages? You sap the foundations of all that is great & independant. Oh send the young to Brothels & intemperance.... You who have steadily stood for the *rights* of the slave are riveting his chains & pursuing the fugitive with increasing the rage the mania for wealth. Were you poor (and the papers speak of your high taxes) what a beautifull vision you might have drawn of its baseless fabrick while you awakened charity in its depths and glory. Forgive me if I offend, & send me the lecture.

[FEBRUARY 1851]

# Samuel Taylor Coleridge

## Reason Versus Understanding

### (1825, 1829)

Coleridge (1772–1834) was a leading British Romantic poet and one of the most inventive critical thinkers of his age. Along with Thomas Carlyle, he was more influential in interpreting German thought for American audiences than any other early-nineteenth-century British writer. A prime example is Coleridge's restatement of the Kantian distinction between "Reason" and "Understanding," in the face of the prevailing Anglo-American view, which rested on John Locke's contention that all knowledge is derived empirically, from sense experience. In Locke's view, "reason" and "understanding" were synonymous. Coleridge prepared the way for the Transcendentalist conception of Reason as a power of mind or soul that enables a person to grasp divine or Transcendent truth intuitively. (Ironically, Kant himself had explicitly denied the human mind such power. Such are the vagaries of intellectual history.) Coleridge's distinction reached most Transcendentalists through the American edition of his *Aids to Reflection* (1829), edited by Vermont Calvinist James Marsh (1794–1842). This indeed was "the decisive event in establishing respect" for Coleridge "as a thinker," as the authoritative modern scholarly edition of *Aids* declares. Marsh's prefatory remarks chastised Locke and seconded the importance of the Reason-Understanding distinction in ways that prompted both foes and friends to lump Marsh with the Transcendentalists—to his acute irritation.

SOURCE: *Aids to Reflection,* ed. James Marsh. Burlington, Vermont: Chauncey Goodrich, 1829. Reprinted from the original English edition of 1825.

Reason is the Power of universal and necessary Convictions, the Source and Substance of Truths above Sense, and having their evidence in themselves.... Contemplated distinctively in reference to *formal* (or abstract) truth, it is the *speculative Reason;* but in reference to *actual* (or moral) truth, as the fountain of ideas and the *Light* of the Conscience, we name it the *Practical* Reason. Whenever by self-subjection to this universal Light, the Will of the Individual, the *particular* Will, has become a Will of Reason, the man is regenerate: and Reason is then the *Spirit* of the regenerated man, whereby the Person is capable of a quickening inter-communication with the Divine Spirit....

On the other hand, the Judgments of the Understanding are binding only in relation to the objects of our Senses, which we *reflect* under the forms of the Understanding....

To apply these remarks for our present purpose, we have only to describe Understanding and Reason, each by its characteristic qualities. The comparison will show the difference.

| UNDERSTANDING | REASON |
|---|---|
| 1. Understanding is discursive. | 1. Reason is fixed. |
| 2. The Understanding in all its judgments refers to some other faculty as its ultimate authority. | 2. The Reason in all its decisions appeals to itself as the ground and *substance* of their truth. |
| 3. Understanding is the faculty of *Reflection*. | 3. Reason of Contemplation.... Reason is a direct Aspect of Truth, an inward Beholding, having a similar relation to the Intelligible or Spiritual, as Sense has to the Material or Phenomenal. |

# 3.

# WILLIAM ELLERY CHANNING
## HUMANITY'S LIKENESS TO GOD
### (1828)

William Ellery Channing (1780–1842) was the most charismatic and liberal of the early Unitarian ministers, and by far the most inspiring figure among them for Transcendentalism's early advocates. Most of the Transcendentalist ministers started out thinking of themselves as "Channing Unitarians." Even as religiously conservative a person as Mary Moody Emerson so admired Channing's fervent piety that she urged her nephew to study privately with him rather than bother with the Harvard Divinity School. The following selection comes from Channing's most spiritually radical performance, "Likeness to God." In it he anticipates the Transcendentalist claim that the human self is inherently divine, although not the movement's more radical disavowal of the Bible as a primary authority in matters of the spirit. Channing later pressed against the limits of Unitarian liberalism in another direction by coming out more vehemently against slavery than any Unitarian leader had done before. Although neither in his theology nor in his social reform thought did he go as far as the more radical Transcendentalists did, they still tended to think of him as "our bishop," as Emerson called him.

SOURCE: *A Discourse Delivered at the Ordination of the Rev. Frederick A. Farley...September 10, 1828*. Boston: Bowles and Dearborn, 1828.

I begin with observing, what all indeed will understand, that the likeness to God, of which I propose to speak, belongs to man's higher or spiritual nature. It has its foundation in the original and essential capacities of the mind. In proportion as these are unfolded by right and vigorous exertion, it is extended and brightened. In proportion as these lie dormant, it is obscured. In proportion as they are perverted and overpowered by the appetites and passions, it is blotted out. In truth, moral evil, if unresisted and habitual, may so blight and lay waste these capacities, that the image of God in man may seem to be wholly destroyed.

The importance of this assimilation to our Creator, is a topic, which needs no labored discussion. All men, of whatever name, or sect, or opinion, will meet me on this ground. All, I presume, will allow, that no good in the compass of the universe, or within the gift of omnipotence, can be compared to a resemblance of God, or to a participation of his attributes. I fear no contradiction here. Likeness to God is the supreme gift. He can communicate nothing so precious, glorious, blessed as himself. To hold intellectual and moral affinity with the Supreme Being, to partake his spirit, to be his children by derivations of kindred excellence, to bear a growing conformity to the perfection which we adore, this is a felicity which obscures and annihilates all other good.

It is only in proportion to this likeness that we can enjoy either God, or the universe. That God can be known and enjoyed only through sympathy or kindred attributes, is a doctrine which even Gentile philosophy discerned. That the pure in heart can alone see and commune with the pure Divinity, was the sublime instruction of ancient sages as well as of inspired prophets. It is indeed the lesson of daily experience. To understand a great and good being, we must have the seeds of the same excellence. How quickly, by what an instinct, do accordant minds recognise one another! No attraction is so powerful as that which subsists between the truly wise, and good; whilst the brightest excellence is lost on those who have nothing congenial in their own breasts. God becomes a real being to us, in proportion as his own nature is unfolded within us. To a man who is growing in the likeness of God, faith begins even here to change into vision. He carries within himself a proof of a Deity, which can only be understood by experience. He more than believes, he feels the divine presence; and gradually rises to an intercourse with his Maker, to which it is not irreverent to apply the name of friendship and intimacy. The apostle John intended to express this truth, when he tells us that he, in whom a principle of divine charity or benevolence has become a habit and life, "dwells in God and God in him."

It is plain, too, that likeness to God is the true and only preparation for the enjoyment of the universe. In proportion as we approach and resemble the mind of God, we are brought into harmony with the creation; for, in that proportion we possess the principles from which the universe sprung; we carry within ourselves the perfections of which, its beauty, magnificence, order, benevolent adaptations, and boundless purposes, are the results and manifestations. God unfolds himself in his works to a kindred mind. It is possible, that the brevity of these hints may expose to the charge of mysticism, what seems to me the calmest and clearest truth. I think, however, that every reflecting man will feel, that likeness to God must be a principle of sympathy or accordance with his creation; for the creation is a birth and shining forth of the Divine Mind, a work through which his spirit breathes. In proportion as we receive this spirit, we possess within ourselves the explanation of what we see. We discern more and more of God in everything, from the frail flower to the everlasting stars. Even in evil, that dark cloud which hangs over the creation, we discern rays of light and hope, and gradually come to see in suffering and temptation, proofs and instruments of the sublimest purposes of Wisdom and Love.

I have offered these very imperfect views, that I may show the great importance of the doctrine which I am solicitous to enforce. I would teach, that likeness to God is a good so unutterably surpassing all other good, that whoever admits it as attainable, must acknowledge it to be the chief aim of life. I would show that the highest and happiest office of religion, is to bring the mind into growing accordance with God, and that by the tendency of religious systems to this end their truth and worth are to be chiefly tried.

———

I am aware that it may be said, that the scriptures, in speaking of man as made in the image of God, and in calling us to imitate him, use bold and figurative language. It may be said, that there is danger from too literal an interpretation; that God is an unapproachable being; that I am not warranted in ascribing to man a like nature to the Divine; that we and all things illustrate the Creator by contrast, not by resemblance; that religion manifests itself chiefly in convictions and acknowledgments of utter worthlessness; and that to talk of the greatness and divinity of the human soul, is to inflate that pride through which Satan fell, and through which man involves himself in that fallen spirit's ruin.

I answer, that, to me, scripture and reason hold a different language. In Christianity particularly, I meet perpetual testimonies to the divinity of human nature. This whole religion expresses an infinite concern of God for the human soul, and teaches that he deems no methods too expensive for its recovery and exaltation. Christianity, with one voice, calls me to turn my regards and care to the spirit within me, as of more worth than the whole outward world. It calls us to "be perfect as our Father in heaven is perfect;" and everywhere, in the sublimity of its precepts, it implies and recognises the sublime capacities of the being to whom they are addressed. It assures us that human virtue is "in the sight of God of great price," and speaks of the return of a human being to virtue as an event which increases the joy of heaven. In the New Testament, Jesus Christ, the Son of God, the brightness of his glory, the express and unsullied image of the Divinity, is seen mingling with men as a friend and brother, offering himself as their example, and promising to his true followers a share in all his splendors and joys. In the New Testament, God is said to communicate his own spirit, and all his fulness to the human soul. In the New Testament man is exhorted to aspire after "honor, glory, and immortality;" and Heaven, a word expressing the nearest approach to God, and a divine happiness, is everywhere proposed as the end of his being. In truth, the very essence of christian faith is, that we trust in God's mercy, as revealed in Jesus Christ, for a state of celestial purity, in which we shall grow forever in the likeness, and knowledge, and enjoyment of the Infinite Father. Lofty views of the nature of man are bound up and interwoven with the whole christian system. Say not, that these are at war with humility; for who was ever humbler than Jesus, and yet who ever possessed such a consciousness of greatness and divinity? Say not that man's business is to think of his sin, and not of his dignity; for great sin implies a great capacity; it is the abuse of a noble nature; and no man can be deeply and rationally contrite, but he who feels, that in wrong doing he has resisted a divine voice, and warred against a divine principle, in his own soul.—I need not, I trust, pursue the argument from revelation. There is an argument from nature and reason, which seems to me so convincing, and is at the same time so fitted to explain what I mean by man's possession of a like nature to God, that I shall pass at once to its exposition.

That man has a kindred nature with God, and may bear most important and ennobling relations to him, seems to me to be established by a striking proof. This proof you will understand, by considering, for a moment, how we obtain our ideas of God. Whence come the conceptions which we include under that august name? Whence do we derive our knowledge of the attributes and perfections which constitute the Supreme Being? I answer, we derive them from our own souls. The divine attributes are first developed in ourselves, and thence transferred to our Creator. The idea of God, sublime and awful as it is, is the idea of our own spiritual nature, purified and enlarged to infinity. In ourselves are the elements of the Divinity. God then does not sustain a figurative resemblance to man. It is the resemblance of a parent to a child, the likeness of a kindred nature.

We call God a Mind. He has revealed himself as a spirit. But what do we know of mind, but through the unfolding of this principle in our own breasts? That unbounded spiritual energy which we call God, is conceived by us only through consciousness, through the knowledge of ourselves.—We ascribe thought or intelligence to the Deity as one of his most glorious attributes. And what means this language? These terms we have framed to express operations or faculties of our own souls. The Infinite Light would be forever hidden from us, did not kindred rays dawn and brighten within us. God is another name for human intelligence, raised above all error and imperfection, and extended to all possible truth.

# 4.

# THOMAS CARLYLE

## THE AGE OF MACHINERY

### (1829)

Thomas Carlyle (1795–1881) was Britain's foremost cultural critic during the second quarter of the nineteenth century, especially for American readers. The Transcendentalists were particularly impressed by his journalistic accounts of German literature and thought, which helped make German philosophy seem accessible and directed them to the significance of Goethe. Emerson sought Carlyle out during his 1833 visit to England after resigning his pastorate and struck up a life-long—though at times strained—friendship with this fellow lapsed-Protestant iconoclast. Later they became each other's literary agent in their home countries.

Carlyle was also the first prominent Anglo-American critic to diagnose the wrenching change ushered in by the industrial revolution. The combination of wonder and severity with which he viewed its disruption of traditional social arrangements struck a responsive chord throughout the English-speaking world. The social reform thrust within Transcendentalism had a distinctly Carlylean ring. Orestes Brownson, Theodore Parker, Henry David Thoreau, and others all wrote about the mechanization of labor and exploitation of the working man with Carlyle's charges at least partially in mind. Both the substance and the sarcasm of Thoreau's assertion, in *Walden*, that "men have become the tools of their tools" goes right back to Carlyle—on whom Thoreau had earlier written an appreciative essay. When Carlyle's jeremiads later turned reactionary, siding, for example, with masters against slaves, even his forbearing friend Emerson objected.

But his early discourses on the consequences of industrialization left a permanent mark.

In this particular reading, Carlyle's satire is directed not so much at concerns about economic or material conditions as more abstractly—or profoundly—at the mechanization of thought and social activity that industrialization seemed to portend: the displacement of individual initiative by corporatism and of individual creativity by the efficiency ethic. The emerging Transcendentalist movement would have been additionally gratified by the link Carlyle draws between the age of machinery and the "mechanical" philosophy of Locke.

SOURCE: "Signs of the Times," *Edinburgh Review,* 49 ( June 1829).

Were we required to characterise this age of ours by any single epithet, we should be tempted to call it, not an Heroical, Devotional, Philosophical, or Moral Age, but, above all others, the Mechanical Age. It is the Age of Machinery, in every outward and inward sense of that word; the age which, with its whole undivided might, forwards, teaches, and practices the greater art of adapting means to ends. Nothing is now done directly, or by hand; all is by rule and calculated contrivance. For the simplest operation, some helps and accompaniments, some cunning, abbreviating process is in readiness. Our old modes of exertion are all discredited, and thrown aside. On every hand, the living artisan is driven from his workshop, to make room for a speedier, inanimate one. The shuttle drops from the fingers of the weaver, and falls into iron fingers that ply it faster. The sailor furls his sail, and lays down his oar, and bids a strong, unwearied servant, on vaporous wings, bear him through the waters. Men have crossed oceans by steam; the Birmingham Fire-king has visited the fabulous East; and the genius of the Cape, were there any Camoens now to sing it, has again been alarmed, and with far stranger thunders than Gama's. There is no end to machinery. Even the horse is stripped of his harness, and finds a fleet fire-horse yoked in his stead. Nay, we have an artist that hatches chickens by steam—the very brood-hen is to be superseded! For all earthly, and for some unearthly purposes, we have machines and mechanic furtherances; for mincing our cabbages; for casting us into magnetic sleep. We remove mountains, and make seas our smooth highway; nothing can resist us. We war with rude nature; and, by our resistless engines, come off always victorious, and loaded with spoils.

What wonderful accessions have thus been made, and are still making, to the physical power of mankind; how much better fed, clothed, lodged, and, in all outward respects, accommodated, men now are, or might be, by a given quantity of labour, is a grateful reflection which forces itself on every one. What changes, too, this addition of power is introducing into the social system; how wealth has more and more increased, and at the same time gathered itself more and more into masses, strangely altering the old relations, and increasing the distance between the rich and the poor, will be a question for Political Economists—and a much more complex and important one than any they have yet engaged with. But leaving these matters for the present, let us observe how the mechanical genius of our time has diffused itself into quite other provinces. Not the external and physical alone is now managed by machinery, but the internal and spiritual also. Here, too, nothing follows its spontaneous course, nothing is left to be accomplished by old, natural methods. Every thing has its cunningly devised implements, its pre-established apparatus; it is not done by hand, but by machinery. Thus we have machines for Education: Lancastrian machines; Hamiltonian machines—Monitors, maps, and emblems. Instruction, that mysterious communing of Wisdom with Ignorance, is no longer an indefinable tentative process, requiring a study of individual aptitudes, and a perpetual variation of means and methods, to attain the same end; but a secure, universal, straight-forward business, to be conducted in the gross, by proper mechanism, with such intellect as comes to hand. Then, we have Religious machines, of all imaginable varieties—the Bible Society, professing a far higher and heavenly structure, is found, on enquiry, to be altogether an earthly contrivance, supported by collection of monies, by fomenting of vanities, by puffing, intrigue, and chicane—and yet, in effect, a very excellent machine for converting the heathen. It is the same in all other departments. Has any man, or any society of men, a truth to speak, a piece of spiritual work to do, they can no-wise proceed at once, and with the mere natural organs, but must first call a public meeting, appoint committees, issue prospectuses, eat a public dinner; in a word, construct or borrow machinery, wherewith to speak it and do it.

———

From Locke's time downwards, our whole Metaphysics have been physical; not a spiritual Philosophy, but a material one. The singular estimation in which his Essay was so long held as a scientific work, (for the character of the man entitled all he said to veneration,) will one day be thought a curious indication of the spirit of these times. His whole doctrine is mechanical, in its aim and origin, in its method and its results. It is a mere discussion concerning the origin of our consciousness, or ideas, or whatever else they are called; a genetic history of what we see *in* the mind. But the grand secrets of Necessity and Free-will, of the mind's vital or non-vital dependence on matter, of our mysterious relations to Time and Space, to God, to the universe, are not, in the faintest degree, touched on in their enquiries; and seem not to have the smallest connexion with them.

# RALPH WALDO EMERSON

## A YOUNG MINISTER REFUSES TO PERFORM A CRUCIAL DUTY

### (1832)

Of the 164 sermons Emerson composed during his short career as a parish minister (1828–32), this one was the most uniquely argued and deservedly the most famous. In it Emerson explains his refusal to administer any longer the eucharist, or ritual of communion, a decision that split the church and—as he expected and probably also hoped—led immediately to his resignation. For most of the sermon, Emerson presents theological and historical reasons for his stance, with an almost scholastic precision quite atypical of his customary speaking and writing style. But in the section printed here, he abruptly changes tone and becomes much more subjective and fervent. Here for the first time, as it were, Emerson becomes Emerson—the voice that will make him Transcendentalism's most compelling spokesperson. His conviction that the source of spiritual authority must come from one's inmost being—later summed up in his Divinity School Address (see Section III) and his essay on Self-Reliance (Section IV-A)—is here expressed in public for the first time. So too is Emerson's contempt for the worthlessness of mere forms as nothing better than "the dead leaves that are falling around us"—an allusion to the September landscape.

The connection between Emerson's religious discontent and the declarations of Coleridge and Channing is much more obvious than the link with Carlyle's disquisition on the age of machinery. But it is no less important in its own way. Why would a "Channing Unitarian" go so far as to renounce his post, as Channing never would? (Indeed,

"Likeness to God" was a sermon preached on the occasion of a young minister's ordination, his entry into the procession Emerson would soon forsake.) A good part of the answer lies in Emerson's conclusion, recorded in his journal, that the profession itself had become "antiquated." Carlyle's portrait of the present age as one of dizzying change in which the power of individuality was increasingly hemmed in by social institutions was calculated to aggravate any reader's discontent with existing social arrangements, but especially for someone like Emerson, whose feelings about committing himself to the traditional family profession had been profoundly mixed from the start.

SOURCE: *The Complete Sermons of Ralph Waldo Emerson,* ed. Wesley T. Mott. Columbia: University of Missouri Press, vol. 4 (1992), Sermon CLXII.

To pass by other objections, I come to this: that the *use of the elements,* however suitable to the people and the modes of thought in the East where it originated, is foreign and unsuited to affect us. Whatever long usage and strong association may have done in some individuals to deaden this repulsion I apprehend that their use is rather tolerated than loved by any of us. We are not accustomed to express our thoughts or emotions by symbolical actions. Most men find the bread and wine no aid to devotion and to some persons it is an impediment. To eat bread is one thing; to love the precepts of Christ and resolve to obey them is quite another. It is of the greatest importance that whatever forms we use should be animated by our feelings; that our religion through all its acts should be living and operative.

The statement of this objection leads me to say that I think this difficulty, wherever it is felt, to be entitled to the greatest weight. It is alone a sufficient objection to the ordinance. It is my own objection. This mode of commemorating Christ is not suitable to me. That is reason enough why I should abandon it. If I believed that it was enjoined by Jesus, on his disciples, and that he even contemplated to make permanent this mode of commemoration every way agreeable to an Eastern mind, and yet on trial it was disagreeable to my own feelings, I should not adopt it. I should choose other ways which he would approve more. For what could he wish to be commemorated for? Only that men might be filled with his spirit. I find that other modes comport with my education and habits of thought. For I chuse that my remembrances of him should be pleasing, affecting, religious. I love him as a glorified friend after the free way of friendship and not pay him a stiff sign of respect as men do to those whom they fear. A passage read from his discourses, the provoking each other to works like his, any act or meeting which tends to awaken a pure thought, a glow of love, an original design of virtue I call a worthy, a true commemoration.

In the last place the importance ascribed to this particular ordinance is not consistent with the spirit of Christianity. The general object and effect of this ordinance is unexceptionable. It has been and is, I doubt not, the occasion of indefinite good, but an importance is given by the friends of the rite to it which never can belong to any form. My friends, the kingdom of God is not meat and drink. Forms are as essential as bodies. It would be foolish to declaim against them, but to adhere to one form a moment after it is outgrown is foolish. That form only is good and Christian which answers its end. Jesus came to take the load of ceremonies from the shoulders of men and substitute principles. If I understand the distinction of Christianity, the reason why it is to be preferred over all other systems and is divine is this, that it is a moral system; that it presents men with truths which are their own reason, and enjoins practices that are their own justification; that if miracles may be said to have been its evidence to the first Christians they are not its evidence to us, but the doctrines themselves; that every practice is Christian which praises itself and every practice unchristian which condemns itself. I am not engaged to Christianity by decent forms; it is not saving ordinances, it is not usage, it is not what I do not understand that engages me to it—let these be the sandy foundation of falsehoods. What I revere and obey in it is its reality, its boundless charity, its deep interior life, the rest it gives to my mind, the echo it returns to my thoughts, the perfect accord it makes with my reason, the persuasion and courage that come out of it to lead me upward and onward.

Freedom is the essence of Christianity. It has for its object simply to make men good and wise. Its institutions should be as flexible as the wants of men. That form out of which the life and suitableness have departed should be as worthless in its eyes as the dead leaves that are falling around us.

# 6.

# Frederic Henry Hedge
## The Significance of Kantian Philosophy
### (1834)

Frederic Henry Hedge (1805–90) was one of the most powerful early Transcendentalist thinkers: its most systematic reasoner, the only one to have studied in Germany, and the first-generation Transcendentalist most deeply versed in German philosophy. Mary Moody Emerson called him the movement's Moses. The Transcendentalist coterie that congealed into a periodic discussion group in 1836 was at first called Hedge's Club, since its meetings were timed to coincide with Hedge's visits to Boston from his pastorate in Bangor, Maine. Hedge was by disposition a loyal Unitarian, however. Unlike Emerson, Orestes Brownson, George Ripley, and others, Hedge never left the ministry and indeed never rocked the clerical boat with anything like the vigor of a Channing, much less an Emerson or a Parker. After the 1830s, Hedge largely parted company with the movement. But his essay on Coleridge's literary character was of landmark significance for its attempted "vindication of German metaphysics," as Hedge later put it: "the *first word*, so far as I know, which any American had uttered in respectful recognition of the claims of Transcendentalism." Here is Hedge's climactic summation.

SOURCE: "Coleridge's Literary Character," *Christian Examiner*, 14 (March 1833).

If now it be asked, as probably it will be asked, whether any definite and substantial good has resulted from the labors of Kant and his followers, we answer, Much. More than metaphysics ever before accomplished, these men have done for the advancement of the human intellect. It is true the immediate, and if we may so speak, the calculable results of their speculations are not so numerous nor so evident as might have been expected: these are chiefly comprised under the head of method. Yet even here we have enough to make us rejoice that such men have been, and that they have lived and spoken in our day. We need mention only the sharp and rightly dividing lines that have been drawn within and around the kingdom of human knowledge; the strongly marked distinctions of subject and object, reason and understanding, phenomena and noumena;—the categories established by Kant; the moral liberty proclaimed by him as it had never been proclaimed by any before; the authority and evidence of law and duty set forth by Fichte; the universal harmony illustrated by Schelling. But in mentioning these things, which are the direct results of the critical philosophy, we have by no means exhausted all that that philosophy has done for liberty and truth. The preeminence of Germany among the nations of our day in respect of intellectual culture, is universally acknowledged; and we do fully believe that whatever excellence that nation has attained in science, in history, or poetry is mainly owing to the influence of her philosophy, to the faculty which that philosophy has imparted of seizing on the spirit of every question, and determining at once the point of view from which each subject should be regarded—in one word, to the transcendental method. In theology this influence has been most conspicuous. We are indebted to it for that dauntless spirit of inquiry which has investigated, and for that amazing erudition which has illustrated, every corner of biblical lore. Twice it has saved the religion of Germany—once from the extreme of fanatic extravagance, and again, from the verge of speculative infidelity. But, though most conspicuous in theology, this influence has been visible in every department of intellectual exertion to which the Germans have applied themselves for the last thirty years. It has characterized each science and each art, and all bear witness to its quickening power. A philosophy which has given such an impulse to mental culture and scientific research, which has done so much to establish and to extend the spiritual in man, and the ideal in nature, needs no apology; it commends itself by its fruits, it lives in its fruits, and must ever live, though the name of its founder be forgotten, and not one of its doctrines survive.

# GEORGE RIPLEY

## VICTOR COUSIN AND THE FUTURE OF AMERICAN PHILOSOPHY

### (1838)

Next to Hedge, George Ripley (1802–80) was the first-generation Transcendentalist most committed to establishing a philosophical grounding for the movement in European thought. But Ripley's bent was more practical than theoretical. It was symptomatic of the difference between them that Hedge ended his professional career as a Harvard professor and a writer of scholarly books, whereas Ripley became a book reviewer and encyclopedist. From the start, to disseminate the new thought and make it accessible was more important to Ripley than to analyze philosophical positions with rigorous precision. So Ripley's early signature contributions to the movement were a pastoral treatise, *Discourses on the Philosophy of Religion Addressed to Doubters Who Wish to Believe* (1836), and the editorship of a fourteen-volume series of translations by himself and others, *Specimens of Foreign Standard Literature* (1838–42). Significantly, its first volume did not feature German thinkers but the more accessible French popularizers of German thought, particularly Victor Cousin, the founder of Eclecticism. No less significant is Ripley's populist defense of this redirection of focus, as better suited to the needs of a democratic society. This defense was both sincere and canny. It expressed the Transcendentalists' central conviction in the inherent divinity of the individual person, and it also countered mounting conservative attacks, like Andrews Norton's (see Section III), on the new thought as German mystagoguery. At the same time, Ripley's insistence that philosophy must be made easily digestible for American consumption is unconsciously revealing and slightly pathetic testimony to the comparative intellectual amateurism that prevailed in the United States of his day, even among the intelligentsia.

SOURCE: "Introductory Note" by George Ripley to *Philosophical Miscellanies, Translated from the French of Cousin, Jouffroy, and B. Constant,* vol. 1. Boston: Hilliard, Gray, 1838.

I may venture to say that there is no living philosopher who has a greater number of readers in this country, and none whose works have met with a more genuine sympathy, a more cordial recognition....

I do not mean that Cousin will ever be regarded as the founder of a philosophical sect among thinkers of this nation. This is forbidden by the whole character of his system. It does not contain a single element which can lead to the establishment of an exclusive school. The happiest effort which he produces on the minds of his disciples is to lead them to think no less independently of him, than of others.... The aim of his philosophy is to furnish a criterion, taken from the actual observation of human nature, by which to estimate both the phenomena of daily experience, and the speculative systems which have been constructed for their explanation in every age of the world....

This characteristic is adapted to give his philosophy a favorable reception among ourselves. The reign of authoritative, dogmatic systems has never been firmly established over the mind of this nation; every exclusive faith has called forth a host in dissent; and the time appears to have arrived when no opinions can gain a general reception unless they appeal to the spirit of inquiry, and disdain the aid of prescription or restraint....

... In point of orderly arrangement, of continuous and systematic reasoning, and of admirable taste in the selection of terms, Cousin presents a favorable contrast to the most eminent philosophers of Germany.... Called upon to exhibit the reasonings and conclusions of the German philosophy to a promiscuous audience in the metropolis of France, he has addressed the popular mind with singular success, and solved the cardinal problem of presenting the highest truths of speculation in a form adapted to the average intelligence of enlightened society....

Th[is] characteristic ... in the writings of Cousin presents an additional claim upon the attention of our countrymen. Our national taste—as far as it is formed,—may certainly be said to repudiate all mystery and concealment.... We forgive any thing sooner than those entanglements of words which leave us to guess at the meaning of the writer, and at last to remain doubtful whether we have read his riddle aright. For this reason, the German philosophers, in their native costume, will never become extensively popular in this country. . . . Their writings will be studied by all who love philosophy for its own sake. . . . But they cannot be made the direct foundation of philosophical culture in a country like our own. We must start with the freer, more popular, more concrete, and more finished productions of the great French writers who have been formed in the German school; who retain its vigor and depth and combine with it the graceful ease of their own beautiful literature.

Intimately connected with its distinctness of expression, is another essential characteristic of the philosophy of Cousin, which will serve to facilitate its advancement among the intelligent thinkers of this nation. I allude to the substantial basis which it gives to the instinctive convictions of the human mind. This is the ultimate aim of all genuine philosophy. No system can be of any permanent utility which does not reproduce and legitimate the indestructible faith, that is cherished by the common sense of the mass of humanity. . . . Of this fact, Cousin is not only fully aware himself; but he takes unwearied pains to explain its origin, to justify its importance, and to urge its consequences upon the attention of the reader. . . . He gives us the true key to the meaning of those remarkable expressions, which in almost every language, indicate the conviction that the voice of God is uttered in the heart of man, that the light of the soul is a light from Heaven.

II

# MANIFESTOS
# AND
# DEFINITIONS

# 1.

# RALPH WALDO EMERSON
## NATURE
### (1836)

Eighteen thirty-six has rightly been called Transcendentalism's annus mirabilis. Emerson's first book was the most talked about and by far the most enduringly influential of the year's half dozen major manifestos, including our next two items by Bronson Alcott and Orestes Brownson, as well as George Ripley's *Discourses on the Philosophy of Religion*, William Henry Furness's *Remarks on the Four Gospels,* and Convers Francis's *Christianity as a Purely Internal Principle*. For these writers as a group, religious concerns predominate. All six authors except Alcott began professional life as Unitarian ministers, Furness and Francis remaining so lifelong. But the issues they broach range widely from spirituality to epistemology to education to social reform to poetics. Emerson's *Nature* touches on the full range. After two introductory chapters, Emerson moves through an inventory of nature's multiple "uses": as raw material, as source and definer of beauty, as a language or vocabulary, as an arena of moral and mental education. These chapters in turn become a platform for the more far-reaching philosophical claim that physical nature is a mystic counterpart of human nature that offers both a mirror of humankind's untapped potential and the means for individual and social redemption. This led some to quip that *Nature* should have been titled *Man* instead, and in fact it explicitly invokes a seventeenth-century metaphysical poem of that title by George Herbert. But more than any of the movement's other early defining works, *Nature* makes the Romanticist case for nature as a source of inspiration and authority superior to the weight of historical precedent and human institutions, churchly or otherwise. Henry Thoreau drew heavily on Emerson's theory of the "correspondence" between the realms of nature and spirit even as he took Emerson's poetic-philosophical view of nature in a more empirical, proto-environmentalist direction. *Nature* is also obviously the manifesto of a "poetic" thinker. Despite its show of carefully outlining an agenda of topics with subparts, it set the tone for Emerson's mature style of discontinuous, strongly metaphorical, "inspired" expression. As such, it also set the tone for the movement's insiders and critics alike to associate Transcendentalism with the realms of art and rhapsodics.

The source text used here is *Nature*'s first edition (Boston: James Munroe, 1836), the one in circulation during the movement's formative years. When Emerson revised *Nature* for republication in 1849, he made numerous small-scale but, in a few cases, significant changes. The most important, in keeping with the overall drift of his thought and of the century in which he lived, was the replacement of the opening motto from the Neoplatonist philosopher Plotinus with a short poem of his own composition that defined nature in proto-evolutionary terms, not as the soul's servant but as an active, shaping force behind the creation of all life forms, including humankind.

"Nature is but an image or imitation of wisdom, the last
thing of the soul; nature being a thing which doth only do,
but not know."

PLOTINUS.

## INTRODUCTION

OUR age is retrospective. It builds the sepulchres of the fathers. It
writes biographies, histories, and criticism. The foregoing generations
beheld God and nature face to face; we, through their eyes. Why
should not we also enjoy an original relation to the universe? Why
should not we have a poetry and philosophy of insight and not of tradition, and a religion by revelation to us, and not the history of theirs?
Embosomed for a season in nature, whose floods of life stream around
and through us, and invite us by the powers they supply, to action proportioned to nature, why should we grope among the dry bones of the
past, or put the living generation into masquerade out of its faded
wardrobe? The sun shines to-day also. There is more wool and flax in
the fields. There are new lands, new men, new thoughts. Let us demand our own works and laws and worship.

Undoubtedly we have no questions to ask which are unanswerable.
We must trust the perfection of the creation so far, as to believe that
whatever curiosity the order of things has awakened in our minds, the
order of things can satisfy. Every man's condition is a solution in hieroglyphic to those inquiries he would put. He acts it as life, before he
apprehends it as truth. In like manner, nature is already, in its forms
and tendencies, describing its own design. Let us interrogate the great
apparition, that shines so peacefully around us. Let us inquire, to what
end is nature?

All science has one aim, namely, to find a theory of nature. We have
theories of races and of functions, but scarcely yet a remote approxi-
mation to an idea of creation. We are now so far from the road to truth,
that religious teachers dispute and hate each other, and speculative
men are esteemed unsound and frivolous. But to a sound judgment,
the most abstract truth is the most practical. Whenever a true theory

appears, it will be its own evidence. Its test is, that it will explain all phenomena. Now many are thought not only unexplained but inexplicable; as language, sleep, dreams, beasts, sex.

Philosophically considered, the universe is composed of Nature and the Soul. Strictly speaking, therefore, all that is separate from us, all which Philosophy distinguishes as the NOT ME, that is, both nature and art, all other men and my own body, must be ranked under this name, NATURE. In enumerating the values of nature and casting up their sum, I shall use the word in both senses;—in its common and in its philosophical import. In inquiries so general as our present one, the inaccuracy is not material; no confusion of thought will occur. *Nature*, in the common sense, refers to essences unchanged by man; space, the air, the river, the leaf. *Art* is applied to the mixture of his will with the same things, as in a house, a canal, a statue, a picture. But his operations taken together are so insignificant, a little chipping, baking, patching, and washing, that in an impression so grand as that of the world on the human mind, they do not vary the result.

# CHAPTER I

To go into solitude, a man needs to retire as much from his chamber as from society. I am not solitary whilst I read and write, though nobody is with me. But if a man would be alone, let him look at the stars. The rays that come from those heavenly worlds, will separate between him and vulgar things. One might think the atmosphere was made transparent with this design, to give man, in the heavenly bodies, the perpetual presence of the sublime. Seen in the streets of cities, how great they are! If the stars should appear one night in a thousand years, how would men believe and adore, and preserve for many generations the remembrance of the city of God which had been shown! But every night come out these preachers of beauty, and light the universe with their admonishing smile.

The stars awaken a certain reverence, because though always present, they are always inaccessible; but all natural objects make a kindred impression, when the mind is open to their influence. Nature never wears a mean appearance. Neither does the wisest man extort all her secret, and lose his curiosity by finding out all her perfection. Nature never became a toy to a wise spirit. The flowers, the animals, the mountains, reflected all the wisdom of his best hour, as much as they had delighted the simplicity of his childhood.

When we speak of nature in this manner, we have a distinct but most poetical sense in the mind. We mean the integrity of impression made by manifold natural objects. It is this which distinguishes the stick of timber of the wood-cutter, from the tree of the poet. The charming landscape which I saw this morning, is indubitably made up of some twenty or thirty farms. Miller owns this field, Locke that, and Manning the woodland beyond. But none of them owns the landscape. There is a property in the horizon which no man has but he whose eye can integrate all the parts, that is, the poet. This is the best part of these men's farms, yet to this their land-deeds give them no title.

To speak truly, few adult persons can see nature. Most persons do not see the sun. At least they have a very superficial seeing. The sun illuminates only the eye of the man, but shines into the eye and the heart of the child. The lover of nature is he whose inward and outward senses are still truly adjusted to each other; who has retained the spirit of infancy even into the era of manhood. His intercourse with heaven and earth, becomes part of his daily food. In the presence of nature, a wild delight runs through the man, in spite of real sorrows. Nature says,—he is my creature, and maugre all his impertinent griefs, he shall be glad with me. Not the sun or the summer alone, but every hour and season yields its tribute of delight; for every hour and change corresponds to and authorizes a different state of the mind, from breathless noon to grimmest midnight. Nature is a setting that fits equally well a comic or a mourning piece. In good health, the air is a cordial of incredible virtue. Crossing a bare common, in snow puddles, at twilight, under a clouded sky, without having in my thoughts any occurrence of special good fortune, I have enjoyed a perfect exhilaration. Almost I fear to think how glad I am. In the woods too, a man casts off his years, as the snake his slough, and at what period soever of life, is always a child. In the woods, is perpetual youth. Within these plantations of God, a decorum and sanctity reign, a perennial festival is dressed, and the guest sees not how he should tire of them in a thousand years. In the woods, we return to reason and faith. There I feel that nothing can befal me in life,—no disgrace, no calamity, (leaving me my eyes), which nature cannot repair. Standing on the bare ground,—my head bathed by the blithe air, and uplifted into infinite space,—all mean egotism vanishes. I become a transparent eye-ball. I am nothing. I see all. The currents of the Universal Being circulate through me; I am part or particle of God. The name of the nearest friend sounds then foreign and accidental. To be brothers, to be acquaintances,—master or servant, is then a trifle and a disturbance. I am the lover of uncontained and immortal beauty. In the wilderness I find something more dear and connate than in streets or villages. In the tranquil landscape, and especially in the distant line of the horizon, man beholds somewhat as beautiful as his own nature.

The greatest delight which the fields and woods minister, is the suggestion of an occult relation between man and the vegetable. I am not alone and unacknowledged. They nod to me and I to them. The waving of the boughs in the storm, is new to me and old. It takes me by surprise, and yet is not unknown. Its effect is like that of a higher thought or a better emotion coming over me, when I deemed I was thinking justly or doing right.

Yet it is certain that the power to produce this delight, does not reside in nature, but in man, or in a harmony of both. It is necessary to use these pleasures with great temperance. For, nature is not always tricked in holiday attire, but the same scene which yesterday breathed perfume and glittered as for the frolic of the nymphs, is overspread with melancholy today. Nature always wears the colors of the spirit. To a man laboring under calamity, the heat of his own fire hath sadness in it. Then, there is a kind of contempt of the landscape felt by him who has just lost by death a dear friend. The sky is less grand as it shuts down over less worth in the population.

## CHAPTER II
### COMMODITY

WHOEVER considers the final cause of the world, will discern a multitude of uses that enter as parts into that result. They all admit of being thrown into one of the following classes: Commodity; Beauty; Language; and Discipline.

Under the general name of Commodity, I rank all those advantages which our senses owe to nature. This, of course, is a benefit which is temporary and mediate, not ultimate, like its service to the soul. Yet although low, it is perfect in its kind, and is the only use of nature which all men apprehend. The misery of man appears like childish petulance, when we explore the steady and prodigal provision that has been made for his support and delight on this green ball which floats him through the heavens. What angels invented these splendid ornaments, these rich conveniences, this ocean of air above, this ocean of water beneath, this firmament of earth between? this zodiac of lights, this tent of dropping clouds, this striped coat of climates, this fourfold year? Beasts, fire, water, stones, and corn serve him. The field is at once his floor, his work-yard, his play-ground, his garden, and his bed.

> "More servants wait on man
> Than he'll take notice of."——

Nature, in its ministry to man, is not only the material, but is also the process and the result. All the parts incessantly work into each other's hands for the profit of man. The wind sows the seed; the sun evaporates the sea; the wind blows the vapor to the field; the ice, on the other side of the planet, condenses rain on this; the rain feeds the plant; the plant feeds the animal; and thus the endless circulations of the divine charity nourish man.

The useful arts are but reproductions or new combinations by the wit of man, of the same natural benefactors. He no longer waits for favoring gales, but by means of steam, he realizes the fable of Æolus's bag, and carries the two and thirty winds in the boiler of his boat. To diminish friction, he paves the road with iron bars, and, mounting a coach with a ship-load of men, animals, and merchandise behind him, he darts through the country, from town to town, like an eagle or a swallow through the air. By the aggregate of these aids, how is the face of the world changed, from the era of Noah to that of Napoleon! The private poor man hath cities, ships, canals, bridges, built for him. He goes to the post-office, and the human race run on his errands; to the book-shop, and the human race read and write of all that happens, for him; to the court-house, and nations repair his wrongs. He sets his house upon the road, and the human race go forth every morning, and shovel out the snow, and cut a path for him.

But there is no need of specifying particulars in this class of uses. The catalogue is endless, and the examples so obvious, that I shall leave them to the reader's reflection, with the general remark, that this mercenary benefit is one which has respect to a farther good. A man is fed, not that he may be fed, but that he may work.

## CHAPTER III

### BEAUTY

A NOBLER want of man is served by nature, namely, the love of Beauty.

The ancient Greeks called the world κοσμος, beauty. Such is the constitution of all things, or such the plastic power of the human eye, that the primary forms, as the sky, the mountain, the tree, the animal, give us a delight *in and for themselves;* a pleasure arising from outline, color, motion, and grouping. This seems partly owing to the eye itself. The eye is the best of artists. By the mutual action of its structure and of the laws of light, perspective is produced, which integrates every mass of objects, of what character soever, into a well colored and shaded globe, so that where the particular objects are mean and unaffecting, the landscape which they compose, is round and symmetrical. And as the eye is the best composer, so light is the first of painters. There is no object so foul that intense light will not make beautiful. And the stimulus it affords to the sense, and a sort of infinitude which it hath, like space and time, make all matter gay. Even the corpse hath its own beauty. But beside this general grace diffused over nature, almost all the individual forms are agreeable to the eye, as is proved by our endless imitations of some of them, as the acorn, the grape, the pine-cone, the wheat-ear, the egg, the wings and forms of most birds, the lion's claw, the serpent, the butterfly, sea-shells, flames, clouds, buds, leaves, and the forms of many trees, as the palm.

For better consideration, we may distribute the aspects of Beauty in a threefold manner.

1. First, the simple perception of natural forms is a delight. The influence of the forms and actions in nature, is so needful to man, that, in its lowest functions, it seems to lie on the confines of commodity and beauty. To the body and mind which have been cramped by noxious work or company, nature is medicinal and restores their tone. The tradesman, the attorney comes out of the din and craft of the street, and sees the sky and the woods, and is a man again. In their eternal calm, he finds himself. The health of the eye seems to demand a horizon. We are never tired, so long as we can see far enough.

But in other hours, Nature satisfies the soul purely by its loveliness, and without any mixture of corporeal benefit. I have seen the spectacle of morning from the hilltop over against my house, from day-break to sun-rise, with emotions which an angel might share. The long slender bars of cloud float like fishes in the sea of crimson light. From the earth, as a shore, I look out into that silent sea. I seem to partake its rapid transformations: the active enchantment reaches my dust, and I dilate and conspire with the morning wind. How does Nature deify us with a few and cheap elements! Give me health and a day, and I will make the pomp of emperors ridiculous. The dawn is my Assyria; the sun-set and moon-rise my Paphos, and unimaginable realms of faerie; broad noon shall be my England of the senses and the understanding; the night shall be my Germany of mystic philosophy and dreams.

Not less excellent, except for our less susceptibility in the after-noon, was the charm, last evening, of a January sunset. The western clouds divided and subdivided themselves into pink flakes modulated with tints of unspeakable softness; and the air had so much life and sweetness, that it was a pain to come within doors. What was it that nature would say? Was there no meaning in the live repose of the val-ley behind the mill, and which Homer or Shakspeare could not re-form for me in words? The leafless trees become spires of flame in the sunset, with the blue east for their background, and the stars of the dead calices of flowers, and every withered stem and stubble rimed with frost, contribute something to the mute music.

The inhabitants of cities suppose that the country landscape is pleasant only half the year. I please myself with observing the graces of the winter scenery, and believe that we are as much touched by it as by the genial influences of summer. To the attentive eye, each moment of the year has its own beauty, and in the same field, it beholds, every hour, a picture which was never seen before, and which shall never be seen again. The heavens change every moment, and reflect their glory or gloom on the plains beneath. The state of the crop in the surround-ing farms alters the expression of the earth from week to week. The succession of native plants in the pastures and roadsides, which make the silent clock by which time tells the summer hours, will make even the divisions of the day sensible to a keen observer. The tribes of birds and insects, like the plants punctual to their time, follow each other, and the year has room for all. By water-courses, the variety is greater. In July, the blue pontederia or pickerel-weed blooms in large beds in the shallow parts of our pleasant river, and swarms with yellow butter-flies in continual motion. Art cannot rival this pomp of purple and gold. Indeed the river is a perpetual gala, and boasts each month a new ornament.

But this beauty of Nature which is seen and felt as beauty, is the least part. The shows of day, the dewy morning, the rainbow, mountains, orchards in blossom, stars, moonlight, shadows in still water, and the like, if too eagerly hunted, become shows merely, and mock us with their unreality. Go out of the house to see the moon, and 't is mere tinsel; it will not please as when its light shines upon your necessary journey. The beauty that shimmers in the yellow afternoons of October, who ever could clutch it? Go forth to find it, and it is gone: 't is only a mirage as you look from windows of diligence.

2. The presence of a higher, namely, of the spiritual element is essential to its perfection. The high and divine beauty which can be loved without effeminacy, is that which is found in combination with the human will, and never separate. Beauty is the mark God sets upon virtue. Every natural action is graceful. Every heroic act is also decent, and causes the place and the bystanders to shine. We are taught by great actions that the universe is the property of every individual in it. Every rational creature has all nature for his dowry and estate. It is his, if he will. He may divest himself of it; he may creep into a corner, and abdicate his kingdom, as most men do, but he is entitled to the world by his constitution. In proportion to the energy of his thought and will, he takes up the world into himself. "All those things for which men plough, build, or sail, obey virtue," said an ancient historian. "The winds and waves," said Gibbon, "are always on the side of the ablest navigators." So are the sun and moon and all the stars of heaven. When a noble act is done—perchance in a scene of great natural beauty; when Leonidas and his three hundred martyrs consume one day in dying, and the sun and moon come each and look at them once in the steep defile of Thermopylæ; when Arnold Winkelried, in the high Alps, under the shadow of the avalanche, gathers in his side a sheaf of Austrian spears to break the line for his comrades; are not these heroes entitled to add the beauty of the scene to the beauty of the deed? When the bark of Columbus nears the shore of America;—before it, the beach lined with savages, fleeing out of all their huts of cane; the sea behind; and the purple mountains of the Indian Archipelago around, can we separate the man from the living picture? Does not the New World clothe his form with her palm-groves and savannahs as fit drapery? Ever does natural beauty steal in like air, and envelope great actions. When Sir Harry Vane was dragged up the Tower-hill, sitting on a sled, to suffer death, as the champion of the English laws, one of the multitude cried out to him, "You never sate on so glorious a seat." Charles II., to intimidate the citizens of London, caused the patriot

Lord Russel to be drawn in an open coach, through the principal streets of the city, on his way to the scaffold. "But," to use the simple narrative of his biographer, "the multitude imagined they saw liberty and virtue sitting by his side." In private places, among sordid objects, an act of truth or heroism seems at once to draw to itself the sky as its temple, the sun as its candle. Nature stretcheth out her arms to embrace man, only let his thoughts be of equal greatness. Willingly does she follow his steps with the rose and the violet, and end her lines of grandeur and grace to the decoration of her darling child. Only let his thoughts be of equal scope, and the frame will suit the picture. A virtuous man is in unison with her works, and makes the central figure of the visible sphere. Homer, Pindar, Socrates, Phocion, associate themselves fitly in our memory with the whole geography and climate of Greece. The visible heavens and earth sympathize with Jesus. And in common life, whosoever has seen a person of powerful character and happy genius, will have remarked how easily he took all things along with him,—the persons, the opinions, and the day, and nature became ancillary to a man.

3. There is still another aspect under which the beauty of the world may be viewed, namely, as it becomes an object of the intellect. Beside the relation of things to virtue, they have a relation to thought. The intellect searches out the absolute order of things as they stand in the mind of God, and without the colors of affection. The intellectual and the active powers seem to succeed each other in man, and the exclusive activity of the one, generates the exclusive activity of the other. There is something unfriendly in each to the other, but they are like the alternate periods of feeding and working in animals; each prepares and certainly will be followed by the other. Therefore does beauty, which, in relation to actions, as we have seen, comes unsought, and comes because it is unsought, remain for the apprehension and pursuit of the intellect; and then again, in its turn, of the active power. Nothing divine dies. All good is eternally reproductive. The beauty of nature reforms itself in the mind, and not for barren contemplation, but for new creation.

All men are in some degree impressed by the face of the world. Some men even to delight. This love of beauty is Taste. Others have the same love in such excess, that, not content with admiring, they seek to embody it in new forms. The creation of beauty is Art.

The production of a work of art throws a light upon the mystery of humanity. A work of art is an abstract or epitome of the world. It is the result or expression of nature, in miniature. For although the works of nature are innumerable and all different, the result or the expression of them all is similar and single. Nature is a sea of forms radically alike and even unique. A leaf, a sun-beam, a landscape, the ocean, make an analogous impression on the mind. What is common to them all,—that perfectness and harmony, is beauty. Therefore the standard of beauty is the entire circuit of natural forms,—the totality of nature; which the Italians expressed by defining beauty "il piu nell' uno." Nothing is quite beautiful alone: nothing but is beautiful in the whole. A single object is only so far beautiful as it suggests this universal grace. The poet, the painter, the sculptor, the musician, the architect, seek each to concentrate this radiance of the world on one point, and each in his several work to satisfy the love of beauty which stimulates him to produce. Thus is Art, a nature passed through the alembic of man. Thus in art, does nature work through the will of a man filled with the beauty of her first works.

The world thus exists to the soul to satisfy the desire of beauty. Extend this element to the uttermost, and I call it an ultimate end. No reason can be asked or given why the soul seeks beauty. Beauty, in its largest and profoundest sense, is one expression for the universe. God is the all-fair. Truth, and goodness, and beauty, are but different faces of the same All. But beauty in nature is not ultimate. It is the herald of inward and eternal beauty, and is not alone a solid and satisfactory good. It must therefore stand as a part and not as yet the last or highest expression of the final cause of Nature.

## CHAPTER IV
### LANGUAGE

A THIRD use which Nature subserves to man is that of Language. Nature is the vehicle of thought, and in a simple, double, and threefold degree.

1. Words are signs of natural facts.
2. Particular natural facts are symbols of particular spiritual facts.
3. Nature is the symbol of spirit.

1. Words are signs of natural facts. The use of natural history is to give us aid in supernatural history. The use of the outer creation is to give us language for the beings and changes of the inward creation. Every word which is used to express a moral or intellectual fact, if

traced to its root, is found to be borrowed from some material appearance. *Right* originally means *straight; wrong* means *twisted. Spirit* primarily means *wind; transgression,* the crossing of a *line; supercilious,* the *raising of the eye-brow.* We say the *heart* to express emotion, the *head* to denote thought; and *thought* and *emotion* are, in their turn, words borrowed from sensible things, and now appropriated to spiritual nature. Most of the process by which this transformation is made, is hidden from us in the remote time when language was framed; but the same tendency may be daily observed in children. Children and savages use only nouns or names of things, which they continually convert into verbs, and apply to analogous mental acts.

2. But this origin of all words that convey a spiritual import,—so conspicuous a fact in the history of language,—is our least debt to nature. It is not words only that are emblematic; it is things which are emblematic. Every natural fact is a symbol of spiritual fact. Every appearance in nature corresponds to some state of the mind, and that state of the mind can only be described by presenting that natural appearance as its picture. An enraged man is a lion, a cunning man is a fox, a firm man is a rock, a learned man is a torch. A lamb is innocence; a snake is subtle spite; flowers express to us the delicate affections. Light and darkness are our familiar expression for knowledge and ignorance; and heat for love. Visible distance behind and before us, is respectively our image of memory and hope.

Who looks upon a river in a meditative hour, and is not reminded of the flux of all things? Throw a stone into the stream, and the circles that propagate themselves are the beautiful type of all influence. Man is conscious of a universal soul within or behind his individual life, wherein, as in a firmament, the natures of Justice, Truth, Love, Freedom, arise and shine. This universal soul, he calls Reason: it is not mine or thine or his, but we are its; we are its property and men. And the blue sky in which the private earth is buried, the sky with its eternal calm, and full of everlasting orbs, is the type of Reason. That which, intellectually considered, we call Reason, considered in relation to nature, we call Spirit. Spirit is the Creator. Spirit hath life in itself. And man in all ages and countries, embodies it in his language, as the FATHER.

It is easily seen that there is nothing lucky or capricious in these analogies, but that they are constant, and pervade nature. These are not the dreams of a few poets, here and there, but man is an analogist, and studies relations in all objects. He is placed in the centre of beings, and a ray of relation passes from every other being to him. And neither can man be understood without these objects, nor these objects without man. All the facts in natural history taken by themselves, have no value, but are barren like a single sex. But marry it to human history, and it is full of life. Whole Floras, all Linnæus' and Buffon's volumes, are but dry catalogues of facts; but the most trivial of these facts, the habit of a plant, the organs, or work, or noise of an insect, applied to the illustration of a fact in intellectual philosophy, or, in any way associated to human nature, affects us in the most lively and agreeable manner. The seed of a plant,—to what affecting analogies in the nature of man, is that little fruit made use of, in all discourse, up to the voice of Paul, who calls the human corpse a seed,—"It is sown a natural body; it is raised a spiritual body." The motion of the earth round its axis, and round the sun, makes the day, and the year. These are certain amounts of brute light and heat. But is there no intent of an analogy between man's life and the seasons? And do the seasons gain no grandeur or pathos from that analogy? The instincts of the ant are very unimportant considered as the ant's; but the moment a ray of relation is seen to extend from it to man, and the little drudge is seen to be a monitor, a little body with a mighty heart, then all its habits, even that said to be recently observed, that it never sleeps, become sublime.

Because of this radical correspondence between visible things and human thoughts, savages, who have only what is necessary, converse in figures. As we go back in history, language becomes more picturesque, until its infancy, when it is all poetry; or, all spiritual facts are represented by natural symbols. The same symbols are found to make the original elements of all languages. It has moreover been observed, that the idioms of all languages approach each other in passages of the greatest eloquence and power. And as this is the first language, so is it the last. This immediate dependence of language upon nature, this conversion of an outward phenomenon into a type of somewhat in human life, never loses its power to affect us. It is this which gives that piquancy to the conversation of a strong-natured farmer or backwoodsman, which all men relish.

Thus is nature an interpreter, by whose means man converses with his fellow men. A man's power to connect his thought with its proper symbol, and so utter it, depends on the simplicity of his character, that is, upon his love of truth and his desire to communicate it without loss. The corruption of man is followed by the corruption of language.

When simplicity of character and the sovereignty of ideas is broken up by the prevalence of secondary desires, the desire of riches, the desire of pleasure, the desire of power, the desire of praise,—and duplicity and falsehood take place of simplicity and truth, the power over nature as an interpreter of the will, is in a degree lost; new imagery ceases to be created, and old words are perverted to stand for things which are not; a paper currency is employed when there is no bullion in the vaults. In due time, the fraud is manifest, and words lose all power to stimulate the understanding or the affections. Hundreds of writers may be found in every long-civilized nation, who for a short time believe, and make others believe, that they see and utter truths, who do not of themselves clothe one thought in its natural garment, but who feed unconsciously upon the language created by the primary writers of the country, those, namely, who hold primarily on nature.

But wise men pierce this rotten diction and fasten words again to visible thing; so that picturesque language is at once a commanding certificate that he who employs it, is a man in alliance with truth and God. The moment our discourse rises above the ground line of familiar facts, and is inflamed with passion or exalted by thought, it clothes itself in images. A man conversing in earnest, if he watch his intellectual processes, will find that always a material image, more or less luminous, arises in his mind, cotemporaneous with every thought, which furnishes the vestment of the thought. Hence, good writing and brilliant discourse are perpetual allegories. This imagery is spontaneous. It is the blending of experience with the present action of the mind. It is proper creation. It is the working of the Original Cause through instruments he has already made.

These facts may suggest the advantage which the country-life possesses for a powerful mind, over the artificial and curtailed life of cities. We know more from nature than we can at will communicate. Its light flows into the mind evermore, and we forget its presence. The poet, the orator, bred in the woods, whose senses have been nourished by their fair and appeasing changes, year after year, without design and without heed,—shall not lose their lesson altogether, in the roar of cities or the broil of politics. Long hereafter, amidst agitation and terror in national councils,—in the hour of revolution,—these solemn images shall reappear in their morning lustre, as fit symbols and words of the thoughts which the passing events shall awaken. At the call of a noble sentiment, again the woods wave, the pines murmur, the river rolls and shines, and the cattle low upon the mountains, as he saw and heard them in his infancy. And with these forms, the spells of persuasion, the keys of power are put into his hands.

3. We are thus assisted by natural objects in the expression of particular meanings. But how great a language to convey such pepper-corn informations! Did it need such noble races of creatures, this profusion of forms, this host of orbs in heaven, to furnish man with the dictionary and grammar of his municipal speech? Whilst we use this grand cipher to expedite the affairs of our pot and kettle, we feel that we have not yet put it to its use, neither are able. We are like travellers using the cinders of a volcano to roast their eggs. Whilst we see that it always stands ready to clothe what we would say, we cannot avoid the question, whether the characters are not significant of themselves. Have mountains, and waves, and skies, no significance but what we consciously give them, when we employ them as emblems of our thoughts? The world is emblematic. Parts of speech are metaphors because the whole of nature is a metaphor of the human mind. The laws of moral nature answer to those of matter as face to face in a glass. "The visible world and the relation of its parts, is the dial plate of the invisible." The axioms of physics translate the laws of ethics. Thus, "the whole is greater than its part;" "reaction is equal to action;" "the smallest weight may be made to lift the greatest, the difference of weight being compensated by time;" and many the like propositions, which have an ethical as well as physical sense. These propositions have a much more extensive and universal sense when applied to human life, than when confined to technical use.

In like manner, the memorable words of history, and the proverbs of nations, consist usually of a natural fact, selected as a picture or parable of a moral truth. Thus; A rolling stone gathers no moss; A bird in the hand is worth two in the bush; A cripple in the right way, will beat a racer in the wrong; Make hay whilst the sun shines; 'T is hard to carry a full cup even; Vinegar is the son of wine; The last ounce broke the camel's back; Long-lived trees make roots first;—and the like. In their primary sense these are trivial facts, but we repeat them for the value of their analogical import. What is true of proverbs, is true of all fables, parables, and allegories.

This relation between the mind and matter is not fancied by some poet, but stands in the will of God, and so is free to be known by all men. It appears to men, or it does not appear. When in fortunate hours we ponder this miracle, the wise man doubts, if, at all other times, he is not blind and deaf;

> ——"Can these things be,
> And overcome us like a summer's cloud,
> Without our special wonder?"

for the universe becomes transparent, and the light of higher laws than its own, shines through it. It is the standing problem which has exercised the wonder and the study of every fine genius since the world began; from the era of the Egyptians and the Brahmins, to that of Pythagoras, of Plato, of Bacon, of Leibnitz, of Swedenborg. There sits the Sphinx at the road-side, and from age to age, as each prophet comes by, he tries his fortune at reading her riddle. There seems to be a necessity in spirit to manifest itself in material forms; and day and night, river and storm, beast and bird, acid and alkali, preëxist in necessary Ideas in the mind of God, and are what they are by virtue of preceding affections, in the world of spirit. A Fact is the end or last issue of spirit. The visible creation is the terminus or the circumference of the invisible world. "Material objects," said a French philosopher, "are necessarily kinds of *scoriæ* of the substantial thoughts of the Creator, which must always preserve an exact relation to their first origin; in other words, visible nature must have a spiritual and moral side."

This doctrine is abstruse, and though the images of "garment," "scoriæ," "mirror," &c., may stimulate the fancy, we must summon the aid of subtler and more vital expositors to make it plain. "Every scripture is to be interpreted by the same spirit which gave it forth,"—is the fundamental law of criticism. A life in harmony with nature, the love of truth and of virtue, will purge the eyes to understand her text. By degrees we may come to know the primitive sense of the permanent objects of nature, so that the world shall be to us an open book, and every form significant of its hidden life and final cause.

A new interest surprises us, whilst, under the view now suggested, we contemplate the fearful extent and multitude of objects; since "every object rightly seen, unlocks a new faculty of the soul." That which was unconscious truth, becomes, when interpreted and defined in an object, a part of the domain of knowledge,—a new amount to the magazine of power.

# CHAPTER V
## DISCIPLINE

IN view of this significance of nature, we arrive at once at a new fact, that nature is a discipline. This use of the world includes the preceding uses, as parts of itself.

Space, time, society, labor, climate, food, locomotion, the animals, the mechanical forces, give us sincerest lessons, day by day, whose meaning is unlimited. They educate both the Understanding and the Reason. Every property of matter is a school for the understanding,— its solidity or resistance, its inertia, its extension, its figure, its divisibility. The understanding adds, divides, combines, measures, and finds everlasting nutriment and room for its activity in this worthy scene. Meantime, Reason transfers all these lessons into its own world of thought, by perceiving the analogy that marries Matter and Mind.

1. Nature is a discipline of the understanding in intellectual truths. Our dealing with sensible objects is a constant exercise in the necessary lessons of difference, of likeness, of order, of being and seeming, of progressive arrangement; of ascent from particular to general; of combination to one end of manifold forces. Proportioned to the importance of the organ to be formed, is the extreme care with which its tuition is provided,—a care pretermitted in no single case. What tedious training, day after day, year after year, never ending, to form the common sense; what continual reproduction of annoyances, inconveniences, dilemmas; what rejoicing over us of little men; what disputing of prices, what reckonings of interest,—and all to form the Hand of the mind;—to instruct us that "good thoughts are no better than good dreams, unless they be executed!"

The same good office is performed by Property and its filial systems of debt and credit. Debt, grinding debt, whose iron face the widow, the orphan, and the sons of genius fear and hate;—debt, which consumes so much time, which so cripples and disheartens a great spirit with cares that seem so base, is a preceptor whose lessons cannot be foregone, and is needed most by those who suffer from it most. Moreover, property, which has been well compared to snow,—"if it fall level to-day, it will be blown into drifts to-morrow,"—is merely the surface action of internal machinery, like the index on the face of a clock. Whilst now it is the gymnastics of the understanding, it is hiving in the foresight of the spirit, experience in profounder laws.

The whole character and fortune of the individual are affected by the least inequalities in the culture of the understanding; for example, in the perception of differences. Therefore is Space, and therefore Time, that man may know that things are not huddled and lumped, but sundered and individual. A bell and a plough have each their use, and neither can do the office of the other. Water is good to drink, coal to burn, wool to wear; but wool cannot be drunk, nor water spun, nor coal eaten. The wise man shows his wisdom in separation, in gradation, and his scale of creatures and of merits, is as wide as nature. The foolish have no range in their scale, but suppose every man is as every other man. What is not good they call the worst, and what is not hateful, they call the best.

In like manner, what good heed, nature forms in us! She pardons no mistakes. Her yea is yea, and her nay, nay.

The first steps in Agriculture, Astronomy, Zoölogy, (those first steps which the farmer, the hunter, and the sailor take,) teach that nature's dice are always loaded; that in her heaps and rubbish are concealed sure and useful results.

How calmly and genially the mind apprehends one after another the laws of physics! What noble emotions dilate the mortal as he enters into the counsels of the creation, and feels by knowledge the privilege to BE! His insight refines him. The beauty of nature shines in his own breast. Man is greater that he can see this, and the universe less, because Time and Space relations vanish as laws are known.

Here again we are impressed and even daunted by the immense Universe to be explored. "What we know, is a point to what we do not know." Open any recent journal of science, and weigh the problems suggested concerning Light, Heat, Electricity, Magnetism, Physiology, Geology, and judge whether the interest of natural science is likely to be soon exhausted.

Passing by many particulars of the discipline of nature we must not omit to specify two.

The exercise of the Will or the lesson of power is taught in every event. From the child's successive possession of his several senses up to the hour when he saith, "thy will be done!" he is learning the secret, that he can reduce under his will, not only particular events, but great classes, nay the whole series of events, and so conform all facts to his character. Nature is thoroughly mediate. It is made to serve. It receives the dominion of man as meekly as the ass on which the Saviour rode. It offers all its kingdoms to man as the raw material which he may mould into what is useful. Man is never weary of working it up. He forges the subtile and delicate air into wise and melodious words, and gives them wing as angels of persuasion and command. More and more, with every thought, does his kingdom stretch over things, until the world becomes, at last, only a realized will,—the double of the man.

2. Sensible objects conform to the premonitions of Reason and reflect the conscience. All things are moral; and in their boundless changes have an unceasing reference to spiritual nature. Therefore is nature glorious with form, color, and motion, that every globe in the remotest heaven; every chemical change from the rudest crystal up to the laws of life; every change of vegetation from the first principle of growth in the eye of a leaf, to the tropical forest and antediluvian coal-mine; every animal function from the sponge up to Hercules, shall hint or thunder to man the laws of right and wrong, and echo the Ten Commandments. Therefore is nature always the ally of Religion: lends all her pomp and riches to the religious sentiment. Prophet and priest, David, Isaiah, Jesus, have drawn deeply from this source.

This ethical character so penetrates the bone and marrow of nature, as to seem the end for which it was made. Whatever private purpose is answered by any member or part, this is its public and universal function, and is never omitted. Nothing in nature is exhausted in its first use. When a thing has served an end to the uttermost, it is wholly new for an ulterior service. In God, every end is converted into a new means. Thus the use of Commodity, regarded by itself, is mean and squalid. But it is to the mind an education in the great doctrine of Use, namely, that a thing is good only so far as it serves; that a conspiring of parts and efforts to the production of an end, is essential to any being. The first and gross manifestation of this truth, is our inevitable and hated training in values and wants, in corn and meat.

It has already been illustrated, in treating of the significance of material things, that every natural process is but a version of a moral sentence. The moral law lies at the centre of nature and radiates to the circumference. It is the pith and marrow of every substance, every relation, and every process. All things with which we deal, preach to us. What is a farm but a mute gospel! The chaff and the wheat, weeds and plants, blight, rain, insects, sun,—it is a sacred emblem from the first furrow of spring to the last stack which the snow of winter overtakes in the fields. But the sailor, the shepherd, the miner, the merchant, in their several resorts, have each an experience precisely parallel and leading to the same conclusions. Because all organizations are radically alike. Nor can it be doubted that this moral sentiment which thus scents the air, and grows in the grain, and impregnates the waters of the world, is caught by man and sinks into his soul. The moral influence of nature upon every individual is that amount of truth which it illustrates to him. Who can estimate this? Who can guess how much firmness the sea-beaten rock has taught the fisherman? how much tranquillity has been reflected to man from the azure sky, over whose unspotted deeps the winds forevermore drive flocks of stormy clouds, and leave no wrinkle or stain? how much industry and providence and affection we have caught from the pantomime of brutes? What a searching preacher of self-command is the varying phenomenon of Health!

Herein is especially apprehended the Unity of Nature,—the Unity in Variety,—which meets us everywhere. All the endless variety of things make a unique, an identical impression. Xenophanes complained in his old age, that, look where he would, all things hastened back to Unity. He was weary of seeing the same entity in the tedious variety of forms. The fable of Proteus has a cordial truth. Every particular in nature, a leaf, a drop, a crystal, a moment of time is related to the whole, and partakes of the perfection of the whole. Each particle is a microcosm, and faithfully renders the likeness of the world.

Not only resemblances exist in things whose analogy is obvious, as when we detect the type of the human hand in the flipper of the fossil saurus, but also in objects wherein there is great superficial unlikeness. Thus architecture is called "frozen music," by De Stael and Goethe. "A Gothic church," said Coleridge, "is a petrified religion." Michael Angelo maintained, that, to an architect, a knowledge of anatomy is essential. In Haydn's oratorios, the notes present to the imagination not only motions, as, of the snake, the stag, and the elephant, but colors also; as the green grass. The granite is differenced in its laws only by the more or less of heat, from the river that wears it away. The river, as it flows, resembles the air that flows over it; the air resembles the light which traverses it with more subtle currents; the light resembles the heat which rides with it through Space. Each creature is only a modification of the other; the likeness in them is more than the difference, and their radical law is one and the same. Hence it is, that a rule of one art, or a law of one organization, holds true throughout nature. So intimate is this Unity, that, it is easily seen, it lies under the undermost garment of nature, and betrays its source in universal Spirit. For, it pervades Thought also. Every universal truth which we express in words, implies or supposes every other truth. *Omne verum vero consonat.* It is like a great circle on a sphere, comprising all possible circles; which, however, may be drawn, and comprise it, in like manner. Every such truth is the absolute Ens seen from one side. But it has innumerable sides.

The same central Unity is still more conspicuous in actions. Words are finite organs of the infinite mind. They cannot cover the dimensions of what is in truth. They break, chop, and impoverish it. An action is the perfection and publication of thought. A right action seems to fill the eye, and to be related to all nature. "The wise man, in doing one thing, does all; or, in the one thing he does rightly, he sees the likeness of all which is done rightly."

Words and actions are not the attributes of mute and brute nature. They introduce us to that singular form which predominates over all other forms. This is the human. All other organizations appear to be degradations of the human form. When this organization appears among so many that surround it, the spirit prefers it to all others. It says, "From such as this, have I drawn joy and knowledge. In such as this, have I found and beheld myself. I will speak to it. It can speak again. It can yield me thought already formed and alive." In fact, the eye,—the mind,—is always accompanied by these forms, male and female; and these are incomparably the richest informations of the power and order that lie at the heart of things. Unfortunately, every one of them bears the marks as of some injury; is marred and superficially defective. Nevertheless, far different from the deaf and dumb nature around them, these all rest like fountain-pipes on the unfathomed sea of thought and virtue whereto they alone, of all organizations, are the entrances.

It were a pleasant inquiry to follow into detail their ministry to our education, but where would it stop? We are associated in adolescent and adult life with some friends, who, like skies and waters, are coextensive with our idea; who, answering each to a certain affection of the soul, satisfy our desire on that side; whom we lack power to put at such focal distance from us, that we can mend or even analyze them. We cannot chuse but love them. When much intercourse with a friend has supplied us with a standard of excellence, and has increased our respect for the resources of God who thus sends a real person to outgo our ideal; when he has, moreover, become an object of thought, and, whilst his character retains all its unconscious effect, is converted in the mind into solid and sweet wisdom,—it is a sign to us that his office is closing, and he is commonly withdrawn from our sight in a short time.

## CHAPTER VI
### IDEALISM

THUS is the unspeakable but intelligible and practicable meaning of the world conveyed to man, the immortal pupil, in every object of sense. To this one end of Discipline, all parts of nature conspire.

A noble doubt perpetually suggests itself, whether this end be not the Final Cause of the Universe; and whether nature outwardly exists. It is a sufficient account of that Appearance we call the World, that God will teach a human mind, and so makes it the receiver of a certain number of congruent sensations, which we call sun and moon, man and woman, house and trade. In my utter impotence to test the authenticity of the report of my senses, to know whether the impressions they make on me correspond with outlying objects, what difference does it make, whether Orion is up there in heaven, or some god paints the image in the firmament of the soul? The relations of parts and the end of the whole remaining the same, what is the difference, whether land and sea interact, and worlds revolve and intermingle without number or end,—deep yawning under deep, and galaxy balancing galaxy, throughout absolute space, or, whether, without relations of time and space, the same appearances are inscribed in the constant faith of man. Whether nature enjoy a substantial existence without, or is only in the apocalypse of the mind, it is alike useful and alike venerable to me. Be it what it may, it is ideal to me, so long as I cannot try the accuracy of my senses.

The frivolous make themselves merry with the Ideal theory, as if its consequences were burlesque; as if it affected the stability of nature. It surely does not. God never jests with us, and will not compromise the end of nature, by permitting any inconsequence in its procession. Any distrust of the permanence of laws, would paralyze the faculties of man. Their permanence is sacredly respected, and his faith therein is perfect. The wheels and springs of man are all set to the hypothesis of the permanence of nature. We are not built like a ship to be tossed, but like a house to stand. It is a natural consequence of this structure, that, so long as the active powers predominate over the reflective, we resist with indignation any hint that nature is more short-lived or mutable than spirit. The broker, the wheelwright, the carpenter, the tollman, are much displeased at the intimation.

But whilst we acquiesce entirely in the permanence of natural laws, the question of the absolute existence of nature, still remains open. It is the uniform effect of culture on the human mind, not to shake our faith in the stability of particular phenomena, as of heat, water, azote; but to lead us to regard nature as a phenomenon, not a substance; to attribute necessary existence to spirit; to esteem nature as an accident and an effect.

To the senses and the unrenewed understanding, belongs a sort of instinctive belief in the absolute existence of nature. In their view, man and nature are indissolubly joined. Things are ultimates, and they never look beyond their sphere. The presence of Reason mars this faith. The first effort of thought tends to relax this despotism of the senses, which binds us to nature as if we were a part of it, and shows us nature aloof, and, as it were, afloat. Until this higher agency inter-vened, the animal eye sees, with wonderful accuracy, sharp outlines and colored surfaces. When the eye of Reason opens, to outline and surface are at once added, grace and expression. These proceed from imagination and affection, and abate somewhat of the angular distinct-ness of objects. If the Reason be stimulated to more earnest vision, out-lines and surfaces become transparent, and are no longer seen; causes and spirits are seen through them. The best, the happiest moments of life, are these delicious awakenings of the higher powers, and the rev-erential withdrawing of nature before its God.

Let us proceed to indicate the effects of culture. 1. Our first institu-tion in the Ideal philosophy is a hint from nature herself.

Nature is made to conspire with spirit to emancipate us. Certain mechanical changes, a small alteration in our local position apprizes us of a dualism. We are strangely affected by seeing the shore from a moving ship, from a balloon, or through the tints of an unusual sky. The least change in our point of view, gives the whole world a pictorial air. A man who seldom rides, needs only to get into a coach and tra-verse his own town, to turn the street into a puppet-show. The men, the women,—talking, running, bartering, fighting,—the earnest mechanic, the lounger, the beggar, the boys, the dogs, are unrealized at once, or, at least, wholly detached from all relation to the observer, and seen as apparent, not substantial beings. What new thoughts are suggested by seeing a face of country quite familiar, in the rapid movement of the rail-road car! Nay, the most wonted objects, (make a very slight change in the point of vision,) please us most. In a camera obscura, the butcher's cart, and the figure of one of our own family amuse us. So a portrait of a well-known face gratifies us. Turn the eyes upside down, by looking at the landscape through your legs, and how agreeable is the picture, though you have seen it any time these twenty years!

In these cases, by mechanical means, is suggested the difference between the observer and the spectacle,—between man and nature. Hence arises a pleasure mixed with awe; I may say, a low degree of the sublime is felt from the fact, probably, that man is hereby apprized, that, whilst the world is a spectacle, something in himself is stable.

2. In a higher manner, the poet communicates the same pleasure. By a few strokes he delineates, as on air, the sun, the mountain, the camp, the city, the hero, the maiden, not different from what we know them, but only lifted from the ground and afloat before the eye. He unfixes the land and the sea, makes them revolve around the axis of his primary thought, and disposes them anew. Possessed himself by a heroic passion, he uses matter as symbols of it. The sensual man conforms thoughts to things; the poet conforms things to his thoughts. The one esteems nature as rooted and fast; the other, as fluid, and impresses his being thereon. To him, the refractory world is ductile and flexible; he invests dust and stones with humanity, and makes them the words of the Reason. The imagination may be defined to be, the use which the Reason makes of the material world. Shakspeare possesses the power of subordinating nature for the purposes of expression, beyond all poets. His imperial muse tosses the creation like a bauble from hand to hand, to embody any capricious shade of thought that is uppermost in his mind. The remotest spaces of nature are visited, and the farthest sundered things are brought together, by a subtile spiritual connexion. We are made aware that magnitude of material things is merely relative, and all objects shrink and expand to serve the passion of the poet. Thus, in his sonnets, the lays of birds, the scents and dyes of flowers, he finds to be the *shadow* of his beloved; time, which keeps her from him, is his *chest;* the suspicion she has awakened, is her *ornament;*

The ornament of beauty is Suspect,
A crow which flies in heaven's sweetest air.

His passion is not the fruit of chance; it swells, as he speaks, to a city, or a state.

No, it was builded far from accident;
It suffers not in smiling pomp, nor falls
Under the brow of thralling discontent;
It fears not policy, that heretic,
That works on leases of short numbered hours,
But all alone stands hugely politic.

In the strength of his constancy, the Pyramids seem to him recent and transitory. And the freshness of youth and love dazzles him with its resemblance to morning.

Take those lips away
Which so sweetly were forsworn;
And those eyes,—the break of day,
Lights that do mislead the morn.

The wild beauty of this hyperbole, I may say, in passing, it would not be easy to match in literature.

This transfiguration which all material objects undergo through the passion of the poet,—this power which he exerts, at any moment, to magnify the small, to micrify the great,—might be illustrated by a thousand examples from his Plays. I have before me the Tempest, and will cite only these few lines.

ARIEL. The strong based promontory
Have I made shake, and by the spurs plucked up
The pine and cedar.

Prospero calls for music to sooth the frantic Alonzo, and his companions;

A solemn air, and the best comforter
To an unsettled fancy, cure thy brains
Now useless, boiled within thy skull.

Again;

> The charm dissolves apace
> And, as the morning steals upon the night,
> Melting the darkness, so their rising senses
> Begin to chase the ignorant fumes that mantle
> Their clearer reason.
> Their understanding
> Begins to swell: and the approaching tide
> Will shortly fill the reasonable shores
> That now lie foul and muddy.

The perception of real affinities between events, (that is to say, of *ideal* affinities, for those only are real,) enables the poet thus to make free with the most imposing forms and phenomena of the world, and to assert the predominance of the soul.

3. Whilst thus the poet delights us by animating nature like a creator, with his own thoughts, he differs from the philosopher only herein, that the one proposes Beauty as his main end; the other Truth. But, the philosopher, not less than the poet, postpones the apparent order and relations of things to the empire of thought. "The problem of philosophy," according to Plato, "is, for all that exists conditionally, to find a ground unconditioned and absolute." It proceeds on the faith that a law determines all phenomena, which being known, the phenomena can be predicted. That law, when in the mind, is an idea. Its beauty is infinite. The true philosopher and the true poet are one, and a beauty, which is truth, and a truth, which is beauty, is the aim of both. Is not the charm of one of Plato's or Aristotle's definitions, strictly like that of the Antigone of Sophocles? It is, in both cases, that a spiritual life has been imparted to nature; that the solid seeming block of matter has been pervaded and dissolved by a thought; that this feeble human being has penetrated the vast masses of nature with an informing soul, and recognised itself in their harmony, that is, seized their law. In physics, when this is attained, the memory disburthens itself of its cumbrous catalogues of particulars, and carries centuries of observation in a single formula.

Thus even in physics, the material is ever degraded before the spiritual. The astronomer, the geometer, rely on their irrefragable analysis, and disdain the results of observation. The sublime remark of Euler on his law of arches, "This will be found contrary to all experience, yet is true;" had already transferred nature into the mind, and left matter like an outcast corpse.

4. Intellectual science has been observed to beget invariably a doubt of the existence of matter. Turgot said, "He that has never doubted the existence of matter, may be assured he has no aptitude for metaphysical inquiries." It fastens the attention upon immortal necessary uncreated natures, that is, upon Ideas; and in their beautiful and majestic presence, we feel that our outward being is a dream and a shade. Whilst we wait in this Olympus of gods, we think of nature as an appendix to the soul. We ascend into their region, and know that these are the thoughts of the Supreme Being. "These are they who were set up from everlasting, from the beginning, or ever the earth was. When he prepared the heavens, they were there; when he established the clouds above, when he strengthened the fountains of the deep. Then they were by him, as one brought up with him. Of them took he counsel."

Their influence is proportionate. As objects of science, they are accessible to few men. Yet all men are capable of being raised by piety or by passion, into their region. And no man touches these divine natures, without becoming, in some degree, himself divine. Like a new soul, they renew the body. We become physically nimble and lightsome; we tread on air; life is no longer irksome, and we think it will never be so. No man fears age or misfortune or death, in their serene company, for he is transported out of the district of change. Whilst we behold unveiled the nature of Justice and Truth, we learn the difference between the absolute and the conditional or relative. We apprehend the absolute. As it were, for the first time, *we exist*. We become immortal, for we learn that time and space are relations of matter; that, with a perception of truth, or a virtuous will, they have no affinity.

5. Finally, religion and ethics, which may be fitly called,—the practice of ideas, or the introduction of ideas into life,—have an analogous effect with all lower culture, in degrading nature and suggesting its dependence on spirit. Ethics and religion differ herein; that the one is the system of human duties commencing from man; the other, from God. Religion includes the personality of God; Ethics does not. They are one to our present design. They both put nature under foot. The first and last lesson of religion is, "The things that are seen, are temporal; the things that are unseen are eternal." It puts an affront upon nature. It does that for the unschooled, which philosophy does for Berkeley

and Viasa. The uniform language that may be heard in the churches of the most ignorant sects, is,—"Contemn the unsubstantial shows of the world; they are vanities, dreams, shadows, unrealities; seek the realities of religion." The devotee flouts nature. Some theosophists have arrived at a certain hostility and indignation towards matter, as the Manichean and Plotinus. They distrusted in themselves any looking back to these flesh-pots of Egypt. Plotinus was ashamed of his body. In short, they might all better say of matter, what Michael Angelo said of external beauty, "it is the frail and weary weed, in which God dresses the soul, which he has called into time."

It appears that motion, poetry, physical and intellectual science, and religion, all tend to affect our convictions of the reality of the external world. But I own there is something ungrateful in expanding too curiously the particulars of the general proposition, that all culture tends to imbue us with idealism. I have no hostility to nature, but a child's love to it. I expand and live in the warm day like corn and melons. Let us speak her fair. I do not wish to fling stones at my beautiful mother, nor soil my gentle nest. I only wish to indicate the true position of nature in regard to man, wherein to establish man, all right education tends; as the ground which to attain is the object of human life, that is, of man's connexion with nature. Culture inverts the vulgar views of nature, and brings the mind to call that apparent, which it uses to call real, and that real, which it uses to call visionary. Children, it is true, believe in the external world. The belief that it appears only, is an afterthought, but with culture, this faith will as surely arise on the mind as did the first.

The advantage of the ideal theory over the popular faith, is this, that it presents the world in precisely that view which is most desirable to the mind. It is, in fact, the view which Reason, both speculative and practical, that is, philosophy and virtue, take. For, seen in the light of thought, the world always is phenomenal; and virtue subordinates it to the mind. Idealism sees the world in God. It beholds the whole circle of persons and things, of actions and events, of country and religion, not as painfully accumulated, atom after atom, act after act, in an aged creeping Past, but as one vast picture, which God paints on the instant eternity, for the contemplation of the soul. Therefore the soul holds itself off from a too trivial and microscopic study of the universal tablet. It respects the end too much, to immerse itself in the means. It sees something more important in Christianity, than the scandals of ecclesiastical history or the niceties of criticism; and, very incurious concerning persons or miracles, and not at all disturbed by chasms of historical evidence, it accepts from God the phenomenon, as it finds it, as the pure and awful form of religion in the world. It is not hot and passionate at the appearance of what it calls its own good or bad fortune, at the union or opposition of other persons. No man is its enemy. It accepts whatsoever befals, as part of its lesson. It is a watcher more than a doer, and it is a doer, only that it may the better watch.

## CHAPTER VII
### SPIRIT

IT is essential to a true theory of nature and of man, that it should contain somewhat progressive. Uses that are exhausted or that may be, and facts that end in the statement, cannot be all that is true of this brave lodging wherein man is harbored, and wherein all his faculties find appropriate and endless exercise. And all the uses of nature admit of being summed in one, which yields the activity of man an infinite scope. Through all its kingdoms, to the suburbs and outskirts of things, it is faithful to the cause whence it had its origin. It always speaks of Spirit. It suggests the absolute. It is a perpetual effect. It is a great shadow pointing always to the sun behind us.

The aspect of nature is devout. Like the figure of Jesus, she stands with bended head, and hands folded upon the breast. The happiest man is he who learns from nature the lesson of worship.

Of that ineffable essence which we call Spirit, he that thinks most, will say least. We can foresee God in the coarse and, as it were, distant phenomena of matter; but when we try to define and describe himself, both language and thought desert us, and we are as helpless as fools and savages. That essence refuses to be recorded in propositions, but when man has worshipped him intellectually, the noblest ministry of nature is to stand as the apparition of God. It is the great organ through which the universal spirit speaks to the individual, and strives to lead back the individual to it.

When we consider Spirit, we see that the views already presented do not include the whole circumference of man. We must add some related thoughts.

Three problems are put by nature to the mind; What is matter? Whence is it? and Whereto? The first of these questions only, the ideal theory answers. Idealism saith: matter is a phenomenon, not a substance. Idealism acquaints us with the total disparity between the evidence of our own being, and the evidence of the world's being. The one is perfect; the other, incapable of any assurance; the mind is a part of the nature of things; the world is a divine dream, from which we may presently awake to the glories and certainties of day. Idealism is a hypothesis to account for nature by other principles than those of carpentry and chemistry. Yet, if it only deny the existence of matter, it does not satisfy the demands of the spirit. It leaves God out of me. It leaves me in the splendid labyrinth of my perceptions, to wander without end. Then the heart resists it, because it baulks the affections in denying substantive being to men and women. Nature is so pervaded with human life, that there is something of humanity in all, and in every particular. But this theory makes nature foreign to me, and does not account for that consanguinity which we acknowledge to it.

Let it stand then, in the present state of our knowledge, merely as a useful introductory hypothesis, serving to apprize us of the eternal distinction between the soul and the world.

But when, following the invisible steps of thought, we come to inquire, Whence is matter? and Whereto? many truths arise to us out of the recesses of consciousness. We learn that the highest is present to the soul of man, that the dread universal essence, which is not wisdom, or love, or beauty, or power, but all in one, and each entirely, is that for which all things exist, and that by which they are; that spirit creates; that behind nature, throughout nature, spirit is present; that spirit is one and not compound; that spirit does not act upon us from without, that is, in space and time, but spiritually, or through ourselves. Therefore, that spirit, that is, the Supreme Being, does not build up nature around us, but puts it forth through us, as the life of the tree puts forth new branches and leaves through the pores of the old. As a plant upon the earth, so a man rests upon the bosom of God; he is nourished by unfailing fountains, and draws, at his need, inexhaustible power. Who can set bounds to the possibilities of man? Once inspire the infinite, by being admitted to behold the absolute natures of justice and truth, and we learn that man has access to the entire mind of the Creator, is himself the creator in the finite. This view, which admonishes me where the sources of wisdom and power lie, and points to virtue as to

> "The golden key
> Which opes the palace of eternity,"

carries upon its face the highest certificate of truth, because it animates me to create my own world through the purification of my soul.

The world proceeds from the same spirit as the body of man. It is a remoter and inferior incarnation of God, a projection of God in the unconscious. But it differs from the body in one important respect. It is not, like that, now subjected to the human will. Its serene order is inviolable by us. It is therefore, to us, the present expositor of the divine mind. It is a fixed point whereby we may measure our departure. As we degenerate, the contrast between us and our house is more evident. We are as much strangers in nature, as we are aliens from God. We do not understand the notes of birds. The fox and the deer run away from us; the bear and tiger rend us. We do not know the uses of more than a few plants, as corn and the apple, the potato and the vine. Is not the landscape, every glimpse of which hath a grandeur, a face of him? Yet this may show us what discord is between man and nature, for you cannot freely admire a noble landscape, if laborers are digging in the field hard by. The poet finds something ridiculous in his delight, until he is out of the sight of men.

## CHAPTER VIII
### PROSPECTS

IN inquiries respecting the laws of the world and the frame of things, the highest reason is always the truest. That which seems faintly possible—it is so refined, is often faint and dim because it is deepest seated in the mind among the eternal verities. Empirical science is apt to cloud the sight, and, by the very knowledge of functions and processes, to bereave the student of the manly contemplation of the whole. The savant becomes unpoetic. But the best read naturalist who lends an entire and devout attention to truth, will see that there remains much to learn of his relation to the world, and that it is not to be learned by any addition or subtraction or other comparison of known quantities, but is arrived at by untaught sallies of the spirit, by a continual self-recovery, and by entire humility. He will perceive that there are far more excellent qualities in the student than preciseness and infallibility; that a guess is often more fruitful than an indisputable affirmation, and that a dream may let us deeper into the secret of nature than a hundred concerted experiments.

For, the problems to be solved are precisely those which the physiologist and the naturalist omit to state. It is not so pertinent to man to know all the individuals of the animal kingdom, as it is to know whence and whereto is this tyrannizing unity in his constitution, which evermore separates and classifies things, endeavouring to reduce the most diverse to one form. When I behold a rich landscape, it is less to my purpose to recite correctly the order and superposition of the strata, than to know why all thought of multitude is lost in a tranquil sense of unity. I cannot greatly honor minuteness in details, so long as there is no hint to explain the relation between things and thoughts; no ray upon the *metaphysics* of conchology, of botany, of the arts, to show the relation of the forms of flowers, shells, animals, architecture, to the mind, and build science upon ideas. In a cabinet of natural history, we become sensible of a certain occult recognition and sympathy in regard to the most bizarre forms of beast, fish, and insect. The American who has been confined, in his own country, to the sight of buildings designed after foreign models, is surprised on entering York Minster or St. Peter's at Rome, by the feeling that these structures are imitations also,—faint copies of an invisible archetype. Nor has science sufficient humanity, so long as the naturalist overlooks that wonderful congruity which subsists between man and the world; of which he is lord, not because he is the most subtile inhabitant, but because he is its head and heart, and finds something of himself in every great and small thing, in every mountain stratum, in every new law of color, fact of astronomy, or atmospheric influence which observation or analysis lays open. A perception of this mystery inspires the muse of George Herbert, the beautiful psalmist of the seventeenth century. The following lines are part of his little poem on Man.

> "Man is all symmetry,
> Full of proportions, one limb to another,
> And to all the world besides.
> Each part may call the farthest, brother;
> For head with foot hath private amity,
> And both with moons and tides.
>
> "Nothing hath got so far
> But man hath caught and kept it as his prey;
> His eyes dismount the highest star;
> He is in little all the sphere.
> Herbs gladly cure our flesh, because that they
> Find their acquaintance there.

"For us, the winds do blow,
The earth doth rest, heaven move, and fountains flow;
Nothing we see, but means our good,
As our delight, or as our treasure;
The whole is either our cupboard of food,
Or cabinet of pleasure.

"The stars have us to bed:
Night draws the curtain; which the sun withdraws.
Music and light attend our head.
All things unto our flesh are kind,
In their descent and being; to our mind,
In their ascent and cause.

"More servants wait on man
Than he'll take notice of. In every path,
He treads down that which doth befriend him
When sickness makes him pale and wan.
Oh mighty love! Man is one world, and hath
Another to attend him."

The perception of this class of truths makes the eternal attraction which draws men to science, but the end is lost sight of in attention to the means. In view of this half-sight of science, we accept the sentence of Plato, that, "poetry comes nearer to vital truth than history." Every surmise and vaticination of the mind is entitled to a certain respect, and we learn to prefer imperfect theories, and sentences, which contain glimpses of truth, to digested systems which have no one valuable suggestion. A wise writer will feel that the ends of study and composition are best answered by announcing undiscovered regions of thought, and so communicating, through hope, new activity to the torpid spirit.

I shall therefore conclude this essay with some traditions of man and nature, which a certain poet sang to me; and which, as they have always been in the world, and perhaps reappear to every bard, may be both history and prophecy.

"The foundations of man are not in matter, but in spirit. But the element of spirit is eternity. To it, therefore, the longest series of events, the oldest chronologies are young and recent. In the cycle of the universal man, from whom the known individuals proceed, centuries are points, and all history is but the epoch of one degradation.

"We distrust and deny inwardly our sympathy with nature. We own and disown our relation to it, by turns. We are, like Nebuchadnezzar, dethroned, bereft of reason, and eating grass like an ox. But who can set limits to the remedial force of spirit?

"A man is a god in ruins. When men are innocent, life shall be longer, and shall pass into the immortal, as gently as we awake from dreams. Now, the world would be insane and rabid, if these disorganizations should last for hundreds of years. It is kept in check by death and infancy. Infancy is the perpetual Messiah, which comes into the arms of fallen men, and pleads with them to return to paradise.

"Man is the dwarf of himself. Once he was permeated and dissolved by spirit. He filled nature with his overflowing currents. Out from him sprang the sun and moon; from man, the sun; from woman, the moon. The laws of his mind, the periods of his actions externized themselves into day and night, into the year and the seasons. But, having made for himself this huge shell, his waters retired; he no longer fills the veins and veinlets; he is shrunk to a drop. He sees, that the structure still fits him, but fits him colossally. Say, rather, once it fitted him, now it corresponds to him from far and on high. He adores timidly his own work. Now is man the follower of the sun, and woman the follower of the moon. Yet sometimes he starts in his slumber, and wonders at himself and his house, and muses strangely at the resemblance betwixt him and it. He perceives that if his law is still paramount, if still he have elemental power, 'if his word is sterling yet in nature,' it is not conscious power, it is not inferior but superior to his will. It is Instinct." Thus my Orphic poet sang.

At present, man applies to nature but half his force. He works on the world with his understanding alone. He lives in it, and masters it by a penny-wisdom; and he that works most in it, is but a half-man, and whilst his arms are strong and his digestion good, his mind is imbruted and he is a selfish savage. His relation to nature, his power over it, is through the understanding; as by manure; the economic use of fire, wind, water, and the mariner's needle; steam, coal, chemical agriculture; the repairs of the human body by the dentist and the surgeon. This is such a resumption of power, as if a banished king should buy his territories inch by inch, instead of vaulting at once into his throne. Meantime, in the thick darkness, there are not wanting gleams of a better light,—occasional examples of the action of man upon nature with his entire force,—with reason as well as understanding. Such examples are; the traditions of miracles in the earliest antiquity of all nations; the history of Jesus Christ; the achievement of a principle, as in religious and political revolutions, and in the abolition of the Slave-trade; the miracles of enthusiasm, as those reported of Swedenborg, Hohenlohe, and the Shakers; many obscure and yet contested facts, now arranged under the name of Animal Magnetism; prayer; eloquence; self-healing; and the wisdom of children. These are examples of Reason's momentary grasp of the sceptre; the exertions of a power which exists not in time or space, but an instantaneous instreaming causing power. The difference between the actual and the ideal force of man is happily figured by the schoolmen, in saying, that the knowledge of man is an evening knowledge, *vespertina cognitio,* but that of God is a morning knowledge, *matutina cognitio.*

The problem of restoring to the world original and eternal beauty, is solved by the redemption of the soul. The ruin or the blank, that we see when we look at nature, is in our own eye. The axis of vision is not coincident with the axis of things, and so they appear not transparent but opake. The reason why the world lacks unity, and lies broken and in heaps, is, because man is disunited with himself. He cannot be a naturalist, until he satisfies all the demands of the spirit. Love is as much its demand, as perception. Indeed, neither can be perfect without the other. In the uttermost meaning of the words, thought is devout, and devotion is thought. Deep calls unto deep. But in actual life, the marriage is not celebrated. There are innocent men who worship God after the tradition of their fathers, but their sense of duty has not yet extended to the use of all their faculties. And there are patient naturalists, but they freeze their subject under the wintry light of understanding. Is not prayer also a study of truth,—a sally of the soul into the unfound infinite? No man ever prayed heartily, without learning something. But when a faithful thinker, resolute to detach every object from personal relations, and see it in the light of thought, shall, at the same time, kindle science with the fire of the holiest affections, then will God go forth anew into the creation.

It will not need, when the mind is prepared for study, to search for objects. The invariable mark of wisdom is to see the miraculous in the common. What is a day? What is a year? What is summer? What is woman? What is a child? What is sleep? To our blindness, these things seem unaffecting. We make fables to hide the baldness of the fact and conform it, as we say, to the higher law of the mind. But when the fact is seen under the light of an idea, the gaudy fable fades and shrivels. We behold the real higher law. To the wise, therefore, a fact is true poetry, and the most beautiful of fables. These wonders are brought to our own door. You also are a man. Man and woman, and their social life, poverty, labor, sleep, fear, fortune, are known to you. Learn that none of these things is superficial, but that each phenomenon hath its roots in the faculties and affections of the mind. Whilst the abstract question occupies your intellect, nature brings it in the concrete to be solved by your hands. It were a wise inquiry for the closet, to compare, point by point, especially at remarkable crises in life, our daily history, with the rise and progress of ideas in the mind.

So shall we come to look at the world with new eyes. It shall answer the endless inquiry of the intellect,—What is truth? and of the affections,—What is good? by yielding itself passive to the educated Will. Then shall come to pass what my poet said; "Nature is not fixed but fluid. Spirit alters, moulds, makes it. The immobility or bruteness of nature, is the absence of spirit; to pure spirit, it is fluid, it is volatile, it is obedient. Every spirit builds itself a house; and beyond its house, a world; and beyond its world, a heaven. Know then, that the world exists for you. For you is the phenomenon perfect. What we are, that only can we see. All that Adam had, all that Cæsar could, you have and can do. Adam called his house, heaven and earth; Cæsar called his house, Rome; you perhaps call yours, a cobler's trade; a hundred acres of ploughed land; or a scholar's garret. Yet line for line and point for point, your dominion is as great as theirs, though without fine names. Build, therefore, your own world. As fast as you conform your life to the pure idea in your mind, that will unfold its great proportions. A correspondent revolution in things will attend the influx of the spirit. So fast will disagreeable appearances, swine, spiders, snakes, pests, mad-houses, prisons, enemies, vanish; they are temporary and shall be no more seen. The sordor and filths of nature, the sun shall dry up, and the wind exhale. As when the summer comes from the south, the snow-banks melt, and the face of the earth becomes green before it, so shall the advancing spirit create its ornaments along its path, and carry with it the beauty it visits, and the song which enchants it; it shall draw beautiful faces, and warm hearts, and wise discourse, and heroic acts, around its way, until evil is no more seen. The kingdom of man over nature, which cometh not with observation,—a dominion such as now is beyond his dream of God,—he shall enter without more wonder than the blind man feels who is gradually restored to perfect sight."

# Amos Bronson Alcott

## from *The Doctrine and Discipline of Human Culture*

### (1836)

One of the few leading Transcendentalists of humble social origins, Amos Bronson Alcott (1799–1888) was a grandly utopian thinker with a special interest in educational reform. For Nathaniel Hawthorne and others at or beyond the movement's edges, Alcott became a byword for Transcendentalism's silly abstruseness (see his "Orphic Sayings," Section V-B) and for lack of common sense. "Emerson is a seer. Alcott is a seer-sucker," snorted another Concord neighbor. Even Emerson, his closest intellectual companion, grumbled that Alcott was "a tedious archangel" and chided him for impracticality and for wooden prose. Yet Alcott also seemed to Emerson and other sympathetic associates a kind of homespun Plato, whose speculative bent energized even when it ran to extremes.

Prone to monologue, Alcott was also at best a memorable conversationalist and, what is more, a philosopher of conversation ahead of his time in holding that the key to education lay not in drill but in interactive dialogue. As the following selection shows, Alcott took with utmost seriousness the Wordsworthian idea that young children are especially close to the Divine, and the model of conversational instruction that he thought he saw in the life and teachings of Jesus. Although the attempt to put these principles into practice in elementary education failed spectacularly (Section IV-B), Alcott was prophetic in holding that the essence of "human culture" (i.e., education) is "mind leaping to meet mind" and "not of force acting on opposing force."

The echoes here with Emerson's *Nature* show the start of their lifelong symbiosis.

SOURCE: *The Doctrine and Discipline of Human Culture.* Boston: James Munroe, 1836.

## IDEA OF MAN

Man is the noblest of the Creator's works. He is the most richly gifted of all his creatures. His sphere of action is the broadest; his influence the widest; and to him is given Nature and Life for his heritage and his possession. He holds dominion over the Outward. He is the rightful Sovereign of the Earth, fitted to subdue all things to himself, and to know of no superior, save God. And yet he enters upon the scene of his labors, a feeble and wailing Babe, at first unconscious of the place assigned him, and needs years of tutelage and discipline to fit him for the high and austere duties that await him.

## IDEA OF EDUCATION

The Art, which fits such a being to fulfil his high destiny, is the first and noblest of arts. Human Culture is the art of revealing to a man the true Idea of his Being—his endowments—his possessions—and of fitting him to use these for the growth, renewal, and perfection of his Spirit. It is the art of completing a man. It includes all those influences, and disciplines, by which his faculties are unfolded and perfected. It is that agency which takes the helpless and pleading Infant from the hands of its Creator; and, apprehending its entire nature, tempts it forth—now by austere, and now by kindly influences and disciplines—and thus moulds it at last into the Image of a Perfect Man; armed at all points, to use the Body, Nature, and Life, for its growth and renewal, and to hold dominion over the fluctuating things of the Outward. It seeks to realize in the Soul the Image of the Creator.—Its end is a perfect man. Its aim, through every stage of influence and discipline, is self-renewal. The body, nature, and life are its instruments and materials. Jesus is its worthiest Ideal. Christianity its purest Organ. The Gospels its fullest Text-Book. Genius its Inspiration. Holiness its Law. Temperance its Discipline. Immortality its Reward.

## HISTORY AND TYPE OF THIS IDEA

This divine Art, including all others, or subordinating them to its Idea, was never apprehended, in all its breadth and depth of significance, till the era of Jesus of Nazareth. He it was that first revealed it. Over his Divine Intellect first flitted the Idea of man's endowments and destiny. He set no limits to the growth of our nature. "Be Ye Perfect even as my Father in Heaven is Perfect," was the high aim which he placed before his disciples; and in this he was true to our nature, for the sentiment lives in every faculty and function of our being. It is the ever-sounding Trump of Duty, urging us to the perpetual work of self-renewal. It is the deep instinct of the spirit. And his Life gives us the promise of its realization. In his attributes and endowments he is a Type of our common nature. His achievements are a glimpse of the Apotheosis of Humanity. They are a glorious unfolding of the Godlike in man. They disclose the Idea of Spirit. And if he was not, in himself, the complete fulfilment of Spirit, he apprehended its law, and set forth its conditions. He bequeathed to us the phenomena of its manifestation; for in the Gospels we have the history of Spirit accomplishing its mission on the earth. We behold the Incarnate One, dealing with flesh and blood—tempted, and suffering—yet baffling and overcoming the ministries of Evil and of Pain.

## IDEA AND TYPE MISAPPREHENDED

Still this Idea, so clearly announced, and so fully demonstrated in the being and life of Jesus, has made but little advance in the minds of men. Men have not subdued it to themselves. It has not become the ground and law of human consciousness. They have not married their nature to it by a living Faith. Nearly two millenniums have elapsed since its announcement, and yet, so slow of apprehension have been the successors of this Divine Genius, that even at this day, the deep and universal significance of his Idea has not been fully taken in. It has been restricted to himself alone. He stands in the minds of this generation, as a Phenomenon, which God, in the inscrutable designs of his Providence, saw fit to present, to the gaze and wonder of mankind, yet as a being of unsettled rank in the universe, whom men may venture to imitate, but dare not approach. In him, the Human Nature is feebly apprehended, while the Divine is lifted out of sight, and lost in the ineffable light of the Godhead. Men do not deem him as the harmonious unfolding of Spirit into the Image of a Perfect Man—as a worthy Symbol of the Divinity, wherein Human Nature is revealed in its Fulness. Yet, as if by an inward and irresistible Instinct, all men have been drawn to him; and, while diverse in their opinions; explaining his Idea in different types, they have given him the full and unreserved homage of their hearts. They have gathered around the altars, inscribed with his perfections, and, through his name, delighted to address the God and Father of Spirits. Disowning him in their minds, unable to grasp his Idea, they have deified him in their hearts. They have worshipped the Holiness which they could not define.

## ERA OF ITS REVIVAL

It is the mission of this Age, to revive his Idea, give it currency, and reinstate it in the faith of men. By its quickening agency, it is to fructify our common nature, and reproduce its like. It is to unfold our being into the same divine likeness. It is to reproduce Perfect Men. The faded Image of Humanity is to be restored, and man reappear in his original brightness. It is to mould anew our Institutions, our Manners, our Men. It is to restore Nature to its rightful use; purify Life; hallow the functions of the Human Body, and regenerate Philosophy, Literature, Art, Society. The Divine Idea of a Man is to be formed in the common consciousness of this age, and genius mould all its products in accordance with it.

## MEANS OF ITS REVIVAL

The means for reinstating this Idea in the common mind, in order to conduce to these results, are many. Yet all are simple. And the most direct and effectual are by apprehending the Genius of this Divine Man, from the study of those Records wherein his career is delineated with so much fidelity, simplicity, and truth. Therein have we a manifestation of Spirit, while undergoing the temptations of this corporeal life; yet faithful to the laws of its renovation and its end. The Divine Idea of Humanity gleams forth through every circumstance of his terrestrial career. The fearful agencies of the Spirit assert their power. In him Nature and Life are subordinated to the spiritual force. The Son of God appears on Earth, enrobed in Flesh, and looks forth serenely upon Man. We feel the significance of the Incarnation; the grandeur of our nature. We associate Jesus with our holiest aspirations, our deepest affections; and thus does he become a fit Mediator between the last age and the new era, of which he was the herald and the pledge. He is to us the Prophet of two millenniums. He is the brightest Symbol of a Man that history affords, and points us to yet fuller manifestations of the Godhead.

## IDEAL OF A TEACHER

And the Gospels are not only a fit Text-Book for the study of Spirit, in its corporeal relations, but they are a specimen also of the true method of imparting instruction. They give us the practice of Jesus himself. They unfold the means of addressing human nature. Jesus was a Teacher; he sought to renovate Humanity. His method commends itself to us. It is a beautiful exhibition of his Genius, bearing the stamp of naturalness, force, and directness. It is popular. Instead of seeking formal and austere means, he rested his influence chiefly on the living word, rising spontaneously in the soul, and clothing itself at once, in the simplest, yet most commanding forms. He was a finished extemporaneous speaker. His manner and style are models. In these, his Ideas became like the beautiful, yet majestic Nature, whose images he wove so skilfully into his diction. He was an Artist of the highest order. More perfect specimens of address do not elsewhere exist. View him in his conversation with his disciples. Hear him in his simple colloquies with the people. Listen to him when seated at the well-side discoursing with the Samaritan woman, on the IDEA OF WORSHIP; and at night with Nicodemus, on SPIRITUAL RENEWAL. From facts and objects the most familiar, he slid easily and simply into the highest and holiest themes, and, in this unimposing guise, disclosed the great Doctrines, and stated the Divine Ideas, that it was his mission to bequeath to his race. Conversation was the form of utterance that he sought. Of formal discourse but one specimen is given, in his Sermon on the Mount; yet in this the inspiration bursts all forms, and he rises to the highest efforts of genius, at its close.

## ORGAN OF INSTRUCTION

This preference of Jesus for Conversation, as the fittest organ of utterance, is a striking proof of his comprehensive Idea of Education. He knew what was in man, and the means of perfecting his being. He saw the superiority of this exercise over others for quickening the Spirit. For, in this all the instincts and faculties of our being are touched. They find full and fair scope. It tempts forth all the powers. Man faces his fellow man. He holds a living intercourse. He feels the quickening life and light. The social affections are addressed; and these bring all the faculties in train. Speech comes unbidden. Nature lends her images. Imagination sends abroad her winged words. We see thought as it springs from the soul, and in the very process of growth and utterance. Reason plays under the mellow light of fancy. The Genius of the Soul is waked, and eloquence sits on her tuneful lip. Wisdom finds an organ worthy her serene, yet imposing products. Ideas stand in beauty and majesty before the Soul.

## SELF-APPREHENSION

Man's mission is to subdue Nature; to hold dominion over his own Body; and use both these, and the ministries of Life, for the growth, renewal, and perfection of his Being. As did Jesus, he must overcome the World, by passing through its temptations, and vanquishing the Tempter. But before he shall attain this mastery he must apprehend himself. In his Nature is wrapt up the problem of all Power reduced to a simple unity. The knowledge of his own being includes, in its endless circuit, the Alphabet of all else. It is a Universe, wherein all else is imaged. God—Nature—are the extremes, of which he is the middle term, and through his Being flow these mighty Forces, if, perchance, he shall stay them as they pass over his Consciousness, apprehend their significance—their use—and then conforming his being to the one; he shall again conform the other to himself.

## CHILDHOOD A TYPE OF THE GODHEAD

Yet, dimmed as is the Divine Image in Man, it reflects not the full and fair Image of the Godhead. We seek it alone in Jesus in its fulness; yet sigh to behold it with our corporeal senses. And this privilege God ever vouchsafes to the pure and undefiled in heart; for he ever sends it upon the earth in the form of the Child. Herein have we a Type of the Divinity. Herein is our Nature yet despoiled of none of its glory. In flesh and blood he reveals his Presence to our senses, and pleads with us to worship and revere.

## MISAPPREHENSION OF CHILDHOOD

Yet few there are who apprehend the significance of the Divine Type. Childhood is yet a problem that we have scarce studied. It has been and still is a mystery to us. Its pure and simple nature; its faith and its hope, are all unknown to us. It stands friendless and alone, pleading in vain for sympathy and aid. And, though wronged and slighted, it still retains its trustingness; still does it cling to the Adult for renovation and light.—But thus shall it not be always. It shall be apprehended. It shall not be a mystery and made to offend. "Light is springing up, and the day-spring from on high is again visiting us." And, as in times sacred to our associations, the Star led the Wise Men to the Infant Jesus, to present their reverent gifts, and was, at once, both the herald and the pledge of the advent of the Son of God on the earth; even so is the hour approaching, and it lingers not on its errand, when the Wise and the Gifted, shall again surround the cradles of the New Born Babe, and there proffer, as did the Magi, their gifts of reverence and of love to the Holiness that hath visited the earth, and shines forth with a celestial glory around their heads;—and these, pondering well, as did Mary, the Divine Significance, shall steal from it the Art—so long lost in our Consciousness—of unfolding its powers into the fulness of the God.

## RENOVATION OF NATURE

And thus Man, repossessing his Idea, shall conform Nature to himself. Institutions shall bear the fruits of his regenerate being. They shall flourish in vigor and beauty. They shall circulate his Genius through Nature and Life, and repeat the story of his renewal.

## HUMAN RENEWAL

Say not that this Era is distant. Verily, it is near. Even at this moment the heralds of the time are announcing its approach. Omens of Good hover over us. A deeper and holier Faith is quickening the Genius of our Time. Humanity awaits the hour of its renewal. The renovating Fiat has gone forth, to revive our Institutions, and remould our Men. Faith is lifting her voice, and, like Jesus near the Tomb of Lazarus, is uttering the living words, "I am the Resurrection and the Life, and he that Believeth, though dead in doubts and sins, shall be reassured of his Immortality, and shall flourish in unfading Youth! I will mould Nature and Man according to my Will. I will transfigure all things into the Image of my Ideal."—And by such Faith, and such Vision, shall Education work its mission on the Earth. Apprehending the Divine Significance of Jesus—yet filled with the assurance of coming Messiahs to meet the growing nature of Man—shall inspired Genius go forth to renovate his Era; casting out the unclean spirits and the demons that yet afflict the Soul. And then shall Humanity, leaving her infirmities, her wrongs, her sufferings, and her sins, in the corrupting grave, reappear in the consciousness of Physical Purity; Inspired Genius; and Spotless Holiness. Men shall be one with God, as was the Man of Nazareth.

# ORESTES BROWNSON

## THE RECONCILIATION OF GOD, HUMANITY, STATE, AND CHURCH

(1836)

Among all the first-generation Transcendentalists, Orestes Brownson (1803–76) and Bronson Alcott were the two social and geographical outsiders. Brownson suffered through an impoverished boyhood in Vermont and points west. But whereas Alcott was one of the most even tempered of the group, Brownson was testy and restless. Until midlife he was a spiritual quester, entering the Unitarian ministry in the early 1830s after cycling through a series of other faiths and nonfaiths. Quickly he became one of the most outspoken critics of its theological and political mainstreams until converting to Catholicism a dozen years later, to the astonishment of his Transcendentalist colleagues. But the following selections show they should not have been quite so surprised. They come from chapters eight and nine of another major manifesto of the Transcendentalist annus mirabilis, on "Indications of the Atonement" and "The Atonement."

This term requires some translation. "Limited Atonement" had for centuries been one of the so-called five points of Calvinist doctrine, according to which Jesus' death on the cross was designed to satisfy or compensate for the original sin of Adam and Eve so that God's elect could be saved. The elect were presumed to be a small fraction of professing Christians, let alone of humanity at large. Nineteenth-century religious liberals tried to redefine away what they took to be the cruelty of the doctrine that Jesus died to appease a wrathful God but also to retain the idea of necessary reconciliation between humankind and the divine. Such is Brownson's strategy here, but his grand vision of humankind's prospects for exaltation goes far beyond the more cautious, humbly pietistic tone of the average liberal revision, far beyond even those of William Ellery Channing, whose "Likeness to God" (Section I) Brownson praises as the most remarkable sermon since Jesus' Sermon on the Mount.

Even more striking is Brownson's emphasis on the human collective, as against the transformation of single individuals. Emerson and Alcott speak generically of individual "man," but Brownson is far more invested in societal institutions, in bonds that conjoin people, in the transformation of humanity as a whole. This illustrates the range, and wrangling, among Transcendentalists over whether the idea of the God-human connection that excited them all should be thought of in single-person-first terms or social-renovation-first terms. Brownson's preference for the latter would subsequently lead to his being viewed as Karl Marx's closest American forerunner and would give added bite to his prophecy here that "Church and State will become one" after he converted from Unitarianism to Catholicism in 1844. Note how Brownson absorbs but inverts Carlyle's analysis of the Age of Machinery (Section I) by invoking "association" as a term of praise.

SOURCE: *New Views of Christianity, Society, and the Church*. Boston: Little, Brown, 1836.

The time has come for a new Church, for a new synthesis of the elements of the life of Humanity. The end to be attained is Union. How would an inspiration designed to give the energy, the power to attain this end be most likely to manifest itself; in what way could it manifest itself but by giving the people an irresistible longing for union, and a tendency to unite, to associate on all occasions and for all purposes not inconsistent with union itself? And what is the most striking characteristic of this age? Is it not the tendency to association, a tendency so strong that it appears to the cool spectator like a monomania?

This tendency shows itself every where. All over Christendom, men seem mad for associations. They associate for almost every thing, to promote science, literature, art and industry, to circulate the Bible, to distribute religious tracts, to diffuse useful knowledge, to improve and extend education, to meliorate governments and laws, to soften the rigors of the prison-house, to aid the sick, to relieve the poor, to prevent pauperism, to free the slave, to send out missionaries, and to evangelize the world. And—what deserves to be remarked—all these associations, various as they are, really propose in every instance a great and glorious end. They all are formed for useful, moral, religious, philosophical, philanthropical or humane purposes. They may be badly managed, they may fail in accomplishing what they propose, but that which they propose deserves to be accomplished. Sectarians may control them; but in all cases their ends are broader than any sect, than all sects, and they alike commend themselves to the consciences and the prayers of mankind. In some of these associations, sects long and widely separated come together, and find to their mutual satisfaction that they have a common ground, and a ground which each one instinctively admits to be higher and holier than any merely sectarian ground.

—

... In this country more than in any other is the man of thought united in the same person with the man of action. The people here have a strong tendency to profound and philosophic thought, as well as to skilful, energetic and persevering action. The time is not far distant when our whole population will be philosophers, and all our philosophers will be practical men. This is written on almost every man's brow in characters so plain that he who runs may read. This characteristic of our population fits us above all other nations to bring out and realize great and important ideas. Here too is the freedom which other nations want, and the faith in ideas which can be found nowhere else. Philosophers in other countries may think and construct important theories, but they can realize them only to a very limited extent. But here every idea may be at once put to a practical test, and if true it will be realized. We have the field, the liberty, the disposition and the faith to work with ideas. It is here then that must first be brought out and realized the true idea of the Atonement. We already seem to have a consciousness of this, and it is therefore that we are not and cannot be surprised to find the union of popular inspiration with profound philosophical thought manifesting itself more clearly here than any where else.

The representative of this union here is a body of individuals rather than a single individual. The many with us are every thing, the individual almost nothing. One man, however, stands out from this body, a more perfect type of the synthesis of Eclecticism and inspiration than any one else. I need not name him. Philosophers consult him, and the people hear his voice and follow him. His connexion with a particular denomination may have exposed him to some unfriendly criticism, but he is in truth one of the most popular men of the age. His voice finds a response in the mind and in the heart of Humanity....

When Rationalism was attacked he appeared in its defence and proclaimed, in a language which still rings in our ears, the imprescriptible rights of the mind. After the first shock of the war upon Rationalism had been met, and a momentary truce tacitly declared, he brought out in an Ordination Sermon the great truth which destroys all antagonism and realizes the Atonement. In that Sermon—the most remarkable since the Sermon on the Mount—he distinctly recognises and triumphantly vindicates the God-Man. "In ourselves are the elements of the Divinity. God then does not sustain a figurative resemblance to man. It is the resemblance of a parent to a child, THE LIKENESS OF A KINDRED NATURE." In this sublime declaration, the Son of God is owned. Humanity, after so many years of vain search for a Father, finds itself here openly proclaimed the true child of God.

This declaration gives us the hidden sense of the symbol of the God-Man. By asserting the Divinity of Humanity, it teaches us that we should not view that symbol as the symbol of two natures in one person, but of kindred natures in two persons. The God-Man indicates not the antithesis of God and man; nor does it stand for a being alone of its kind; but it indicates the homogeneousness of the human and divine natures, and shows that they can dwell together in love and peace. The Son of Man and the Son of God are not two persons but one—a mystery which becomes clear the very moment that the human nature is discovered to have a sameness with the Divine.

—

Hitherto we have considered man as the antithesis of all good. We have loaded him with reproachful epithets and made it a sin in him even to be born. We have uniformly deemed it necessary to degrade him in order to exalt his Creator. But this will end. The slave will become a son. Man is hereafter to stand erect before God as a child before its father. Human nature, at which we have pointed our wit and vented our spleen, will be clothed with a high and commanding worth. It will be seen to be a lofty and deathless nature. It will be felt to be Divine, and Infinite will be found traced in living characters on all its faculties.

We shall not treat one another then as we do now. Man will be sacred in the eyes of man. To wrong him will be more than crime, it will be sin. To labor to degrade him will seem like laboring to degrade the Divinity. Man will reverence man.

Slavery will cease. Man will shudder at the bare idea of enslaving so

noble a being as man. It will seem to him hardly less daring than to presume to task the motions of the Deity and to compel him to come and
go at our bidding. When man learns the true value of man, the chains
of the captive must be unloosed and the fetters of the slave fall off.

Wars will fail. The sword will be beaten into the ploughshare and
the spear into the pruning hook. Man will not dare to mar and mangle
the shrine of the Divinity. The God looking out from human eyes will
disarm the soldier and make him kneel to him he had risen up to slay.
The warhorse will cease to bathe his fetlocks in human gore. He will
snuff the breeze in the wild freedom of his native plains, or quietly submit to be harnessed to the plough. The hero's occupation will be gone,
and heroism will be found only in saving and blessing human life.

Education will destroy the empire of ignorance. The human mind,
allied as it is to the Divine, is too valuable to lie waste or to be left to
breed only briars and thorns. Those children, ragged and incrusted
with filth, which throng our streets, and for whom we must one day
build prisons, forge bolts and bars, or erect gibbets, are not only our
children, our brother's children, but they are children of God, they
have in themselves the elements of the Divinity and powers which
when put forth will raise them above what the tallest archangel now is.
And when this is seen and felt, will those children be left to fester in
ignorance or to grow up in vice and crime? The whole energy of man's
being cries out against such folly, such gross injustice.

Civil freedom will become universal. It will be every where felt that
one man has no right over another which that other has not over him.
All will be seen to be brothers and equals in the sight of their common
Father. All will love one another too much to desire to play the tyrant.
Human nature will be reverenced too much not to be allowed to have
free scope for the full and harmonious development of all its faculties.
Governments will become sacred; and while on the one hand they are
respected and obeyed, on the other it will be felt to be a religious right
and a religious duty, to labor to make them as perfect as they can be.

Religion will not stop with the command to obey the laws, but it
will bid us make just laws, such laws as befit a being divinely endowed
like man. The Church will be on the side of progress, and Spiritualism
and Materialism will combine to make man's earthly condition as near
like the lost Eden of the Eastern poets, as is compatible with the
growth and perfection of his nature.

Industry will be holy. The cultivation of the earth will be the worship of God. Working-men will be priests, and as priests they will be

reverenced, and as priests they will reverence themselves and feel that they must maintain themselves undefiled. He that ministers at the altar must be pure, will be said of the mechanic, the agriculturist, the common laborer, as well as of him who is technically called a priest.

The earth itself and the animals which inhabit it will be counted sacred. We shall study in them the manifestation of God's goodness, wisdom, and power, and be careful that we make of them none but a holy use.

Man's body will be deemed holy. It will be called the temple of the Living God. As a temple it must not be desecrated. Men will beware of defiling it by sin, by any excessive or improper indulgence, as they would of defiling the temple or the altar consecrated to the service of God. Man will reverence himself too much, he will see too much of the Holy in his nature ever to pervert it from the right line of Truth and Duty.

———

Church and State will become one. The State will be holy, and the Church will be holy. Both will aim at the same thing, and the existence of one as separate from the other will not be needed. The Church will not be then an outward visible power, coexisting with the State, sometimes controlling it and at other times controlled by it; but it will be within, a true spiritual—not spiritualistic—Church, regulating the heart, the conscience and the life.

And when this all takes place the glory of the Lord will be manifested until the ends of the earth, and all flesh will see it and rejoice together. The time is yet distant before this will be fully realized. We are now realizing it in our theory. We assert the holiness of all things. This assertion becomes an idea, and ideas, if they are true, are omnipotent. As soon as Humanity fully possesses this idea, it will lose no time in reducing it to practice. Men will conform their practice to it. They will become personally holy. Holiness will be written on all their thoughts, emotions and actions, on their whole lives. And then will Christ really be formed within, the hope of glory. He will be truly incarnated in universal Humanity, and God and man will be one.

# 4.

# RALPH WALDO EMERSON
## "THE AMERICAN SCHOLAR"
### (1837)

This lecture-essay was first given to a generally enthusiastic audience of Boston-area notables at Harvard's annual Phi Beta Kappa Society oration. It was and remains one of the texts by which Emerson is best known, as well as being the most widely read and influential speech ever given at Harvard. The Phi Beta Kappa Society later named its magazine *The American Scholar* in Emerson's honor.

Emerson here addresses the already hackneyed topic of America's lingering intellectual and cultural dependence on European models. This had long been the expected topic of such orations, as Emerson states at the outset. But he breathes fresh life into it by using the occasion to unfold his distinctive ideas in a more accessible way than *Nature* had. Emerson's portrait of "the scholar" is a portrait of the kind of figure he himself wanted to be. It was also his favorite and indeed perennial subject when speaking to academic audiences. As such, "The American Scholar" sets the template for a score of lectures and orations delivered at various colleges over the next thirty years. During his long career as a public speaker, Emerson held forth on an astonishing range of topics, from art history to the chemistry of water; but none appealed to him more strongly than this.

Emerson's definition of "the scholar" in nonparochial terms as "Man Thinking" rather than strictly as an academic, his threefold recipe of nature-books-action as the scholar's key resources, his insistence that the scholar's principal duty is "self-trust," and the argument that the spirit of the age is summed up by a new respect for the commonplace and for the single person—all these were faithful to the vision of the social role of the thinking person laid out in *Nature,* "Self-Reliance," and later essays. They were also calculated to speak to the condition of a nation that tended to value intellectual power insofar as it served the interests of social practicality. Emerson's theory of the scholar meets this prejudice halfway, but only halfway.

Another example of strategic compromise is how the oration both does and does not play the cultural nationalism card. It does so vigorously only at the start and the close. In between, Emerson might easily have made a point of stressing that his prescription of nature-books-action is a distinctively "American" recipe. But he refrains. And the examples he cites of auspicious signs of the times are all Anglo-European. In short, Emerson was no jingoist. Although Emerson and Transcendentalism generally had a stronger influence within the United States than beyond it, Transcendentalist thought is more marked for its cosmopolitan eclecticism than for its investment in the purely national.

SOURCE: *An Oration, Delivered before the Phi Beta Kappa Society, at Cambridge, August 31, 1837.* Boston: James Munroe, 1837.


MR. PRESIDENT, AND GENTLEMEN,

I greet you on the re-commencement of our literary year. Our anniversary is one of hope, and, perhaps, not enough of labor. We do not meet for games of strength or skill, for the recitation of histories, tragedies and odes, like the ancient Greeks; for parliaments of love and poesy, like the Troubadours; nor for the advancement of science, like our cotemporaries in the British and European capitals. Thus far, our holiday has been simply a friendly sign of the survival of the love of letters amongst a people too busy to give to letters any more. As such, it is precious as the sign of an indestructible instinct. Perhaps the time is already come, when it ought to be, and will be something else; when the sluggard intellect of this continent will look from under its iron lids and fill the postponed expectation of the world with something better than the exertions of mechanical skill. Our day of dependence, our long apprenticeship to the learning of other lands, draws to a close. The millions that around us are rushing into life, cannot always be fed on the sere remains of foreign harvests. Events, actions arise, that must be sung, that will sing themselves. Who can doubt that poetry will revive and lead in a new age, as the start in the constellation Harp which now flames in our zenith, astronomers announce, shall one day be the pole-star for a thousand years.

In the light of this hope, I accept the topic which not only usage, but the nature of our association, seem to prescribe to this day,—the AMERICAN SCHOLAR. Year by year, we come up hither to read one more chapter of his biography. Let us inquire what new lights, new events and more days have thrown on his character, his duties and his hopes.

It is one of those fables, which out of an unknown antiquity, convey an unlooked for wisdom, that the gods, in the beginning, divided Man into men, that he might be more helpful to himself; just as the hand was divided into fingers, the better to answer its end.

The old fable covers a doctrine ever new and sublime; that there is One Man,—present to all particular men only partially, or through one faculty; and that you must take the whole society to find the whole man. Man is not a farmer, or a professor, or an engineer, but he is all. Man is priest, and scholar, and statesman, and producer, and soldier. In the *divided* or social state, these functions are parcelled out to individuals, each of whom aims to do his stint of the joint work, whilst each other performs his. The fable implies that the individual to possess himself, must sometimes return from his own labor to embrace all the other laborers. But unfortunately, this original unit, this fountain of power, has been so distributed to multitudes, has been so minutely subdivided and peddled out, that it is spilled into drops, and cannot be gathered. The state of society is one in which the members have suffered amputation from the trunk, and strut about so many walking monsters,—a good finger, a neck, a stomach, an elbow, but never a man.

Man is thus metamorphosed into a thing, into many things. The planter, who is Man sent out into the field to gather food, is seldom cheered by any idea of the true dignity of his ministry. He sees his bushel and his cart, and nothing beyond, and sinks into the farmer, instead of Man on the farm. The tradesman scarcely ever gives an ideal worth to his work, but is ridden by the routine of his craft, and the soul is subject to dollars. The priest becomes a form; the attorney, a statute-book; the mechanic, a machine; the sailor, a rope of a ship.

In this distribution of functions, the scholar is the delegated intellect. In the right state, he is, *Man Thinking*. In the degenerate state, when the victim of society, he tends to become a mere thinker, or, still worse, the parrot of other men's thinking.

In this view of him, as Man Thinking, the whole theory of his office is contained. Him nature solicits, with all her placid, all her monitory pictures. Him the past instructs. Him the future invites. Is not, indeed, every man a student, and do not all things exist for the student's behoof? And, finally, is not the true scholar the only true master? But, as the old oracle said, "All things have two handles. Beware of the wrong one." In life, too often, the scholar errs with mankind and forfeits his privilege. Let us see him in his school, and consider him in reference to the main influences he receives.

I. The first in time and the first in importance of the influences upon the mind is that of nature. Every day, the sun; and, after sunset, night and her stars. Ever the winds blow; ever the grass grows. Every day, men and women, conversing, beholding and beholden. The scholar must needs stand wistful and admiring before this great spectacle. He must settle its value in his mind. What is nature to him? There is never a beginning, there is never an end to the inexplicable continuity of this web of God, but always circular power returning into itself. Therein it resembles his own spirit, whose beginning, whose ending he never can find—so entire, so boundless. Far, too, as her splendors shine, system on system shooting like rays, upward, downward, without centre, without circumference,—in the mass and in the particle nature hastens to render account of herself to the mind. Classification begins. To the young mind, every thing is individual, stands by itself. By and by, it finds how to join two things, and see in them one nature; then three, then three thousand; and so, tyrannized over by its own unifying instinct, it goes on tying things together, diminishing anomalies, discovering roots running under ground, whereby contrary and remote things cohere, and flower out from one stem. It presently learns, that, since the dawn of history, there has been a constant accumulation and classifying of facts. But what is classification but the perceiving that these objects are not chaotic, and are not foreign, but have a law which is also a law of the human mind? The astronomer discovers that geometry, a pure abstraction of the human mind, is the measure of planetary motion. The chemist finds proportions and intelligible method throughout matter: and science is nothing but the finding of analogy, identity in the most remote parts. The ambitious soul sits down before each refractory fact; one after another, reduces all strange constitutions, all new powers, to their class and their law, and goes on forever to animate the last fibre of organization, the outskirts of nature, by insight.

Thus to him, to this school-boy under the bending dome of day, is suggested, that he and it proceed from one root; one is leaf and one is flower; relation, sympathy, stirring in every vein. And what is that Root? Is not that the soul of his soul?—A thought too bold—a dream too wild. Yet when this spiritual light shall have revealed the law of more earthly natures,—when he has learned to worship the soul, and to see that the natural philosophy that now is, is only the first gropings of its gigantic hand, he shall look forward to an ever expanding knowledge as to a becoming creator. He shall see that nature is the opposite of the soul answering to it part for part. One is seal, and one is print. Its beauty is the beauty of his own mind. Its laws are the laws of his own mind. Nature then becomes to him the measure of his attainments. So much of nature as he is ignorant of, so much of his own mind does he not yet possess. And, in fine, the ancient precept, "Know thyself," and the modern precept, "Study nature," become at last one maxim.

II. The next great influence into the spirit of the scholar, is, the mind of the Past,—in whatever form, whether of literature, of art, of institutions, that mind is inscribed. Books are the best type of the influence of the past, and perhaps we shall get at the truth—learn the amount of this influence more conveniently—by considering their value alone.

The theory of books is noble. The scholar of the first age received into him the world around; brooded thereon; gave it the new arrangement of his own mind, and uttered it again. It came into him—life; it went out from him—truth. It came to him—short-lived actions; it went out from him—immortal thoughts. It came to him—business; it went from him—poetry. It was—dead fact; now, it is quick thought. It can stand, and it can go. It now endures, it now flies, it now inspires. Precisely in proportion to the depth of mind from which it issued, so high does it soar, so long does it sing.

Or, I might say, it depends on how far the process had gone, of transmuting life into truth. In proportion to the completeness of the distillation, so will the purity and imperishableness of the product be. But none is quite perfect. As no air-pump can by any means make a perfect vacuum, so neither can any artist entirely exclude the conventional, the local, the perishable from his book, or write a book of pure thought that shall be as efficient, in all respects, to a remote posterity, as to cotemporaries, or rather to the second age. Each age, it is found, must write its own books; or rather, each generation for the next succeeding. The books of an older period will not fit this.

Yet hence arises a grave mischief. The sacredness which attaches to the act of creation,—the act of thought,—is instantly transferred to the record. The poet chanting, was felt to be a divine man. Henceforth the chant is divine also. The writer was a just and wise spirit. Henceforward it is settled, the book is perfect; as love of the hero corrupts into worship of his statue. Instantly, the book becomes noxious. The guide is a tyrant. We sought a brother, and lo, a governor. The sluggish and perverted mind of the multitude, always slow to open to the incursions of Reason, having once so opened, having once received this book, stands upon it, and makes an outcry, if it is disparaged. Colleges are built on it. Books are written on it by thinkers, not by Man Thinking; by men of talent, that is, who start wrong, who set out from accepted dogmas, not from their own sight of principles. Meek young men grow up in libraries, believing it their duty to accept the views which Cicero, which Locke, which Bacon have given, forgetful that Cicero, Locke and Bacon were only young men in libraries when they wrote these books.

Hence, instead of Man Thinking, we have the bookworm. Hence, the book-learned class, who value books, as such; not as related to nature and the human constitution, but as making a sort of Third Estate with the world and the soul. Hence, the restorers of readings, the emendators, the bibliomaniacs of all degrees.

This is bad; this is worse than it seems. Books are the best of things, well used; abused, among the worst. What is the right use? What is the one end which all means go to effect? They are for nothing but to inspire. I had better never see a book than to be warped by its attraction clean out of my own orbit, and made a satellite instead of a system. The one thing in the world of value, is, the active soul,—the soul, free, sovereign, active. This every man is entitled to; this every man contains within him, although in almost all men, obstructed, and as yet unborn. The soul active sees absolute truth; and utters truth, or creates. In this action, it is genius; not the privilege of here and there a favorite, but the sound estate of every man. In its essence, it is progressive. The book, the college, the school of art, the institution of any kind, stop with some past utterance of genius. This is good, say they,— let us hold by this. They pin me down. They look backward and not forward. But genius always looks forward. The eyes of man are set in his forehead, not in his hindhead. Man hopes. Genius creates. To create,—to create,—is the proof of a divine presence. Whatever talents may be, if the man create not, the pure efflux of the Deity is not his:—

cinders and smoke, there may be, but not yet flame. There are creative manners, there are creative actions, and creative words; manners, actions, words, that is, indicative of no custom or authority, but springing spontaneous from the mind's own sense of good and fair.

On the other part, instead of being its own seer, let it receive always from another mind its truth, though it were in torrents of light, without periods of solitude, inquest and self-recovery, and a fatal disservice is done. Genius is always sufficiently the enemy of genius by over influence. The literature of every nation bear me witness. The English dramatic poets have Shakspearized now for two hundred years.

Undoubtedly there is a right way of reading,—so it be sternly subordinated. Man Thinking must not be subdued by his instruments. Books are for the scholar's idle times. When he can read God directly, the hour is too precious to be wasted in other men's transcripts of their readings. But when the intervals of darkness come, as come they must,—when the soul seeth not, when the sun is hid, and the stars withdraw their shining,—we repair to the lamps which were kindled by their ray to guide our steps to the East again, where the dawn is. We hear that we may speak. The Arabian proverb says, "A fig tree looking on a fig tree, becometh fruitful."

It is remarkable, the character of the pleasure we derive from the best books. They impress us ever with the conviction that one nature wrote and the same reads. We read the verses of one of the great English poets, of Chaucer, of Marvell, of Dryden, with the most modern joy,—with a pleasure, I mean, which is in great part caused by the abstraction of all *time* from their verses. There is some awe mixed with the joy of our surprise, when this poet, who lived in some past world, two or three hundred years ago, says that which lies close to my own soul, that which I also had well nigh thought and said. But for the evidence thence afforded to the philosophical doctrine of the identity of all minds, we should suppose some pre-established harmony, some foresight of souls that were to be, and some preparation of stores for their future wants, like the fact observed in insects, who lay up food before death for the young grub they shall never see.

I would not be hurried by any love of system, by any exaggeration of instincts, to underrate the Book. We all know, that as the human body can be nourished on any food, though it were boiled grass and the broth of shoes, so the human mind can be fed by any knowledge. And great and heroic men have existed, who had almost no other information than by the printed page. I only would say, that it needs a strong head to bear that diet. One must be an inventor to read well. As the proverb says, "He that would bring home the wealth of the Indies, must carry out the wealth of the Indies." There is then creative reading, as well as creative writing. When the mind is braced by labor and invention, the page of whatever book we read becomes luminous with manifold allusion. Every sentence is doubly significant, and the sense of our author is as broad as the world. We then see, what is always true, that as the seer's hour of vision is short and rare among heavy days and months, so is its record, perchance, the least part of his volume. The discerning will read in his Plato or Shakspeare, only that least part,— only the authentic utterances of the oracle,—and all the rest he rejects, were it never so many times Plato's and Shakspeare's.

Of course, there is a portion of reading quite indispensable to a wise man. History and exact science he must learn by laborious reading. Colleges, in like manner, have their indispensable office,—to teach elements. But they can only highly serve us, when they aim not to drill, but to create; when they gather from far every ray of various genius to their hospitable halls, and, by the concentrated fires, set the hearts of their youth on flame. Thought and knowledge are natures in which apparatus and pretension avail nothing. Gowns, and pecuniary foundations, though of towns of gold, can never countervail the least sentence or syllable of wit. Forget this, and our American colleges will recede in their public importance whilst they grow richer every year.

III. There goes in the world a notion that the scholar should be a recluse, a valetudinarian,—as unfit for any handiwork or public labor, as a penknife for an axe. The so called "practical men" sneer at speculative men, as if, because they speculate or *see,* they could do nothing. I have heard it said that the clergy,—who are always more universally than any other class, the scholars of their day,—are addressed as women: that the rough, spontaneous conversation of men they do not hear, but only a mincing and diluted speech. They are often virtually disfranchised; and, indeed, there are advocates for their celibacy. As far as this is true of the studious classes, it is not just and wise. Action is with the scholar subordinate, but it is essential. Without it, he is not yet man. Without it, thought can never ripen into truth. Whilst the world hangs before the eye as a cloud of beauty, we cannot even see its beauty. Inaction is cowardice, but there can be no scholar without the heroic mind. The preamble of thought, the transition through which it passes from the unconscious to the conscious, is action. Only so much do I know, as I have lived. Instantly we know whose words are loaded with life, and whose not.

The world,—this shadow of the soul, or *other me,* lies wide around. Its attractions are the keys which unlock my thoughts and make me acquainted with myself. I launch eagerly into this resounding tumult. I grasp the hands of those next me, and take my place in the ring to suffer and to work, taught by an instinct that so shall the dumb abyss be vocal with speech. I pierce its order; I dissipate its fear; I dispose of it within the circuit of my expanding life. So much only of life as I know by experience, so much of the wilderness have I vanquished and planted, or so far have I extended my being, my dominion. I do not see how any man can afford, for the sake of his nerves and his nap, to spare any action in which he can partake. It is pearls and rubies to his discourse. Drudgery, calamity, exasperation, want, are instructers in eloquence and wisdom. The true scholar grudges every opportunity of action past by, as a loss of power.

It is the raw material out of which the intellect moulds her splendid products. A strange process too, this, by which experience is converted into thought, as a mulberry leaf is converted into satin. The manufacture goes forward at all hours.

The actions and events of our childhood and youth are now matters of calmest observation. They lie like fair pictures in the air. Not so with our recent actions,—with the business which we now have in hand. On this we are quite unable to speculate. Our affections as yet circulate through it. We no more feel or know it, than we feel the feet, or the hand, or the brain of our body. The new deed is yet a part of life,—remains for a time immersed in our unconscious life. In some contemplative hour, it detaches itself from the life like a ripe fruit, to become a thought of the mind. Instantly, it is raised, transfigured; the corruptible has put on incorruption. Always now it is an object of beauty, however base its origin and neighborhood. Observe, too, the impossibility of antedating this act. In its grub state, it cannot fly, it cannot shine,—it is a dull grub. But suddenly, without observation, the selfsame thing unfurls beautiful wings, and is an angel of wisdom. So is there no fact, no event, in our private history, which shall not, sooner or later, lose its adhesive inert form, and astonish us by soaring from our body into the empyrean. Cradle and infancy, school and playground, the fear of boys, and dogs, and ferules, the love of little maids and berries, and many another fact that once filled the whole sky, are gone already; friend and relative, profession and party, town and country, nation and world, must also soar and sing.

Of course, he who has put forth his total strength in fit actions, has the richest return of wisdom. I will not shut myself out of this globe of action and transplant an oak into a flower pot, there to hunger and pine; nor trust the revenue of some single faculty, and exhaust one vein of thought, much like those Savoyards, who, getting their livelihood by carving shepherds, shepherdesses, and smoking Dutchmen, for all Europe, went out one day to the mountain to find stock, and discovered that they had whittled up the last of their pine trees. Authors we have in numbers, who have written out their vein, and who, moved by a commendable prudence, sail for Greece or Palestine, follow the trapper into the prairie, or ramble round Algiers to replenish their merchantable stock.

If it were only for a vocabulary the scholar would be covetous of action. Life is our dictionary. Years are well spent in country labors; in town—in the insight into trades and manufactures; in frank intercourse with many men and women; in science; in art; to the one end of mastering in all their facts a language, by which to illustrate and embody our perceptions. I learn immediately from any speaker how much he has already lived, through the poverty or the splendor of his speech. Life lies behind us as the quarry from whence we get tiles and copestones for the masonry of to-day. This is the way to learn grammar. Colleges and books only copy the language which the field and the work-yard made.

But the final value of action, like that of books, and better than books, is, that it is a resource. That great principle of Undulation in nature, that shows itself in the inspiring and expiring of the breath; in desire and satiety; in the ebb and flow of the sea, in day and night, in heat and cold, and as yet more deeply ingrained in every atom and every fluid is known to us under the name of Polarity,—these "fits of easy transmission and reflection," as Newton called them, are the law of nature because they are the law of spirit.

The mind now thinks; now acts; and each fit reproduces the other. When the artist has exhausted his materials, when the fancy no longer paints, when thoughts are no longer apprehended, and books are a weariness,—he has always the resource *to live*. Character is higher than intellect. Thinking is the function. Living is the functionary. The stream retreats to its source. A great soul will be strong to live, as well as strong to think. Does he lack organ or medium to impart his truths? He can still fall back on this elemental force of living them. This is a total act. Thinking is a partial act. Let the grandeur of justice shine in his affairs. Let the beauty of affection cheer his lowly roof. Those "far from fame" who dwell and act with him, will feel the force of his constitution in the doings and passages of the day better than it can be measured by any public and designed display. Time shall teach him that the scholar loses no hour which the man lives. Herein he unfolds the sacred germ of his instinct, screened from influence. What is lost in seemliness is gained in strength. Not out of those on whom systems of education have exhausted their culture, comes the helpful giant to destroy the old or to build the new, but out of unhandselled savage nature, out of terrible Druids and Berserkirs, come at last Alfred and Shakspeare.

I hear therefore with joy whatever is beginning to be said of the dignity and necessity of labor to every citizen. There is virtue yet in the hoe and the spade, for learned as well as for unlearned hands. And labor is every where welcome; always we are invited to work; only be this limitation observed, that a man shall not for the sake of wider activity sacrifice any opinion to the popular judgments and modes of action.

I have now spoken of the education of the scholar by nature, by books, and by action. It remains to say somewhat of his duties.

They are such as become Man Thinking. They may all be comprised in self-trust. The office of the scholar is to cheer, to raise, and to guide men by showing them facts amidst appearances. He plies the slow, unhonored, and unpaid task of observation. Flamsteed and Herschel, in their glazed observatory, may catalogue the stars with the praise of all men, and, the results being splendid and useful, honor is sure. But he, in his private observatory, cataloguing obscure and nebulous stars of the human mind, which as yet no man has thought of as such,— watching days and months, sometimes, for a few facts; correcting still his old records;—must relinquish display and immediate fame. In the long period of his preparation, he must betray often an ignorance and shiftlessness in popular arts, incurring the disdain of the able who shoulder him aside. Long he must stammer in his speech; often forego the living for the dead. Worse yet, he must accept—how often! poverty and solitude. For the ease and pleasure of treading the old road, accepting the fashions, the education, the religion of society, he takes the cross of making his own, and, of course, the self-accusation, the faint heart, the frequent uncertainty and loss of time which are the nettles and tangling vines in the way of the self-relying and self-directed; and the state of virtual hostility in which he seems to stand to society, and especially to educated society. For all this loss and scorn, what offset? He is to find consolation in exercising the highest functions of human nature. He is one who raises himself from private considerations, and breathes and lives on public and illustrious thoughts. He is the world's eye. He is the world's heart. He is to resist the vulgar prosperity that retrogrades ever to barbarism, by preserving and communicating heroic sentiments, noble biographies, melodious verse, and the conclusions of history. Whatsoever oracles the human heart in all emergencies, in all solemn hours has uttered as its commentary on the world of actions,—these he shall receive and impart. And whatsoever new verdict Reason from her inviolable seat pronounces on the passing men and events of to-day,—this he shall hear and promulgate.

These being his functions, it becomes him to feel all confidence in himself, and to defer never to the popular cry. He and he only knows the world. The world of any moment is the merest appearance. Some great decorum, some fetish of a government, some ephemeral trade, or war, or man, is cried up by half mankind and cried down by the other half, as if all depended on this particular up or down. The odds are that the whole question is not worth the poorest thought which the scholar has lost in listening to the controversy. Let him not quit his belief that a popgun is a popgun, though the ancient and honorable of the earth affirm it to be the crack of doom. In silence, in steadiness, in severe abstraction, let him hold by himself; add observation to observation; patient of neglect, patient of reproach, and bide his own time,—happy enough if he can satisfy himself alone that this day he has seen something truly. Success treads on every right step. For the instinct is sure that prompts him to tell his brother what he thinks. He then learns that in going down into the secrets of his own mind, he has descended into the secrets of all minds. He learns that he who has mastered any law in his private thoughts, is master to that extent of all men whose language he speaks, and of all into whose language his own can be translated. The poet in utter solitude remembering his spontaneous thoughts and recording them, is found to have recorded that which men in "cities vast" find true for them also. The orator distrusts at first the fitness of his frank confessions,—his want of knowledge of the persons he addresses,—until he finds that he is the complement of his hearers;—that they drink his words because he fulfils for them their own nature;

the deeper he dives into his privatest secretest presentiment,—to his wonder he finds, this is the most acceptable, most public, and universally true. The people delight in it; the better part of every man feels, This is my music: this is myself.

In self-trust, all the virtues are comprehended. Free should the scholar be,—free and brave. Free even to the definition of freedom, "without any hindrance that does not arise out of his own constitution." Brave; for fear is a thing which a scholar by his very function puts behind him. Fear always springs from ignorance. It is a shame to him if his tranquillity, amid dangerous times, arise from the presumption that like children and women, his is a protected class; or if he seek a temporary peace by the diversion of his thoughts from politics or vexed questions, hiding his head like an ostrich in the flowering bushes, peeping into microscopes, and turning rhymes, as a boy whistles to keep his courage up. So is the danger a danger still: so is the fear worse. Manlike let him turn and face it. Let him look into its eye and search its nature, inspect its origin,—see the whelping of this lion,—which lies no great way back; he will then find in himself a perfect comprehension of its nature and extent; he will have made his hands meet on the other side, and can henceforth defy it, and pass on superior. The world is his who can see through its pretension. What deafness, what stone-blind custom, what overgrown error you behold, is there only by sufferance,—by your sufferance. See it to be a lie, and you have already dealt it its mortal blow.

Yes, we are the cowed,—we the trustless. It is a mischievous notion that we are come late into nature; that the world was finished a long time ago. As the world was plastic and fluid in the hands of God, so it is ever to so much of his attributes as we bring to it. To ignorance and sin, it is flint. They adapt themselves to it as they may; but in proportion as a man has anything in him divine, the firmament flows before him, and takes his signet and form. Not he is great who can alter matter, but he who can alter my state of mind. They are the kings of the world who give the color of their present thought to all nature and all art, and persuade men by the cheerful serenity of their carrying the matter, that this thing which they do, is the apple which the ages have desired to pluck, now at last ripe, and inviting nations to the harvest. The great man makes the great thing. Wherever Macdonald sits, there is the head of the table. Linnæus makes botany the most alluring of studies and wins it from the farmer and the herb-woman. Davy, chemistry: and Cuvier, fossils. The day is always his, who works in it with serenity and great aims. The unstable estimates of men crowd to him whose mind is filled with a truth, as the heaped waves of the Atlantic follow the moon.

For this self-trust, the reason is deeper than can be fathomed,—darker than can be enlightened. I might not carry with me the feeling of my audience in stating my own belief. But I have already shown the ground of my hope, in adverting to the doctrine that man is one. I believe man has been wronged: he has wronged himself. He has almost lost the light that can lead him back to his prerogatives. Men are become of no account. Men in history, men in the world of to-day are bugs, are spawn, and are called "the mass" and "the herd." In a century, in a millennium, one or two men; that is to say,—one or two approximations to the right state of every man. All the rest behold in the hero or the poet their own green and crude being—ripened; yes, and are content to be less, so *that* may attain to its full stature. What a testimony—full of grandeur, full of pity, is borne to the demands of his own nature, by the poor clansman, the poor partisan, who rejoices in the glory of his chief. The poor and the low find some amends to their immense moral capacity, for their acquiescence in a political and social inferiority. They are content to be brushed like flies from the path of a great person, so that justice shall be done by him to that common nature which it is the dearest desire of all to see enlarged and glorified. They sun themselves in the great man's light, and feel it to be their own element. They cast the dignity of man from their downtrod selves upon the shoulders of a hero, and will perish to add one drop of blood to make that great heart beat, those giant sinews combat and conquer. He lives for us, and we live in him.

Men such as they are, very naturally seek money or power; and power because it is as good as money,—the "spoils," so called, "of office." And why not? for they aspire to the highest, and this, in their sleepwalking, they dream is highest. Wake them, and they shall quit the false good and leap to the true, and leave governments to clerks and desks. This revolution is to be wrought by the gradual domestication of the idea of Culture. The main enterprise of the world for splendor, for extent, is the upbuilding of a man. Here are the materials strown along the ground. The private life of one man shall be a more illustrious monarchy,—more formidable to its enemy, more sweet and serene in its influence to its friend, than any kingdom in history. For a man, rightly viewed, comprehendeth the particular natures of all men. Each philosopher, each bard, each actor, has only done for me, as by a delegate, what one day I can do for myself. The books which once we valued more than the apple of the eye, we have quite exhausted. What is that but saying that we have come up with the point of view which the universal mind took through the eyes of that one scribe; we have been that man, and have passed on. First, one; then, another; we drain all cisterns, and waxing greater by all these supplies, we crave a better and more abundant food. The man has never lived that can feed us ever. The human mind cannot be enshrined in a person who shall set a barrier on any one side to this unbounded, unboundable empire. It is one central fire which flaming now out of the lips of Etna, lightens the capes of Sicily; and now out of the throat of Vesuvius, illuminates the towers and vineyards of Naples. It is one light which beams out of a thousand stars. It is one soul which animates all men.

But I have dwelt perhaps tediously upon this abstraction of the Scholar. I ought not to delay longer to add what I have to say, of nearer reference to the time and to this country.

Historically, there is thought to be a difference in the ideas which predominate over successive epochs, and there are data for making the genius of the Classic, of the Romantic, and now of the Reflective or Philosophical age. With the views I have intimated of the oneness or the identity of the mind through all individuals, I do not much dwell on these differences. In fact, I believe each individual passes through all three. The boy is a Greek; the youth, romantic; the adult, reflective. I deny not, however, that a revolution in the leading idea may be distinctly enough traced.

Our age is bewailed as the age of Introversion. Must that needs be evil? We, it seems, are critical. We are embarrassed with second thoughts. We cannot enjoy any thing for hankering to know whereof the pleasure consists. We are lined with eyes. We see with our feet. The time is infected with Hamlet's unhappiness,—

"Sicklied o'er with the pale cast of thought."

Is it so bad then? Sight is the last thing to be pitied. Would we be blind? Do we fear lest we should outsee nature and God, and drink truth dry? I look upon the discontent of the literary class as a mere announcement of the fact that they find themselves not in the state of mind of their fathers, and regret the coming state as untried; as a boy dreads the water before he has learned that he can swim. If there is any period one would desire to be born in,—is it not the age of Revolution; when the old and the new stand side by side, and admit of being compared; when the energies of all men are searched by fear and by hope; when the historic glories of the old, can be compensated by the rich possibilities of the new era? This time, like all times, is a very good one, if we but know what to do with it.

I read with joy some of the auspicious signs of the coming days as they glimmer already through poetry and art, through philosophy and science, through church and state.

One of these signs is the fact that the same movement which effected the elevation of what was called the lowest class in the state, assumed in literature a very marked and as benign an aspect. Instead of the sublime and beautiful, the near, the low, the common, was explored and poetised. That which had been negligently trodden under foot by those who were harnessing and provisioning themselves for long journies into far countries, is suddenly found to be richer than all foreign parts. The literature of the poor, the feelings of the child, the philosophy of the street, the meaning of household life, and the topics of the time. It is a great stride. It is a sign—is it not? of new vigor, when the extremities are made active, when currents of warm life run into the hands and the feet. I ask not for the great, the remote, the romantic; what is doing in Italy or Arabia; what is Greek art, or Provencal Minstrelsy; I embrace the common, I explore and sit at the feet of the familiar, the low. Give me insight into to-day, and you may have the antique and future worlds. What would we really know the meaning of? The meal in the firkin; the milk in the pan; the ballad in the street; the news of the boat; the glance of the eye; the form and the gait of the body;—show me the ultimate reason of these matters;—show me the sublime presence of the highest spiritual cause lurking, as always it does lurk, in these suburbs and extremities of nature; let me see every trifle bristling with the polarity that ranges it instantly on an eternal law; and the shop, the plough, and the ledger, referred to the like cause by which light undulates and poets sing;—and the world lies no longer a dull miscellany and lumber room, but has form and order; there is no trifle; there is no puzzle; but one design unites and animates the farthest pinnacle and the lowest trench.

This idea has inspired the genius of Goldsmith, Burns, Cowper, and, in a newer time, of Goethe, Wordsworth, and Carlyle. This idea they have differently followed and with various success. In contrast with their writing, the style of Pope, of Johnson, of Gibbon, looks cold and pedantic. This writing is blood-warm. Man is surprised to find that things near are not less beautiful and wondrous than things remote.

The near explains the far. The drop is a small ocean. A man is related to all nature. This perception of the worth of the vulgar, is fruitful in discoveries. Goethe, in this very thing the most modern of the moderns, has shown us, as none ever did, the genius of the ancients.

There is one man of genius who has done much for this philosophy of life, whose literary value has never yet been rightly estimated;— I mean Emanuel Swedenborg. The most imaginative of men, yet writing with the precision of a mathematician, he endeavored to engraft a purely philosophical Ethics on the popular Christianity of his time. Such an attempt, of course, must have difficulty which no genius could surmount. But he saw and showed the connexion between nature and the affections of the soul. He pierced the emblematic or spiritual character of the visible, audible, tangible world. Especially did his shade-loving muse hover over and interpret the lower parts of nature; he showed the mysterious bond that allies moral evil to the foul material forms, and has given in epical parables a theory of insanity, of beasts, of unclean and fearful things.

Another sign of our times, also marked by an analogous political movement is, the new importance given to the single person. Every thing that tends to insulate the individual,—to surround him with barriers of natural respect, so that each man shall feel the world is his, and man shall treat with man as a sovereign state with a sovereign state;— tends to true union as well as greatness. "I learned," said the melancholy Pestalozzi, "that no man in God's wide earth is either willing or able to help any other man." Help must come from the bosom alone. The scholar is that man who must take up into himself all the ability of the time, all the contributions of the past, all the hopes of the future. He must be an university of knowledges. If there be one lesson more than another which should pierce his ear, it is, The world is nothing, the man is all; in yourself is the law of all nature, and you know not yet how a globule of sap ascends; in yourself slumbers the whole of Reason; it is for you to know all, it is for you to dare all. Mr. President and Gentlemen, this confidence in the unsearched might of man, belongs by all motives, by all prophecy, by all preparation, to the American Scholar. We have listened too long to the courtly muses of Europe. The spirit of the American freeman is already suspected to be timid, imitative, tame. Public and private avarice make the air we breathe thick and fat. The scholar is decent, indolent, complaisant. See already the tragic consequence. The mind of this country taught to aim at low objects, eats upon itself. There is no work for any but the decorous and the complaisant. Young men of the fairest promise, who begin life upon our shores, inflated by the mountain winds, shined upon by all the stars of God, find the earth below not in unison with these,—but are hindered from action by the disgust which the principles on which business is managed inspire, and turn drudges, or die of disgust,—some of them suicides. What is the remedy? They did not yet see, and thousands of young men as hopeful now crowding to the barriers for the career, do not yet see, that if the single man plant himself indomitably on his instincts, and there abide, the huge world will come round to him. Patience—patience;—with the shades of all the good and great for company; and for solace, the perspective of your own infinite life; and for work, the study and the communication of principles, the making those instincts prevalent, the conversion of the world. Is it not the chief disgrace in the world, not to be an unit;—not to be reckoned one character;—not to yield that peculiar fruit which each man was created to bear, but to be reckoned in the gross, in the hundred, or the thousand, of the party, the section, to which we belong; and our opinion predicted geographically, as the north, or the south. Not so, brothers and friends,—please God, ours shall not be so. We will walk on our own feet; we will work with our own hands; we will speak our own minds. Then shall man be no longer a name for pity, for doubt, and for sensual indulgence. The dread of man and the love of man shall be a wall of defence and a wreath of love around all. A nation of men will for the first time exist, because each believes himself inspired by the Divine Soul which also inspires all men.

# CHRISTOPHER PEARSE CRANCH

## FROM "TRANSCENDENTALISM"

### (1839)

Son of a prominent Washington, D.C., judge, Christopher Cranch (1813–92) was a prolific Transcendentalist poet and artist, remembered today for a few remarkable poems (see Section V-C) and for his droll cartoons of Emersonian passages, especially his drawings of the "transparent eyeball" rapturously striding through nature (see Chapter I of *Nature*, this section). But Cranch started his career with a stint as a liberal Unitarian minister, out of which came the following attempt to explain Transcendentalism to an audience mainly of diasporic New Englanders in the midwest. The magazine that printed the essay fifteen months later was the leading journal of trans-Appalachian Unitarianism, but much more open to the "new thought" than the eastern Unitarian magazines and newspapers were. Cranch's definition shows more pointedly than any other item in this section how hard it was for the Transcendentalists to avoid getting beyond a mirror-opposite approach to countering their detractors' charges. Their commonest tactic, as here, was to "refute" the charge of copycat imitation of foreign ideas ("the latest form of infidelity," as mainstream Unitarian spokesman Andrews Norton had stigmatized it) by redescribing themselves in terms of a more lumping generalization: the perennial quest for new truth. The variety of Transcendentalist opinion tended to be praised rather than described.

SOURCE: "Transcendentalism," *The Western Messenger*, 8 (January 1841).

Much is said of late by persons not knowing whereof they speak, of what has been termed "Transcendentalism." Now, though not one in a hundred of these talkers can tell what this hard word means, or even explain their own vague idea of its meaning, it is a very convenient word. In the minds of most persons, it signifieth (being interpreted) "new doctrine,"—a modern synonyme for "Heresy." Strangely enough, all the "New Lights" of Philosophy and Theology, in foreign countries as well as in our own, however independent in thought, are, by a singular mode of generalizing, lumped together into a "Sect," honoured with the cognomen of "New School," and "Transcendental-ists." It might amuse almost, to see how this love of wholesale classifi-cation melts down obvious differences—persuading us that this new movement which is commencing on both sides of the Atlantic, for reviving the old well-nigh obscured truths of philosophy and theology, and is going forward in so many ways and by so many minds—is not a many-headed monster, a hydra whose heads will grow again, though ever so well lopped off; but is *one*-headed, and may and must die, as only "the latest form of infidelity." It might amuse, to see how Kant, Cousin, Carlyle, Emerson, and about half Germany, are placed side by side, as if reading like schoolboys, out of the same book—stereotyping each other's thoughts—a sort of co-partnership for vending mysti-cisms, and turning brains. As if the "New School," as it is termed, *could* be a sect, with a fixed creed before it: as if it were not its glory that it is *many*-headed and progressive . . .

Hence the charge we so often hear, of Imitation, and of the too enthusiastic reception which young and fresh spirits are apt to give to new views. How superficial this charge of stiff barren conservatives. . . . As if this word *Imitation* settled anything. A convenient word it is, we allow, but what does it prove? Is it anything more than a superficial term for a phenomenon, to the eternal foundations of which, as it looms up from the infinite deep of the Spiritual, those narrow observers will not or cannot look? If this phenomenon—this dawning of truths over the earth, be nothing more than a paroxysm, a temporary enchant-ment, a spoiled child's cry after whatever is *new*—then why so eagerly received? . . . I speak not now of any opinions or speculations in partic-ular. There is every variety of such, as there should be. But I speak of that fresh, earnest, truth-loving and truth-seeking SPIRIT, which is abroad;—of that heart's thirst, not of the fever-dream, but of the sober waking vision of soundest health, after something *always* new and lovely and true,—something always adapted to the soul's deep demands.... The true Transcendentalism is that living and always new *spirit* of truth, which is ever going forth on its conquests into the world, and leading all captivity captive; but which at times arms itself as with new splendors of victory,—which is thus in the only sense *transcendental*, when it labors to *transcend* itself, and soar ever higher and nearer the great source of Truth, Himself.

# 6.

# George Ripley
## Letter of Intent to Resign
### (1840)

Ripley began his ministry at almost exactly the same time as Emerson, but he stayed much longer within the fold, being a more devoted pastor though less gifted as a public speaker. But Ripley, too, came to feel irksomely constrained. His sense of constraint was all the greater given the mainstream Unitarian reaction of the 1830s against the Transcendentalist challenges with which he himself deeply sympathized. Ripley had written some of the best "new school" retorts to conservative Unitarianism, including its denunciation of Emerson's 1838 Divinity School Address (see Section III). Ripley's letter contains echoes of Emerson's address, of *Nature*, and of Emerson's own resignation sermon, as well as the marks of Ripley's extensive knowledge of continental philosophy, which he invokes in order to add force to his charge that the Unitarian backlash was out of step with enlightened opinion throughout the Atlantic world.

Among all the Transcendentalist ministers' position statements, this one argues most winningly for the position that the Transcendental "radicals" are the true exemplars of principles of free inquiry for which early Unitarianism stood. Unitarianism's backtracking has forced him to the reluctant conclusion that he should withdraw from the ministry. (Ripley actually wound up issuing several different statements of intent to resign over the course of nearly a year before he and his small but fond congregation could finally bring themselves to part.)

Ripley's letter is also notable for its identification of Transcendentalism as a mode of *thought* rather than the social activism of the other "class of persons" he goes on to describe. That was a distinction his friend Orestes Brownson would not have accepted. Nor indeed would Ripley himself, just a few months later, influenced as he also was by the criticisms of the social status quo of Channing, Brownson, and others. Contrary to this letter's explicit disavowal of intent to join "any public association," he and his wife, Sophia, soon went on to found Brook Farm, the most successful of Transcendentalism's experiments in alternative living, on which see Section IV-A.

SOURCE: *A Letter Addressed to the Congregational Church in Purchase Street.* Boston: privately printed for the church, 1840.

I will confess ... that I was somewhat influenced in the decision at which I had arrived by the present aspect of the times. This is very different from what it was when I became your minister. ...

The essential principles of liberal Christianity, as I have always understood them, made religion to consist, not in any speculative doctrines, but in a divine life; they asserted the unlimited freedom of the human mind, and not only the right, but the duty of private judgment; they established the kingdom of God, not in the dead past, but in the living present; gave the spirit a supremacy over the letter; insisted on the necessity of pointing out the corruptions of the church, of sweeping away the traditions which obscured the simplicity of truth, and urged every soul to press on to the highest attainment, to forget what was behind, and never to be kept back from expressing its convictions by the voice of authority or the fear of man. A portion of the liberal clergy felt it their duty to carry out these views. ... They could not linger around the grave of the past; the experiences of manhood enlarged the conception of their pupilage; they had been taught that no system of divinity monopolized the truth; and they were no more willing to be bound by the prevailing creed of Boston and Cambridge, than their fathers had been by the prescriptions of Rome or Geneva. But in these convictions they were divided from some of their brethren. It was thought dangerous to continue the progress which had been commenced. Liberal churches began to fear liberality, and the most heretical sect in Christendom to bring the charge of heresy against those who carried out its own principles. They who defended the progress as well as the freedom of thought were openly denounced as infidels. ...

---

There is a class of persons who desire a reform in the prevailing philosophy of the day. These are called Transcendentalists, because they believe in an order of truths which transcends the sphere of the external sense. Their leading idea is the supremacy of mind over matter. Hence they maintain that the truth of religion does not depend on tradition, nor historical facts, but has an unerring witness in the soul. There is a light, they believe, which enlighteneth every man that cometh into the world; there is a faculty in all—the most degraded, the most ignorant, the most obscure—to perceive spiritual truth, when distinctly presented; and the ultimate appeal on all moral questions is not to a jury of scholars, a hierarchy of divines, or the prescriptions of a creed, but to the common sense of the human race. These views I have always adopted; they have been at the foundation of my preaching from the first time that I entered the pulpit until now. The experience and reflection of nearly twenty years have done much to confirm, nothing to shake them; and if my discourses in this house, or in my lectures in yonder vestry, have in any instance displayed the vitality of truth, impressed on a single heart a genuine sense of religion, disclosed to you a new prospect of the resources of your own nature, made you feel more deeply your responsibility to God, cheered you in the sublime hope of immortality, and convinced your reason of the reality and worth of the Christian revelation, it was because my mind has been trained in the principles of Transcendental Philosophy,—a philosophy which is now taught in every Protestant university on the Continent of Europe, which is the common creed of the most enlightened nations, and the singular misunderstanding of which among ourselves illustrates more forcibly, I am ashamed to say, the heedless confidence than the literary culture or the just discrimination of some of the leaders of public opinion in this country. If you ask, Why I have not preached this philosophy in the pulpit, I answer that I could not have preached without it; but my main business as a minister, I conceive, has been not to preach philosophy or politics or medicine or mathematics, but the Gospel of Christ. If you ask, Whether I embrace every unintelligible production of the mind that is quoted from mouth to mouth as Transcendentalism, I answer that if any man writes so as not to be understood, be he Transcendentalist or Materialist, it is his own fault, not another's. . . .

There is another class of persons who are devoted to the removal of the abuses that prevail in modern society. They witness the oppressions that are done under the sun, and they cannot keep silence.... They look forward to a more pure, more lovely, more divine state of society than was ever realized on earth. With these views, I rejoice to say, I strongly and entirely sympathize. While I do not feel it my duty to unite with any public association for the promotion of these ideas, it is not because I would disavow their principles, but because in many cases the cause of truth is carried forward better by individual testimony than by combined action. I would not be responsible for the measures of a society; I would have no society responsible for me; but in public and in private, by word and by deed, by persuasion and example, I would endeavor to help the progress of the great principles which I have at heart. The purpose of Christianity, as I firmly believe, is to redeem society as well as the individual from all sin. As a Christian, then, I feel bound to do what I can for the promotion of universal temperance, to persuade men to abandon every habit which is at war with their physical welfare and their moral improvement, and to produce, by appeals to the reason and conscience, that love of inward order which is beyond the reach of legal authority. As a Christian, I would aid in the overthrow of every form of slavery; I would free the mind from bondage and the body from chains; I could not feel that my duty was accomplished while there was one human being, within the sphere of my influence, held to unrequited labor at the will of another, destitute of the means of education, or doomed to penury, degradation, and vice by the misfortune of his birth.

# RALPH WALDO EMERSON

## "THE TRANSCENDENTALIST"

### (1841)

Emerson's most extended definitional statement of Transcendentalism was delivered as a lecture in December 1841, then printed in the
movement's leading magazine, *The Dial*, of which he was then the editor. Emerson published it again in book form in 1849 together with the
slightly revised *Nature*, "The American Scholar," the Divinity School
Address, and other lectures. Like Ripley, Emerson counters hostile
criticism by portraying Transcendentalism as a persuasion far more
basic and universal than just a present-day German-instigated movement. Emerson is much more emphatic, however, in typing Transcendentalists as thinkers rather than doers. Note how different this
emphasis also is from his own tactic in "The American Scholar" of
broadening what counts as "action" so as to include the power of mental activity. Here, by contrast, Emerson makes light of what he characterizes as the indecisive, Hamlet-like standoffishness of the model
Transcendentalist, who emerges as something of a cartoon character.
Why this difference? To some extent it is simply part of a rhetorical
strategy to create a pair of entertaining portraits of opposite character
types, the opposite number to "The Conservative," a companion lecture also printed in *The Dial* and reprinted in 1849. To some extent, the
essay should be read as a self-caricature of "The American Scholar" and
its insistence that the scholar should never defer "to the popular cry"
but "hold by himself" in "silence, in steadiness, in severe abstraction."
But "The Transcendentalist" also reflects Emerson's increasing desire
to put himself at a critical, though still sympathetic, distance from

what seemed to him the narcissistic tendencies of some of his younger-generation imitators. Significantly, Emerson never embraced the Transcendentalist label as Thoreau did (item 9 below). On the other hand, it would be wrong to take this lecture-essay—as some have done—as a farewell to the movement that Emerson had done so much to ignite, or as a sign that the movement's force was already waning.

SOURCE: "The Transcendentalist," *The Dial,* 3 (January 1843), amended in a few places in light of Emerson's later corrections.

THE first thing we have to say respecting what are called *new views* here in New England, at the present time, is, that they are not new, but the very oldest of thoughts cast into the mould of these new times. The light is always identical in its composition, but it falls on a great variety of objects, and by so falling is first revealed to us, not in its own form, for it is formless, but in theirs; in like manner, thought only appears in the objects it classifies. What is popularly called Transcendentalism among us, is Idealism; Idealism as it appears in 1842. As thinkers, mankind have ever divided into two sects, Materialists and Idealists; the first class founding on experience, the second on consciousness; the first class beginning to think from the data of the senses, the second class perceive that the senses are not final, and say, the senses give us representations of things, but what are the things themselves, they cannot tell. The materialist insists on facts, on history, on the force of circumstances, and the animal wants of man; the idealist on the power of Thought and of Will, on inspiration, on miracle, on individual culture. These two modes of thinking are both natural, but the idealist contends that his way of thinking is in higher nature. He concedes all that the other affirms, admits the impression of sense, admits their coherency, their use and beauty, and then asks the materialist for his grounds of assurance that things are as his senses represent them. But I, he says, affirm facts not affected by the illusions of sense, facts which are of the same nature as the faculty which reports them, and not liable to doubt; facts which in their first appearance to us assume a native superiority to material facts, degrading these into a language by which the first are to be spoken; facts which it only needs a retirement from the senses to discern. Every materialist will be an idealist; but an idealist can never go backward to be a materialist.

The idealist, in speaking of events, sees them as spirits. He does not deny the sensuous fact; by no means; but he will not see that alone. He does not deny the presence of this table, this chair, and the walls of this room, but he looks at these things as the reverse side of the tapestry, as the *other end,* each being a sequel or completion of a spiritual fact which nearly concerns him. This manner of looking at things, transfers every object in nature from an independent and anomalous position without there, into the consciousness. Even the materialist Condillac, perhaps the most logical expounder of materialism, was constrained to say, "Though we should soar into the heavens, though we should sink into the abyss, we never go out of ourselves; it is always our own thought that we perceive." What more could an idealist say?

The materialist, secure in the certainty of sensation, mocks at fine-spun theories, at star-gazers and dreamers, and believes that his life is solid, that he at least takes nothing for granted, but knows where he stands, and what he does. Yet how easy it is to show him, that he also is a phantom walking and working amid phantoms, and that he need only ask a question or two beyond his daily questions, to find his solid universe growing dim and impalpable before his sense. The sturdy capitalist, no matter how deep and square on blocks of Quincy granite he lays the foundations of his banking-house or Exchange, must set it, at last, not on a cube corresponding to the angles of his structure, but on a mass of unknown materials and solidity, red-hot or white-hot, perhaps at the core, which rounds off to an almost perfect sphericity, and lies floating in soft air, and goes spinning away, dragging bank and banker with it at a rate of thousands of miles the hour, he knows not whither,—a bit of bullet, now glimmering, now darkling through a small cubic space on the edge of an unimaginable pit of emptiness. And this wild baloon, in which his whole venture is embarked, is a just symbol of his whole state and faculty. One thing, at least, he says is certain, and does not give me the headache, that figures do not lie; the multiplication table has been hitherto found unimpeachable truth; and, moreover, if I put a gold eagle in my safe, I find it again to-morrow;— but for these thoughts, I know not whence they are. They change and pass away. But ask him why he believes that an uniform experience will continue uniform, or on what grounds he founds his faith in his figures, and he will perceive that his mental fabric is built up on just as strange and quaking foundations as his proud edifice of stone.

In the order of thought, the materialist takes his departure from the external world, and esteems a man as one product of that. The idealist takes his departure from his consciousness, and reckons the world as an appearance. The materialist respects sensible masses, Society,

Government, social art, and luxury, every establishment, every mass, whether majority of numbers, or extent of space, or amount of objects, every social action. The idealist has another measure, which is metaphysical, namely, the *rank* which things themselves take in his consciousness; not at all, the size or appearance. Mind is the only reality, of which men and all other natures are better or worse reflectors. Nature, literature, history, are only subjective phenomena. Although in his action overpowered by the laws of action, and so, warmly coöperating with men, even preferring them to himself, yet when he speaks scientifically, or after the order of thought, he is constrained to degrade persons into representatives of truths. He does not respect labor, or the products of labor, namely, property, otherwise than as a manifold symbol, illustrating with wonderful fidelity of details the laws of being; he does not respect government, except as far as it reiterates the law of his mind; nor the church; nor charities; nor arts, for themselves; but hears, as at a vast distance, what they say, as if his consciousness would speak to him through a pantomimic scene. His thought,—that is the Universe. His experience inclines him to behold the procession of facts you call the world, as flowing perpetually outward from an invisible, unsounded centre in himself, centre alike of him and of them, and necessitating him to regard all things as having a subjective or relative existence, relative to that aforesaid Unknown Centre of him.

From this transfer of the world into the consciousness, this beholding of all things in the mind, follows easily his whole ethics. It is simpler to be self-dependent. The height, the deity of man is to be self-sustained, to need no gift, no foreign force. Society is good when it does not violate me; but best when it is likest to solitude. Everything real is self-existent. Everything divine shares the self-existence of Deity. All that you call the world is the shadow of that substance which you are, the perpetual creation of the powers of thought, of those that are dependent and of those that are independent of your will. Do not cumber yourself with fruitless pains to mend and remedy remote effects; let the soul be erect, and all things will go well. You think me the child of my circumstances: I make my circumstance. Let any thought or motive of mine be different from that they are, the difference will transform my whole condition and economy. I—this thought which is called I,—is the mould into which the world is poured like melted wax. The mould is invisible, but the world betrays the shape of the mould. You call it the power of circumstance, but it is the power of me. Am I in harmony with myself? my position will seem to you just and commanding. Am I vicious and insane? my fortunes will seem to you obscure and descending. As I am, so shall I associate; as I am, so shall I act; Cæsar's history will paint out Cæsar. Jesus acted so, because he thought so. I do not wish to overlook or to gainsay any reality; I say, I make my circumstance: but if you ask me, Whence am I? I feel like other men my relation to that Fact which cannot be spoken, or defined, nor even thought, but which exists, and will exist.

The Transcendentalist adopts the whole connexion of spiritual doctrine. He believes in miracle, in the perpetual openness of the human mind to new influx of light and power; he believes in inspiration, and in ecstasy. He wishes that the spiritual principle should be suffered to demonstrate itself to the end, in all possible applications to the state of man, without the admission of anything unspiritual; that is, anything positive, dogmatic, personal. Thus, the spiritual measure of inspiration is the depth of the thought, and never, *who* said it? And so he resists all attempts to palm other rules and measures on the spirit than its own.

In action, he easily incurs the charge of antinomianism by his avowal that he, who has the Lawgiver, may with safety not only neglect, but even contravene every written commandment. In the play of Othello, the expiring Desdemona absolves her husband of the murder, to her attendant Emilia. Afterwards, when Emilia charges him with the crime, Othello exclaims,

> "You heard her say herself it was not I."

Emilia replies,

> "The more angel she, and thou the blacker devil."

Of this fine incident, Jacobi, the Transcendental moralist, makes use, with other parallel instances, in his reply to Fichte. Jacobi, refusing all measure of right and wrong except the determinations of the private spirit, remarks that there is no crime but has sometimes been a virtue. "I," he says, "am that atheist, that godless person who, in opposition to an imaginary doctrine of calculation, would lie as the dying Desdemona lied; would lie and deceive as Pylades when he personated Orestes; would assassinate like Timoleon; would perjure myself like Epaminondas, and John de Witt; I would resolve on suicide like

Cato; I would commit sacrilege with David; yea, and pluck ears of corn on the Sabbath, for no other reason than that I was fainting for lack of food. For, I have assurance in myself that in pardoning these faults according to the letter, man exerts the sovereign right which the majesty of his being confers on him; he sets the seal of his divine nature to the grace he accords."

In like manner, if there is anything grand and daring in human thought or virtue, any reliance on the vast, the unknown; any presentiment; any extravagance of faith, the spiritualist adopts it as most in nature. The oriental mind has always tended to this largeness. Buddhism is an expression of it. The Buddhist who thanks no man, who says, "do not flatter your benefactors," but who in his conviction that every good deed can by no possibility escape its reward, will not deceive the benefactor by pretending that he has done more than be should, is a Transcendentalist.

You will see by this sketch that there is no such thing as a Transcendental *party;* that there is no pure Transcendentalist; that we know of none but the prophets and heralds of such a philosophy; that all who by strong bias of nature have leaned to the spiritual side in doctrine, have stopped short of their goal. We have had many harbingers and forerunners; but of a purely spiritual life, history has yet afforded no example. I mean, we have yet no man who has leaned entirely on his character, and eaten angels' food; who, trusting to his sentiments, found life made of miracles; who, working for universal aims, found himself fed, he knew not how; clothed, sheltered, and weaponed, he knew not how, and yet it was done by his own hands. Only in the instinct of the lower animals we find the suggestion of the methods of it, and something higher than our understanding. The squirrel hoards nuts, and the bee gathers honey, without knowing what they do, and they are thus provided for without selfishness or disgrace.

Shall we say, then, that Transcendentalism is the Saturnalia or excess of Faith; the presentiment of a faith proper to man in his integrity, excessive only when his imperfect obedience hinders the satisfaction of his wish. Nature is transcendental, exists primarily, necessarily, ever works and advances, yet takes no thought for the morrow. Man owns the dignity of the life which throbs around him in chemistry, and tree, and animal, and in the involuntary functions of his own body; yet he is baulked when he tries to fling himself into this enchanted circle, where all is done without degradation. Yet genius and virtue predict in man the same absence of private ends, and of condescension to circumstances, united with every trait and talent of beauty and power.

This way of thinking, falling on Roman times, made Stoic philosophers; falling on despotic times, made patriot Catos and Brutuses; falling on superstitious times, made prophets and apostles; on popish times, made protestants and ascetic monks, preachers of Faith against the preachers of Works; on prelatical times, made Puritans and Quakers; and falling on Unitarian and conservative times, makes the peculiar shades of Idealism which we know.

It is well known to most of my audience, that the Idealism of the present day acquired the name of Transcendental, from the use of that term by Immanuel Kant, of Konigsberg, who replied to the skeptical philosophy of Locke, which insisted that there was nothing in the intellect which was not previously in the experience of the senses, by showing that there was a very important class of ideas, or imperative forms, which did not come by experience, but through which experience was acquired; that these were intuitions of the mind itself; and he denominated them *Transcendental* forms. The extraordinary profoundness and precision of that man's thinking have given vogue to his nomenclature, in Europe and America, to that extent, that whatever belongs to the class of intuitive thought, is popularly called at the present day *Transcendental*.

Although, as we have said, there is no pure transcendentalist, yet the tendency to respect the intuitions, and to give them, at least in our creed, all authority over our experience, has deeply colored the conversation and poetry of the present day; and the history of genius and of religion in these times, though impure, and as yet not incarnated in any powerful individual, will be the history of this tendency.

It is a sign of our times, conspicuous to the coarsest observer, that many intelligent and religious persons withdraw themselves from the common labors and competitions of the market and the caucus, and betake themselves to a certain solitary and critical way of living, from which no solid fruit has yet appeared to justify their separation. They hold themselves aloof: they feel the disproportion between their faculties and the work offered them, and they prefer to ramble in the country and perish of ennui, to the degradation of such charities and such ambitions as the city can propose to them. They are striking work, and crying out for somewhat worthy to do! What they do, is done only because they are overpowered by the humanities that speak on all sides; and they consent to such labor as is open to them, though to their lofty dream the writing of Iliads or Hamlets, or the building of cities or empires seems drudgery.

Now every one must do after his kind, be he asp or angel, and these must. The question, which a wise man and a student of modern history will ask, is, what that kind is? And truly, as in ecclesiastical history we take so much pains to know what the Gnostics, what the Essenes, what the Manichees, and what the Reformers believed, it would not misbecome us to inquire nearer home, what these companions and contemporaries of ours think and do, at least so far as these thoughts and actions appear to be not accidental and personal, but common to many, and so the inevitable flower of the Tree of Time. Our American literature and spiritual history are, we confess, in the optative mood; but whoso knows these seething brains, these admirable radicals, these unsocial worshippers, these talkers who talk the sun and moon away, will believe that this heresy cannot pass away without leaving its mark.

They are lonely; the spirit of their writing and conversation is lonely; they shed influences; they shun general society; they incline to shut themselves in their chamber in the house, to live in the country rather than in the town, and to find their tasks and amusements in solitude. Society, to be sure, does not like this very well; it saith, Whoso goes to walk alone, accuses the whole world; he declareth all to be unfit to be his companions; it is very uncivil, nay, insulting; Society will retaliate. Meantime, this retirement does not proceed from any whim on the part of these separators; but if any one will take pains to talk with them, he will find that this part is chosen both from temperament and from principle; with some unwillingness, too, and as a choice of the less of two evils; for these persons are not by nature melancholy, sour, and unsocial,—they are not stockish or brute,—but joyous, susceptible, affectionate; they have even more than others a great wish to be loved. Like the young Mozart, they are rather ready to cry ten times a day, "But are you sure you love me?" Nay, if they tell you their whole thought, they will own that love seems to them the last and highest gift of nature; that there are persons whom in their hearts they daily thank for existing,—persons whose faces are perhaps unknown to them, but whose fame and spirit have penetrated their solitude,—and for whose sake they wish to exist. To behold the beauty of another character, which inspires a new interest in our own; to behold the beauty lodged in a human being, with such vivacity of apprehension, that I am instantly forced home to inquire if I am not deformity itself; to behold in another the expression of a love so high that it assures itself,—assures itself also to me against every possible casualty except my unworthiness;—these are degrees on the scale of human happiness, to which they have ascended; and it is a fidelity to this sentiment which has made common association distasteful to them. They wish a just and even fellowship, or none. They cannot gossip with you, and they do not wish, as they are sincere and religious, to gratify any mere curiosity which you may entertain. Like fairies, they do not wish to be spoken of. Love me, they say, but do not ask who is my cousin and my uncle. If you do not need to hear my thought, because you can read it in my face and behavior, then I will tell it you from sunrise to sunset. If you cannot divine it, you would not understand what I say. I will not molest myself for you. I do not wish to be profaned.

And yet, when you see them near, it seems as if this loneliness, and not this love, would prevail in their circumstances, because of the extravagant demand they make on human nature. That, indeed, constitutes a new feature in their portrait, that they are the most exacting and extortionate critics. Their quarrel with every man they meet, is not with his kind, but with his degree. There is not enough of him,—that is the only fault. They prolong their privilege of childhood in this wise, of doing nothing,—but making immense demands on all the gladiators in the lists of action and fame. They make us feel the strange disappointment which overcasts every human youth. So many promising youths, and never a finished man! The profound nature will have a savage rudeness; the delicate one will be shallow, or the victim of sensibility; the richly accomplished will have some capital absurdity; and so every piece has a crack. 'T is strange, but this masterpiece is a result of such an extreme delicacy, that the most unobserved flaw in the boy will neutralize the most aspiring genius, and spoil the work. Talk with a seaman of the hazards to life in his profession, and he will ask you, "Where are the old sailors? do you not see that all are young men?" And we, on this sea of human thought, in like manner inquire, Where are the old idealists? where are they who represented to the last generation that extravagant hope, which a few happy aspirants suggest to ours? In looking at the class of counsel, and power, and wealth, and at the matronage of the land, amidst all the prudence and all the triviality, one asks, Where are they who represented genius, virtue, the invisible and heavenly world, to these? Are they dead,—taken in early ripeness to the gods,—as ancient wisdom foretold their fate? Or did the high idea die out of them, and leave their unperfumed body as its tomb and tablet, announcing to all that the celestial inhabitant, who once gave them beauty, had departed? Will it be better with the new generation? We easily predict a fair future to each new candidate who enters the lists, but we are frivolous and volatile, and by low aims and ill example do what we can to defeat this hope. Then these youths bring us a rough but effectual aid. By their unconcealed dissatisfaction, they expose our poverty, and the insignificance of man to man. A man is a poor limitary benefactor. He ought to be a shower of benefits—a great influence, which should never let his brother go, but should refresh old merits continually with new ones; so that, though absent, he should never be out of my mind, his name never far from my lips; but if the earth should open at my side, or my last hour were come, his name should be the prayer I should utter to the Universe. But in our experience, man is cheap, and friendship wants its deep sense. We affect to dwell with our friends in their absence, but we do not; when deed, word, or letter comes not, they let us go. These exacting children advertise us of our wants. There is no compliment, no smooth speech with them; they pay you only this one compliment, of insatiable expectation; they aspire, they severely exact, and if they only stand fast in this watch-tower, and persist in demanding unto the end, and without end, then are they terrible friends, whereof poet and priest cannot choose but stand in awe; and what if they eat clouds, and drink wind, they have not been without service to the race of man.

With this passion for what is great and extraordinary, it cannot be wondered at, that they are repelled by vulgarity and frivolity in people. They say to themselves, It is better to be alone than in bad company. And it is really a wish to be met,—the wish to find society for their hope and religion,—which prompts them to shun what is called society. They feel that they are never so fit for friendship, as when they have quit mankind, and taken themselves to friend. A picture, a book, a favorite spot in the hills or the woods, which they can people with the fair and worthy creation of the fancy, can give them often forms so vivid, that these for the time shall seem real, and society the illusion.

But their solitary and fastidious manners not only withdraw them from the conversation, but from the labors of the world; they are not good citizens, not good members of society; unwillingly they bear their part of the public and private burdens; they do not willingly share in the public charities, in the public religious rites, in the enterprises of education, of missions foreign or domestic, in the abolition of the slave-trade, or in the temperance-society. They are inactive; they do not even like to vote. The philanthropists inquire whether Transcendentalism does not mean sloth. They had as lief hear that their friend was dead as that he was a Transcendentalist; for then is he paralyzed, and can never do anything for humanity. What right, cries the good world, has the man of genius to retreat from work, and indulge himself? The popular literary creed seems to be, "I am a sublime genius; I ought not therefore to labor." But genius is the power to labor better and more availably than others. Deserve thy genius: exalt it. The good, the illuminated, sit apart from the rest, censuring their dulness and vices, as if they thought that, by sitting very grand in their chairs, the very brokers, attorneys, and congressmen would see the error of their ways, and flock to them. But the good and wise must learn to act, and carry salvation to the combatants and demagogues in the dusty arena below.

On the part of these children, it is replied, that life and their faculty seem to them gifts too rich to be squandered on such trifles as you propose to them. What you call your fundamental institutions, your great and holy causes, seem to them great abuses, and, when nearly seen, paltry matters. Each "Cause," as it is called,—say Abolition, Temperance, say Calvinism, or Unitarianism,—becomes speedily a little shop, where the article, let it have been at first never so subtle and ethereal, is now made up into portable and convenient cakes, and retailed in small quantities to suit purchasers. You make very free use of these words "great and holy," but few things appear to them such. Few persons have any magnificence of nature to inspire enthusiasm, and the philanthropies and charities have a certain air of quackery. As to the general course of living, and the daily employments of men, they cannot see much virtue in these, since they are parts of this vicious circle; and, as no great ends are answered by the men, there is nothing noble in the arts by which they are maintained. Nay, they have made the experiment, and found that from the liberal professions to the coarsest manual labor, and from the courtesies of the academy and the college to the conventions of the cotillon-room and the morning call, there is a spirit of cowardly compromise and seeming, which intimates a frightful skepticism, a life without love, and an activity without an aim.

Unless the action is necessary, unless it is adequate, I do not wish to perform it. I do not wish to do one thing but once. I do not love routine.

Once possessed of the principle, it is equally easy to make four or forty thousand applications of it. A great man will be content to have indicated in any the slightest manner his perception of the reigning Idea of his time, and will leave to those who like it the multiplication of examples. When he has hit the white, the rest may shatter the target. Every thing admonishes us how needlessly long life is. Every moment of a hero so raises and cheers us, that a twelve-month is an age. All that the brave Xanthus brings home from his wars, is the recollection that, at the storming of Samos, "in the heat of the battle, Pericles smiled on me, and passed on to another detachment." It is the quality of the moment, not the number of days, of events, or of actors, that imports.

New, we confess, and by no means happy, is our condition: if you want the aid of our labor, we ourselves stand in greater want of the labor. We are miserable with inaction. We perish of rest and rust. But we do not like your work.

"Then," says the world, "show me your own."

"We have none."

"What will you do, then?" cries the world.

"We will wait."

"How long?"

"Until the Universe rises up and calls us to work."

"But whilst you wait, you grow old and useless."

"Be it so: I can sit in a corner and *perish*, (as you call it,) but I will not move until I have the highest command. If no call should come for years, for centuries, then I know that the want of the Universe is the attestation of faith by this my abstinence. Your virtuous projects, so called, do not cheer me. I know that which shall come will cheer me. If I cannot work, at least I need not lie. All that is clearly due to-day is not to lie. In other places, other men have encountered sharp trials, and have behaved themselves well. The martyrs were sawn asunder, or hung alive on meat hooks. Cannot we screw our courage to patience and truth, and without complaint, or even with good-humor, await our turn of action in the Infinite Counsels?"

But, to come a little closer to the secret of these persons, we must say, that to them it seems a very easy matter to answer the objections of the man of the world, but not so easy to dispose of the doubts and objections that occur to themselves. They are exercised in their own spirit with queries, which acquaint them with all adversity, and with the trials of the bravest heroes. When I asked them concerning their private experience, they answered somewhat in this wise: It is not to be denied that there must be some wide difference between my faith and other faith; and mine is a certain brief experience, which surprised me in the highway or in the market, in some place, at some time,— whether in the body or out of the body, God knoweth,—and made me aware that I had played the fool with fools all this time, but that law existed for me and for all; that to me belonged trust, a child's trust and obedience, and the worship of ideas, and I should never be fool more. Well, in the space of an hour, probably, I was let down from this height; I was at my old tricks, the selfish member of a selfish society. My life is superficial, takes no root in the deep world; I ask, When shall I die, and be relieved of the responsibility of seeing an Universe which I do not use? I wish to exchange this flash-of-lightning faith for continuous daylight, this fever-glow for a benign climate.

These two states of thought diverge every moment, and stand in wild contrast. To whom who looks at his life from these moments of illumination, it will seem that he skulks and plays a mean, shiftless and subaltern part in the world. That is to be done which he has not skill to do, or to be said which others can say better, and he lies by, or occupies his hands with some plaything, until his hour comes again. Much of our reading, much of our labor, seems mere waiting: it was not that we were born for. Any other could do it as well, or better. So little skill enters into these works, so little do they mix with the divine life, that it really signifies little what we do, whether we turn a grindstone, or ride, or run, or make fortunes, or govern the state. The worst feature of this double consciousness is, that the two lives, of the understanding and of the soul, which we lead, really show very little relation to each other, never meet and measure each other: one prevails now, all buzz and din; and the other prevails then, all infinitude and paradise; and, with the progress of life, the two discover no greater disposition to reconcile themselves. Yet, what is my faith? What am I? What but a thought of serenity and independence, an abode in the deep blue sky? Presently the clouds shut down again; yet we retain the belief that this pretty web we weave will at last be overshot and reticulated with veins of the blue, and that the moments will characterize the days. Patience, then, is for us, is it not? Patience, and still patience. When we pass, as presently we shall, into some new infinitude, out of this Iceland of negations, it will please us to reflect that, though we had few virtues or consolations, we bore with our indigence, nor once strove to repair it with hypocrisy or false heat of any kind.

But this class are not sufficiently characterized, if we omit to add that they are lovers and worshippers of Beauty. In the eternal trinity of Truth, Goodness, and Beauty, each in its perfection including the three, they prefer to make Beauty the sign and head. Something of the same taste is observable in all the moral movements of the time, in the religious and benevolent enterprises. They have a liberal, even an æsthetic spirit. A reference to Beauty in action sounds, to be sure, a little hollow and ridiculous in the ears of the old church. In politics, it has often sufficed, when they treated of justice, if they kept the bounds of selfish calculation. If they granted restitution, it was prudence which granted it. But the justice which is now claimed for the black, and the pauper, and the drunkard, is for Beauty—is for a necessity to the soul of the agent, not of the beneficiary. I say this is the tendency, not yet the realization. Our virtue totters and trips, does not yet walk firmly. Its representatives are austere; they preach and denounce; their rectitude is not yet a grace. They are still liable to that slight taint of burlesque which, in our strange world, attaches to the zealot. A saint should be as dear as the apple of the eye. Yet we are tempted to smile, and we flee from the working to the speculative reformer, to escape that same slight ridicule. Alas for these days of derision and criticism! We call the Beautiful the highest, because it appears to us the golden mean, escaping the dowdiness of the good, and the heartlessness of the true.—They are lovers of nature also, and find an indemnity in the inviolable order of the world for the violated order and grace of man.

There is, no doubt, a great deal of well-founded objection to be spoken or felt against the sayings and doings of this class, some of whose traits we have selected; no doubt, they will lay themselves open to criticism and to lampoons, and as ridiculous stories will be to be told to them as of any. There will be cant and pretension; there will be subtility and moonshine. These persons are of unequal strength, and do not all prosper. They complain that everything around them must be denied; and if feeble, it takes all their strength to deny, before they can begin to lead their own life. Grave seniors insist on their respect to this institution, and that usage; to an obsolete history; to some vocation, or college, or etiquette, or beneficiary, or charity, or morning or evening call, which they resist, as what does not concern them. But it costs such sleepless nights, and alienations and misgivings,—they have so many moods about it;—these old guardians never changed *their* minds; they have but one mood on the subject, namely, that Antony is very perverse,—that it is quite as much as Antony can do, to assert his rights, abstain from what he thinks foolish, and keep his temper. He cannot help the reaction of this injustice in his own mind. He is braced-up and stilted; all freedom and flowing genius, all sallies of wit and frolic nature are quite out of the question; it is well if he can keep from lying, injustice, and suicide. This is no time for gayety and grace. His strength and spirits are wasted in rejection. But the strong spirits over-power those around them without effort. Their thought and emotion comes in like a flood, quite withdraws them from all notice of these carping critics; they surrender themselves with glad heart to the heav-enly guide, and only by implication reject the clamorous nonsense of the hour. Grave seniors talk to the deaf,—church and old book mumble and ritualize to an unheeding, preoccupied and advancing mind, and thus they by happiness of greater momentum lose no time, but take the right road at first.

But all these of whom I speak are not proficients, they are novices; they only show the road in which man should travel, when the soul has greater health and prowess. Yet let them feel the dignity of their charge, and deserve a larger power. Their heart is the ark in which the fire is concealed, which shall burn in a broader and universal flame. Let them obey the Genius then most when his impulse is wildest; then most when he seems to lead to uninhabitable desarts of thought and life; for the path which the hero travels alone is the highway of health and benefit to mankind. What is the privilege and nobility of our nature, but its persistency, through its power to attach itself to what is permanent?

Society also has its duties in reference to this class, and must behold them with what charity it can. Possibly some benefit may yet accrue from them to the state. In our Mechanics' Fair, there must be not only bridges, ploughs, carpenters' planes, and baking troughs, but also some few finer instruments,—raingauges, thermometers, and telescopes; and in society, besides farmers, sailors, and weavers, there must be a few persons of purer fire kept specially as gauges and meters of charac-ter; persons of a fine, detecting instinct, who betray the smallest accu-mulations of wit and feeling in the bystander. Perhaps too there might be room for the exciters and monitors; collectors of the heavenly spark with power to convey the electricity to others. Or, as the storm-tossed vessel at sea speaks the frigate or "line-packet" to learn its longitude, so it may not be without its advantage that we should now and then encounter rare and gifted men, to compare the points of our spiritual compass, and verify our bearings from superior chronometers.

Amidst the downward tendency and proneness of things, when

every voice is raised for a new road or another statute, or a subscription of stock, for an improvement in dress, or in dentistry, for a new house or a larger business, for a political party, or the division of an estate,—will you not tolerate one or two solitary voices in the land, speaking for thoughts and principles not marketable or perishable? Soon these improvements and mechanical inventions will be superseded; these modes of living lost out of memory; these cities rotted, ruined by war, by new inventions, by new seats of trade, or the geologic changes:—all gone, like the shells which sprinkle the seabeach with a white colony to-day, forever renewed to be forever destroyed. But the thoughts which these few hermits strove to proclaim by silence, as well as by speech, not only by what they did, but by what they forbore to do, shall abide in beauty and strength, to reorganize themselves in nature, to invest themselves anew in other, perhaps higher endowed and happier mixed clay than ours, in fuller union with the surrounding system.

# Charles Dickens
## On Boston Transcendentalism
### (1842)

Charles Dickens (1812–70) was already the most popular novelist of his age in the English-speaking world at the time of his first of two lecture tours to the United States in 1842. His book about his travels irritated many of his American readers with its often sarcastic portrayal of the manners and pretensions of the still-new nation. But he had complimentary things to say about his stay in Boston, including this sympathetically bemused cameo portrait of Transcendentalism. It testified to the movement's growing fame abroad, thanks especially to Emerson—and to Carlyle's promotion of his work.

SOURCE: *American Notes for General Circulation.* London: Chapman and Hall, 1842.

… there has sprung up in Boston a sect of philosophers known as Transcendentalists. On inquiring what its appellation might be supposed to signify, I was given to understand that whatever was unintelligible would be certainly transcendental. Not deriving much comfort from this elucidation, I pursued the inquiry still further, and found that the Transcendentalists are followers of my friend Mr. Carlyle, or I should rather say, of a follower of his, Mr. Ralph Waldo Emerson. This gentleman has written a volume of Essays, in which, among much that is dreamy and fanciful (if he will pardon me for saying so), there is much more that is true and manly, honest and bold. Transcendentalism has its occasional vagaries (what school has not?) but it has good healthful qualities in spite of them, not least among the number a hearty disgust of Cant, and an aptitude to detect her in all the million varieties of her everlasting wardrobe. And therefore, if I were a Bostonian, I think I would be a Transcendentalist.

# 9.

# HENRY DAVID THOREAU
## A TRANSCENDENTALIST'S PROFESSION OF FAITH
### (1853)

This pugnacious passage shows that even in the 1850s, as Emerson had reached the height of his fame and as activism by Transcendentalist sympathizers was making a significant impact within the antislavery movement, to be classified as a "Transcendentalist" was still far from being mainstream. Even Henry David Thoreau was prepared to talk tougher to his *Journal* than to the scientific community. He dutifully filled out the form that the American Association for Advancement of Science sent, listing as his particular branch of interest in science "The Manners and Customs of the Indians of the Algonquin Group previous to contact with the civilized man." He remained a member of the Association, which memorialized him after his death with a short obituary in its official journal.

SOURCE: *The Journal of Henry David Thoreau*, ed. Bradford Torrey and Francis Allen. Boston: Houghton-Mifflin, 1906, volume 5, slightly corrected. For the sake of readability, I use this text as a basis rather than the more minutely accurate Princeton University scholarly edition (*Journal 5: 1852–53*, pp. 469–70), for the language is identical except for two word endings that I have restored here, and Thoreau's dash-ridden manuscript punctuation (reminiscent of Emily Dickinson's manuscript poems and letters) is herky-jerky and often also confusing. Only in two instances, also corrected here, does Thoreau's punctuation seem essential to the sense.

The secretary of the Association for the Advancement of Science requested me, as he probably has thousands of others, by a printed circular letter from Washington the other day, to fill in the blanks against certain questions, among which the most important one was what branch of science I was especially interested in, using the term science in the most comprehensive sense possible. Now, though I could state to a select few that department of human inquiry which engages me, and should be rejoiced at an opportunity to do so, I felt that it would be to make myself the laughing-stock of the scientific community to describe or attempt to describe to them that branch of science which especially interests me, inasmuch as they do not believe in a science which deals with the higher law. So I was obliged to speak to their condition and describe to them that poor part of me which alone they can understand. The fact is I am a mystic—a transcendentalist—and a natural philosopher to boot. Now I think of it, I should have told them at once that I was a transcendentalist. That would have been the shortest way of telling them that they would not understand my explanations.

How absurd that, though I probably stand as near to nature as any of them, and am by constitution as good an observer as most, yet a true account of my relation to nature itself should excite their ridicule only. If it had been the secretary of an association of which Plato or Aristotle was the president, I should not have hesitated to describe my studies at once and particularly.

# III

# SPIRITUAL FERMENT
# AND
# RELIGIOUS REFORM

# Ralph Waldo Emerson
## Divinity School Address
### (1838)

This is Emerson's most incendiary work. It was delivered as a commencement oration at the behest of the graduating class of the Harvard Divinity School, Unitarianism's academic home base and Emerson's own graduate alma mater. Emerson takes aim at the two related arguments on which Unitarian theology chiefly rested its case for being a distinctive form of "rational" Christianity: that the Gospel narratives of Jesus' miracles proved the authenticity of Christianity, and that Jesus was God's unique and authoritative messenger. After this comes an equally acerbic denunciation of ineffective preaching, in which Emerson charges each graduate to think of himself by contrast as "a newborn bard of the Holy Ghost" and preach prophetically. The address caused an irreversible rift between Unitarian liberals and radicals. Emerson was not invited back again to speak at Harvard for nearly thirty years. Indeed, his choice of venue, Unitarianism's inner sanctum, in the presence of its oligarchs, was as important in giving offense as the things he said and the lofty, ironic tone in which he said them. Emerson professed surprise and alarm at the ensuing fallout, of which the next two items are examples; and no doubt some conservatives did overreact. The poet Henry Wadsworth Longfellow, himself a moderate Unitarian, couldn't understand all the fuss over what seemed to him nothing more scandalous than a "stout humanitarian discourse." But it is clear from Emerson's Journal reflections before the event that he knew he would be pushing the limits. The address itself is clearly provocative from the very start, with its distinctly unclerical opening paean to the "luxury" of summer.

SOURCE: *An Address Delivered Before the Senior Class in Divinity College, Cambridge, Sunday Evening, 15 July, 1838.* Boston: James Munroe, 1838.

In this refulgent summer it has been a luxury to draw the breath of life. The grass grows, the buds burst, the meadow is spotted with fire and gold in the tint of flowers. The air is full of birds, and sweet with the breath of the pine, the balm-of-Gilead, and the new hay. Night brings no gloom to the heart with its welcome shade. Through the transparent darkness pour the stars their almost spiritual rays. Man under them seems a young child, and his huge globe a toy. The cool night bathes the world as with a river, and prepares his eyes again for the crimson dawn. The mystery of nature was never displayed more happily. The corn and the wine have been freely dealt to all creatures, and the never-broken silence with which the old bounty goes forward, has not yielded yet one word of explanation. One is constrained to respect the perfection of this world, in which our senses converse. How wide; how rich; what invitation from every property it gives to every faculty of man! In its fruitful soils; in its navigable sea; in its mountains of metal and stone; in its forests of all woods; in its animals; in its chemical ingredients; in the powers and path of light, heat, attraction, and life, is it well worth the pith and heart of great men to subdue and enjoy it. The planters, the mechanics, the inventors, the astronomers, the builders of cities, and the captains, history delights to honor.

But the moment the mind opens, and reveals the laws which traverse the universe, and make things what they are, then shrinks the great world at once into a mere illustration and fable of this mind. What am I? and What is? asks the human spirit with a curiosity newkindled, but never to be quenched. Behold these outrunning laws, which our imperfect apprehension can see tend this way and that, but not come full circle. Behold these infinite relations, so like, so unlike; many, yet one. I would study, I would know, I would admire forever. These works of thought have been the entertainments of the human spirit in all ages.

A more secret, sweet, and overpowering beauty appears to man when his heart and mind open to the sentiment of virtue. Then instantly he is instructed in what is above him. He learns that his being is without bound; that, to the good, to the perfect, he is born, low as he now lies in evil and weakness. That which he venerates is still his own, though he has not realized it yet. *He ought.* He knows the sense of that grand word, though his analysis fails entirely to render account of it. When in innocency, or when by intellectual perception, he attains to say,—"I love the Right; Truth is beautiful within and without, forevermore. Virtue, I am thine: save me: use me: thee will I serve, day and night, in great, in small, that I may be not virtuous, but virtue;"—then is the end of the creation answered, and God is well pleased.

The sentiment of virtue is a reverence and delight in the presence of certain divine laws. It perceives that this homely game of life we play, covers, under what seem foolish details, principles that astonish. The child amidst his baubles, is learning the action of light, motion, gravity, muscular force; and in the game of human life, love, fear, justice, appetite, man, and God, interact. These laws refuse to be adequately stated. They will not by us or for us be written out on paper, or spoken by the tongue. They elude, evade our persevering thought, and yet we read them hourly in each other's faces, in each other's actions, in our own remorse. The moral traits which are all globed into every virtuous act and thought,—in speech, we must sever, and describe or suggest by painful enumeration of many particulars. Yet, as this sentiment is the essence of all religion, let me guide your eye to the precise objects of the sentiment, by an enumeration of some of those classes of facts in which this element is conspicuous.

The intuition of the moral sentiment is an insight of the perfection of the laws of the soul. These laws execute themselves. They are out of time, out of space, and not subject to circumstance. Thus; in the soul of man there is a justice whose retributions are instant and entire. He who does a good deed, is instantly ennobled himself. He who does a mean deed, is by the action itself contracted. He who puts off impurity, thereby puts on purity. If a man is at heart just, then in so far is he God; the safety of God, the immortality of God, the majesty of God do enter into that man with justice. If a man dissemble, deceive, he deceives himself, and goes out of acquaintance with his own being. A man in the view of absolute goodness, adores, with total humility. Every step so downward, is a step upward. The man who renounces himself, comes to himself by so doing.

See how this rapid intrinsic energy worketh everywhere, righting wrongs, correcting appearances, and bringing up facts to a harmony with thoughts. Its operation in life, though slow to the senses, is, at last, as sure as in the soul. By it, a man is made the Providence to himself dispensing good to his goodness, and evil to his sin. Character is always known. Thefts never enrich; alms never impoverish; murder will speak out of stone walls. The least admixture of a lie,—for example, the smallest mixture of vanity, the least attempt to make a good impression, a favorable appearance,—will instantly vitiate the effect. But speak the truth, and all nature and all spirits help you with unexpected furtherance. Speak the truth, and all things alive or brute are vouchers, and the very roots of the grass underground there, do seem to stir and move to bear you witness. See again the perfection of the Law as it applies itself to the affections, and becomes the law of society. As we are, so we associate. The good, by affinity, seek the good; the vile, by affinity, the vile. Thus of their own volition, souls proceed into heaven, into hell.

These facts have always suggested to man the sublime creed, that the world is not the product of manifold power, but of one will, of one mind; and that one mind is everywhere, in each ray of the star, in each wavelet of the pool, active; and whatever opposes that will, is everywhere baulked and baffled, because things are made so, and not otherwise. Good is positive. Evil is merely privative, not absolute. It is like cold, which is the privation of heat. All evil is so much death or nonentity. Benevolence is absolute and real. So much benevolence as a man hath, so much life hath he. For all things proceed out of this same spirit, which is differently named love, justice, temperance, in its different applications, just as the ocean receives different names on the several shores which it washes. All things proceed out of the same spirit, and all things conspire with it. Whilst a man seeks good ends, he is strong by the whole strength of nature. In so far as he roves from these ends, he bereaves himself of power, of auxiliaries; his being shrinks out of all remote channels, he becomes less and less, a mote, a point, until absolute badness is absolute death.

The perception of this law of laws always awakens in the mind a sentiment which we call the religious sentiment, and which makes our highest happiness. Wonderful is its power to charm and to command. It is a mountain air. It is the embalmer of the world. It is myrrh and storax, and chlorine and rosemary. It makes the sky and the hills sublime, and the silent song of the stars is it. By it, is the universe made safe and habitable, not by science or power. Thought may work cold and intransitive in things, and find no end or unity. But the dawn of the sentiment of virtue on the heart, gives and is the assurance that Law is sovereign over all natures; and the worlds, time, space, eternity, do seem to break out into joy.

This sentiment is divine and deifying. It is the beatitude of man. It makes him illimitable. Through it, the soul first knows itself. It corrects the capital mistake of the infant man, who seeks to be great by following the great, and hopes to derive advantages *from another*,—by showing the fountain of all good to be in himself, and that he, equally with every man, is a door into the deeps of Reason. When he says, "I ought;" when love warms him; when he chooses, warned from on high, the good and great deed; then, deep melodies wander through his soul from Supreme Wisdom. Then he can worship, and be enlarged by his worship; for he can never go behind this sentiment. In the sublimest flights of the soul, rectitude is never surmounted, love is never outgrown.

This sentiment lies at the foundation of society, and successively creates all forms of worship. The principle of veneration never dies out. Man fallen into superstition, into sensuality, is never wholly without the visions of the moral sentiment. In like manner, all the expressions of this sentiment are sacred and permanent in proportion to their purity. The expressions of this sentiment affect us deeper, greatlier, than all other compositions. The sentences of the oldest time, which ejaculate this piety, are still fresh and fragrant. This thought dwelled always deepest in the minds of men in the devout and contemplative East; not alone in Palestine, where it reached its purest expression, but in Egypt, in Persia, in India, in China. Europe has always owed to oriental genius, its divine impulses. What these holy bards said, all sane men found agreeable and true. And the unique impression of Jesus upon mankind, whose name is not so much written as ploughed into the history of this world, is proof of the subtle virtue of this infusion.

Meantime, whilst the doors of the temple stand open, night and day, before every man, and the oracles of this truth cease never, it is guarded by one stern condition; this, namely; It is an intuition. It cannot be received at second hand. Truly speaking, it is not instruction, but provocation, that I can receive from another soul. What he announces, I must find true in me, or wholly reject; and on his word, or as his second, be he who he may, I can accept nothing. On the contrary, the absence of this primary faith is the presence of degradation. As is the flood so is the ebb. Let this faith depart, and the very words it spake, and the things it made, become false and hurtful. Then falls the church, the state, art, letters, life. The doctrine of the divine nature being forgotten, a sickness infects and dwarfs the constitution. Once man was all; now he is an appendage, a nuisance. And because the indwelling Supreme Spirit cannot wholly be got rid of, the doctrine of it suffers this perversion, that the divine nature is attributed to one or two persons, and denied to all the rest, and denied with fury. The doctrine of inspiration is lost; the base doctrine of the majority of voices, usurps the place of the doctrine of the soul. Miracles, prophecy, poetry, the ideal life, the holy life, exist as ancient history merely; they are not in the belief, nor in the aspiration of society; but, when suggested, seem ridiculous. Life is comic or pitiful, as soon as the high ends of being fade out of sight, and man becomes near-sighted, and can only attend to what addresses the senses.

These general views, which, whilst they are general, none will contest, find abundant illustration in the history of religion, and especially in the history of the Christian church. In that, all of us have had our birth and nurture. The truth contained in that, you, my young friends, are now setting forth to teach. As the Cultus, or established worship of the civilized world, it has great historical interest for us. Of its blessed words, which have been the consolation of humanity, you need not that I should speak. I shall endeavor to discharge my duty to you, on this occasion, by pointing out two errors in its administration, which daily appear more gross from the point of view we have just now taken.

Jesus Christ belonged to the true race of prophets. He saw with open eye the mystery of the soul. Drawn by its severe harmony, ravished with its beauty, he lived in it, and had his being there. Alone in all history, he estimated the greatness of man. One man was true to what is in you and me. He saw that God incarnates himself in man, and evermore goes forth anew to take possession of his world. He said, in this jubilee of sublime emotion, "I am divine. Through me, God acts; through me, speaks. Would you see God, see me; or, see thee, when thou also thinkest as I now think." But what a distortion did his doctrine and memory suffer in the same, in the next, and the following ages! There is no doctrine of the Reason which will bear to be taught by the Understanding. The understanding caught this high chant from the poet's lips, and said, in the next age, "This was Jehovah come down out of heaven. I will kill you, if you say he was a man." The idioms of his language, and the figures of his rhetoric, have usurped the place of his truth; and churches are not built on his principles, but on his tropes. Christianity became a Mythus, as the poetic teaching of Greece and of Egypt, before. He spoke of miracles; for he felt that man's life was a miracle, and all that man doth, and he knew that this daily miracle shines, as the man is diviner. But the very word Miracle, as pronounced by Christian churches, gives a false impression; it is Monster. It is not one with the blowing clover and the falling rain.

He felt respect for Moses and the prophets; but no unfit tenderness at postponing their initial revelations, to the hour and the man that now is; to the eternal revelation in the heart. Thus was he a true man. Having seen that the law in us is commanding, he would not suffer it to be commanded. Boldly, with hand, and heart, and life, he declared it was God. Thus was he a true man. Thus is he, as I think, the only soul in history who has appreciated the worth of a man.

1. In thus contemplating Jesus, we become very sensible of the first defect of historical Christianity. Historical Christianity has fallen into the error that corrupts all attempts to communicate religion. As it appears to us, and as it has appeared for ages, it is not the doctrine of the soul, but an exaggeration of the personal, the positive, the ritual. It has dwelt, it dwells, with noxious exaggeration about the *person* of Jesus. The soul knows no persons. It invites every man to expand to the full circle of the universe, and will have no preferences but those of spontaneous love. But by this eastern monarchy of a Christianity, which indolence and fear have built, the friend of man is made the injurer of man. The manner in which his name is surrounded with expressions, which were once sallies of admiration and love, but are now petrified into official titles, kills all generous sympathy and liking. All who hear me, feel, that the language that describes Christ to Europe and America, is not the style of friendship and enthusiasm to a good and noble heart, but is appropriated and formal,—paints a demigod, as the Orientals or the Greeks would describe Osiris or Apollo. Accept the injurious impositions of our early catechetical instruction, and even honesty and self-denial were but splendid sins, if they did not wear the Christian name. One would rather be

"A pagan suckled in a creed outworn,"

than to be defrauded of his manly right in coming into nature, and finding not names and places, not land and professions, but even virtue and truth foreclosed and monopolized. You shall not be a man even.

You shall not own the world; you shall not dare, and live after the infinite Law that is in you, and in company with the infinite Beauty which heaven and earth reflect to you in all lovely forms; but you must subordinate your nature to Christ's nature; you must accept our interpretations; and take his portrait as the vulgar draw it.

That is always best which gives me to myself. The sublime is excited in me by the great stoical doctrine, Obey thyself. That which shows God in me, fortifies me. That which shows God out of me, makes me a wart and a wen. There is no longer a necessary reason for my being. Already the long shadows of untimely oblivion creep over me, and I shall decease forever.

The divine bards are the friends of my virtue, of my intellect, of my strength. They admonish me, that the gleams which flash across my mind, are not mine, but God's; that they had the like, and were not disobedient to the heavenly vision. So I love them. Noble provocations go out from them, inviting me also to emancipate myself; to resist evil; to subdue the world; and to Be. And thus by his holy thoughts, Jesus serves us, and thus only. To aim to convert a man by miracles, is a profanation of the soul. A true conversion, a true Christ, is now, as always, to be made, by the reception of beautiful sentiments. It is true that a great and rich soul, like his, falling among the simple, does so preponderate, that, as his did, it names the world. The world seems to them to exist for him, and they have not yet drunk so deeply of his sense, as to see that only by coming again to themselves, or to God in themselves, can they grow forevermore. It is a low benefit to give me something; it is a high benefit to enable me to do somewhat of myself. The time is coming when all men will see, that the gift of God to the soul is not a vaunting, overpowering, excluding sanctity, but a sweet, natural goodness, a goodness like thine and mine, and that so invites thine and mine to be and to grow.

The injustice of the vulgar tone of preaching is not less flagrant to Jesus, than it is to the souls which it profanes. The preachers do not see that they make his gospel not glad, and shear him of the locks of beauty and the attributes of heaven. When I see a majestic Epaminondas, or Washington; when I see among my contemporaries, a true orator, an upright judge, a dear friend; when I vibrate to the melody and fancy of a poem; I see beauty that is to be desired. And so lovely, and with yet more entire consent of my human being, sounds in my ear the severe music of the bards that have sung of the true God in all ages. Now do not degrade the life and dialogues of Christ out of the circle of this charm, by insulation and peculiarity. Let them lie as they befel, alive and warm, part of human life, and of the landscape, and of the cheerful day.

2. The second defect of the traditionary and limited way of using the mind of Christ is a consequence of the first; this, namely; that the Moral Nature, that Law of laws, whose revelations introduce greatness,—yea, God himself, into the open soul, is not explored as the fountain of the established teaching in society. Men have come to speak of the revelation as somewhat long ago given and done, as if God were dead. The injury to faith throttles the preacher; and the goodliest of institutions becomes an uncertain and inarticulate voice.

It is very certain that it is the effect of conversation with the beauty of the soul, to beget a desire and need to impart to others the same knowledge and love. If utterance is denied, the thought lies like a burden on the man. Always the seer is a sayer. Somehow his dream is told. Somehow he publishes it with solemn joy. Sometimes with pencil on canvas; sometimes with chisel on stone; sometimes in towers and aisles of granite, his soul's worship is builded; sometimes in anthems of indefinite music; but clearest and most permanent, in words.

The man enamored of this excellency, becomes its priest or poet. The office is coeval with the world. But observe the condition, the spiritual limitation of the office. The spirit only can teach. Not any profane man, not any sensual, not any liar, not any slave can teach, but only he can give, who has; he only can create, who is. The man on whom the soul descends, through whom the soul speaks, alone can teach. Courage, piety, love, wisdom, can teach; and every man can open his door to these angels, and they shall bring him the gift of tongues. But the man who aims to speak as books enable, as synods use, as the fashion guides, and as interest commands, babbles. Let him hush.

To this holy office, you propose to devote yourselves. I wish you may feel your call in throbs of desire and hope. The office is the first in the world. It is of that reality, that it cannot suffer the deduction of any falsehood. And it is my duty to say to you, that the need was never greater of new revelation than now. From the views I have already expressed, you will infer the sad conviction, which I share, I believe, with numbers, of the universal decay and now almost death of faith in society. The soul is not preached. The Church seems to totter to its fall, almost all life extinct. On this occasion, any complaisance, would be criminal, which told you, whose hope and commission it is to preach the faith of Christ, that the faith of Christ is preached.

It is time that this ill-suppressed murmur of all thoughtful men against the famine of our churches; this moaning of the heart because it is bereaved of the consolation, the hope, the grandeur, that come alone out of the culture of the moral nature; should be heard through the sleep of indolence, and over the din of routine. This great and perpetual office of the preacher is not discharged. Preaching is the expression of the moral sentiment in application to the duties of life. In how many churches, by how many prophets, tell me, is man made sensible that he is an infinite Soul; that the earth and heavens are passing into his mind; that he is drinking forever the soul of God? Where now sounds the persuasion, that by its very melody imparadises my heart, and so affirms its own origin in heaven? Where shall I hear words such as in elder ages drew men to leave all and follow,—father and mother, house and land, wife and child? Where shall I hear these august laws of moral being so pronounced, as to fill my ear, and I feel ennobled by the offer of my uttermost action and passion? The test of the true faith, certainly, should be its power to charm and command the soul, as the laws of nature control the activity of the hands,—so commanding that we find pleasure and honor in obeying. The faith should blend with the light of rising and of setting suns, with the flying cloud, the singing bird, and the breath of flowers. But now the priest's Sabbath has lost the splendor of nature; it is unlovely; we are glad when it is done; we can make, we do make, even sitting in our pews, a far better, holier, sweeter, for ourselves.

Whenever the pulpit is usurped by a formalist, then is the worshipper defrauded and disconsolate. We shrink as soon as the prayers begin, which do not uplift, but smite and offend us. We are fain to wrap our cloaks about us, and secure, as best we can, a solitude that hears not. I once heard a preacher who sorely tempted me to say, I would go to church no more. Men go, thought I, where they are wont to go, else had no soul entered the temple in the afternoon. A snowstorm was falling around us. The snowstorm was real; the preacher merely spectral; and the eye felt the sad contrast in looking at him, and then out of the window behind him, into the beautiful meteor of the snow. He had lived in vain. He had no one word intimating that he had laughed or wept, was married or in love, had been commended, or cheated, or chagrined. If he had ever lived and acted, we were none the wiser for it.

The capital secret of his profession, namely, to convert life into truth, he had not learned. Not one fact in all his experience, had he yet imported into his doctrine. This man had ploughed, and planted, and talked, and bought, and sold; he had read books; he had eaten and drunken; his head aches; his heart throbs; he smiles and suffers; yet was there not a surmise, a hint, in all the discourse, that he had ever lived at all. Not a line did he draw out of real history. The true preacher can always be known by this, that he deals out to the people his life,—life passed through the fire of thought. But of the bad preacher, it could not be told from his sermon, what age of the world he fell in; whether he had a father or a child; whether he was a freeholder or a pauper; whether he was a citizen or a countryman; or any other fact of his biography.

It seemed strange that the people should come to church. It seemed as if their houses were very unentertaining, that they should prefer this thoughtless clamor. It shows that there is a commanding attraction in the moral sentiment, that can lend a faint tint of light to dulness and ignorance, coming in its name and place. The good hearer is sure he has been touched sometimes; is sure there is somewhat to be reached, and some word that can reach it. When he listens to these vain words, he comforts himself by their relation to his remembrance of better hours, and so they clatter and echo unchallenged.

I am not ignorant that when we preach unworthily, it is not always quite in vain. There is a good ear, in some men, that draws supplies to virtue out of very indifferent nutriment. There is poetic truth concealed in all the common-places of prayer and of sermons, and though foolishly spoken, they may be wisely heard; for, each is some select expression that broke out in a moment of piety from some stricken or jubilant soul, and its excellency made it remembered. The prayers and even the dogmas of our church, are like the zodiac of Denderah, and the astronomical monuments of the Hindoos, wholly insulated from anything now extant in the life and business of the people. They mark the height to which the waters once rose. But this docility is a check upon the mischief from the good and devout. In a large portion of the community, the religious service gives rise to quite other thoughts and emotions. We need not chide the negligent servant. We are struck with pity, rather, at the swift retribution of his sloth. Alas for the unhappy man that is called to stand in the pulpit, and *not* give bread of life. Everything that befals, accuses him. Would he ask contributions for the missions, foreign or domestic? Instantly his face is suffused with shame, to propose to his parish, that they should send money a hundred or a thousand miles, to furnish such poor fare as they have at home, and would do well to go the hundred or the thousand miles, to escape. Would he urge people to a godly way of living;—and can he ask a fellow creature to come to Sabbath meetings, when he and they all know what is the poor uttermost they can hope for therein? Will he invite them privately to the Lord's Supper? He dares not. If no heart warm this rite, the hollow, dry, creaking formality is too plain, than that he can face a man of wit and energy, and put the invitation without terror. In the street, what has he to say to the bold village blasphemer? The village blasphemer sees fear in the face, form, and gait of the minister.

Let me not taint the sincerity of this plea by any oversight of the claims of good men. I know and honor the purity and strict conscience of numbers of the clergy. What life the public worship retains, it owes to the scattered company of pious men, who minister here and there in the churches, and who, sometimes accepting with too great tenderness the tenet of the elders, have not accepted from others, but from their own heart, the genuine impulses of virtue, and so still command our love and awe, to the sanctity of character. Moreover, the exceptions are not so much to be found in a few eminent preachers, as in the better hours, the truer inspirations of all,—nay, in the sincere moments of every man. But with whatever exception, it is still true, that tradition characterizes the preaching of this country; that it comes out of the memory, and not out of the soul; that it aims at what is usual, and not at what is necessary and eternal; that thus, historical Christianity destroys the power of preaching, by withdrawing it from the exploration of the moral nature of man, where the sublime is, where are the resources of astonishment and power. What a cruel injustice it is to that Law, the joy of the whole earth, which alone can make thought dear and rich; that Law whose fatal sureness the astronomical orbits poorly emulate, that it is travestied and depreciated, that it is behooted and behowled, and not a trait, not a word of it articulated. The pulpit in losing sight of this Law, loses all its inspiration, and gropes after it knows not what. And for want of this culture, the soul of the community is sick and faithless. It wants nothing so much as a stern, high, stoical, Christian discipline, to make it know itself and the divinity that speaks through it. Now man is ashamed of himself; he skulks and sneaks through the world, to be tolerated, to be pitied, and scarcely in a thousand years does any man dare to be wise and good, and so draw after him the tears and blessings of his kind.

Certainly there have been periods when, from the inactivity of the intellect on certain truths, a greater faith was possible in names and persons. The Puritans in England and America, found in the Christ of the Catholic Church, and in the dogmas inherited from Rome, scope for their austere piety, and their longings for civil freedom. But their creed is passing away, and none arises in its room. I think no man can go with his thoughts about him, into one of our churches, without feeling that what hold the public worship had on men, is gone or going. It has lost its grasp on the affection of the good, and the fear of the bad. In the country,—neighborhoods, half parishes are *signing off*,—to use the local term. It is already beginning to indicate character and religion to withdraw from the religious meetings. I have heard a devout person, who prized the Sabbath, say in bitterness of heart, "On Sundays, it seems wicked to go to church." And the motive, that holds the best there, is now only a hope and a waiting. What was once a mere circumstance, that the best and the worst men in the parish, the poor and the rich, the learned and the ignorant, young and old, should meet one day as fellows in one house, in sign of an equal right in the soul,—has come to be a paramount motive for going thither.

My friends, in these two errors, I think, I find the causes of that calamity of a decaying church and a wasting unbelief, which are casting malignant influences around us, and making the hearts of good men sad. And what greater calamity can fall upon a nation, than the loss of worship? Then all things go to decay. Genius leaves the temple, to haunt the senate, or the market. Literature becomes frivolous. Science is cold. The eye of youth is not lighted by the hope of other worlds, and age is without honor. Society lives to trifles, and when men die, we do not mention them.

And now, my brothers, you will ask, What in these desponding days can be done by us? The remedy is already declared in the ground of our complaint of the Church. We have contrasted the Church with the Soul. In the soul, then, let the redemption be sought. In one soul, in your soul, there are resources for the world. Wherever a man comes, there comes revolution. The old is for slaves. When a man comes, all books are legible, all things transparent, all religions are forms. He is religious. Man is the wonderworker. He is seen amid miracles. All men bless and curse. He saith yea and nay, only. The stationariness of religion; the assumption that the age of inspiration is past, that the Bible is closed; the fear of degrading the character of Jesus by representing him as a man; indicate with sufficient clearness the falsehood of our theology. It is the office of a true teacher to show us that God is, not was; that He speaketh, not spake. The true Christianity,—a faith like Christ's in the infinitude of man,—is lost. None believeth in the soul of man, but only in some man or person old and departed. Ah me! no man goeth alone. All men go in flocks to this saint or that poet, avoiding the God who seeth in secret. They cannot see in secret; they love to be blind in public. They think society wiser than their soul; and know not that one soul, and their soul, is wiser than the whole world. See how nations and races flit by on the sea of time, and leave no ripple to tell where they floated or sunk, and one good soul shall make the name of Moses, or of Zeno, or of Zoroaster, reverend forever. None assayeth the stern ambition to be the Self of the nation, and of nature, but each would be an easy secondary to some Christian scheme, or sectarian connexion, or some eminent man. Once leave your own knowledge of God, your own sentiment, and take secondary knowledge, as St. Paul's, or George Fox's, or Swedenborg's, and you get wide from God with every year this secondary form lasts, and if, as now, for centuries,—the chasm yawns to that breadth, that men can scarcely be convinced there is in them anything divine.

Let me admonish you, first of all, to go alone; to refuse the good models, even those most sacred in the imagination of men, and dare to love God without mediator or veil. Friends enough you shall find who will hold up to your emulation Wesleys and Oberlins, Saints and Prophets. Thank God for these good men, but say, "I also am a man." Imitation cannot go above its model. The imitator dooms himself to hopeless mediocrity. The inventor did it, because it was natural to him, and so in him it has a charm. In the imitator, something else is natural, and he bereaves himself of his own beauty, to come short of another man's.

Yourself a newborn bard of the Holy Ghost,—cast behind you all conformity, and acquaint men at first hand with Deity. Be to them a man. Look to it first and only, that you are such; that fashion, custom, authority, pleasure, and money are nothing to you,—are not bandages over your eyes, that you cannot see,—but live with the privilege of the immeasurable mind. Not too anxious to visit periodically all families and each family in your parish connexion,—when you meet one of these men or women, be to them a divine man; be to them thought and virtue; let their timid aspirations find in you a friend; let their trampled instincts be genially tempted out in your atmosphere; let their doubts know that you have doubted, and their wonder feel that you have wondered. By trusting your own soul, you shall gain a greater confidence in other men. For all our penny-wisdom, for all our soul-destroying slavery to habit, it is not to be doubted, that all men have sublime thoughts; that all men do value the few real hours of life; they love to be heard; they love to be caught up into the vision of principles. We mark with light in the memory the few interviews, we have had in the dreary years of routine and of sin, with souls that made our souls wiser; that spoke what we thought; that told us what we knew; that gave us leave to be what we inly were. Discharge to men the priestly office, and, present or absent, you shall be followed with their love as by an angel.

And, to this end, let us not aim at common degrees of merit. Can we not leave, to such as love it, the virtue that glitters for the commendation of society, and ourselves pierce the deep solitudes of absolute ability and worth? We easily come up to the standard of goodness in society. Society's praise can be cheaply secured, and almost all men are content with those easy merits; but the instant effect of conversing with God, will be, to put them away. There are sublime merits; persons who are not actors, not speakers, but influences; persons too great for fame, for display; who disdain eloquence; to whom all we call art and artist, seems too nearly allied to show and by-ends, to the exaggeration of the finite and selfish, and loss of the universal. The orators, the poets, the commanders encroach on us only as fair women do, by our allowance and homage. Slight them by preoccupation of mind, slight them, as you can well afford to do, by high and universal aims, and they instantly feel that you have right, and that it is in lower places that they must shine. They also feel your right; for they with you are open to the influx of the all-knowing Spirit, which annihilates before its broad noon the little shades and gradations of intelligence in the compositions we call wiser and wisest.

In such high communion, let us study the grand strokes of rectitude: a bold benevolence, an independence of friends, so that not the unjust wishes of those who love us, shall impair our freedom, but we shall resist for truth's sake the freest flow of kindness, and appeal to sympathies far in advance; and,—what is the highest form in which we know this beautiful element,—a certain solidity of merit, that has nothing to do with opinion, and which is so essentially and manifestly virtue, that it is taken for granted, that the right, the brave, the generous step will be taken by it, and nobody thinks of commending it. You would compliment a coxcomb doing a good act, but you would not praise an angel. The silence that accepts merit as the most natural thing in the world, is the highest applause. Such souls, when they appear, are the Imperial Guard of Virtue, the perpetual reserve, the dictators of fortune. One needs not praise their courage,—they are the heart and soul of nature. O my friends, there are resources in us on which we have not drawn. There are men who rise refreshed on hearing a threat; men to whom a crisis which intimidates and paralyzes the majority—demanding not the faculties of prudence and thrift, but comprehension, immovableness, the readiness of sacrifice,—comes graceful and beloved as a bride. Napoleon said of Massena, that he was not himself until the battle began to go against him; then, when the dead began to fall in ranks around him, awoke his powers of combination, and he put on terror and victory as a robe. So it is in rugged crises, in unweariable endurance, and in aims which put sympathy out of question, that the angel is shown. But these are heights that we can scarce remember and look up to, without contrition and shame. Let us thank God that such things exist.

And now let us do what we can to rekindle the smouldering, nigh quenched fire on the altar. The evils of that church that now is, are manifest. The question returns, What shall we do? I confess, all attempts to project and establish a Cultus with new rites and forms, seem to me vain. Faith makes us, and not we it, and faith makes its own forms. All attempts to contrive a system, are as cold as the new worship introduced by the French to the goddess of Reason,—to-day, pasteboard and fillagree, and ending to-morrow in madness and murder. Rather let the breath of new life be breathed by you through the forms already existing. For, if once you are alive, you shall find they shall become plastic and new. The remedy to their deformity is, first, soul, and second, soul, and evermore, soul. A whole popedom of forms, one pulsation of virtue can uplift and vivify. Two inestimable advantages Christianity has given us; first; the Sabbath, the jubilee of the whole world; whose light dawns welcome alike into the closet of the philosopher, into the garret of toil, and into prison cells, and everywhere suggests, even to the vile, a thought of the dignity of spiritual being. Let it stand forevermore, a temple, which new love, new faith, new sight shall restore to more than its first splendor to mankind. And secondly, the institution of preaching,—the speech of man to men,—essentially the most flexible of all organs, of all forms. What hinders that now, everywhere, in pulpits, in lecture-rooms, in houses, in fields, wherever the invitation of men or your own occasions lead you, you speak the very truth, as your life and conscience teach it, and cheer the waiting, fainting hearts of men with new hope and new revelation.

I look for the hour when that supreme Beauty, which ravished the souls of those Eastern men, and chiefly of those Hebrews, and through their lips spoke oracles to all time, shall speak in the West also. The Hebrew and Greek Scriptures contain immortal sentences, that have been bread of life to millions. But they have no epical integrity; are fragmentary; are not shown in their order to the intellect. I look for the new Teacher, that shall follow so far those shining laws, that he shall see them come full circle; shall see their rounding complete grace; shall see the world to be the mirror of the soul; shall see the identity of the law of gravitation with purity of heart; and shall show that the Ought, that Duty, is one thing with Science, with Beauty, and with Joy.

2.

# Andrews Norton

## from "The New School in Literature and Religion"

(1838)

This is the first of two retorts to Emerson's Divinity School Address by the incarnation of mainstream academic Unitarianism, one of Emerson's former divinity school teachers who was now immersed in what would become his magnum opus, *The Evidences of the Genuineness of the Gospels* (1837–44). In this and in his *Discourse on the Latest Form of Infidelity* (1839), Andrews Norton (1786–1853) accuses Emerson and his "school" of heresy, sloppy thinking, mawkish writing, and bad manners. This assault by the Unitarian "pope," as Norton was sometimes satirically called, was both a cause and effect of the contemporary caricature of Transcendentalists as Germanized aliens. Norton's hostility to unwanted foreign influences of all sorts is evident from his opening swipe at English Unitarian author Harriet Martineau, whose recently published impressions of the United States had complimentary things to say about Emerson.

SOURCE: *Boston Daily Advertiser*, August 27, 1838.

There is a strange state of things existing about us in the literary and religious world, of which none of our larger periodicals has yet taken notice. It is the result of this restless craving for notoriety and excitement, which, in one way or another, is keeping our community in a perpetual stir. It has shown itself, we think, particularly since that foolish woman, Miss Martineau, was among us, and stimulated the vanity of her flatterers by loading them in return with the copper coin of her praise, which they easily believed was as good as gold. She was accustomed to talk about her mission, as if she were a special dispensation of Providence, and they too thought that they must all have their missions, and began to "vaticinate," as one of their number has expressed it. But though her genial warmth may have caused the new school to bud and bloom, it was not planted by her.—It owes its origin in part to ill-understood notions, obtained by blundering through the crabbed and disgusting obscurity of some of the worst German speculatists, which notions, however, have been received by most of its disciples at second hand, through an interpreter. The atheist Shelley has been quoted and commented in a professedly religious work, called the Western Messenger, but he is not, we conceive, to be reckoned among the patriarchs of the sect. But this honor is due to that hasher up of German metaphysics, the Frenchman, Cousin; and, of late, that hyper-Germanized Englishman, Carlyle, has been the great object of admiration and model of style. Cousin and Carlyle indeed seem to have been transformed into idols to be publicly worshipped; the former for his philosophy, and the latter both for his philosophy and his fine writing; while the veiled image of the German pantheist, Schleiermacher, is kept in the sanctuary.

The characteristics of this school are the most extraordinary assumption, united with great ignorance, and incapacity for reasoning. There is indeed a general tendency among its disciples to disavow learning and reasoning as sources of their higher knowledge.—The mind must be its own unassisted teacher. It discerns transcendental truths by immediate vision, and these truths can no more be communicated to another by addressing his understanding, than the power of *clairvoyance* can be given to one not magnetized. They announce themselves as the prophets and priests of a new future, in which all is to be changed, all old opinions done away, and all present forms of society abolished. But by what process this joyful revolution is to be effected as are not told; nor how human happiness and virtue is to be saved from the universal wreck, and regenerated in their Medea's caldron. There are great truths with which they are laboring, but they are unutterable in words to be understood by common minds. To such minds they seem nonsense, oracles as obscure as those of Delphi.

The rejection of reasoning is accompanied with an equal contempt for good taste. All modesty is laid aside. The writer of an article for an obscure periodical, or a religious newspaper, assumes a tone as if he were one of the chosen enlighteners of a dark age.—He continually obtrudes himself upon his reader, and announces his own convictions, as if from their having that character, they were necessarily indisputable.—He floats about magnificently on bladders, which he would have it believed are swelling with ideas.—Common thoughts, sometimes true, oftener false, and "Neutral nonsense, neither false nor true," are exaggerated, and twisted out of shape, and forced into strange connexions, to make them look like some grand and new conception. To produce a more striking effect, our common language is abused; antic tricks are played with it; inversions, exclamations, anomalous combinations of words, unmeaning, but coarse and violent, metaphors abound, and withal a strong infusion of German barbarians. Such is the style of Carlyle, a writer of some talent; for his great deficiency is not in this respect, it is in good sense, good taste and soundness of principle; but a writer, who, through his talents, such as they are, through that sort of buffoonery and affectation of manner which throws the reader off his guard, through the indisputable novelty of his way of writing, and through a somewhat too prevalent taste among us for an over-excited and *convulsionary* style, which we mistake for eloquence, has obtained a degree of fame in this country, very disproportioned to what he enjoys at home, out of the Westminister Review. Carlyle, however, as an original, might be tolerated, if one could forget his admirers and imitators.

The state of things described might seem a matter of no great concern, a mere insurrection of folly, a sort of Jack Cade rebellion; which in the nature of things must soon be put down, if those engaged in it were not gathering confidence from neglect, and had not proceeded to attack principles which are the foundation of human society and human happiness. "Silly women," it has been said, and silly young men, it is to be feared, have been drawn away from their christian faith, if not divorced from all that can properly be called religion. The evil is becoming, for the time, disastrous and alarming; and of this fact there could hardly be a more extraordinary and ill boding evidence, than is afforded by a publication, which has just appeared, entitled an "Address, delivered before the Senior class in Divinity College, Cambridge," upon the occasion of that class taking leave of the Institution, "By Ralph Waldo Emerson."

It is not necessary to remark particularly on this composition. It will be sufficient to state generally, that the author professes to reject all belief in Christianity as a revelation, that he makes a general attack upon the Clergy, on the ground that they preach what he calls "Historical Christianity," and that if he believe in God in the proper sense of the term, which one passage might have led his hearers to suppose, his language elsewhere is very ill-judged and indecorous. But what *his* opinions may be is a matter of minor concern; the main question is how it has happened, that religion has been insulted by the delivery of these opinions in the Chapel of the Divinity College at Cambridge, as the last instruction which those were to receive, who were going forth from it, bearing the name of christian preachers. This is a question in which the community is deeply interested. No one can doubt for a moment of the disgust and strong disapprobation with which it must have been heard by the highly respectable officers of that Institution. They must have felt it not only as an insult to religion, but as personal insult to themselves. But this renders the fact of its having been so delivered only the more remarkable. We can proceed but a step in accounting for it. The preacher was invited to occupy the place he did, not by the officers of the Divinity College, but by the members of the graduating class. These gentlemen, therefore, have become accessories, perhaps innocent accessories, to the commission of a great offence; and the public must be desirous of learning what exculpation or excuse they can offer.

It is difficult to believe that they thought this incoherent rhapsody a specimen of fine writing, that they listened with admiration, for instance, when they were told that the religious sentiment "is myrrh, and storax and chlorine and rosemary;" or that they wondered at the profound views of their present Teacher, when he announced to them that "the new Teacher," for whom he is looking, would "see the identity of the law of gravitation with purity of heart;" or that they had not some suspicion of inconsistency, when a new Teacher was talked of, after it had been declared to them, that religious truth "is an intuition," and "cannot be received at second hand."

But the subject is to be viewed under a far more serious aspect. The words God, Religion, Christianity, have a definite meaning, well understood.... The community know what they require when they ask for a Christian Teacher; and should any one approving the doctrines of this discourse assume that character, he would deceive his hearers; he would be guilty of a practical falsehood for the most paltry of temptations; he would consent to live, a lie, for the sake of being maintained by those whom he had cheated. . . .

# Henry Ware Jr.

## God's Personhood Vindicated

### (1838)

Henry Ware Jr. (1794–1843) was Emerson's predecessor and his one-time senior colleague as pastor of Boston's Second Church. His relation to Emerson was much more cordial and avuncular than was Norton's, not only because of their previous acquaintance but also because of Ware's kind and gracious personality. Emerson was genuinely fond of him, although not uncritical. Unlike Norton, Ware took the trouble to initiate contact with Emerson in order to sound him out further on his views. Later, Ware sent Emerson his pamphlet with another friendly letter again desiring classification of the basis of Emerson's views. Emerson was cordial but standoffish, refusing to be drawn into debate. He even went so far as to protest that "I do not know . . . what arguments mean in reference to any expression of a thought." That must have flabbergasted Ware. Nonetheless, much more perceptively than either Norton's previous aspersion of Emerson's bad manners or his later objections to Emerson's contempt for the Unitarian doctrine of miracles, Ware strikes at the heart of what would have been most disturbing about the Divinity School Address for Unitarian believers, if not to Unitarian theologues: Emerson's aversion to *personalizing* Jesus or God. Here Emerson was at odds with the tide of mainstream nineteenth-century Protestantism as a whole, which increasingly invoked the image of God as parent to displace the traditional image of God as judge. Indeed, some of his closest associates, like Bronson Alcott, disagreed with him on this point. But for Emerson, it was a profanation of "absolute truth, absolute goodness" to insist that they "leave their infinity" and take on "fingers and head and hair."

SOURCE: *The Personality of the Deity. A Sermon, Preached in the Chapel of Harvard University, September 23, 1838.* Boston: James Munroe, 1838.

In treating the doctrine respecting God, the mind is deeply impressed with a sense of its importance in its bearing on human duty and happiness. It is the doctrine of a Creator, the Governor and Father of man. The discussion relates not merely to the laws of the universe and the principles by which its affairs are directed, but to the character and dispositions of the Being, who presides over those laws, and by whose will those affairs are determined. It teaches, not only that there is a wise and holy order to which it is for every man's interest to conform; but that that order is ordained and upheld by an active, overruling Intelligence; and that hence virtue is not merely conformity to a rule, but allegiance to a rightful Lawgiver; and happiness not the result merely of obedience to a command, but of affectionate subjection to a Parent.

The importance of this consideration to a true and happy virtue cannot be overestimated. The difference between conformity to a statute and obedience to a father is a difference not to be measured in words, but to be realized in the experience of the soul. It is slightly represented in the difference between the condition of a little child that lives in the presence of a judicious and devoted mother, an object of perpetual affection, and of another that is placed under the charge of a public institution, which knows nothing but a set of rules. Each is alike provided for and governed; but the one enjoys the satisfactions of a trusting and loving heart, while the other, deprived of the natural objects of affection, knows nothing but a life of order and restraint. Take away the Father of the universe, and, though every ordinance remain unchanged, mankind becomes but a company of children in an orphan asylum; clothed, fed, governed, but objects of pity rather than congratulation, because deprived of those resting-places for the affections, without which the soul is not happy.

## 4.

## ANDREWS NORTON

FROM *A DISCOURSE ON THE LATEST FORM OF INFIDELITY*

(1839)

In his second attempt to confute the "new school," Norton stops sling-
ing mud and makes a concerted attempt to pinpoint the fallacy inherent in what he takes to be Transcendentalist "infidelity." Norton
contends that the proof of Christianity, of religion in general, is a matter of probability and not of certainty. It can only be established by
informed and laborious reasoning from evidence—in short, by biblical
scholars like Norton himself. Norton's "reason," in other words, is not
the Transcendentalists' Reason, or Truth-intuiting power, but Locke's
reason with a small *r,* which the Transcendentalists were discounting as mere "understanding." Norton's denial of certainty is a perfect
example of what Emerson scornfully called the "pale negations" of
Boston Unitarianism. Just as we have seen Ware deploring Emersonian
spirituality for perpetrating its own sort of coldheartedness, so we
shall soon see Ripley exposing the dehydrated mandarinism of Norton's view that the evidential basis of faith must be left to the experts to
decide. But it is going too far to type Norton as an arrogant bigot and
nothing more, a dogged pedant of the kind Emerson had in mind in
"The American Scholar" (Section II) when he warned that the true
scholar is not a bookworm. For one thing, Norton writes here not
simply in truculence or exasperation as he did before, but with a searching earnestness about the ultimate unknowability of spiritual truth,
obviously as sincere in its own way as Ware's piety and Emerson's
prophetic fervor. Although Norton attached no significance to feeling
in his theory, he certainly *shows* deep feeling here. Note too the odd

family resemblance between Norton's and Emerson's heavy reliance on the power of the emphatic statement to carry the day.

SOURCE: *A Discourse on the Latest Form of Infidelity.* Cambridge, MA: John Owen, 1839.

The latest form of infidelity is distinguished by assuming the Christian name, while it strikes directly at the root of faith in Christianity, and indirectly of all religion, by denying the miracles attesting the divine mission of Christ....

Nothing is left that can be called Christianity, if its miraculous character be denied. Its essence is gone; its evidence is annihilated. Its truths, involving the highest interests of man, the facts which it makes known, and which are implied in its very existence as a divine revelation, rest no longer on the authority of God....

... This evidence, it is said, consists only of probabilities. We want certainty. The dwellers in the regions of shadows complain, that the solid earth is not stable enough for them to rest on. They have firm footing in the clouds.

To the demand for certainty, let it come from whom it may, I answer, that I know of no absolute certainty, beyond the limit of momentary consciousness, a certainty that vanishes the instant it exists, and is lost in the region of metaphysical doubt. Beyond this limit, absolute certainty, so far as human reason may judge, cannot be the privilege of any finite being. When we talk of certainty, a wise man will remember what he is, and the narrow bounds of his wisdom and of his powers ... There can be no intuition, no direct perception, of the truth of Christianity, no metaphysical certainty....

———

There is, then, no mode of establishing religious belief, but by the exercise of reason, by investigation, by forming a probable judgment upon facts....

But we have not, it may be said, yet removed the difficulty, that the evidence and character of Christianity, in order to be properly understood, require investigations which are beyond the capacity or the opportunities of a great majority of men....

... On what ground is the truth of Christianity to be received by those who are unable to give themselves to a full study of its evidences? The reply is, that it is to be received on the same ground as we receive all other truths, of which we have not ourselves mastered the evidences; for the same reason that we do not reject all that vast amount of knowledge which is not the result of our own deductions. Our belief in those truths, the evidence of which we cannot fully examine for ourselves, is founded in a greater or less degree on the testimony of others, who have examined their evidence, and whom we regard as intelligent and trustworthy.... The admission of this principle does not weaken the force of its evidences in the mind of any man of correct judgment. In maintaining, therefore, that the thorough investigation of the evidences and character of our religion requires much knowledge and much thought, and the combined and continued labor of different minds, we maintain nothing that gives to Christianity a different character from what belongs to all the higher and more important branches of knowledge, and nothing inconsistent with its being in its nature a universal religion....

# 5.

# George Ripley

## from "The Latest Form of Infidelity" Examined
### (1839)

Ripley here attacks Norton at his most vulnerable point: Norton's insistence that ordinary Christians must be guided by the superior knowledge and reasoning powers of the theological experts. For Ripley as for Emerson, this insistence missed the point that religious "sentiment" counts for much more than logic-chopping. That was the underlying point of Emerson's waspish but somewhat cryptic declaration that to attempt to convert a man by miracles was "a profanation of the soul." But Ripley gives his argument a more overtly populist turn than Emerson did. First, Ripley simply takes pains to be more lucid. Here as always, he is the patient explainer, the gentle, egalitarian pastor rather than the elite academic—even though Ripley also makes it clear in other parts of this pamphlet that he knows contemporary theology better than Norton does. Second and more important, the principle that all persons have direct access to spiritual insight is paramount for Ripley. That is what Jesus stood for. That was the distinctive spirit of early Unitarianism. Upon that the bond between minister and people depends. That is what makes a community of the spirit possible. Ripley's position here is entirely consistent with his earlier claim that Cousin's accessibility is more suited to the ethos of a democratic society than is esoteric Kantian philosophical discourse (Section I) and with the affirmation he will soon make to his church (Section II) that Unitarianism has lost sight of its original mission.

SOURCE: *"The Latest Form of Infidelity" Examined. A Letter to Mr. Andrews Norton.* Boston: James Munroe, 1839.

In the course of the inquiries which [Unitarianism's first leaders] had entered into, for their own satisfaction and the good of their people, they had become convinced of the superiority of the testimony of the soul to the evidence of the external senses.... No difference of speculation had estranged them from the hearts of their brethren; no breach had been made in the sympathy which was the pervading principle of their association; the understanding had been sacredly observed, if not formally expressed, that a profession of faith in Christ and a sincere and virtuous character were the conditions of fellowship, rather than any agreement in theological opinion....

———

... As liberal Christians, ... we have claimed the right of private judgment, as essential to Christian freedom.... We have not presumed to sit in judgment on any Christian's claim to discipleship; we have refused to entertain the question, whether he were entitled to the Christian name; we have felt that it was not ours to give or to withhold; and that the decision in all cases, must rest with himself....

The doctrine, that miracles are the only evidence of a divine revelation, if generally admitted, would ... separate the pastor of a church from the sympathies of his people, confine him in a sphere of thought remote from their usual interests, and give an abstract and scholastic character to his services in the pulpit. The great object of his endeavors would be to demonstrate the truth of the Christian history; the weapons of his warfare would be carnal, and not spiritual; drawn from grammars, and lexicons, and mouldy traditions, not from the treasures of the human heart.... The minister would rely for success on his skill in argument, rather than on his sympathy with man; on the knowledge he gains within the walls of the University, rather than on the experience which may be learned in the homes of his people. He would trust more to his logical demonstration of the evidences of Christianity, than to the faithful exhibition of Christian truth to the naked human heart....

... If you confine [a man] to the demonstration of the miracles; if you deny him intimate access to the soul, by the truth which he bears; if you virtually tell him that the internal evidence of Christianity is a delusion, that our personal experience of its power is no proof of its divinity, and that the glorious Gospel of the blessed God is to be believed only because learned men vouchsafe to assure the humble Christian of its truth, you deprive the minister of all inward force; you make him little better than a logical machine; and much as I value a sound logic in its proper place, I am sure it is not the instrument which is mighty through God to the pulling down of the strong holds of sin.... It may refute fallacies; but it cannot bind the heart to the love of holiness.... Christ honored man. He felt the worth of the soul. He knew its intimate connexion with God. He believed in the omnipresence of the Deity; but taught, that of all temples the "upright heart and pure" was the most acceptable. He saw that the parade of wisdom which books impart was as nothing before "the light that enlighteneth every human mind."... Christ established no college of Apostles; he did not revive the school of the prophets which had died out; he paid no distinguished respect to the pride of learning; indeed, he sometimes intimates that it is an obstacle to the perception of truth...

... I honor the learned, when they devote their attainments to the service of society; when they cherish a stronger interest in the welfare of their brethren, than in the luxury of their books; when they bring the researches of science to the illustration of truth, the correction of abuses, and the aid of the sufferer; but if they do not acknowledge a higher light than that which comes from the printed page; if they confound the possession of erudition with the gift of wisdom; and above all, if they presume to interfere in the communion of the soul with God, and limit the universal bounty of Heaven within their "smoky cells," I can only utter my amazement.

Christian truth has always been addressed to the "intuitive perceptions" of the common mind.... The sword of the Spirit is not wielded after the tactics of a University; and even a shepherd's sling has often proved more powerful than the spear of a giant.

# MARGARET FULLER

## RECOLLECTION OF MYSTICAL EXPERIENCES

### (1840)

When Ripley wrote of "the communion of the soul with God," he might have been thinking of such moments as his friend Margaret Fuller (1810–50) describes in the following passage. Although Fuller did not keep so voluminous a private journal as Emerson, Thoreau, and Alcott, the portions of it that survive often show a greater sense of emotional and spiritual intensity. What Ripley and Emerson theorized, Fuller seems more often actually to have *felt*—or at least to have admitted feeling it. "Why should we not also enjoy an original relation to the universe?" Emerson asks at the start of *Nature*. The Divinity School Address insists that one can be acquainted "at first hand with Deity," and Ripley seconds the point in less flamboyant language. Yet none of the Transcendentalists with the exception of Jones Very (Section V-C) recorded many of these experiences. Emerson's thirty published volumes of private journals, notebooks, and letters report no more than two or three such events. Much more common throughout Transcendentalist writing are laments about the unpredictability and brevity of peak experiences. If there is such a thing as a "Transcendentalist tragedy," this is it. "Our faith comes in moments; our vice is habitual," as Emerson mournfully puts it in his essay "The Over-Soul." "Yet," he adds, "there is a depth in those brief moments, which constrains us to ascribe more reality to them than to all other experiences." For Fuller, however, such moments evidently came oftener than they did for Emerson, although not enough to keep her from similar self-reproaches.

SOURCE: *Memoirs of Margaret Fuller Ossoli*, ed. James Freeman Clarke, Ralph Waldo Emerson, and William Henry Channing. Boston: Phillips, Sampson, 1852, vol. 1.

It was Thanksgiving day, (Nov., 1831,) and I was obliged to go to church, or exceedingly displease my father. I almost always suffered much in church from a feeling of disunion with the hearers and dissent from the preacher; but to-day, more than ever before, the services jarred upon me from their grateful and joyful tone. I was wearied out with mental conflicts, and in a mood of most childish, child-like sadness. I felt within myself great power, and generosity, and tenderness; but it seemed to me as if they were all unrecognized, and as if it was impossible that they should be used in life. I was only one-and-twenty; the past was worthless, the future hopeless; yet I could not remember ever voluntarily to have done a wrong thing, and my aspiration seemed very high. I looked round the church, and envied all the little children; for I supposed they had parents who protected them, so that they could never know this strange anguish, this dread uncertainty. I knew not, then, that none could have any father but God. I knew not, that I was not the only lonely one, that I was not the selected Œdipus, the special victim of an iron law. I was in haste for all to be over, that I might get into the free air. . . .

I walked away over the fields as fast as I could walk. This was my custom at that time, when I could no longer bear the weight of my feelings, and fix my attention on any pursuit; for I do believe I never voluntarily gave way to these thoughts one moment. The force I exerted I think, even now, greater than I ever knew in any other character. But when I could bear myself no longer, I walked many hours, till the anguish was wearied out, and I returned in a state of prayer. Today all seemed to have reached its height. It seemed as if I could never return to a world in which I had no place,—to the mockery of humanities. I could not act a part, nor seem to live any longer. It was a sad and sallow day of the late autumn. Slow processions of sad clouds were passing over a cold blue sky; the hues of earth were dull, and gray, and brown, with sickly struggles of late green here and there; sometimes a moaning gust of wind drove late, reluctant leaves across the path;— there was no life else. In the sweetness of my present peace, such days seem to me made to tell man the worst of his lot; but still that November wind can bring a chill of memory.

I paused beside a little stream, which I had envied in the merry

fulness of its spring life. It was shrunken, voiceless, choked with withered leaves. I marvelled that it did not quite lose itself in the earth.
There was no stay for me, and I went on and on, till I came to where
the trees were thick about a little pool, dark and silent. I sat down
there. I did not think; all was dark, and cold, and still. Suddenly the sun
shone out with that transparent sweetness, like the last smile of a dying
lover, which it will use when it has been unkind all a cold autumn day.
And, even then, passed into my thought a beam from its true sun, from
its native sphere, which has never since departed from me. I remembered how, a little child, I had stopped myself one day on the stairs,
and asked, how came I here? How is it that I seem to be this Margaret
Fuller? What does it mean? What shall I do about it? I remembered all
the times and ways in which the same thought had returned. I saw how
long it must be before the soul can learn to act under these limitations
of time and space, and human nature; but I saw, also, that it MUST do
it,—that it must make all this false true,—and sow new and immortal
plants in the garden of God, before it could return again. I saw there
was no self; that selfishness was all folly, and the result of circumstance;
that it was only because I thought self real that I suffered; that I had
only to live in the idea of the ALL, and all was mine. This truth came to
me, and I received it unhesitatingly; so that I was for that hour taken up
into God. In that true ray most of the relations of earth seemed mere
films, phenomena.

My earthly pain at not being recognized never went deep after this
hour. I had passed the extreme of passionate sorrow; and all check, all
failure, all ignorance, have seemed temporary ever since. When I consider that this will be nine years ago next November, I am astonished
that I have not gone on faster since; that I am not yet sufficiently purified to be taken back to God. Still, I did but touch then on the only
haven of Insight. You know what I would say. I was dwelling in the
ineffable, the unutterable. But the sun of earth set, and it grew dark
around; the moment came for me to go. I had never been accustomed
to walk alone at night, for my father was very strict on that subject, but
now I had not one fear. When I came back, the moon was riding clear
above the houses. I went into the churchyard, and there offered a
prayer as holy, if not as deeply true, as any I know now; a prayer, which
perhaps took form as the guardian angel of my life. If that word in the
Bible, Selah, means what gray-headed old men think it does, when
they read aloud, it should be written here,—Selah!

Since that day, I have never more been completely engaged in self;

but the statue has been emerging, though slowly, from the block. Others may not see the promise even of its pure symmetry, but I do, and am learning to be patient. I shall be all human yet; and then the hour will come to leave humanity, and live always in the pure ray.

This first day I was taken up; but the second time the Holy Ghost descended like a dove. I went out again for a day, but this time it was spring. I walked in the fields of Groton. But I will not describe that day; its music still sounds too sweetly near. Suffice it to say, I gave it all into our Father's hands, and was no stern-weaving Fate more, but one elected to obey, and love, and at last know. Since then I have suffered, as I must suffer again, till all the complex be made simple, but I have never been in discord with the grand harmony.

# THEODORE PARKER

## FROM *A DISCOURSE OF THE TRANSIENT AND PERMANENT IN CHRISTIANITY*

### (1841)

This discourse, preached at the ordination of a younger Boston minister, marks the emergence of Theodore Parker (1810–60) as the most powerful voice in radical theology for second-generation Transcendentalism. It is Parker's equivalent of Emerson's Divinity School Address, an unprecedentedly pugnacious statement of the historical relativism of religious forms and traditions that put Parker beyond the Christian pale in the eyes of many fellow Unitarian ministers. Parker himself did not see it that way. He saw himself as getting at the essence of Christianity by sorting out the indispensable from the merely contingent. Parker went on to publish his *summa theologica* the following year, *A Discourse of Matters Pertaining to Religion* (1842), which added to the pressure on him to resign. His outspoken social radicalism, particularly on the slavery issue (Section IV-E), increased the pressure further. But Parker did not relent. He succeeded in winning a considerable measure of public support for his radicalism, too. By the mid-1840s, he had moved to Boston from his small parish in West Roxbury and was on the way to building the largest congregation of any Unitarian or Congregational church in New England.

SOURCE: *A Discourse of the Transient and Permanent in Christianity; Preached at the Ordination of Mr. Charles C. Shackford, in the Hawes Place Church in Boston, May 19, 1841.* Boston: the Author, 1841.

> Heaven and Earth shall pass away:
> but my word shall not pass away.
> —LUKE XXI. 33.

Christ says, his Word shall never pass away. Yet at first sight nothing seems more fleeting than a word. It is an evanescent impulse of the most fickle element. It leaves no track where it went through the air. Yet to this, and this only, did Jesus entrust the truth wherewith he came laden, to the earth; truth for the salvation of the world. He took no pains to perpetuate his thoughts; they were poured forth where occasion found him an audience,—by the side of the lake, or a well; in a cottage, or the temple; in a fisher's boat, or the synagogue of the Jews. He founds no institution as a monument of his words. He appoints no order of men to preserve his bright and glad revelations. He only bids his friends give freely the truth they had freely received. He did not even write his words in a book. With a noble confidence, the result of his abiding faith, he scattered them, broad-cast, on the world, leaving the seed to its own vitality. He knew, that what is of God cannot fail, for God keeps his own. He sowed his seed in the heart, and left it there, to be watered and warmed by the dew and the sun which heaven sends. He felt his words were for eternity. So he trusted them to the uncertain air; and for eighteen hundred years that faithful element has held them good,—distinct as when first warm from his lips. . . .

———

Looking at the Word of Jesus, at real Christianity, the pure religion he taught, nothing appears more fixed and certain. Its influence widens as light extends; it deepens as the nations grow more wise. But, looking at the history of what men call Christianity, nothing seems more uncertain and perishable. While true religion is always the same thing, in each century and every land, in each man that feels it, the Christianity of the Pulpit, which is the religion taught; the Christianity of the People, which is the religion that is accepted and lived out, has never been the same thing in any two centuries or lands, except only in name. The difference between what is called Christianity by the Unitarians in our times, and that of some ages past, is greater than the difference between Mahomet and the Messiah. The difference at this day between opposing classes of Christians; the difference between the Christianity of some sects and that of Christ himself, is deeper and more vital than that between Jesus and Plato, Pagan as we call him. The Christianity of the seventh century has passed away. We recognise only the ghost of Superstition in its faded features, as it comes up at our call. It is one of the things which has been, and can be no more, for neither God nor the world goes back. Its terrors do not frighten, nor its hopes allure us. We rejoice that it has gone. But how do we know that our Christianity shall not share the same fate? Is there that difference between the nineteenth century, and some seventeen that have gone before it, since Jesus, to warrant the belief that our notion of Christianity shall last forever? The stream of time has already beat down Philosophies and Theologies, Temple and Church, though never so old and revered. How do we know there is not a perishing element in what we call Christianity? Jesus tells us, *his* Word is the word of God, and so shall never pass away. But who tells us, that *our* word shall never pass away? that *our notion* of his Word shall stand forever?

Let us look at this matter a little more closely. In actual Christianity, that is, in that portion of Christianity which is preached and believed, there seem to have been, ever since the time of its earthly founder, two elements, the one transient, the other permanent. The one is the thought, the folly, the uncertain wisdom, the theological notions, the impiety of man; the other the eternal truth of God. These two bear perhaps the same relation to each other that the phenomena of outward nature, such as sunshine and cloud, growth, decay and reproduction, bear to the great law of nature, which underlies and supports them all. As in that case, more attention is commonly paid to the particular phenomena than to the general law, so in this case, more is generally given to the transient in Christianity than to the permanent therein.

It must be confessed, though with sorrow, that transient things form a great part of what is commonly taught as Religion. An undue place has often been assigned to forms and doctrines, while too little stress has been laid on the divine life of the soul, love to God, and love to man. Religious forms may be useful, and beautiful. They are so, whenever they speak to the soul, and answer a want thereof. In our present state some forms are perhaps necessary. But they are only the accident of Christianity; not its substance. They are the robe, not the angel, who may take another robe, quite as becoming and useful. One sect has many forms; another none. Yet both may be equally Christian, in spite of the redundance or the deficiency. They are a part of the language in which religion speaks, and exist, with few exceptions, wherever man is found. In our calculating nation, in our rationalizing sect, we have retained but two of the rites so numerous in the early Christian church, and even these we have attenuated to the last degree, leaving them little more than a spectre of the ancient form. Another age may continue or forsake both; may revive old forms, or invent new ones to suit the altered circumstances of the times, and yet be Christians quite as good as we, or our fathers of the dark ages. Whether the Apostles designed these rites to be perpetual, seems a question which belongs to scholars and antiquarians, not to us, as Christian men and women. So long as they satisfy or help the pious heart, so long they are good. Looking behind, or around us, we see that the forms and rites of the Christians are quite as fluctuating as those of the heathens; from whom some of them have been, not unwisely, adopted by the earlier church.

Again, the doctrines that have been connected with Christianity, and taught in its name, are quite as changeable as the form. This also takes place unavoidably. If observations be made upon Nature, which must take place so long as man has senses and understanding, there will be a philosophy of Nature, and philosophical doctrines. These will differ as the observations are just or inaccurate, and as the deductions from observed facts are true or false. Hence there will be different schools of natural philosophy, so long as men have eyes and understandings of different clearness and strength. And if men observe and reflect upon Religion, which will be done so long as man is a religious and reflective being, there must also be a philosophy of Religion, a theology and theological doctrines. These will differ, as men have felt much or little of religion, as they analyze their sentiments correctly or otherwise, and as they have reasoned right or wrong. Now the true system of Nature which exists in the outward facts, whether discovered or not, is always the same thing, though the philosophy of Nature, which men invent, change every month, and be one thing at London and the opposite at Berlin. Thus there is but one system of Nature as it exists in fact, though many theories of Nature, which exist in our imperfect notions of that system, and by which we may approximate and at length reach it. Now there can be but one Religion which is absolutely true, existing in the facts of human nature, and the ideas of Infinite God. That, whether acknowledged or not, is always the same thing and never changes. So far as a man has any real religion—either the principle or the sentiment thereof—so far he has that, by whatever name he may call it. For strictly speaking there is but one kind of religion as there is but one kind of love, though the manifestations of this religion, in forms, doctrines and life, be never so diverse. It is through these, men approximate to the true expression of this religion. Now while this religion is one and always the same thing, there may be numerous systems of theology or philosophies of religion. These with their creeds, confessions and collections of doctrines, deduced by reasoning upon the facts observed, may be baseless and false, either because the observation was too narrow in extent, or otherwise defective in point of accuracy, or because the reasoning was illogical and therefore the deduction spurious. Each of these three faults is conspicuous in the systems of theology. Now the solar system as it exists in fact is permanent, though the notions of Thales and Ptolemy, of Copernicus and Descartes about this system, prove transient, imperfect approximations to the true expression. So the Christianity of Jesus is permanent, though what passes for Christianity with Popes and catechisms, with sects and churches, in the first century or in the nineteenth century, prove transient also. Now it has sometimes happened that a man took his philosophy of Nature at second hand, and then attempted to make his observations conform to his theory, and Nature ride in his panniers. Thus some philosophers refused to look at the Moon through Galileo's telescope, for according to their theory of vision, such an instrument would not aid the sight. Thus their preconceived notions stood up between them and Nature. Now it has often happened that men took their theology thus at second hand, distorted the history of the world and man's nature besides, to make Religion conform to their notions. Their theology stood between them and God. Those obstinate philosophers have disciples in no small number.

What another has said of false systems of science, will apply equally to theology: "It is barren in effects, fruitful in questions, slow and languid in its improvement, exhibiting in its generality the counterfeit of perfection, but ill filled up in its details, popular in its choice, but suspected by its very promoters, and therefore bolstered up and countenanced with artifices. Even those who have been determined to try for themselves, to add their support to learning, and to enlarge its limits, have not dared entirely to desert received opinions, nor to seek the spring-head of things. But they think they have done a great thing if they intersperse and contribute something of their own; prudently considering, that by their assent they can save their modesty, and by their contributions, their liberty. Neither is there, nor ever will be, an end or limit to these things. One snatches at one thing, another is pleased with another; there is no dry nor clear sight of any thing. Every one plays the philosopher out of the small treasures of his own fancy. The more sublime wits more acutely and with better success; the duller with less success but equal obstinacy, and, by the discipline of some learned men, sciences are bounded within the limits of some certain authors which they have set down, imposing them upon old men and instilling them into young. So that now, (as Tully cavilled upon Cæsar's consulship) the star Lyra riseth by an edict, and authority is taken for truth and not truth for authority; which kind of order and discipline is very convenient for our present use, but banisheth those which are better."

Any one who traces the history of what is called Christianity, will see that nothing changes more from age to age than the doctrines taught as Christian and insisted on as essential to Christianity and personal salvation. What is falsehood in one province passes for truth in another. The heresy of one age is the orthodox belief and "only infallible rule" of the next. Now Arius, and now Athanasius is Lord the ascendant. Both were excommunicated in their turn; each for affirming what the other denied. Men are burned for professing what men are burned for denying. For centuries the doctrines of the Christians were no better, to say the least, than those of their contemporary pagans. The theological doctrines derived from our fathers, seem to have come from Judaism, Heathenism, and the caprice of philosophers, far more than they have come from the principle and sentiment of Christianity. The doctrine of the Trinity, the very Achilles of theological dogmas, belongs to philosophy and not religion; its subtleties cannot even be expressed in our tongue. As old religions became superannuated and died out, they left to the rising faith, as to a residuary legatee, their forms, and their doctrines; or rather, as the giant in the fable left his poisoned garment to work the overthrow of his conqueror. Many tenets that pass current in our theology, seem to be the refuse of idol temples....

... It must of necessity be the case that our reasonings, and therefore our theological doctrines, are imperfect and so, perishing. It is only gradually that we approach to the true system of Nature by observation and reasoning, and work out our philosophy and theology by the toil of the brain. But mean time, if we are faithful, the great truths of morality and religion, the deep sentiment of love to man and love to God, are perceived intuitively, and by instinct, as it were, though our theology be imperfect and miserable. The theological notions of Abraham, to take the story as it stands, were exceedingly gross, yet a greater than Abraham has told us Abraham desired to see my day, saw it and was glad. Since these notions are so fleeting, why need we accept the commandment of men, as the doctrine of God?

This transitoriness of doctrines appears, in many instances, of which two may be selected for a more attentive consideration. First, the doctrine respecting the origin and authority of the Old and New Testament. There has been a time when men were burned for asserting doctrines of natural philosophy, which rested on evidence the most incontestable, because those doctrines conflicted with sentences in the Old Testament. Every word of that Jewish record was regarded as miraculously inspired and therefore as infallibly true. It was believed that the Christian religion itself rested thereon, and must stand or fall with the immaculate Hebrew text. He was deemed no small sinner who found mistakes in the manuscripts. On the authority of the written Word, man was taught to believe impossible legends, conflicting assertions; to take fiction for fact; a dream for a miraculous revelation of God; an oriental poem for a grave history of miraculous events; a collection of amatory idyls for a serious discourse "touching the mutual love of Christ and the Church;" they have been taught to accept a picture sketched by some glowing eastern imagination, never intended to be taken for a reality, as a proof that the Infinite God spoke in human words, appeared in the shape of a cloud, a flaming bush, or a man who ate and drank, and vanished into smoke; that he gave counsels to-day, and the opposite to-morrow; that he violated his own laws, was angry, and was only dissuaded by a mortal man from destroying at once a whole nation—millions of men who rebelled against their leader in a moment of anguish. Questions in philosophy, questions in the Christian religion, have been settled by an appeal to that book. The inspiration of its authors has been assumed as infallible. Every fact in the early Jewish history, has been taken as a type of some analogous fact in Christian history. The most distant events, even such as are still in the arms of time, were supposed to be clearly foreseen and foretold by pious Hebrews several centuries before Christ. It has been assumed at the outset, with no shadow of evidence, that those writers held a miraculous communication with God, such as he has granted to no other man....

... But modern Criticism is fast breaking to pieces this idol which men have made out of the Scriptures. It has shown that here are the most different works thrown together. That their authors, wise as they sometimes were; pious as we feel often their spirit to have been, had only that inspiration which is common to other men equally pious and wise; that they were by no means infallible; but were mistaken in faces or in reasoning; uttered predictions which time has not fulfilled; men who in some measure partook of the darkness and limited notions of their age, and were not always above its mistakes or its corruptions.

The history of opinions on the New Testament is quite similar. It has been assumed at the outset, it would seem with no sufficient reason, without the smallest pretence on its writers' part, that all of its authors were infallibly and miraculously inspired, so that they could commit no error of doctrine or fact....

But the current notions respecting the infallible inspiration of the Bible have no foundation in the Bible itself. Which Evangelist, which Apostle of the New Testament, what Prophet or Psalmist of the Old Testament, ever claims infallible authority for himself or for others? Which of them does not in his own writings show that he was finite and with all his zeal and piety, possessed but a limited inspiration, the bound whereof we can sometimes discover? Did Christ ever demand that men should assent to the doctrines of the Old Testament, credit its stories, and take its poems for histories, and believe equally two accounts that contradict one another? Has he ever told you that all the truths of his religion, all the beauty of a Christian life should be contained in the writings of those men, who, even after his resurrection, expected him to be a Jewish king; of men who were sometimes at variance with one another and misunderstood his divine teachings? Would not those modest writers themselves be confounded at the idolatry we pay them? Opinions may change on these points, as they have often changed—changed greatly and for the worse since the days of Paul. They are changing now, and we may hope for the better; for God makes man's folly as well as his wrath to praise Him, and continually brings good out of evil.

———

Another instance of the transitoriness of doctrines taught as Christian is found in those which relate to the nature and authority of Christ.

One ancient party has told us, that he is the infinite God; another, that he is both God and man; a third, that he was a man, the son of Joseph and Mary,—born as we are; tempted like ourselves; inspired, as we may be, if we will pay the price. Each of the former parties believed its doctrine on this head was infallibly true, and formed the substance of Christianity, and was one of the essential conditions of salvation, though scarce any two distinguished teachers, of ancient or modern times, agree in their expression of this truth.

Almost every sect that has ever been, makes Christianity rest on the personal authority of Jesus, and not the immutable truth of the doctrines themselves, or the authority of God, who sent him into the world. Yet it seems difficult to conceive any reason why moral and religious truths should rest for their support on the personal authority of their revealer, any more than the truths of science on that of him who makes them known first or most clearly. It is hard to see why the great truths of Christianity rest on the personal authority of Jesus, more than the axioms of geometry rest on the personal authority of Euclid, or Archimedes. The authority of Jesus, as of all teachers, one would naturally think, must rest on the truth of his words, and not their truth on his authority.

Opinions respecting the nature of Christianity seem to be constantly changing. In the three first centuries after Christ, it appears, great latitude of speculation prevailed. Some said he was God, with nothing of human nature, his body only an illusion; others, that he was man, with nothing of the divine nature, his miraculous birth having no foundation in fact. In a few centuries it was decreed by councils that he was God, thus honoring the divine element; next, that he was man also, thus admitting the human side. For some ages the Catholic Church seems to have dwelt chiefly on the divine nature that was in him, leaving the human element to mystics and other heretical persons, whose bodies served to flesh the swords of orthodox believers. . . .

Now it seems clear, that the notions men form about the origin and nature of the scriptures; respecting the nature and authority of Christ, have nothing to do with Christianity except as its aids or its adversaries; they are not the foundation of its truths. These are theological questions, not religious questions. Their connection with Christianity appears accidental; for if Jesus had taught at Athens, and not at Jerusalem; if he had wrought no miracle, and none but the human nature had ever been ascribed to him; if the Old Testament had forever perished at his birth,—Christianity would still have been the Word of God; it would have lost none of its truths. It would be just as true, just as beautiful, just as lasting, as now it is; though we should have lost so many a blessed word, and the work of Christianity itself would have been, perhaps, a long time retarded.

To judge the future by the past, the former authority of the Old Testament can never return. Its present authority cannot stand. It must be taken for what it is worth. The occasional folly and impiety of its authors pass for no more than their value;—while the religion, the wisdom, the love, which make fragrant its leaves, will still speak to the best hearts as hitherto, and in accents even more divine, when Reason is allowed her rights. The ancient belief in the infallible inspiration of each sentence of the New Testament, is fast changing; very fast. One writer, not a skeptic, but a Christian of unquestioned piety, sweeps off the beginning of Matthew; another, of different church and equally religious, the end of John. Numerous critics strike off several epistles. The Apocalypse itself is not spared, notwithstanding its concluding curse. Who shall tell us the work of retrenchment is to stop here; that others will not demonstrate, what some pious hearts have long felt, that errors of doctrine and errors of fact may be found in many parts of the law, here and there, from the beginning of Matthew to the end of Acts! We see how opinions have changed ever since the apostles' time; and who shall assure us that they were not sometimes mistaken in historical, as well as doctrinal matters; did not sometimes confound the actual with the imaginary, and that the fancy of these pious writers never stood in the place of their recollection?

But what if this should take place? Is Christianity then to perish out of the heart of the nations, and vanish from the memory of the world, like the religions that were before Abraham? It must be so, if it rest on a foundation which a scoffer may shake, and a score of pious critics shake down. But this is the foundation of a theology, not of Christianity. That does not rest on the decision of Councils. It is not to stand or fall with the infallible inspiration of a few Jewish fishermen, who have writ their names in characters of light all over the world. It does not continue to stand through the forbearance of some critic, who can cut when he will the thread on which its life depends. Christianity does not rest on the infallible authority of the New Testament. It depends on this collection of books for the historical statement of its facts. In this we do not require infallible inspiration on the part of the writers, more than in the record of other historical facts. To me it seems as presumptuous on the one hand for the believer to claim this evidence for the truth of Christianity, as it is absurd on the other hand, for the skeptic to demand such evidence to support these historical statements. I cannot see that it depends on the personal authority of Jesus. He was the organ through which the Infinite spoke. It is God that was manifested in the flesh by him, on whom rests the truth which Jesus brought to light and made clear and beautiful in his life; and if Christianity be true, it seems useless to look for any other authority to uphold it, as for some one to support Almighty God. So if it could be proved,—as it cannot,—in opposition to the greatest amount of historical evidence ever collected on any similar point, that the gospels were the fabrication of designing and artful men, that Jesus of Nazareth had never lived, still Christianity would stand firm, and fear no evil. None of the doctrines of that religion would fall to the ground, for if true, they stand by themselves. But we should lose,—oh, irreparable loss!—the example of that character, so beautiful, so divine, that no human genius could have conceived it, as none, after all the progress and refinement of eighteen centuries, seems fully to have comprehended its lustrous life. If Christianity were true, we should still think it was so, not because its record was written by infallible pens; nor because it was lived out by an infallible teacher,—but that it is true, like the axioms of geometry, because it is true, and is to be tried by the oracle God places in the breast. If it rest on the personal authority of Jesus alone, then there is no certainty of its truth, if he were ever mistaken in the smallest matter, as some Christians have thought he was, in predicting his second coming. . . .

. . . In him, as in a mirror, we may see the image of God, and go on from glory to glory, till we are changed into the same image, led by the spirit which enlightens the humble. Viewed in this way, how beautiful is the life of Jesus. Heaven has come down to earth, or, rather, earth has become heaven. The Son of God, come of age, has taken possession of his birthright. The brightest revelation is this,—of what is possible for all men, if not now at least hereafter. How pure is his spirit, and how encouraging its words. "Lowly sufferer," he seems to say, "see how I bore the cross. Patient laborer, be strong; see how I toiled for the unthankful and the merciless. Mistaken sinner, see of what thou art capable. Rise up, and be blessed."

But if, as some early Christians began to do, you take a heathen view, and make him a God, the Son of God in a peculiar and exclusive sense—much of the significance of his character is gone. His virtue has no merit; his love no feeling; his cross no burden; his agony no pain.

His death is an illusion; his resurrection but a show. For if he were not a man, but a god, what are all these things; what his words, his life, his excellence of achievement?—It is all nothing, weighed against the illimitable greatness of Him who created the worlds and fills up all time and space! Then his resignation is no lesson; his life no model; his death no triumph to you or me,—who are not gods, but mortal men, that know not what a day shall bring forth, and walk by faith "dim sounding on our perilous way." Alas, we have despaired of man, and so cut off his brightest hope.

———

To turn away from the disputes of the Catholics and the Protestants, of the Unitarian and the Trinitarian, of Old School and New School, and come to the plain words of Jesus of Nazareth, Christianity is a simple thing; very simple. It is absolute, pure morality; absolute, pure religion; the love of man; the love of God acting without let or hindrance. The only creed it lays down, is the great truth which springs up spontaneous in the holy heart—there is a God. Its watchword is, be perfect as your Father in Heaven. The only form it demands is a divine life; doing the best thing, in the best way, from the highest motives; perfect obedience to the great law of God. Its sanction is the voice of God in your heart; the perpetual presence of Him, who made us and the stars over our head; Christ and the Father abiding within us. All this is very simple; a little child can understand it; very beautiful, the loftiest mind can find nothing so lovely. Try it by Reason, Conscience and Faith—things highest in man's nature—we see no redundance, we feel no deficiency. Examine the particular duties it enjoins; humility, reverence, sobriety, gentleness, charity, forgiveness, fortitude, resignation, faith and active love; try the whole extent of Christianity so well summed up in the command, "Thou shalt love the Lord thy God, with all thy heart, and with all thy soul and with all thy mind—thou shalt love thy neighbor as thyself," and is there any thing therein that can perish? No, the very opponents of Christianity have rarely found fault with the teachings of Jesus. The end of Christianity seems to be to make all men one with God as Christ was one with Him; to bring them to such a state of obedience and goodness, that we shall think divine thoughts and feel divine sentiments, and so keep the law of God by living a life of truth and love. Its means are Purity and Prayer; getting strength from God and using it for our fellow men as well as ourselves. It allows perfect freedom. It does not demand all men to *think* alike, but to think uprightly, and get as near as possible at truth; not all men to *live* alike, but to live holy and get as near as possible to a life perfectly divine. Christ set up no pillars of Hercules, beyond which men must not sail the sea in quest of Truth. He says "I have many things to say unto you, but ye cannot bear them now ... Greater works than these shall ye do." Christianity lays no rude hand on the sacred peculiarity of individual genius and character. But there is no Christian sect which does not fetter a man. It would make all men think alike, or smother their conviction in silence. Were all men Quakers or Catholics, Unitarians or Baptists, there would be much less diversity of thought, character and life: less of truth active in the world than now. But Christianity gives us the largest liberty of the sons of God, and were all men Christians after the fashion of Jesus, this variety would be a thousand times greater than now, for Christianity is not a system of doctrines, but rather a method of attaining oneness with God. It demands, therefore, a good life of piety within, of purity without, and gives the promise that whoso does God's will, shall know of God's doctrine. . . .

———

Such, then, is the Transient, and such the Permanent in Christianity. What is of absolute value never changes; we may cling round it and grow to it forever. No one can say his notions shall stand. But we may all say, the Truth, as it is in Jesus, shall never pass away. Yet there are always some even religious men, who do not see the permanent element, so they rely on the fleeting; and, what is also an evil, condemn others for not doing the same. They mistake a defence of the Truth for an attack upon the Holy of Holies; the removal of a theological error for the destruction of all religion. Already men of the same sect eye one another with suspicion, and lowering brows that indicate a storm, and, like children who have fallen out in their play, call hard names. Now, as always, there is a collision between these two elements. The question puts itself to each man, "Will you cling to what is perishing, or embrace what is eternal?" This question each must answer for himself.

# 8.

# LIDIAN EMERSON
## "TRANSCENDENTAL BIBLE"
### (1841?)

Lidian Jackson Emerson (1802–92) was Emerson's second wife and the mother of all his children. Waldo insisted on changing her name from Lydia to avoid the sound of the New England drawl ("Lydiar"). He did not succeed in converting her to Emersonianism, however. She remained more religiously orthodox than he, although occasionally he was able to draw her over the line. She was the source of the sardonic one-liner quote in the Divinity School Address: "On Sundays, it seems wicked to go to church." Often Emerson's iconoclasm troubled her, however. Sometimes they sparred over their differences. Though Waldo was the luminary and Lidian the homebody, she was fully as arresting a personality in her own way as he—as this selection shows: a reductio ad absurdum of the Emersonian gospel of "Self-Reliance." Her "Transcendental Bible" also takes satiric aim at Transcendental rarefactions, returning in kind the contempt Emerson and especially Parker displayed toward what they took to be benighted religious conservatism.

SOURCE: Delores Bird Carpenter, ed., "Lidian Emerson's 'Transcendental Bible,'" *Studies in the American Renaissance*, 1980: 91–92.

## WHOLE DUTY OF MAN

Never hint at a Providence, Particular or Universal. It is narrow to believe that the Universal Being concerns itself with particular affairs, egotistical to think it regards your own. Never speak of sin. It is of no consequence to "the Being" whether *you* are good or bad. It is egotistical to consider it yourself; who are you?

Never confess a fault. You should not have committed it and who cares whether you are sorry?

Never speak of Happiness as a consequence of Holiness. Do you need any bribe to well-doing? Cannot you every hour practise holiness for its own sake? Are you not ashamed to wish to be happy? It is egotistical—mean.

Never speak of the hope of Immortality. What do you know about it? It is egotistical to cling to it. Enough for the great to know that "Being" Is. He is quite content to drop into annihilation at the death of the body.

Never speak of affliction being sent and sent in kindness; that is an old wives' fable. What do you know about it? And what business is it of ours whether it is for our good or not?

## DUTY TO YOUR NEIGHBOUR

Loathe and shun the sick. They are in bad taste, and may untune us for writing the poem floating through our mind.

Scorn the infirm of character and omit no opportunity of insulting and exposing them. They ought not to be infirm and should be punished by contempt and avoidance.

Despise the unintellectual, and make them feel that you do by not noticing their remark and question lest they presume to intrude into your conversation.

Abhor those who commit certain crimes because they indicate stupidity, want of intellect which is the one thing needful.

Justify those who commit certain other crimes. Their commission is consistent with the possession of intellect. We should not judge the intellectual as common men. It is mean enough to wish to put a great mind into the strait-jacket of morality.

It is mean and weak to seek for sympathy; it is mean and weak to give it. Great souls are self-sustained and stand ever erect, saying only to the prostrate sufferer "Get up, and stop your complaining." Never wish to be loved. Who are you to expect that? Besides, the great never value being loved.

If any seek to believe that their sorrows are sent or sent in love, do your best to dispel the silly egotistical delusion.

If you scorn happiness (though you value a pleasant talk or walk, a tasteful garment, a comfortable dinner), if you wish not for immortal consciousness (though you bear with impatience the loss of an hour of thought or study), if you care not for the loss of your soul (though you deprecate the loss of your house), if you care not how much you sin (though in pain at the commission of a slight indiscretion), if you ask not a wise Providence over the earth in which you live (although wishing a wise manager of the house in which you live), if you care not that a benign Divinity shapes your ends (though you seek a good tailor to shape your coat), if you scorn to believe your affliction cometh not from the dust (though bowed to the dust by it), then, if there is such a thing as duty, you have done your whole duty to your noble self-sustained, impeccable, infallible Self.

If you have refused all sympathy to the sorrowful, all pity and aid to the sick, all toleration to the infirm of character, if you have condemned the unintellectual and loathed such sinners as have discovered want of intellect by their sin, then are you a perfect specimen of Humanity.

Let us all aspire after this Perfection! So be it.

# 9.

# HENRY DAVID THOREAU
## CHRISTIANITY AND HINDUISM COMPARED
### (1849)

Transcendentalism oscillated between skeptical and affirming views of religious tradition. Emerson's Divinity School Address and especially Parker's *Transient and Permanent* discourse concentrate on exposing Judaeo-Christianity as just another mythology. Yet implicit in Emerson if not also in Parker is a more sympathetic revaluation of *all* mythic traditions as symbolically significant. Emerson in particular laid the ground for a more inclusive view of religion. He was particularly struck by the Hindu *Bhagavad Gita*, "the first of books," as he once called it. Thoreau was even more so. In fact, Thoreau took the lead in editing a series of "Ethnical Scriptures" for *The Dial*—excerpts from sacred texts of Asian and Mediterranean antiquity (see Section V-B). His meditation below on the relative merits of two great religions shows both a typical limit of Transcendentalist thinking—the tendency to work within stereotypical contrasts between "east" and "west"—and a more searching attempt to take the great ancient religious and philosophical texts of Asia seriously. Although none of the Transcendentalists ever learned Sanskrit or Chinese, they were the first group of American intelligentsia to make anything like a systematic attempt at comparative religious studies.

SOURCE: *A Week on the Concord and Merrimack Rivers.* Boston: James Munroe, 1849, slightly revised in light of 1868 edition.

The wisest conservatism is that of the Hindoos. "Immemorial custom is transcendent law," says Menu. That is, it was the custom of the gods before men used it. The fault of our New England custom is that it is memorial. What is morality but immemorial custom? Conscience is the chief of conservatives. "Perform the settled functions," says Kreeshna in the Bhagvat-Geeta; "action is preferable to inaction. The journey of thy mortal frame may not succeed from inaction."—"A man's own calling with all its faults, ought not to be forsaken. Every undertaking is involved in its faults as the fire in its smoke."—"The man who is acquainted with the whole, should not drive those from their works who are slow of comprehension, and less experienced than himself."—"Wherefore, O Arjoon, resolve to fight," is the advice of the God to the irresolute soldier who fears to slay his best friends. It is a sublime conservatism; as wide as the world, and as unwearied as time; preserving the universe with Asiatic anxiety, in that state in which it appeared to their minds. These philosophers dwell on the inevitability and unchangeableness of laws, on the power of temperament and constitution, the three *goon* or qualities, and the circumstances of birth and affinity. The end is an immense consolation; eternal absorption in Brahma. Their speculations never venture beyond their own table-lands, though they are high and vast as they. Buoyancy, freedom, flexibility, variety, possibility, which also are qualities of the Unnamed, they deal not with. The undeserved reward is to be earned by an ever-lasting moral drudgery; the incalculable promise of the morrow is, as it were, weighed. And who will say that their conservatism has not been effectual? "Assuredly," says a French translator, speaking of the antiquity and durability of the Chinese and Indian nations, and of the wisdom of their legislators, "there are there some vestiges of the eternal laws which govern the world."

Christianity, on the other hand, is humane, practical, and, in a large sense, radical. So many years and ages of the gods those Eastern sages sat contemplating Brahm, uttering in silence the mystic "Om," being absorbed into the essence of the Supreme Being, never going out of themselves, but subsiding farther and deeper within; so infinitely wise, yet infinitely stagnant; until, at last, in that same Asia, but in the western part of it, appeared a youth, wholly unforetold by them,—not being absorbed into Brahm, but bringing Brahm down to earth and to mankind; in whom Brahm had awaked from his long sleep, and exerted himself, and the day began,—a new avatar. The Brahman had never thought to be a brother of mankind as well as a child of God. Christ is the prince of Reformers and Radicals. Many expressions in the New Testament come naturally to the lips of all Protestants, and it furnishes the most pregnant and practical texts. There is no harmless dreaming, no wise speculation in it, but everywhere a substratum of good sense. It never *reflects,* but it *repents.* There is no poetry in it, we may say, nothing regarded in the light of beauty merely, but moral truth is its object. All mortals are convicted by its conscience.

The New Testament is remarkable for its pure morality; the best of the Hindo Scripture, for its pure intellectuality. The reader is nowhere raised into and sustained in a higher, purer, or *rarer* region of thought than in the Bhagvat-Geeta. Warren Hastings, in his sensible letter recommending the translation of this book to the Chairman of the East India Company, declares the original to be "of a sublimity of conception, reasoning, and diction almost unequalled," and that the writings of the Indian philosophers "will survive when the British dominion in India shall have long ceased to exist, and when the sources which it once yielded of wealth and power are lost to remembrance." It is unquestionably one of the noblest and most sacred scriptures which have come down to us. Books are to be distinguished by the grandeur of their topics, even more than by the manner in which they are treated. The Oriental philosophy approaches, easily, loftier themes than the modern aspires to; and no wonder if it sometimes prattle about them. *It* only assigns their due rank respectively to Action and Contemplation, or rather does full justice to the latter. Western philosophers have not conceived of the significance of Contemplation in their sense. . . .

———

To an American reader, who, by the advantage of his position, can see over that strip of Atlantic coast to Asia and the Pacific, who, as it were, sees the shore slope upward over the Alps to the Himmaleh Mountains, the comparatively recent literature of Europe often appears partial and clannish, and, notwithstanding the limited range of his own sympathies and studies, the European writer who presumes that he is speaking for the world, is perceived by him to speak only for that corner of it which he inhabits. One of the rarest of England's scholars and critics, in his classification of the worthies of the world, betrays the narrowness of his European culture and the exclusiveness of his reading. None of her children has done justice to the poets and philosophers of Persia or of India. They have even been better known to her merchant scholars than to her poets and thinkers by profession. You may look in vain through English poetry for a single memorable verse inspired by these themes. Nor is Germany to be excepted, though her philological industry is indirectly serving the cause of philosophy and poetry. Even Goethe wanted that universality of genius which could have appreciated the philosophy of India, if he had more nearly approached it. His genius was more practical, dwelling much more in the regions of the understanding, and was less native to contemplation than the genius of those sages. It is remarkable that Homer and a few Hebrews are the most Oriental names which modern Europe, whose literature has taken its rise since the decline of the Persian, has admitted into her list of Worthies, and perhaps the *worthiest* of mankind, and the fathers of modern thinking,—for the contemplations of those Indian sages have influenced, and still influence, the intellectual development of mankind,—whose works even yet survive in wonderful completeness, are, for the most part, not recognized as ever having existed. If the lions had been the painters it would have been otherwise. In every one's youthful dreams philosophy is still vaguely but inseparably, and with singular truth, associated with the East, nor do after years discover its local habitation in the Western world. In comparison with the philosophers of the East, we may say that modern Europe has yet given birth to none. Beside the vast and cosmogonal philosophy of the Bhagvat-Geeta, even our Shakespeare seems sometimes youthfully green and practical merely. Some of these sublime sentences, as the Chaldæan oracles of Zoroaster, still surviving after a thousand revolutions and translations, alone make us doubt if the poetic form and dress are not transitory, and not essential to the most effective and enduring expression of thought. *Ex oriente lux* may still be the motto of scholars, for the Western world has not yet derived from the East all the light which it is destined to receive thence.

It would be worthy of the age to print together the collected Scriptures or Sacred Writings of the several nations, the Chinese, the Hindoos, the Persians, the Hebrews, and others, as the Scripture of mankind. The New Testament is still, perhaps, too much on the lips and in the hearts of men to be called a Scripture in this sense. Such a juxtaposition and comparison might help to liberalize the faith of men. This is a work which Time will surely edit, reserved to crown the labors of the printing-press. This would be the Bible, or Book of Books, which let the missionaries carry to the uttermost parts of the earth.

# 10.

# THOMAS WENTWORTH HIGGINSON

## FROM "THE SYMPATHY OF RELIGIONS"

### (1871)

Higginson (1823–1911) is best known for his memoir of Civil War service, *Army Life in a Black Regiment* (1870), and for his later career as a mildly liberal man of letters. A feminist of sorts, Higginson wrote an early biography of Margaret Fuller and served, to his infinite perplexity, as Emily Dickinson's chosen literary advisor. (During their long correspondence, Dickinson mostly ignored his advice.) After her death he helped ensure publication of (a doctored version of) her poems. But Higginson was also closely allied with the Transcendentalist group, an admirer of Emerson, Parker, and also Thoreau. He was a liberal minister by training who maintained an interest in comparative religion long after he left the ministry. This selection, a magazine article later printed as a pamphlet, was the first of a series of increasingly ambitious attempts by younger-generation Transcendentalists to define religion in global terms, among which *Ten Great Religions* (1871, 1883), by Margaret Fuller's old friend James Freeman Clarke, was the most widely read. Most of these attempts at comparison were marked by a lingering judgmentalism of one or both of the following sorts: either Christianity came out more or less on top, as the highest stage to which world religious consciousness had yet advanced, or the particularities of all religious traditions were more or less written off in the course of arguing for a bedrock religious consciousness inherent in the human spirit. Higginson avoided the first pitfall remarkably well, if not the second.

SOURCE: "The Sympathy of Religions," *The Radical*, 8 (February 1871).

OUR true religious life begins when we discover that there is an Inner Light, not infallible but invaluable, which "lighteth every man that cometh into the world." Then we have something to steer by; and it is chiefly this, and not an anchor, that we need. The human soul, like any other noble vessel, was not built to be anchored, but to sail. An anchorage may, indeed, be at times a temporary need, in order to make some special repairs, or to take fresh cargo in; yet the natural destiny of both ship and soul is not the harbor, but the ocean; to cut with even keel the vast and beautiful expanse; to pass from island on to island of more than Indian balm, or to continents fairer than Columbus won; or, best of all, steering close to the wind, to extract motive power from the greatest obstacles. Men must forget the eternity through which they have yet to sail, when they talk of anchoring here upon this bank and shoal of time. It would be a tragedy to see the shipping of the world whitening the seas no more, and idly riding at anchor in Atlantic ports; but it would be more tragic to see a world of souls fascinated into a fatal repose and renouncing their destiny of motion.

And as with individuals, so with communities. The great historic religions of the world are not so many stranded hulks left to perish. The best of them are all in motion. All over the world the divine influence moves men. There is a sympathy in religions, and this sympathy is shown alike in their origin, their records, and their progress. Men are ceasing to disbelieve, and learning to believe more. I have worshiped in an Evangelical church when thousands rose to their feet at the motion of one hand. I have worshiped in a Roman Catholic church when the lifting of one finger broke the motionless multitude into twinkling motion, till the magic sign was made, and all was still once more. But I never for an instant have supposed that this concentrated moment of devotion was more holy or more beautiful than when one cry from a minaret hushes a Mohammedan city to prayer, or when, at sunset, the low invocation, "Oh! the gem in the lotus—oh! the gem in the lotus," goes murmuring, like the cooing of many doves, across the vast surface of Thibet. True, "the gem in the lotus" means nothing to us, but it means as much to the angels as "the Lamb of God," for it is a symbol of aspiration.

Every year brings new knowledge of the religions of the world, and every step in knowledge brings out the sympathy between them. They all show the same aim, the same symbols, the same forms, the same weaknesses, the same aspirations. Looking at these points of unity, we might say there is but one religion under many forms, whose essential creed is the Fatherhood of God, and the Brotherhood of Man,— disguised by corruptions, symbolized by mythologies, ennobled by virtues, degraded by vices, but still the same. Or if, passing to a closer analysis, we observe the shades of difference, we shall find in these varying faiths the several instruments which perform what Cudworth calls "the Symphony of Religions." And though some may stir like drums, and others soothe like flutes, and others like violins command the whole range of softness and of strength, yet they are all alike instruments, and nothing in any one of them is so wondrous as the great laws of sound which equally control them all....

———

The greatest of modern scholars, Von Humboldt, asserted in middle life and repeated the assertion in old age, that "all positive religions contain three distinct parts. First, a code of morals, very fine, and nearly the same in all. Second, a geological dream, and, third, a myth or historical novelette, which last becomes the most important of all." And though this observation may be somewhat roughly stated, its essential truth is seen when we compare the different religions of the world, side by side. With such startling points of similarity, where is the difference? The main difference lies here, that each fills some blank space in its creed with the name of a different teacher. For instance, the Oriental Parsee wears a fine white garment, bound around him with a certain knot; and whenever this knot is undone, at morning or night, he repeats the four main points of his creed, which are as follows:—

"To believe in one God, and hope for mercy from him only."

"To believe in a future state of existence."

"To do as you would be done by."

Thus far the Parsee keeps on the universal ground of religion. Then he drops into the language of his sect and adds,—

"To believe in Zoroaster as lawgiver, and to hold his writings sacred."

The creed thus furnishes a formula for all religions. It might be printed in blank like a circular, leaving only the closing name to be filled in. For Zoroaster read Christ, and you have Christianity; read Buddha, and you have Buddhism; read Mohammed, and you have Mohammedanism. Each of these, in short, is Natural Religion *plus* an individual name. It is by insisting on that *plus* that each religion stops short of being universal.

In this religion of the human race, thus variously disguised, we find everywhere the same leading features. The same great doctrines, good or bad,—regeneration, predestination, atonement, the future life, the final judgment, the Divine Reason or Logos, and the Trinity. The same religious institutions,—monks, missionaries, priests, and pilgrims. The same ritual,—prayers, liturgies, sacrifices, sermons, hymns. The same implements,—frankincense, candles, holy water, relics, amulets, votive offerings. The same symbols,—the cross, the ball, the triangle, the serpent, the all-seeing eye, the halo of rays, the tree of life. The same saints, angels, and martyrs. The same holiness attached to particular cities, rivers, and mountains. The same prophecies and miracles,—the dead restored and evil spirits cast out. The self-same holy days; for Easter and Christmas were kept as spring and autumn festivals, centuries before our era, by Egyptians, Persians, Saxons, Romans. The same artistic designs, since the mother and child stand depicted, not only in the temples of Europe, but in those of Etruria and Arabia, Egypt and Thibet. In ancient Christian art, the evangelists were represented with the same heads of eagles, oxen, and lions, upon which we gaze with amazement in Egyptian tombs. Nay, the very sects and subdivisions of all historic religions have been the same, and each supplies us with mystic and rationalist, formalist and philanthropist, ascetic and epicurean. The simple fact is, that all these things are as indigenous as grass and mosses; they spring up in every soil, and only the microscope can tell them apart.

And, as all these inevitably recur, so comes back again and again the idea of incarnation,—the Divine Man. Here, too, all religions sympathize, and, with slight modifications, each is the copy of the other. As in the dim robing-rooms of foreign churches are kept rich stores of sacred vestments, ready to be thrown over every successive generation of priests, so the world has kept in memory the same stately traditions to decorate each new Messiah. He is predicted by prophecy, hailed by sages, born of a virgin, attended by miracle, borne to heaven without tasting death, and with promise of return. Zoroaster and Confucius have no human father. Osiris is the Son of God, he is called the Revealer of Life and Light; he first teaches one chosen race; he then goes with his apostles to teach the Gentiles, conquering the world by peace; he is slain by evil powers; after death he descends into hell, then rises again, and presides at the last judgment of all mankind: those who call upon his name shall be saved. Buddha is born of a virgin; his name means the Word, the Logos, but he is known more tenderly as the Saviour of Man; he embarrasses his teachers, when a child, by his understanding and his answers; he is tempted in the wilderness, when older; he goes with his apostles to redeem the world; he abolishes caste and cruelty, and teaches forgiveness; he receives among his followers outcasts whom Pharisaic pride despises, and he only says, "My law is a law of mercy to all." Slain by enemies, he descends into hell, rising without tasting death, and still lives to make intercession for man.

———

The one unpardonable sin is exclusiveness. Any form of religion is endangered when we bring it to the test of facts; for none on earth can bear that test. There never existed a person, nor a book, nor an institution, which did not share the merits and the drawbacks of its rivals. Granting all that can be established as to the debt of the world to the very best dispensation, the fact still remains, that there is not a single maxim, nor idea, nor application, nor triumph, that any single religion can claim as exclusively its own. Neither faith, nor love, nor truth, nor disinterestedness, nor forgiveness, nor patience, nor peace, nor equality, nor education, nor missionary effort, nor prayer, nor honesty, nor the sentiment of brotherhood, nor reverence for woman, nor the spirit of humility, nor the fact of martyrdom, nor any other good thing, is monopolized by any one or any half dozen forms of faith. . . .

What religion stands highest in moral results if not Christianity? Yet the slave-trader belongs to Christendom as well as the saint. If we say that Christendom was not truly represented by the slaves in the hold of John Newton's slave-ship, but only by the prayers which he read every day, as he narrates, in the cabin,—then we must admit that Buddhism is not to be judged merely by the prostrations before Fo, but by the learning of its lamaseries and the beneficence of its people. The reformed Brahmoes of India complain that Christian nations force alcoholic drinks on their nation, despite their efforts; and the greater humanity of Hindoos towards animals has been, according to Dr. Hedge, a serious embarrassment to our missionaries. So men interrupt the missionaries in China, according to Coffin's late book, by asking them why, if their doctrines be true, Christian nations forced opium on an unwilling emperor, who refused to the last to receive money from the traffic? What a history has been our treatment of the American Indians? "Instead of virtues," said Cadwallader Colden, writing as early as 1727, "we have taught them vices that they were entirely free from before that time." The delegation from the Society of Friends reported last year that an Indian chief brought a young Indian before a white commissioner to give evidence, and the commissioner hesitated a little in receiving a part of the testimony, when the chief said with great emphasis, "Oh! you may believe what he says: he tells the truth: *he has never seen a white man before!*" In Southey's Wesley there is an account of an Indian whom Wesley met in Georgia, and who thus summed up his objections to Christianity: "Christian much drunk! Christian beat man! Christian tell lies! Devil Christian! Me no Christian!" What then? All other religions show the same disparity between belief and practice, and each is safe till it tries to exclude the rest. . . .

It is our happiness to live in a time when all religions are at last out-growing their mythologies, and emancipated men are stretching out their hands to share together "the luxury of a religion that does not degrade." The progressive Brahmoes of India, the Jewish leaders in America, the Free Religious Association among ourselves, are teaching essentially the same principles, seeking the same ends. The Jewish congregations in Baltimore were the first to contribute for the education of the freedmen; the Buddhist Temple, in San Francisco, was the first edifice of that city draped in mourning after the murder of President Lincoln; the Parsees of the East sent contributions to the Sanitary Commission. The great religions of the world are but larger sects; they come together, like the lesser sects, for works of benevolence; they share the same aspirations, and every step in the progress of each brings it nearer to all the rest. For us, the door out of superstition and sin may be called Christianity; that is an historical name only, the accident of a birthplace. But other nations find other outlets; they must pass through their own doors, not through ours; and all will come at last upon the broad ground of God's providing, which bears no man's name. The reign of heaven on earth will not be called the Kingdom of Christ nor of Buddha,—it will be called the Church of God, or the Commonwealth of Man. I do not wish to belong to a religion only, but to *the* religion; it must not include less than the piety of the world. . . .

IV

# SECULAR REFORM

# A.
# Reform as Individual Transformation Versus Reform as Systemic Social Change

# ORESTES BROWNSON
## FROM "THE LABORING CLASSES"
### (1840)

Before the Transcendentalist social conscience began to mobilize on behalf of communitarianism and abolitionism in the 1840s, Orestes Brownson was the group's most outspoken social radical. This is Brownson at his most vehement. Published in a magazine Brownson edited and largely wrote himself, "The Laboring Classes" starts with a review of Thomas Carlyle's *Chartism,* praising its concern for the working class but contending that its proposed reforms do not begin to go far enough. Brownson proceeds to expose the immiseration of labor by capital in the new industrial era. The essay is written at the height of the "log cabin and hard cider" presidential campaign of 1840 and in bitter opposition to the mercantile-class-supported Whig Party, whose candidate, William Henry Harrison, eventually won. The essay has deeper roots in Brownson's own hardscrabble background ("we were born and reared in the class of proletaries," he writes elsewhere). But Brownson goes far beyond fellow Transcendentalists, and fellow Democrats as well, in arguing for not only the "distruction" (*sic*) of "the Banks" but also for the abolition of hereditary property. In the process, Brownson explicitly opposes reform initiatives primarily directed toward reform of individuals. To him, these abet existing social hierarchy rather than offer the necessary systemic reform. As a long section not printed here makes clear, Brownson's target is "priestcraft" in general and Unitarian minister William Ellery Channing's gospel of "self-culture" in particular. But he might have said—and on other occasions did—much the same about Emersonian individualism. At the same time, as Brownson's sequel in the next issue of his magazine emphasizes, he had no sympathy with communitarian experimentations of the kind that Ripley was in the process of organizing at Brook Farm. For Brownson, the key to social amelioration lies in legislative activism to overhaul the existing system of finance and property, not in the abolition of property or secession from mainstream society.

SOURCE: "The Laboring Classes," *Boston Quarterly Review*, 3 (July 1840).

No one can observe the signs of the times with much care, without perceiving that a crisis as to the relation of wealth and labor is approaching. It is useless to shut our eyes to the fact, and like the ostrich fancy ourselves secure because we have so concealed our heads that we see not the danger. We or our children will have to meet this crisis. The old war between the King and the Barons is well nigh ended, and so is that between the Barons and the Merchants and Manufacturers,—landed capital and commercial capital. The business man has become the peer of my Lord. And now commences the new struggle between the operative and his employer, between wealth and labor. Every day does this struggle extend further and wax stronger and fiercer; what or when the end will be God only knows. . . .

What we would ask is, throughout the Christian world, the actual condition of the laboring classes, viewed simply and exclusively in their capacity of laborers? . . .

. . . We have no means of ascertaining their precise proportion to the whole number of the race; but we think we may estimate them at one half. In any contest they will be as two to one, because the large class of proprietors who are not employers, but laborers on their own lands or in their own shops will make common cause with them.

Now we will not so belie our acquaintance with political economy, as to allege that these alone perform all that is necessary to the production of wealth. We are not ignorant of the fact, that the merchant, who is literally the common carrier and exchange dealer, performs a useful service, and is therefore entitled to a portion of the proceeds of labor. But make all necessary deductions on his account, and then ask what portion of the remainder is retained, either in kind or in its equivalent, in the hands of the original producer, the workingman? All over the world this fact stares us in the face, the workingman is poor and depressed, while a large portion of the non-workingmen, in the sense we now use the term, are wealthy. It may be laid down as a general rule, with but few exceptions, that men are rewarded in an inverse ratio to the amount of actual service they perform. Under every government on earth the largest salaries are annexed to those offices, which demand of their incumbents the least amount of actual labor either mental or manual. And this is in perfect harmony with the whole system of repartition of the fruits of industry, which obtains in every department of society. Now here is the system which prevails, and here is its result. The whole class of simple laborers are poor, and in general unable to procure anything beyond the bare necessaries of life....

———

We pass through our manufacturing villages, most of them appear neat and flourishing. The operatives are well dressed, and we are told, well paid. They are said to be healthy, contented, and happy. This is the fair side of the picture; the side exhibited to distinguished visitors. There is a dark side, moral as well as physical. Of the common operatives, few, if any, by their wages, acquire a competence.... The great mass wear out their health, spirits, and morals, without becoming one whit better off than when they commenced labor. The bills of mortality in these factory villages are not striking, we admit, for the poor girls when they can toil no longer go home to die. The average life, working life we mean, of the girls that come to Lowell, for instance, from Maine, New Hampshire, and Vermont, we have been assured, is only about three years. What becomes of them then? Few of them ever marry; fewer still ever return to their native places with reputations unimpaired. "She has worked in a Factory," is almost enough to damn to infamy the most worthy and virtuous girl. We know no sadder sight on earth than one of our factory villages presents, when the bell at break of day, or at the hour of breakfast, or dinner, calls out its hundreds or thousands of operatives. We stand and look at these hard working men and women hurrying in all directions, and ask ourselves, where go the proceeds of their labors? The man who employs them, and for whom they are toiling as so many slaves, is one of our city nabobs, revelling in luxury; or he is a member of our legislature, enacting laws to put money in his own pocket; or he is a member of Congress, contending for a high Tariff to tax the poor for the benefit of the rich; or in these times he is shedding crocodile tears over the deplorable condition of the poor laborer, while he docks his wages twenty-five per cent....

---

Now, what is the prospect of those who fall under the operation of this system? We ask, is there a reasonable chance that any considerable portion of the present generation of laborers, shall ever become owners of a sufficient portion of the funds of production, to be able to sustain themselves by laboring on their own capital, that is, as independent laborers? We need not ask this question, for everybody knows there is not. Well, is the condition of a laborer at wages the best that the great mass of the working people ought to be able to aspire to? Is it a condition,—nay can it be made a condition,—with which a man should be satisfied; in which he should be contented to live and die?

In our own country this condition has existed under its most favorable aspects, and has been made as good as it can be. It has reached all the excellence of which it is susceptible. It is now not improving but growing worse. The actual condition of the working-man to-day, viewed in all its bearings, is not so good as it was fifty years ago. If we have not been altogether misinformed, fifty years ago, health and industrious habits, constituted no mean stock in trade, and with them almost any man might aspire to competence and independence. But it is so no longer. The wilderness has receded, and already the new lands are beyond the reach of the mere laborer, and the employer has him at his mercy. If the present relation subsist, we see nothing better for him in reserve than what he now possesses, but something altogether worse.

We are not ignorant of the fact that men born poor become wealthy, and that men born to wealth become poor; but this fact does not necessarily diminish the numbers of the poor, nor augment the numbers of the rich. The relative numbers of the two classes remain, or may remain, the same. But be this as it may; one fact is certain, no man born poor has ever, by his wages, as a simple operative, risen to the class of the wealthy. Rich he may have become, but it has not been by his own manual labor. He has in some way contrived to tax for his benefit the labor of others. He may have accumulated a few dollars which he has placed at usury, or invested in trade; or he may, as a master workman, obtain a premium on his journeymen; or he may have from a clerk passed to a partner, or from a workman to an overseer. The simple market wages for ordinary labor, has never been adequate to raise him from poverty to wealth. This fact is decisive of the whole controversy, and proves that the system of wages must be supplanted by some other system, or else one half of the human race must forever be the virtual slaves of the other.

Now the great work for this age and the coming, is to raise up the laborer, and to realize in our own social arrangements and in the actual condition of all men, that equality between man and man, which God has established between the rights of one and those of another. In other words, our business is to emancipate the proletaries, as the past has emancipated the slaves. This is our work. There must be no class of our fellow men doomed to toil through life as mere workmen at wages. If wages are tolerated it must be, in the case of the individual operative, only under such conditions that by the time he is of a proper age to settle in life, he shall have accumulated enough to be an independent laborer on his own capital,—on his own farm or in his own shop. Here is our work. How is it to be done?

Reformers in general answer this question, or what they deem its equivalent, in a manner which we cannot but regard as very unsatisfactory. They would have all men wise, good, and happy; but in order to make them so, they tell us that we want not external changes, but internal; and therefore instead of declaiming against society and seeking to disturb existing social arrangements, we should confine ourselves to the individual reason and conscience; seek merely to lead the individual to repentance, and to reformation of life; make the individual a practical, a truly religious man, and all evils will either disappear, or be sanctified to the spiritual growth of the soul. . . .

———

The truth is, the evil we have pointed out is not merely individual in its character. It is not, in the case of any single individual, of any one man's procuring, nor can the efforts of any one man, directed solely to his own moral and religious perfection, do aught to remove it. What is purely individual in its nature, efforts of individuals to perfect themselves, may remove. But the evil we speak of is inherent in all our social arrangements, and cannot be cured without a radical change of those arrangements. Could we convert all men to Christianity in both theory and practice, as held by the most enlightened sect of Christians among us, the evils of the social state would remain untouched. Continue our present system of trade, and all its present evil consequences will follow, whether it be carried on by your best men or your worst. Put your best men, your wisest, most moral, and most religious men, at the head of your paper money banks, and the evils of the present banking system will remain scarcely diminished. The only way to get rid of its evils is to change the system, not its managers. The evils of slavery do not result from the personal characters of slave masters. They are inseparable from the system, let who will be masters. Make all your rich men good Christians, and you have lessened not the evils of existing inequality in wealth. The mischievous effects of this inequality do not result from the personal characters of either rich or poor, but from itself, and they will continue, just so long as there are rich men and poor men in the same community. You must abolish the system or accept its consequences. No man can serve both God and Mammon. If you will serve the devil, you must look to the devil for your wages; we know no other way....

———

But what shall government do? Its first doing must be an *un*doing. There has been thus far quite too much government, as well as government of the wrong kind. The first act of government we want, is a still further limitation of itself. It must begin by circumscribing within narrower limits its powers. And then it must proceed to repeal all laws which bear against the laboring classes, and then to enact such laws as are necessary to enable them to maintain their equality. We have no faith in those systems of elevating the working classes, which propose to elevate them without calling in the aid of the government. We must have government, and legislation expressly directed to this end.

But again what legislation do we want so far as this country is concerned? We want first the legislation which shall free the government, whether State or Federal, from the control of the Banks. The Banks represent the interest of the employer, and therefore of necessity interests adverse to those of the employed; that is, they represent the interests of the business community in opposition to the laboring community. So long as the government remains under the control of the Banks, so long it must be in the hands of the natural enemies of the laboring classes, and may be made, nay, will be made, an instrument of depressing them yet lower. It is obvious then that, if our object be the elevation of the laboring classes, we must destroy the power of the Banks over the government, and place the government in the hands of laboring classes themselves, or in the hands of those, if such there be, who have an identity of interest with them. But this cannot be done so long as the Banks exist. Such is the subtle influence of credit, and such the power of capital, that a banking system like ours, if sustained, necessarily and inevitably becomes the real and efficient government of the country. We have been struggling for ten years in this country against the power of the banks, struggling to free merely the Federal government from their grasp, but with humiliating success. At this moment, the contest is almost doubtful,—not indeed in our mind, but in the minds of a no small portion of our countrymen. The partizans of the Banks count on certain victory. The Banks discount freely to build "log cabins," to purchase "hard cider," and to defray the expense of manufacturing enthusiasm for a cause which is at war with the interests of the people. That they will succeed, we do not for one moment believe; but that they could maintain the struggle so long, and be as strong as they now are, at the end of ten years' constant hostility, proves but all too well the power of the Banks, and their fatal influence on the political action of the community. The present character, standing, and resources of the Bank party, prove to a demonstration that the Banks must be destroyed, or the laborer not elevated. Uncompromising hostility to the whole banking system should therefore be the motto of every working man, and of every friend of Humanity. The system must be destroyed. On this point there must be no misgiving, no subterfuge, no palliation. The system is at war with the rights and interest of labor, and it must go. Every friend of the system must be marked as an enemy to his race, to his country, and especially to the laborer. No matter who he is, in what party he is found, or what name he bears, he is, in our judgment, no true democrat, as he can be no true Christian.

Following the distruction of the Banks, must come that of all monopolies, of all PRIVILEGE. There are many of these. We cannot specify them all; we therefore select only one, the greatest of them all, the privilege which some have of being born rich while others are born poor. It will be seen at once that we allude to the hereditary descent of property, an anomaly in our American system, which must be removed, or the system itself will be destroyed. We cannot now go into a discussion of this subject, but we promise to resume it at our earliest opportunity. We only say now, that as we have abolished hereditary monarchy and hereditary nobility, we must complete the work by abolishing hereditary property. A man shall have all he honestly acquires, so long as he himself belongs to the world in which he acquires it. But his power over his property must cease with his life, and his property must then become the property of the state, to be disposed of by some equitable law for the use of the generation which takes his place. Here is the principle without any of its details, and this is the grand legislative measure to which we look forward. We see no means of elevating the laboring classes which can be effectual without this. And is this a measure to be easily carried? Not at all. It will cost infinitely more than it cost to abolish either hereditary monarchy or hereditary nobility. It is a great measure, and a startling. The rich, the business community, will never voluntarily consent to it, and we think we know too much of human nature to believe that it will ever be effected peaceably. It will be effected only by the strong arm of physical force. It will come, if it ever come at all, only at the conclusion of war, the like of which the world as yet has never witnessed, and from which, however inevitable it may seem to the eye of philosophy, the heart of Humanity recoils with horror.

We are not ready for this measure yet. There is much previous work to be done, and we should be the last to bring it before the legislature. The time, however, has come for its free and full discussion. It must be canvassed in the public mind, and society prepared for acting on it. No doubt they who broach it, and especially they who support it, will experience a due share of contumely and abuse. They will be regarded by the part of the community they oppose, or may be thought to oppose, as "graceless varlets," against whom every man of substance should set his face. But this is not, after all, a thing to disturb a wise man, nor to deter a true man from telling his whole thought. He who is worthy of the name of man, speaks what he honestly believes the interests of his race demand, and seldom disquiets himself about what may be the consequences to himself. Men have, for what they believed the cause of God or man, endured the dungeon, the scaffold, the stake, the cross, and they can do it again, if need be. This subject must be freely, boldly, and fully discussed, whatever may be the fate of those who discuss it.

# RALPH WALDO EMERSON DECLINES GEORGE RIPLEY'S INVITATION TO JOIN BROOK FARM
## (1840)

While Brownson was zealously advocating social reform, George and Sophia Ripley were quietly but energetically trying to put reform into practice. Ripley did his best to persuade his friend Emerson to join their new utopian socialist commune (see below for a statement of its principles), on a 170-acre farm along the Charles River in what was then the village of West Roxbury, eight miles from the center of Boston. The participation of Transcendentalism's most eminent figure would have been a prize acquisition. But Ripley would never have made his appeal without having the greatest personal respect for Emerson. Emerson also thought well of Ripley. Upon reading his resignation letter early this same year (Section II), Emerson praised it to Margaret Fuller as a brave step that put Ripley "at the head of the Church militant" and "cannot be without an important sequel." This was the sequel. Emerson hated to disappoint Ripley, partly because he, too, believed that major renovation of society was needed. But the communitarian scheme left him cold. It seemed both too utilitarian and unrealistic. "Shall I raise the siege of this hencoop & march baffled away to a pretended siege of Babylon?" he asks his Journal the day after the Ripleys visited him, together with Fuller and Alcott, both of whom were more sympathetic to the project even though they never joined up, either. (Alcott later started a disastrously short-lived commune of his own, at Fruitlands, an hour northwest of Boston.) But Emerson stood firm in his settled conviction that "to join this body would be to traverse all my long trumpeted theory, and the instinct which spoke from it, that one man is a counterpoise to a city . . . that his solitude is more prevalent & beneficent than the concert of crowds." This was to be the core idea of his great essay "Self-Reliance."

SOURCE: Octavius B. Frothingham, *George Ripley.* Boston: Houghton, 1882. Emerson's reply, which Frothingham calls an "unfinished sketch," may be compared with the two drafts dated from early December 1840, in *The Letters of Ralph Waldo Emerson* (New York: Columbia University Press, 1939, 1990–95), volumes 3 and 7. Frothingham's version is considerably longer than either. He may have fused two different manuscripts together.

*Ripley to Emerson, 9 November 1840*

MY DEAR SIR,—Our conversation in Concord was of such a general nature, that I do not feel as if you were in complete possession of the idea of the Association which I wish to see established. As we have now a prospect of carrying it into effect, at an early period, I wish to submit the plan more distinctly to your judgment, that you may decide whether it is one that can have the benefit of your aid and coöperation.

Our objects, as you know, are to insure a more natural union between intellectual and manual labor than now exists; to combine the thinker and the worker, as far as possible, in the same individual; to guarantee the highest mental freedom, by providing all with labor, adapted to their tastes and talents, and securing to them the fruits of their industry; to do away the necessity of menial services, by opening the benefits of education and the profits of labor to all; and thus to prepare a society of liberal, intelligent, and cultivated persons, whose relations with each other would permit a more simple and wholesome life, than can be led amidst the pressure of our competitive institutions.

To accomplish these objects, we propose to take a small tract of land, which, under skillful husbandry, uniting the garden and the farm, will be adequate to the subsistence of the families; and to connect with this a school or college, in which the most complete instruction shall be given, from the first rudiments to the highest culture. Our farm would be a place for improving the race of men that lived on it; thought would preside over the operations of labor, and labor would contribute to the expansion of thought; we should have industry without drudgery, and true equality without its vulgarity.

An offer has been made to us of a beautiful estate, on very reasonable terms, on the borders of Newton, West Roxbury, and Dedham. I am very familiar with the premises, having resided on them a part of last summer, and we might search the country in vain for anything more eligible. Our proposal now is for three or four families to take possession on the first of April next, to attend to the cultivation of the farm and the erection of buildings, to prepare for the coming of as many more in the autumn, and thus to commence the institution in the simplest manner, and with the smallest number, with which it can go into operation at all. It would thus be not less than two or three years, before we should be joined by all who mean to be with us; we should not fall to pieces by our own weight; we should grow up slowly and strong; and the attractiveness of our experiment would win to us all whose society we should want.

The step now to be taken at once is the procuring of funds for the necessary capital. According to the present modification of our plan, a much less sum will be required than that spoken of in our discussions at Concord. We thought then $50,000 would be needed; I find now, after a careful estimate, that $30,000 will purchase the estate and buildings for ten families, and give the required surplus for carrying on the operations for one year.

We propose to raise this sum by a subscription to a joint stock company, among the friends of the institution, the payment of a fixed interest being guaranteed to the subscribers, and the subscription itself secured by the real estate. No man then will be in danger of losing; he will receive as fair an interest as he would from any investment, while at the same time he is contributing towards an institution, in which while the true use of money is retained, its abuses are done away. The sum required cannot come from rich capitalists; their instinct would protest against such an application of their coins; it must be obtained from those who sympathize with our ideas, and who are willing to aid their realization with their money, if not by their personal coöperation. There are some of this description on whom I think we can rely; among ourselves we can produce perhaps $10,000; the remainder must be subscribed for by those who wish us well, whether they mean to unite with us or not.

I can imagine no plan which is suited to carry into effect so many divine ideas as this. If wisely executed, it will be a light over this country and this age. If not the sunrise, it will be the morning star. As a practical man, I see clearly that we must have some such arrangement, or all changes less radical will be nugatory. I believe in the divinity of labor; I wish to "harvest my flesh and blood from the land;" but to do this, I must either be insulated and work to disadvantage, or avail myself of the services of hirelings, who are not of my order, and whom I can scarce make friends; for I must have another to drive the plough, which I hold. I cannot empty a cask of lime upon my grass alone. I wish to see a society of educated friends, working, thinking, and living together, with no strife, except that of each to contribute the most to the benefit of all.

Personally, my tastes and habits would lead me in another direction. I have a passion for being independent of the world, and of every man in it. This I could do easily on the estate which is now offered, and which I could rent at a rate, that with my other resources, would place me in a very agreeable condition, as far as my personal interests were involved. I should have a city of God, on a small scale of my own; and please God, I should hope one day to drive my own cart to market and sell greens. But I feel bound to sacrifice this private feeling, in the hope of a great social good. I shall be anxious to hear from you. Your decision will do much towards settling the question with me, whether the time has come for the fulfillment of a high hope, or whether the work belongs to a future generation. All omens now are favorable; a singular union of diverse talents is ready for the enterprise; everything indicates that we ought to arise and build; and if we let slip this occasion, the unsleeping Nemesis will deprive us of the boon we seek. For myself, I am sure that I can never give so much thought to it again; my mind must act on other objects, and I shall acquiesce in the course of fate, with grief that so fair a light is put out. A small pittance of the wealth which has been thrown away on ignoble objects, during this wild contest for political supremacy, would lay the cornerstone of a house, which would ere long become the desire of nations.

I almost forgot to say that our friends, the "Practical Christians," insist on making their "Standard,"—a written document,—a prescribed test. This cuts them off. Perhaps we are better without them. They are good men; they have salt, which we needed with our spice; but we might have proved too liberal, too comprehensive, too much attached to the graces of culture, to suit their ideas. Instead of them, we have the offer of ten or twelve "Practical Men," from Mr. S. G. May, who himself is deeply interested in the proposal, and would like one day to share in its concerns. Pray write me with as much frankness as I have used towards you, and believe me ever your friend and faithful servant,

GEORGE RIPLEY.

P.S. I ought to add, that in the present stage of the enterprise no proposal is considered as binding. We wish only to know what can probably be relied on, provided always, that no pledge will be accepted until the articles of association are agreed on by all parties.

I recollect you said that if you were sure of compeers of the right stamp you might embark yourself in the adventure: as to this, let me suggest the inquiry, whether our Association should not be composed of various classes of men? If we have friends whom we love and who love us, I think we should be content to join with others, with whom our personal sympathy is not strong, but whose general ideas coincide with ours, and whose gifts and abilities would make their services important. For instance, I should like to have a good washerwoman in my parish admitted into the plot. She is certainly not a Minerva or a Venus; but we might educate her two children to wisdom and varied accomplishments, who otherwise will be doomed to drudge through life. The same is true of some farmers and mechanics, whom we should like with us.

### Emerson to Ripley, December 1840

MY DEAR SIR,—It is quite time I made an answer to your proposition that I should venture into your new community. The design appears to me noble and generous, proceeding, as I plainly see, from nothing covert, or selfish, or ambitious, but from a manly and expanding heart and mind. So it makes all men its friends and debtors. It becomes a matter of conscience to entertain it in a friendly spirit, and examine what it has for us.

I have decided not to join it, and yet very slowly and I may almost say with penitence. I am greatly relieved by learning that your coadjutors are now so many that you will no longer attach that importance to the defection of individuals which, you hinted in your letter to me, I or others might possess,—the painful power I mean of preventing the execution of the plan.

My feeling is that the community is not good for me, that it has little to offer me, which, with resolution I cannot procure for myself; that it would not be worth my while to make the difficult exchange of my property in Concord for a share in the new household. I am in many respects placed as I wish to be, in an agreeable neighborhood, in a town which I have some reason to love, and which has respected my freedom so far that I have reason to hope it will indulge me further when I demand it. I cannot accuse my townsmen or my neighbors of my domestic grievances, only my own sloth and conformity. It seems to me a circuitous and operose way of relieving myself to put upon your community the emancipation which I ought to take on myself. I must assume my own vows.

The institution of domestic hired service is to me very disagreeable. I should like to come one step nearer to nature than this usage permits. But surely I need not sell my house and remove my family to Newton in order to make the experiment of labor and self help. I am already in the act of trying some domestic and social experiments which would gain nothing.

I ought to say that I do not put much trust in any arrangements or combinations, only in the spirit which dictates them. Is that benevolent and divine, they will answer their end. Is there any alloy in that, it will certainly appear in the result.

I have the same answer to make to the proposition of the school. According to my ability and according to your's, you and I do now keep school for all comers, and the energy of our thought and of our will measures our influence.

I do not think I should gain anything, I, who have little skill to converse with people, by a plan of so many parts, and which I comprehend so slowly and bluntly.

I almost shudder to make any statement of my objections to our ways of living, because I see how slowly I shall mend them. My own health and habits of living and those of my wife and my mother are not of that robustness that should give any pledge of enterprise and ability in reform. Nor can I insist with any heat on new methods when I am at work in my study on any literary composition. Yet I think that all I shall solidly do, I must do alone, and I am so ignorant and uncertain in my improvements that I would fain hide my attempts and failures in solitude where they shall perplex none or very few beside myself. The result of our secretest attempts will certainly have as much renown as shall be due to it.

I do not look on myself as a valuable member to any community which is not either very large or very small and select. I fear that your's would not find me as profitable and pleasant an associate as I should wish to be, and as so important a project seems imperatively to require in all its constituents.

Mr. Edmund Hosmer, a very intelligent farmer and a very upright man in my neighborhood, to whom I read your letter, admired the spirit of the plan but distrusted all I told him of the details as far as they concerned the farm.

1. He said, as a general rule nothing was gained by coöperation in a farm, except in those few pieces of work which cannot be done alone, like getting in a load of hay, which takes three men. In every other case, it is better to separate the workmen. His own boys (all good boys) work better separately than with him.

2. He thought Mr. Ripley should put no dependence on the results of gentlemen farmers such as Mr. P—— and others who were named. If his (Mr. Hosmer's) farm had been managed in the way of Mr. P——'s, it would have put himself and family in the poor-house long ago. If Mr. P——'s farm should be exhibited in an accurate account of debt and credit from his beginning until now, it would probably show a great deficit. Another consideration: The gentlemen farmers are obliged to conduct their operations by means of a foreman whom they choose because he has skill to make ends meet, and sell the produce without any scrupulous inquiry on the part of the employer as to his methods. That foreman buys cheap and sells dear, in a manner which Mr. Ripley and his coadjutors will not sanction. The same thing is true of many farmers, whose praise is in the agricultural reports. If they were honest there would be no brilliant results. And Mr. Hosmer is sure that no large property can ever be made by honest farming.

3. Mr. Hosmer thinks the equal payment of ten cents per hour to every laborer unjust. One man brings capital to the community and receives his interest. He has little skill to labor. A farmer also comes who has no capital but can do twice as much as Mr. Hosmer in a day. His skill is his capital. It would be unjust to pay him no interest on that.

4. Mr. Hosmer disbelieves that good work will continue to be done for the community if the worker is not directly benefited. His boys receive a cent a basket for the potatoes they bring in, and that makes them work, though they know very well that the whole produce of the farm is for them.

# Ralph Waldo Emerson

## "Self-Reliance"

### (1841)

Together with *Nature,* "The American Scholar," and the Divinity School Address, this was the essay by which Emerson is best known, both in his day and in ours. And for good reason. It sums up the quintessence of Emersonianism. "I have only one doctrine," he once declared in his Journal, "the infinitude of the private man." "Self-Reliance" lays this out more pointedly and memorably than anything else he wrote. Although Emerson later stressed to a much greater degree the importance of recognizing the fallibility of the self and the constraints imposed upon individualism by the forces of history, tradition, and biology, he remained convinced that the key to reform of any sort lay in the activation of the individual person first, not the group first. His view was a unique fusion of several different intellectual legacies, including the Puritan emphasis on conversion of the individual soul by divine grace; the importance attached to individual perception in Kantian philosophy and Romantic poetry; and Republican-Democratic political theory, which helps account for Emerson's egalitarian view that all individuals are capable of rising above their ordinary selves, even if few do so in practice.

In order to understand the complexities of this essay's fusion of these various strands of individualism, two further points also are crucial to bear in mind. First, Emersonian Self-Reliance really *is* "better than whim at last," as he puts it in a famously elusive phrase. Emerson is counseling reliance on a Self that is higher or deeper than one's everyday self. He conceives of that higher Self as resting on a moral and spiritual bedrock that is universally shared by all humans, whether or not they realize it. Second, and related, despite his assertive tone Emerson is under no illusions that his Self-Reliance ethic will be easy to achieve. His essay is targeted not at already-confident people, much less for the arrogant, but for those—the great majority of people, he believes—who tend to doubt themselves and be overawed by public opinion. Ironically, Emerson saw himself, especially his younger self, as precisely this kind of person: too dutiful, too easily influenced. Nor does Emerson underestimate the price that Self-Reliance must extract in terms of the loneliness and misunderstanding that one must endure in order to be truly self-reliant. The Latin motto at the start of the essay is quoted (inexactly) from Persius' first satire: "Seek not outside yourself." The third motto is by Emerson himself.

SOURCE: "Self-Reliance," *Essays, First Series.* Boston: James Munroe, 1841.

Ne te quæsiveris extra.
—PERSIUS *SATIRES*, I, 7

"Man is his own star; and the soul that can
Render an honest and a perfect man,
Command all light, all influence, all fate;
Nothing to him falls early or too late.
Our acts our angels are, or good or ill,
Our fatal shadows that walk by us still."
—EPILOGUE TO BEAUMONT AND FLETCHER'S
HONEST MAN'S FORTUNE (1647)

Cast the bantling on the rocks,
Suckle him with the she-wolf's teat:
Wintered with the hawk and fox,
Power and speed be hands and feet.

I read the other day some verses written by an eminent painter which were original and not conventional. Always the soul hears an admonition in such lines, let the subject be what it may. The sentiment they instil is of more value than any thought they may contain. To believe your own thought, to believe that what is true for you in your private heart, is true for all men,—that is genius. Speak your latent conviction and it shall be the universal sense; for always the inmost becomes the outmost,—and our first thought is rendered back to us by the trumpets of the Last Judgment. Familiar as the voice of the mind is to each, the highest merit we ascribe to Moses, Plato, and Milton, is that they set at naught books and traditions, and spoke not what men but what they thought. A man should learn to detect and watch that gleam of light which flashes across his mind from within, more than the lustre of the firmament of bards and sages. Yet he dismisses without notice his thought, because it is his. In every work of genius we recognise our own rejected thoughts: they come back to us with a certain alienated majesty. Great works of art have no more affecting lesson for us than this. They teach us to abide by our spontaneous impression with good-humored inflexibility then most when the whole cry of voices is on the other side. Else, to-morrow a stranger will say with masterly good sense precisely what we have thought and felt all the time, and we shall be forced to take with shame our own opinion from another.

There is a time in every man's education when he arrives at the conviction that envy is ignorance; that imitation is suicide; that he must take himself for better, for worse, as his portion; that though the wide universe is full of good, no kernel of nourishing corn can come to him but through his toil bestowed on that plot of ground which is given to him to till. The power which resides in him is new in nature, and none but he knows what that is which he can do, nor does he know until he has tried. Not for nothing one face, one character, one fact makes much impression on him, and another none. It is not without preëstablished harmony, this sculpture in the memory. The eye was placed where one ray should fall, that it might testify of that particular ray. Bravely let him speak the utmost syllable of his confession. We but half express ourselves, and are ashamed of that divine idea which each of us represents. It may be safely trusted as proportionate and of good issues, so it be faithfully imparted, but God will not have his work made manifest by cowards. It needs a divine man to exhibit any thing divine. A man is relieved and gay when he has put his heart into his work and done his best; but what he has said or done otherwise, shall give him no peace. It is a deliverance which does not deliver. In the attempt his genius deserts him; no muse befriends; no invention, no hope.

Trust thyself: every heart vibrates to that iron string. Accept the place the divine Providence has found for you; the society of your contemporaries, the connexion of events. Great men have always done so and confided themselves childlike to the genius of their age, betraying their perception that the Eternal was stirring at their heart, working through their hands, predominating in all their being. And we are now men, and must accept in the highest mind the same transcendent destiny; and not pinched in a corner, not cowards fleeing before a revolution, but redeemers and benefactors, pious aspirants to be noble clay plastic under the Almighty effort, let us advance and advance on Chaos and the Dark.

What pretty oracles nature yields us on this text in the face and behavior of children, babes and even brutes. That divided and rebel mind, that distrust of a sentiment because our arithmetic has computed the strength and means opposed to our purpose, these have not.

Their mind being whole, their eye is as yet unconquered, and when we look in their faces, we are disconcerted. Infancy conforms to nobody: all conform to it, so that one babe commonly makes four or five out of the adults who prattle and play to it. So God has armed youth and puberty and manhood no less with its own piquancy and charm, and made it enviable and gracious and its claims not to be put by, if it will stand by itself. Do not think the youth has no force because he cannot speak to you and me. Hark! in the next room, who spoke so clear and emphatic? Good Heaven! it is he! it is that very lump of bashfulness and phlegm which for weeks has done nothing but eat when you were by, that now rolls out these words like bell-strokes. It seems he knows how to speak to his contemporaries. Bashful or bold, then, he will know how to make us seniors very unnecessary.

The nonchalance of boys who are sure of a dinner, and would disdain as much as a lord to do or say aught to conciliate one, is the healthy attitude of human nature. How is a boy the master of society; independent, irresponsible, looking out from his corner on such people and facts as pass by, he tries and sentences them on their merits, in the swift summary way of boys, as good, bad, interesting, silly, eloquent, troublesome. He cumbers himself never about consequences, about interests: he gives an independent, genuine verdict. You must court him: he does not court you. But the man is, as it were, clapped into jail by his consciousness. As soon as he has once acted or spoken with eclat, he is a committed person, watched by the sympathy or the hatred of hundreds whose affections must now enter into his account. There is no Lethe for this. Ah, that he could pass again into his neutral, godlike independence! Who can thus lose all pledge, and having observed, observe again from the same unaffected, unbiased, unbribable, unaffrighted innocence, must always be formidable, must always engage the poet's and the man's regards. Of such an immortal youth the force would be felt. He would utter opinions on all passing affairs, which being seen to be not private but necessary, would sink like darts into the ear of men, and put them in fear.

These are the voices which we hear in solitude, but they grow faint and inaudible as we enter into the world. Society everywhere is in conspiracy against the manhood of every one of its members. Society is a joint-stock company in which the members agree for the better securing of his bread to each shareholder, to surrender the liberty and culture of the eater. The virtue in most request is conformity. Self-reliance is its aversion. It loves not realities and creators, but names and customs.

Whoso would be a man must be a nonconformist. He who would gather immortal palms must not be hindered by the name of goodness, but must explore if it be goodness. Nothing is at last sacred but the integrity of your own mind. Absolve you to yourself, and you shall have the suffrage of the world. I remember an answer which when quite young I was prompted to make to a valued adviser who was wont to importune me with the dear old doctrines of the church. On my saying, What have I to do with the sacredness of traditions, if I live wholly from within? my friend suggested—"But these impulses may be from below, not from above." I replied, "They do not seem to me to be such; but if I am the devil's child, I will live then from the devil." No law can be sacred to me but that of my nature. Good and bad are but names very readily transferable to that or this; the only right is what is after my constitution, the only wrong what is against it. A man is to carry himself in the presence of all opposition as if every thing were titular and ephemeral but he. I am ashamed to think how easily we capitulate to badges and names, to large societies and dead institutions. Every decent and well-spoken individual affects and sways me more than is right. I ought to go upright and vital, and speak the rude truth in all ways. If malice and vanity wear the coat of philanthropy, shall that pass? If an angry bigot assumes this bountiful cause of Abolition, and comes to me with his last news from Barbadoes, why should I not say to him, "Go love thy infant; love thy wood-chopper: be good-natured and modest: have that grace; and never varnish your hard, uncharitable ambition with this incredible tenderness for black folk a thousand miles off. Thy love afar is spite at home." Rough and graceless would be such greeting, but truth is handsomer than the affectation of love. Your goodness must have some edge to it—else it is none. The doctrine of hatred must be preached as the counteraction of the doctrine of love when that pules and whines. I shun father and mother and wife and brother, when my genius calls me. I would write on the lintels of the door-post, *Whim.* I hope it is somewhat better than whim at last, but we cannot spend the day in explanation. Expect me not to show cause why I seek or why I exclude company. Then, again, do not tell me, as a good man did to-day, of my obligation to put all poor men in good situations. Are they *my* poor? I tell thee, thou foolish philanthropist, that I grudge the dollar, the dime, the cent I give to such men as do not belong to me and to whom I do not belong. There is a class of persons to whom by all spiritual affinity I am bought and sold; for them I will go to prison, if need be; but your miscellaneous popular charities; the education at college of fools; the building of meeting-houses to the vain end to which many now stand; alms to sots; and the thousandfold Relief Societies;—though I confess with shame I sometimes succumb and give the dollar, it is a wicked dollar which by-and-by I shall have the manhood to withhold.

Virtues are in the popular estimate rather the exception than the rule. There is the man *and* his virtues. Men do what is called a good action, as some piece of courage or charity, much as they would pay a fine in expiation of daily non-appearance on parade. Their works are done as an apology or extenuation of their living in the world,—as invalids and the insane pay a high board. Their virtues are penances. I do not wish to expiate, but to live. My life is not an apology, but a life. It is for itself and not for a spectacle. I much prefer that it should be of a lower strain, so it be genuine and equal, than that it should be glittering and unsteady. I wish it to be sound and sweet, and not to need diet and bleeding, My life should be unique; it should be an alms, a battle, a conquest, a medicine. I ask primary evidence that you are a man, and refuse this appeal from the man to his actions. I know that for myself it makes no difference whether I do or forbear those actions which are reckoned excellent. I cannot consent to pay for a privilege where I have intrinsic right. Few and mean as my gifts may be, I actually am, and do not need for my own assurance or the assurance of my fellows any secondary testimony.

What I must do, is all that concerns me, not what the people think. This rule, equally arduous in actual and in intellectual life, may serve for the whole distinction between greatness and meanness. It is the harder, because you will always find those who think they know what is your duty better than you know it. It is easy in the world to live after the world's opinion; it is easy in solitude to live after our own; but the great man is he who in the midst of the crowd keeps with perfect sweetness the independence of solitude.

The objection to conforming to usages that have become dead to you, is, that it scatters your force. It loses your time and blurs the impression of your character. If you maintain a dead church, contribute to a dead Bible-Society, vote with a great party either for the Government or against it, spread your table like base housekeepers,— under all these screens, I have difficulty to detect the precise man you are. And, of course, so much force is withdrawn from your proper life. But do your thing, and I shall know you. Do your work, and you shall reinforce yourself. A man must consider what a blind-man's-buff is this game of conformity. If I know your sect, I anticipate your argument. I hear a preacher announce for his text and topic the expediency of one of the institutions of his church. Do I not know beforehand that not possibly can he say a new and spontaneous word? Do I not know that with all this ostentation of examining the grounds of the institution, he will do no such thing? Do I not know that he is pledged to himself not to look but at one side; the permitted side, not as a man, but as a parish minister? He is a retained attorney, and these airs of the bench are the emptiest affectation. Well, most men have bound their eyes with one or another handkerchief, and attached themselves to some one of these communities of opinion. This conformity makes them not false in a few particulars, authors of a few lies, but false in all particulars. Their every truth is not quite true. Their two is not the real two, their four not the real four: so that every word they say chagrins us, and we know not where to begin to set them right. Meantime nature is not slow to equip us in the prison-uniform of the party to which we adhere. We come to wear one cut of face and figure, and acquire by degrees the gentlest asinine expression. There is a mortifying experience in particular which does not fail to wreak itself also in the general history; I mean, "the foolish face of praise," the forced smile which we put on in company where we do not feel at ease in answer to conversation which does not interest us. The muscles, not spontaneously moved, but moved by a low usurping wilfulness, grow tight about the outline of the face and make the most disagreeable sensation, a sensation of rebuke and warning which no brave young man will suffer twice.

For nonconformity the world whips you with its displeasure. And therefore a man must know how to estimate a sour face. The bystanders look askance on him in the public street or in the friend's parlor. If this aversation had its origin in contempt and resistance like his own, he might well go home with a sad countenance; but the sour faces of the multitude, like their sweet faces, have no deep cause,—disguise no god, but are put on and off as the wind blows, and a newspaper directs. Yet is the discontent of the multitude more formidable than that of the senate and the college. It is easy enough for a firm man who knows the world to brook the rage of the cultivated classes. Their rage is decorous and prudent, for they are timid as being very vulnerable themselves. But when to their feminine rage the indignation of the people is added, when the ignorant and the poor are aroused, when the unintelligent brute force that lies at the bottom of society is made to growl and mow, it needs the habit of magnanimity and religion to treat it godlike as a trifle of no concernment.

The other terror that scares us from self-trust is our consistency; a reverence for our past act or word, because the eyes of others have no other data for computing our orbit than our past acts, and we are loath to disappoint them.

But why should you keep your head over your shoulder? Why drag about this monstrous corpse of your memory, lest you contradict somewhat you have stated in this or that public place? Suppose you should contradict yourself; what then? It seems to be a rule of wisdom never to rely on your memory alone, scarcely even in acts of pure memory, but bring the past for judgment into the thousand-eyed present, and live ever in a new day. Trust your emotion. In your metaphysics you have denied personality to the Deity: yet when the devout motions of the soul come, yield to them heart and life, though they should clothe God with shape and color. Leave your theory as Joseph his coat in the hand of the harlot, and flee.

A foolish consistency is the hobgoblin of little minds, adored by little statesmen and philosophers and divines. With consistency a great soul has simply nothing to do. He may as well concern himself with his shadow on the wall. Out upon your guarded lips! Sew them up with packthread, do. Else, if you would be a man, speak what you think to-day in words as hard as cannon balls, and to-morrow speak what to-morrow thinks in hard words again, though it contradict every thing you said to-day. Ah, then, exclaim the aged ladies, you shall be sure to be misunderstood. Misunderstood! It is a right fool's word. Is it so bad then to be misunderstood? Pythagoras was misunderstood, and Socrates, and Jesus, and Luther, and Copernicus, and Galileo, and Newton, and every pure and wise spirit that ever took flesh. To be great is to be misunderstood.

I suppose no man can violate his nature. All the sallies of his will are rounded in by the law of his being as the inequalities of Andes and Himmaleh are insignificant in the curve of the sphere. Nor does it matter how you gauge and try him. A character is like an acrostic or Alexandrian stanza;—read it forward, backward, or across, it still spells the same thing. In this pleasing contrite wood-life which God allows me, let me record day by day my honest thought without prospect or retrospect, and, I cannot doubt, it will be found symmetrical, though I mean it not, and see it not. My book should smell of pines and resound with the hum of insects. The swallow over my window should interweave that thread or straw he carries in his bill into my web also. We pass for what we are. Character teaches above our wills. Men imagine that they communicate their virtue or vice only by overt actions and do not see that virtue or vice emit a breath every moment.

Fear never but you shall be consistent in whatever variety of actions, so they be each honest and natural in their hour. For of one will, the actions will be harmonious, however unlike they seem. These varieties are lost sight of when seen at a little distance, at a little height of thought. One tendency unites them all. The voyage of the best ship is a zigzag line of a hundred tacks. This is only microscopic criticism. See the line from a sufficient distance, and it straightens itself to the average tendency. Your genuine action will explain itself and will explain your other genuine actions. Your conformity explains nothing. Act singly, and what you have already done singly, will justify you now. Greatness always appeals to the future. If I can be great enough now to do right and scorn eyes, I must have done so much right before, as to defend me now. Be it how it will, do right now. Always scorn appearances, and you always may. The force of character is cumulative. All the foregone days of virtue work their health into this. What makes the majesty of the heroes of the senate and the field, which so fills the imagination? The consciousness of a train of great days and victories behind. There they all stand and shed an united light on the advancing actor. He is attended as by a visible escort of angels to every man's eye. That is it which throws thunder into Chatham's voice, and dignity into Washington's port, and America into Adams's eye. Honor is venerable to us because it is no ephemeris. It is always ancient virtue. We worship it to-day, because it is not of to-day. We love it and pay it homage, because it is not a trap for our love and homage, but is self-dependent, self-derived, and therefore of an old immaculate pedigree, even if shown in a young person.

I hope in these days we have heard the last of conformity and consistency. Let the words be gazetted and ridiculous henceforward. Instead of the gong for dinner, let us hear a whistle from the Spartan fife. Let us bow and apologize never more. A great man is coming to eat at my house. I do not wish to please him: I wish that he should wish to please me. I will stand here for humanity, and though I would make it kind, I would make it true. Let us affront and reprimand the smooth mediocrity and squalid contentment of the times, and hurl in the face of custom, and trade, and office, the fact which is the upshot of all history, that there is a great responsible Thinker and Actor moving wherever moves a man; that a true man belongs to no other time or place, but is the centre of things. Where he is, there is nature. He measures you, and all men, and all events. You are constrained to accept his standard. Ordinarily every body in society reminds us of somewhat else or of some other person. Character, reality, reminds you of nothing else. It takes place of the whole creation. The man must be so much that he must make all circumstances indifferent,—put all means into the shade. This all great men are and do. Every true man is a cause, a country, and an age; requires infinite spaces and numbers and time fully to accomplish his thought;—and posterity seem to follow his steps as a procession. A man Cæsar is born, and for ages after, we have a Roman Empire. Christ is born, and millions of minds so grow and cleave to his genius, that he is confounded with virtue and the possible of man. An institution is the lengthened shadow of one man; as, the Reformation, of Luther; Quakerism, of Fox; Methodism, of Wesley, Abolition, of Clarkson. Scipio, Milton called "the height of Rome;" and all history resolves itself very easily into the biography of a few stout and earnest persons.

Let a man then know his worth, and keep things under his feet. Let him not peep or steal, or skulk up and down with the air of a charity-boy, a bastard, or an interloper, in the world which exists for him. But the man in the street finding no worth in himself which corresponds to the force which built a tower or sculptured a marble god, feels poor when he looks on these. To him a palace, a statue, or a costly book have an alien and forbidding air, much like a gay equipage, and seem to say like that, "Who are you, sir?" Yet they all are his, suitors for his notice, petitioners to his faculties that they will come out and take possession. The picture waits for my verdict: it is not to command me, but I am to settle its claims to praise. That popular fable of the sot who was picked up dead drunk in the street, carried to the duke's house, washed and dressed and laid in the duke's bed, and, on his waking, treated with all obsequious ceremony like the duke, and assured that he had been insane,—owes its popularity to the fact, that it symbolizes so well the state of man, who is in the world a sort of sot, but now and then wakes up, exercises his reason, and finds himself a true prince.

Our reading is mendicant and sycophantic. In history, our imagination makes fools of us, plays us false. Kingdom and lordship, power and estate are a gaudier vocabulary than private John and Edward in a small house and common day's work: but the things of life are the same to both: the sum total of both is the same. Why all this deference to Alfred, and Scanderbeg, and Gustavus? Suppose they were virtuous: did they wear out virtue? As great a stake depends on your private act to-day, as followed their public and renowned steps. When private men shall act with vast views, the lustre will be transferred from the actions of kings to those of gentlemen.

The world has indeed been instructed by its kings, who have so magnetized the eyes of nations. It has been taught by this colossal symbol the mutual reverence that is due from man to man. The joyful loyalty with which men have every where suffered the king, the noble, or the great proprietor to walk among them by a law of his own, make his own scale of men and things, and reverse theirs, pay for benefits not with money but with honor, and represent the Law in his person, was the hieroglyphic by which they obscurely signified their consciousness of their own right and comeliness, the right of every man.

The magnetism which all original action exerts is explained when we inquire the reason of self-trust. Who is the Trustee? What is the aboriginal Self on which a universal reliance may be grounded? What is the nature and power of that science-baffling star, without parallax, without calculable elements, which shoots a ray of beauty even into trivial and impure actions, if the least mark of independence appear? The inquiry leads us to that source, at once the essence of genius, the essence of virtue, and the essence of life, which we call Spontaneity or Instinct. We denote this primary wisdom as Intuition, whilst all later teachings are tuitions. In that deep force, the last fact behind which analysis cannot go, all things find their common origin. For the sense of being which in calm hours rises, we know not how, in the soul, is not diverse from things, from space, from light, from time, from man, but one with them, and proceedeth obviously from the same source whence their life and being also proceedeth. We first share the life by which things exist, and afterwards see them as appearances in nature, and forget that we have shared their cause. Here is the fountain of action and the fountain of thought. Here are the lungs of that inspiration which giveth man wisdom, of that inspiration of man which cannot be denied without impiety and atheism. We lie in the lap of immense intelligence, which makes us organs of its activity and receivers of its truth. When we discern justice, when we discern truth, we do nothing of ourselves, but allow a passage to its beams. If we ask whence this comes, if we seek to pry into the soul that causes,—all metaphysics, all philosophy is at fault. Its presence or its absence is all we can affirm. Every man discerns between the voluntary acts of his mind, and his involuntary perceptions. And to his involuntary perceptions, he knows a perfect respect is due. He may err in the expression of them, but he knows that these things are so, like day and night, not to be disputed. All my wilful actions and acquisitions are but roving;— the most trivial reverie, the faintest native emotion are domestic and divine. Thoughtless people contradict as readily the statement of perceptions as of opinions, or rather much more readily; for, they do not distinguish between perception and notion. They fancy that I choose to see this or that thing. But perception is not whimsical, but fatal. If I see a trait, my children will see it after me, and in course of time, all mankind,—although it may chance that no one has seen it before me. For my perception of it is as much a fact as the sun.

The relations of the soul to the divine spirit are so pure that it is profane to seek to interpose helps. It must be that when God speaketh, he should communicate not one thing, but all things; should fill the world with his voice; should scatter forth light, nature, time, souls, from the centre of the present thought; and new date and new create the whole. Whenever a mind is simple, and receives a divine wisdom, then old things pass away,—means, teachers, texts, temples fall; it lives now and absorbs past and future into the present hour. All things are made sacred by relation to it,—one thing as much as another. All things are dissolved to their centre by their cause, and in the universal miracle petty and particular miracles disappear. This is and must be. If, therefore, a man claims to know and speak of God, and carries you backward to the phraseology of some old mouldered nation in another country, in another world, believe him not. Is the acorn better than the oak which is its fulness and completion? Is the parent better than the child into whom he has cast his ripened being? Whence then this worship of the past? The centuries are conspirators against the sanity and majesty of the soul. Time and space are but physiological colors which the eye maketh, but the soul is light; where it is, is day; where it was, is night; and history is an impertinence and an injury, if it be anything more than a cheerful apologue or parable of my being and becoming.

Man is timid and apologetic. He is no longer upright. He dares not say "I think," "I am," but quotes some saint or sage. He is ashamed before the blade of grass or the blowing rose. These roses under my window make no reference to former roses or to better ones; they are for what they are; they exist with God to-day. There is no time to them. There is simply the rose; it is perfect in every moment of its existence. Before a leaf-bud has burst, its whole life acts; in the full-blown flower, there is no more; in the leafless root, there is no less. Its nature is satisfied, and it satisfies nature, in all moments alike. There is no time to it. But man postpones or remembers; he does not live in the present, but with reverted eye laments the past, or, heedless of the riches that surround him, stands on tiptoe to foresee the future. He cannot be happy and strong until he too lives with nature in the present, above time.

This should be plain enough. Yet see what strong intellects dare not yet hear God himself, unless he speak the phraseology of I know not what David, or Jeremiah, or Paul. We shall not always set so great a price on a few texts, on a few lives. We are like children who repeat by rote the sentences of grandames and tutors, and, as they grow older, of the men of talents and character they chance to see,—painfully recollecting the exact words they spoke; afterwards, when they come into the point of view which those had who uttered these sayings, they understand them, and are willing to let the words go; for, at any time, they can use words as good, when occasion comes. So was it with us, so will it be, if we proceed. If we live truly, we shall see truly. It is as easy for the strong man to be strong, as it is for the weak to be weak. When we have new perception, we shall gladly disburthen the memory of its hoarded treasures as old rubbish. When a man lives with God, his voice shall be as sweet as the murmur of the brook and the rustle of the corn.

And now at last the highest truth on this subject remains unsaid; probably, cannot be said; for all that we say is the far off remembering of the intuition. That thought, by what I can now nearest approach to say it, is this. When good is near you, when you have life in yourself,— it is not by any known or appointed way; you shall not discern the footprints of any other; you shall not see the face of man; you shall not hear any name;—the way, the thought, the good shall be wholly strange and new. It shall exclude all other being. You take the way from man, not to man. All persons that ever existed are its fugitive ministers. There shall be no fear in it. Fear and hope are alike beneath it. It asks nothing. There is somewhat low even in hope. We are then in vision. There is nothing that can be called gratitude nor properly joy. The soul is raised over passion. It seeth identity and eternal causation. It is a perceiving that Truth and Right are. Hence it becomes a Tranquillity out of the knowing that all things go well. Vast spaces of nature; the Atlantic Ocean, the South Sea; vast intervals of time, years, centuries, are of no account. This which I think and feel, underlay that former state of life and circumstances, as it does underlie my present, and will always all circumstance, and what is called life, and what is called death.

Life only avails, not the having lived. Power ceases in the instant of repose; it resides in the moment of transition from a past to a new state; in the shooting of the gulf; in the darting to an aim. This one fact the world hates, that the soul *becomes;* for, that forever degrades the past; turns all riches to poverty; all reputation to a shame; confounds the saint with the rogue; shoves Jesus and Judas equally aside. Why then do we prate of self-reliance? Inasmuch as the soul is present, there will be power not confident but agent. To talk of reliance, is a poor external way of speaking. Speak rather of that which relies, because it works and is. Who has more soul than I, masters me, though he should not raise his finger. Round him I must revolve by the gravitation of spirits; who has less, I rule with like facility. We fancy it rhetoric when we speak of eminent virtue. We do not yet see that virtue is Height, and that a man or a company of men plastic and permeable to principles, by the law of nature must overpower and ride all cities, nations, kings, rich men, poets, who are not.

This is the ultimate fact which we so quickly reach on this as on every topic, the resolution of all into the ever blessed ONE. Virtue is the governor, the creator, the reality. All things real are so by so much of virtue as they contain. Hardship, husbandry, hunting, whaling, war, eloquence, personal weight, are somewhat, and engage my respect as examples of the soul's presence and impure action. I see the same law working in nature for conservation and growth. The poise of a planet, the bended tree recovering itself from the strong wind, the vital resources of every vegetable and animal, are also demonstrations of the self-sufficing, and therefore self-relying soul. All history from its highest to its trivial passages is the various record of this power.

Thus all concentrates; let us not rove; let us sit at home with the cause. Let us stun and astonish the intruding rabble of men and books and institutions by a simple declaration of the divine fact. Bid them take the shoes from off their feet, for God is here within. Let our simplicity judge them, and our docility to our own law demonstrate the poverty of nature and fortune beside our native riches.

But now we are a mob. Man does not stand in awe of man, nor is the soul admonished to stay at home, to put itself in communication with the internal ocean, but it goes abroad to beg a cup of water of the urns of men. We must go alone. Isolation must precede true society. I like the silent church before the service begins, better than any preaching. How far off, how cool, how chaste the persons look, begirt each one with a precinct or sanctuary. So let us always sit. Why should we assume the faults of our friend, or wife, or father, or child, because they sit around our hearth, or are said to have the same blood? All men have my blood, and I have all men's. Not for that will I adopt their petulance or folly, even to the extent of being ashamed of it. But your isolation must not be mechanical, but spiritual, that is, must be elevation. At times the whole world seems to be in conspiracy to importune you with emphatic trifles. Friend, client, child, sickness, fear, want, charity, all knock at once at thy closet door and say, "Come out unto us."—Do not spill thy soul; do not all descend; keep thy state; stay at home in thine own heaven; come not for a moment into their facts, into their hubbub of conflicting appearances, but let in the light of thy law on their confusion. The power men possess to annoy me, I give them by a weak curiosity. No man can come near me but through my act. "What we love that we have, but by desire we bereave ourselves of the love."

If we cannot at once rise to the sanctities of obedience and faith, let us at least resist our temptations, let us enter into the state of war, and wake Thor and Woden, courage and constancy in our Saxon breasts. This is to be done in our smooth times by speaking the truth. Check this lying hospitality and lying affection. Live no longer to the expectation of these deceived and deceiving people with whom we converse. Say to them, O father, O mother, O wife, O brother, O friend, I have lived with you after appearances hitherto. Henceforward I am the truth's. Be it known unto you that henceforward I obey no law less than the eternal law. I will have no covenants but proximities. I shall endeavor to nourish my parents, to support my family, to be the chaste husband of one wife,—but these relations I must fill after a new and unprecedented way. I appeal from your customs. I must be myself. I cannot break myself any longer for you, or you. If you can love me for what I am, we shall be the happier. If you cannot, I will still seek to deserve that you should. I must be myself. I will not hide my tastes or aversions. I will so trust that what is deep is holy, that I will do strongly before the sun and moon whatever inly rejoices me, and the heart appoints. If you are noble, I will love you; if you are not, I will not hurt you and myself by hypocritical attentions. If you are true, but not in the same truth with me, cleave to your companions; I will seek my

own. I do this not selfishly, but humbly and truly. It is alike your interest and mine and all men's, however long we have dwelt in lies, to live
in truth. Does this sound harsh to-day? You will soon love what is dictated by your nature as well as mine, and if we follow the truth, it will
bring us out safe at last.—But so you may give these friends pain. Yes,
but I cannot sell my liberty and my power, to save their sensibility.
Besides, all persons have their moments of reason when they look out
into the region of absolute truth; then will they justify me and do the
same thing.

The populace think that your rejection of popular standards is a
rejection of all standard, and mere antinomianism; and the bold sensu-
alist will use the name of philosophy to gild his crimes. But the law of
consciousness abides. There are two confessionals, in one or the other
of which we must be shriven. You may fulfil your round of duties by
clearing yourself in the *direct*, or, in the *reflex* way. Consider whether
you have satisfied your relations to father, mother, cousin, neighbor,
town, cat, and dog; whether any of these can upbraid you. But I may
also neglect this reflex standard, and absolve me to myself. I have my
own stern claims and perfect circle. It denies the name of duty to many
offices that are called duties. But if I can discharge its debts, it enables
me to dispense with the popular code. If any one imagines that this law
is lax, let him keep its commandment one day.

And truly it demands something godlike in him who has cast off the
common motives of humanity, and has ventured to trust himself for a
task-master. High be his heart, faithful his will, clear his sight, that he
may in good earnest be doctrine, society, law to himself, that a simple
purpose may be to him as strong as iron necessity is to others.

If any man consider the present aspects of what is called by distinction *society*, he will see the need of these ethics. The sinew and heart of
man seem to be drawn out, and we are become timorous desponding
whimperers. We are afraid of truth, afraid of fortune, afraid of death,
and afraid of each other. Our age yields no great and perfect persons.
We want men and women who shall renovate life and our social state,
but we see that most natures are insolvent; cannot satisfy their own
wants, have an ambition out of all proportion to their practical force,
and so do lean and beg day and night continually. Our housekeeping is
mendicant, our arts, our occupations, our marriages, our religion we
have not chosen, but society has chosen for us. We are parlor soldiers.
The rugged battle of fate, where strength is born, we shun.

If our young men miscarry in their first enterprizes, they lose all heart. If the young merchant fails, men say he is *ruined*. If the finest genius studies at one of our colleges, and is not installed in an office within one year afterwards in the cities or suburbs of Boston or New York, it seems to his friends and to himself that he is right in being disheartened and in complaining the rest of his life. A sturdy lad from New Hampshire or Vermont, who in turn tries all the professions, who *teams it, farms it, peddles,* keeps a school, preaches, edits a newspaper, goes to Congress, buys a township, and so forth, in successive years, and always, like a cat, falls on his feet, is worth a hundred of these city dolls. He walks abreast with his days, and feels no shame in not "studying a profession," for he does not postpone his life, but lives already. He has not one chance, but a hundred chances. Let a stoic arise who shall reveal the resources of man, and tell men they are not leaning willows, but can and must detach themselves; that with the exercise of self-trust, new powers shall appear; that a man is the word made flesh, born to shed healing to the nations, that he should be ashamed of our compassion, and that the moment he acts from himself, tossing the laws, the books, idolatries, and customs out of the window,—we pity him no more but thank and revere him,—and that teacher shall restore the life of man to splendor, and make his name dear to all History.

It is easy to see that a greater self-reliance,—a new respect for the divinity in man,—must work a revolution in all the offices and relations of men; in their religion; in their education; in their pursuits; their modes of living; their association; in their property; in their speculative views.

1. In what prayers do men allow themselves! That which they call a holy office, is not so much as brave and manly. Prayer looks abroad and asks for some foreign addition to come through some foreign virtue, and loses itself in endless mazes of natural and supernatural, and mediatorial and miraculous. Prayer that craves a particular commodity—any thing less than all good, is vicious. Prayer is the contemplation of the facts of life from the highest point of view. It is the soliloquy of a beholding and jubilant soul. It is the spirit of God pronouncing his works good. But prayer as a means to effect a private end, is theft and meanness. It supposes dualism and not unity in nature and consciousness. As soon as the man is at one with God, he will not beg. He will then see prayer in all action. The prayer of the farmer kneeling in his field to weed it, the prayer of the rower kneeling with the stroke of his

oar, are true prayers heard throughout nature, though for cheap ends. Caratach, in Fletcher's *Bonduca*, when admonished to inquire the mind of the god Audate, replies,

> His hidden meaning lies in our endeavors,
> Our valors are our best gods.

Another sort of false prayers are our regrets. Discontent is the want of self-reliance: it is infirmity of will. Regret calamities, if you can thereby help the sufferer; if not, attend your own work, and already the evil begins to be repaired. Our sympathy is just as base. We come to them who weep foolishly, and sit down and cry for company, instead of imparting to them truth and health in rough electric shocks, putting them once more in communication with the soul. The secret of fortune is joy in our hands. Welcome evermore to gods and men is the self-helping man. For him all doors are flung wide. Him all tongues greet, all honors crown, all eyes follow with desire. Our love goes out to him and embraces him, because he did not need it. We solicitously and apologetically caress and celebrate him, because he held on his way and scorned our disapprobation. The gods love him because men hated him. "To the persevering mortal," said Zoroaster, "the blessed Immortals are swift."

As men's prayers are a disease of the will, so are their creeds a disease of the intellect. They say with those foolish Israelites, "Let not God speak to us, lest we die. Speak thou, speak any man with us, and we will obey." Everywhere I am bereaved of meeting God in my brother, because he has shut his own temple doors, and recites fables merely of his brother's, or his brother's brother's God. Every new mind is a new classification. If it prove a mind of uncommon activity and power, a Locke, a Lavoisier, a Hutton, a Bentham, a Spurzheim, it imposes its classification on other men, and lo! a new system. In proportion always to the depth of the thought, and so to the number of the objects it touches and brings within reach of the pupil, is his complacency. But chiefly is this apparent in creeds and churches, which are also classifications of some powerful mind acting on the great elemental thought of Duty, and man's relation to the Highest. Such is Calvinism, Quakerism, Swedenborgianism. The pupil takes the same delight in subordinating every thing to the new terminology that a girl does who has just learned botany, in seeing a new earth and new seasons thereby. It will happen for a time, that the pupil will feel a real debt to the teacher,—will find his intellectual power has grown by the study of his writings. This will continue until he has exhausted his master's mind. But in all unbalanced minds, the classification is idolized, passes for the end, and not for a speedily exhaustible means, so that the walls of the system blend to their eye in the remote horizon with the walls of the universe; the luminaries of heaven seem to them hung on the arch their master built. They cannot imagine how you aliens have any right to see,—how you can see; "It must be somehow that you stole the light from us." They do not yet perceive, that, light unsystematic, indomitable, will break into any cabin, even into theirs. Let them chirp awhile and call it their own. If they are honest and do well, presently their neat new pinfold will be too strait and low, will crack, will lean, will rot and vanish, and the immortal light, all young and joyful, million-orbed, million-colored, will beam over the universe as on the first morning.

2. It is for want of self-culture that the idol of Travelling, the idol of Italy, of England, of Egypt, remains for all educated Americans. They who made England, Italy, or Greece venerable in the imagination, did so not by rambling round creation as a moth round a lamp, but by sticking fast where they were, like an axis of the earth. In manly hours, we feel that duty is our place, and that the merrymen of circumstance should follow as they may. The soul is no traveller: the wise man stays at home with the soul, and when his necessities, his duties, on any occasion call him from his house, or into foreign lands, he is at home still, and is not gadding abroad from himself, and shall make men sensible by the expression of his countenance, that he goes the missionary of wisdom and virtue, and visits cities and men like a sovereign, and not like an interloper or a valet.

I have no churlish objection to the circumnavigation of the globe, for the purposes of art, of study, and benevolence, so that the man is first domesticated, or does not go abroad with the hope of finding somewhat greater than he knows. He who travels to be amused, or to get somewhat which he does not carry, travels away from himself, and grows old even in youth among old things. In Thebes, in Palmyra, his will and mind have become old and dilapidated as they. He carries ruins to ruins.

Travelling is a fool's paradise. We owe to our first journeys the discovery that place is nothing. At home I dream that at Naples, at Rome, I can be intoxicated with beauty, and lose my sadness. I pack my trunk, embrace my friends, embark on the sea, and at last wake up in Naples, and there beside me is the stern Fact, the sad self, unrelenting, identical, that I fled from. I seek the Vatican, and the palaces. I affect to be intoxicated with sights and suggestions, but I am not intoxicated. My giant goes with me wherever I go.

3. But the rage of travelling is itself only a symptom of a deeper unsoundness affecting the whole intellectual action. The intellect is vagabond, and the universal system of education fosters restlessness. Our minds travel when our bodies are forced to stay at home. We imitate; and what is imitation but the travelling of the mind? Our houses are built with foreign taste; our shelves are garnished with foreign ornaments; our opinions, our tastes, our whole minds lean, and follow the Past and the Distant, as the eyes of a maid follow her mistress. The soul created the arts wherever they have flourished. It was in his own mind that the artist sought his model. It was an application of his own thought to the thing to be done and the conditions to be observed. And why need we copy the Doric or the Gothic model? Beauty, convenience, grandeur of thought, and quaint expression are as near to us as to any, and if the American artist will study with hope and love the precise thing to be done by him, considering the climate, the soil, the length of the day, the wants of the people, the habit and form of the government, he will create a house in which all these will find themselves fitted, and taste and sentiment will be satisfied also.

Insist on yourself; never imitate. Your own gift you can present every moment with the cumulative force of a whole life's cultivation; but of the adopted talent of another, you have only an extemporaneous, half possession. That which each can do best, none but his Maker can teach him. No man yet knows what it is, nor can, till that person has exhibited it. Where is the master who could have taught Shakspeare? Where is the master who could have instructed Franklin, or Washington, or Bacon, or Newton. Every great man is an unique. The Scipionism of Scipio is precisely that part he could not borrow. If any body will tell me whom the great man imitates in the original crisis when he performs a great act, I will tell him who else than himself can teach him. Shakespeare will never be made by the study of Shakspeare. Do that which is assigned thee, and thou canst not hope too much or dare too much. There is at this moment, there is for me an utterance bare and grand as that of the colossal chisel of Phidias, or trowel of the Egyptians, or the pen of Moses, or Dante, but different from all these. Not possibly will the soul all rich, all eloquent, with thousand-cloven tongue, deign to repeat itself; but if I can hear what these patriarchs say, surely I can reply to them in the same pitch of voice: for the ear and the tongue are two organs of one nature. Dwell up there in the simple and noble regions of thy life, obey thy heart, and thou shalt reproduce the Foreworld again.

4. As our Religion, our Education, our Art look abroad, so does our spirit of society. All men plume themselves on the improvement of society, and no man improves.

Society never advances. It recedes as fast on one side as it gains on the other. Its progress is only apparent, like the workers of a treadmill. It undergoes continual changes: it is barbarous, it is civilized, it is christianized, it is rich, it is scientific; but this change is not amelioration. For every thing that is given, something is taken. Society acquires new arts and loses old instincts. What a contrast between the well-clad, reading, writing, thinking American, with a watch, a pencil, and a bill of exchange in his pocket, and the naked New Zealander, whose property is a club, a spear, a mat, and an undivided twentieth of a shed to sleep under. But compare the health of the two men, and you shall see that his aboriginal strength the white man has lost. If the traveller tell us truly, strike the savage with a broad axe, and in a day or two the flesh shall unite and heal as if you struck the blow into soft pitch, and the same blow shall send the white to his grave.

The civilized man has built a coach, but has lost the use of his feet. He is supported on crutches, but loses so much support of muscle. He has got a fine Geneva watch, but he has lost the skill to tell the hour by the sun. A Greenwich nautical almanac he has, and so being sure of the information when he wants it, the man in the street does not know a star in the sky. The solstice he does not observe; the equinox he knows as little; and the whole bright calendar of the year is without a dial in his mind. His note-books impair his memory; his libraries overload his wit; the insurance office increases the number of accidents; and it may be a question whether machinery does not encumber; whether we have not lost by refinement some energy, by a christianity entrenched in establishments and forms, some vigor of wild virtue. For every stoic was a stoic; but in Christendom where is the Christian?

There is no more deviation in the moral standard than in the standard of height or bulk. No greater men are now than ever were. A singular equality may be observed between the great men of the first and of the last ages; nor can all the science, art, religion and philosophy of the nineteenth century avail to educate greater men than Plutarch's heroes, three or four and twenty centuries ago. Not in time is the race progressive. Phocion, Socrates, Anaxagoras, Diogenes, are great men, but they leave no class. He who is really of their class will not be called by their name, but be wholly his own man, and, in his turn the founder of a sect. The arts and inventions of each period are only its costume, and do not invigorate men. The harm of the improved machinery may compensate its good. Hudson and Behring accomplished so much in their fishing-boats, as to astonish Parry and Franklin, whose equipment exhausted the resources of science and art. Galileo, with an opera-glass, discovered a more splendid series of facts than any one since. Columbus found the New World in an undecked boat. It is curious to see the periodical disuse and perishing of means and machinery which were introduced with loud laudation, a few years or centuries before. The great genius returns to essential man. We reckoned the improvements of the art of war among the triumphs of science, and yet Napoleon conquered Europe by the Bivouac, which consisted of falling back on naked valor, and disencumbering it of all aids. The Emperor held it impossible to make a perfect army, says Las Cases, "without abolishing our arms, magazines, commissaries, and carriages, until in imitation of the Roman custom, the soldier should receive his supply of corn, grind it in his hand-mill, and bake his bread himself."

Society is a wave. The wave moves onward, but the water of which it is composed, does not. The same particle does not rise from the valley to the ridge. Its unity is only phenomenal. The persons who make up a nation to-day, next year die, and their experience with them.

And so the reliance on Property, including the reliance on governments which protect it, is the want of self-reliance. Men have looked away from themselves and at things so long, that they have come to esteem what they call the soul's progress, namely, the religious, learned, and civil institutions, as guards of property, and they deprecate assaults on these, because they feel them to be assaults on property. They measure their esteem of each other, by what each has, and not by what each is. But a cultivated man becomes ashamed of his property, ashamed of what he has, out of new respect for his being. Especially he hates what he has, if he see that it is accidental,—came to him by inheritance, or gift, or crime; then he feels that it is not having; it does not belong to him, has no root in him, and merely lies there, because no revolution or no robber takes it away. But that which a man is, does always by necessity acquire, and what the man acquires is permanent and living property, which does not wait the beck of rulers, or mobs, or revolutions, or fire, or storm, or bankruptcies, but perpetually renews itself wherever the man is put. "Thy lot or portion of life," said the Caliph Ali, "is seeking after thee; therefore be at rest from seeking after it." Our dependence on these foreign goods leads us to our slavish respect for numbers. The political parties meet in numerous conventions; the greater the concourse, and with each new uproar of announcement, The delegation from Essex! The Democrats from New Hampshire! The Whigs of Maine! the young patriot feels himself stronger than before by a new thousand of eyes and arms. In like manner the reformers summon conventions, and vote and resolve in multitude. But not so, O friends! will the God deign to enter and inhabit you, but by a method precisely the reverse. It is only as a man puts off from himself all external support, and stands alone, that I see him to be strong and to prevail. He is weaker by every recruit to his banner. Is not a man better than a town? Ask nothing of men, and in the endless mutation, thou only firm column must presently appear the upholder of all that surrounds thee. He who knows that power is in the soul, that he is weak only because he has looked for good out of him and elsewhere, and so perceiving, throws himself unhesitatingly on his thought, instantly rights himself, stands in the erect position, commands his limbs, works miracles; just as a man who stands on his feet is stronger than a man who stands on his head.

So use all that is called Fortune. Most men gamble with her, and gain all, and lose all, as her wheel rolls. But do thou leave as unlawful these winnings, and deal with Cause and Effect, the chancellors of God. In the Will work and acquire, and thou hast chained the wheel of Chance, and shalt always drag her after thee. A political victory, a rise of rents, the recovery of your sick, or the return of your absent friend, or some other quite external event, raises your spirits, and you think good days are preparing for you. Do not believe it. It can never be so. Nothing can bring you peace but yourself. Nothing can bring you peace but the triumph of principles.

# Elizabeth Palmer Peabody
## from "Plan of the West Roxbury Community"
### (1842)

This sympathetic yet nonpartisan and somewhat quizzical appraisal for *The Dial* by a Transcendentalist visitor to Brook Farm gives a flavor of the commune in its earlier years before it committed itself decisively to the more programmatic socialism of Charles Fourier. As Peabody indicates, Brook Farm was established as a kind of joint stock company whose members would be supported by a combination of reimbursement for work and profits from the community. The truly utopian elements in the original design were the principle of equal pay for every kind of work, the option to work as many hours as one chose, and the expectation that all "body" labor for everyone would be curtailed for the sake of ennobling intellectual and social pursuits. Viewing the community with an educator's eye, Peabody sensed that its potential lay not in its prospects as a working farm but as an educational project. Misled by the naive idealization of rustic pursuits that many other Transcendentalists also shared, Peabody was comically mistaken in anticipating that Brook Farm would become a model training ground for "young agriculturalists." But she was correct in predicting that the community's greatest success would be its experimental school.

SOURCE: "Plan of the West Roxbury Community," *The Dial*, 2 (January 1842).

The plan of the Community, as an Economy, is in brief this; for all who have property to take stock, and receive a fixed interest thereon; then to keep house or board in commons, as they shall severally desire, at the cost of provisions purchased at wholesale, or raised on the farm; and for all to labor in community, and be paid at a certain rate an hour, choosing their own number of hours, and their own kind of work. With the results of this labor, and their interest, they are to pay their board, and also purchase whatever else they require at cost, at the warehouse of the Community, which are to be filled by the Community as such. To perfect this economy, in the course of time they must have all trades, and all modes of business carried on among themselves, from the lowest mechanical trade, which contributes to the health and comfort of life, to the finest art which adorns it with food or drapery for the mind.

All labor, whether bodily or intellectual, is to be paid at the same rate of wages; on the principle, that as the labor becomes merely bodily, it is a greater sacrifice to the individual laborer, to give his time to it; because time is desirable for the cultivation of the intellect, in exact proportion to ignorance. Besides, intellectual labor involves in itself higher pleasures, and is more its own reward, than bodily labor.

Another reason for setting the same pecuniary value on every kind of labor is to give outward expression to the great truth that all labor is sacred, when done for a common interest.... The community will have nothing done within its precincts but what is done by its own members, who stand in social equality.... Minds incapable of refinement will not be attracted into this association. It is an Ideal community, and only to the ideally inclined will it be attractive; but these are to be found in every rank of life, under every shadow of circumstance. Even among the diggers in the ditch are to be found some, who through religious cultivation can look down, in meek superiority, upon the outwardly refined, and the book-learned.

Besides, after becoming members of the community, none will be engaged merely in bodily labor. The hours of labor for the Association will be limited by a general law, and can be curtailed at the will of the individual still more; and means will be given to all for intellectual improvement and for social intercourse, calculated to refine and expand. The hours redeemed from labor by community, will not be reapplied to the acquisition of wealth, but to the production of intellectual goods. This community aims to be rich, not in the metallic representative of wealth, but in the wealth itself, which money should represent; namely, LEISURE TO LIVE IN ALL THE FACULTIES OF THE SOUL. As a community, it will traffic with the world at large, in the produces of Agricultural labor; and it will sell education to as many young persons as can be domesticated in the families, and enter into the common life with their own children. In the end, it hopes to be enabled to provide not only the necessaries but all the elegances desirable for bodily and for spiritual health: books, apparatus, collections for science, works of art, means of beautiful amusement. These things are to be common to all. . . .

———

It seems impossible that the little organization can be looked on with any unkindness by the world without it. Those who have not the faith that the principles of Christ's kingdom are applicable to real life in the world will smile at it, as a visionary attempt. But even they must acknowledge it can do no harm, in any event. If it realizes the hopes of its founders, it will immediately become a manifold blessing. Its moral *aura* must be salutary. As long as it lasts, it will be an example of the beauty of brotherly love. If it succeeds in uniting successful labor with improvement in mind and manners, it will teach a noble lesson to the agricultural population, and do something to check that rush from the country to the city which is now stimulated by ambition, and by something better, even a desire for learning. Many a young man leaves the farmer's life, because only by so doing can he have intellectual companionship and opportunity; and yet, did he but know it, professional life is ordinarily more unfavorable to the perfection of the mind, than the farmer's life; if the latter is lived with wisdom and moderation, and labor mingled as it might with study. This community will be a school for young agriculturalists, who may learn within its precincts, not only the skillful practice, but the scientific reasons of their work, and be enabled afterwards to improve their art continuously. It will also prove the best of normal schools, and as such, may claim the interest of those, who mourn over the inefficiency of our common school system, with its present ill-instructed teachers. . . .

# George Ripley et al.
## Brook Farm's (First Published) Constitution
### (1844)

Here the Brook Farmers speak for themselves, in a document at once designed as a constitution, an interim progress report, and a fund-raising promotional. The document conveys mixed signals. On the one hand, it offers the promise of individual freedom, security, and mutuality in the service of a community that is determined—but gently—to reform society. On the other hand, it alludes to early difficulties not yet overcome and announces the plan of "ultimate expansion into a perfect Phalanx." "Phalanx," as socially aware readers of this document would have known, was the technical term used by utopian socialist Charles Fourier to denote a more stringently regulated kind of community than this one describes itself as being. Brook Farm was in fact on the verge of hitching its wagon, for better and for worse, to Fourier's star. The more detailed, second edition of the Brook Farm constitution, issued later the same year, stipulates a more draconian set of regulations, eliminating some of the guarantees of individual freedom.

SOURCE: *Constitution of the Brook Farm Association for Industry and Education, West Roxbury, Mass. With an Introductory Statement,* Brook Farm Association for Industry and Education. Boston: I. R. Butts, 1844.

The Association at Brook Farm, has now been in existence upwards of two years. Originating in the thought and experience of a few individuals, it has hitherto worn, for the most part, the character of a private experiment, and has avoided rather than sought, the notice of the public. It has, until the present time, seemed fittest to those engaged in this enterprise to publish no statements of their purposes or methods, to make no promises or declarations, but quietly and sincerely to realise, as far as might be possible, the great ideas which gave the central impulse to their movement. It has been thought that a steady endeavor to embody these ideas more and more perfectly in life, would give the best answer, both to the hopes of the friendly and the cavils of the sceptical, and furnish in its results the surest grounds for any larger efforts.

———

Meanwhile every step has strengthened the faith with which we set out; our belief in a divine order of human society, has in our own minds become an absolute certainty; and considering the present state of humanity and of social science, we do not hesitate to affirm, that the world is much nearer the attainment of such a condition than is generally supposed.

The deep interest in the doctrine of Association, which now fills the minds of intelligent persons every where, indicates plainly that the time has passed when even initiative movements ought to be prosecuted in silence, and makes it imperative on all who have either a theoretical or practical knowledge of the subject to give their share to the stock of public information.

Accordingly, we have taken occasion at several public meetings recently held in Boston, to state some of the results of our studies and experience, and we desire here to say emphatically, that while on the one hand we yield an unqualified assent to that doctrine of universal unity which Fourier teaches, so on the other, our whole observation has shown us the truth of the practical arrangements which he deduces therefrom. The law of groups and series is, as we are convinced, the law of human nature, and when men are in true social relations their industrial organization will necessarily assume those forms.

But beside the demand for information respecting the principles of association, there is a deeper call for action in the matter. We wish, therefore, to bring Brook Farm before the public, as a location offering at least as great advantages for a thorough experiment as can be found in the vicinity of Boston. It is situated in West Roxbury, three miles from the depot of the Dedham Branch Rail Road, and about eight miles from Boston, and combines a convenient nearness to the city with a degree of retirement and freedom from unfavorable influences, unusual even in the country. The place is one of great natural beauty, and indeed the whole landscape is so rich and various as to attract the notice even of casual visitors. The farm now owned by the Association contains two hundred and eight acres, of as good quality as any land in the neighborhood of Boston, and can be enlarged by the purchase of land adjoining to any necessary extent. The property now in the hands of the Association is worth nearly or quite thirty thousand dollars, of which about twenty-two thousand dollars is invested either in the stock of the company, or in permanent loans at six per cent., which can remain as long as the Association may wish.

The fact that so large an amount of capital is already invested and at our service as the basis of more extensive operations, furnishes a reason why Brook Farm should be chosen as the scene of that practical trial of association which the public feeling calls for in this immediate vicinity, instead of forming an entirely new organization for that purpose. The completeness of our educational department is also not to be overlooked. This has hitherto received our greatest care, and in forming it we have been particularly successful. In any new Association it must be many years before so many accomplished and skilful teachers in the various branches of intellectual culture could be enlisted. Another strong reason is to be found in the degree of order our organization has already attained, by the help of which a large Association might be formed without the losses and inconveniences which would otherwise necessarily occur. The experience of nearly three years in all the misfortunes and mistakes incident to an undertaking so new and so little understood, carried on throughout by persons not entirely fitted for the duties they have been compelled to perform, has, as we think, prepared us to assist in the safe conduct of an extensive and complete Association.

Such an institution, as will be plain to all, cannot by any sure means, be brought at once and full grown into existence. It must at least in the present state of society, begin with a comparatively small number of select and devoted persons, and increase by natural and gradual aggregations. With a view to an ultimate expansion into a perfect Phalanx, we desire without any delay to organize the three primary departments of labor, namely, Agriculture, Domestic Industry, and the Mechanic Arts.

For this purpose additional capital will be needed, which it is most desirable should be invested by those who propose to connect themselves personally with the institution. These should be men and women accustomed to labor, skilful, careful, in good health, and more than all imbued with the idea of Association, and ready to consecrate themselves without reserve to its realization. For it ought to be known that the work we propose is a difficult one, and except to the most entire faith and resolution will offer insurmountable obstacles and discouragements. Neither will it be possible to find in Association at the outset the great outward advantages it ultimately promises. The first few years must be passed in constant and unwearied labor, heightened chiefly by the consciousness of high aims and the inward content that devotion to a universal object cannot fail to bring. Still there are certain tangible compensations which Association guaranties immediately. These are freedom from pecuniary anxiety, and the evils of competitive industry, free and friendly society, and the education of children. How great these are, those who have felt the terrible burdens which the present civilized society imposes in these respects will not need to be informed.

Those who may wish to further this course by investments of money only will readily perceive that their end is not likely to be lost in an Association whose means are devoted mainly to productive industry, and where nothing will ever be risked in uncertain speculations.

The following Constitution is the same as that under which we have hitherto acted, with such alterations as on a careful revision seemed needful. All persons who are not familiar with the purposes of Association, will understand from this document that we propose a radical and universal reform, rather than to redress any particular wrong or to remove the sufferings of any single class of human beings. We do this in the light of universal principles, in which all differences, whether of religion, or politics, or philosophy, are reconciled, and the dearest and most private hope of every man has the promise of fulfilment. Herein, let it be understood, we would remove nothing that is truly beautiful or venerable; we reverence the religious sentiment in all its forms, the family, and whatever else has its foundation either in human nature or the Divine Providence. The work we are engaged in is not destruction, but true conservation: it is not a mere revolution, but, as we are assured, a necessary step in the course of social progress which no one can be blind enough to think has yet reached its limit. We believe that humanity, trained by these long centuries of suffering and struggle, led onward by so many saints and heroes and sages, is at length prepared to enter into that universal order, toward which it has perpetually moved. Thus we recognize the worth of the whole Past and of every doctrine and institution it has bequeathed us; thus also we perceive that the Present has its own high mission, and we shall only say what is beginning to be seen by all sincere thinkers, when we declare that the imperative duty of this time and this country, nay more, that its only salvation, and the salvation of all civilized countries, lies in the Reorganization of Society, according to the unchanging laws of human nature and of universal harmony.

We look, then, to the generous and hopeful of all classes for sympathy, for encouragement and for actual aid, not to ourselves only, but to all those who are engaged in this great work. And whatever may be the result of any special efforts, we can never doubt that the object we have in view will finally be attained; that human life shall yet be developed, not in discord and misery, but in harmony and joy, and that the perfected earth shall at last bear on her bosom a race of men worthy of the name.

GEORGE RIPLEY,
MINOT PRATT, } *Directors.*
CHARLES A. DANA,

*Brook Farm, West Roxbury, Mass.,* }
*January 18, 1844.*

## CONSTITUTION.

In order more effectually to promote the great purposes of human culture; to establish the external relations of life on a basis of wisdom and purity; to apply the principles of justice and love to our social organization in accordance with the laws of Divine Providence; to substitute a system of brotherly coöperation for one of selfish competition; to secure to our children and those who may be entrusted to our care the benefits of the highest physical, intellectual and moral education, which in the progress of knowledge the resources at our command will permit; to institute an attractive, efficient, and productive system of industry; to prevent the exercise of worldly anxiety, by the competent supply of our necessary wants; to diminish the desire of excessive accumulation, by making the acquisition of individual property subservient to upright and disinterested uses; to guarantee to each other forever the means of physical support, and of spiritual progress; and thus to impart a greater freedom, simplicity, truthfulness, refinement, and moral dignity, to our mode of life;—we the undersigned do unite in a voluntary Association, and adopt and ordain the following articles of agreement, to wit:

### ARTICLE I. NAME AND MEMBERSHIP.

SEC. 1. The name of this Association shall be "THE BROOK-FARM ASSOCIATION FOR INDUSTRY AND EDUCATION." All persons who shall hold one or more shares in its stock, or whose labor and skill shall be considered an equivalent for capital, may be admitted by the vote of two-thirds of the Association, as members thereof.

SEC. 2. No member of the Association shall ever be subjected to any religious test; nor shall any authority be assumed over individual freedom of opinion by the Association, nor by one member over another; nor shall any one be held accountable to the Association, except for such overt acts, or omissions of duty, as violate the principles of justice, purity, and love, on which it is founded; and in such cases the relation of any member may be suspended or discontinued, at the pleasure of the Association.

### ARTICLE II. CAPITAL STOCK.

SEC. 1. The members of this Association shall own and manage such real and personal estate in joint stock proprietorship, divided into shares of one hundred dollars each, as may from time to time be agreed on.

SEC. 2. No share-holder shall be liable to any assessment whatever on the shares held by him; nor shall he be held responsible individually in his private property on account of the Association; nor shall the Trustees or any officer or agent of the Association have any authority to do any thing which shall impose personal responsibility on any share-holder, by making any contracts or incurring any debts for which the share-holders shall be individually or personally responsible.

SEC. 3. The Association guaranties to each share-holder the interest of five per cent. annually on the amount of stock held by him in the Association, and this interest may be paid in certificates of stock and credited on the books of the Association; provided that each share-holder may draw on the funds of the Association for the amount of interest due at the third annual settlement from the time of investment.

SEC. 4. The share-holders on their part for themselves, their heirs and assigns, do renounce all claim on any profits accruing to the Association for the use of their capital invested in the stock of the Association, except five per cent. interest on the amount of stock held by them, payable in the manner described in the preceding section.

### ARTICLE III. GUARANTIES.

SEC. 1. The Association shall provide such employment for all its members as shall be adapted to their capacities, habits, and tastes; and each member shall select and perform such operations of labor, whether corporal or mental, as shall be deemed best suited to his own endowments and the benefit of the Association.

SEC. 2. The Association guaranties to all its members, their children and family dependents, house-rent, fuel, food, and clothing, and the other necessaries of life, without charge, not exceeding a certain fixed amount to be decided annually by the Association; no charge shall ever be made for support during inability to labor from sickness or old age, or for medical or nursing attendance, except in case of shareholders, who shall be charged therefor, and also for the food and clothing of children, to an amount not exceeding the interest due to them on settlement; but no charge shall be made to any member for education or the use of library and public rooms.

SEC. 3. Members may withdraw from labor, under the direction of the Association, and in that case, they shall not be entitled to the benefit of the above guaranties.

SEC. 4. Children over ten years of age shall be provided with employment in suitable branches of industry; they shall be credited for such portions of each annual dividend, as shall be decided by the Association, and on the completion of their education in the Association at the age of twenty, shall be entitled to a certificate of stock to the amount of credits in their favor, and may be admitted as members of the Association.

### ARTICLE IV. DISTRIBUTION OF PROFITS.

SEC. 1. The nett profits of the Association, after the payment of all expenses, shall be divided into a number of shares corresponding to the number of day's labor; and every member shall be entitled to one share for every day's labor performed by him.

SEC. 2. A full settlement shall be made with every member once a year, and certificates of stock given for all balances due; but in case of need to be decided by himself, every member may be permitted to draw on the funds in the Treasury to an amount not exceeding the credits in his favor for labor performed.

### ARTICLE V. GOVERNMENT.

SEC. 1. The government of the Association shall be vested in a board of Directors, divided into four departments, as follows: 1st, General Direction; 2d, Direction of Education; 3d, Direction of Industry; 4th, Direction of Finance; consisting of three persons each, provided that the same person may be elected member of each Direction.

SEC. 2. The General Direction and Direction of Education shall be chosen annually, by the vote of a majority of the members of the Association. The Direction of Finance shall be chosen annually, by the vote of a majority of the share-holders and members of the Association. The Direction of Industry shall consist of the chiefs of the three primary series.

SEC. 3. The chairman of the General Direction shall be the President of the Association, and together with the Direction of Finance, shall constitute a board of Trustees, by whom the property of the Association shall be held and managed.

SEC. 4. The General Direction shall oversee and manage the affairs of the Association, so that every department should be carried on in an orderly and efficient manner.

SEC. 5. The departments of Education and Finance shall be under the control each of its own Direction, which shall select, and in concurrence with the General Direction, shall appoint such teachers, officers, and agents, as shall be necessary to the complete and systematic organization of the department. No Directors or other officers shall be deemed to possess any rank superior to the other members of the Association, nor shall they receive any extra remuneration for their official services.

SEC. 6. The department of Industry shall be arranged in groups and series, as far as practicable, and shall consist of three primary series, to wit, Agricultural, Mechanical, and Domestic Industry. The chief of each series shall be elected every two months by the members thereof, subject to the approval of the General Direction. The chief of each group shall be chosen weekly by its members.

### ARTICLE VI. MISCELLANEOUS.

SEC. 1. The Association may from time to time adopt such bye-laws, not inconsistent with the spirit and purpose of these articles, as shall be found expedient or necessary.

SEC. 2. In order to secure to the Association the benefits of the highest discoveries in social science, and to preserve its fidelity to the principles of progress and reform, on which it is founded, any amendment may be proposed to this Constitution at a meeting called for the purpose; and if approved by two-thirds of the members at a subsequent meeting, at least one month after the date of the first, shall be adopted.

# THEODORE PARKER

## FROM "A SERMON OF MERCHANTS"

### (1846)

When Parker moved from West Roxbury, near Brook Farm, to an urban ministry in Boston, he began to preach more vigorously against social abuses. More than any other Transcendentalist minister, Parker influenced the Social Gospel movement a generation later, according to which remediation of social injustice became the practical test of one's Christian faith. Eventually, Parker channeled his activist efforts almost exclusively into abolitionism. But at first he placed even greater emphasis on a Brownson-like indictment of systemic inequalities of wealth and class. (Brownson, now a Catholic convert turned bitterly hostile to Transcendentalist theological radicalism of the Parker stamp, accused him of plagiarism.) Parker was another of those relatively few leading Transcendentalists of yeoman background, and he was commensurately harsher on institutionalized wealth and power than Emerson was. This particular discourse was a complement to a previous sermon on "the perishing classes in Boston." Typically for Parker's published sermons, both texts are heavily researched performances, packed with facts and statistics. But the fiery zeal that led Emerson to call Parker "Our Savanarola" pervades throughout. Parker dramatizes the formidable power, temptations, and corruptions of the mercantile class, diagnosing it as the contemporary equivalent to feudal aristocracy. The sermon thereby becomes a forceful statement of American and particularly New England distinctiveness as defined by the transatlantic bourgeois revolution. Throughout Parker stresses the mercantile interests' perversion of democratic promise—even blaming this for the underdevelopment of American literature!—and gives only scant attention to the new establishment's positive accomplishments. But neither does he join Brownson or the Brook Farmers in calling for social revolution. Rather he exhorts merchants to use their power honorably. This concluding call helps show why Parker insisted on remaining in the Unitarian ministry, even as conservative fellow clergy tried to drive him out of it.

SOURCE: *Speeches, Addresses, and Occasional Sermons,* 2 vols. Boston: Crosby and Nichols, 1852.

Now the merchants in America occupy the place which was once held by the fighters and next by the nobles. In our country we have balanced into harmony the centrifugal power of the government, and the centrifugal power of the people: so have national unity of action, and individual variety of action—personal freedom. Therefore a vast amount of talent is active here which lies latent in other countries, because that harmony is not established there. Here the army and navy offer few inducements to able and aspiring young men. They are fled to as the last resort of the desperate, or else sought for their traditional glory, not their present value. In Europe, the army, the navy, the parliament or the court, the church and the learned professions offer brilliant prizes to ambitious men. Thither flock the able and the daring. Here such men go into trade. It is better for a man to have set up a mill than to have won a battle. I deny not the exceptions. I speak only of the general rule. Commerce and manufactures offer the most brilliant rewards—wealth, and all it brings. Accordingly the ablest men go into the class of merchants. The strongest men in Boston, taken as a body, are not lawyers, doctors, clergymen, bookwrights, but merchants. . . .

———

In virtue of its strength and position, this class is the controlling one in politics. It mainly enacts the laws of this State and the nation; makes them serve its turn. Acting consciously or without consciousness, it buys up legislators when they are in the market; breeds them when the market is bare. It can manufacture governors, senators, judges, to suit its purposes, as easily as it can make cotton cloth. It pays them money and honors; pays them for doing its work, not another's. It is fairly and faithfully represented by them. Our popular legislators are made in its image; represent its wisdom, foresight, patriotism and conscience. Your Congress is its mirror.

This class is the controlling one in the churches, none the less, for with us fortunately the churches have no existence independent of the wealth and knowledge of the people. In the same way it buys up the clergymen, hunting them out all over the land; the clergymen who will do its work, putting them in comfortable places. It drives off such as interfere with its work, saying; "Go starve, you and your children!" It raises or manufactures others to suit its taste.

The merchants build mainly the churches, endow theological schools; they furnish the material sinews of the church. Hence the metropolitan churches are in general as much commercial as the shops....

———

This class owns the machinery of society, in great measure,—the ships, factories, shops, water privileges, houses and the like. This brings into their employment large masses of working men, with no capital but muscles or skill. The law leaves the employed at the employer's mercy. Perhaps this is unavoidable. One wishes to sell his work dear, the other to get it cheap as he can. It seems to me no law can regulate this matter, only conscience, reason, the Christianity of the two parties. One class is strong, the other weak. In all encounters of these two, on the field of battle, or in the market-place, we know the result: the weaker is driven to the wall. When the earthen and iron vessel strike together, we know beforehand which will go to pieces. The weaker class can seldom tell their tale, so their story gets often suppressed in the world's literature, and told only in outbreaks and revolutions. Still the bold men who wrote the Bible, Old Testament and New, have told truths on this theme which others dared not tell—terrible words which it will take ages of Christianity to expunge from the world's memory.

There is a strong temptation to use one's power of nature or position to the disadvantage of the weak. This may be done consciously or unconsciously. There are examples enough of both. Here the merchant deals in the labor of men. This is a legitimate article of traffic, and dealing in it is quite indispensable in the present condition of affairs. In the Southern States, the merchant, whether producer, manufacturer or trader, owns men and deals in their labor, or their bodies. He uses their labor, giving them just enough of the result of that labor to keep their bodies in the most profitable working state; the rest of that result he steals for his own use, and by that residue becomes rich and famous. He owns their persons and gets their labor by direct violence, though sanctioned by law. That is slavery. He steals the man and his labor.

Here it is possible to do a similar thing: I mean it is possible to employ men and give them just enough of the result of their labor to keep up a miserable life, and yourself take all the rest of the result of that labor. This may be done consciously or otherwise, but legally, without direct violence, and without owning the person. This is not slavery, though only one remove from it. This is the tyranny of the strong over the weak; the feudalism of money; stealing a man's work, and not his person. The merchants as a class are exposed to this very temptation. Sometimes it is yielded to. Some large fortunes have been made in this way. Let me mention some extreme cases; one from abroad, one near at home. In Belgium the average wages of men in manufactories is less than twenty-seven cents a day. The most skilful women in that calling can only earn twenty cents a day, and many very much less. In that country almost every seventh man receives charity from the public: the mortality of operatives, in some of the cities, is ten per cent a year! Perhaps that is the worst case which you can find on a large scale even in Europe. How much better off are many women in Boston who gain their bread by the needle? yes, a large class of women in all our great cities? The ministers of the poor can answer that; your police can tell of the direful crime to which necessity sometimes drives women whom honest labor cannot feed! . . .

Then, too, there is a temptation to abuse their political power to the injury of the nation, to make laws which seem good for themselves, but are baneful to the people; to control the churches, so that they shall not dare rebuke the actual sins of the nation, or the sins of trade, and so the churches be made apologizers for lowness, practising infidelity as their sacrament, but in the name of Christ and God. The ruling power in England once published a volume of sermons, as well as a book of prayers, which the clergy were commanded to preach. What sort of a gospel got recommended therein, you may easily guess; and what is recommended by the class of merchants in New England, you may as easily hear. . . .

---

There is always a conservative element in society; yes, an element which resists the further application of Christianity to public affairs. Once the fighters and their children were uppermost, and represented that element. Then the merchants were reformatory, radical, in collision with the nobles. They were "Whigs"—the nobles were "Tories." The merchants formed themselves into companies, and got power from the crown to protect themselves against the nobles, whom the crown also feared. It is so in England now. The great revolution in the laws of trade lately effected there, was brought about by the merchants, though opposed by the lords. The anti-corn law league was a trades-union of merchants contending against the owners of the soil. There the lord of land, and by birth, is slowly giving way to the lord of money, who is powerful by his knowledge or his wealth. There will always be such an element in society. Here I think it is represented by the merchants. They are backward in all reforms, excepting such as their own interest demands. Thus they are blind to the evils of slavery, at least silent about them. How few commercial or political newspapers in the land ever seriously oppose this great national wickedness! Nay, how many of them favor its extension and preservation! . . . A merchant of this city says publicly, that a large majority of his brethren would kidnap a fugitive slave in Boston; says it with no blush and without contradiction. It was men of this class who opposed the abolition of the slave-trade, and had it guaranteed them for twenty years after the formation of the Constitution; through their instigation that this foul blot was left to defile the Republic and gather blackness from age to age; through their means that the nation stands before the world pledged to maintain it. They could end slavery at once, at least could end the national connection with it, but it is through their support that it continues; that it acquires new strength, new boldness, new territory, darkens the nation's fame and hope, delays all other reformations in Church and State and the mass of the people. Yes, it is through their influence that the chivalry, the wisdom, patriotism, eloquence, yea, religion of the free States, are all silent when the word slavery is pronounced. . . .

———

Would that my words could reach all of this class. Think not I love to speak hard words, and so often; say not that I am setting the poor against the rich. It is no such thing. I am trying to set the strong in favor of the weak. I speak for man. Are you not all brothers, rich or poor? I am here to gratify no vulgar ambition, but in Religion's name to tell their duty to the most powerful class in all this land. I must speak the truth I know, though I may recoil with trembling at the words I speak; yes, though their flame should scorch my own lips. Some of the evils I complain of are your misfortune, not your fault. Perhaps the best hearts in the land, no less than the ablest heads, are yours. If the evils be done unconsciously, then it will be greatness to be higher than society, and with your good overcome its evil. All men see your energy, your honor, your disciplined intellect. Let them see your goodness, justice, Christianity. The age demands of you a development of religion proportionate with the vigor of your mind and arms. Trade is silently making a wonderful revolution. We live in the midst of it, and therefore see it not. All property has become movable, and therefore power departs from the family of the first-born, and comes to the family of mankind. God only controls this revolution, but you can help it forward, or retard it. The freedom of labor, and the freedom of trade, will work wonders little dreamed of yet; one is now uniting all men of the same nation; the other, some day, will weave all tribes together into one mighty family. Then who shall dare break its peace? I cannot now stop to tell half the proud achievements I foresee resulting from the fierce energy that animates your yet unconscious hearts. Men live faster than ever before. Life, like money, like mechanical power, is getting intensified and condensed. The application of science to the arts, the use of wind, water, steam, electricity, for human works, is a wonderful fact, far greater than the fables of old time. . . . It is for you, who own the machinery of society, to see that no class appropriates to itself what God meant for all. Remember it is as easy to tyrannize by machinery as by armies, and as wicked; that it is greater now to bless mankind thereby, than it was of old to conquer new realms. Let men not curse you, as the old nobility, and shake you off, smeared with blood and dust. Turn your power to goodness, its natural transfiguration, and men shall bless your name, and God bless your soul. If you control the nation's politics, then it is your duty to legislate for the nation,—for man. You may develope the great national idea, the equality of all men; may frame a government which shall secure man's unalienable rights. It is for you to organize the rights of man, thus balancing into harmony the man and the many, to organize the rights of the hand, the head, and the heart. If this be not done, the fault is yours. If the nation play the tyrant over her weakest child, if she plunder and rob the feeble Indian, the feebler Mexican, the Negro, feebler yet, why the blame is yours. Remember there is a God who deals justly with strong and weak. The poor and the weak have loitered behind in march of man; our cities yet swarm with men half-savage. It is for you, ye elder brothers, to lead forth the weak and poor! If you do the national duty that devolves on you, then are you the saviours of your country, and shall bless not that alone, but all the thousand million sons of men. Toil then for that. . . .

For these great works you may labor; yes, you are laboring, when you help forward justice, industry, when you promote the education of the people; when you practise, public and private, the virtues of a Christian man; when you hinder these seemingly little things, you hinder also the great. You are the nation's head, and if the head be wilful and wicked, what shall its members do and be? To this class let me say: Remember your Position at the head of the nation; use it not as pirates, but Americans, Christians, men. Remember your Temptations, and be warned in time. Remember your opportunities—such as no men ever had before. God and man alike call on you to do your duty. Elevate your calling still more; let its nobleness appear in you. Scorn a mean thing. Give the world more than you take. You are to serve the nation, not it you; to build the church, not make it a den of thieves, nor allow it to apologize for your crime, or sloth. Try this experiment and see what comes of it. In all things govern yourselves by the eternal law of right. You shall build up not a military despotism, nor a mercantile oligarchy, but a State, where the government is of all, by all, and for all; you shall found not a feudal theocracy, nor a beggarly sect, but the church of mankind, and that Christ which is the same yesterday, to-day and for ever, will dwell in it, to guide, to warn, to inspire, and to bless all men.

# 7.

# MARGARET FULLER
## ON THE ITALIAN REVOLUTION
### (1847-50)

During the 1840s, Margaret Fuller left Boston to embark on a career as a freelance journalist for the most influential liberal American newspaper of the day, Horace Greeley's *New York Tribune,* which later promoted Thoreau's work and employed George Ripley as its lead book reviewer after the demise of Brook Farm. After contributing articles and reviews on a wide range of social, cultural, and artistic issues, Fuller embarked on an extended journey to England and Europe that finally took her to Italy on the eve of the revolution of 1848. She became a confidante of the Risorgimento's leader, Giuseppe Mazzini, and the lover and probably also the wife of a revolutionary partisan among the minor nobility, Giovanni Ossoli, by whom she had a son. Returning to the United States in 1850 after the revolution failed, all three drowned in a shipwreck off Long Island. Fuller's journalistic letters on the revolutionary uprising in Italy are her most sustained and pointed work of political commentary, although she never ceased to notice and care deeply about matters of art and culture as well. Her late journalism is also her most incisive prose, still impressionistic but far less abstract and circuitous than much of her early writing.

Fuller's European journalism and most especially her Italian letters are unique among Transcendentalist writing as a participant-observer's on-the-spot involvement with transatlantic political upheavals at a critical moment, and as a dramatic example of a person accustomed to the status of independent critic being drawn into solidarity with a resistance movement. Fuller's desire for U.S. intervention in the cause of democracy at this time of crisis contrasts strikingly with Thoreau's hostility toward federal solutions of any sort. Both Fuller's commentary and Thoreau's, however, show the shift in thinking among a number of Transcendentalists as the 1840s unfolded, from an early individual-centeredness to a keener social conscience and attentiveness to hard political realities. On the home front, the particular issue that had already begun to emerge as the "reform among reforms," as one historian put it, was the fight against slavery, Thoreau's central concern in the next reading.

SOURCE: *New York Tribune* (1847–50), published on the dates noted below, each column entitled "Things and Thoughts in Europe," except the last, which was titled "Italy."

I earnestly hope some expression of sympathy from my country toward Italy. Take a good change and do something.... This cause is OURS, above all others; we ought to show that we feel it to be so. At present there is no likelihood of war, but in case of it I trust the United States would not fail in some noble token of sympathy toward this country. The Soul of our Nation need not wait for its Government; these things are better done by the effort of individuals.... In many ways [Italy] is of kin to us; she is the country of Columbus, of Amerigo, of Cabot. It would please me much to see a cannon here bought by the contributions of Americans, at whose head should stand the name of Cabot, to be used by the Guard for salutes on festive occasions, if they should be so happy as to have no more serious need.... I should like the gift of America to be called the AMERICA, the COLUMBO, or the WASHINGTON. Please think of this, some of my friends, who still care for the Eagle, the 4th July, and the old cries of Hope and Honor.   [NOVEMBER 27, 1847]

—

Yet, oh Eagle, whose early flight showed this clear sight of the Sun, how often dost thou near the ground, how show the vulture in these later days! Thou wert to be the advance-guard of Humanity, the herald of all Progress; how often hast thou betrayed this high commission! Fain would the tongue in clear triumphant accents draw example from thy story, to encourage the hearts who almost faint and die beneath the old oppressions. But we must stammer and blush when we speak of many things. I take pride here that I may really say the Liberty of the

Press works well, and that checks and balances naturally evolve from it which suffice to its government. I may say that the minds of our people are alert, and that Talent has a free chance to rise. It is much. But dare I say that political ambition is not as darkly sullied as in other countries? Dare I say that men of most influence in political life are those who represent most virtue or even intellectual power? . . . Must I not confess in my country to a boundless lust of gain. Must I not confess to the weakest vanity, which bristles and blusters at each foolish taunt of the foreign press. . . . Can I say our social laws are generally better, or show a nobler insight into the wants of man and woman? I do, indeed, say what I believe, that voluntary association for improvement in these particulars will be the grand means for my nation to grow and give a nobler harmony to the coming age. But it is only of a small minority that I can say they as yet seriously take to heart these things; that they earnestly meditate on what is wanted for their country,—for mankind,—for our cause is, indeed the cause of all mankind. . . . Then there is this horrible cancer of Slavery, and this wicked War [against Mexico], that has grown out of it. How dare I speak of these things here? I listen to the same arguments against the emancipation of Italy, that are used against the emancipation of our blacks; the same arguments in favor of the spoilation of Poland as for the conquest of Mexico. I find the cause of tyranny and wrong everywhere the same—and lo! my Country the darkest offender, because with the least excuse, foresworn to the high calling which she was called,—no champion of the rights of men, but a robber and a jailer; the scourge hid behind her banner; her eyes fixed, not on the stars, but on the possessions of other men.

How it pleases me here to think of the Abolitionists! I could never endure to be with them at home, they were so tedious, often so narrow, always so rabid and exaggerated in their tone.

But, after all, they had a high motive, something eternal in their desire and life; and, if it was not the only thing worth thinking of it was really something worth living and dying for to free a great nation from such a terrible blot, such a threatening plague. God strengthen them and make them wise to achieve their purpose! . . .

I have found many among the youth of England, of France—of Italy also—full of high desire, but will they have courage and purity to fight the battle through in the sacred, the immortal band? Of some of them I believe it and await the proof. If a few succeed amid the trial, we have not lived and loved in vain. [JANUARY 1, 1848]

---

Rome is all full of effigies of those over whom violence had no power. There is an early Pope about to be thrown into the Tiber; violence had no power to make him say what he did not mean. Delicate girls, men in the prime of hope and pride of power—they were all alike about that. They could be done to death in boiling oil, roasted on coals, or cut to pieces; but they could not say what they did not mean. These formed the true Church. . . .

And my country, what does she? You have chosen a new President [Zachary Taylor] from a Slave State, representative of the Mexican War. But he seems to be honest, a man that can be esteemed, and is one really known to the people; which is a step upward after having sunk last time to choosing a mere took of party [James K. Polk].

Pray send here a good Ambassador—one that has experience of foreign life, that he may act with good judgment; and, if possible, a man that has knowledge and views which extend beyond the cause of party politics in the United States; a man of unity in principles, but capable of understanding variety in forms. And send a man capable to prize the luxury of living in, or knowing Rome: it is one that should not be thrown away on a person who cannot prize or use it. Another century, and I might ask to be made Ambassador myself ('tis true, like other Ambassadors, I would employ clerks to do the most of the duty,) but woman's day has not come yet. . . .   [JANUARY 26, 1849]

---

The Americans here are not in a pleasant situation. Mr. [Lewis] Cass, the Chargé [d'Affaires] of the United States, stays here without recognizing the Government. Of course, he holds no position at the present moment than can enable him to act for us. Beside, it gives us pain that our country, whose policy it justly is to avoid physical interference with the affairs of Europe, should not use a moral influence. Rome has, as we did, thrown off a Government no longer tolerable; she has made use of the suffrage to form another; she stands on the same basis as ourselves. . . .   [MARCH 20, 1849]

---

I met an American. He "had no confidence in the Republic." Why? Because he "had no confidence in the People." Why? Because "they were not like *our* People." Ah! Jonathan and John—excuse me, but I must say the Italian has a decided advantage over you in the power of quickly feeling generous sympathy. . . .

How I wish my country would show some noble sympathy when an experience so like her own is going on. Politically she cannot interfere; but formerly when Greece and Poland were struggling, they were at least aided by private contributions. Italy, naturally so rich, but long racked and improverished by her oppressors, greatly needs money to arm and clothe her troops. Some token of sympathy, too, from America would be so welcome to her now. If there were a circle of persons inclined to trust such to me, I might venture to promise the trust should be used to the advantage of Italy. It would make me proud to have my country show a religious faith in the progress of ideas, and make some small sacrifice of its own great resources in aid of a sister cause, now.   [MARCH 31, 1849]

---

. . . It is most unfortunate that we should have an envoy here for the first time, just to offend and disappoint the Romans. When all the other ambassadors are at Gaesta ours is in Rome, as if by his presence to discountenance the Republican Government which he does not recognize. Mr. Cass, it seems, is limited by his instructions not to recognize the Government till sure it can be sustained. Now, it seems to me the only dignified ground for our Government, the only legitimate ground for any Republican Government, is to recognize for any nation the Government chosen by itself. The suffrage had been correct here, and the proportion of votes to the whole population was much larger, it was said, by Americans here, than it is in our country at the time of contested elections. . . . The Roman people claims once more to have a national existence. It declines farther serfdom to an ecclesiastical court. It claims liberty of conscience, of action and of thought. Should it fall from its present position, it will not be from internal dissent, but from foreign oppression.   [JUNE 23, 1849]

---

. . . Too often . . . [Americans in Europe] disdain the "people," forgetting that if they have risen to peculiar privileges it was owing to freedom which kept the career open to talent; they stand cap in hand to the dignities of the old world and quote with contemptible delight opinions backed only by inherited rank. It is very painful to see how stupidly they abase themselves, apparently unhappy till they can present their breasts for a ribbon, forgetful that the same implies readiness of the forehead for the rod of the absolving priest, or of the back for the knout. The position of an American is so glorious, if he has simple good sense and manly dignity to uphold it, that it is lamentable indeed to see it thus forfeited on every-day occasions. ... America is the star of hope to the enslaved nations[;] bitter indeed were the night of the world if that star were hid from its sight by foul vapors.

[JANUARY 9, 1850]

---

At this moment all the worst men are in power, and the best betrayed and exiled. All the falsities, the abuses of the old political forms, the old social compact, seem confirmed. Yet it is not so: the struggle that is now to begin will be fearful, but even from the first hours not doubtful. Bodies rotten and trembling cannot long contend with swelling life. Tongue and hand cannot be permanently employed to keep down hearts. ... Do you laugh, Roman Cardinal, as you shut the prison-door on woman weeping for her son martyred in the cause of his country? Do you laugh, Austrian officer, as you drill the Hungarian and Lombard youth to tremble at your baton? Soon you, all of you, shall *"believe and tremble."*   [FEBRUARY 13, 1850]

# 8.

# HENRY DAVID THOREAU
## "RESISTANCE TO CIVIL GOVERNMENT"
### (1849)

Under its better-known title of "Civil Disobedience," substituted when the essay was collected in book form after Thoreau's death, "Resistance" has become by far the most famous and influential of all Transcendentalist social reform writings. Here Thoreau describes and justifies his refusal to pay his poll tax, for which he was arrested and briefly jailed during the time he was living at Walden (1846), as a protest against the injustice of the U.S. war against Mexico (1845–47), which Thoreau and many other New Englanders saw as having been imposed upon the country as a whole by supporters of the expansion of slaveholding territory. The essay is especially memorable for its tenacious and pithy defense of the legitimacy and the potential power of individual acts of principled refusal to obey unjust laws. Thoreau here applies the principles of Emersonian Self-Reliance with a literalness and moral intensity that went beyond what even his mentor could then accept. Thoreau's actual experience of one-night incarceration, also described here in bemusingly pastoral terms, led to nothing in the short run except local anecdote. In the long run, however, it bore out the truth of Emerson's adage that "an institution is the lengthened shadow of one man." "Civil Disobedience" supplied Mohandas Gandhi with the name and a good deal of the rationale for his nonviolent resistance movement against the British raj in India; and the essay also helped inspire Martin Luther King's civil rights campaign in the 1950s and 1960s.

SOURCE: "Resistance to Civil Government," *Aesthetic Papers*, ed. Elizabeth Palmer Peabody. Boston: The Editor; New York: Putnam, 1849.

I HEARTILY accept the motto,—"That government is best which governs least;" and I should like to see it acted up to more rapidly and systematically. Carried out, it finally amounts to this, which also I believe,—"That government is best which governs not at all;" and when men are prepared for it, that will be the kind of government which they will have. Government is at best but an expedient; but most governments are usually, and all governments are sometimes, inexpedient. The objections which have been brought against a standing army, and they are many and weighty, and deserve to prevail, may also at last be brought against a standing government. The standing army is only an arm of the standing government. The government itself, which is only the mode which the people have chosen to execute their will, is equally liable to be abused and perverted before the people can act through it. Witness the present Mexican war, the work of comparatively a few individuals using the standing government as their tool; for, in the outset, the people would not have consented to this measure.

This American government,—what is it but a tradition, though a recent one, endeavoring to transmit itself unimpaired to posterity, but each instant losing some of its integrity? It has not the vitality and force of a single living man; for a single man can bend it to his will. It is a sort of wooden gun to the people themselves; and, if ever they should use it in earnest as a real one against each other, it will surely split. But it is not the less necessary for this; for the people must have some complicated machinery or other, and hear its din, to satisfy that idea of government which they have. Governments show thus how successfully men can be imposed on, even impose on themselves, for their own advantage. It is excellent, we must all allow; yet this government never of itself furthered any enterprise, but by the alacrity with which it got out of its way. *It* does not keep the country free. *It* does not settle the West. *It* does not educate. The character inherent in the American people has done all that has been accomplished; and it would have done somewhat more, if the government had not sometimes got in its way. For government is an expedient by which men would fain succeed in letting one another alone; and, as has been said, when it is most expedient, the governed are most let alone by it. Trade and commerce, if they were not made of India rubber, would never manage to bounce over the obstacles which legislators are continually putting in their way; and, if one were to judge these men wholly by the effects of their actions, and not partly by their intentions, they would deserve to be classed and punished with those mischievous persons who put obstructions on the railroads.

But, to speak practically and as a citizen, unlike those who call themselves no-government men, I ask for, not at once no government, but *at once* a better government. Let every man make known what kind of government would command his respect, and that will be one step toward obtaining it.

After all, the practical reason why, when the power is once in the hands of the people, a majority are permitted, and for a long period continue, to rule, is not because they are most likely to be in the right, nor because this seems fairest to the minority, but because they are physically the strongest. But a government in which the majority rule in all cases cannot be based on justice, even as far as men understand it. Can there not be a government in which majorities do not virtually decide right and wrong, but conscience?—in which majorities decide only those questions to which the rule of expediency is applicable? Must the citizen ever for a moment, or in the least degree, resign his conscience to the legislator? Why has every man a conscience, then? I think that we should be men first, and subjects afterward. It is not desirable to cultivate a respect for the law, so much as for the right. The only obligation which I have a right to assume, is to do at any time what I think right. It is truly enough said, that a corporation has no conscience; but a corporation of conscientious men is a corporation *with* a conscience. Law never made men a whit more just; and, by means of their respect for it, even the well-disposed are daily made the agents of injustice. A common and natural result of an undue respect for law is, that you may see a file of soldiers, colonel, captain, corporal, privates, powder-monkeys and all, marching in admirable order over hill and dale to the wars, against their wills, aye, against their common sense and consciences, which makes it very steep marching indeed, and produces a palpitation of the heart. They have no doubt that it is a damnable business in which they are concerned; they are all peaceably inclined. Now, what are they? Men at all? or small moveable forts and magazines, at the service of some unscrupulous man in power? Visit the Navy Yard, and behold a marine, such a man as an American government can make, or such as it can make a man with its black arts, a mere shadow and reminiscence of humanity, a man laid out alive and standing, and already, as one may say, buried under arms with funeral accompaniments, though it may be

> "Not a drum was heard, nor a funeral note,
>     As his corse to the ramparts we hurried;
> Not a soldier discharged his farewell shot
>     O'er the grave where our hero we buried."

The mass of men serve the State thus, not as men mainly, but as machines, with their bodies. They are the standing army, and the militia, jailers, constables, *posse comitatus*, &c. In most cases there is no free exercise whatever of the judgment or of the moral sense; but they put themselves on a level with wood and earth and stones; and wooden men can perhaps be manufactured that will serve the purpose as well. Such command no more respect than men of straw, or a lump of dirt. They have the same sort of worth only as horses and dogs. Yet such as these even are commonly esteemed good citizens. Others, as most legislators, politicians, lawyers, ministers, and office-holders, serve the State chiefly with their heads; and, as they rarely make any moral distinctions, they are as likely to serve the devil, without intending it, as God. A very few, as heroes, patriots, martyrs, reformers in the great sense, and *men,* serve the State with their consciences also, and so necessarily resist it for the most part; and they are commonly treated by it as enemies. A wise man will only be useful as a man, and will not submit to be "clay," and "stop a hole to keep the wind away," but leave that office to his dust at least:—

> "I am too high-born to be propertied,
>     To be a secondary at control,
>     Or useful serving-man and instrument
> To any sovereign state throughout the world."

He who gives himself entirely to his fellow-men appears to them useless and selfish; but he who gives himself partially to them is pronounced a benefactor and philanthropist.

How does it become a man to behave toward this American government to-day? I answer that he cannot without disgrace be associated with it. I cannot for an instant recognize that political organization as *my* government which is the *slave's* government also.

261 Secular Reform: Individual Transformation Vs. Systemic Social Change · 261

All men recognize the right of revolution; that is, the right to refuse allegiance to and to resist the government, when its tyranny or its inefficiency are great and unendurable. But almost all say that such is not the case now. But such was the case, they think, in the Revolution of '75. If one were to tell me that this was a bad government because it taxed certain foreign commodities brought to its ports, it is most probable that I should not make an ado about it, for I can do without them: all machines have their friction; and possibly this does enough good to counterbalance the evil. At any rate, it is a great evil to make a stir about it. But when the friction comes to have its machine, and oppression and robbery are organized, I say, let us not have such a machine any longer. In other words, when a sixth of the population of a nation which has undertaken to be the refuge of liberty are slaves, and a whole country is unjustly overrun and conquered by a foreign army, and subjected to military law, I think that it is not too soon for honest men to rebel and revolutionize. What makes this duty the more urgent is the fact, that the country so overrun is not our own, but ours is the invading army.

Paley, a common authority with many on moral questions, in his chapter on the "Duty of Submission to Civil Government," resolves all civil obligation into expediency; and he proceeds to say, "that so long as the interest of the whole society requires it, that is, so long as the established government cannot be resisted or changed without public inconveniency, it is the will of God that the established government be obeyed, and no longer."—"This principle being admitted, the justice of every particular case of resistance is reduced to a computation of the quantity of the danger and grievance on the one side, and of the probability and expense of redressing it on the other." Of this, he says, every man shall judge for himself. But Paley appears never to have contemplated those cases to which the rule of expediency does not apply, in which a people, as well as an individual, must do justice, cost what it may. If I have unjustly wrested a plank from a drowning man, I must restore it to him though I drown myself. This, according to Paley, would be inconvenient. But he that would save his life, in such a case, shall lose it. This people must cease to hold slaves, and to make war on Mexico, though it cost them their existence as a people.

In their practice, nations agree with Paley; but does any one think that Massachusetts does exactly what is right at the present crisis?

"A drab of state, a cloth-o'-silver slut,
   To have her train borne up, and her soul trail in the dirt."

Practically speaking, the opponents to a reform in Massachusetts are
not a hundred thousand politicians at the South, but a hundred thousand merchants and farmers here, who are more interested in commerce and agriculture than they are in humanity, and are not prepared
to do justice to the slave and to Mexico, *cost what it may*. I quarrel not
with far-off foes, but with those who, near at home, co-operate with,
and do the bidding of those far away, and without whom the latter
would be harmless. We are accustomed to say, that the mass of men are
unprepared; but improvement is slow, because the few are not materi-
ally wiser or better than the many. It is not so important that many
should be as good as you, as that there be some absolute goodness
somewhere; for that will leaven the whole lump. There are thousands
who are *in opinion* opposed to slavery and to the war, who yet in effect
do nothing to put an end to them; who, esteeming themselves children
of Washington and Franklin, sit down with their hands in their pockets, and say that they know not what to do, and do nothing; who even
postpone the question of freedom to the question of free-trade, and
quietly read the prices-current along with the latest advices from
Mexico, after dinner, and, it may be, fall asleep over them both. What is
the price-current of an honest man and patriot today? They hesitate,
and they regret, and sometimes they petition; but they do nothing in
earnest and with effect. They will wait, well disposed, for others to
remedy the evil, that they may no longer have it to regret. At most,
they give only a cheap vote, and a feeble countenance and Godspeed,
to the right, as it goes by them. There are nine hundred and ninety-
nine patrons of virtue to one virtuous man; but it is easier to deal with
the real possessor of a thing than with the temporary guardian of it.

All voting is a sort of gaming, like chequers or backgammon, with a
slight moral tinge to it, a playing with right and wrong, with moral
questions; and betting naturally accompanies it. The character of the
voters is not staked. I cast my vote, perchance, as I think right; but I am
not vitally concerned that that right should prevail. I am willing to
leave it to the majority. Its obligation, therefore, never exceeds that of
expediency. Even voting *for the right* is *doing* nothing for it. It is only
expressing to men feebly your desire that it should prevail. A wise man
will not leave the right to the mercy of chance, nor wish it to prevail

through the power of the majority. There is but little virtue in the action of masses of men. When the majority shall at length vote for the abolition of slavery, it will be because they are indifferent to slavery, or because there is but little slavery left to be abolished by their vote. *They* will then be the only slaves. Only *his* vote can hasten the abolition of slavery who asserts his own freedom by his vote.

I hear of a convention to be held at Baltimore, or elsewhere, for the selection of a candidate for the Presidency, made up chiefly of editors, and men who are politicians by profession; but I think, what is it to any independent, intelligent, and respectable man what decision they may come to, shall we not have the advantage of his wisdom and honesty, nevertheless? Can we not count upon some independent votes? Are there not many individuals in the country who do not attend conventions? But no: I find that the respectable man, so called, has immediately drifted from his position, and despairs of his country, when his country has more reason to despair of him. He forthwith adopts one of the candidates thus selected as the only *available* one, thus proving that he is himself *available* for any purposes of the demagogue. His vote is of no more worth than that of any unprincipled foreigner or hireling native, who may have been bought. Oh for a man who is a *man*, and, as my neighbor says, has a bone in his back which you cannot pass your hand through! Our statistics are at fault: the population has been returned too large. How many *men* are there to a square thousand miles in this country? Hardly one. Does not America offer any inducement for men to settle here? The American has dwindled into an Odd Fellow,—one who may be known by the development of his organ of gregariousness, and a manifest lack of intellect and cheerful self-reliance; whose first and chief concern, on coming into the world, is to see that the alms-houses are in good repair; and, before yet he has lawfully donned the virile garb, to collect a fund for the support of the widows and orphans that may be; who, in short, ventures to live only by the aid of the mutual insurance company, which has promised to bury him decently.

It is not a man's duty, as a matter of course, to devote himself to the eradication of any, even the most enormous wrong; he may still properly have other concerns to engage him; but it is his duty, at least, to wash his hands of it, and, if he gives it no thought longer, not to give it practically his support. If I devote myself to other pursuits and contemplations, I must first see, at least, that I do not pursue them sitting upon another man's shoulders. I must get off him first, that he may pursue his contemplations too. See what gross inconsistency is tolerated. I have heard some of my townsmen say, "I should like to have them order me out to help put down an insurrection of the slaves, or to march to Mexico,—see if I would go;" and yet these very men have each, directly by their allegiance, and so indirectly, at least, by their money, furnished a substitute. The soldier is applauded who refuses to serve in an unjust war by those who do not refuse to sustain the unjust government which makes the war; is applauded by those whose own act and authority he disregards and sets at nought; as if the State were penitent to that degree that it hired one to scourge it while it sinned, but not to that degree that it left off sinning for a moment. Thus, under the name of order and civil government, we are all made at last to pay homage to and support our own meanness. After the first blush of sin, comes its indifference; and from immoral it becomes, as it were, *un*moral, and not quite unnecessary to that life which we have made.

The broadest and most prevalent error requires the most disinterested virtue to sustain it. The slight reproach to which the virtue of patriotism is commonly liable, the noble are most likely to incur. Those who, while they disapprove of the character and measures of a government, yield to it their allegiance and support, are undoubtedly its most conscientious supporters, and so frequently the most serious obstacles to reform. Some are petitioning the State to dissolve the Union, to disregard the requisitions of the President. Why do they not dissolve it themselves,—the union between themselves and the State,— and refuse to pay their quota into its treasury? Do not they stand in the same relation to the State, that the State does to the Union? And have not the same reasons prevented the State from resisting the Union, which have prevented them from resisting the State?

How can a man be satisfied to entertain an opinion merely, and enjoy *it?* Is there any enjoyment in it, if his opinion is that he is aggrieved? If you are cheated out of a single dollar by your neighbor, you do not rest satisfied with knowing that you are cheated, or with saying that you are cheated, or even with petitioning him to pay you your due; but you take effectual steps at once to obtain the full amount, and see that you are never cheated again. Action from principle,—the perception and the performance of right,—changes things and relations; it is essentially revolutionary, and does not consist wholly with any thing which was. It not only divides states and churches, it divides families; aye, it divides the *individual,* separating the diabolical in him from the divine.

Unjust laws exist: shall we be content to obey them, or shall we endeavor to amend them, and obey them until we have succeeded, or shall we transgress them at once? Men generally, under such a government as this, think that they ought to wait until they have persuaded the majority to alter them. They think that, if they should resist, the remedy would be worse than the evil. But it is the fault of the government itself that the remedy *is* worse than the evil. *It* makes it worse. Why is it not more apt to anticipate and provide for reform? Why does it not cherish its wise minority? Why does it cry and resist before it is hurt? Why does it not encourage its citizens to be on the alert to point out its faults, and *do* better than it would have them? Why does it always crucify Christ, and excommunicate Copernicus and Luther, and pronounce Washington and Franklin rebels?

One would think, that a deliberate and practical denial of its authority was the only offence never contemplated by government; else, why has it not assigned its definite, its suitable and proportionate penalty? If a man who has no property refuses but once to earn nine shillings for the State, he is put in prison for a period unlimited by any law that I know, and determined only by the discretion of those who placed him there; but if he should steal ninety times nine shillings from the State, he is soon permitted to go at large again.

If the injustice is part of the necessary friction of the machine of government, let it go, let it go: perchance it will wear smooth,—certainly the machine will wear out. If the injustice has a spring, or a pulley, or a rope, or a crank, exclusively for itself, then perhaps you may consider whether the remedy will not be worse than the evil; but if it is of such a nature that it requires you to be the agent of injustice to another, then, I say, break the law. Let your life be a counter friction to stop the machine. What I have to do is to see, at any rate, that I do not lend myself to the wrong which I condemn.

As for adopting the ways which the State has provided for remedying the evil, I know not of such ways. They take too much time, and a man's life will be gone. I have other affairs to attend to. I came into this world, not chiefly to make this a good place to live in, but to live in it, be it good or bad. A man has not every thing to do, but something; and because he cannot do *every thing,* it is not necessary that he should do *something* wrong. It is not my business to be petitioning the governor or the legislature any more than it is theirs to petition me; and, if they should not hear my petition, what should I do then? But in this case the State has provided no way: its very Constitution is the evil. This may seem to be harsh and stubborn and unconciliatory; but it is to treat with the utmost kindness and consideration the only spirit that can appreciate or deserves it. So is all change for the better, like birth and death which convulse the body.

I do not hesitate to say, that those who call themselves abolitionists should at once effectually withdraw their support, both in person and property, from the government of Massachusetts, and not wait till they constitute a majority of one, before they suffer the right to prevail through them. I think that it is enough if they have God on their side, without waiting for that other one. Moreover, any man more right than his neighbors, constitutes a majority of one already.

I meet this American government, or its representative the State government, directly, and face to face, once a year, no more, in the person of its tax-gatherer; this is the only mode in which a man situated as I am necessarily meets it; and it then says distinctly, Recognize me; and the simplest, the most effectual, and, in the present posture of affairs, the indispensablest mode of treating with it on this head, of expressing your little satisfaction with and love for it, is to deny it then. My civil neighbor, the tax-gatherer, is the very man I have to deal with,—for it is, after all, with men and not with parchment that I quarrel,—and he has voluntarily chosen to be an agent of the government. How shall he ever know well what he is and does as an officer of the government, or as a man, until he is obliged to consider whether he shall treat me, his neighbor, for whom he has respect, as a neighbor and well-disposed man, or as a maniac and disturber of the peace, and see if he can get over this obstruction to his neighborliness without a ruder and more impetuous thought or speech corresponding with his action? I know this well, that if one thousand, if one hundred, if ten men whom I could name,—if ten *honest* men only,—aye, if *one* HONEST man, in this State of Massachusetts, *ceasing to hold slaves,* were actually to withdraw from this copartnership, and be locked up in the county jail therefor, it would be the abolition of slavery in America. For it matters not how small the beginning may seem to be: what is once well done is done for ever. But we love better to talk about it: that we say is our mission. Reform keeps many scores of newspapers in its service, but not one man. If my esteemed neighbor, the State's ambassador, who will devote his days to the settlement of the question of human rights in the Council Chamber, instead of being threatened with the prisons of Carolina, were to sit down the prisoner of Massachusetts, that State which is so anxious to foist the sin of slavery upon her sister,—though at present she can discover only an act of inhospitality to be the ground of a quarrel with her,—the Legislature would not wholly waive the subject the following winter.

Under a government which imprisons any unjustly, the true place for a just man is also a prison. The proper place to-day, the only place which Massachusetts has provided for her freer and less desponding spirits, is in her prisons, to be put out and locked out of the State by her own act, as they have already put themselves out by their principles. It is there that the fugitive slave, and the Mexican prisoner on parole, and the Indian come to plead the wrongs of his race, should find them; on that separate, but more free and honorable ground, where the State places those who are not *with* her but *against* her,—the only house in a slave-state in which a free man can abide with honor. If any think that their influence would be lost there, and their voices no longer afflict the ear of the State, that they would not be as an enemy within its walls, they do not know by how much truth is stronger than error, nor how much more eloquently and effectively he can combat injustice who has experienced a little in his own person. Cast your whole vote, not a strip of paper merely, but your whole influence. A minority is powerless while it conforms to the majority; it is not even a minority then; but it is irresistible when it clogs by its whole weight. If the alternative is to keep all just men in prison, or give up war and slavery, the State will not hesitate which to choose. If a thousand men were not to pay their tax-bills this year, that would not be a violent and bloody measure, as it would be to pay them, and enable the State to commit violence and shed innocent blood. This is, in fact, the definition of a peaceable revolution, if any such is possible. If the tax-gatherer, or any other public officer, asks me, as one has done, "But what shall I do?" my answer is, "If you really wish to do any thing, resign your office." When the subject has refused allegiance, and the officer has resigned his office, then the revolution is accomplished. But even suppose blood should flow. Is there not a sort of blood shed when the conscience is wounded? Through this wound a man's real manhood and immortality flow out, and he bleeds to an everlasting death. I see this blood flowing now.

I have contemplated the imprisonment of the offender, rather than the seizure of his goods,—though both will serve the same purpose,—

because they who assert the purest right, and consequently are most dangerous to a corrupt State, commonly have not spent much time in accumulating property. To such the State renders comparatively small service, and a slight tax is wont to appear exorbitant, particularly if they are obliged to earn it by special labor with their hands. If there were one who lived wholly without the use of money, the State itself would hesitate to demand it of him. But the rich man—not to make any invidious comparison—is always sold to the institution which makes him rich. Absolutely speaking, the more money, the less virtue; for money comes between a man and his objects, and obtains them for him; and it was certainly no great virtue to obtain it. It puts to rest many questions which he would otherwise be taxed to answer; while the only new question which it puts is the hard but superfluous one, how to spend it. Thus his moral ground is taken from under his feet. The opportunities of living are diminished in proportion as what are called the "means" are increased. The best thing a man can do for his culture when he is rich is to endeavour to carry out those schemes which he entertained when he was poor. Christ answered the Herodians according to their condition. "Show me the tribute-money," said he;— and one took a penny out of his pocket;—If you use money which has the image of Cæsar on it, and which he has made current and valuable, that is, *if you are men of the State*, and gladly enjoy the advantages of Cæsar's government, then pay him back some of his own when he demands it; "Render therefore to Cæsar that which is Cæsar's, and to God those things which are God's,"—leaving them no wiser than before as to which was which; for they did not wish to know.

When I converse with the freest of my neighbors, I perceive that, whatever they may say about the magnitude and seriousness of the question, and their regard for the public tranquillity, the long and the short of the matter is, that they cannot spare the protection of the existing government, and they dread the consequences of disobedience to it to their property and families. For my own part, I should not like to think that I ever rely on the protection of the State. But, if I deny the authority of the State when it presents its tax-bill, it will soon take and waste all my property, and so harass me and my children without end. This is hard. This makes it impossible for a man to live honestly and at the same time comfortably in outward respects. It will not be worth the while to accumulate property; that would be sure to go again. You must hire or squat somewhere, and raise but a small crop, and eat that soon. You must live within yourself, and depend upon yourself, always tucked up and ready for a start, and not have many affairs. A man may grow rich in Turkey even, if he will be in all respects a good subject of the Turkish government. Confucius said,—"If a State is governed by the principles of reason, poverty and misery are subjects of shame; if a State is not governed by the principles of reason, riches and honors are the subjects of shame." No: until I want the protection of Massachusetts to be extended to me in some distant southern port, where my liberty is endangered, or until I am bent solely on building up an estate at home by peaceful enterprise, I can afford to refuse allegiance to Massachusetts, and her right to my property and life. It costs me less in every sense to incur the penalty of disobedience to the State, than it would to obey. I should feel as if I were worth less in that case.

Some years ago, the State met me in behalf of the church, and commanded me to pay a certain sum toward the support of a clergyman whose preaching my father attended, but never I myself. "Pay it," it said, "or be locked up in the jail." I declined to pay. But, unfortunately, another man saw fit to pay it. I did not see why the schoolmaster should be taxed to support the priest, and not the priest the schoolmaster; for I was not the State's schoolmaster, but I supported myself by voluntary subscription. I did not see why the lyceum should not present its tax-bill, and have the State to back its demand, as well as the church. However, at the request of the selectmen, I condescended to make some such statement as this in writing:—"Know all men by these presents, that I, Henry Thoreau, do not wish to be regarded as a member of any incorporated society which I have not joined." This I gave to the town-clerk; and he has it. The State, having thus learned that I did not wish to be regarded as a member of that church, has never made a like demand on me since; though it said that it must adhere to its original presumption that time. If I had known how to name them, I should then have signed off in detail from all the societies which I never signed on to; but I did not know where to find a complete list.

I have paid no poll-tax for six years. I was put into a jail once on this account, for one night; and, as I stood considering the walls of solid stone, two or three feet thick, the door of wood and iron, a foot thick, and the iron grating which strained the light, I could not help being struck with the foolishness of that institution which treated me as if I were mere flesh and blood and bones, to be locked up. I wondered that it should have concluded at length that this was the best use it could put me to, and had never thought to avail itself of my services in some

way. I saw that, if there was a wall of stone between me and my townsmen, there was a still more difficult one to climb or break through,
before they could get to be as free as I was. I did not for a moment feel
confined, and the walls seemed a great waste of stone and mortar. I felt
as if I alone of all my townsmen had paid my tax. They plainly did not
know how to treat me, but behaved like persons who are underbred. In
every threat and in every compliment there was a blunder; for they
thought that my chief desire was to stand the other side of that stone
wall. I could not but smile to see how industriously they locked the
door on my meditations, which followed them out again without let or
hinderance, and *they* were really all that was dangerous. As they could
not reach me, they had resolved to punish my body; just as boys, if they
cannot come at some person against whom they have a spite, will
abuse his dog. I saw that the State was half-witted, that it was timid as a
lone woman with her silver spoons, and that it did not know its friends
from its foes, and I lost all my remaining respect for it, and pitied it.

Thus the State never intentionally confronts a man's sense, intellectual or moral, but only his body, his senses. It is not armed with superior wit or honesty, but with superior physical strength. I was not born
to be forced. I will breathe after my own fashion. Let us see who is the
strongest. What force has a multitude? They only can force me who
obey a higher law than I. They force me to become like themselves. I
do not hear of *men* being *forced* to live this way or that by masses of men.
What sort of life were that to live? When I meet a government which
says to me, "Your money or your life," why should I be in haste to give
it my money? It may be in a great strait, and not know what to do: I
cannot help that. It must help itself; do as I do. It is not worth the while
to snivel about it. I am not responsible for the successful working of the
machinery of society. I am not the son of the engineer. I perceive that,
when an acorn and a chestnut fall side by side, the one does not remain
inert to make way for the other, but both obey their own laws, and
spring and grow and flourish as best they can, till one, perchance, overshadows and destroys the other. If a plant cannot live according to its
nature, it dies; and so a man.

The night in prison was novel and interesting enough. The prisoners in
their shirt-sleeves were enjoying a chat and the evening air in the door-
way, when I entered. But the jailer said, "Come, boys, it is time to lock up;"
and so they dispersed, and I heard the sound of their steps returning into
the hollow apartments. My room-mate was introduced to me by the jailer,

as "a first-rate fellow and a clever man." When the door was locked, he showed me where to hang my hat, and how he managed matters there. The rooms were whitewashed once a month; and this one, at least, was the whitest, most simply furnished, and probably the neatest apartment in the town. He naturally wanted to know where I came from, and what brought me there; and, when I had told him, I asked him in my turn how he came there, presuming him to be an honest man, of course; and, as the world goes, I believe he was. "Why," said he, "they accuse me of burning a barn; but I never did it." As near as I could discover, he had probably gone to bed in a barn when drunk, and smoked his pipe there; and so a barn was burnt. He had the reputation of being a clever man, had been there some three months waiting for his trial to come on, and would have to wait as much longer; but he was quite domesticated and contented, since he got his board for nothing, and thought that he was well treated.

He occupied one window, and I the other; and I saw, that, if one stayed there long, his principal business would be to look out the window. I had soon read all the tracts that were left there, and examined where former prisoners had broken out, and where a grate had been sawed off, and heard the history of the various occupants of that room; for I found that even here there was a history and a gossip which never circulated beyond the walls of the jail. Probably this is the only house in the town where verses are composed, which are afterward printed in a circular form, but not published. I was shown quite a long list of verses which were composed by some young men who had been detected in an attempt to escape, who avenged themselves by singing them.

I pumped my fellow-prisoner as dry as I could, for fear I should never see him again; but at length he showed me which was my bed, and left me to blow out the lamp.

It was like travelling into a far country, such as I had never expected to behold, to lie there for one night. It seemed to me that I never had heard the town-clock strike before, nor the evening sounds of the village; for we slept with the windows open, which were inside the grating. It was to see my native village in the light of the middle ages, and our Concord was turned into a Rhine stream, and visions of knights and castles passed before me. They were the voices of old burghers that I heard in the streets. I was an involuntary spectator and auditor of whatever was done and said in the kitchen of the adjacent village-inn,—a wholly new and rare experience to me. It was a closer view of my native town. I was fairly inside of it. I never had seen its institutions before. This is one of its peculiar institutions; for it is a shire town. I began to comprehend what its inhabitants were about.

In the morning, our breakfasts were put through the hole in the door, in small oblong-square tin pans, made to fit, and holding a pint of chocolate, with brown bread, and an iron spoon. When they called for the vessels again, I was green enough to return what bread I had left; but my comrade seized it, and said that I should lay that up for lunch or dinner. Soon after, he was let out to work at haying in a neighboring field, whither he went every day, and would not be back till noon; so he bade me good-day, saying that he doubted if he should see me again.

When I came out of prison,—for some one interfered, and paid the tax,—I did not perceive that great changes had taken place on the common, such as he observed who went in a youth, and emerged a tottering and gray-headed man; and yet a change had to my eyes come over the scene,—the town, and State, and country,—greater than any that mere time could effect. I saw yet more distinctly the State in which I lived. I saw to what extent the people among whom I lived could be trusted as good neighbors and friends; that their friendship was for summer weather only; that they did not greatly purpose to do right; that they were a distinct race from me by their prejudices and superstitions, as the Chinamen and Malays are; that, in their sacrifices to humanity, they ran no risks, not even to their property; that, after all, they were not so noble but they treated the thief as he had treated them, and hoped, by a certain outward observance and a few prayers, and by walking in a particular straight though useless path from time to time, to save their souls. This may be to judge my neighbors harshly; for I believe that most of them are not aware that they have such an institution as the jail in their village.

It was formerly the custom in our village, when a poor debtor came out of jail, for his acquaintances to salute him, looking through their fingers, which were crossed to represent the grating of a jail window, "How do ye do?" My neighbors did not thus salute me, but first looked at me, and then at one another, as if I had returned from a long journey. I was put into jail as I was going to the shoemaker's to get a shoe which was mended. When I was let out the next morning, I proceeded to finish my errand, and, having put on my mended shoe, joined a huckleberry party, who were impatient to put themselves under my conduct; and in half an hour,—for the horse was soon tackled,—was in the midst of a huckleberry field, on one of our highest hills, two miles off; and then the State was nowhere to be seen.

This is the whole history of "My Prisons."

———

I have never declined paying the highway tax, because I am as desirous of being a good neighbor as I am of being a bad subject; and, as for supporting schools, I am doing my part to educate my fellow-countrymen now. It is for no particular item in the tax-bill that I refuse to pay it. I simply wish to refuse allegiance to the State, to withdraw and stand aloof from it effectually. I do not care to trace the course of my dollar, if I could, till it buys a man, or a musket to shoot one with,—the dollar is innocent,—but I am concerned to trace the effects of my allegiance. In fact, I quietly declare war with the State, after my fashion, though I will still make what use and get what advantage of her I can, as is usual in such cases.

If others pay the tax which is demanded of me, from a sympathy with the State, they do but what they have already done in their own case, or rather they abet injustice to a greater extent than the State requires. If they pay the tax from a mistaken interest in the individual taxed, to save his property or prevent his going to jail, it is because they have not considered wisely how far they let their private feelings interfere with the public good.

This, then, is my position at present. But one cannot be too much on his guard in such a case, lest his action be biassed by obstinacy, or an undue regard for the opinions of men. Let him see that he does only what belongs to himself and to the hour.

I think sometimes, Why, this people mean well; they are only ignorant; they would do better if they knew how: why give your neighbors this pain to treat you as they are not inclined to? But I think, again, this is no reason why I should do as they do, or permit others to suffer much greater pain of a different kind. Again, I sometimes say to myself, When many millions of men, without heat, without ill-will, without personal feeling of any kind, demand of you a few shillings only, without the possibility, such is their constitution, of retracting or altering their present demand, and without the possibility, on your side, of appeal to any other millions, why expose yourself to this overwhelming brute force? You do not resist cold and hunger, the winds and the waves, thus obstinately; you quietly submit to a thousand similar necessities. You do not put your head into the fire. But just in proportion as I regard this as not wholly a brute force, but partly a human force, and consider that I have relations to those millions as to so many millions of men, and not of mere brute or inanimate things, I see that appeal is possible, first and instantaneously, from them to the Maker of them, and, secondly, from them to themselves. But, if I put my head deliberately into the fire, there is no appeal to fire or to the Maker of fire, and I have only myself to blame. If I could convince myself that I have any right to be satisfied with men as they are, and to treat them accordingly, and not according, in some respects, to my requisitions and expectations of what they and I ought to be, then, like a good Mussulman and fatalist, I should endeavor to be satisfied with things as they are, and say it is the will of God. And, above all, there is this difference between resisting this and a purely brute or natural force, that I can resist this with some effect; but I cannot expect, like Orpheus, to change the nature of the rocks and trees and beasts.

I do not wish to quarrel with any man or nation. I do not wish to split hairs, to make fine distinctions, or set myself up as better than my neighbors. I seek rather, I may say, even an excuse for conforming to the laws of the land. I am but too ready to conform to them. Indeed I have reason to suspect myself on this head; and each year, as the tax-gatherer comes round, I find myself disposed to review the acts and position of the general and state governments, and the spirit of the people, to discover a pretext for conformity. I believe that the State will soon be able to take all my work of this sort out of my hands, and then I shall be no better a patriot than my fellow-countrymen. Seen from a lower point of view, the Constitution, with all its faults, is very good; the law and the courts are very respectable; even this State and this American government are, in many respects, very admirable and rare things, to be thankful for, such as a great many have described them; but seen from a point of view a little higher, they are what I have described them; seen from a higher still, and the highest, who shall say what they are, or that they are worth looking at or thinking of at all?

However, the government does not concern me much, and I shall bestow the fewest possible thoughts on it. It is not many moments that I live under a government, even in this world. If a man is thought-free, fancy-free, imagination-free, that which *is not* never for a long time appearing *to be* to him, unwise rulers or reformers cannot fatally interrupt him.

I know that most men think differently from myself; but those whose lives are by profession devoted to the study of these or kindred subjects, content me as little as any. Statesmen and legislators, standing so completely within the institution, never distinctly and nakedly behold it. They speak of moving society, but have no resting-place without it. They may be men of a certain experience and discrimination, and have no doubt invented ingenious and even useful systems, for which we sincerely thank them; but all their wit and usefulness lie within certain not very wide limits. They are wont to forget that the world is not governed by policy and expediency. Webster never goes behind government, and so cannot speak with authority about it. His words are wisdom to those legislators who contemplate no essential reform in the existing government; but for thinkers, and those who leg-islate for all time, he never once glances at the subject. I know of those whose serene and wise speculations on this theme would soon reveal the limits of his mind's range and hospitality. Yet, compared with the cheap professions of most reformers, and the still cheaper wisdom and eloquence of politicians in general, his are almost the only sensible and valuable words, and we thank Heaven for him. Comparatively, he is always strong, original, and, above all, practical. Still his quality is not wisdom, but prudence. The lawyer's truth is not Truth, but consis-tency, or a consistent expediency. Truth is always in harmony with herself, and is not concerned chiefly to reveal the justice that may con-sist with wrong-doing. He well deserves to be called, as he has been called, the Defender of the Constitution. There are really no blows to be given by him but defensive ones. He is not a leader, but a follower. His leaders are the men of '87. "I have never made an effort," he says, "and never propose to make an effort; I have never countenanced an effort, and never mean to countenance an effort, to disturb the ar-rangement as originally made, by which the various States came into the Union." Still thinking of the sanction which the Constitution gives to slavery, he says, "Because it was a part of the original compact,—let it stand." Notwithstanding his special acuteness and ability, he is unable to take a fact out of its merely political relations, and behold it as it lies absolutely to be disposed of by the intellect,—what, for instance, it behoves a man to do here in America to-day with regard to slavery, but ventures, or is driven, to make some such desperate answer as the following, while professing to speak absolutely, and as a private man,—from which what new and singular code of social duties might be inferred?—"The manner," says he, "in which the government of those States where slavery exists are to regulate it, is for their own con-sideration, under their responsibility to their constituents, to the gen-eral laws of propriety, humanity, and justice, and to God. Associations formed elsewhere, springing from a feeling of humanity, or any other cause, have nothing whatever to do with it. They have never received any encouragement from me, and they never will."

They who know of no purer sources of truth, who have traced up its stream no higher, stand, and wisely stand, by the Bible and the Constitution, and drink at it there with reverence and humility; but they who behold where it comes trickling into this lake or that pool, gird up their loins once more, and continue their pilgrimage toward its fountain-head.

No man with a genius for legislation has appeared in America. They are rare in the history of the world. There are orators, politicians, and eloquent men, by the thousand; but the speaker has not yet opened his mouth to speak, who is capable of settling the much-vexed questions of the day. We love eloquence for its own sake, and not for any truth which it may utter, or any heroism it may inspire. Our legislators have not yet learned the comparative value of free-trade and of freedom, of union, and of rectitude, to a nation. They have no genius or talent for comparatively humble questions of taxation and finance, commerce and manufactures and agriculture. If we were left solely to the wordy wit of legislators in Congress for our guidance, uncorrected by the seasonable experience and the effectual complaints of the people, America would not long retain her rank among the nations. For eighteen hundred years, though perchance I have no right to say it, the New Testament has been written; yet where is the legislator who has wisdom and practical talent enough to avail himself of the light which it sheds on the science of legislation?

The authority of government, even such as I am willing to submit to,—for I will cheerfully obey those who know and can do better than I, and in many things even those who neither know nor can do so well,—is still an impure one: to be strictly just, it must have the sanction and consent of the governed. It can have no pure right over my person and property but what I concede to it. The progress from an absolute to a limited monarchy, from a limited monarchy to a democracy, is a progress toward a true respect for the individual. Is a democracy, such as we know it, the last improvement possible in government? Is it not possible to take a step further towards recognizing and organizing the rights of man? There will never be a really free and enlightened State, until the State comes to recognize the individual as a higher and independent power, from which all its own power and authority are derived, and treats him accordingly. I please myself with imagining a State at last which can afford to be just to all men, and to treat the individual with respect as a neighbor; which even would not think it inconsistent with its own repose, if a few were to live aloof from it, not meddling with it, nor embraced by it, who fulfilled all the duties of neighbors and fellow-men. A State which bore this kind of fruit, and suffered it to drop off as fast as it ripened, would prepare the way for a still more perfect and glorious State, which also I have imagined, but not yet anywhere seen.

# B.
# EDUCATION

# ELIZABETH PEABODY AND AMOS BRONSON ALCOTT

## A CONTROVERSIAL EXPERIMENT IN PROGRESSIVE EDUCATION: PART ONE

### (1835-36)

Upon moving from Philadelphia to Boston in 1834, Bronson Alcott established the Temple School, an experimental school for young children run contrary to the rote education of the day, according to the vision later outlined in his *Doctrine and Discipline of Human Culture* (see Section II). Alcott taught in an inductive and Socratic rather than authoritarian way, seeking to draw out what he trusted was the divinity within his pupils—although, like Socrates, he also applied considerable direction through his way of framing questions and responses. When a pupil misbehaved, instead of administering corporal punishment, Alcott either simply excluded the child from the group for a cooling-off period, or else insisted that he himself be punished instead—a tactic that produced immediate and dramatic results. Elizabeth Peabody served as his assistant and also as "recorder" or transcriber of the class sessions. At first all went well. But soon Alcott's experimental pedagogy began to create uneasiness in his assistant and among the public at large. Disaster struck when Alcott not only pressed discussion imprudently far into the delicate subjects of religion and sex but published the class proceedings in an insouciantly provocative way (see next reading). The contrasts between the two editions of this first volume show editor Peabody's growing anxiety about some of Alcott's methods. The second edition's "Explanatory Preface" is more guarded than the first edition's concluding statement of Alcott's "Principles." Yet Peabody's record and analysis also show that Alcott's pedagogy got some positive results. A sense of energy and excitement among students and adults is clearly visible here.

SOURCES: (1–2) *Record of a School: Exemplifying the General Principles of Spiritual Culture*, 1st ed., ed. Elizabeth Palmer Peabody. Boston: James Munroe, 1835. (3) *Record of a School* . . . 2nd ed., ed. Elizabeth Palmer Peabody. Boston: Russell, Shattuck; New York: Leavitt, Lord, 1836.

## (1) A CONVERSATION ON OBEDIENCE AND CONSCIENCE

[Alcott questions "a little boy of five years old."] What makes us good? Conscience. What is conscience? It is the spirit speaking. Have you any conscience? Yes. How do you know? My mother told me so. When? Why once she was washing my face and hands, and I did not want to have her; and she told me that people would think my conscience was dirty, if my body is dirty; and so I asked her what my conscience was, and she said it was what told us right and wrong. Well, did you look in then, and find there was conscience? Yes. Such of you as think you were told of conscience, before you found it out, hold up your hands. Most of them did. How many of you think your conscience began to be, when you were told of it? Some did; and the little boy added, there was a spirit before. Well, said Mr. Alcott, was not this the way; there was a feeling before, and your mother made a thought of the feeling? Oh yes. Some, however, thought there was a time when there was neither a feeling or a thought. Can you conceive that the spirit lived before your bodies were made? Most of them said yes. About a half dozen[,] including the older ones, thought it was not possible.

Mr. Alcott then said, I observe that those who cannot conceive of spirit without body, existing in God before it comes out upon the earth, are the very ones who have required the most discipline and punishment, and have the least love of obedience. The rest are those who exercise most self-control, and seem to have the most conscience. You all have conscience? Yes. How did you get it? No one knew. At last a boy of seven . . . said, God gives us our conscience. When? Why, when we have learned right and wrong, God sends us conscience to make us right. So I think, said the oldest boy in school. Is it born out of the soul, said Mr. Alcott, or does God add it to the soul? He adds it. Is it something new? Yes. Do the rest think so? No one agreed. And the oldest boy said, it is in the soul but it does not act, till there is knowledge. Does it ever act,

then, fully? True; there is much in the spirit that can never be represented in thought probably, nor acted out, at least on earth. . . .

Who was the very best man in the world? Lafayette. Was he the very
best? Oh no, it was Jesus Christ; I am surprised I could forget that! How
many of you think, said Mr. Alcott, that you can be as good as Jesus
Christ, at least in another world? Several held up their hands. Do any
of you feel in despair, as if you could never be what you want to be?
Several held up their hands. One said he was in despair of doing what
he wanted to do with his mind. What do you want to do with it? He
could not explain. Several said they wanted to be good. One said he
would go through a fire for it. Another said he wanted to have a strong
mind. Strong thoughts or feelings? Strong thoughts. Another wanted to
be good, and to do good. Yes, said Mr. Alcott, part of being good is
doing good. I cannot conceive of being good without the goodness
shaping itself out in actions. Several wanted to have self-knowledge.
One wanted self-control. Another wanted to be generous. Such of you,
said Mr. Alcott, as think you came into the world to do all these things
you have spoken of, hold up your hands. All held up their hands. Do
you know recess-time has passed, half an hour? No, said all, with great
surprise, looking at the clock. . . .

## (2) FROM PEABODY'S CONCLUDING SUMMATION OF ALCOTT'S "GENERAL PRINCIPLES"

The lessons on self-analysis . . . are not merely of a fine moral influence, in showing the grounds of self-estimation, and of righteous judgment of others, but in laying a foundation of accurate knowledge of
language in its most spiritual vein. It has been seen how the life of
Christ is used as the standard in self-analysis; but Mr. Alcott has arranged the Gospels of this Life, in such a way as to illustrate the whole
Career of Spirit on earth; and this he intends now to go upon, and read,
with conversations in place of the lessons on self-analysis.

Biography is the right study for the young. But there is very little
biography written, which gives an insight into the life of the mind, and
especially into its formation. It is only occasionally, that we find a
philosopher who can read other men's experience; and to whom the
incidents of a life are transparent. . . . Autobiography will however increase, as men grow enlightened enough by the revival of the spiritual

philosophy, to look upon themselves as objects, without egotism, and to consider the facts of a soul's development, as the best gift which philanthropy can contribute to the cause of general improvement.

To supply the want of biography, Mr. Alcott relies a great deal upon journal writing, which is autobiography, while it hardly seems so to the writer. . . . He knows he is also assisting them in the art of composition, in a way that the rules of Rhetoric could never do. Every one knows that a technical memory of words, and of rules of composition, gives very little command of language; while a rich consciousness, a quick imagination and force of feeling, seem to unlock the treasury; and even so vulgar a passion as anger, produces eloquence, and quickens the perception to the slightest innuendo.

Self-analysis, biography, and journal-writing, leading therefore, immediately, into the knowledge of language, are as truly the initiation of intellectual as of moral education.

### (3) FROM PEABODY'S "EXPLANATORY PREFACE" TO SECOND EDITION

The work now put to the press, for the second time, has, in several particulars, been misunderstood. And I am told that I must ascribe this to my own want of perspicacity,—especially in the last chapter, in which I undertook to sum up the general principles of Spiritual Culture, deduced from a view of the soul, that some persons say is unintelligible. On this account, I here attempt another explanation of the psychology, which is made the basis of Mr. Alcott's School, with the principles and methods, which are evolved from it; intending to alter that chapter considerably, although there is nothing in it, which I wish to take back, or by which I did not mean something important.

To contemplate Spirit in the Infinite Being, has ever been acknowledged to be the only ground of true Religion. To contemplate Spirit in External nature, is universally allowed to be the only true Science. To contemplate Spirit in ourselves, and in our fellow men, is obviously the only means of understanding social duty, and quickening within ourselves a wise Humanity.—In general terms,—Contemplation of Spirit is the first principle of Human Culture; the foundation of Self-education.

This principle, Mr. Alcott begins with applying to the education of the youngest children. Considering early education as a leading of the young mind to self-education, he would have it proceed on the same principles. And few will disagree with him, in drawing this inference from the premises.

But it is not pretended, that it is peculiar to the system of education, developed in the following pages, to aim at the contemplation of Spirit, at least in theory. But perhaps it will be admitted that Mr. Alcott is somewhat peculiar in the faith which he puts in this principle, in his fearless and persevering application of it; and especially, in his not setting the child to look for Spirit, *first,* in the vast and varied field of external nature; as seems to be the sole aim of common education. For, in common education as is well known, the attention is primarily and principally directed to the part of language which consists of the names of outward things; as well as to books which scientifically class and explain them; or, which narrate events in a matter-of-fact manner.

One would think that there has been proof enough, that this common plan is a bad one, in the universally acknowledged difficulty, of making children study those things to which they are first put, without artificial stimulus;—also, in the absolute determination, with which so many fine minds turn aside, from word-knowledge and dry science, to play and fun, and to whatever interests the imagination or heart;—and, finally, in the very small amount of acquisition, which after all the pains taken, is generally laid up, from school days. Besides, is it not *a priori* absurd? Is not external nature altogether too vast a field for the eye of childhood to command? And is it not impossible for the mind to discover the Spirit in unity, unless the field is, as it were, commanded? The result of the attempt, has generally been that no spiritual culture has taken place at school. In most cases, the attention has been bewildered, discouraged, or dissipated by a variety of objects and in the best cases, the mind has become onesided and narrow, by being confined to some particular department. Naturalists are generally full of oddities.

Instead, therefore, of making it his aim to make children investigate External nature, after Spirit, Mr. Alcott leads them in the first place, to the contemplation of Spirit as it unveils itself within themselves. He thinks there is no intrinsic difficulty in doing this, inasmuch as a child can as easily perceive and name pleasure, pain, love, anger, hate and any other exercises of soul, to which himself is subjected, as he can see the objects before his eyes, and thus a living knowledge of that part of language, which expresses intellectual and moral ideas, and involves the study of his own consciousness of feelings and moral law, may be gained, External nature being only made use of, as imagery, to express the inward life which he experiences. Connected with this self contemplation, and constantly checking any narrowing effect of egotism, or self complacency, which it may be supposed to engender, is the contemplation of God, that can so easily be associated with it. For as the word finite gives meaning to the word infinite, so the finite virtue always calls up in the mind, an Idea which is henceforth named, and becomes an attribute to the Eternal Spirit. Thus a child, having felt what a just action is, either in himself or another, henceforth has an Idea of Justice, which is pure and perfect, in the same ratio, as he is unsophisticated; and is more and more comprehensive of particular applications, as his Reason unfolds. How severe and pure it often is, in a child, thousands have felt!

So when a cause is named,—the First Cause becomes the immediate object of inquiry. Who taught the hen to lay its eggs, said a little boy to his mother. The hen's mother, was the reply. Who taught the hen's mother? That mother had a mother. But who taught the first hen that ever laid an egg in the world?—he exclaimed impatiently. This child had never heard of a God. What mother or nurse, will not recognize that this is the way children talk? It is proverbial, that children ask questions so deep, that they cannot be answered. The perception of the finite, seems with them, to be followed immediately, by a plunge into the infinite. A wise observer will see this, even through the broken language of infancy, and often through its voiceless silence. And a deep reasoner on such facts, will see, that a plan of education, founded on the idea of studying Spirit in their own consciousness, and in God,—is one that will meet children just where they are,—much more than will the common plan of pursuing the laws of nature, as exhibited in movements of the external world.

But some say, that the philosophy of the Spirit is a disputed philosophy;—that the questions,—what are its earliest manifestations upon earth? and what are the means and laws of its growth?—are unsettled; and therefore it is not a subject for dogmatic teaching.

Mr. Alcott replies to this objection, that his teaching is not dogmatic; that nothing more is assumed by him, than that Spirit exists, bearing a relation to the body in which it is manifested, analogous to the relation which God bears to the external creation. And it is only those persons who are spiritualists, so far as to admit this, whom he expects to place children under his care.

At this point, his dogmatic teaching ends; and here he takes up the Socratic mode. He begins with asking questions upon the meanings of the words, which the children use in speaking, and which they find in their spelling lessons, requiring illustrations of them, in sentences composed or remembered. This involves the study of Spirit. He one day began with the youngest of thirty scholars, to ask illustrations of the word brute; and there were but three literal answers. A brute, was a man who killed another; a drunken man; a man who beat his wife; a man without any love; but it was always a man. In one instance, it was a boy beating a dog. Which is the brute, said Mr. Alcott, the boy or the dog? The boy; said the little girl, with the gravest face. This case indicates a general tendency of childhood, and is an opening therefore, for speaking of the outward as the sign of the inward, and for making all the reading and spelling lessons, exercises for defining and illustrating words.—The lessons on language, given in the Record, have generally been admitted to be most valuable. Most persons seem to be struck with the advantages, necessarily to be derived from the habit of inquiring into the history of words from their material origin, and throughout the spiritual applications of them, which the Imagination makes.

It is true, that one person, in leading such an exercise, may sometimes give a cast to the whole inquiry, through the influence of his own idiosyncracies and favorite doctrines; and Mr. Alcott's definitions may not be defensible in every instance. I am not myself prepared to say, that I entirely trust his associations. But he is so successful, in arousing the activity of the children's own minds, and he gives such free scope to their associations, that his personal peculiarities are likely to have much less influence than those of most instructors. Not by any means, so much objection could be made to his school, on this account, as can be made to Johnson's Dictionary; for the manner in which the words are studied and talked about in school, is such, that the children must be perpetually reminded, that nothing connected with spiritual subjects can be finally settled into any irreversible formula of doctrine, by finite and unperfected minds;—excepting, perhaps the two moral laws, on which hang the law and the prophets.

———

But some of his methods of discipline have been questioned. Before I had had an opportunity of observing their operation with my own eyes, I was very much inclined to question some of them myself; and perhaps it will be the best means of doing both him and myself justice, to relate my own views upon this subject, and the modifications they have undergone, since I have been a spectator of his School.

I will begin with saying, that I have no doubt at all, that as far as regards this particular school, the methods have been in every respect salutary, and the best possible for the members of it. General intelligence, order, self-control, and goodwill, have been produced to a degree that is marvellous to see; especially, when we consider that his scholars' ages range from three years to twelve, and none are older, and most of them only eight or nine years old. I can indeed conceive of something quite equal, if not superior, in moral beauty, that may be gained on a different plan, supposing the school is composed of older scholars; and the education is a more private one, from the beginning. I do not know, however, but that my differing methods are applicable, more especially and exclusively, to girls.

The point from which I diverge from Mr. Alcott, in theory, is this: I think that a private conscience in the young will naturally be the highest. Mr. Alcott thinks a common conscience is to be cultivated in a school, and that this will be higher in all, than any one conscience would be, if it were private.

Pursuing my own idea in my own school, my method has, in theory, been this. I have begun with every individual, by taking it for granted, in the first place, that there is a predominating sense of duty. This is not artificial on my part; for the germ of the principle of duty, lies in every mind, I know; and generally, it is accompanied by a wish, at least, to follow duty. With this I would sympathise, and let my sympathy be felt, by showing my scholars that I can find the wish out, even when enveloped in many shadows. All derelictions from duty, I would meet with surprise, as accidental mistakes or indisputable misfortunes, according as the fact might be, and offer my advice, endeavoring to win a confidential exposure of the individual's own moral condition, as it appears to themselves, in order that I might wisely and tenderly give suitable advice. Thus would I establish a separate understanding with each particular scholar, and act the part of a religious friend, with each; while in general assembly, no reference should be made to any moral wrong-doing of any one; but it be courteously and charitably taken for granted, that all mean to act conscientiously and religiously. . . .

———

. . . I am frequently asked,—will children ever be willing to study from books, who have been educated by Mr. Alcott? I have always answered to this question, and I will here repeat it, they will study from books more intelligently, thoroughly and profoundly, just in proportion as they imbibe the spirit of his instructions; for they will have an object whenever they open a book, and the beautiful things, Mr. Alcott constantly reads to them, have a tendency to make them feel what treasures are locked up in books.—Yet they may not be bookworms. They learn that there are other sources of knowledge, and especially, that thought is the chief source of wisdom. There is much illusion concerning children's reading; the book-devouring, which is frequently seen, nowadays, in children, is of no advantage to them. There is a great deal, in the spirit of that maxim of Aquinas, "Read one book to be learned." Mr. Alcott's scholars may show less interest, than some other children, in the miserable juvenile literature, which cheats so many poor little things, into the idea that they know the sciences, history, biography, and the creations of the imagination, and if it be so, it is a blessing to their minds. But many of the parents of the children, have told me, that they read over and over again, at home, the books of classical literature, which he reads to them in school. And what can be finer than this effect?

# Amos Bronson Alcott and Elizabeth Peabody

## A Controversial Experiment in Progressive Education: Part Two

### (1836-37)

Alcott himself edited this second record of class proceedings: conversations about the life and teachings of Jesus, based on the four Christian gospels. Peabody tried but was unable to convince Alcott to delete certain passages she knew would be objectionable, such as a conversation about the nature of conception. Alcott "complied" by striking them from the text and then haplessly putting them in notes marked "restored by the editor" that guaranteed they would not be missed. A furor ensued, and so many parents withdrew their children that the school had to be closed. Even if Alcott had followed Peabody's advice, however, he would probably still have run into trouble simply by having encroached on subjects that ministers would have considered rightfully theirs, and all the more so given that he prefaced this book of conversations with not one but two disquisitions (including *Doctrine and Discipline*) that insistently hammered home the point that the mission of "the true Teacher, like Jesus" was to "awaken the Godlike" in his pupils. On the other hand, the conversational records themselves suggest that Alcott earnestly sought to keep the discussion of delicate subjects on the highest possible plane of conversation and that the children in the class continued to be deeply engaged by Alcott's method, though they were also sometimes perplexed, cornered, and resistant. From a twenty-first-century standpoint, the specific offenses here look tepid indeed, although the possibility of community outrage over schoolteachers meddling with the subjects of sex and religion continues to be as great as ever. Of the two selections below, the first is an excerpt from one of the most controversial conversations, having to do with the Gospel accounts of Jesus' conception. The third, on conscience, exemplifies Alcott's strong, continuing concern with the subject of moral education.

SOURCE: *Conversations with Children on the Gospels,* conducted and edited by A. Bronson Alcott, 2 vols. Boston: James Munroe, 1836–37. In items (1) and (2) below, the "restored" passages are bracketed with { } marks.

## (1) FROM CONVERSATION VII: INCARNATION OF SPIRIT./GESTATION.

MR. ALCOTT.  What does love make?

LUCIA.  Obedience.

GEORGE K.  Happiness.

FRANK.  Holiness.

MR. ALCOTT.  Does it not make something to love?
{If you want love, what must you do?

CHARLES.  You must begin and love.

MR. ALCOTT.  Love begets love, and is not a baby love made flesh and shaped to the eyes? Love forms babies. Could bad passions make the soul of a baby?

CHARLES.  Bad people have children.

MR. ALCOTT.  But would not the children be better if their parents were better?

CHARLES.  Yes; after they were born and could follow their example.

GEORGE K.  I think that the baby's goodness has something to do with the goodness of the father and mother, and their badness makes its badness.

SAMUEL R.  I don't think there are any bad babies.

MR. ALCOTT.  No bad spirits; but if the spirits are surrounded with bodies diseased, do you think they have as good chance to be immediately good?

CHARLES.  Oh no; I think the spirit will not have near so good a chance if it has a bad body.

MR. ALCOTT.  Suppose you want to have a beautiful flower; you have the seed and you want to plant it; do you think nothing of the soil in which it is to grow? do you not fill your flower pot with the finest, freshest soil, and put it in the sun-shine?

CHARLES.   Yes; and water it and tend it, and watch over it very carefully.

MR. ALCOTT.   And do you not think it is equally important in what soil a soul is planted?

SEVERAL.   Yes.

MR. ALCOTT.   The parents have much to do in regard to the body of a child. God helps, as he does about the rose seed. The Body is the Soil of the Soul.}

{MR. ALCOTT.   The heart, when thus full of life and joy, is said to be quickened. Mothers feel this when they know children are to be given them. The angel of love first tells a mother that a child is coming. Sometime after she has other signs. "Blessed is she that believed, for there shall be a performance to her of those things told by the Lord." What does that mean?

*No answer.*

Resolution and faith, lead to success. Faith brings out what it planted in the spirit into the external world.}

## (2) FROM CONVERSATION XLVII: CONSCIENCE RECONSIDERED

MR. ALCOTT.   Is there no internal evidence of the truth or falsehood of any thing?

CHARLES.   Yes; Reason.

MR. ALCOTT.   Is Reason unerring?

GEORGE K.   Conscience.

MR. ALCOTT.   How many think it is Conscience that testifies to the truth?

*All held up hands.*

RECORDER.   Is there no such thing as a morbid or mistaken conscience?

MR. ALCOTT.   A little while ago I heard two persons discussing the subject; one said Conscience never erred; but that Reason mistook its decisions; the other that Conscience erred. What is your opinion—is it your conscience that errs, or your other faculties?

*Most said Conscience never erred.*

CHARLES. I know your opinion; for you often tell us that Conscience should be obeyed.

MR. ALCOTT. Yes; I hope that I have always told you to obey Conscience. Do you think that Jesus' Conscience always spoke, and that his Reason always understood it; and that he always obeyed it?

*All held up hands.*

How is it that some people do not hear the Conscience?

CHARLES. Because they leave off obeying it, so that they cannot understand it. Intemperance dims the perception of Conscience.

MR. ALCOTT. Tell some instance.

GEORGE K. Conscience does not speak to me when I am doing a thing, but afterwards.

MR. ALCOTT. Does it not speak, or do you not hear? Do you suppose you could hear it before, or when you were doing it, if you listened?

GEORGE K. Yes.

EMMA. Mr. Alcott, I very often do wrong things; but I always hear my conscience; it speaks low even at first, and while I am doing wrong.

MR. ALCOTT. Those boys, who hear the voice of Conscience sometimes speaking loud and of punishment, may rise.

*Many rose.*

Why does it speak loud?

SUSAN. Because it wants to keep us from doing wrong.

GEORGE K. When you first begin to do wrong, it begins to speak low; then it becomes loud; and at last it gets tired, and the voice dies away.

MR. ALCOTT. What makes the voice die away?

CHARLES. Because you get deafened.

MR. ALCOTT. There is a friend at a distance, whose lips are moving, and I hear him speak low words of warning; I approach him and he grows louder, clearer, and more distinct. Again I see him speak to me, and I turn away from him. He raises his voice to make me hear; but I walk away, and away, till at last his loudest voice cannot be heard. Is Conscience your friend?

CHARLES. Yes, it is our friend, though we are sometimes its foe.

MR. ALCOTT. Have you all heard the voice of conscience?

CHARLES. I might as well pretend not to hear a cannon.

# C.

## FEMINISM

# Elizabeth Peabody (?)

## A Margaret Fuller Conversation on Gender
### (1840)

Fuller, who briefly assisted Alcott in his Temple School venture, became an even more powerful teacher in her own right. Schoolteaching never appealed to her; she did it in the later 1830s in order to make ends meet while working on her writing and the study and translation of Goethe and other works of German literature. Much more successful and personally fulfilling was her adaptation of Alcott's Socratic pedagogy in a series of conversations for adults, first for a circle of (already well-educated) Boston-area women (1839–44) and eventually also for mixed audiences. By all accounts, the former went especially well. At her best, Fuller was a compelling improviser, with a "singular gift of speech," her friend and fellow Transcendentalist James Freeman Clarke recalled. "Conversation is my natural element," she agreed. "I need to be called out, and never think alone, without imagining some companion." She herself feared that this was the sign of a "second-rate mind." Yet others reaped the benefit. "The companion was made a thinker," as Emerson put it, "and went away quite other than he came." This gift, combined with the power to make even shy people open up, made her an exceptionally magnetic presence as a discussion leader. Here is one example, from a session probably originally recorded by Peabody, though the handwriting is another's.

SOURCE: "Margaret Fuller's Boston Conversations," ed. Nancy Simmons, *Studies in the American Renaissance 1994*, 215–16.

Miss Fuller's 17<sup>th</sup> conversation began with reading the articles upon the intellectual differences between men & women.— The first made the difference to consist in the fineness & delicacy of organization—the greater openness to impressions—&c. Margaret remarked that this made no essential difference—it was only more or less. Ellen Hooper asked if the difference of organization were not essential—if it did not begin in the mind—& if this was not the author's idea? Margaret looked again & thought it was—but still said that she did not find that the author made any quality belong to the one mind that did not belong to the other— Ellen asked if she thought that there was any quality in the masculine or in the feminine mind that did not belong to the other— Margaret said no—she did not—& therefore she wished to see if the others fully admitted this, because if all admitted it, it would follow of course that we should hear no more of repressing or subduing faculties because they were not fit for women to cultivate. She desired that whatever faculty we felt to be moving within us, that we should consider a principle of our perfection, & cultivate it accordingly.— & not excuse ourselves from any duty on the ground that we had not the intellectual powers for it; that it was not for women to do, *on an intellectual ground*— Some farther remarks were made on the point of the want of objectiveness of woman, as the cause of her not giving herself to the fine arts. It was also attributed to her want of isolation. The physical inconveniences of sculpture, architecture & even of painting were adverted to— But why not music & poetry? Miss Fuller said it had troubled her to think there was no great musical composer among women. It is true that at the period of life when men gave themselves to their pursuit most women became mothers—but there were some women who never married. I suggested that these too often spent the rest of their lives in mourning over this fact—& society spoke so uniformly of woman as more respectable for being married— that it was long before she entirely despaired. This caused some lively talk all round—& Margaret averred that there came a time however when every one *must give up*. I might have answered that then it was but too common for youth to be past—& the mind to have wedded itself to that mediocrity, which is too commonly the result of disappointed hope, especially if hopes are not the highest.—

The second piece that was read spoke of the subtlety of woman's mind. Miss Fuller summed it up after she had finished it, with the words— Woman more pervasive— Man more prominent.— While speaking of this piece the question came up whether Brutus' great action could have been performed by a woman. It was decided that if there were no doubt about the duty in Brutus' case there could be none about the duty being obligatory on a woman who had the same general office; else the moral nature could not be the same in man & woman. A great deal of talk arose here—and Margaret repelled the sentimentalism that took away woman's moral power of performing stern duty. In answer to one thing she said that as soon as we began to calculate our condition & to make allowances for it, we sank into the depths of sentimentalism. And again— Nothing I hate to hear of so much as *woman's lot*. I wish I never could hear that word *lot*. Something must be wrong where there is a universal lamentation. Youth ought not to be mourned—for it ought to be replaced with something better.— Miss F. then read her own piece as she said that otherwise she should say every thing that was in it, which would make it duller when it came— It was a constant contrast of man & woman— Man had more genius—woman more taste— Man more determination of purpose— woman more delicacy of rejection— Man more versatility—woman more power of adaptation. Maryann Jackson disputed the proposition that woman had less genius—*as woman*. Is it not so? said Miss Fuller— Is not man's intellect the fire caught from heaven—woman's the flower called forth from earth by the ray? Mrs. Park—Anna Shaw—Ellen Hooper seemed inclined also to doubt this proposition— Somewhere here Margaret defined *taste* the reasoning of beauty—& woman the interpreter of genius.

Then came Sally Gardner's piece of which Miss Fuller remarked that it was the aspiration which is prophecy, and all seemed charmed with it & spoke of its beautiful composition. Here it is.

"I recognise between man & woman a necessary difference of position, of which the results are accidental or arbitrary. It was founded, in the origin of society, on the difference of physical strength, when materials were scanty & the labour which procured & made them available was all-important. The first lyrics, doubtless among the earliest mental efforts, celebrated the deeds of the strongest. The first Epics sung 'arms & the men' who wielded them. Now we vastly overrate the progress we have made since those early times. Still *might* makes *right* & other remnants of barbarism linger amongst us. The thousand forms by which we write as in hieroglyphics, our present characters, are far enough from showing that harmonious developement of the faculties of which we sometimes read the prophecy in our own souls. Let men & women be gentle & firm; brave & tender; instinctive but confirming their instincts by reason; let judgment & taste exercise their selecting & rejecting power among the stores of imagination & fancy; let reflection preserve women from folly; the stern 'I ought' produce in them a concentration of intellectual effort, forbid the apathy & self-indulgence which their physical constitution induces, & bind on them the necessity to use, cultivate, elevate all that self-consciousness reveals to them, let them listen to their heart's dictates not fearing that they will lead them astray & we shall no longer hear of masculine women or effeminate men. Scattered up & down in the world's history there are women who have set aside the accidents of position, & left their mark on the ages. Some of them in whom was an imperfect moral developement were guided only by a strong will; in others a holy purpose inspired noble deeds. These instances are not so rare as to be a sort of lusus naturae, they prove that reflection & the power of concentration which predominate in men exist in women, and only require a more earnest culture. And what if our necessary position our proper sphere prevents the production of the Epic & the Drama, influence in the Council or the Camp—how do we know that in the possible future woman's intellect may not manifest itself in forms beautiful as poetry & art, permanent as empires, all emanating from her home—created out of it, from her relations as daughter, sister, wife, & mother? Out of these relations may yet rise a beauty & a power which shall bless & heal the nations. Then the progress of the race will be harmonious & universal; the Hebrew seer said truly, 'Men shall learn war no more.'"

# Margaret Fuller

## from "The Great Lawsuit"

### (1843)

This essay is the basis of Fuller's most important book, *Woman in the Nineteenth Century* (1845), the first major feminist manifesto written in the United States. The peculiar subtitle (see source note) is meant to suggest that so long as actual men and women fall short of the human ideal, humankind as a whole will remain divided, men and women likewise. Fuller likens discrimination against women to slavery, but she also stresses her hope and belief that history was tending toward the juster recognition of women's right to autonomy and opportunity that had been celebrated since antiquity in myth and literature. Fuller's argument, which alternates tauntingly between satire and playfulness, often baffles first-time readers with its allusive learning and generalizing abstraction. But these tactics make better sense when we realize how important it was to Fuller to put her subject in the broadest cultural-historical context possible and to stress the gap between the relation between the sexes as they are versus the ideal as pictured by inspired human imagination through the ages.

Fuller's feminism is more "cultural" than "political" in aiming to revolutionize attitudes rather than to revolutionize society at the ballot box. Yet this does not make "The Great Lawsuit" any less audacious. For example, Fuller's praise of Mary Wollstonecraft and George Sand was a bold and daring move in Victorian America. No less significant is her strong defense of the legitimacy of women staying single. The German couplet below is by Friedrich Schiller (1759–1805), next to Goethe the greatest German literary figure of his day. "Miranda" is one of Fuller's numerous stylized self-images, as seen in the fact that the transition back from Miranda's voice to the author's is imperceptible.

SOURCE: "The Great Lawsuit: Man *Versus* Men. Woman *Versus* Women," *The Dial,* 4 ( July 1843).

It is worthy of remark, that as the principle of liberty is better understood and more nobly interpreted, a broader protest is made in behalf of woman. As men become aware that all men have not had their fair chance, they are inclined to say that no women have had a fair chance. The French revolution, that strangely disguised angel, bore witness in favor of woman, but interpreted her claims no less ignorantly than those of man. Its idea of happiness did not rise beyond outward enjoyment, unobstructed by the tyranny of others. The title it gave was Citoyen, Citoyenne, and it is not unimportant to woman that even this species of equality was awarded her. Before, she could be condemned to perish on the scaffold for treason, but not as a citizen, but a subject. The right, with which this title then invested a human being, was that of bloodshed and license. The Goddess of Liberty was impure. Yet truth was prophesied in the ravings of that hideous fever induced by long ignorance and abuse. Europe is conning a valued lesson from the blood-stained page. The same tendencies, farther unfolded, will bear good fruit in this country.

Yet, in this country, as by the Jews, when Moses was leading them to the promised land, everything has been done that inherited depravity could, to hinder the promise of heaven from its fulfilment. The cross, here as elsewhere, has been planted only to be blasphemed by cruelty and fraud. The name of the Prince of Peace has been profaned by all kinds of injustice towards the Gentile whom he said he came to save. But I need not speak of what has been done towards the red man, the black man. These deeds are the scoff of the world; and they have been accompanied by such pious words, that the gentlest would not dare to intercede with, "Father forgive them, for they know not what they do."

Here, as elsewhere, the gain of creation consists always in the growth of individual minds, which live and aspire, as flowers bloom and birds sing, in the midst of morasses; and in the continual development of that thought, the thought of human destiny, which is given to eternity to fulfil, and which ages of failure only seemingly impede. Only seemingly, and whatever seems to the contrary, this country is as surely destined to elucidate a great moral law, as Europe was to promote the mental culture of man.

Though the national independence be blurred by the servility of individuals; though freedom and equality have been proclaimed only to leave room for a monstrous display of slave dealing and slave keeping; though the free American so often feels himself free, like the Roman, only to pamper his appetites and his indolence through the misery of his fellow beings, still it is not in vain, that the verbal statement has been made, "All men are born free and equal." There it stands, a golden certainty, wherewith to encourage the good, to shame the bad. The new world may be called clearly to perceive that it incurs the utmost penalty, if it reject the sorrowful brother. And if men are deaf, the angels hear. But men cannot be deaf. It is inevitable that an external freedom, such as has been achieved for the nation, should be so also for every member of it. That, which has once been clearly conceived in the intelligence, must be acted out. It has become a law, irrevocable as that of the Medes in their ancient dominion. . . .

. . . We have waited here long in the dust; we are tired and hungry, but the triumphal procession must appear at last.

Of all its banners, none has been more steadily upheld, and under none has more valor and willingness for real sacrifices been shown, than that of the champions of the enslaved African. And this band it is, which, partly in consequence of a natural following out of principles, partly because many women have been prominent in that cause, makes, just now, the warmest appeal in behalf of woman.

Though there has been a growing liberality on this point, yet society at large is not so prepared for the demands of this party, but that they are, and will be for some time, coldly regarded as the Jacobins of their day.

"Is it not enough," cries the sorrowful trader, "that you have done all you could to break up the national Union, and thus destroy the prosperity of our country, but now you must be trying to break up family union, to take my wife away from the cradle, and the kitchen hearth, to vote at polls, and preach from a pulpit? Of course, if she does such things, she cannot attend to those of her own sphere. She is happy enough as she is. She has more leisure than I have, every means of improvement, every indulgence."

"Have you asked her whether she was satisfied with these indulgences?"

"No, but I know she is. She is too amiable to wish what would make me unhappy, and too judicious to wish to step beyond the sphere of her sex. I will never consent to have our peace disturbed by any such discussions."

"'Consent'—you? it is not consent from you that is in question, it is assent from your wife."

"Am I not the head of my house?"

"You are not the head of your wife. God has given her a mind of her own."

"I am the head and she the heart."

"God grant you play true to one another then. If the head represses no natural pulse of the heart, there can be no question as to your giving your consent. Both will be of one accord, and there needs but to present any question to get a full and true answer. There is no need of precaution, of indulgence, or consent. But our doubt is whether the heart consents with the head, or only acquiesces in its decree; and it is to ascertain the truth on this point, that we propose some liberating measures."

Thus vaguely are these questions proposed and discussed at present. But their being proposed at all implies much thought, and suggests more. Many women are considering within themselves what they need that they have not, and what they can have, if they find they need it. Many men are considering whether women are capable of being and having more than they are and have, and whether, if they are, it will be best to consent to improvement in their condition.

The numerous party, whose opinions are already labelled and adjusted too much to their mind to admit of any new light, strive, by lectures on some model-woman of bridal-like beauty and gentleness, by writing or lending little treatises, to mark out with due precision the limits of woman's sphere, and woman's mission, and to prevent other than the rightful shepherd from climbing the wall, or the flock from using any chance gap to run astray.

Without enrolling ourselves at once on either side, let us look upon the subject from that point of view which to-day offers. No better, it is to be feared, than a high house-top. A high hill-top, or at least a cathedral spire, would be desirable.

It is not surprising that it should be the Anti-Slavery party that pleads for woman, when we consider merely that she does not hold property on equal terms with men; so that, if a husband dies without a will, the wife, instead of stepping at once into his place as head of the family, inherits only a part of his fortune, as if she were a child, or ward only, not an equal partner.

We will not speak of the innumerable instances, in which profligate or idle men live upon the earnings of industrious wives; or if the wives leave them and take with them the children, to perform the double duty of mother and father, follow from place to place, and threaten to rob them of the children, if deprived of the rights of a husband, as they call them, planting themselves in their poor lodgings, frightening them into paying tribute by taking from them the children, running into debt at the expense of these otherwise so overtasked helots. Though such instances abound, the public opinion of his own sex is against the man, and when cases of extreme tyranny are made known, there is private action in the wife's favor. But if woman be, indeed, the weaker party, she ought to have legal protection, which would make such oppression impossible.

And knowing that there exists, in the world of men, a tone of feeling towards women as towards slaves, such as is expressed in the common phrase, "Tell that to women and children;" that the infinite soul can only work through them in already ascertained limits; that the prerogative of reason, man's highest portion, is allotted to them in a much lower degree; that it is better for them to be engaged in active labor, which is to be furnished and directed by those better able to think, &c. &c.; we need not go further, for who can review the experience of last week, without recalling words which imply, whether in jest or earnest, these views, and views like these? Knowing this, can we wonder that many reformers think that measures are not likely to be taken in behalf of women, unless their wishes could be publicly represented by women?

That can never be necessary, cry the other side. All men are privately influenced by women; each has his wife, sister, or female friends, and is too much biassed by these relations to fail of representing their interests. And if this is not enough, let them propose and enforce their wishes with the pen. The beauty of home would be destroyed, the delicacy of the sex be violated, the dignity of halls of legislation destroyed, by an attempt to introduce them there. Such duties are inconsistent with those of a mother; and then we have ludicrous pictures of ladies in hysterics at the polls, and senate chambers filled with cradles.

But if, in reply, we admit as truth that woman seems destined by nature rather to the inner circle, we must add that the arrangements of civilized life have not been as yet such as to secure it to her. Her circle, if the duller, is not the quieter. If kept from excitement, she is not from drudgery. Not only the Indian carries the burdens of the camp, but the favorites of Louis the Fourteenth accompany him in his journeys, and the washerwoman stands at her tub and carries home her work at all seasons, and in all states of health.

As to the use of the pen, there was quite as much opposition to woman's possessing herself of that help to free-agency as there is now to her seizing on the rostrum or the desk; and she is likely to draw, from a permission to plead her cause that way, opposite inferences to what might be wished by those who now grant it.

As to the possibility of her filling, with grace and dignity, any such position, we should think those who had seen the great actresses, and heard the Quaker preachers of modern times, would not doubt, that woman can express publicly the fulness of thought and emotion, without losing any of the peculiar beauty of her sex.

As to her home, she is not likely to leave it more than she now does for balls, theatres, meetings for promoting missions, revival meetings, and others to which she flies, in hope of an animation for her existence, commensurate with what she sees enjoyed by men. Governors of Ladies' Fairs are no less engrossed by such a charge, than the Governor of the State by his; presidents of Washingtonian societies, no less away from home than presidents of conventions. If men look straitly to it, they will find that, unless their own lives are domestic, those of the women will not be. The female Greek, of our day, is as much in the street as the male, to cry, What news? We doubt not it was the same in Athens of old. The women, shut out from the market-place, made up for it at the religious festivals. For human beings are not so constituted, that they can live without expansion; and if they do not get it one way, must another, or perish.

And, as to men's representing women fairly, at present, while we hear from men who owe to their wives not only all that is comfortable and graceful, but all that is wise in the arrangement of their lives, the frequent remark, "You cannot reason with a woman," when from those of delicacy, nobleness, and poetic culture, the contemptuous phrase, "Women and children," and that in no light sally of the hour, but in works intended to give a permanent statement of the best experiences, when not one man in the million, shall I say, no, not in the hundred million, can rise above the view that woman was made *for man*, when such traits as these are daily forced upon the attention, can we feel that man will always do justice to the interests of woman? Can we think that he takes a sufficiently discerning and religious view of her office and destiny, ever to do her justice, except when prompted by sentiment; accidentally or transiently, that is, for his sentiment will vary according to the relations in which he is placed. The lover, the poet, the artist, are likely to view her nobly. The father and the philosopher have some chance of liberality; the man of the world, the legislator for expediency, none.

Under these circumstances, without attaching importance in themselves to the changes demanded by the champions of woman, we hail them as signs of the times. We would have every arbitrary barrier thrown down. We would have every path laid open to woman as freely as to man. Were this done, and a slight temporary fermentation allowed to subside, we believe that the Divine would ascend into nature to a height unknown in the history of past ages, and nature, thus instructed, would regulate the spheres not only so as to avoid collision, but to bring forth ravishing harmony.

Yet then, and only then, will human beings be ripe for this, when inward and outward freedom for woman, as much as for man, shall be acknowledged as a right, not yielded as a concession. As the friend of the negro assumes that one man cannot, by right, hold another in bondage, should the friend of woman assume that man cannot, by right, lay even well-meant restrictions on woman. If the negro be a soul, if the woman be a soul, apparelled in flesh, to one master only are they accountable. There is but one law for all souls, and, if there is to be an interpreter of it, he comes not as man, or son of man, but as Son of God.

Were thought and feeling once so far elevated that man should esteem himself the brother and friend, but nowise the lord and tutor of woman, were he really bound with her in equal worship, arrangements as to function and employment would be of no consequence. What woman needs is not as a woman to act or rule, but as a nature to grow, as an intellect to discern, as a soul to live freely, and unimpeded to unfold such powers as were given her when we left our common home. If fewer talents were given her, yet, if allowed the free and full employment of these, so that she may render back to the giver his own with usury, she will not complain, nay, I dare to say she will bless and rejoice in her earthly birth-place, her earthly lot.

Let us consider what obstructions impede this good era, and what signs give reason to hope that it draws near.

I was talking on this subject with Miranda, a woman, who, if any in the world, might speak without heat or bitterness of the position of her sex. Her father was a man who cherished no sentimental reverence for woman, but a firm belief in the equality of the sexes. She was his eldest child, and came to him at an age when he needed a companion. From the time she could speak and go alone, he addressed her not as a plaything, but as a living mind. Among the few verses he ever wrote were a copy addressed to this child, when the first locks were cut from her head, and the reverence expressed on this occasion for that cherished head he never belied. It was to him the temple of immortal intellect. He respected his child, however, too much to be an indulgent parent. He called on her for clear judgment, for courage, for honor and fidelity, in short for such virtues as he knew. In so far as he possessed the keys to the wonders of this universe, he allowed free use of them to her, and by the incentive of a high expectation he forbade, as far as possible, that she should let the privilege lie idle.

Thus this child was early led to feel herself a child of the spirit. She took her place easily, not only in the world of organized being, but in the world of mind. A dignified sense of self-dependence was given as all her portion, and she found it a sure anchor. Herself securely anchored, her relations with others were established with equal security. She was fortunate, in a total absence of those charms which might have drawn to her bewildering flatteries, and of a strong electric nature, which repelled those who did not belong to her, and attracted those who did. With men and women her relations were noble; affectionate without passion, intellectual without coldness. The world was free to her, and she lived freely in it. Outward adversity came, and inward conflict, but that faith and self-respect had early been awakened, which must always lead at last to an outward serenity, and an inward peace.

Of Miranda I had always thought as an example, that the restraints upon the sex were insuperable only to those who think them so, or who noisily strive to break them. She had taken a course of her own, and no man stood in her way. Many of her acts had been unusual, but excited no uproar. Few helped, but none checked her; and the many men, who knew her mind and her life, showed to her confidence as to a brother, gentleness as to a sister. And not only refined, but very coarse men approved one in whom they saw resolution and clearness of design. Her mind was often the leading one, always effective.

When I talked with her upon these matters, and had said very much what I have written, she smilingly replied, And yet we must admit that

I have been fortunate, and this should not be. My good father's early trust gave the first bias, and the rest followed of course. It is true that I have had less outward aid, in after years, than most women, but that is of little consequence. Religion was early awakened in my soul, a sense that what the soul is capable to ask it must attain, and that, though I might be aided by others, I must depend on myself as the only constant friend. This self-dependence, which was honored in me, is deprecated as a fault in most women. They are taught to learn their rule from without, not to unfold it from within.

This is the fault of man, who is still vain, and wishes to be more important to woman than by right he should be.

Men have not shown this disposition towards you, I said.

No, because the position I early was enabled to take, was one of self-reliance. And were all women as sure of their wants as I was, the result would be the same. The difficulty is to get them to the point where they shall naturally develop self-respect, the question how it is to be done.

Once I thought that men would help on this state of things more than I do now. I saw so many of them wretched in the connections they had formed in weakness and vanity. They seemed so glad to esteem women whenever they could!

But early I perceived that men never, in any extreme of despair, wished to be women. Where they admired any woman they were inclined to speak of her as above her sex. Silently I observed this, and feared it argued a rooted skepticism, which for ages had been fastening on the heart, and which only an age of miracles could eradicate.

Ever I have been treated with great sincerity; and I look upon it as a most signal instance of this, that an intimate friend of the other sex said in a fervent moment, that I deserved in some star to be a man. Another used as highest praise, in speaking of a character in literature, the words "a manly woman."

It is well known that of every strong woman they say she has a masculine mind.

This by no means argues a willing want of generosity towards woman. Man is as generous towards her, as he knows how to be.

Wherever she has herself arisen in national or private history, and nobly shone forth in any ideal of excellence, men have received her, not only willingly, but with triumph. Their encomiums indeed are always in some sense mortifying, they show too much surprise.

In every-day life the feelings of the many are stained with vanity. Each wishes to be lord in a little world, to be superior at least over one;

and he does not feel strong enough to retain a life-long ascendant over a strong nature. Only a Brutus would rejoice in a Portia. Only Theseus could conquer before he wed the Amazonian Queen. Hercules wished rather to rest from his labors with Dejanira, and received the poisoned robe, as a fit guerdon. The tale should be interpreted to all those who seek repose with the weak.

But not only is man vain and fond of power, but the same want of development, which thus affects him morally in the intellect, prevents his discerning the destiny of woman. The boy wants no woman, but only a girl to play ball with him, and mark his pocket handkerchief.

Thus in Schiller's Dignity of Woman, beautiful as the poem is, there is no "grave and perfect man," but only a great boy to be softened and restrained by the influence of girls. Poets, the elder brothers of their race, have usually seen further; but what can you expect of every-day men, if Schiller was not more prophetic as to what women must be? Even with Richter one foremost thought about a wife was that she would "cook him something good."

The sexes should not only correspond to and appreciate one another, but prophesy to one another. In individual instances this happens. Two persons love in one another the future good which they aid one another to unfold. This is very imperfectly done as yet in the general life. Man has gone but little way, now he is waiting to see whether woman can keep step with him, but instead of calling out like a good brother; You can do it if you only think so, or impersonally; Any one can do what he tries to do, he often discourages with school-boy brag; Girls cant do that, girls cant play ball. But let any one defy their taunts, break through, and be brave and secure, they rend the air with shouts.

No! man is not willingly ungenerous. He wants faith and love, because he is not yet himself an elevated being. He cries with sneering skepticism; Give us a sign. But if the sign appears, his eyes glisten, and he offers not merely approval, but homage. . . .

———

Whatever may have been the domestic manners of the ancient nations, the idea of woman was nobly manifested in their mythologies and poems, where she appeared as Sita in the Ramayana, a form of tender purity, in the Egyptian Isis, of divine wisdom never yet surpassed. In Egypt, too, the Sphynx, walking the earth with lion tread, looked out upon its marvels in the calm, inscrutable beauty of a virgin's face, and the Greek could only add wings to the great emblem. In Greece, Ceres and Proserpine, significantly termed "the great goddesses," were seen seated, side by side. They needed not to rise for any worshipper or any change; they were prepared for all things, as those initiated to their mysteries knew. More obvious is the meaning of those three forms, the Diana, Minerva, and Vesta. Unlike in the expression of their beauty, but alike in this,—that each was self-sufficing. Other forms were only accessories and illustrations, none the complement to one like these. Another might indeed be the companion, and the Apollo and Diana set off one another's beauty. Of the Vesta, it is to be observed, that not only deep-eyed deep-discerning Greece, but ruder Rome, who represents the only form of good man (the always busy warrior) that could be indifferent to woman, confided the permanence of its glory to a tutelary goddess, and her wisest legislator spoke of Meditation as a nymph.

In Sparta, thought, in this respect as all others, was expressed in the characters of real life, and the women of Sparta were as much Spartans as the men. The Citoyen, Citoyenne, of France, was here actualized. Was not the calm equality they enjoyed well worth the honors of chivalry? They intelligently shared the ideal life of their nation.

Generally, we are told of these nations, that women occupied there a very subordinate position in actual life. It is difficult to believe this, when we see such range and dignity of thought on the subject in the mythologies, and find the poets producing such ideals as Cassandra, Iphigenia, Antigone, Macaria, (though it is not unlike our own day, that men should revere those heroines of their great princely houses at theatres from which their women were excluded,) where Sibylline priestesses told the oracle of the highest god, and he could not be content to reign with a court of less than nine Muses. Even Victory wore a female form.

But whatever were the facts of daily life, I cannot complain of the age and nation, which represents its thought by such a symbol as I see before me at this moment. It is a zodiac of the busts of gods and goddesses, arranged in pairs. The circle breathes the music of a heavenly order. Male and female heads are distinct in expression, but equal in beauty, strength, and calmness. Each male head is that of a brother and a king, each female of a sister and a queen. Could the thought, thus expressed, be lived out, there would be nothing more to be desired. There would be unison in variety, congeniality in difference.

Coming nearer our own time, we find religion and poetry no less true in their revelations. The rude man, but just disengaged from the sod, the Adam, accuses woman to his God, and records her disgrace to their posterity. He is not ashamed to write that he could be drawn from heaven by one beneath him. But in the same nation, educated by time, instructed by successive prophets, we find woman in as high a position as she has ever occupied. And no figure, that has ever arisen to greet our eyes, has been received with more fervent reverence than that of the Madonna. Heine calls her the Dame du Comptoir of the Catholic Church, and this jeer well expresses a serious truth.

And not only this holy and significant image was worshipped by the pilgrim, and the favorite subject of the artist, but it exercised an immediate influence on the destiny of the sex. The empresses, who embraced the cross, converted sons and husbands. Whole calendars of female saints, heroic dames of chivalry, binding the emblem of faith on the heart of the best beloved, and wasting the bloom of youth in separation and loneliness, for the sake of duties they thought it religion to assume, with innumerable forms of poesy, trace their lineage to this one. Nor, however imperfect may be the action, in our day, of the faith thus expressed, and though we can scarcely think it nearer this ideal than that of India or Greece was near their ideal, is it in vain that the truth has been recognised, that woman is not only a part of man, bone of his bone and flesh of his flesh, born that men might not be lonely, but in themselves possessors of and possessed by immortal souls. This truth undoubtedly received a greater outward stability from the belief of the church, that the earthly parent of the Saviour of souls was a woman.

The Assumption of the Virgin, as painted by sublime artists, Petrarch's Hymn to the Madonna, cannot have spoken to the world wholly without result, yet oftentimes those who had ears heard not.

Thus, the Idea of woman has not failed to be often and forcibly represented. So many instances throng on the mind, that we must stop here, lest the catalogue be swelled beyond the reader's patience. . . .

———

Ye cannot believe it, men; but the only reason why women ever assume what is more appropriate to you, is because you prevent them from finding out what is fit for themselves. Were they free, were they wise fully to develop the strength and beauty of woman, they would never wish to be men, or manlike. The well-instructed moon flies not from her orbit to seize on the glories of her partner. No; for she knows that one law rules, one heaven contains, one universe replies to them alike. It is with women as with the slave.

> "Vor dem Sklaven, wenn er die Kette bricht,
>   Vor dem freien Menschen erzittert nicht."

Tremble not before the free man, but before the slave who has chains to break.

In slavery, acknowledged slavery, women are on a par with men. Each is a work-tool, an article of property,—no more! In perfect freedom, such as is painted in Olympus, in Swedenborg's angelic state, in the heaven where there is no marrying nor giving in marriage, each is a purified intelligence, an enfranchised soul,—no less! . . .

That an era approaches which shall approximate nearer to such a temper than any has yet done, there are many tokens, indeed so many that only a few of the most prominent can here be enumerated.

The reigns of Elizabeth of England and Isabella of Castile foreboded this era. They expressed the beginning of the new state, while they forwarded its progress. These were strong characters, and in harmony with the wants of their time. One showed that this strength did not unfit a woman for the duties of a wife and mother; the other, that it could enable her to live and die alone. Elizabeth is certainly no pleasing example. In rising above the weakness, she did not lay aside the weaknesses ascribed to her sex; but her strength must be respected now, as it was in her own time.

We may accept it as an omen for ourselves, that it was Isabella who furnished Columbus with the means of coming hither. This land must pay back its debt to woman, without whose aid it would not have been brought into alliance with the civilized world. . . .

———

Where the thought of equality has become pervasive, it shows itself in four kinds.

The household partnership. In our country the woman looks for a "smart but kind" husband, the man for a "capable, sweet-tempered" wife.

The man furnishes the house, the woman regulates it. Their relation is one of mutual esteem, mutual dependence. Their talk is of business, their affection shows itself by practical kindness. They know that life goes more smoothly and cheerfully to each for the other's aid; they are grateful and content. The wife praises her husband as a "good provider," the husband in return compliments her as a "capital housekeeper." This relation is good as far as it goes.

Next comes a closer tie which takes the two forms, either of intellectual companionship, or mutual idolatry. The last, we suppose, is to no one a pleasing subject of contemplation. The parties weaken and narrow one another; they lock the gate against all the glories of the universe that they may live in a cell together. To themselves they seem the only wise, to all others steeped in infatuation, the gods smile as they look forward to the crisis of cure, to men the woman seems an unlovely syren, to women the man an effeminate boy.

The other form, of intellectual companionship, has become more and more frequent. Men engaged in public life, literary men, and artists have often found in their wives companions and confidants in thought no less than in feeling. And, as in the course of things the intellectual development of woman has spread wider and risen higher, they have, not unfrequently, shared the same employment. As in the case of Roland and his wife, who were friends in the household and the nation's councils, read together, regulated home affairs, or prepared public documents together indifferently.

It is very pleasant, in letters begun by Roland and finished by his wife, to see the harmony of mind and the difference of nature, one thought, but various ways of treating it.

This is one of the best instances of a marriage of friendship. It was only friendship, whose basis was esteem; probably neither party knew love, except by name.

Roland was a good man, worthy to esteem and be esteemed, his wife as deserving of admiration as able to do without it. Madame Roland is the fairest specimen we have yet of her class, as clear to discern her aim, as valiant to pursue it, as Spenser's Britomart, austerely set apart from all that did not belong to her, whether as woman or as mind. She is an antetype of a class to which the coming time will afford a field, the Spartan matron, brought by the culture of a book-furnishing age to intellectual consciousness and expansion.

Self-sufficing strength and clear-sightedness were in her combined with a power of deep and calm affection. The page of her life is one of unsullied dignity.

Her appeal to posterity is one against the injustice of those who committed such crimes in the name of liberty. She makes it in behalf of herself and her husband. I would put beside it on the shelf a little volume, containing a similar appeal from the verdict of contemporaries to that of mankind, that of Godwin in behalf of his wife, the celebrated, the by most men detested Mary Wolstonecraft. In his view it was an appeal from the injustice of those who did such wrong in the name of virtue.

Were this little book interesting for no other cause, it would be so for the generous affection evinced under the peculiar circumstances. This man had courage to love and honor this woman in the face of the world's verdict, and of all that was repulsive in her own past history. He believed he saw of what soul she was, and that the thoughts she had struggled to act out were noble. He loved her and he defended her for the meaning and intensity of her inner life. It was a good fact.

Mary Wolstonecraft, like Madame Dudevant (commonly known as George Sand) in our day, was a woman whose existence better proved the need of some new interpretation of woman's rights, than anything she wrote. Such women as these, rich in genius, of most tender sympathies, and capable of high virtue and a chastened harmony, ought not to find themselves by birth in a place so narrow, that in breaking bonds they become outlaws. Were there as much room in the world for such, as in Spenser's poem for Britomart, they would not run their heads so wildly against its laws. They find their way at last to purer air, but the world will not take off the brand it has set upon them. The champion of the rights of woman found in Godwin one who plead her own cause like a brother. George Sand smokes, wears male attire, wishes to be addressed as Mon frère; perhaps, if she found those who were as brothers indeed, she would not care whether she were brother or sister.

We rejoice to see that she, who expresses such a painful contempt for men in most of her works, as shows she must have known great wrong from them, in La Roche Mauprat depicting one raised, by the workings of love, from the depths of savage sensualism to a moral and intellectual life. It was love for a pure object, for a steadfast woman, one of those who, the Italian said, could make the stair to heaven.

Women like Sand will speak now, and cannot be silenced; their characters and their eloquence alike foretell an era when such as they shall easier learn to lead true lives. But though such forebode, not such shall be the parents of it. Those who would reform the world must show that they do not speak in the heat of wild impulse; their lives must be unstained by passionate error; they must be severe lawgivers to themselves. As to their transgressions and opinions, it may be observed, that the resolve of Eloisa to be only the mistress of Abelard, was that of one who saw the contract of marriage a seal of degradation. Wherever abuses of this sort are seen, the timid will suffer, the bold protest. But society is in the right to outlaw them till she has revised her law, and she must be taught to do so, by one who speaks with authority, not in anger and haste.

If Godwin's choice of the calumniated authoress of the "Rights of Woman," for his honored wife, be a sign of a new era, no less so is an article of great learning and eloquence, published several years since in an English review, where the writer, in doing full justice to Eloisa, shows his bitter regret that she lives not now to love him, who might have known better how to prize her love than did the egotistical Abelard.

These marriages, these characters, with all their imperfections, express an onward tendency. They speak of aspiration of soul, of energy of mind, seeking clearness and freedom. Of a like promise are the tracts now publishing by Goodwyn Barmby (the European Pariah as he calls himself) and his wife Catharine. Whatever we may think of their measures, we see them in wedlock, the two minds are wed by the only contract that can permanently avail, of a common faith, and a common purpose.

We might mention instances, nearer home, of minds, partners in work and in life, sharing together, on equal terms, public and private interests, and which have not on any side that aspect of offence which characterizes the attitude of the last named; persons who steer straight onward, and in our freer life have not been obliged to run their heads against any wall. But the principles which guide them might, under petrified or oppressive institutions, have made them warlike, paradoxical, or, in some sense, Pariahs. The phenomenon is different, the law the same, in all these cases. Men and women have been obliged to build their house from the very foundation. If they found stone ready in the quarry, they took it peaceably, otherwise they alarmed the country by pulling down old towers to get materials.

These are all instances of marriage as intellectual companionship. The parties meet mind to mind, and a mutual trust is excited which can buckler them against a million. They work together for a common purpose, and, in all these instances, with the same implement, the pen. . . .

———

Yet even this acknowledgment, rather obtained by woman than proffered by man, has been sullied by the usual selfishness. So much is said of women being better educated that they may be better companions and mothers *of men!* They should be fit for such companionship, and we have mentioned with satisfaction instances where it has been established. Earth knows no fairer, holier relation than that of a mother. But a being of infinite scope must not be treated with an exclusive view to any one relation. Give the soul free course, let the organization be freely developed, and the being will be fit for any and every relation to which it may be called. The intellect, no more than the sense of hearing, is to be cultivated, that she may be a more valuable companion to man, but because the Power who gave a power by its mere existence signifies that it must be brought out towards perfection.

In this regard, of self-dependence and a greater simplicity and fulness of being, we must hail as a preliminary the increase of the class contemptuously designated as old maids.

We cannot wonder at the aversion with which old bachelors and old maids have been regarded. Marriage is the natural means of forming a sphere, of taking root on the earth: it requires more strength to do this without such an opening, very many have failed of this, and their imperfections have been in every one's way. They have been more partial, more harsh, more officious and impertinent than others. Those, who have a complete experience of the human instincts, have a distrust as to whether they can be thoroughly human and humane, such as is hinted at in the saying, "Old maids' and bachelors' children are well cared for," which derides at once their ignorance and their presumption.

Yet the business of society has become so complex, that it could now scarcely be carried on without the presence of these despised auxiliaries, and detachments from the army of aunts and uncles are wanted to stop gaps in every hedge. They rove about, mental and moral Ishmaelites, pitching their tents amid the fixed and ornamented habitations of men.

They thus gain a wider, if not so deep, experience. They are not so intimate with others, but thrown more upon themselves, and if they do not there find peace and incessant life, there is none to flatter them that they are not very poor and very mean.

A position, which so constantly admonishes, may be of inestimable benefit. The person may gain, undistracted by other relationships, a closer communion with the One. Such a use is made of it by saints and sibyls. Or she may be one of the lay sisters of charity, or more humbly only the useful drudge of all men, or the intellectual interpreter of the varied life she sees.

Or she may combine all these. Not "needing to care that she may please a husband," a frail and limited being, all her thoughts may turn to the centre, and by steadfast contemplation enter into the secret of truth and love, use it for the use of all men, instead of a chosen few, and interpret through it all the forms of life.

Saints and geniuses have often chosen a lonely position, in the faith that, if undisturbed by the pressure of near ties they could give themselves up to the inspiring spirit, it would enable them to understand and reproduce life better than actual experience could.

How many old maids take this high stand, we cannot say; it is an unhappy fact that too many of those who come before the eye are gossips rather, and not always good-natured gossips. But, if these abuse, and none make the best of their vocation, yet, it has not failed to produce some good fruit. It has been seen by others, if not by themselves, that beings likely to be left alone need to be fortified and furnished within themselves, and education and thought have tended more and more to regard beings as related to absolute Being, as well as to other men. It has been seen that as the loss of no bond ought to destroy a human being, so ought the missing of none to hinder him from growing. And thus a circumstance of the time has helped to put woman on the true platform. Perhaps the next generation will look deeper into this matter, and find that contempt is put on old maids, or old women at all, merely because they do not use the elixir which will keep the soul always young. No one thinks of Michael Angelo's Persican Sibyl, or St. Theresa, or Tasso's Leonora, or the Greek Electra as an old maid, though all had reached the period in life's course appointed to take that degree.

Even among the North American Indians, a race of men as completely engaged in mere instinctive life as almost any in the world, and where each chief, keeping many wives as useful servants, of course looks with no kind eye on celibacy in woman, it was excused in the following instance mentioned by Mrs. Jameson. A woman dreamt in youth that she was betrothed to the sun. She built her a wigwam apart, filled it with emblems of her alliance and means of an independent life. There she passed her days, sustained by her own exertions, and true to her supposed engagement.

In any tribe, we believe, a woman, who lived as if she was betrothed to the sun, would be tolerated, and the rays which made her youth blossom sweetly would crown her with a halo in age.

There is on this subject a nobler view than heretofore, if not the noblest, and we greet improvement here, as much as on the subject of marriage. Both are fertile themes, but time permits not here to explore them....

———

The especial genius of woman I believe to be electrical in movement, intuitive in function, spiritual in tendency. She is great not so easily in classification, or re-creation, as in an instinctive seizure of causes, and a simple breathing out of what she receives that has the singleness of life, rather than the selecting or energizing of art.

More native to her is it to be the living model of the artist, than to set apart from herself any one form in objective reality; more native to inspire and receive the poem than to create it. In so far as soul is in her completely developed, all soul is the same; but as far as it is modified in her as woman, it flows, it breathes, it sings, rather than deposits soil, or finishes work, and that which is especially feminine flushes in blossom the face of earth, and pervades like air and water all this seeming solid globe, daily renewing and purifying its life. Such may be the especially feminine element, spoken of as Femality. But it is no more the order of nature that it should be incarnated pure in any form, than that the masculine energy should exist unmingled with it in any form.

Male and female represent the two sides of the great radical dualism. But, in fact, they are perpetually passing into one another. Fluid hardens to solid, solid rushes to fluid. There is no wholly masculine man, no purely feminine woman.

History jeers at the attempts of physiologists to bind great original laws by the forms which flow from them. They make a rule; they say from observation what can and cannot be. In vain! Nature provides exceptions to every rule. She sends women to battle, and sets Hercules spinning; she enables women to bear immense burdens, cold, and frost; she enables the man, who feels maternal love, to nourish his infant like a mother. Of late she plays still gayer pranks. Not only she deprives organizations, but organs, of a necessary end. She enables people to read with the top of the head, and see with the pit of the stomach. Presently she will make a female Newton, and a male Syren.

Man partakes of the feminine in the Apollo, woman of the Masculine as Minerva.

Let us be wise and not impede the soul. Let her work as she will. Let us have one creative energy, one incessant revelation. Let it take what form it will, and let us not bind it by the past to man or woman, black or white. Jove sprang from Rhea, Pallas from Jove. So let it be.

If it has been the tendency of the past remarks to call woman rather to the Minerva side,—if I, unlike the more generous writer, have spoken from society no less than the soul,—let it be pardoned. It is love that has caused this, love for many incarcerated souls, that might be freed could the idea of religious self-dependence be established in them, could the weakening habit of dependence on others be broken up.

Every relation, every gradation of nature, is incalculably precious, but only to the soul which is poised upon itself, and to whom no loss, no change, can bring dull discord, for it is in harmony with the central soul.

If any individual live too much in relations, so that he becomes a stranger to the resources of his own nature, he falls after a while into a distraction, or imbecility, from which he can only be cured by a time of isolation, which gives the renovating fountains time to rise up. With a society it is the same. Many minds, deprived of the traditionary or instinctive means of passing a cheerful existence, must find help in self-impulse or perish. It is therefore that while any elevation, in the view of union, is to be hailed with joy, we shall not decline celibacy as the great fact of the time. It is one from which no vow, no arrangement, can at present save a thinking mind. For now the rowers are pausing on their oars, they wait a change before they can pull together. All tends to illustrate the thought of a wise contemporary. Union is only possible to those who are units. To be fit for relations in time, souls, whether of man or woman, must be able to do without them in the spirit.

It is therefore that I would have woman lay aside all thought, such as she habitually cherishes, of being taught and led by men. I would have her, like the Indian girl, dedicate herself to the Sun, the Sun of Truth, and go no where if his beams did not make clear the path. I would have her free from compromise, from complaisance, from helplessness, because I would have her good enough and strong enough to love one and all beings, from the fulness, not the poverty of being. . . .

# D.

# NATURE AND THE HEALTH
# OF BODY AND SPIRIT

# RALPH WALDO EMERSON
## WHY CONCORD? ("MUSKETAQUID")
### (1843-44, 1847)

Emerson was responsible for making nature a major topic for Transcendentalist writers. He largely left it to Thoreau to study nature intensively on its own terms and to bear out his Romantic assertions that the natural world is more indispensable to human well-being than as a storehouse of raw material for manufacture and perception. Yet Emerson himself profoundly believed that a country village setting offered the best mode of life for both body and spirit. For him, that village was, of course, Concord, Massachusetts, and his lifelong attachment to it was crucial to making Concord the Transcendentalist movement's social and spiritual center. Emerson summed up his attachment in his poem "Musketaquid," written about 1843–44, which takes its title from the Indian name for the flat, low-lying landscape's most prominent feature, the convergence of the Sudbury and Assabet rivers to form the Concord, or "Musketaquid" ("Grass-ground River" was Thoreau's translation). Emerson conjures up Concord's legacy as the place where the fight for American independence began in order to make the point that voluntary submission to the conditions of life in this superficially tame but deeply meaningful rural setting defines liberty's very meaning. This poem's sense of Concord life as pastoral idyll also comports with the difference between Emerson's status as lord of a comfortable brookside property and Thoreau's role as his sometime handyman.

SOURCE: *Poems.* Boston: James Munroe, 1847.

## MUSKETAQUID

Because I was content with these poor fields,
Low, open meads, slender and sluggish streams,
And found a home in haunts which others scorned,
The partial wood-gods overpaid my love,
And granted me the freedom of their state,
And in their secret senate have prevailed
With the dear, dangerous lords that rule our life,
Made moon and planets parties to their bond,
And through my rock-like, solitary wont
Shot million rays of thought and tenderness.
For me, in showers, in sweeping showers, the spring
Visits the valley;—break away the clouds,—
I bathe in the morn's soft and silvered air,
And loiter willing by yon loitering stream.
Sparrows far off, and nearer, April's bird,
Blue-coated,—flying before from tree to tree,
Courageous, sing a delicate overture
To lead the tardy concert of the year.
Onward and nearer rides the sun of May;
And wide around, the marriage of the plants
Is sweetly solemnized. Then flows amain
The surge of summer's beauty; dell and crag,
Hollow and lake, hill-side, and pine arcade,
Are touched with genius. Yonder ragged cliff
Has thousand faces in a thousand hours.

Beneath low hills, in the broad interval
Through which at will our Indian rivulet
Winds mindful still of sannup and of squaw,
Whose pipe and arrow oft the plough unburies,
Here in pine houses built of new fallen trees,
Supplanters of the tribe, the farmers dwell.
Traveller, to thee, perchance, a tedious road,
Or, it may be, a picture; to these men,
The landscape is an armory of powers,
Which, one by one, they know to draw and use.

They harness beast, bird, insect, to their work;
They prove the virtues of each bed of rock,
And, like the chemist mid his loaded jars,
Draw from each stratum its adapted use
To drug their crops or weapon their arts withal.
They turn the frost upon their chemic heap,
They set the wind to winnow pulse and grain,
They thank the spring-flood for its fertile slime,
And, on cheap summit-levels of the snow,
Slide with the sledge to inaccessible woods
O'er meadows bottomless. So, year by year,
They fight the elements with elements,
(That one would say, meadow and forest walked,
Transmuted in these men to rule their like,)
And by the order in the field disclose
The order regnant in the yeoman's brain.

What these strong masters wrote at large in miles,
I followed in small copy in my acre;
For there's no rood has not a star above it;
The cordial quality of pear or plum
Ascends as gladly in a single tree
As in broad orchards resonant with bees;
And every atom poises for itself,
And for the whole. The gentle deities
Showed me the lore of colors and of sounds,
The innumerable tenements of beauty,
The miracle of generative force,
Far-reaching concords of astronomy
Felt in the plants, and in the punctual birds;
Better, the linked purpose of the whole,
And, chiefest prize, found I true liberty
In the glad home plain-dealing nature gave.
The polite found me impolite; the great
Would mortify me, but in vain; for still
I am a willow of the wilderness,
Loving the wind that bent me. All my hurts
My garden spade can heal. A woodland walk,
A quest of river-grapes, a mocking thrush,
A wild-rose, or rock-loving columbine,

Salve my worst wounds.
For thus the wood-gods murmured in my ear:
"Dost love our manners? Canst thou silent lie?
Canst thou, thy pride forgot, like nature pass
Into the winter night's extinguished mood?
Canst thou shine now, then darkle,
And being latent feel thyself no less?
As, when the all-worshipped moon attracts the eye,
The river, hill, stems, foliage are obscure
Yet envies none, none are unenviable."

# Charles Lane

## from "Life in the Woods"

### (1844)

Charles Lane (1800–70) was Bronson Alcott's coadjutor in the short-lived commune at Fruitlands (1843–44). A man of ascetic tendencies, Lane lived thereafter with the Shakers for a time. In some ways, his essay uncannily anticipates Thoreau's Walden experiment the next year. Thoreau doubtless read it; and he may well have been thinking about it years later when he titled his book about the experience *Walden; or, Life in the Woods* (1854). This is not to say that Thoreau would have seen eye to eye with Lane on all points. Although Lane was strongly drawn to a life of seclusion from mundane society, he was but no less convinced that for most people the right way to go was through "association" rather than solitude. Still, Thoreau might well have been more heartened than otherwise by this fellow Transcendentalist's interest in imagining a form of viable "amalgamation" of secession from versus retention of ties with society. One can also think of *Walden* as a direct retort to Lane's practical objections to a solo retreat.

SOURCE: "Life in The Woods," *The Dial*, 4 (April 1844).

. . . The experiment of a true wilderness life by a white person must . . . be very rare. He is not born for it; he is not natured for it. He lacks the essential qualities as well as the physical substance for such a life, and the notion of entering on it must be considered merely an interesting dream. Some amalgamation may, however, be possible; and to unite the advantages of the two modes has doubtless been the aim of many.

Even now we hear of some individuals, on whom the world might hopefully rely to become eminent even amongst the worthy, betaking themselves from the busy haunts of men to a more select and secluded life.

But will they succeed in wrestling against their increased natural needs, and their remaining civic wants, diminished as these may be? On trial, as on due consideration, it will be found that this is not a very promising course. By the time the hut is built, the rudest furniture constructed, the wood chopped, the fire burning, the bread grown and prepared, the whole time will be exhausted, and no interval remain for comfortably clothing the body, for expansion in art, or for recreation by the book or pen. This but faintly promises to be the mode, by which the pure in heart shall escape the pressures and burdens, which prevent the full and happy development of the soul.

Of those who have sought a recluse life on a religious basis, it has been remarked that solitude is a state suitable only to the best or the worst. The average cast of humanity cannot be much benefitted by it. It is not a condition in which human beings can be brought into the world, and it is rarely a condition in which they should attempt to remain in it. The austerities pertaining to silence and solitude may improve the very bad; they may leave uninjured the very good; but such as are in the process of improvement, an association of some kind seems more suitable, as it is evidently more natural. . . .

# Henry David Thoreau

## from "Walking"

### (1850-62)

While Thoreau was writing his greatest book, *Walden,* he was also laying the groundwork for what his best biographer calls his "central
essay" on the same subject of excursions into nature. In 1850–51 he
gave public lectures on both "The Wild" and "The Walking," originally part of a single discourse that was later reassembled and finally
published as "Walking" after Thoreau's death. The opening section of
Thoreau's essay makes a revealing counterpoint to Emerson's "Musketaquid," both its opposite number and its counterpart. On the one
hand, Emerson sounds sedentary; Thoreau sounds restless. Yet each
text echoes the other as well. Walking is also vital to Emerson's regime,
even if secondary. Often they took walks together. Having a home base
in Concord was no more vital for Emerson than it was for Thoreau,
even though his prescription for the good life meant dedicating many
more of his hours to roaming in woodsy seclusion.

With the transportation revolution, which brought the railroad to
Transcendental Concord in 1844, long-distance walking had started to
become more of a pastime than a subsistence necessity. That helps
explain the rise of a large body of Romantic walking literature in the
nineteenth century, of which this essay is a leading example. But
Thoreau gives a special edge to the genre with his metaphor of walking as pilgrimage and his insistence on it as a way of putting a person in
contact with "absolute freedom and wildness."

Thoreau's Latin motto means "the walker is born, not made." The
poetic quotation is from a fifteenth-century narrative poem about

English folk hero Robin Hood. Toward the end, Thoreau plays upon his local reputation as a land surveyor, a day job he didn't particularly care for although he took pride in his expertise.

SOURCE: "Walking," *The Atlantic Monthly,* 9 ( June 1862).

I wish to speak a word for Nature, for absolute freedom and wildness, as contrasted with a freedom and culture merely civil—to regard man as an inhabitant, or a part and parcel of Nature, rather than a member of society. I wish to make an extreme statement, if so I may make an emphatic one, for there are enough champions of civilization: the minister, and the school-committee, and every one of you will take care of that.

I have met with but one or two persons in the course of my life who understood the art of Walking, that is, of taking walks,—who had a genius, so to speak, for *sauntering:* which word is beautifully derived "from idle people who roved about the country, in the Middle Ages, and asked charity, under pretence of going *à la Sainte Terre,*" to the Holy Land, till the children exclaimed, "There goes a *Sainte-Terrer,*" a Saunterer—a Holy-Lander. They who never go to the Holy Land in their walks, as they pretend, are indeed mere idlers and vagabonds; but they who do go there are saunterers in the good sense, such as I mean. Some, however, would derive the word from *sans terre,* without land or a home, which, therefore, in the good sense, will mean, having no particular home, but equally at home everywhere. For this is the secret of successful sauntering. He who sits still in a house all the time may be the greatest vagrant of all; but the saunterer, in the good sense, is no more vagrant than the meandering river, which is all the while sedulously seeking the shortest course to the sea. But I prefer the first, which, indeed, is the most probable derivation. For every walk is a sort of crusade, preached by some Peter the Hermit in us, to go forth and reconquer this Holy Land from the hands of the Infidels.

It is true, we are but faint-hearted crusaders, even the walkers, nowadays, who undertake no persevering, never-ending enterprises. Our expeditions are but tours, and come round again at evening to the old hearth-side from which we set out. Half the walk is but retracing our steps. We should go forth on the shortest walk, perchance, in the spirit of undying adventure, never to return,—prepared to send back our embalmed hearts only as relics to our desolate kingdoms. If you are ready to leave father and mother, and brother and sister, and wife and child and friends, and never see them again,—if you have paid your debts, and made your will, and settled all your affairs, and are a free man, then you are ready for a walk.

To come down to my own experience, my companion and I, for I sometimes have a companion, take pleasure in fancying ourselves knights of a new, or rather an old, order,—not Equestrians or Chevaliers, not Ritters or Riders, but Walkers, a still more ancient and honorable class, I trust. The chivalric and heroic spirit which once belonged to the Rider seems now to reside in, or perchance to have subsided into, the Walker,—not the Knight, but Walker Errant. He is a sort of fourth estate, outside of Church and State and People.

We have felt that we almost alone hereabouts practised this noble art; though, to tell the truth, at least, if their own assertions are to be received, most of my townsmen would fain walk sometimes, as I do, but they cannot. No wealth can buy the requisite leisure, freedom, and independence, which are the capital in this profession. It comes only by the grace of God. It requires a direct dispensation from Heaven to become a walker. You must be born into the family of the Walkers. *Ambulator nascitur, non fit.* Some of my townsmen, it is true, can remember and have described to me some walks which they took ten years ago, in which they were so blessed as to lose themselves for half an hour in the woods; but I know very well that they have confined themselves to the highway ever since, whatever pretensions they may make to belong to this select class. No doubt they were elevated for a moment as by the reminiscence of a previous state of existence, when even they were foresters and outlaws.

> "When he came to grene wode,
>     In a mery mornynge,
> There he herde the notes small
>     Of byrdes mery syngynge.
> "It is ferre gone, sayd Robyn,
>     That I was last here;
> Me lyste a lytell for to shote
>     At the donne dere."

I think that I cannot preserve my health and spirits, unless I spend four hours a day at least—and it is commonly more than that—sauntering through the woods and over the hills and fields, absolutely free from all worldly engagements. You may safely say, A penny for your thoughts, or a thousand pounds. When sometimes I am reminded that the mechanics and shopkeepers stay in their shops not only all the forenoon, but all the afternoon too, sitting with crossed legs, so many of them,—as if the legs were made to sit upon, and not to stand or walk upon,—I think that they deserve some credit for not having all committed suicide long ago.

I, who cannot stay in my chamber for a single day without acquiring some rust, and when sometimes I have stolen forth for a walk at the eleventh hour of four o'clock in the afternoon, too late to redeem the day, when the shades of night were already beginning to be mingled with the daylight, have felt as if I had committed some sin to be atoned for,—I confess that I am astonished at the power of endurance, to say nothing of the moral insensibility, of my neighbors who confine themselves to shops and offices the whole day for weeks and months, ay, and years almost together. I know not what manner of stuff they are of,—sitting there now at three o'clock in the afternoon, as if it were three o'clock in the morning. Bonaparte may talk of the three-o'clock-in-the-morning courage, but it is nothing to the courage which can sit down cheerfully at this hour in the afternoon over against one's self whom you have known all the morning, to starve out a garrison to whom you are bound by such strong ties of sympathy. I wonder that about this time, or say between four and five o'clock in the afternoon, too late for the morning papers and too early for the evening ones, there is not a general explosion heard up and down the street, scattering a legion of antiquated and house-bred notions and whims to the four winds for an airing,—and so the evil cure itself.

How womankind, who are confined to the house still more than men, stand it I do not know; but I have ground to suspect that most of them do not *stand* it at all. When, early in a summer afternoon, we have been shaking the dust of the village from the skirts of our garments, making haste past those houses with purely Doric or Gothic fronts, which have such an air of repose about them, my companion whispers that probably about these times their occupants are all gone to bed. Then it is that I appreciate the beauty and the glory of architecture, which itself never turns in, but forever stands out and erect, keeping watch over the slumberers.

No doubt temperament, and, above all, age, have a good deal to do with it. As a man grows older, his ability to sit still and follow in-door occupations increases. He grows vespertinal in his habits as the evening of life approaches, till at last he comes forth only just before sun-down, and gets all the walk that he requires in half an hour.

But the walking of which I speak has nothing in it akin to taking exercise, as it is called, as the sick take medicine at stated hours,—as the swinging of dumbbells or chairs; but is itself the enterprise and adventure of the day. If you would get exercise, go in search of the springs of life. Think of a man's swinging dumbbells for his health, when those springs are bubbling up in far-off pastures unsought by him!

Moreover, you must walk like a camel, which is said to be the only beast which ruminates when walking. When a traveller asked Words-worth's servant to show him her master's study, she answered, "Here is his library, but his study is out of doors."

Living much out of doors, in the sun and wind, will no doubt produce a certain roughness of character,—will cause a thicker cuticle to grow over some of the finer qualities of our nature, as on the face and hands, or as severe manual labor robs the hands of some of their delicacy of touch. So staying in the house, on the other hand, may produce a softness and smoothness, not to say thinness of skin, accompanied by an increased sensibility to certain impressions. Perhaps we should be more susceptible to some influences important to our intellectual and moral growth, if the sun had shone and the wind blown on us a little less; and no doubt it is a nice matter to proportion rightly the thick and thin skin. But methinks that is a scurf that will fall off fast enough,—that the natural remedy is to be found in the proportion which the night bears to the day, the winter to the summer, thought to experience. There will be so much the more air and sunshine in our thoughts. The callous palms of the laborer are conversant with finer tissues of self-respect and heroism, whose touch thrills the heart, than the languid fingers of idleness. That is mere sentimentality that lies abed by day and thinks itself white, far from the tan and callus of experience.

When we walk, we naturally go to the fields and woods: what would become of us, if we walked only in a garden or a mall? Even some sects of philosophers have felt the necessity of importing the woods to themselves, since they did not go to the woods. "They planted groves and walks of Plantanes," where they took *subdiales ambulationes* in porticos open to the air. Of course it is of no use to direct our steps to the woods, if they do not carry us thither. I am alarmed when it happens that I have walked a mile into the woods bodily, without getting there in spirit. In my afternoon walk I would fain forget all my morning occupations and my obligations to society. But it sometimes happens that I cannot easily shake off the village. The thought of some work will run in my head, and I am not where my body is,—I am out of my senses. In my walks I would fain return to my senses. What business have I in the woods, if I am thinking of something out of the woods? I suspect myself, and cannot help a shudder, when I find myself so implicated even in what are called good works,—for this may sometimes happen.

My vicinity affords many good walks; and though for so many years I have walked almost every day, and sometimes for several days together, I have not yet exhausted them. An absolutely new prospect is a great happiness, and I can still get this any afternoon. Two or three hours' walking will carry me to as strange a country as I expect ever to see. A single farm-house which I had not seen before is sometimes as good as the dominions of the King of Dahomey. There is in fact a sort of harmony discoverable between the capabilities of the landscape within a circle of ten miles' radius, or the limits of an afternoon walk, and the threescore years and ten of human life. It will never become quite familiar to you.

Nowadays almost all man's improvements, so called, as the building of houses, and the cutting down of the forest and of all large trees, simply deform the landscape, and make it more and more tame and cheap. A people who would begin by burning the fences and let the forest stand! I saw the fences half consumed, their ends lost in the middle of the prairie, and some worldly miser with a surveyor looking after his bounds, while heaven had taken place around him, and he did not see the angels going to and fro, but was looking for an old post-hole in the midst of paradise. I looked again, and saw him standing in the middle of a boggy, stygian fen, surrounded by devils, and he had found his bounds without a doubt, three little stones, where a stake had been driven, and looking nearer, I saw that the Prince of Darkness was his surveyor.

I can easily walk ten, fifteen, twenty, any number of miles, commencing at my own door, without going by any house, without crossing a road except where the fox and the mink do: first along by the river, and then the brook, and then the meadow and the wood-side. There are square miles in my vicinity which have no inhabitant. From many a hill I can see civilization and the abodes of man afar. The farmers and their works are scarcely more obvious than woodchucks and their burrows. Man and his affairs, church and state and school, trade and commerce, and manufactures and agriculture, even politics, the most alarming of them all,—I am pleased to see how little space they occupy in the landscape. Politics but a narrow field, and that still narrower highway yonder leads to it. I sometimes direct the traveller thither. If you would go to the political world, follow the great road,—follow that market-man, keep his dust in your eyes, and it will lead you straight to it; for it, too, has its place merely, and does not occupy all space. I pass from it as from a beanfield into the forest, and it is forgotten. In one half-hour I can walk off to some portion of the earth's surface where a man does not stand from one year's end to another, and there, consequently, politics are not . . .

# HENRY DAVID THOREAU
## TWO PROPOSALS FOR LAND PRESERVATION
### (1858, 1859)

Thoreau has been called a prophet of American environmentalism, which did not become an organized movement until a generation after his death. The Sierra Club (founded 1892) took for its motto Thoreau's pronouncement "In wildness is the preservation of the world." A loner himself, Thoreau confined his advocacy of wilderness—and the near-home wild spaces that concerned him most—to his writing. But he did venture some farsighted suggestions about the creation of forest preserves and town parks. Here are two examples. The first selection is the concluding paragraph of "Chesuncook" (1858), a narrative of the second of three excursions to northeastern New England that were later collected as *The Maine Woods* (1864). The second, from Thoreau's *Journal,* was evidently intended to form one of the closing paragraphs of the unfinished *Wild Fruits* (New York: Norton, 1999, ed. Bradley P. Dean), unbeknownst even to most Thoreau scholars for more than a century. Thoreau was hardly the first American to envision park preservation, but he was well ahead of the curve. Note especially how he anticipates and rebuts the idea that parks are only for the elite.

SOURCES: (1) *The Maine Woods.* Boston: Ticknor & Fields, 1864. (2) *The Journal of Henry D. Thoreau,* ed. Bradford Torrey and Francis Allen. Boston: Houghton, 1906.

( 1 )

The kings of England formerly had their forests "to hold the king's game," for sport or food, sometimes destroying villages to create or extend them; and I think that they were impelled by a true instinct. Why should not we, who have renounced the king's authority, have our national preserves, where no villages need be destroyed, in which the bear and panther, and some even of the hunter race, may still exist, and not be "civilized off the face of the earth,"—our forests, not to hold the king's game merely, but to hold and preserve the king himself also, the lord of creation,—not for idle sport or food, but for inspiration and our own true recreation? or shall we, like villains, grub them all up, poaching on our own national domains?

( 2 )

[October 15, 1859] Each town should have a park, or rather a primitive forest, of five hundred or a thousand acres, where a stick should never be cut for fuel, a common possession forever, for instruction and recreation. We hear of cow-commons and ministerial lots, but we want *men*-commons and lay lots, inalienable forever. Let us keep the New World *new,* preserve all the advantages of living in the country. There is meadow and pasture and wood-lot for the town's poor. Why not a forest and huckleberry-field for the town's rich? All Walden Wood might have been preserved for our park forever, with Walden in its midst, and the Easterbrooks Country, an unoccupied area of some four square miles, might have been our huckleberry-field. If any owners of these tracts are about to leave the world without natural heirs who need or deserve to be specially remembered, they will do wisely to abandon their possession to all, and not will them to some individual who perhaps has enough already. As some give to Harvard College or another institution, why might not another give a forest or huckleberry-field to Concord? . . . We boast of our system of education, but why stop at schoolmasters and schoolhouses? We are all schoolmasters, and our school-house is the universe. To attend chiefly to the desk or school-house while we neglect the scenery in which it is placed is absurd. If we do not look out we shall find our fine schoolhouse standing in a cow-yard at last.

# 5.

# Thomas Wentworth Higginson

## from "Saints, and Their Bodies"
### (1858)

Higginson was the first Transcendentalist other than Thoreau to argue strenuously for the merits of physical culture as such. He deplored what he saw as a general declension of American vigor and strength since colonial times. As a minister with a passion for the outdoors and for testing his own physical limits, Higginson was perturbed by the public perception of ministers as an effete class, and of the supposed correlation between saintliness and sickliness, or denial of the body. Such was the aura that invested William Ellery Channing, "the little saint with the flaming heart" revered by liberal Unitarians. So, too, a fictional figure like Hawthorne's Reverend Arthur Dimmesdale in *The Scarlet Letter* (1850). Higginson, by contrast, advocated what the Victorian era came to call "muscular Christianity." His praise of exercise as necessary to the perfection of the complete man—and woman!—synchronizes with Thoreau's protestation that he needed as much daily walking time as indoor study time, and with Emerson's praise of Thoreau's physical dexterity and keen senses. Indeed, "outdoors" meant much more to Higginson than sports and exercise, as his later remarks make clear. He shared Thoreau's zest for nature and for natural history. In fact, almost half of the other chapters in the book from which this selection comes are nature essays. "Saints, and Their Bodies" also foreshadows the satisfaction Higginson took as an officer during the Civil War (see his *Army Life in a Black Regiment*) in acts of physical courage and endurance.

SOURCE: "Saints, and Their Bodies," *Out-Door Papers.* Boston: Houghton, 1863.

Ever since the time of that dyspeptic heathen, Plotinus, the saints have been "ashamed of their bodies." What is worse, they have usually had reason for the shame. Of the four famous Latin fathers, Jerome describes his own limbs as misshapen, his skin as squalid, his bones as scarcely holding together; while Gregory the Great speaks in his Epistles of his own large size, as contrasted with his weakness and infirmities. Three of the four Greek fathers—Chrysostom, Basil, and Gregory Nazianzen—ruined their health early, and were invalids for the remainder of their days. Three only of the whole eight were able-bodied men,—Ambrose, Augustine, and Athanasius; and the permanent influence of these three has been far greater, for good or for evil, than that of all the others put together. . . .

———

It would be tedious to analyze the causes of this modern deterioration of the saints. The fact is clear. There is in the community an impression that physical vigor and spiritual sanctity are incompatible. Recent ecclesiastical history records that a young Orthodox divine lost his parish by swimming the Merrimac River, and that another was compelled to ask a dismissal in consequence of vanquishing his most influential parishioner in a game of ten-pins; it seemed to the beaten party very unclerical. The writer further remembers a match, in a certain seaside bowling-alley, in which two brothers, young divines, took part. The sides being made up, with the exception of these two players, it was necessary to find places for them also. The head of one side accordingly picked his man, on the avowed presumption that the best preacher would naturally be the worst bowler. The athletic capacity, he thought, would be in inverse ratio to the sanctity. It is a satisfaction to add, that in this case his hopes were signally disappointed. But it shows which way the popular impression lies.

———

. . . so far there is a deficiency in these respects among us, this generation must not shrink from the responsibility. It is unfair to charge it on the Puritans. They are not even answerable for Massachusetts; for there is no doubt that athletic exercises, of some sort, were far more generally practised in this community before the Revolution than at present. A state of almost constant Indian warfare then created an obvious demand for muscle and agility. At present there is no such immediate necessity. And it has been supposed that a race of shop-keepers, brokers, and lawyers could live without bodies. Now that the terrible records of dyspepsia and paralysis are disproving this, one may hope for a reaction in favor of bodily exercises. And when we once begin the competition, there seems no reason why any other nation should surpass us. The wide area of our country, and its variety of surface and shore, offer a corresponding range of physical training. Contrast our various aquatic opportunities, for instance. It is one thing to steer a pleasure-boat with a rudder, and another to steer a dory with an oar; one thing to paddle a birch-canoe, and another to paddle a ducking-float; in a Charles River club-boat, the post of honor is in the stern,—in a Penobscot *bateau*, in the bow; and each of these experiences educates a different set of muscles. Add to this the constitutional American receptiveness, which welcomes new pursuits without distinction of origin,—unites German gymnastics with English sports and sparring, and takes the red Indians for instructors in paddling and running. With these various aptitudes, we certainly ought to become a nation of athletes.

Thus it is that, in one way or another, American schoolboys obtain active exercise. The same is true, in a very limited degree, even of girls. They are occasionally, in our larger cities, sent to gymnasiums,—the more the better. Dancing-schools are better than nothing, though all the attendant circumstances are usually unfavorable. A fashionable young lady is estimated to traverse her three hundred miles a season on foot; and this needs training. But out-door exercise for girls is terribly restricted, first by their costume, and secondly by the social proprieties. All young female animals unquestionably require as much motion as their brothers, and naturally make as much noise; but what mother would not be shocked, in the case of her girl of twelve, by one tenth part the activity and uproar which are recognized as being the breath of life to her twin brother? Still, there is a change going on, which is tantamount to an admission that there is an evil to be remedied. Twenty years ago, if we mistake not, it was by no means considered "proper" for little girls to play with their hoops and balls on Boston Common; and swimming and skating have hardly been recognized as "lady-like" for half that period of time. . . .

But even among American men, how few carry athletic habits into manhood! The great hindrance, no doubt, is absorption in business; and we observe that this winter's hard times and consequent leisure have given a great stimulus to out-door sports. But in most places there is the further obstacle, that a certain stigma of boyishness goes with them. So early does this begin, that the writer remembers, in his teens, to have been slightly reproached with juvenility, for still clinging to foot-ball, though a Senior Sophister. Juvenility! He only wishes he had the opportunity now. Mature men are, of course, intended to take not only as much, but far more active exercise than boys. Some physiologists go so far as to demand six hours of out-door life daily; and it is absurd to complain that we have not the healthy animal happiness of children, while we forswear their simple sources of pleasure....

—

... Vishnu Sarma gives, in his apologues, the characteristics of the fit place for a wise man to live in, and enumerates among its necessities first "a Rajah" and then "a river." Democrats can dispense with the first, but not with the second. A square mile even of pond water is worth a year's schooling to any intelligent boy. A boat is a kingdom. I personally own one,—a mere flat-bottomed "float," with a centre-board. It has seen service,—it is eight years old,—has spent two winters under the ice, and been fished in by boys every day for as many summers. It grew at last so hopelessly leaky, that even the boys disdained it. It cost seven dollars originally, and I would not sell it to-day for seventeen. To own the poorest boat is better than hiring the best. It is a link to Nature; without a boat, one is so much the less a man.

Sailing is of course delicious; it is as good as flying to steer anything with wings of canvas, whether one stand by the wheel of a clipper-ship, or by the clumsy stern-oar of a "gundalow." But rowing has also its charms; and the Indian noiselessness of the paddle, beneath the fringing branches of the Assabeth or Artichoke, puts one into Fairyland at once, and Hiawatha's *cheemaun* becomes a possible possession. Rowing is peculiarly graceful and appropriate as a feminine exercise, and any able-bodied girl can learn to handle one light oar at the first lesson, and two at the second.

Swimming has also a birdlike charm of motion. The novel element, the free action, the abated drapery, give a sense of personal contact with Nature which nothing else so fully bestows. No later triumph of existence is so fascinating, perhaps, as that in which the boy first wins his panting way across the deep gulf that severs one green bank from another, (ten yards, perhaps,) and feels himself thenceforward lord of the watery world. The Athenian phrase for a man who knew nothing was, that he could "neither read nor swim." Yet there is a vast amount of this ignorance; the majority of sailors, it is said, cannot swim a stroke; and in a late lake disaster, many able-bodied men perished by drowning, in calm water, only half a mile from shore. At our watering-places it is rare to see a swimmer venture out more than a rod or two, though this proceeds partly from the fear of sharks,—as if sharks of the dangerous order were not far more afraid of the rocks than the swimmers of being eaten. But the fact of the timidity is unquestionable; and I was told by a certain clerical frequenter of a watering-place, himself an athlete, that he had never met but two companions who would swim boldly out with him, both being ministers, and one a distinguished Ex-President of Brown University. This fact must certainly be placed to the credit of the bodies of our saints. . . .

———

. . . the secret charm of all these sports and studies is simply this,—that they bring us into more familiar intercourse with Nature. They give us that *vitam sub divo* in which the Roman exulted,—those out-door days, which, say the Arabs, are not to be reckoned in the length of life. Nay, to a true lover of the open air, night beneath its curtain is as beautiful as day. The writer has personally camped out under a variety of auspices,—before a fire of pine logs in the forests of Maine, beside a blaze of faya-boughs on the steep side of a foreign volcano, and beside no fire at all (except a possible one of Sharp's rifles), in that domestic volcano, Kansas; and every such remembrance is worth many nights of in-door slumber. There is never a week in the year, nor an hour of day or night, which has not, in the open air, its own special interest. One need not say, with Reade's Australians, that the only use of a house is to sleep in the lee of it; but they might do worse. As for rain, it is chiefly formidable in-doors. Lord Bacon used to ride with uncovered head in a shower, and loved "to feel the spirit of the universe upon his brow"; and I once knew an enthusiastic hydropathic physician who loved to expose himself in thunder-storms at midnight, without a shred of earthly clothing between himself and the atmosphere. Some prudent persons may possibly regard this as being rather an extreme, while yet their own extreme of avoidance of every breath from heaven is really the more extravagantly unreasonable of the two.

It is easy for the sentimentalist to say, "But if the object is, after all, the enjoyment of Nature, why not go and enjoy her, without any collateral aim?" Because it is the universal experience of man, that, if we have a collateral aim, we enjoy her far more. He knows not the beauty of the universe, who has not learned the subtle mystery, that Nature loves to work on us by *indirections.* Astronomers say, that, when observing with the naked eye, you see a star less clearly by looking at it, than by looking at the next one. Margaret Fuller's fine saying touches the same point,—"Nature will not be stared at." Go out merely to enjoy her, and it seems a little tame, and you begin to suspect yourself of affectation. There are persons who, after years of abstinence from athletic sports or the pursuits of the naturalist or artist, have resumed them, simply in order to restore to the woods and the sunsets the zest of the old fascination. Go out under pretence of shooting on the marshes or botanizing in the forests; study entomology, that most fascinating, most neglected of all the branches of natural history; go to paint a red maple-leaf in autumn, or watch a pickerel-line in winter; meet Nature on the cricket-ground or at the regatta; swim with her, ride with her, run with her, and she gladly takes you back once more within the horizon of her magic, and your heart of manhood is born again into more than the fresh happiness of the boy.

# E.
## ANTISLAVERY

# 1.

# RALPH WALDO EMERSON

## THE SIGNIFICANCE OF BRITISH WEST INDIAN EMANCIPATION

### (1844)

Emerson always hated slavery, but the early aversion to institutionalized reform that he voices in "Self-Reliance" (1841) made him a tardy convert to antislavery activism. This is his first strong public statement on the subject, delivered in Concord at a meeting attended by Frederick Douglass as well as various white abolitionist notables, on the tenth anniversary of British abolition of slavery in the West Indies (August 1, 1834), the date that the African-American community was already celebrating as Black Independence Day. The abolitionist establishment Emerson had previously satirized he now began to embrace. His extensive reading in the long history of British imperial slavery and emancipation efforts aroused as never before Emerson's moral outrage at the abuses of the system and his admiration for the reformers. Although he himself did not become a consistent antislavery activist until after 1850, from this point on American abolitionists counted him as one of their own. Printed below is the culminating portion of the address, in which Emerson, eloquently if somewhat paradoxically, praises first "the civilization of the negro" and then "the genius of the Saxon race, friendly to liberty."

SOURCE: *An Address Delivered in the Court-House in Concord, Massachusetts, on 1st August, 1844, on the Anniversary of the Emancipation of the Negroes in the British West Indies.* Boston: James Munroe, 1844.

This event was a moral revolution. The history of it is before you. Here was no prodigy, no fabulous hero, no Trojan horse, no bloody war, but all was achieved by plain means of plain men, working not under a leader, but under a sentiment. Other revolutions have been the insurrection of the oppressed; this was the repentence of the tyrant. It was the masters revolting from their mastery. The slave-holder said, I will not hold slaves. The end was noble, and the means were pure. Hence, the elevation and pathos of this chapter of history. The lives of the advocates are pages of greatness, and the connexion of the eminent senators with this question, constitutes the immortalizing moments of those men's lives. The bare enunciation of the theses, at which the lawyers and legislators arrived, gives a glow to the heart of the reader. Lord Chancellor Northington is the author of the famous sentence, "As soon as any man puts his foot on English ground, he becomes free." "I was a slave," said the counsel of Somerset, speaking for his client, "for I was in America: I am now in a country, where the common rights of mankind are known and regarded." Granville Sharp filled the ear of the judges with the sound principles, that had from time to time been affirmed by the legal authorities. "Derived power cannot be superior to the power from which it is derived." "The reasonableness of the law is the soul of the law." "It is better to suffer every evil, than to consent to any." Out it would come, the God's truth, out it came, like a bolt from a cloud, for all the mumbling of the lawyers. One feels very sensibly in all this history that a great heart and soul are behind there, superior to any man, and making use of each, in turn, and infinitely attractive to every person according to the degree of reason in his own mind, so that this cause has had the power to draw to it every particle of talent and of worth in England, from the beginning. . . .

I will say further, that we are indebted mainly to this movement, and to the continuers of it, for the popular discussion of every point of practical ethics, and a reference of every question to the absolute standard. It is notorious, that the political, religious, and social schemes, with which the minds of men are now most occupied, have been matured, or at least broached, in the free and daring discussions of these assemblies. Men have become aware through the emancipation, and kindred events, of the presence of powers, which, in their days of darkness, they had overlooked. Virtuous men will not again rely on political agents. They have found out the deleterious effect of political association. Up to this day, we have allowed to statesmen a paramount social standing, and we bow low to them as to the great. We cannot extend this deference to them any longer. The secret cannot be kept, that the seats of power are filled by underlings, ignorant, timid, and selfish, to a degree to destroy all claim, excepting that on compassion, to the society of the just and generous. What happened notoriously to an American ambassador in England, that he found himself compelled to palter, and to disguise the fact that he was a slave-breeder, happens to men of state. Their vocation is a presumption against them, among well-meaning people. The superstition respecting power and office, is going to the ground. The stream of human affairs flows its own way, and is very little affected by the activity of legislators. What great masses of men wish done, will be done; and they do not wish it for a freak, but because it is their state and natural end. There are now other energies than force, other than political, which no man in future can allow himself to disregard. There is direct conversation and influence. A man is to make himself felt, by his proper force. The tendency of things runs steadily to this point, namely, to put every man on his merits, and to give him so much power as he naturally exerts—no more, no less. Of course, the timid and base persons, all who are conscious of no worth in themselves, and who owe all their place to the opportunities which the old order of things allowed them to deceive and defraud men, shudder at the change, and would fain silence every honest voice, and lock up every house where liberty and innovation can be pleaded for. They would raise mobs, for fear is very cruel. But the strong and healthy yeomen and husbands of the land, the self-sustaining class of inventive and industrious men, fear no competition or superiority. Come what will, their faculty cannot be spared.

The First of August marks the entrance of a new element into modern politics, namely, the civilization of the negro. A man is added to the human family. Not the least affecting part of this history of abolition, is, the annihilation of the old indecent nonsense about the nature of the negro. In the case of the ship Zong, in 1781, whose master had thrown one hundred and thirty-two slaves alive into the sea, to cheat the underwriters, the first jury gave a verdict in favor of the master and owners: they had a right to do what they had done. Lord Mansfield is reported to have said on the bench, "The matter left to the jury is,— Was it from necessity? For they had no doubt,—though it shocks one very much,—that the case of slaves was the same as if horses had been thrown overboard. It is a very shocking case." But a more enlightened and humane opinion began to prevail. Mr. Clarkson, early in his career, made a collection of African productions and manufactures, as specimens of the arts and culture of the negro; comprising cloths and loom, weapons, polished stones and woods, leather, glass, dyes, ornaments, soap, pipe-bowls, and trinkets. These he showed to Mr. Pitt, who saw and handled them with extreme interest. "On sight of these," says Clarkson, "many sublime thoughts seemed to rush at once into his mind, some of which he expressed;" and hence appeared to arise a project which was always dear to him, of the civilization of Africa,— a dream which forever elevates his fame. In 1791, Mr. Wilberforce announced to the House of Commons, "We have already gained one victory: we have obtained for these poor creatures the recognition of their human nature, which, for a time, was most shamefully denied them." It was the sarcasm of Montesquieu, "it would not do to suppose that negroes were men, lest it should turn out that whites were not;" for, the white has, for ages, done what he could to keep the negro in that hoggish state. His laws have been furies. It now appears, that the negro race is, more than any other, susceptible of rapid civilization. The emancipation is observed, in the islands, to have wrought for the negro a benefit as sudden as when a thermometer is brought out of the shade into the sun. It has given him eyes and ears. If, before, he was taxed with such stupidity, or such defective vision, that he could not set a table square to the walls of an apartment, he is now the principal, if not the only mechanic, in the West Indies; and is, besides, an architect, a physician, a lawyer, a magistrate, an editor, and a valued and increasing political power. The recent testimonies of Sturge, of Thome and Kimball, of Gurney, of Phillippo, are very explicit on this point, the capacity and the success of the colored and the black population in employments of skill, of profit, and of trust; and, best of all, is the testimony to their moderation. They receive hints and advances from the whites, that they will be gladly received as subscribers to the Exchange, as members of this or that committee of trust. They hold back, and say to each other, that "social position is not to be gained by pushing."

I have said that this event interests us because it came mainly from the concession of the whites; I add, that in part it is the earning of the blacks. They won the pity and respect which they have received, by their powers and native endowments. I think this a circumstance of the highest import. Their whole future is in it. Our planet, before the age of written history, had its races of savages, like the generations of sour paste, or the animalcules that wriggle and bite in a drop of putrid water. Who cares for these or for their wars? We do not wish a world of bugs or of birds; neither afterward of Scythians, Caraibs, or Feejees. The grand style of nature, her great periods, is all we observe in them. Who cares for oppressing whites, or oppressed blacks, twenty centuries ago, more than for bad dreams? Eaters and food are in the harmony of nature; and there too is the germ forever protected, unfolding gigantic leaf after leaf, a newer flower, a richer fruit, in every period, yet its next product is never to be guessed. It will only save what is worth saving; and it saves not by compassion, but by power. It appoints no police to guard the lion, but his teeth and claws; no fort or city for the bird, but his wings; no rescue for flies and mites, but their spawning numbers, which no ravages can overcome. It deals with men after the same manner. If they are rude and foolish, down they must go. When at last in a race, a new principle appears, an idea;—*that* conserves it; ideas only save races. If the black man is feeble, and not important to the existing races not on a parity with the best race, the black man must serve, and be exterminated. But if the black man carries in his bosom an indispensable element of a new and coming civilization, for the sake of that element, no wrong, nor strength, nor circumstance, can hurt him: he will survive and play his part. So now, the arrival in the world of such men as Toussaint, and the Haytian heroes, or of the leaders of their race in Barbadoes and Jamaica, outweighs in good omen all the English and American humanity. The anti-slavery of the whole world, is dust in the balance before this,—is a poor squeamishness and nervousness: the might and the right are here: here is the anti-slave: here is man: and if you have man, black or white is an insignificance. The intellect,—that is miraculous! Who has it, has the talisman: his skin and bones, though they were of the color of night, are transparent, and the everlasting stars shine through, with attractive beams. But a compassion for that which is not and cannot be useful or lovely, is degrading and futile. All the songs, and newspapers, and money-subscriptions, and vituperation of such as do not think with us, will avail nothing against a fact. I say to you, you must save yourself, black or white, man or woman; other help is none. I esteem the occasion of this jubilee to be the proud discovery, that the black race can contend with the white; that, in the great anthem which we call history, a piece of many parts and vast compass, after playing a long time a very low and subdued accompaniment, they perceive the time arrived when they can strike in with effect, and take a master's part in the music. The civility of the world has reached that pitch, that their more moral genius is becoming indispensable, and the quality of this race is to be honored for itself. For this, they have been preserved in sandy deserts, in rice-swamps, in kitchens and shoe-shops, so long: now let them emerge, clothed and in their own form.

There remains the very elevated consideration which the subject opens, but which belongs to more abstract views than we are now taking, this namely, that the civility of no race can be perfect whilst another race is degraded. It is a doctrine alike of the oldest, and of the newest philosophy, that, man is one, and that you cannot injure any member, without a sympathetic injury to all the members. America is not civil, whilst Africa is barbarous.

These considerations seem to leave no choice for the action of the intellect and the conscience of the country. There have been moments in this, as well as in every piece of moral history, when there seemed room for the infusions of a skeptical philosophy; when it seemed doubtful, whether brute force would not triumph in the eternal struggle. I doubt not, that sometimes a despairing negro, when jumping over the ship's sides to escape from the white devils who surrounded him, has believed there was no vindication of right; it is horrible to think of, but it seemed so. I doubt not, that sometimes the negro's friend, in the face of scornful and brutal hundreds of traders and drivers, has felt his heart sink. Especially, it seems to me, some degree of despondency is pardonable, when he observes the men of conscience and of intellect, his own natural allies and champions,— those whose attention should be nailed to the grand objects of this cause, so hotly offended by whatever incidental petulances or infirmities of indiscreet defenders of the negro, as to permit themselves to be ranged with the enemies of the human race; and names which should be the alarums of liberty and the watchwords of truth, are mixed up with all the rotten rabble of selfishness and tyranny. I assure myself that this coldness and blindness will pass away. A single noble wind of sentiment will scatter them forever. I am sure that the good and wise elders, the ardent and generous youth will not permit what is incidental and exceptional to withdraw their devotion from the essential and permanent characters of the question. There have been moments, I said, when men might be forgiven, who doubted. Those moments are past. Seen in masses, it cannot be disputed, there is progress in human society. There is a blessed necessity by which the interest of men is always driving them to the right; and, again, making all crime mean and ugly. The genius of the Saxon race, friendly to liberty; the enterprise, the very muscular vigor of this nation, are inconsistent with slavery. The Intellect, with blazing eye, looking through history from the beginning onward, gazes on this blot, and it disappears. The sentiment of Right, once very low and indistinct, but ever more articulate, because it is the voice of the universe, pronounces Freedom. The Power that built this fabric of things affirms it in the heart; and in the history of the First of August, has made a sign to the ages, of his will.

# 2.

# Margaret Fuller

## On *The Narrative of Frederick Douglass*
### (1845)

Fuller makes clear her antislavery convictions in this review of the most famous and one of the most accomplished of all antebellum slave narratives. Douglass might have been composing it at the time of Emerson's antislavery address, which Douglass heard but is not known to have said anything about. Had he seen Fuller's review, it would likely have gratified him without fully satisfying him. Like most northern white opponents of slavery, including Emerson and Parker, Fuller continued to think in racialist terms of the distinctive traits of "the African race." More seriously—for Douglass sometimes used racialist rhetoric, too, for his own purposes—Fuller carefully distances herself here from abolitionist zealotry, almost as much as Emerson did in "Self-Reliance," and she carefully distinguishes her detestation for the institution of slavery from her attitude toward slaveholders. Fuller seems even a bit regretful that Douglass's activism kept him from manifesting more of the "torrid energy" and "saccharine fulness" that she sees as distinctive marks of "African" genius. Later in the 1840s, and particularly after the Compromise of 1850 (the year of Fuller's death), Transcendentalist reformers moved more decisively into the abolitionist camp. In her last dispatches from Italy (Section IV-A), Fuller took back her harsh words about abolitionists, as Emerson had begun to do.

SOURCE: "Frederick Douglass," *New York Daily Tribune,* June 10, 1845.

Frederick Douglass has been for some time a prominent member of the Abolition party. He is said to be an excellent speaker—can speak from a thorough personal experience—and has upon the audience, beside, the influence of a strong character and uncommon talents. In the book before us he has put into the story of his life the thoughts, the feelings and the adventures that have been so affecting through the living voice; nor are they less so from the printed page. He has had the courage to name the persons, times and places, thus exposing himself to obvious danger, and setting the seal on his deep convictions as to the religious need of speaking the whole truth. Considered merely as a narrative, we have never read one more simple, true, coherent, and warm with genuine feeling. It is an excellent piece of writing, and on that score to be prized as a specimen of the powers of the Black Race, which Prejudice persists in disputing. We prize highly all evidence of this kind, and it is becoming more abundant. The Cross of the Legion of Honor has just been conferred in France on Dumas and Soulie, both celebrated in the paths of light literature. Dumas, whose father was a General in the French Army, is a Mulatto; Soulie, a Quadroon. He went from New-Orleans, where, though to the eye a white man, yet, as known to have African blood in his veins, he could never have enjoyed the privileges due to a human being. Leaving the land of Freedom, he found himself free to develope the powers that God had given.

Two wise and candid thinkers,—the Scotchman, Kinmont, prematurely lost to this country, of which he was so faithful and generous a student, and the late Dr. Channing,—both thought that the African Race had in them a peculiar element, which, if it could be assimilated with those imported among us from Europe, would give to genius a development, and to the energies of character a balance and harmony beyond what has been seen heretofore in the history of the world. Such an element is indicated in their lowest estate by a talent for melody, a ready skill at imitation and adaptation, an almost indestructible elasticity of nature. It is to be remarked in the writings both of Soulie and Dumas, full of faults but glowing with plastic life and fertile invention. The same torrid energy and saccharine fulness may be felt in the writings of this Douglass, though his life being one of action or resistance, was less favorable to *such* powers than one of a more joyous flow might have been.

The book is prefaced by two communications,—one from Garrison, and one from Wendell Phillips. That from the former is in his usual over emphatic style. His motives and his course have been noble and generous. We look upon him with high respect, but he has indulged in violent invective and denunciation till he has spoiled the temper of his mind. Like a man who has been in the habit of screaming himself hoarse to make the deaf hear, he can no longer pitch his voice on a key agreeable to common ears. Mr. Phillips's remarks are equally decided, without this exaggeration in the tone. Douglass himself seems very just and temperate. We feel that his view, even of those who have injured him most, may be relied upon. He knows how to allow for motives and influences. Upon the subject of Religion, he speaks with great force, and not more than our own sympathies can respond to. The inconsistencies of Slaveholding professors of religion cry to Heaven. We are not disposed to detest, or refuse communion with them. Then blindness is but one form of that prevalent fallacy which substitutes a creed for a faith, a ritual for a life. We have seen too much of this system of atonement not to know that those who adopt it often began with good intentions, and are, at any rate, in their mistakes worthy of the deepest pity. But that is no reason why the truth should not be uttered, trumpet-tongued, about the thing.

# Theodore Parker

## from "The Function of Conscience"
### (1850)

### and

## "The Fugitive Slave Law"
### (1851)

Nothing did more to intensify northern liberals' detestation of slavery and draw them into the radical abolitionist camp than the passage and the enforcement of a more stringent federal Fugitive Slave Law, as part of the so-called Compromise of 1850. It imposed more draconian requirements on the northern states to assist slave masters in recapturing escapees. This outraged figures like Parker, Emerson, and Thoreau as a violation of human rights, as a capitulation of north to south, and as a blow to New England's proud heritage of moral rectitude. Many Transcendentalists had long held that conscience was, in principle, a higher authority than public opinion or the imperfect laws of the state. This had been the basis of their religious radicalism. Now they linked this vision more firmly than ever before to a secular reform; and as the broader tide of opinion in the north gradually swung from the 1850s into the 1860s in favor of antislavery activism, Transcendentalism started to become almost mainstream. During this time, no Transcendentalist was more outspoken on behalf of abolition than Theodore Parker, as the next two selections show. The first is from a sermon arguing for the priority of conscience over Constitution in general terms. The second gives a more specific idea of what Parker was up against in his own backyard. Always vehement, he was made even more so by the recalcitrance of conservative clerical brethren and by his sense of responsibility to his heterogeneous congregation, which included some fugitives. We see both these motives at work in the following selections: the first from a sermon, the second from a speech delivered at an 1851 meeting of a ministerial conference in Boston. Although he had previously preached against war, Parker now disowns "non-resistance" (the current term for pacifism) and declares himself ready to use violence if necessary to protect fugitives against slave catchers.

SOURCES: (1) *Speeches, Addresses, and Occasional Sermons.* Boston: Crosby and Nichols, 1852; (2) *The Rights of Man in America.* Boston: American Unitarian Association, 1911.

( 1 )

Suppose a man has sworn to keep the Constitution of the United States, and the Constitution is found to be wrong in certain particulars: then his oath is not morally binding, for before his oath, by his very existence, he is morally bound to keep the law of God as fast as he learns it. No oath can absolve him from his natural allegiance to God. Yet I see not how a man can knowingly, and with a good conscience, swear to keep what he deems wrong to keep, and will not keep, and does not intend to keep.

It seems to me very strange that men so misunderstand the rights of conscience and their obligations to obey their country. Not long ago, an eminent man taunted one of his opponents, telling him he had better adhere to the "higher law." The newspapers echoed the sneer, as if there were no law higher than the Constitution. Latterly, the democratic party, even more completely than the whig party, seems to have forgotten that there is any law higher than the Constitution, any rights above vested rights.

An eminent theologian of New England, who has hitherto done good and great service in his profession, grinding off the barb of Calvinism, wrote a book in defence of slave-catching, on "Conscience and the Constitution," a book which not only sins against the sense of the righteous in being wicked, but against the worldliness of the world in being weak,—and he puts the official business of keeping "a compact" far before the natural duty of keeping a conscience void of offence, and serving God. But suppose forty thieves assemble on Fire Island, and make a compact to rob every vessel wrecked on their coast, and reduce the survivors to bondage. Suppose I am born amongst that brotherhood of pirates, am I morally bound to keep that compact, or to perform any function which grows out of it? Nay, I am morally bound to violate the compact, to keep the pirates from their plunder and their prey. Instead of forty thieves on Fire Island, suppose twenty millions of men in the United States make a compact to enslave every sixth man—the dark men—am I morally bound to heed that compact, or to perform any function which grows out of it? Nay, I am morally bound to violate the compact, in every way that is just and wise. The very men who make such a compact are morally discharged from it as soon as they see it is wrong. The forty Jews who bound themselves by wicked oath to kill Paul before they broke their fast,—were they morally bound to keep their word? Nay, morally bound to break it.

I will tell you a portion of the story of a fugitive slave whom I have known. I will call his name Joseph, though he was in worse than Egyptian bondage. He was "owned" by a notorious gambler, and once ran away, but was retaken. His master proceeded to punish him for that crime, took him to a chamber, locked the door and lighted a fire; he then beat the slave severely. After that he put the branding-iron in the fire, took a knife,—I am not telling of what took place in Algiers, but in Alabama,—and proceeded to cut off the ears of his victim! The owner's wife, alarmed at the shrieks of the sufferer, beat down the door with a sledge-hammer, and prevented that catastrophe. Afterwards, two slaves of this gambler, for stealing their master's sheep, were beaten so that they died of the stripes. The "Minister" came to the funeral, told the others that those were wicked slaves, who deserved their fate; that they would never "rise" in the general resurrection, and were not fit to be buried! Accordingly their bodies were thrown into a hole and left there. Joseph ran away again; he came to Boston; was sheltered by a man whose charity never fails; he has been in my house, and often has worshipped here with us. Shall I take that man and deliver him up?— do it "with alacrity?" Shall I suffer that gambler to carry his prey from this city? Will you allow it—though all the laws and constitutions of men give the commandment? God do so unto us if we suffer it.

( 2 )

A little while ago we were told we must not preach on this matter of slavery, because it was "an abstraction;" then because the North was "all right on that subject;" and then because we had "nothing to do with it," we "must go to Charleston or New Orleans to see it." But now it is a most concrete thing. We see what public opinion is on the matter of slavery; what it is in Boston; nay, what it is with members of this Conference. It favors slavery and this wicked law! We need not go to Charleston and New Orleans to see slavery; our own court-house was a barracoon; our officers of this city were slave-hunters, and members of Unitarian churches in Boston are kidnappers.

I have in my church black men, fugitive slaves. They are the crown of my apostleship, the seal of my ministry. It becomes me to look after their bodies in order to "save their souls." This law has brought us into the most intimate connection with the sin of slavery. I have been obliged to take my own parishioners into my house to keep them out of the clutches of the kidnapper. Yes, gentlemen, I have been obliged to do that; and then to keep my door guarded by day as well as by night. Yes, I have had to arm myself. I have written my sermons with a pistol in my desk,—loaded, a cap on the nipple, and ready for action. Yea, with a drawn sword within reach of my right hand. This I have done in Boston; in the middle of the nineteenth century; been obliged to do it to defend the [innocent] members of my own church, women as well as men!

You know that I do not like fighting. I am no non-resistant, "that nonsense never went down with me." But it is no small matter which will compel me to shed human blood. But what could I do? I was born in the little town where the fight and bloodshed of the Revolution began. The bones of the men who first fell in that war are covered by the monument at Lexington, it is "sacred to liberty and the rights of man kind;" those men fell "in the sacred cause of God and their country." This is the first inscription that I ever read. These men were my kindred. My grandfather drew the first sword in the Revolution; my fathers fired the first shot; the blood which flowed there was kindred to this which courses in my veins to-day. Besides that, when I write in my library at home, on the one side of me is the Bible which my fathers prayed over, their morning and evening prayer, for nearly a hundred years. On the other side there hangs the firelock my grandfather fought with in the old French war, which he carried at the taking of Quebec, which he zealously used at the battle of Lexington, and beside it is another, a trophy of that war, the first gun taken in the Revolution, taken also by my grandfather. With these things before me, these symbols; with these memories in me, when a parishioner, a fugitive from slavery, a woman, pursued by the kidnappers, came to my house, what could I do less than take her in and defend her to the last? But who sought her life—or liberty? A parishioner of my brother Gannett came to kidnap a member of my church; Mr. Gannett preaches a sermon to justify the Fugitive Slave Law, demanding that it should be obeyed; yes, calling on his church members to kidnap mine, and sell them into bondage forever.

Yet all this while Mr. Gannett calls himself a "Christian," and me an "infidel;" his doctrine is "Christianity," mine only "infidelity," "deism, at the best!"

O my brothers, I am not afraid of men, I can offend them. I care nothing for their hate, or their esteem. I am not very careful of my reputation. But I should not dare to violate the eternal law of God. You have called me "infidel." Surely I differ widely enough from you in my theology. But there is one thing I cannot fail to trust; that is the Infinite God, Father of the white man, Father also of the white man's slave. I should not dare violate His laws, come what may come;—should you? Nay, I can love nothing so well as I love my God.

# RALPH WALDO EMERSON

## FROM "THE FUGITIVE SLAVE LAW"

### (1854)

During the 1850s and 1860s, Emerson's visibility on the national scene as an antislavery campaigner came to equal and ultimately surpass even Parker's. But Emerson's method of attack was quite different. Emerson preferred suppressed rage to open indignation, to combine moral fervor with cutting irony and insinuation, limiting passion and vitriol to short flashes, as this speech shows.

Emerson delivered it in New York City on the fourth anniversary of the controversial oration by Daniel Webster (1782–1852) in defense of the Compromise of 1850, anathema to the growing abolitionist community. For the younger Emerson, Webster had seemed the personification of eloquence, force of character, and—at best—public rectitude. Webster's betrayal of the antislavery principles that he once had advocated seemed all the more shocking and opportunistic to Emerson and fellow Transcendentalist antislavery advocates. Notice how both the previous selection and this one refer in scorn to Webster's taunting of the "higher law."

Emerson begins on the peculiar but distinctive note of stressing extreme reluctance to speak on the topic he is about to take up. This was a sincere expression of his long inner debate on whether social activism compromised the proper mission of a scholar (see also his earlier "Ode," Section V-C). But it was also a shrewd tactic. Only a crisis of the first magnitude, he insinuates, could have dragged me from my study into the arena. In calling attention to his own belated activism, furthermore, Emerson models the broader awakening he claims is taking place within northern society, and which he obviously seeks to further. True to his customary idealism, Emerson appeals especially to the power of principle. He indicts Webster and those who side with him for moral turpitude, and insists on the irresistible power of antislavery values to overcome all political obstacles, including the flawed U.S. Constitution. For "the Eternal constitution of the universe," as Emerson puts it, will always be on the side of the man of principle. This transformation of what he seems to have diagnosed as a losing battle into the guarantee of a winning one—provided his listeners rise to the challenge—is another Emerson hallmark.

SOURCE: "The Fugitive Slave Law," *Emerson's Antislavery Writings,* ed. Len Gougeon and Joel Myerson. New Haven: Yale University Press, 1995.

I do not often speak to public questions. They are odious and hurtful and it seems like meddling or leaving your work. I have my own spirits in prison,—spirits in deeper prisons, whom no man visits, if I do not. And then I see what havoc it makes with any good mind this dissipated philanthropy. The one thing not to be given to intellectual persons is not to know their own task, or to take their ideas from others and believe in the ideas of others. From this want of manly rest in their own, and foolish acceptance of other people's watchwords, comes the imbecility and fatigue of their conversation. For they cannot affirm these from any original experience, and of course, not with the natural movement and whole power of their nature and talent, but from their memory, only from the cramp position of standing for their teacher.— They say, what they would have you believe, but which they do not quite know.

My own habitual view is to the well-being of students or scholars, and it is only when the public event affects them, that it very seriously affects me. And what I have to say is to them. For every man speaks mainly to a class whom he works with, and more or less fitly represents. It is to them I am beforehand related and engaged,—in this audience or out of this audience,—to them and not to others. And yet when I say the class of scholars and students,—that is a class which comprises in some sort all mankind,—comprises every man in the best hours of his life:—and in these days not only virtually, but actually. For who are the readers and thinkers of 1854?

Owing to the silent revolution which the newspaper has wrought, this class has come in this country to take in all classes. Look into the morning trains, which, from every suburb carry the businessmen into the city, to their shops, counting-rooms, work-yards, and warehouses. With them, enters the car the humble priest of politics, philosophy, and religion in the shape of the newsboy. He unfolds his magical sheets, two pence a head his bread of knowledge costs, and instantly the entire rectangular assembly fresh from their breakfast, are bending as one man to their second breakfast. There is, no doubt, chaff enough, in what he brings, but there is fact and thought and wisdom in the crudeness from all regions of the world.

Now I have lived all my life without suffering any known inconvenience from American slavery. I never saw it; never heard the whip; I never felt the check on my free speech and action; until the other day when Mr. Webster by his personal influence brought the Fugitive Slave law on the country. I say Mr. Webster, for though the bill was not his, yet it is notorious that he was the life and soul of it, that he gave all he had, it cost him his life. And under the shadow of his great name, inferior men sheltered themselves, and threw their ballots for it, and made the law. I say inferior men; there were all sorts of what are called brilliant men, accomplished men, men of high office, a President of the United States, senators, and of eloquent speech, but men without self-respect, without character, and it was droll to see that office, age, fame, talent, even a repute for honesty, all count for nothing. They had no opinions, they had no memory for what they had been saying like the Lord's prayer, all their lifetime; they were only looking to what their great captain did, and if he jumped, they jumped,—if he stood on his head, they did. In ordinary, the supposed sense of the district and state is their guide, and this keeps them to liberty and justice. But it is always a little difficult to decipher what this public sense is: and when a great man comes, who knots up into himself the opinions and wishes of his people, it is so much easier to follow him as an exponent of this. He, too, is responsible, they will not be. It will always suffice to say,—I followed him. I saw plainly that the great show their legitimate power in nothing more than in their power to misguide us. I saw that a great man, deservedly esteemed and admired for his powers and their general right direction, was able, fault of the total want of stamina in public men, when he failed, to break them all with him, to carry parties with him.

It showed much. It ended a great deal of nonsense we had been accustomed to hear and to repeat, on the 22nd December, 19th April, 17th June, and 4th July. It showed what reputations are made of; what straw we dignify by office and title, and how competent they are to give counsel and help in a day of trial: the shallowness of leaders; showed the divergence of parties from their alleged grounds, and that men would not stick to what they had said: that the resolutions of public bodies, and the pledges never so often given and put on record, of public men,—will not bind them. The fact comes out more plainly, that you cannot rely on any man for the defence of truth who is not constitutionally, or by blood and temperament, on that side.

In what I have to say of Mr. Webster I do not confound him with vulgar politicians of his own time or since. There is always base ambition enough, men who calculate on the immense ignorance of masses of men;—that is their quarry and farm,—they use the constituencies at home only for their shoes. And of course they can drive out from the contest any honorable man. The low can best win the low, and all men like to be made much of. There are those too who have power and inspiration only to do ill. Their talent or their faculty deserts them when they undertake anything right.

Mr. Webster had a natural ascendancy of aspect and carriage, which distinguished him over all his contemporaries. His countenance, his figure, and his manners, were all in so grand a style, that he was, without effort, as superior to his most eminent rivals, as they were to the humblest, so that his arrival in any place was an event which drew crowds of people, who went to satisfy their eyes, and could not see him enough. I think they looked at him as the representative of the American continent. He was there in his Adamitic capacity, as if he alone of all men did not disappoint the eye and ear, but was a fit figure in the landscape. I remember his appearance at Bunker Hill. There was the monument, and here was Webster. He knew well that a little more or less of rhetoric signified nothing; he was only to say plain and equal things;—grand things, if he had them,—and, if he had them not, only to abstain from saying unfit things;—and the whole occasion was answered by his presence. It was a place for behavior, much more than for speech; and Webster walked through his part with entire success....

—

Four years ago tonight, [however] on one of those critical moments in history when great issues are determined,—when the powers of right and wrong are mustered for conflict, and it lies with one man to give a casting vote,—Mr. Webster most unexpectedly threw his whole weight on the side of slavery, and caused by his personal and official authority the passage of the Fugitive Slave Bill....

In the final hour, when he was forced by the peremptory necessity of the closing armies to take a side, did he take the side of great principles, the side of humanity and justice, or the side of abuse and oppression and chaos? Mr. Webster decided for slavery; and *that,* when the aspect of the institution was no longer doubtful, no longer feeble and apologetic, and proposing soon to end itself, but when it was strong and aggressive and threatening an illimitable increase, then he listened to state reasons and hopes and left with much complacency, we are told, the testament of his speech to the astonished State of Massachusetts. *Vera pro gratis.* A ghastly result of all those years of experience in affairs, this, that there was nothing better for the foremost man, the most American man in America, to tell his countrymen, than, that slavery was now at that strength, that they must beat down their conscience and become kidnappers for it. This was like the doleful speech falsely ascribed to the patriot Brutus, "Virtue, I have followed thee through life, and I find thee but a shadow."

Here was a question of an immoral law, a question agitated for ages, and settled always in the same way by every great jurist, that an immoral law cannot be valid. Cicero, Grotius, Coke, Blackstone, Burlamaqui, Vattel, Burke, Jefferson do all affirm this, and I cite them not that they can give plainness to what is so clear, but because though lawyers and practical statesmen, they could not hide from themselves this truth. Here was the question: Are you for man, and for the god of man; or are you for the hurt and harm of man? It was a question, whether man shall be treated as leather? Whether the negroes shall be, as the Indians were in Spanish America, a species of money? Whether this institution, which is a kind of mill or factory for converting men into monkeys, shall be upheld and enlarged? And Mr. Webster and the country went for quadruped law. Immense mischief was done. People were all expecting a totally different course from Mr. Webster. If any man had in that hour possessed the weight with the country which he had acquired, he would have brought the whole country to its senses. But not a moment's pause was allowed. Angry parties went from bad to worse, and the decision of Webster was accompanied with every thing offensive to freedom and good morals.

There was something like an attempt to debauch the moral sentiment of the clergy and of the youth. The immense power of rectitude is apt to be forgotten in politics. But they who brought this great wrong on the country, did not forget it. They wished to avail themselves of the names of men of known probity and honor to endorse the statute.

The ancient maxim is still true, that never was any injustice effected except by the help of justice. Burke said, "he would pardon something to the spirit of liberty"—but the opposition was sharply called *treason*, by Webster and prosecuted so. He told the people at Boston, "they must conquer their prejudices," that "agitation of the subject of Slavery must be suppressed." He did, as immoral men usually do, make very low bows to the Christian Church, and went through all the Sunday decorums; but when allusion was made to the sanctions of morality, he very frankly said, at Albany, "Some higher law, something existing somewhere between here and the third heaven,—I do not know where,"—and, if the reporters say true, this wretched atheism found some laughter in the company.

I said I had never in my life suffered before from the slave institution. It was like slavery in Africa or in Japan for me. There was a fugitive law, but it had become, or was fast becoming, a dead letter; and, by the genius and laws of Massachusetts inoperative. The new Bill made it operative; required me to hunt slaves; and it found citizens in Massachusetts willing to act as judges and captors. Moreover, it disclosed the secret of the new times; that slavery was no longer mendicant, but was become aggressive and dangerous. . . .

———

What is the use of admirable law forms and political forms if a hurricane of party feeling and a combination of monied interests can beat them to the ground? What is the use of courts, if judges only quote authorities, and no judge exerts original jurisdiction, or recurs to first principles? What is the use of guaranties provided by the jealousy of ages for the protection of liberty,—if these are made of no effect, when a bad act of Congress finds a willing commissioner? You relied on the Missouri Compromise: that is ridden over. You relied on state sovereignty in the free states to protect their citizens. They are driven with contempt out of the courts, and out of the territory of the slave states, if they are so happy as to get out with their lives. And now, you relied on these dismal guaranties infamously made in 1850, and before the body of Webster is yet crumbled, it is found that they have crumbled: this eternal monument at once of his fame and of common Union, is rotten in four years. They are no guaranty to the free states. They are a guaranty to the slave states; that as they have hitherto met with no repulse, they shall meet with none. I fear there is no reliance to be had on any kind of form or covenant, no, not on sacred forms,—none on churches, none on bibles. For one would have said that a Christian would not keep slaves, but the Christians keep slaves. Of course, they will not dare read the bible. Won't they? They quote the bible and Christ and Paul to maintain slavery. If slavery is a good, then is lying, theft, arson, incest, homicide, each and all goods and to be maintained by union societies. These things show that no forms, neither Constitutions nor laws nor covenants nor churches nor bibles, are of any use in themselves; the devil nestles comfortably into them all. There is no help but in the head and heart and hamstrings of a man. Covenants are of no use without honest men to keep them. Laws are of no use, but with loyal citizens to obey them. To interpret Christ, it needs Christ in the heart. The teachings of the spirit can be apprehended only by the same spirit that gave them forth. To make good the cause of Freedom you must draw off from all these foolish trusts on others. You must be citadels and warriors, yourselves Declarations of Independence, the charter, the battle, and the victory. Cromwell said, "We can only resist the superior training of the king's soldiers, by having godly men." And no man has a right to hope that the laws of New York will defend him from the contamination of slaves another day, until he has made up his mind that he will not owe his protection to the laws of New York, but to his own sense and spirit. Then he protects New York. He only who is able to stand alone, is qualified for society. And that I understand to be the end for which a soul exists in this world, to be himself the counterbalance of all falsehood and all wrong. "The army of unright is encamped from pole to pole, but the road of victory is known to the just." Everything may be taken away, he may be poor, he may be homeless, yet he will know out of his arms to make a pillow and out of his breast a bolster. Why have the minority no influence? because they have not a real minority of one.

I conceive that thus to detach a man, and make him feel that he is to owe all to himself, is the way to make him strong and rich. And here the optimist must find if anywhere the benefit of slavery. We have many teachers. We are in this world for nothing else than Culture: to be instructed in nature, in realities; in the laws of moral and intelligent nature; and surely our education is not conducted by toys and luxuries,—but by austere and rugged masters,—by poverty, solitude, passions, war, slavery,—to know that paradise is under the shadow of swords; that divine sentiments, which are always soliciting us, are breathed into us from on high and are a counterbalance to an universe of suffering and crime,—that self-reliance, the height and perfection of man, is reliance on God. The insight of the religious sentiment will disclose to him unexpected aids in the nature of things. The Persian Saadi said "Beware of hurting the orphan. When the orphan sets a crying the throne of the Almighty is rocked from side to side."

Whenever a man has come to this mind, that there is no church for him but his humble morning prayer; no constitution, but his talent of dealing well and justly with his neighbor; no liberty, but his invincible will to do right, then certain aids and allies will promptly appear. For the Eternal constitution of the universe is on his side. It is of no use to vote down gravitation or morals. What is useful will last; whilst that which is hurtful to the world will sink beneath all the opposing forces which it must exasperate. . . .

———

. . . It is not possible to extricate oneself from the questions in which your age is involved. I hate that we should be content with standing on the defensive. Liberty is aggressive. Liberty is the Crusade of all brave and conscientious men. It is the epic poetry, the new religion, the chivalry of all gentlemen. This is the oppressed Lady whom true knights on their oath and honor must rescue and save.

Now at last we are disenchanted and shall have no more false hopes. I respect the Anti-Slavery Society. It is the Cassandra that has foretold all that has befallen, fact for fact, years ago,—foretold it all, and no man laid it to heart. It seemed, as the Turks say, "Fate makes that a man should not believe his own eyes." But the Fugitive Law did much to unglue the eyes of men, and now the Nebraska Bill leaves us staring. The Anti-Slavery Society will add many members this year. The Whig party will join it. The Democrats will join it. The population of the Free States will join it. I doubt not, at last, the Slave States will join it. But be that sooner or later,—and whoever comes or stays away,— I hope we have come to an end of our unbelief, have come to a belief that there is a Divine Providence in the world which will not save us but through our own co-operation.

# Henry David Thoreau
## from "A Plea for Captain John Brown"
### (1859)

John Brown (1800–59), a militant abolitionist whose guerrilla activities as an antislavery partisan in Kansas had been supported by Transcendentalist radicals, in October 1859 led a small group of followers in a surprise attack on the arsenal at Harper's Ferry, Virginia. Brown hoped to incite a broader uprising among slaves. He failed and was executed soon after, but his death made him an abolitionist martyr, hardened north-south divisions, and helped precipitate the Civil War. None of the several Transcendental eulogies of Brown was as fervent as this one, nor as witheringly critical of Brown's critics and denouncers. Indeed, Thoreau never lauded another human being in such exalted terms as this. He was irresistibly drawn by Brown's combination of homespun shrewdness, zeal in a righteous cause, and above all his willingness to take decisive, self-sacrificing action for conscience's sake while the rest of the country dithered. Thoreau characterizes Brown here as a larger-than-life figure squarely in the Puritan-Revolutionary-Transcendentalist tradition: as a latter-day Oliver Cromwell, the leader of the seventeenth-century Puritan revolutionaries. Although Thoreau exaggerated Brown's virtues, he was certainly right in sensing that his act bore out the claims in "Resistance to Civil Government" of the power of a single person's self-reliant action. He was also right in thinking that Brown would have a more powerful impact on national history dead than alive. Hence Thoreau's strange-seeming expression of "fear" toward the end of the essay that Brown's life might be saved.

SOURCE: "A Plea for Captain John Brown," *Echoes of Harper's Ferry*, ed. James Redpath. Boston: Thayer and Eldridge, 1860.

He was by descent and birth a New England farmer, a man of great common sense, deliberate and practical as that class is, and tenfold more so. He was like the best of those who stood at Concord Bridge once, on Lexington Common, and on Bunker Hill, only he was firmer and higher principled than any that I have chanced to hear of as there. It was no abolition lecturer that converted him. Ethan Allen and Stark, with whom he may in some respects be compared, were rangers in a lower and less important field. They could bravely face their country's foes, but he had the courage to face his country herself, when she was in the wrong. A Western writer says, to account for his escape from so many perils, that he was concealed under a "rural exterior;" as if, in that prairie land, a hero should, by good rights, wear a citizen's dress only.

He did not go to the college called Harvard, good old Alma Mater as she is. He was not fed on the pap that is there furnished. As he phrased it, "I know no more of grammar than one of your calves." But he went to the great university of the West, where he sedulously pursued the study of Liberty, for which he had early betrayed a fondness, and having taken many degrees, he finally commenced the public practice of Humanity in Kansas, as you all know. Such were *his humanities*, and not any study of grammar. He would have left a Greek accent slanting the wrong way, and righted up a falling man.

He was one of that class of whom we hear a great deal, but, for the most part, see nothing at all—the Puritans. It would be in vain to kill him. He died lately in the time of Cromwell, but he reappeared here. Why should he not? Some of the Puritan stock are said to have come over and settled in New England. They were a class that did something else than celebrate their forefathers' day, and eat parched corn in remembrance of that time. They were neither Democrats nor Republicans, but men of simple habits, straightforward, prayerful; not thinking much of rulers who did not fear God, not making many compromises, nor seeking after available candidates.

———

On the whole, my respect for my fellow-men, except as one may outweigh a million, is not being increased these days. I have noticed the cold-blooded way in which newspaper writers and men generally speak of this event, as if an ordinary malefactor, though one of unusual "pluck,"—as the Governor of Virginia is reported to have said, using the language of the cock-pit, "the gamest man he ever saw,"—had been caught, and were about to be hung. He was not dreaming of his foes when the governor thought he looked so brave. It turns what sweetness I have to gall, to hear, or hear of, the remarks of some of my neighbors. When we heard at first that he was dead, one of my townsmen observed that "he died as the fool dieth;" which, pardon me, for an instant suggested a likeness in him dying to my neighbor living. Others, craven-hearted, said disparagingly, that "he threw his life away," because he resisted the government. Which way have they thrown *their* lives, pray?—Such as would praise a man for attacking singly an ordinary band of thieves or murderers. I hear another ask, Yankee-like, "What will he gain by it?" as if he expected to fill his pockets by this enterprise. Such a one has no idea of gain but in this worldly sense. If it does not lead to a "surprise" party, if he does not get a new pair of boots, or a vote of thanks, it must be a failure. "But he won't gain any thing by it." Well, no, I don't suppose he could get four-and-sixpence a day for being hung, take the year round; but then he stands a chance to save a considerable part of his soul—and *such* a soul!— when *you* do not. No doubt you can get more in your market for a quart of milk than for a quart of blood, but that is not the market that heroes carry their blood to. . . .

———

Our foes are in our midst and all about us. There is hardly a house but is divided against itself, for our foe is the all but universal woodenness of both head and heart, the want of vitality in man, which is the effect of our vice; and hence are begotten fear, superstition, bigotry, persecution, and slavery of all kinds. We are mere figure-heads upon a hulk, with livers in the place of hearts. The curse is the worship of idols, which at length changes the worshipper into a stone image himself; and the New Englander is just as much an idolater as the Hindoo. This man was an exception, for he did not set up even a political graven image between him and his God.

A church that can never have done with excommunicating Christ while it exists! Away with your broad and flat churches, and your narrow and tall churches! Take a step forward, and invent a new style of out-houses. Invent a salt that will save you, and defend our nostrils.

The modern Christian is a man who has consented to say all the prayers in the liturgy, provided you will let him go straight to bed and sleep quietly afterward. All his prayers begin with "Now I lay me down to sleep," and he is forever looking forward to the time when he shall go to his "*long* rest." He has consented to perform certain old established charities, too, after a fashion, but he does not wish to hear of any new-fangled ones; he doesn't wish to have any supplementary articles added to the contract, to fit it to the present time. He shows the whites of his eyes on the Sabbath, and the blacks all the rest of the week. The evil is not merely a stagnation of blood, but a stagnation of spirit. Many, no doubt, are well disposed, but sluggish by constitution and by habit, and they cannot conceive of a man who is actuated by higher motives than they are. Accordingly they pronounce this man insane, for they know that *they* could never act as he does, as long as they were themselves.

We dream of foreign countries, of other times and races of men, placing them at a distance in history or space; but let some significant event like the present occur in our midst, and we discover, often, this distance and this strangeness between us and our nearest neighbors. *They* are our Austrias, and Chinas, and South Sea Islands. Our crowded society becomes well spaced all at once, clean and handsome to the eye, a city of magnificent distances. We discover why it was that we never got beyond compliments and surfaces with them before; we become aware of as many versts between us and them as there are between a wandering Tartar and a Chinese town. The thoughtful man becomes a hermit in the thoroughfares of the market-place. Impassable seas suddenly find their level between us, or dumb steppes stretch themselves out there. It is the difference of constitution, of intelligence, and faith, and not streams and mountains, that make the true and impassable boundaries between individuals and between states. None but the like-minded can come plenipotentiary to our court.

I read all the newspapers I could get within a week after this event, and I do not remember in them a single expression of sympathy for these men. I have since seen one noble statement, in a Boston paper, not editorial. Some voluminous sheets decided not to print the full report of Brown's words to the exclusion of other matter. It was as if a publisher should reject the manuscript of the New Testament, and print Wilson's last speech. The same journal which contained this pregnant news, was chiefly filled, in parallel columns, with the reports of the political conventions that were being held. But the descent to them was too steep. They should have been spared this contrast, been printed in an extra at least. To turn from the voices and deeds of earnest men to the *cackling* of political conventions! Office-seekers and speech-makers, who do not so much as lay an honest egg, but wear their breasts bare upon an egg of chalk! Their great game is the game of straws, or rather that universal aboriginal game of the platter, at which the Indians cried *hub, bub!* Exclude the reports of religious and political conventions, and publish the words of a living man.

But I object not so much to what they have omitted, as to what they have inserted. Even the *Liberator* called it "a misguided, wild, and apparently insane—effort." As for the herd of newspapers and magazines, I do not chance to know an editor in the country who will deliberately print any thing which he knows will ultimately and permanently reduce the number of his subscribers. They do not believe that it would be expedient. How then can they print truth? If we do not say pleasant things, they argue, nobody will attend to us. And so they do like some travelling auctioneers, who sing an obscene song in order to draw a crowd around them. Republican editors, obliged to get their sentences ready for the morning edition, and accustomed to look at every thing by the twilight of politics, express no admiration, nor true sorrow even, but call these men "deluded fanatics"—"mistaken men"—"insane," or "crazed." It suggests what a *sane* set of editors we are blessed with, *not* "mistaken men"; who know very well on which side their bread is buttered, at least....

———

Prominent and influential editors, accustomed to deal with politicians, men of an infinitely lower grade, say, in their ignorance, that he acted "on the principle of revenge." They do not know the man. They must enlarge themselves to conceive of him. I have no doubt that the time will come when they will begin to see him as he was. They have got to conceive of a man of faith and of religious principle, and not a politician nor an Indian; of a man who did not wait till he was personally interfered with or thwarted in some harmless business before he gave his life to the cause of the oppressed.

... I wish I could say that Brown was the representative of the North. He was a superior man. He did not value his bodily life in comparison with ideal things. He did not recognize unjust human laws, but resisted them as he was bid. For once we are lifted out of the trivialness and dust of politics into the region of truth and manhood. No man in America has ever stood up so persistently and effectively for the dignity of human nature, knowing himself for a man, and the equal of any and all governments. In that sense he was the most American of us all. He needed no babbling lawyer, making false issues, to defend him. He was more than a match for all the judges that American voters, or office-holders of whatever grade, can create. He could not have been tried by a jury of his peers, because his peers did not exist. When a man stands up serenely against the condemnation and vengeance of mankind, rising above them literally *by a whole body*,—even though he were of late the vilest murderer, who has settled that matter with himself,—the spectacle is a sublime one,—didn't ye know it, ye Liberators, ye Tribunes, ye Republicans?—and we become criminal in comparison. Do yourselves the honor to recognize him. He needs none of your respect. . . .

———

"All is quiet at Harper's Ferry," say the journals. What is the character of that calm which follows when the law and the slaveholder prevail? I regard this event as a touchstone designed to bring out, with glaring distinctness, the character of this government. We needed to be thus assisted to see it by the light of history. It needed to see itself. When a government puts forth its strength on the side of injustice, as ours to maintain Slavery and kill the liberators of the slave, it reveals itself a merely brute force, or worse, a demoniacal force. . . .

We talk about a *representative* government; but what a monster of a government is that where the noblest faculties of the mind, and the *whole* heart, are not *represented*. A semi-human tiger or ox, stalking over the earth, with its heart taken out and the top of its brain shot away. Heroes have fought well on their stumps when their legs were shot off, but I never heard of any good done by such a government as that.

The only government that I recognize,—and it matters not how few are at the head of it, or how small its army,—is that power that establishes justice in the land, never that which establishes injustice. What shall we think of a government to which all the truly brave and just men in the land are enemies, standing between it and those whom it oppresses? A government that pretends to be Christian and crucifies a million Christs every day!

Treason! Where does such treason take its rise? I cannot help thinking of you as you deserve, ye governments. Can you dry up the fountains of thought? High treason, when it is resistance to tyranny here below, has its origin in, and is first committed by the power that makes and forever recreates man. When you have caught and hung all these human rebels, you have accomplished nothing but your own guilt, for you have not struck at the fountain head. You presume to contend with a foe against whom West Point cadets and rifled cannon *point* not.

Can all the art of the cannon-founder tempt matter to turn against its maker? Is the form in which the founder thinks he casts it more essential than the constitution of it and of himself?

The United States have a coffle of four millions of slaves. They are determined to keep them in this condition; and Massachusetts is one of the confederated overseers to prevent their escape. Such are not all the inhabitants of Massachusetts, but such are they who rule and are obeyed here. It was Massachusetts, as well as Virginia, that put down this insurrection at Harper's Ferry. She sent the marines there, and she will have to pay the penalty of her sin.

Suppose that there is a society in this State that out of its own purse and magnanimity saves all the fugitive slaves that run to us, and protects our colored fellow-citizens, and leaves the other work to the Government, so-called. Is not that government fast losing its occupation, and becoming contemptible to mankind? If private men are obliged to perform the offices of government, to protect the weak and dispense justice, then the government becomes only a hired man, or clerk, to perform menial or indifferent services. Of course, that is but the shadow of a government whose existence necessitates a Vigilant Committee. What should we think of the oriental Cadi even, behind whom worked in secret a Vigilant Committee? But such is the character of our Northern States generally; each has its Vigilant Committee. And, to a certain extent, these crazy governments recognize and accept this relation. They say, virtually, "We'll be glad to work for you on these terms, only don't make a noise about it." And thus the government, its salary being insured, withdraws into the back shop, taking the constitution with it, and bestows most of its labor on repairing that. When I hear it at work sometimes, as I go by, it reminds me, at best, of those farmers who in winter contrive to turn a penny by following the coopering business. And what kind of spirit is their barrel made to hold? They speculate in stocks, and bore holes in mountains, but they are not competent to lay out even a decent highway. The only *free* road, the Underground Railroad, is owned and managed by the Vigilant Committee. *They* have tunnelled under the whole breadth of the land. Such a government is losing its power and respectability as surely as water runs out of a leaky vessel, and is held by one that can contain it. . . .

———

It was his peculiar doctrine that a man has a perfect right to interfere by force with the slaveholder, in order to rescue the slave. I agree with him. They who are continually shocked by slavery have some right to be shocked by the violent death of the slaveholder, but no others. Such will be more shocked by his life than by his death. I shall not be forward to think him mistaken in his method who quickest succeeds to liberate the slave. I speak for the slave when I say, that I prefer the philanthropy of Captain Brown to that philanthropy which neither shoots me nor liberates me. At any rate, I do not think it is quite sane for one to spend his whole life in talking or writing about this matter, unless he is continuously inspired, and I have not done so. A man may have other affairs to attend to. I do not wish to kill nor to be killed, but I can foresee circumstances in which both these things would be by me unavoidable. We preserve the so-called peace of our community by deeds of petty violence every day. Look at the police-man's billy and handcuffs! Look at the jail! Look at the gallows! Look at the chaplain regiment! We are hoping only to live safely on the out-skirts of *this* provisional army. So we defend ourselves and our hen-roosts, and maintain slavery. I know that the mass of my countrymen think that the only righteous use that can be made of Sharp's rifles and revolvers is to fight duels with them, when we are insulted by other nations, or to hunt Indians, or shoot fugitive slaves with them, or the like. I think that for once the Sharp's rifles and the revolvers were employed in a righteous cause. The tools were in the hands of one who could use them. . . .

————

I am here to plead his cause with you. I plead not for his life, but for his character—his immortal life; and so it becomes your cause wholly, and is not his in the least. Some eighteen hundred years ago Christ was crucified; this morning, perchance, Captain Brown was hung. These are the two ends of a chain which is not without its links. He is not Old Brown any longer; he is an angel of light.

I see now that it was necessary that the bravest and humanest man in all the country should be hung. Perhaps he saw it himself. I *almost fear* that I may yet hear of his deliverance, doubting if a prolonged life, if *any* life, can do as much good as his death.

"Misguided"! "Garrulous"! "Insane"! "Vindictive"! So ye write in your easy chairs, and thus he wounded responds from the floor of the Armory, clear as a cloudless sky, true as the voice of nature is: "No man sent me here; it was my own prompting and that of my Maker. I acknowledge no master in human form."

And in what a sweet and noble strain he proceeds, addressing his captors, who stand over him: "I think, my friends, you are guilty of a great wrong against God and humanity, and it would be perfectly right for any one to interfere with you so far as to free those you willfully and wickedly hold in bondage."

And referring to his movement: "It is, in my opinion, the greatest service a man can render to God."

"I pity the poor in bondage that have none to help them; that is why I am here; not to gratify any personal animosity, revenge, or vindictive spirit. It is my sympathy with the oppressed and the wronged, that are as good as you, and as precious in the sight of God."

You don't know your testament when you see it. . . .

———

I foresee the time when the painter will paint that scene, no longer going to Rome for a subject; the poet will sing it; the historian record it; and, with the Landing of the Pilgrims and the Declaration of Independence, it will be the ornament of some future national gallery, when at least the present form of Slavery shall be no more here. We shall then be at liberty to weep for Captain Brown. Then, and not till then, we will take our revenge.

# V

# LITERATURE
# AND THE
# ARTS

# A.
## CRITICAL STATEMENTS

# 1.

# Ralph Waldo Emerson
## "The Editors to the Reader"
### (1840)

This was the first article in the first issue of the leading Transcendentalist magazine. *The Dial* (1840–44) called itself "A Magazine for Literature, Philosophy, and Religion," and its actual scope was even broader than that. It also wound up publishing a number of articles on social issues, such as on-the-spot accounts of Brook Farm like Elizabeth Peabody's (Section IV-A). This particular call for contributors concentrates especially on the literary, however; and in fact the magazine proved strongest in the area of the arts and especially literature, both creative writing and literary criticism. At the outset, however, Emerson could not have known this for sure. His assertions that the "spirit of the time" had so far been expressed in ferment rather than in solid results, and "in the higher tone of criticism" rather than in literature itself, are typical of him—and a fair diagnosis of the Transcendentalist movement thus far. So too is Emerson's valuation of deeply felt expression above polish—also an important point for him in the next two selections. Although sometimes these views led him into a lofty fastidiousness that inhibited the genius he wanted to help inspire, he clearly meant to sound encouraging, and he was always on the lookout for new talent.

SOURCE: "The Editors to the Reader," *The Dial*, 1 (July 1840).

We invite the attention of our countrymen to a new design. Probably not quite unexpected or unannounced will our Journal appear, though small pains have been taken to secure its welcome. Those, who have immediately acted in editing the present Number, cannot accuse themselves of any unbecoming forwardness in their undertaking, but rather of a backwardness, when they remember how often in many private circles the work was projected, how eagerly desired, and only postponed because no individual volunteered to combine and concentrate the free-will offerings of many coöperators. With some reluctance the present conductors of this work have yielded themselves to the wishes of their friends, finding something sacred and not to be withstood in the importunity which urged the production of a Journal in a new spirit.

As they have not proposed themselves to the work, neither can they lay any the least claim to an option or determination of the spirit in which it is conceived, or to what is peculiar in the design. In that respect, they have obeyed, though with great joy, the strong current of thought and feeling, which, for a few years past, has led many sincere persons in New England to make new demands in literature, and to reprobate that rigor of our conventions of religion and education which is turning us to stone, which renounces hope, which looks only backward, which asks only such a future as the past, which suspects improvement, and holds nothing so much in horror as new views and the dreams of youth.

With these terrors the conductors of the present Journal have nothing to do,—not even so much as a word of reproach to waste. They know that there is a portion of the youth and of the adult population of this country, who have not shared them; who have in secret or in public paid their vows to truth and freedom; who love reality too well to care for names, and who live by a Faith too earnest and profound to suffer them to doubt the eternity of its object, or to shake themselves free from its authority. Under the fictions and customs which occupied others, these have explored the Necessary, the Plain, the True, the Human,—and so gained a vantage ground, which commands the history of the past and the present.

No one can converse much with different classes of Society in New England, without remarking the progress of a revolution. Those who share in it have no eternal organization, no badge, no creed, no name. They do not vote, or print, or even meet together. They do not know each other's faces or names. They are united only in a common love of truth, and love of its work. They are of all conditions and constitutions. Of these acolytes, if some are happily born and well bred, many are no doubt ill dressed, ill placed, ill made—with as many scars of hereditary vice as other men. Without pomp, without trumpet, in lonely and obscure places, in solitude, in servitude, in compunctions and privations, trudging beside the team in the dusty road, or drudging a hireling in other men's cornfields, schoolmasters, who teach a few children rudiments for a pittance, ministers of small parishes of the obscurer sects, lone women in dependent condition, matrons and young maidens, rich and poor, beautiful and hard-favored, without concert or proclamation of any kind, they have silently given in their several adherence to a new hope, and in all companies do signify a greater trust in the nature and resources of man, than the laws or the popular opinions will well allow.

This spirit of the time is felt by every individual with some difference,—to each one casting its light upon the objects nearest to his temper and habits of thought;—to one, coming in the shape of special reforms in the state; to another, in modifications of the various callings of men, and the customs of business; to a third, opening a new scope for literature and art; to a fourth, in philosophical insight; to a fifth, in the vast solitudes of prayer. It is in every form a protest against usage, and a search for principles. In all its movements, it is peaceable, and in the very lowest marked with a triumphant success. Of course, it rouses the opposition of all which it judges and condemns, but it is too confident in its tone to comprehend an objection, and so builds no outworks for possible defence against contingent enemies. It has the step of Fate, and goes on existing like an oak or a river, because it must.

In literature, this influence appears not yet in new books so much as in the higher tone of criticism. The antidote to all narrowness is the comparison of the record with nature, which at once shames the record and stimulates to new attempts. Whilst we look at this, we wonder how any book has been thought worthy to be preserved. There is somewhat in all life untranslatable into language. He who keeps his eye on that will write better than others, and think less of his writing, and of all writing. Every thought has a certain imprisoning as well as uplifting quality, and, in proportion to its energy on the will, refuses to become an object of intellectual contemplation. Thus what is great usually slips through our fingers, and it seems wonderful how a lifelike word ever comes to be written. If our Journal share the impulses of the time, it cannot now prescribe its own course. It cannot foretell in orderly propositions what it shall attempt. All criticism should be poetic; unpredictable; superseding, as every new thought does, all foregone thoughts, and making a new light on the whole world. Its brow is not wrinkled with circumspection, but serene, cheerful, adoring. It has all things to say, and no less than all the world for its final audience.

Our plan embraces much more than criticism; were it not so, our criticism would be naught. Everything noble is directed on life, and this is. We do not wish to say pretty or curious things, or to reiterate a few propositions in varied forms, but, if we can, to give expression to that spirit which lifts men to a higher platform, restores to them the religious sentiment, brings them worthy aims and pure pleasures, purges the inward eye, makes life less desultory, and, through raising man to the level of nature, takes away its melancholy from the landscape, and reconciles the practical with the speculative powers.

But perhaps we are telling our little story too gravely. There are always great arguments at hand for a true action, even for the writing of a few pages. There is nothing but seems near it and prompts it,—the sphere in the ecliptic, the sap in the apple tree,—every fact, every appearance seem to persuade to it.

Our means correspond with the ends we have indicated. As we wish not to multiply books, but to report life, our resources are therefore not so much the pens of practised writers, as the discourse of the living, and the portfolios which friendship has opened to us. From the beautiful recesses of private thought; from the experience and hope of spirits which are withdrawing from all old forms, and seeking in all that is new somewhat to meet their inappeasable longings; from the secret confession of genius afraid to trust itself to aught but sympathy; from the conversation of fervid and mystical pietists; from tearstained diaries of sorrow and passion; from the manuscripts of young poets; and from the records of youthful taste commenting on old works of art; we hope to draw thoughts and feelings, which being alive can impart life.

And so with diligent hands and good intent we set down our Dial on the earth. We wish it may resemble that instrument in its celebrated happiness, that of measuring no hours but those of sunshine. Let it be one cheerful rational voice amidst the din of mourners and polemics. Or to abide by our chosen image, let it be such a Dial, not as the dead face of a clock, hardly even such as the Gnomon in a garden, but rather such a Dial as is the Garden itself, in whose leaves and flowers and fruits the suddenly awakened sleeper is instantly apprised not what part of dead time, but what state of life and growth is now arrived and arriving.

# 2.

# Ralph Waldo Emerson

## Verses of the Portfolio

## (1840)

In *The Dial*'s second issue, Emerson tried to spell out in more detail one kind of art the new magazine wished to encourage—an art of inspired improvisation, work written from the heart rather than for the marketplace. Significantly, Emerson defends such "private and household poetry" on *democratic* grounds, seeing it as a revolutionary extension of the realm of authorship beyond mainstream print culture. In this advocacy of a counterestablishment aesthetic we can hear a slight echo of the revolution in social arrangements that the Ripleys were simultaneously planning for Brook Farm. But only a distant echo at most, because Emerson seems to take for granted that the kind of writing he commends here will be written in solitary detachment from the social arena. As his poster-boy example, Emerson includes eleven poems (omitted here) by an unnamed "youth." This was Ellery Channing, who was soon to become Margaret Fuller's errant brother-in-law and a lifelong Concord resident. (For the first and by far the best of these poems, "Boat Song," see Section IV-C.)

source: "New Poetry," *The Dial*, 1 (October 1840).

The tendencies of the times are so democratical, that we shall soon have not so much as a pulpit or raised platform in any church or townhouse, but each person, who is moved to address any public assembly, will speak from the floor. The like revolution in literature is now giving importance to the portfolio over the book. Only one man in the thousand may print a book, but one in ten or one in five may inscribe his thoughts, or at least with short commentary his favorite readings in a private journal. The philosophy of the day has long since broached a more liberal doctrine of the poetic faculty than our fathers held, and reckons poetry the right and power of every man to whose culture justice is done. We own that, though we were trained in a stricter school of literary faith, and were in all our youth inclined to the enforcement of the straitest restrictions on the admission of candidates to the Parnassian fraternity, and denied the name of poetry to every composition in which the workmanship and the material were not equally excellent, in our middle age we have grown lax, and have learned to find pleasure in verses of a ruder strain,—to enjoy *verses of society,* or those effusions which in persons of a happy nature are the easy and unpremeditated translation of their thoughts and feelings into rhyme. This new taste for a certain private and household poetry for somewhat less pretending than the festal and solemn verses which are written for the nations really indicates, we suppose, that a new style of poetry exists. The number of writers has increased. Every child has been taught the tongues. The universal communication of the arts of reading and writing has brought the works of the great poets into every house, and made all ears familiar with the poetic forms. The progress of popular institutions has favored self-respect, and broken down that terror of the great, which once imposed awe and hesitation on the talent of the masses of society. A wider epistolary intercourse ministers to the ends of sentiment and reflection than ever existed before; the practice of writing diaries is becoming almost general; and every day witnesses new attempts to throw into verse the experiences of private life.

What better omen of true progress can we ask than an increasing intellectual and moral interest of men in each other ? What can be better for the republic than that the Capitol, the White House, and the Court House are becoming of less importance than the farm-house and the bookcloset? If we are losing our interest in public men, and finding that their spell lay in number and size only, and acquiring instead a taste for the depths of thought and emotion as they may be sounded in the soul of the citizen or the countryman, does it not replace man for the state, and character for official power? Men should be treated with solemnity; and when they come to chant their private griefs and doubts and joys, they have a new scale by which to compute magnitude and relation. Art is the noblest consolation of calamity. The poet is compensated for his defects on the street and in society, if in his chamber he has turned his mischance into noble numbers.

Is there not room then for a new department in poetry, namely, *Verses of the Portfolio?* We have fancied that we drew greater pleasure from some manuscript verses than from printed ones of equal talent. For there was herein the charm of character; they were confessions; and the faults, the imperfect parts, the fragmentary verses, the halting rhymes, had a worth beyond that of a high finish; for they testified that the writer was more man than artist, more earnest than vain; that the thought was too sweet and sacred to him, than that he should suffer his ears to hear or his eyes to see a superficial defect in the expression.

The characteristic of such verses is, that being not written for publication, they lack that finish which the conventions of literature require of authors. But if poetry of this kind has merit, we conceive that the prescription which demands a rhythmical polish may be easily set aside; and when a writer has outgrown the state of thought which produced the poem, the interest of letters is served by publishing it imperfect, as we preserve studies, torsos, and blocked statues of the great masters. For though we should be loath to see the wholesome conventions, to which we have alluded, broken down by a general incontinence of publication, and every man's and woman's diary flying into the bookstores, yet it is to be considered, on the other hand, that men of genius are often more incapable than others of that elaborate execution which criticism exacts. Men of genius in general are, more than others, incapable of any perfect exhibition, because however agreeable it may be to them to act on the public, it is always a secondary aim. They are humble, self-accusing, moody men, whose worship is toward the Ideal Beauty, which chooses to be courted not so often in perfect hymns, as in wild ear-piercing ejaculations, or in silent musings. Their face is forward, and their heart is in this heaven. By so much are they disqualified for a perfect success in any particular performance to which they can give only a divided affection. But the man of talents has every advantage in the competition. He can give that cool and commanding attention to the thing to be done, that shall secure its just performance. Yet are the failures of genius better than the victories of talent; and we are sure that some crude manuscript poems have yielded us a more sustaining and a more stimulating diet, than many elaborated and classic productions.

We have been led to these thoughts by reading some verses, which were lately put into our hands by a friend with the remark, that they were the production of a youth, who had long passed out of the mood in which he wrote them, so that they had become quite dead to him. Our first feeling on reading them was a lively joy. So then the Muse is neither dead nor dumb, but has found a voice in these cold Cisatlantic States. Here is poetry which asks no aid of magnitude or number, of blood or crime, but finds theatre enough in the first field or brookside, breadth and depth enough in the flow of its own thought. Here is self-repose, which to our mind is stabler than the Pyramids; here is self-respect which leads a man to date from his heart more proudly than from Rome. Here is love which sees through surface, and adores the gentle nature and not the costume. Here is religion, which is not of the Church of England, nor of the Church of Boston. Here is the good wise heart, which sees that the end of culture is strength and cheerfulness. In an age too which tends with so strong an inclination to the philosophical muse, here is poetry more purely intellectual than any American verses we have yet seen, distinguished from all competition by two merits; the fineness of perception; and the poet's trust in his own genius to that degree, that there is an absence of all conventional imagery, and a bold use of that which the moment's mood had made sacred to him, quite careless that it might be sacred to no other, and might even be slightly ludicrous to the first reader.

We proceed to give our readers some selections, taken without much order from this rich pile of manuscript. . . .

# 3.

# RALPH WALDO EMERSON

## FROM "THE POET"

### (1844)

This is Emerson's most sustained reflection on poetics. It leads off his *Essays, Second Series.* The great essay that immediately follows it, "Experience," is one of his most downbeat. But "The Poet" is one of his most exuberant. This striking juxtaposition was probably intended to dramatize the ironic contrast between moments of inspiration and daily actuality. Inspiration is the true poet's arena. Poetry worthy of the name begins in acts of higher perception; craft is secondary, however indispensable. Since Emerson holds that the key to poetry is perception rather than skill in verse, he sees "the poet" as broadly representative of a certain kind of human power rather than as a specialist in a particular kind of verbal artistry. The essay is therefore both strikingly "elitist" and strikingly "populist." At times Emerson suggests that none but the greatest poets in history can meet his standards, and even they only at special moments. At other times, he insists that all people have at least a touch of the poet in them. Toward the end Emerson issues a ringing call for a national poet worthy of the name to appear: a call that inspired Walt Whitman among many others. (Whitman was in the audience when Emerson delivered an earlier version of "The Poet" as a lecture in New York City.) Along the way, Emerson revises his earlier pronouncements about the mystical importance of symbolic language (see the "Language" chapter of *Nature*) by insisting that there is no permanent one-to-one relation between natural fact and poetic symbol: "the quality of the imagination is to flow and not to freeze." For more on the somewhat prissy "chaste" intoxication that

Emerson commends toward the end, see his poem "Bacchus" in Section V-B.

SOURCE: "The Poet," *Essays, Second Series.* Boston: James Munroe, 1844.

. . . the poet is representative. He stands among partial men for the complete man, and aprises us not of his wealth, but of the commonwealth. The young man reveres men of genius, because, to speak truly, they are more himself than he is. They receive of the soul as he also receives, but they more. Nature enhances her beauty to the eye of loving men, from their belief that the poet is beholding her shows at the same time. He is isolated among his contemporaries, by truth and by his art, but with this consolation in his pursuits, that they will draw all men sooner or later. For all men live by truth, and stand in need of expression. In love, in art, in avarice, in politics, in labor, in games, we study to utter our painful secret. The man is only half himself, the other half is his expression.

Notwithstanding this necessity to be published, adequate expression is rare. I know not how it is that we need an interpreter; but the great majority of men seem to be minors, who have not yet come into possession of their own, or mutes, who cannot report the conversation they have had with nature. There is no man who does not anticipate a supersensual utility in the sun, and stars, earth, and water. These stand and wait to render him a peculiar service. But there is some obstruction, or some excess of phlegm in our constitution, which does not suffer them to yield the due effect. Too feeble fall the impressions of nature on us to make us artists. Every touch should thrill. Every man should be so much an artist, that he could report in conversation what had befallen him. Yet, in our experience, the rays or appulses have sufficient force to arrive at the senses, but not enough to reach the quick, and compel the reproduction of themselves in speech. The poet is the person in whom these powers are in balance, the man without impediment, who sees and handles that which others dream of, traverses the whole scale of experience, and is representative of man, in virtue of being the largest power to receive and to impart.

For the Universe has three children, born at one time, which reappear, under different names, in every system of thought, whether they be called cause, operation, and effect; or, more poetically, Jove, Pluto, Neptune; or, theologically, the Father, the Spirit, and the Son; but which we will call here, the Knower, the Doer, and the Sayer. These stand respectively for the love of truth, for the love of good, and for the love of beauty. These three are equal. Each is that which he is essentially, so that he cannot be surmounted or analyzed, and each of these three has the power of the others latent in him, and his own patent.

The poet is the sayer, the namer, and represents beauty. He is a sovereign, and stands on the centre. For the world is not painted, or adorned, but is from the beginning beautiful; and God has not made some beautiful things, but Beauty is the creator of the universe. Therefore the poet is not any permissive potentate, but is emperor in his own right. Criticism is infested with a cant of materialism, which assumes that manual skill and activity is the first merit of all men, and disparages such as say and do not, overlooking the fact, that some men, namely, poets, are natural sayers, sent into the world to the end of expression, and confounds them with those whose province is action, but who quit it to imitate the sayers. But Homer's words are as costly and admirable to Homer, as Agamemnon's victories are to Agamemnon. The poet does not wait for the hero or the sage, but, as they act and think primarily, so he writes primarily what will and must be spoken, reckoning the others, though primaries also, yet, in respect to him, secondaries and servants; as sitters or models in the studio of a painter, or as assistants who bring building materials to an architect.

For poetry was all written before time was, and whenever we are so finely organized that we can penetrate into that region where the air is music, we hear those primal warblings, and attempt to write them down, but we lose ever and anon a word, or a verse, and substitute something of our own, and thus miswrite the poem. The men of more delicate ear write down these cadences more faithfully, and these transcripts, though imperfect, become the songs of the nations. For nature is as truly beautiful as it is good, or as it is reasonable, and must as much appear, as it must be done, or be known. Words and deeds are quite indifferent modes of the divine energy. Words are also actions, and actions are a kind of words.

The sign and credentials of the poet are, that he announces that which no man foretold. He is the true and only doctor; he knows and tells; he is the only teller of news, for he was present and privy to the appearance which he describes. He is a beholder of ideas, and an utterer of the necessary and causal. For we do not speak now of men of poetical talents, or of industry and skill in metre, but of the true poet. I took part in a conversation the other day, concerning a recent writer of lyrics, a man of subtle mind, whose head appeared to be a music-box of delicate tunes and rhythms, and whose skill, and command of language, we could not sufficiently praise. But when the question arose, whether he was not only a lyrist, but a poet, we were obliged to confess that he is plainly a contemporary, not an eternal man. He does not stand out of our low limitations, like a Chimborazo under the line, running up from the torrid base through all the climates of the globe, with belts of the herbage of every latitude on its high and mottled sides; but this genius is the landscape-garden of a modern house, adorned with fountains and statues, with well-bred men and women standing and sitting in the walks and terraces. We hear, through all the varied music, the ground-tone of conventional life. Our poets are men of talents who sing, and not the children of music. The argument is secondary, the finish of the verses is primary.

For it is not metres, but a metre-making argument, that makes a poem,—a thought so passionate and alive, that, like the spirit of a plant or an animal, it has an architecture of its own, and adorns nature with a new thing. The thought and the form are equal in the order of time, but in the order of genesis the thought is prior to the form. The poet has a new thought: he has a whole new experience to unfold; he will tell us how it was with him, and all men will be the richer in his fortune. For, the experience of each new age requires a new confession, and the world seems always waiting for its poet. I remember, when I was young, how much I was moved one morning by tidings that genius had appeared in a youth who sat near me at table. He had left his work, and gone rambling none knew whither, and had written hundreds of lines, but could not tell whether that which was in him was therein told: he could tell nothing but that all was changed,—man, beast, heaven, earth, and sea. How gladly we listened! how credulous! Society seemed to be compromised. We sat in the aurora of a sunrise which was to put out all the stars. Boston seemed to be at twice the distance it had the night before, or was much farther than that. Rome,—what was Rome? Plutarch and Shakspeare were in the yellow leaf, and Homer no more should be heard of. It is much to know that poetry has been written this very day, under this very roof, by your side. What! that wonderful spirit has not expired! these stony moments are still sparkling and animated! I had fancied that the oracles were all silent, and nature had spent her fires, and behold! all night, from every pore, these fine auroras have been streaming. Every one has some interest in the advent of the poet, and no one knows how much it may concern him. We know that the secret of the world is profound, but who or what shall be our interpreter, we know not. A mountain ramble, a new style of face, a new person, may put the key into our hands. Of course, the value of genius to us is in the veracity of its report. Talent may frolic and juggle; genius realizes and adds. Mankind, in good earnest, have arrived so far in understanding themselves and their work, that the foremost watchman on the peak announces his news. It is the truest word ever spoken, and the phrase will be the fittest, most musical, and the unerring voice of the world for that time. . . .

———

. . . Nature offers all her creatures to him as a picture-language. Being used as a type, a second wonderful value appears in the object, far better than its old value, as the carpenter's stretched cord, if you hold your ear close enough, is musical in the breeze. "Things more excellent than every image," says Jamblichus, "are expressed through images." Things admit of being used as symbols, because nature is a symbol, in the whole, and in every part. . . .

. . . Since everything in nature answers to a moral power, if any phenomenon remains brute and dark, it is that the corresponding faculty in the observer is not yet active.

No wonder, then, if these waters be so deep, that we hover over them with a religious regard. The beauty of the fable proves the importance of the sense; to the poet, and to all others; or, if you please, every man is so far a poet as to be susceptible of these enchantments of nature: for all men have the thoughts whereof the universe is the celebration. I find that the fascination resides in the symbol. Who loves nature? Who does not? Is it only poets, and men of leisure and cultivation, who live with her? No; but also hunters, farmers, grooms, and butchers, though they express their affection in their choice of life, and not in their choice of words. The writer wonders what the coachman or the hunter values in riding, in horses, and dogs. It is not superficial qualities. When you talk with him, he holds these at as slight a rate as you. His worship is sympathetic; he has no definitions, but he is commanded in nature, by the living power which he feels to be there present. No imitation, or playing of these things, would content him; he loves the earnest of the north wind, of rain, of stone, and wood, and iron. A beauty not explicable, is dearer than a beauty which we can see to the end of. It is nature the symbol, nature certifying the supernatural, body overflowed by life, which he worships, with coarse, but sincere rites.

The inwardness, and mystery, of this attachment, drive men of every class to the use of emblems. The schools of poets, and philosophers, are not more intoxicated with their symbols, than the populace with theirs. In our political parties, compute the power of badges and emblems. See the great ball rolled by successive ardent crowds from Baltimore to Bunker hill! In the political processions, Lowell goes in a loom, and Lynn in a shoe, and Salem in a ship. Witness the cider-barrel, the log-cabin, the hickory-stick, the palmetto, and all the cognizances of party. See the power of national emblems. Some stars, lilies, leopards, a crescent, a lion, an eagle, or other figure, which came into credit God knows how, on an old rag of bunting, blowing in the wind, on a fort, at the ends of the earth, shall make the blood tingle under the rudest, or the most conventional exterior. The people fancy they hate poetry, and they are all poets and mystics!

Beyond this universality of the symbolic language, we are apprised of the divineness of this superior use of things, whereby the world is a temple, whose walls are covered with emblems, pictures, and commandments of the Deity, in this, that there is no fact in nature which does not carry the whole sense of nature; and the distinctions which we make in events, and in affairs, of low and high, honest and base, disappear when nature is used as a symbol. Thought makes everything fit for use. The vocabulary of an omniscient man would embrace words and images excluded from polite conversation. What would be base, or even obscene, to the obscene, becomes illustrious, spoken in a new connexion of thought. The piety of the Hebrew prophets purges their grossness. The circumcision is an example of the power of poetry to raise the low and offensive. Small and mean things serve as well as great symbols. The meaner the type by which a law is expressed, the more pungent it is, and the more lasting in the memories of men: just as we choose the smallest box, or case, in which any needful utensil can be carried. Bare lists of words are found suggestive, to an imaginative and excited mind; as it is related of Lord Chatham, that he was accustomed to read in Bailey's Dictionary, when he was preparing to speak in Parliament. The poorest experience is rich enough for all the purposes of expressing thought. Why covet a knowledge of new facts? Day and night, house and garden, a few books, a few actions, serve us as well as would all trades and all spectacles. We are far from having exhausted the significance of the few symbols we use. We can come to use them yet with a terrible simplicity. It does not need that a poem should be long. Every word was once a poem. Every new relation is a new word. Also, we use defects and deformities to a sacred purpose, so expressing our sense that the evils of the world are such only to the evil eye. In the old mythology, mythologists observe, defects are ascribed to divine natures, as lameness to Vulcan, blindness to Cupid, and the like, to signify exuberances.

For, as it is dislocation and detachment from the life of God, that makes things ugly, the poet, who re-attaches things to nature and the Whole,—re-attaching even artificial things, and violations of nature, to nature, by a deeper insight,—disposes very easily of the most disagreeable facts. Readers of poetry see the factory-village, and the railway, and fancy that the poetry of the landscape is broken up by these; for these works of art are not yet consecrated in their reading; but the poet sees them fall within the great Order not less than the bee-hive, or the spider's geometrical web. Nature adopts them very fast into her vital circles, and the gliding train of cars she loves like her own. Besides, in a centred mind, it signifies nothing how many mechanical inventions you exhibit. Though you add millions, and never so surprising, the fact of mechanics has not gained a grain's weight. The spiritual fact remains unalterable, by many or by few particulars; as no mountain is of any appreciable height to break the curve of the sphere. A shrewd country-boy goes to the city for the first time, and the complacent citizen is not satisfied with his little wonder. It is not that he does not see all the fine houses, and know that he never saw such before, but he disposes of them as easily as the poet finds place for the railway. The chief value of the new fact, is to enhance the great and constant fact of Life, which can dwarf any and every circumstance, and to which the belt of wampum, and the commerce of America, are alike.

The world being thus put under the mind for verb and noun, the poet is he who can articulate it. For, though life is great, and fascinates, and absorbs,—and though all men are intelligent of the symbols through which it is named,—yet they cannot originally use them. We are symbols, and inhabit symbols; workmen, work, and tools, words and things, birth and death, all are emblems; but we sympathize with the symbols, and, being infatuated with the economical uses of things, we do not know that they are thoughts. The poet, by an ulterior intellectual perception, gives them a power which makes their old use forgotten, and puts eyes, and a tongue, into every dumb and inanimate object. He perceives the thought's independence of the symbol, the stability of the thought, the accidency and fugacity of the symbol. As the eyes of Lyncæus were said to see through the earth, so the poet turns the world to glass, and shows us all things in their right series and procession. For, through that better perception, he stands one step nearer to things, and sees the flowing or metamorphosis; perceives that thought is multiform; that within the form of every creature is a force impelling it to ascend into a higher form; and, following with his eyes the life, uses the forms which express that life, and so his speech flows with the flowing of nature. All the facts of the animal economy,—sex, nutriment, gestation, birth, growth—are symbols of the passage of the world into the soul of man, to suffer there a change, and reappear a new and higher fact. He uses forms according to the life, and not according to the form. This is true science. The poet alone knows astronomy, chemistry, vegetation, and animation, for he does not stop at these facts, but employs them as signs. He knows why the plain, or meadow of space, was strown with these flowers we call suns, and moons, and stars; why the great deep is adorned with animals, with men, and gods; for, in every word he speaks he rides on them as the horses of thought.

By virtue of this science the poet is the Namer, or Language-maker, naming things sometimes after their appearance, sometimes after their essence, and giving to every one its own name and not another's, thereby rejoicing the intellect, which delights in detachment or boundary. The poets made all the words, and therefore language is the archives of history, and, if we must say it, a sort of tomb of the muses. For, though the origin of most of our words is forgotten, each word was at first a stroke of genius, and obtained currency, because for the moment it symbolized the world to the first speaker and to the hearer. The etymologist finds the deadest word to have been once a brilliant picture. Language is fossil poetry. As the limestone of the continent consists of infinite masses of the shells of animalcules, so language is made up of images, or tropes, which now, in their secondary use, have long ceased to remind us of their poetic origin. But the poet names the thing because he sees it, or comes one step nearer to it than any other. This expression, or naming, is not art, but a second nature, grown out of the first, as a leaf out of a tree. What we call nature, is a certain self-regulated motion, or change; and nature does all things by her own hands, and does not leave another to baptize her, but baptizes herself; and this through the metamorphosis again. . . .

———

... And herein is the legitimation of criticism, in the mind's faith, that the poems are a corrupt version of some text in nature, with which they ought to be made to tally. A rhyme in one of our sonnets should not be less pleasing than the iterated nodes of a sea-shell, or the resembling difference of a group of flowers. The pairing of the birds is an idyl, not tedious as our idyls are; a tempest is a rough ode without falsehood or rant; a summer, with its harvest sown, reaped, and stored, is an epic song, subordinating how many admirably executed parts. Why should not the symmetry and truth that modulate these, glide into our spirits, and we participate the invention of nature?

This insight, which expresses itself by what is called Imagination, is a very high sort of seeing, which does not come by study, but by the intellect being where and what it sees, by sharing the path, or circuit of things through forms, and so making them translucid to others. The path of things is silent. Will they suffer a speaker to go with them? A spy they will not suffer; a lover, a poet, is the transcendency of their own nature,—him they will suffer. The condition of true naming, on the poet's part, is his resigning himself to the divine *aura* which breathes through forms, and accompanying that.

It is a secret which every intellectual man quickly learns, that, beyond the energy of his possessed and conscious intellect, he is capable of a new energy (as of an intellect doubled on itself), by abandonment to the nature of things; that, beside his privacy of power as an individual man, there is a great public power, on which he can draw, by unlocking, at all risks, his human doors, and suffering the ethereal tides to roll and circulate through him: then he is caught up into the life of the Universe, his speech is thunder, his thought is law, and his words are universally intelligible as the plants and animals. The poet knows that he speaks adequately, then only when he speaks somewhat wildly, or, "with the flower of the mind;" not with the intellect, used as an organ, but with the intellect released from all service, and suffered to take its direction from its celestial life; or, as the ancients were wont to express themselves, not with intellect alone, but with the intellect inebriated by nectar. As the traveller who has lost his way, throws his reins on his horse's neck, and trusts to the instinct of the animal to find his road, so must we do with the divine animal who carries us through this world. For if in any manner we can stimulate this instinct, new passages are opened for us into nature, the mind flows into and through things hardest and highest, and the metamorphosis is possible.

This is the reason why bards love wine, mead, narcotics, coffee, tea, opium, the fumes of sandal-wood and tobacco, or whatever other species of animal exhilaration. All men avail themselves of such means as they can, to add this extraordinary power to their normal powers; and to this end they prize conversation, music, pictures, sculpture, dancing, theatres, travelling, war, mobs, fires, gaming, politics, or love, or science, or animal intoxication, which are several coarser or finer *quasi*-mechanical substitutes for the true nectar, which is the ravishment of the intellect by coming nearer to the fact. These are auxiliaries to the centrifugal tendency of a man, to his passage out into free space, and they help him to escape the custody of that body in which he is pent up, and of that jail-yard of individual relations in which he is enclosed. Hence a great number of such as were professionally expressors of Beauty, as painters, poets, musicians, and actors, have been more than others wont to lead a life of pleasure and indulgence; all but the few who receive the true nectar; and, as it was a spurious mode of attaining freedom, as it was an emancipation not into the heavens, but into the freedom of baser places, they were punished for that advantage they won, by a dissipation and deterioration. But never can any advantage be taken of nature by a trick. The spirit of the world, the great calm presence of the creator, comes not forth to the sorceries of opium or of wine. The sublime vision comes to the pure and simple soul in a clean and chaste body. That is not an inspiration which we owe to narcotics, but some counterfeit excitement and fury. Milton says, that the lyric poet may drink wine and live generously, but the epic poet, he who shall sing of the gods, and their descent unto men, must drink water out of a wooden bowl. For poetry is not "Devil's wine," but God's wine. It is with this as it is with toys. We fill the hands and nurseries of our children with all manner of dolls, drums, and horses, withdrawing their eyes from the plain face and sufficing objects of nature, the sun, and moon, the animals, the water, and stones, which should be their toys. So the poet's habit of living should be set on a key so low and plain, that the common influences should delight him. His cheerfulness should be the gift of the sunlight; the air should suffice for his inspiration, and he should be tipsy with water. That spirit which suffices quiet hearts, which seems to come forth to such from every dry knoll of sere grass, from every pine-stump, and half-imbedded stone, on which the dull March sun shines, comes forth to the poor and hungry, and such as are of simple taste. If thou fill thy brain with Boston and New York, with fashion and covetousness, and wilt stimulate thy jaded senses with wine and French coffee, thou shalt find no radiance of wisdom in the lonely waste of the pinewoods.

If the imagination intoxicates the poet, it is not inactive in other men. The metamorphosis excites in the beholder an emotion of joy. The use of symbols has a certain power of emancipation and exhilaration for all men. We seem to be touched by a wand, which makes us dance and run about happily, like children. We are like persons who come out of a cave or cellar into the open air. . . .

The poets are thus liberating gods. The ancient British bards had for the title of their order, "Those who are free throughout the world." They are free, and they make free. An imaginative book renders us much more service at first, by stimulating us through its tropes, than afterward, when we arrive at the precise sense of the author. I think nothing is of any value in books, excepting the transcendental and extraordinary. If a man is inflamed and carried away by his thought, to that degree that he forgets the authors and the public, and heeds only this one dream, which holds him like an insanity, let me read his paper, and you may have all the arguments and histories and criticism. All the value which attaches to Pythagoras, Paracelsus, Cornelius Agrippa, Cardan, Kepler, Swedenborg, Schelling, Oken, or any other who introduces questionable facts into his cosmogony, as angels, devils, magic, astrology, palmistry, mesmerism, and so on, is the certificate we have of departure from routine, and that here is a new witness. That also is the best success in conversation, the magic of liberty, which puts the world, like a ball, in our hands. How cheap even the liberty then seems; how mean to study, when an emotion communicates to the intellect the power to sap and upheave nature: how great the perspective! nations, times, systems, enter and disappear, like threads in tapestry of large figure and many colors; dream delivers us to dream, and, while the drunkenness lasts, we will sell our bed, our philosophy, our religion, in our opulence.

There is good reason why we should prize this liberation. The fate of the poor shepherd, who, blinded and lost in the snowstorm, perishes in a drift within a few feet of his cottage door, is an emblem of the state of man. On the brink of the waters of life and truth, we are miserably dying. The inaccessibleness of every thought but that we are in, is wonderful. What if you come near to it,—you are as remote, when you are nearest, as when you are farthest. Every thought is also a prison; every heaven is also a prison. Therefore we love the poet, the inventor, who in any form, whether in an ode, or in an action, or in looks and behavior, has yielded us a new thought. He unlocks our chains, and admits us to a new scene.

This emancipation is dear to all men, and the power to impart it, as it must come from greater depth and scope of thought, is a measure of intellect. Therefore all books of the imagination endure, all which ascend to that truth, that the writer sees nature beneath him, and uses it as his exponent. Every verse or sentence, possessing this virtue, will take care of its own immortality. The religions of the world are the ejaculations of a few imaginative men.

But the quality of the imagination is to flow, and not to freeze. The poet did not stop at the color, or the form, but read their meaning; neither may he rest in this meaning, but he makes the same objects exponents of his new thought. Here is the difference betwixt the poet and the mystic, that the last nails a symbol to one sense, which was a true sense for a moment, but soon becomes old and false. For all symbols are fluxional; all language is vehicular and transitive, and is good, as ferries and horses are, for conveyance, not as farms and houses are, for homestead. Mysticism consists in the mistake of an accidental and individual symbol for an universal one. The morning-redness happens to be the favorite meteor to the eyes of Jacob Behmen, and comes to stand to him for truth and faith; and he believes should stand for the same realities to every reader. But the first reader prefers as naturally the symbol of a mother and child, or a gardener and his bulb, or a jeweller polishing a gem. Either of these, or of a myriad more, are equally good to the person to whom they are significant. Only they must be held lightly, and be very willingly translated into the equivalent terms which others use. And the mystic must be steadily told,—All that you say is just as true without the tedious use of that symbol as with it. Let us have a little algebra, instead of this trite rhetoric,—universal signs, instead of these village symbols,—and we shall both be gainers. The history of hierarchies seems to show, that all religious error consisted in making the symbol too stark and solid, and, at last, nothing but an excess of the organ of language. . . .

———

I look in vain for the poet whom I describe. We do not, with sufficient plainness, or sufficient profoundness, address ourselves to life, nor dare we chaunt our own times and social circumstance. If we filled the day with bravery, we should not shrink from celebrating it. Time and nature yield us many gifts, but not yet the timely man, the new religion, the reconciler, whom all things await. Dante's praise is, that he dared to write his autobiography in colossal cipher, or into universality. We have yet had no genius in America, with tyrannous eye, which knew the value of our incomparable materials, and saw, in the barbarism and materialism of the times, another carnival of the same gods whose picture he so much admires in Homer; then in the middle age; then in Calvinism. Banks and tariffs, the newspaper and caucus, methodism and unitarianism, are flat and dull to dull people, but rest on the same foundations of wonder as the town of Troy, and the temple of Delphi, and are as swiftly passing away. Our logrolling, our stumps and their politics, our fisheries, our Negroes, and Indians, our boasts, and our repudiations, the wrath of rogues, and the pusillanimity of honest men, the northern trade, the southern planting, the western clearing, Oregon, and Texas, are yet unsung. Yet America is a poem in our eyes; its ample geography dazzles the imagination, and it will not wait long for metres. . . .

# 4.

# MARGARET FULLER

## FROM "AMERICAN LITERATURE"

### (1846)

When Margaret Fuller began writing for the *New York Tribune*, she was already an experienced critic. Not only had she published in *The Dial*, starting with "A Short Essay on Critics" in the first issue, she was also a more exacting editor than Emerson proved to be, as Henry Thoreau, among others, discovered. The section of the essay printed below offers her most comprehensive summation of the state of American literature. Her diagnosis of the national literary scene is much less mystical in tone than Emerson's, although similar in its bottom line. Like Emerson, Fuller is underwhelmed with what American writers have produced thus far, though more hopeful about the future. Unlike Emerson, Fuller also stresses the interdependence of self-reliant originality and the maturity of social institutions, including a public and a marketplace that will support serious authorship. Solitary genius and stern sincerity are indispensable; but they alone cannot suffice in the absence of the right social conditions. Emerson also knew this perfectly well, but he tends to banish it to the edges of his theory of poetic genius, which puts primary emphasis on the innateness of the poetic gift.

SOURCE: "American Literature; Its Position in the Present Time, and Prospects for the Future," *Papers on Literature and Art*. New York: Wiley & Putnam, 1846.

Some thinkers may object to this essay, that we are about to write of that which has, as yet, no existence.

For it does not follow because many books are written by persons born in America that there exists an American literature. Books which imitate or represent the thoughts and life of Europe do not constitute an American literature. Before such can exist, an original idea must animate this nation and fresh currents of life must call into life fresh thoughts along its shores.

We have no sympathy with national vanity. We are not anxious to prove that there is as yet much American literature. Of those who think and write among us in the methods and of the thoughts of Europe, we are not impatient; if their minds are still best adapted to such food and such action. If their books express life of mind and character in graceful forms, they are good and we like them. We consider them as colonists and useful schoolmasters to our people in a transition state; which lasts rather longer than is occupied in passing, bodily, the ocean which separates the new from the old world.

We have been accused of an undue attachment to foreign continental literature, and, it is true, that in childhood, we had well nigh "forgotten our English," while constantly reading in other languages. Still, what we loved in the literature of continental Europe was the range and force of ideal manifestation in forms of national and individual greatness. A model was before us in the great Latins of simple masculine minds seizing upon life with unbroken power. The stamp both of nationality and individuality was very strong upon them; their lives and thoughts stood out in clear and bold relief. The English character has the iron force of the Latins, but not the frankness and expansion. Like their fruits, they need a summer sky to give them more sweetness and a richer flavour. This does not apply to Shakspeare, who has all the fine side of English genius, with the rich colouring, and more fluent life, of the Catholic countries. Other poets, of England also, are expansive more or less, and soar freely to seek the blue sky, but take it as a whole, there is in English literature, as in English character, a reminiscence of walls and ceilings, a tendency to the arbitrary and conventional that repels a mind trained in admiration of the antique spirit. It is only in later days that we are learning to prize the peculiar greatness which a thousand times outweighs this fault, and which has enabled English genius to go forth from its insular position and conquer such vast dominion in the realms both of matter and of mind.

Yet there is, often, between child and parent, a reaction from excessive influence having been exerted, and such an one we have experienced, in behalf of our country, against England. We use her language, and receive, in torrents, the influence of her thought, yet it is, in many respects, uncongenial and injurious to our constitution. What suits Great Britain, with her insular position and consequent need to concentrate and intensify her life, her limited monarchy, and spirit of trade, does not suit a mixed race, continually enriched with new blood from other stocks the most unlike that of our first descent, with ample field and verge enough to range in and leave every impulse free, and abundant opportunity to develope a genius, wide and full as our rivers, flowery, luxuriant and impassioned as our vast prairies, rooted in strength as the rocks on which the Puritan fathers landed.

That such a genius is to rise and work in this hemisphere we are confident; equally so that scarce the first faint streaks of that day's dawn are yet visible. It is sad for those that foresee, to know they may not live to share its glories, yet it is sweet, too, to know that every act and word, uttered in the light of that foresight, may tend to hasten or ennoble its fulfilment.

That day will not rise till the fusion of races among us is more complete. It will not rise till this nation shall attain sufficient moral and intellectual dignity to prize moral and intellectual, no less highly than political, freedom, not till, the physical resources of the country being explored, all its regions studded with towns, broken by the plow, netted together by railways and telegraph lines, talent shall be left at leisure to turn its energies upon the higher department of man's existence. Nor then shall it be seen till from the leisurely and yearning soul of that riper time national ideas shall take birth, ideas craving to be clothed in a thousand fresh and original forms.

Without such ideas all attempts to construct a national literature must end in abortions like the monster of Frankenstein, things with forms, and the instincts of forms, but souless, and therefore revolting. We cannot have expression till there is something to be expressed.

The symptoms of such a birth may be seen in a longing felt here and there for the sustenance of such ideas. At present, it shows itself, where felt, in sympathy with the prevalent tone of society, by attempts at external action, such as are classed under the head of social reform. But it needs to go deeper, before we can have poets, needs to penetrate beneath the springs of action, to stir and remake the soil as by the action of fire.

Another symptom is the need felt by individuals of being even sternly sincere. This is the one great means by which alone progress can be essentially furthered. Truth is the nursing mother of genius. No man can be absolutely true to himself, eschewing cant, compromise, servile imitation, and complaisance, without becoming original, for there is in every creature a fountain of life which, if not choked back by stones and other dead rubbish, will create a fresh atmosphere, and bring to life fresh beauty. And it is the same with the nation as with the individual man.

The best work we do for the future is by such truth. By use of that, in whatever way, we harrow the soil and lay it open to the sun and air. The winds from all quarters of the globe bring seed enough, and there is nothing wanting but preparation of the soil, and freedom in the atmosphere, for ripening of a new and golden harvest.

We are sad that we cannot be present at the gathering in of this harvest. And yet we are joyous, too, when we think that though our name may not be writ on the pillar of our country's fame, we can really do far more towards rearing it, than those who come at a later period and to a seemingly fairer task. *Now,* the humblest effort, made in a noble spirit, and with religious hope, cannot fail to be even infinitely useful. Whether we introduce some noble model from another time and clime, to encourage aspiration in our own, or cheer into blossom the simplest wood-flower that ever rose from the earth, moved by the genuine impulse to grow, independent of the lures of money or celebrity; whether we speak boldly when fear or doubt keep others silent, or refuse to swell the popular cry upon an unworthy occasion, the spirit of truth, purely worshipped, shall turn our acts and forbearances alike to profit, informing them with oracles which the latest time shall bless.

Under present circumstances the amount of talent and labour given to writing ought to surprise us. Literature is in this dim and struggling state, and its pecuniary results exceedingly pitiful. From many well known causes it is impossible for ninety-nine out of the hundred, who wish to use the pen, to ransom, by its use, the time they need. This state of things will have to be changed in some way. No man of genius writes for money; but it is essential to the free use of his powers, that he should be able to disembarrass his life from care and perplexity. This is very difficult here; and the state of things gets worse and worse, as less and less is offered in pecuniary meed for works demanding great devotion of time and labour (to say nothing of the ether engaged) and the publisher, obliged to regard the transaction as a matter of business, demands of the author to give him only what will find an immediate market, for he cannot afford to take any thing else. This will not do! When an immortal poet was secure only of a few copyists to circulate his works, there were princes and nobles to patronize literature and the arts. Here is only the public, and the public must learn how to cherish the nobler and rarer plants, and to plant the aloe, able to wait a hundred years for its bloom, or its garden will contain, presently, nothing but potatoes and pot-herbs. We shall have, in the course of the next two or three years, a convention of authors to inquire into the causes of this state of things and propose measures for its remedy. Some have already been thought of that look promising, but we shall not announce them till the time be ripe; that date is not distant, for the difficulties increase from day to day, in consequence of the system of cheap publication, on a great scale. . . .

# John Sullivan Dwight

## Music Philosophically Considered

### (1849)

For most Transcendentalists, "art" meant chiefly the printed or spoken word. Otherwise, most of them were amateur dabblers at best. But Dwight (1813–93) was—or became—an exception. As with Emerson, Thoreau, and Fuller, his identity took a long time to congeal. He drifted into the ministry and out again, preferring sermons on the religion of beauty to long-term pastoral labors. He then joined Brook Farm, remaining for its entire existence. There he helped to edit *The Harbinger* (1845–49), the journal first of the community and then of the Fourierist associationist movement in general. His early interest in music resurfaced at this time in the form of book reviews and essays. The following selection comes from one of these, a disquisition on music published by his friend Elizabeth Peabody in the same miscellaneous collection as Thoreau's "Resistance to Civil Government." (Dwight may or may not have known that Thoreau was himself something of a musician in a humbler vein, a self-taught flautist who even devised some original compositions.) In the 1850s, Dwight started his own magazine, *Dwight's Journal of Music*, which garnered one thousand subscribers and elevated him to the stature of Boston's leading music critic. But the essay that follows is conceptual rather than practical criticism: a Romantic celebration of music as a universal medium of communication and inspiration. As such it shows, as do Fuller's reflections on painting and sculpture and dance, that the Transcendentalist vision of art extended across a range of different genres even though most of the time it focused on the arts of language.

SOURCE: "Music," *Aesthetic Papers,* ed. Elizabeth Peabody. Boston: The Editor; New York: Putnam, 1849.

Music is a universal language, subtly penetrating all the walls of time and space. It is no more local than the mathematics, which are its impersonal reason, just as sound is its body, and feeling or passion is its soul. The passions of the human heart are radically alike, and answer to the same tones everywhere and always, except as they may be undeveloped; and music has a power to develope them, like an experience of life. It can convey a foretaste of moods and states of feeling yet in reserve for the soul, of loves which yet have never met an object that could call them out. A musical composition is the best expression of its author's inmost life. No persons in all history are so intimately known to those that live away from them or after them, as are Handel, Mozart, Beethoven, Weber, Schubert, Bellini, and others, to those who enter into the spirit of their musical works. For they have each bequeathed the very wine of his peculiar life in this form, that it sparkles still the same as often as it is opened to the air. The sounds may effervesce in each performance; but they may be woke to life again at any time. So it is with the passions and emotions which first dictated the melodious creations.

Hence it is that great composers have no biography, except their music. Theirs is a life of deep, interior sentiment, of ever-active passion and affection, of far-reaching aspiration, rather than of ideas or events; theirs is the wisdom of love; their belief is faith, the felt creed of the heart; and they dwell in the peculiar element of that, in the wondrous *tone-world*, communicating all the strongest, swiftest, and most delicate pulsations of their feeling to the ready vibrations of wood or metal or string, which propagate themselves through the equally ready vibrations of the air, and of every other medium, till they reach the chambers of the ear, and set in motion chords more sensitive, that vibrate on the nervous boundary between matter and the soul; and there, what was vibration becomes sound, and the hearer has caught the spirit of the composer. Yes: the whole soul of a Beethoven thrills through your soul, when you have actually heard one of his great symphonies. There is no other communion of so intimate a nature possible, as that which operates through music. Intimate, and yet most mystical; intimacy not profaned by outward contact of familiarity, but a meeting and communing of the ideal, one with another, which never grows familiar. Why is it but because in sentiment the tendency always is to unity, while thought for ever differentiates and splits? Feeling communicates by sympathy, or fellow-feeling, the earth round; and music is its common language, which admits no dialects, and means the same in Europe and America. Light corresponds to thought; and light is changed and colored by every medium through which it shoots, by every surface which reflects it. Sound, or, which is the same thing, measured motion or vibration, corresponds to feeling, and its vibrations are passed on through every medium unchanged, except as they grow fainter. Light is volatile; but sound is constant: so it is when you compare thought with feeling, which last comes more from the centre where all souls are one.

Music is religious and prophetic. She is the real Sibyl, chanting evermore of unity. Over wild, waste oceans of discord floats her silvery voice, the harbinger of love and hope. Every genuine strain of music is a serene prayer, or bold, inspired demand, to be united with all, at the Heart of all things. Her appeal to the world is more loving than the world can yet appreciate. Kings and statesmen, and men of affairs, and men of theories, would stand aside from their own over-rated occupations to listen to her voice, if they knew how nearly it concerned them, how much more it goes to the bottom of the matter, and how clearly she forefeels humanity's great destiny. The soul that is truly receptive of music learns angelic wisdom, and grows more childlike with experience. The sort of experience which music gives does not plough cunning furrows in the brow of the fresh soul, nor darken its expressive face by knitting there the tangled lines of Satan. Here, the most deeply initiated are in spirit the most youthful; and Hope delights to wait on them.

The native impulses of the soul, or what are variously called the passions, affections, propensities, desires, are, all of them, when considered in their essence and original unwarped tendency, so many divinely implanted loves. Union, harmony of some sort, is their very life. To meet, to unite, to blend, by methods intricate as swift, is their whole business and effort through eternity. As is their attraction, such must be their destiny; not to collision, not to excess followed by exhaustion; not to discord, chaos, and confusion; but to binding ties of fitness and conjunction through all spheres, from the simplest to the most universal accords. Through these (how else?) are the hearts of the human race to be knit into one mutually conscious, undivided whole, one living temple not too narrow, nor too fragmentary for the reception of the Spirit of Good. Is not this foretold in music, the natural language of these passions, which cannot express corruption nor any evil feeling, without ceasing to be music; which has no tone for any bad passion, and translates into harmony and beauty whatever it expresses? The blending of all these passions harmoniously into one becomes the central love, the deepest and most undivided life of man. This is the love of God, as it also, from the first, is the inbreathing of God, who is love; to whom the soul seeks its way, by however blind an instinct, through all these partial harmonies, learning by degrees to understand the universal nature of its desire and aim. The sentiment of unity, the strongest and deepest sentiment of which man is capable, the great affection into which all his affections flow—to find, not lose themselves; which looks to the source when little wants conflict, and straightway they are reconciled in emulous ardor for the glory of the whole; which lifts a man above the thought of self, by making him in every sense fully himself, by reuniting his prismatic, party-colored passions into one which is as clear and universal as the light; the sentiment which seeks only universal harmony and order, so that all things, whether of the inner or of the outer world, may be perfectly transparent to the love in which they have their being, and that the sole condition of all peace and happiness, the consciousness of one in all and all in one, may never more be wanting;—that is what the common sense of mankind means by the *religious* sentiment,—that is the pure essence of religion. Music is its natural language, the chief rite of its worship, the rite which cannot lose its sacredness; for music cannot cease to be harmony, cannot cease to symbolize the sacred relationship of each to all, cannot contract a taint, any more than the sunbeam which shines into all corners. Music cannot narrow or cloak the message which it bears; it cannot lie; it cannot raise questions in the mind, or excite any other than a pure enthusiasm. It is God's alphabet, and not man's; unalterable and unpervertable; suited for the harmony of the human passions and affections; and sent us, in this their long winter of disharmony and strife, to be a perpetual type and monitor, rather say an actual foretaste, of that harmony which must yet come. How could there be religion without music? That sentiment would create it again, would evoke its elements out of the completest jargon of discords, if the scale and the accords, and all the use of instruments, were forgotten. Let that feeling deepen in our nation, and absorb its individual ambitions, and we shall have our music greater than the world has known. There *was* an age of faith, though the doctrinal statements and the forms thereof were narrow. Art, however, freed the spirit which the priest imprisoned. Music, above all, woke to celestial power and beauty in the bosom of a believing though an ignorant age. The Catholic church did not neglect this great secret of expression and of influence; and the beautiful free servant served it in a larger spirit than itself had dreamed of. Where it could not teach the Bible, where its own formal interpretations thereof were perhaps little better than stones for bread, it could breathe the spirit of the Bible and of all love and sanctity into the most ignorant and thoughtless worshipper, through its sublime Masses, at once so joyous and so solemn, so soul-subduing and so soul-exalting, so full of tenderness, so full of rapture uncontrollable, so confident and so devout. In these, the hearer did, for the time being, actually *live* celestial states. The mystery of the cross and the ascension, the glorious doctrine of the kingdom of heaven, were not reasoned out to his understanding, but passed through his very soul, like an experience, in these all-permeating clouds of sound; and so the religion became in him an emotion, which could not so easily become a thought, which had better not become such thought as the opinionated teachers of the visible church would give him. The words of the Credo never yet went down with all minds; but their general tenor is universal, and music is altogether so. Music extracts and embodies only the spirit of the doctrine, that inmost life of it which all feel, and miraculously revivifies and transfigures the cold statements of the understanding with the warm faith of feeling. In music there is no controversy; in music there are no opinions: its springs are deeper than the foundations of any of these partition walls, and its breath floats undivided over all their heads. No danger to the Catholic whose head is clouded by dull superstitions, while his heart is nourished and united with the life of all lives by this refreshing dew!

The growing disposition, here and there, among select musical circles, to cultivate acquaintance with this form of music, is a good sign. What has been called sacred music in this country has been the least sacred in every thing but the name, and the forced reverence paid it. With the superstitions of the past, the soul of nature also was suppressed; and the free spirit of music found small sphere amid our loud *protestings*. A joyless religion of the intellect merely, which could almost find fault with the sun's shining, closed every pore of the self-mortified and frozen soul against the subtle, insinuating warmth of this most eloquent apostle of God. The sublime sincerity of that wintry energy of self-denial having for the most part passed away, and the hearts of the descendants of the Pilgrims having become opened to all worldly influences, why should they not be also visited by the heavenly corrective of holy and enchanting music, which is sure to call forth and to nourish germs of loftier affection? Can the bitter spirit of sectarianism, can the formal preachings of a worldly church which strives to keep religion so distinct from life, can the utilitarian ethics of this great day of trade, give the soul such nourishment and such conviction of the higher life as the great religious music of Mozart and Haydn and Beethoven?

# Walt Whitman

## from Preface to *Leaves of Grass*

### (1855)

Together with Emily Dickinson, Walt Whitman (1819–92) was the foremost American poet of his age. No other figure has so often been called the "father of American poetry." Neither Dickinson nor Whitman was a card-carrying Transcendentalist, but the work of both, particularly Whitman's, reflects the movement's influence. Though Transcendentalism was too idealized and cerebral for his taste, the first two editions of his *Leaves of Grass* (1855, 1856) are steeped in the Transcendentalist spirit. Emerson's influence was particularly crucial. "I was simmering, simmering, simmering. Emerson brought me to a boil," Whitman once affirmed. He was thrilled when Emerson responded to a gift copy of the first edition of *Leaves,* which Whitman sent him out of the blue, with warm praise of the book as "the most remarkable piece of wit and wisdom that America has yet produced." (Notice that Emerson refrained from praising the book specifically as *poetry.*) Emerson then dispatched Alcott and Thoreau to Brooklyn for a memorable encounter with Whitman—edgy but cordial. To Emerson's dismay, Whitman proceeded to use Emerson's tribute for publicity purposes. In the 1856 edition of *Leaves,* he added a long open-letter reply to Emerson, addressing him as "master" but mainly boasting about his own progress as a poet. Nevertheless, the two men developed an amicable, intermittent acquaintance that Whitman especially valued. Many parts of the manifesto with which he opened the first edition of *Leaves of Grass* read like more extravagant recyclings of Emerson's already extravagant portrait of the ideal poet, including the vision of genius as "the larger embodiment of the common heart," as Emerson puts it elsewhere. Indeed, Whitman's account of the *American* poet picks up where *Nature* and "The Poet" leave off. His aggressive literary nationalism also differs from the more tempered views of Emerson and Fuller, for whom artistic genius was universal even more than it was nation-specific.

SOURCE: *Leaves of Grass.* Brooklyn: Walter Whitman, 1855. (Because this text frequently resorts to ellipses when punctuating, I have used a seven-dot sequence [ . . . . . . . ] to mark omitted passages.)

Of all nations the United States with veins full of poetical stuff most need poets and will doubtless have the greatest and use them the greatest. Their Presidents shall not be their common referee so much as their poets shall. Of all mankind the great poet is the equable man. . . . . . . He is the equalizer of his age and land. . . . . . .

The land and sea, the animals fishes and birds, the sky of heaven and the orbs, the forests mountains and rivers, are not small themes . . . but folks expect of the poet to indicate more than the beauty and dignity which always attach to dumb real objects . . . they expect him to indicate the path between reality and their souls. Men and women perceive the beauty well enough . . . probably as well as he. The passionate tenacity of hunters, woodmen, early risers, cultivators of gardens and orchards and fields, the love of healthy women for the manly form, seafaring persons, drivers of horses, the passion for light and the open air, all is an old varied sign of the unfailing perception of beauty and of a residence of the poetic in outdoor people. They can never be assisted by poets to perceive . . . some may but they never can. The poetic quality is not marshalled in rhyme or uniformity or abstract addresses to things nor in melancholy complaints or good precepts, but is the life of these and much else and is in the soul. The profit of rhyme is that it drops seeds of a sweeter and more luxuriant rhyme, and of uniformity that it conveys itself into its own roots in the ground out of sight. The rhyme and uniformity of perfect poems show the free growth of metrical laws and bud from them as unerringly and loosely as lilacs or roses on a bush, and take shapes as compact as the shapes of chestnuts and oranges and melons and pears, and shed the perfume impalpable to form. . . . . . . Who troubles himself about his ornaments or fluency is lost. This is what you shall do: Love the earth and sun and the animals, despise riches, give alms to every one that asks, stand up for the stupid and crazy, devote your income and labor to others, hate tyrants, argue not concerning God, have patience and indulgence toward the people, take off your hat to nothing known or unknown or to any man or number of men, go freely with powerful uneducated persons and with the young and with the mothers of families, read these leaves in the open air every season of every year of your life, reexamine all you have been told at school or in any book, dismiss whatever insults your own soul, and your very flesh shall be a great poem and have the richest fluency not only in its words but in the silent lines of its lips and face and between the lashes of your eyes and in every motion and joint of your body. . . . . . .

The messages of great poets to each man and woman are, Come to us on equal terms, Only then can you understand us, We are no better than you, What we enclose you enclose, What we enjoy you may enjoy. Did you suppose there could be only one Supreme? We affirm there can be unnumbered Supremes, and that one does not countervail another any more than one eyesight countervails another. . . . . . .

A great poem is for ages and ages in common and for all degrees and complexions and all departments and sects and for a woman as much as a man and a man as much as a woman. A great poem is no finish to a man or woman but rather a beginning. Has any one fancied he could sit at last under some due authority and rest satisfied with explanations and realize and be content and full? To no such terminus does the greatest poet bring . . . he brings neither cessation or sheltered fatness and ease. The touch of him tells in action. Whom he takes he takes with firm sure grasp into live regions previously unattained. . . . . . .

# B.

## "IMPROVISED" PROSE

# Amos Bronson Alcott

## selected "Orphic Sayings"

### (1840)

*The Dial* opened itself up to ridicule by printing fifty lofty aphorisms by Bronson Alcott in its very first issue. For anti-Transcendentalists, this "article" seemed proof positive of the vapidness of the magazine— and the movement. Transcendentalist confreres also smirked and cringed. Alcott was indeed a clunky writer. Yet in at least three ways his "Orphic Sayings" are an important index of Transcendentalism's aesthetic *aspiration,* if not its achievement. First, they underscore the importance of the individual pronouncement or aphorism in the best Transcendentalist prose: Emerson's "Trust thyself, every heart vibrates to that iron string," Thoreau's "The mass of men lead lives of quiet desperation." The art of the aphorism was broadly a Romantic inheritance, both advocated and practiced by such prominent figures as Friedrich Schlegel in Germany and Coleridge in England. The Transcendentalists attached extra importance to the memorable encapsulation or fragment as a mark of inspired expression. Even more than the "inspired" but unfinished verse Emerson sought to elicit for *The Dial,* the prose aphorism was the essence of Transcendentalist "portfolio" writing. Emerson, Thoreau, Fuller, Alcott, and others kept voluminous journals that they packed with such nuggets, both from their reading and their own devising. When they shared their journals with one another, they often jotted them down. Second and related, the Transcendentalists saw aphorism as the primal form of expression from which the ancient scriptures of world religion had been built (see

Section V-B-3). If there was such a thing as an "idiom of the sacred," this was it. Alcott used "orphic" advisedly, alluding to the ancient Greek religious movement of which the poet Orpheus was the mythical founder. Third, and most sweepingly important, aphorism was one of a cluster of prose genres along with the conversational dialogue, the private journal, the epistle, and improvised oratory seen as potentially "inspired" relative to more canonical forms of high literary art. This was part of the impetus behind Emerson's call for "portfolio" verse. Of course these "spontaneous" genres could be equally canned, as Alcott's "Orphic Sayings" show. The Transcendentalists' practice of circulating their "private" writing—journals and letters—back and forth also helped ensure a blurring of the boundary between the spontaneous and the premeditated.

SOURCE: "Orphic Sayings," *The Dial*, 1 (July 1840).


I.


Thou art, my heart, a soul-flower, facing ever and following the motions of thy sun, opening thyself to her vivifying ray, and pleading thy affinity with the celestial orbs. Thou dost

> the livelong day
> Dial on time thine own eternity.


## II. ENTHUSIASM.

Believe, youth, that your heart is an oracle; trust her instinctive auguries, obey her divine leadings; nor listen too fondly to the uncertain echoes of your head. The heart is the prophet of your soul, and ever fulfils her prophecies; reason is her historian; but for the prophecy the history would not be. Great is the heart: cherish her; she is big with the future, she forebodes renovations. Let the flame of enthusiasm fire alway your bosom. Enthusiasm is the glory and hope of the world. It is the life of sanctity and genius; it has wrought all miracles since the beginning of time.

## V. VOCATION.

Engage in nothing that cripples or degrades you. Your first duty is self-culture, self-exaltation: you may not violate this high trust. Your self is sacred, profane it not. Forge no chains wherewith to shackle your own members. Either subordinate your vocation to your life, or quit it forever: it is not for you; it is condemnation of your own soul. Your influence on others is commensurate with the strength that you have found in yourself. First cast the demons from your own bosom, and then shall your word exorcise them from the hearts of others.

## VII. SPIRITUALISM.

Piety is not scientific; yet embosoms the fact that reason develops in scientific order to the understanding. Religion, being a sentiment, is science yet in synthetic relations; truth yet undetached from love; thought not yet severed from action. For every fact that eludes the analysis of reason, conscience affirms its root in the supernatural. Every synthetic fact is supernatural and miraculous. Analysis by detecting its law resolves it into science, and renders it a fact of the understanding. Divinely seen, natural facts are symbols of spiritual laws. Miracles are of the heart; not of the head: indigenous to the soul; not freaks of nature, not growths of history. God, man, nature, are miracles.

## X. APOTHEOSIS.

Every soul feels at times her own possibility of becoming a God; she cannot rest in the human, she aspires after the Godlike. This instinctive tendency is an authentic augury of its own fulfilment. Men shall become Gods. Every act of admiration, prayer, praise, worship, desire, hope, implies and predicts the future apotheosis of the soul.

## XXVIII. PRUDENCE.

Prudence is the footprint of Wisdom.

# 2.

# ELIZABETH PEABODY (?)

## REPORT OF MARGARET FULLER
## CONVERSATION ON "LIFE"
### (1841)

Both Alcott and Fuller were committed to the idea that public dialogue, or guided "conversation," was a medium with great potential both as education and as performance. Alcott pioneered this method in his short-lived Boston school in the 1830s (see Section IV-B). Later, both Alcott and Fuller conducted adult classes in this mode. It was their equivalent of the lyceum lecture; indeed, Alcott's public conversations were sometimes lyceum-sponsored. Of the two, Fuller was the more dazzling by far. Section IV-C includes a hybrid example: a conversation on gender in preparation for which discussants were required to write an essay. The session reported below, from a series held the following year, is closer to pure improvisation. Note that this particular report is twice mediated: by its scribe, probably Elizabeth Peabody, and by the editor who prepared it for publication, Emerson. Still, it gives a flavor of the combination of aphorism and disquisition at such meetings.

SOURCE: *Memoirs of Margaret Fuller Ossoli.* Boston: Phillips, Sampson, and Company, 1852. Volume 1.

MARCH 22, 1841.—The question of the day was, What is life?

Let us define, each in turn, our idea of living. Margaret did not believe we had, any of us, a distinct idea of life.

A[nna] S[haw] thought so great a question ought to be given for a written definition. "No," said Margaret, "that is of no use. When we go away to think of anything, we never do think. We all talk of life. We all have some thought now. Let us tell it. C——, what is life?"

C——replied,—"It is to laugh, or cry, according to our organization."

"Good," said Margaret, "but not grave enough. Come, what is life? I know what I think; I want you to find out what you think."

Miss P[eabody] replied,—"Life is division from one's principles of life in order to [attain] a conscious reorganization. We are cut up by time and circumstance, in order to feel our reproduction of the eternal law."

Mrs. E[merson],—"We live by the will of God, and the object of life is to submit," and went on into Calvinism.

Then came up all the antagonisms of Fate and Freedom.

Mrs. H[ooper] said,—"God created us in order to have a perfect sympathy from us as free beings."

Mrs. A[lmira] B[arlow] said she thought the object of life was to attain absolute freedom. At this Margaret immediately and visibly kindled.

C[aroline] S[turgis] said,—"God creates from the fulness of life, and cannot but create; he created us to overflow, without being exhausted, because what he created, necessitated new creation. It is not to make us happy, but creation is his happiness and ours."

Margaret was then pressed to say what she considered life to be.

Her answer was so full, clear, and concise, at once, that it cannot but be marred by being drawn through the scattering medium of my memory. But here are some fragments of her satisfying statement.

She began with God as Spirit, Life, so full as to create and love eternally, yet capable of pause. Love and creativeness are dynamic forces, out of which we, individually, as creatures, go forth bearing his image, that is, having within our being the same dynamic forces, by which we also add constantly to the total sum of existence, and shaking off ignorance, and its effects, and by becoming more ourselves—*i.e.,* more divine—destroying sin in principle, we attain to absolute freedom, we return to God, conscious like himself, and, as his friends, giving, as well as receiving, felicity forevermore. In short, we become gods, and able to give the life which we now feel ourselves only to receive.

On Saturday morning, Mrs. L. E. and Mrs. E[llen] H[ooper] were present, and begged Margaret to repeat the statement concerning life, with which she closed the last conversation. Margaret said she had forgotten every word she said. She must have been inspired by a good genius, to have so satisfied everybody,—but the good genius had left her. She would try, however, to say what she thought, and trusted it would resemble what she had said already. She then went into the matter, and, true enough, she did not use a single word she used before.

# 3.

# HENRY DAVID THOREAU

## FROM "SAYINGS OF CONFUCIUS"

### (1843)

This is one of a series of "Ethnical Scriptures" prepared for *The Dial* by Thoreau, Emerson, and others from ancient texts and designed to represent the "essential" vision of a wide range of religio-philosophical traditions of the Asian and Mediterranean worlds—including also, for example, Hindu, Buddhist, Islamic, Zoroastrian, Chaldaic. The basis for these compilations was a universalistic faith in the unity of the human spirit and a trust in the idiom of proverbial wisdom literature as the aboriginal form of inspired verbal expression. A number of these sayings from the *Analects* of Confucius (one of the classic "four books" of Confucianism) were recycled in Emerson's essays and Thoreau's *Walden.*

SOURCE: "Ethnical Scriptures. Sayings of Confucius," *The Dial,* 3 (April 1843).

Chee says, if in the morning I hear about the right way, and in the evening die, I can be happy.

A man's life is properly connected with virtue. The life of the evil man is preserved by mere good fortune.

Coarse rice for food, water to drink, and the bended arm for a pillow—happiness may be enjoyed even in these. Without virtue, riches and honor seem to me like a passing cloud.

A wise and good man was Hooi. A piece of bamboo was his dish, a cocoa-nut his cup, his dwelling a miserable shed. Men could not sustain the sight of his wretchedness; but Hooi did not change the serenity of his mind. A wise and good man was Hooi.

Chee-koong said, Were they discontented? The sage replies, They sought and obtained complete virtue;—how then could they be discontented?

Chee says, Yaou is the man who, in torn clothes or common apparel, sits with those dressed in furred robes without feeling shame.

To worship at a temple not your own is mere flattery.

Chee says, grieve not that men know not you; grieve that you are ignorant of men.

How can a man remain concealed! How can a man remain concealed! . . .

Having knowledge, to apply it; not having knowledge, to confess your ignorance; this is real knowledge. . . .

Silence is absolutely necessary to the wise man. Great speeches, elaborate discourses, pieces of eloquence, ought to be a language unknown to him; his actions ought to be his language. As for me, I would never speak more. Heaven speaks, but what language does it use to preach to men, that there is a sovereign principle from which all things depend; a sovereign principle which makes them to act and move? Its motion is its language; it reduces the seasons to their time; it agitates nature; it makes it produce. This silence is eloquent.

# 4.

# NATHANIEL HAWTHORNE
## A WALK TO WALDEN
### (1843)

Nathaniel Hawthorne (1804–64) is remembered chiefly as a writer of fiction strongly infused by symbolism and the fantastic. But he was also a meticulous observer of people and places. His *American Notebooks* (1835–53) doubles as a writer's journal of ideas for stories, some fanciful in the extreme, and a record of mundane experiences such as this excursion to Walden Pond from his honeymoon abode in Concord (see Section VI), two years before Thoreau began his twenty-six months of living there. Read alongside *Walden,* the greatest of all Transcendentalist classics, the passage has special interest. It captures both the beauty of the spot that also charmed Thoreau and the bustle of the colony of railroad workers, from one of whom Thoreau later bought a shanty that he recycled into a cabin of his own. The railroad along the west end of the pond was completed by the time Thoreau moved there, but Hawthorne's passage nonetheless alerts us to the fact that the Walden area was not so isolated a spot as *Walden* tends to imply. Conversely, to think of Hawthorne as a meditative diarist who roamed the precincts of Concord shows that he was not as detached from the Transcendentalist circle as he liked to make himself out to be.

SOURCE: *The American Notebooks,* ed. Claude Simpson. Columbus: Ohio State University Press, 1972.

*Friday, October 6th, [1843].*

Yesterday afternoon (leaving wifie with my sister Louisa, who has been with us two or three days) I took a solitary walk to Walden Pond. It was a cool, north-west windy day, with heavy clouds rolling and tumbling about the sky, but still a prevalence of genial autumn sunshine. The fields are still green, and the great masses of the woods have not yet assumed their many-colored garments; but here and there, are solitary oaks of a deep, substantial red, or maples of a more brilliant hue, or chesnuts, either yellow or of a tenderer green than in summer. Some trees seem to return to their hue of May or early June, before they put on the brighter autumnal tints. In some places, along the borders of low and moist land, a whole range of trees were clothed in the perfect gorgeousness of autumn, of all shades of brilliant color, looking like the palette on which Nature was arranging the tints wherewith to paint a picture. These hues appeared to be thrown together without design; and yet there was perfect harmony among them, and a softness and delicacy made up of a thousand different brightnesses. There is not, I think, so much contrast among these colors as might at first appear; the more you consider them, the more they seem to have one element among them all—which is the reason that the most brilliant display of them soothes the observer, instead of exciting him. And I know not whether it be more a moral effect, or a physical one operating merely on the eye, but it is a pensive gaiety, which causes a sigh often, but never a smile. We never fancy, for instance, that these gaily-clad trees should be changed into young damsels in holiday attire, and betake themselves to dancing on the plain. If they were to undergo such a transformation, they would surely arrange themselves in a funeral procession, and go sadly along with their purple, and scarlet, and golden garments trailing over the withering grass. When the sunshine falls upon them, they seem to smile; but it is as if they were heart-broken. But it is in vain for me to attempt to describe these autumnal brilliancies, or to convey the impression which they make on me. I have tried a thousand times, and always without the slightest self-satisfaction. Luckily, there is no need of such a record; for Nature renews the scene, year after year; and even when we shall have passed away from the world, we can spiritually create these scenes; so that we may dispense now and hereafter with all further efforts to put them into words.

Walden Pond was clear and beautiful, as usual. It tempted me to bathe; and though the water was thrillingly cold, it was like the thrill of a happy death. Never was there such transparent water as this. I threw sticks into it, and saw them float suspended on an almost invisible medium; it seemed as if the pure air was beneath them, as well as above. If I were to be baptized, it should be in this pond; but then one would not wish to pollute it by washing off his sins into it. None but angels should bathe there. It would be a fit bathing-place for my little wife; and sometime or other, I hope, our blessed baby shall be dipt into its bosom.

In a small and secluded dell, that opens upon the most beautiful cove of the whole lake, there is a little hamlet of huts or shanties, inhabited by the Irish people who are at work upon the rail-road. There are three or four of these habitations, the very rudest, I should imagine, that civilized men ever made for themselves, constructed of rough boards, with protruding ends. Against some of them the earth is heaped up to the roof, or nearly so; and when the grass has had time to sprout upon them, they will look like small natural hillocks, or a species of ant-hill, or something in which Nature has a larger share than man. These huts are placed, beneath the trees, (oaks, walnuts, and white pines) wherever the trunks give them space to stand; and by thus adapting themselves to natural interstices instead of making new ones, they do not break or disturb the solitude and seclusion of the place. Voices are heard, and the shouts and laughter of children, who play about like the sunbeams that come down through the branches. Women are washing beneath the trees, and long lines of whitened clothes are extended from tree to tree, fluttering and gambolling in the breeze. A pig, in a stye even more extemporary than the shanties, is grunting, and poking his snout through the clefts of his habitation. The household pots and kettles are seen at the doors, and a glance within shows the rough benches that serve for chairs, and the bed upon the floor. The visiter's nose takes note of the fragrance of a pipe. And yet, with all these homely items, the repose and sanctity of the old wood do not seem to be destroyed or prophaned; she overshadows these poor people, and assimilates them, somehow or other, to the character of her natural inhabitants. Their presence did not shock me, any more than if I had merely discovered a squirrel's nest in a tree. To be sure, it is a torment to see the great, high, ugly embankment of the rail-road, which is here protruding itself into the lake, or along its margin, in close vicinity to this picturesque little hamlet. I have seldom seen anything more beautiful than the cove, on the border of which the huts are situated; and the more I looked, the lovelier it grew. The trees overshadowed it deeply; but on one side there was some brilliant shrubbery which seemed to light up the whole picture with the effect of a sweet and melancholy smile. I felt as if spirits were there—or as if these shrubs had a spiritual life—in short, the impression was undefinable; and after gazing and musing a good while, I retraced my steps through the Irish hamlet, and plodded on along a wood-path.

According to my invariable custom, I mistook my way, and emerging upon a road, I turned my back, instead of my face, towards Concord, and walked on very diligently, till a guide-board informed me of my mistake. I then turned about, and was shortly overtaken by an old yeoman in a chaise, who kindly offered me a ride, and shortly set me down in the village.

# 5.

# Henry David Thoreau

## First Days at Walden

## (1845)

Nothing Thoreau wrote is so full of sustained excitement as the journal he kept during his first summer at Walden, after moving into his cabin on the symbolic date of July 4, U.S. Independence Day. It is striking how many of these first jottings worked their way through *Walden*'s multiple drafts into the finished book, published nine years later. To read through this selection in sequence is like fast-forwarding through the first half of *Walden*. Yet Thoreau's special and continued attachment to his impressions of this first summer is not surprising, either. This was indeed a time of extraordinary excitement for him. From the very first, he saw his experiment as a new start in life, a symbolic rebirth. Clearly Thoreau approached his Walden experiment as a mythic or epic quest, seeing himself as "a fellow wanderer and survivor of Ulysses." Even as he fleshed out the book with descriptive elaboration, philosophic musings, and social satire, he never lost the sense of his experiment as a kind of sacred ritual enactment whose tiniest daily details often felt suffused with a larger-than-life intensity. Perhaps more than any other aspect of the book, this gives *Walden* its special character. That Thoreau was so obviously filled with the sense of this from the start corroborates the Transcendentalist idea of great art as starting with inspiration. But the fact that the book took multiple rewritings and nearly a decade to complete also testifies to the fact that inspiration requires hard labor in order to be fully realized.

SOURCE: *Journal, Volume 2: 1842–1848*, ed. Robert Sattelmeyer. Princeton University Press, 1984.

*Walden Sat. July 5th—45*

Yesterday I came here to live. My house makes me think of some mountain houses I have seen, which seemed to have a fresher auroral atmosphere about them as I fancy of the halls of Olympus. I lodged at the house of a saw-miller last summer, on the Caatskills mountains, high up as Pine orchard in the blue-berry & raspberry region, where the quiet and cleanliness & coolness seemed to be all one, which had this ambrosial character. He was the miller of the Kaaterskill Falls, They were a clean & wholesome family inside and out—like their house. The latter was not plastered—only lathed and the inner doors were not hung. The house seemed high placed, airy, and perfumed, fit to entertain a travelling God. It was so high indeed that all the music, the broken strains, the waifs & accompaniments of tunes, that swept over the ridge of the Caatskills, passed through its aisles. Could not man be man in such an abode? And would he ever find out this grovelling life?

It was the very light & atmosphere in which the works of Grecian art were composed, and in which they rest. They have appropriated to themselves a loftier hall than mortals ever occupy, at least on a level with the mountain brows of the world.

There was wanting a little of the glare of the lower vales and in its place a pure twilight as became the precincts of heaven Yet so equable and calm was the season there that you could not tell whether it was morning or noon or evening. Always there was the sound of the morning cricket

*July 6th*

I wish to meet the facts of life—the vital facts, which where the phenomena or actuality the Gods meant to show us,—face to face, And so I came down here. Life! who knows what it is—what it does? If I am not quite right here I am less wrong than before—and now let us see what they will have. The preacher, instead of vexing the ears of drowsy farmers on their day of rest, at the end of the week, (for sunday always seemed to me like a fit conclusion of an ill spent week and not the fresh and brave beginning of a new one) with this one other draggletail and postponed affair of a sermon, from thirdly to 15thly, should teach them with a thundering voice—pause & simplicity.

—

stop— Avast— Why so fast? In all studies we go not forward but rather backward with redoubled pauses, we always study *antiques*— with silence and *re*flection. Even time has a depth, and below its surface the waves do not lapse and roar. I wonder men can be so frivolous almost as to attend to the gross form of negro slavery—there are so many keen and subtle masters, who subject us both. Self-emancipation in the West Indies of a man's thinking and imagining provinces, which should be more than his island territory One emancipated heart & intellect— It would knock off the fetters from a million slaves.

*July 7th*

I am glad to remember tonight as I sit by my door that I too am at least a remote descendent of that heroic race of men of whom there is tradition. I too sit here on the shore of my Ithaca, a fellow wanderer and survivor of Ulysses. How Symbolical, significant of I know not what the pitch pine stands here before my door unlike any glyph I have seen sculptured or painted yet— One of nature's later designs. Yet perfect as her Grecian art. There it is, a done tree. Who can mend it? And now where is the generation of heroes whose lives are to pass amid these our northern pines? Whose exploits shall appear to posterity pictured amid these strong and shaggy forms?

Shall there be only arrows and bows to go with these pines on some pipe stone quarry at length.

If we can forget we have done somewhat, if we can remember we have done somewhat. Let us remember this

The Great spirit of course makes indifferent all times & places. The place where he is seen is always the same, and indescribably pleasant to all our senses. We had allowed only near-lying and transient circumstances to make our occasions— But nearest to all things is that which fashions its being. Next to us the grandest laws are being enacted and administered.

Bread may not always nourish us, but it always does us good   it even takes stiffness out of our joints and makes us supple and boyant when we knew not what ailed us—to share any heroic joy—to recognise any largeness in man or nature, to see and to know— This is all cure and prevention.

Verily a good house is a temple— A clean house—pure and undefiled, as the saying is. I have seen such made of white pine. Seasoned and seasoning still to eternity. Where a Goddess might trail her garment. The less dust we bring in to nature, the less we shall have to pick up. It was a place where one would go in, expecting to find something agreeable; as to a shade—or to a shelter—a more natural place.

I hear the far off lowing of a cow and it seems to heave the firmament. I at first thought it was the voice of a minstrel whom I know, who might be straying over hill and dale this eve—but soon I was not disappointed when it was prolonged into the sweet and natural and withal cheap tone of the cow. This youths brave music is indeed of kin with the music of the cow. They are but one articulation of nature.

Sound was made not so much for convenience, that we might hear when called, as to regale the sense—and fill one of the avenues of life. A healthy organization will never need what are commonly called the sensual gratifications, but will enjoy the daintiest feasts at those tables where there is nothing to tempt the appetite of the sensual.

There are strange affinities in this universe—strange ties stranger harmonies and relationships, what kin am I to some wildest pond among the mountains—high up ones shaggy side—in the gray morning twilight draped with mist—suspended in low wreathes from the dead willows and bare firs that stand here and there in the water, as if here were the evidence of those old contests between the land and water which we read of. But why should I find anything to welcome me in such a nook as this— This faint reflection this dim watery eye— where in some angle of the hills the woods meet the waters edge and a grey tarn lies sleeping

My beans—whose continuous length of row is 7 miles, already planted and now so impatient to be howed—not easily to be put off. What is the meaning of this service this small Hercules labor—of this small warfare—I know not. I come to love my rows—they attatch me to the earth—and so I get new strength and health like Antaeus

—My beans, so many more than I want. This has been my curious labor— Why only heaven knows—to make this surface of the earth, which yielded only blackberries & Johnswort—& cinqfoil—sweet wild fruits & pleasant flowers produce instead this pulse What shall I learn of beans or beans of me— I cherish them— I hoe them early & late I have an eye to them.— And this is my days work. It is a fine broad leaf to look upon.

My auxiliaries are the dews and rains—to water this dry soil—and genial fatness in the soil itself, which for the most part is lean and effoete. My enemies are worms cool days—and most of all wood-chucks. They have nibbled for me an eigth of an acre clean. I plant in faith—and they reap—this is the tax I pay—for ousting Jonswort & the rest But soon the surviving beans will be too tough for woodchucks and then—they will go forward to meet new foes.

### July 14th 1845

What sweet and tender, the most innocent and divinely encouraging society there is in every natural object, and so in universal nature even for the poor misanthrope and most melancholy man. There can be no really *black* melan-choly to him who lives in the midst of nature, and has still his senses. There never was yet such a storm but it was Aeolian music to the innocent ear. Nothing can compel to a vulgar sadness a simple & brave man. While I enjoy the sweet friendship of the seasons I trust that nothing can make life a burden to me. This rain which is now watering my beans, and keeping me in the house waters me too. I needed it as much. And what if most are not hoed—those who send the rain whom I chiefly respect will pardon me.

Sometimes when I compare myself with other men methinks I am favored by the Gods. They seem to whisper joy to me beyond my deserts and that I do have a solid warrant and surety at their hands, which my fellows do not. I do not flatter myself but if it were possible *they* flatter me. I am especially guided and guarded.

And now I think of it—let me remember—

What was seen true once—and sanctioned by the flash of Jove— will always be true, and nothing can hinder it. I have the warrant that no fair dream I have had need fail of its fulfilment.

Here I know I am in good company—here is the world its centre and metropolis, and all the palms of Asia—and the laurels of Greece— and the firs of the Arctic Zones incline thither.

Here I can read Homer if I would have books, as well as in Ionia, and not wish myself in Boston or New-york or London or Rome or

Greece— In such place as this he wrote or sang. Who should come to my lodge Just now—but a true Homeric boor—one of those Paphlagonian men? Alek Therien—he called himself— A Canadian now, a woodchopper—a post maker—makes fifty posts—holes them i.e. in a day, and who made his last supper on a woodchuck which his dog caught— And he too has heard of Homer and *if it were not for books would not know what to do*—rainy days. Some priest once who could read glibly from the Greek itself—taught him reading in a measure his verse at least in his turn—at Nicolet away by the Trois Riviers once.

And now I must read to him while he holds the book—Achilles' reproof of Patrocles on his sad countenance

> "Why are you in tears,—Patrocles? Like a
> young child (girl) &c. &c
>
> Or have you only heard some news from Phthia?
> They say that Menoetius lives yet, son of Actor
> And Peleus lives, son of AEacus, among the Myrmidons,
> Both of whom having died, we should greatly grieve."

He has a neat bundle of white-oak bark under his arm for a sick man—gathered this Sunday morning— "I suppose there's no harm in going after such a thing today."? ? The simple man. May the Gods send him many wood chucks.

And earlier today came 5 Lestrigones—Railroad men who take care of the road, some of them at least. They still represent the bodies of men—transmitting arms and legs—and bowels downward from those remote days to more remote. They have some got a rude wisdom withal—thanks to their dear experience. And one with them a handsome younger man—a sailor like Greek like man—says "Sir I like your notions—I think I shall live so myself Only I should like a wilder country—where there is more game. I have been among the Indians near Apallachecola I have lived with them, I like your kind of life— Good-day I wish you success and happiness."

# C.
## POETRY

# 1.

# WILLIAM ELLERY CHANNING II

Ellery Channing was the prolific but undisciplined talent whose work Emerson used as his example of the "literature of the portfolio" that he hoped to see printed in *The Dial* (see Section V-B). At first Emerson was quite taken by Channing, who was in the process of moving to Concord for the rest of his long life. He proved to be a moody, thriftless being, and a negligent husband to Margaret Fuller's sister. But he was a witty conversationalist and an amusing walking companion, whose writing shows flashes of talent for both lyricism and satire. Unfortunately, he scribbled far too much, taking Emerson's doctrine of inspiration all too literally. His earlier poems were skewered by writer-critic Edgar Allan Poe, no friend to the Transcendentalists in general and particularly severe on Channing. At best, however, Channing wrote with grace and sensitivity. The first two poems included here were originally published in *The Dial*. The third is an excerpt from a long, descriptive rumination from the vantage point of the highest mountain in eastern Massachusetts.

SOURCES: ("Boat Song") *Poems by William Ellery Channing*. Boston: Little Brown, 1843. ("Hymn of the Earth" and "Wachusett") *Poems, Second Series*. Boston: James Munroe, 1847.

## BOAT SONG

The River calmly flows
Through shining banks, through lonely glen,
Where the owl shrieks, though ne'er the cheer of men
Has stirred its mute repose;
Still if you should walk there, you would go there again.

The stream is well alive;
Another passive world you see,
Where downward grows the form of every tree,
Like soft light clouds they thrive;
Like them let us in our pure loves reflected be.

A yellow gleam is thrown
Into the secrets of that maze
Of tangled trees, that late shut out our gaze,
Refusing to be known;
It must its privacy unclose,—its glories blaze.

Sweet falls the summer air
Over her form who sails with me,
Her way like it is beautifully free,
Her nature far more rare,
And is her constant heart of virgin purity.

A quivering star is seen
Keeping its watch above the hill;
Though from the sun's retreat small light is still
Poured on earth's saddening mien:
We all are tranquilly obeying Evening's will.

Thus ever love the Power;
To simplest thoughts dispose the mind;
In each obscure event a worship find
Like that of this dim hour,—
In lights, and airs, and trees, and in all human kind.

We smoothly glide below
The faintly glimmering worlds of light:
Day has a charm, and this deceptive night
Brings a mysterious show;
He shadows our dear earth, but his cool stars are white.


## HYMN OF THE EARTH

My highway is unfeatured air,
My consorts are the sleepless Stars,
And men, my giant arms upbear,
My arms unstained and free from scars.

I rest forever on my way,
Rolling around the happy Sun.
My children love the sunny day,
But noon and night to me are one.

My heart has pulses like their own,
I am their Mother, and my veins
Though built of the enduring stone,
Thrill as do theirs with godlike pains.

The forests and the mountains high,
The foaming ocean and the springs,
The plains,—O pleasant Company,
My voice through all your anthem rings.

Ye are so cheerful in your minds,
Content to smile, content to share,
My being in your Chorus finds
The echo of the spheral air.

No leaf may fall, no pebble roll,
No drop of water lose the road,
The issues of the general Soul
Are mirrored in its round abode.

FROM "WACHUSETT"

And off the summit one sees villages,
Church spires, white houses, and their belts of trees,
Plenty of farmers' clearings, and some woods,
But no remote Sierra solitudes.
I never counted up the list of towns,
That I can see spread on the rolling downs,
Or sought for names of mountains on the map,
As Jackson might who is a Scenery-trap,
But to my notion there is matter here,
As pleasant as if larger or severe.
'T is plain New England, neither more nor less,
Pure Massachusetts-looking, in plain dress;
From every village point at least three spires,
To satiate the good villagers' desires,
Baptist, and Methodist, and Orthodox,
And even Unitarian, creed that shocks
Established church-folk; they are one to me,
Who is in the different creeds the same things see,
But I love dearly to look down at them,
In rocky landscapes like Jerusalem.
The villages gleam out painted with white,
Like paper castles are the houses light,
And every gust that o'er the valley blows,
May scatter them perchance like drifting snows.
The little streams that thread the valleys small,
Make scythes or axes, driving factories all,
The ponds are damned, and e'en the petty brooks,
Convert to sluices swell the River's crooks,
And where the land's so poor, it will not pay
For farming, winds the Railroad's yellow way.

# 2.

# CHRISTOPHER PEARSE CRANCH

Though Cranch is better known for his cartoon illustrations of high-minded passages from Emerson, he also wrote several resonant poems on such hallmark Transcendentalist themes as the mystical rapport between humankind and nature ("Correspondences"), and the emotional cost extracted by the idea of the god within each person. Cranch's "Enosis" (Greek for "union") testifies to how this idea, designed to inspire, could ironically leave one feeling isolated from others and despondent at the sense of everyday life's superficiality and fragmentation. These two poems were both first published in *The Dial*. The third poem, written later in life, revisits the subject of the second, in a more skeptical way.

SOURCES: ("Enosis" and "Correspondences") *Poems*. Philadelphia: Carey and Hart, 1844. ("The Pines and the Sea") *Ariel and Caliban, with Other Poems*. Boston: Houghton, 1887.

# ENOSIS

Thought is deeper than all speech,
Feeling deeper than all thought;
Souls to souls can never teach
What unto themselves was taught.

We are spirits clad in veils;
Man by man was never seen;
All our deep communing fails
To remove the shadowy screen.

Heart to heart was never known;
Mind with mind did never meet;
We are columns left alone,
Of a temple once complete.

Like the stars that gem the sky,
Far apart, though seeming near,
In our light we scattered lie;
All is thus but starlight here.

What is social company
But a babbling summer stream?
What our wise philosophy
But the glancing of a dream?

Only when the sun of love
Melts the scattered stars of thought;
Only when we live above
What the dim-eyed world hath taught;

Only when our souls are fed
By the Fount which gave them birth,
And by inspiration led,
Which they never drew from earth,

We, like parted drops of rain
Swelling till they meet and run,
Shall be all absorbed again,
Melting, flowing into one.

## CORRESPONDENCES

All things in Nature are beautiful types to the soul that can read them;
Nothing exists upon earth, but for unspeakable ends.
Every object that speaks to the senses was meant for the spirit:
Nature is but a scroll; God's hand-writing thereon.
Ages ago, when man was pure, ere the flood overwhelmed him,
While in the image of God every soul yet lived,
Every thing stood as a letter or word of a language familiar,
Telling of truths which now only the angels can read.
Lost to man was the key of those sacred hieroglyphics.
Stolen away by sin, till by heaven restored.
Now with infinite pains we here and there spell out a letter,
Here and there will the sense feebly shine through the dark.
When we perceive the light which breaks through the visible symbol,
What exultation is ours! *We* the discovery have made!
Yet is the meaning the same as when Adam lived sinless in Eden,
Only long hidden is slept, and now again is revealed.
Man unconsciously uses figures of speech every moment,
Little dreaming the cause why to such terms he is prone,
Little dreaming that everything has its own correspondence
Folded within its form, as in the body the soul.
Gleams of the mystery fall on us still, though much is forgotten,
And through our commonest speech, illumine the path of our
 thoughts.

Thus doth the lordly sun shine out a type of the Godhead;
Wisdom and love the beams that stream on a darkened world.
Thus do the sparkling waters flow, giving joy to the desert,
And the fountain of life opens itself to the thirst.
Thus doth the word of God distil like the rain and the dew-drops;

Thus doth the warm wind breathe like to the Spirit of God;
And the green grass and the flowers are signs of the regeneration.

O thou Spirit of Truth, visit our minds once more,
Give us to read in letters of light the language celestial
Written all over the earth, written all over the sky—
Thus may we bring our hearts once more to know our Creator,
Seeing in all things around, types of the Infinite Mind.

## THE PINES AND THE SEA

Beyond the low marsh-meadows and the beach,
Seen through the hoary trunks of windy pines,
The long blue level of the ocean shines.
The distant surf, with hoarse, complaining speech,
Out from its sandy barrier seems to reach;
And while the sun behind the woods declines,
The moaning sea with sighing boughs combines,
And waves and pines make answer, each to each.
O melancholy soul, whom far and near,
In life, faith, hope, the same sad undertone
Pursues from thought to thought! thou needs must hear
An old refrain, too much, too long thine own:
'Tis thy mortality infects thine ear;
The mournful strain was in thyself alone.

# Ralph Waldo Emerson

Emerson was Transcendentalism's leading poet in verse as well as in prose. But his poems have never enjoyed anything like the same influence and acclaim as his essays. Ironically for one who had deprecated meter in "The Poet," when writing verse Emerson often contorted his syntax and watered down his language for the sake of the verse pattern. He sized up his own limitations in portraying himself as a poet with a "husky" voice that sang mostly in prose. Nevertheless, his poems have always had warm admirers among poets more distinguished than he (Emily Dickinson and Robert Frost, to name two), and for good reason. Emerson is capable of striking lines, surprising turns, compressed vehemence, delicate images, teasingly riddlesome tonalities, and greater variety of form and subject matter than is usually supposed. Of the poems below, composed over a period of three decades starting in the mid-1830s, two show him working out his ministerial identity crisis ("The Problem" and "Uriel," the latter a veiled, after-the-fact reflection on the Divinity School Address controversy); two are about the art of poetry ("The Problem" and "Bacchus"); three are nature meditations ("Each and All," "The Rhodora," and "The Snow-Storm"); two are public performance pieces for historic occasions (the two hymns, the latter commemorating the end of slavery in the United States); two are political poems ("Ode" and "Boston Hymn") that take antithetical positions on political activism; one is the rendition of a Sanskrit text ("Brahma"); and another a staged collision of Yankee and "eastern" wisdom ("Hamatreya"). See also Section IV-D for still

another memorable Emerson poem, "Musketaquid," which comple-
ments his celebration of the Concord landscape and history in several
of the selections below.

SOURCES: (First nine poems) *Poems.* Boston: James Munroe, 1847. (Last three
poems) *May-Day and Other Pieces.* Boston: Ticknor and Fields, 1867. Texts are
slightly emended in light of Emerson's later corrections.

## EACH AND ALL

Little thinks, in the field, yon red-cloaked clown,
Of thee from the hill-top looking down;
The heifer that lows in the upland farm,
Far-heard, lows not thine ear to charm;
The sexton, tolling his bell at noon,
Deems not that great Napoleon
Stops his horse, and lists with delight,
Whilst his files sweep round yon Alpine height;
Nor knowest thou what argument
Thy life to thy neighbor's creed has lent.
All are needed by each one;
Nothing is fair or good alone.
I thought the sparrow's note from heaven,
Singing at dawn on the alder bough;
I brought him home, in his nest, at even;
He sings the song, but it pleases not now,
For I did not bring home the river and sky;—
He sang to my ear,—they sang to my eye.
The delicate shells lay on the shore;
The bubbles of the latest wave
Fresh pearls to their enamel gave;
And the bellowing of the savage sea
Greeted their safe escape to me.
I wiped away the weeds and foam,
I fetched my sea-born treasures home;
But the poor, unsightly, noisome things
Had left their beauty on the shore,
With the sun, and the sand, and the wild uproar.
The lover watched his graceful maid,

As 'mid the virgin train she strayed,
Nor knew her beauty's best attire
Was woven still by the snow-white choir.
At last she came to his hermitage,
Like the bird from the woodlands to the cage;—
The gay enchantment was undone,
A gentle wife, but fairy none.
Then I said, "I covet truth;
Beauty is unripe childhood's cheat;
I leave it behind with the games of youth."—
As I spoke, beneath my feet
The ground-pine curled its pretty wreath,
Running over the club-moss burrs;
I inhaled the violet's breath;
Around me stood the oaks and firs;
Pine-cones and acorns lay on the ground,
Over me soared the eternal sky,
Full of fight and of deity;
Again I saw, again I heard,
The rolling river, the morning bird;—
Beauty through my senses stole;
I yielded myself to the perfect whole.

## THE PROBLEM

I like a church; I like a cowl;
I love a prophet of the soul;
And on my heart monastic aisles
Fall like sweet strains, or pensive smiles;
Yet not for all his faith can see
Would I that cowled churchman be.

Why should the vest on him allure,
Which I could not on me endure?

Not from a vain or shallow thought
His awful Jove young Phidias brought;

Never from lips of cunning fell
The thrilling Delphic oracle;
Out from the heart of nature rolled
The burdens of the Bible old;
The litanies of nations came,
Like the volcano's tongue of flame,
Up from the burning core below,—
The canticles of love and woe;
The hand that rounded Peter's dome,
And groined the aisles of Christian Rome,
Wrought in a sad sincerity;
Himself from God he could not free;
He builded better than he knew;—
The conscious stone to beauty grew.

Know'st thou what wove yon woodbird's nest
Of leaves, and feathers from her breast?
Or how the fish outbuilt her shell,
Painting with morn each annual cell?
Or how the sacred pine-tree adds
To her old leaves new myriads?
Such and so grew these holy piles,
Whilst love and terror laid the tiles.
Earth proudly wears the Parthenon,
As the best gem upon her zone;
And Morning opes with haste her lids,
To gaze upon the Pyramids;
O'er England's abbeys bends the sky,
As on its friends, with kindred eye;
For, out of Thought's interior sphere,
These wonders rose to upper air;
And Nature gladly gave them place,
Adopted them into her race,
And granted them an equal date
With Andes and with Ararat.

These temples grew as grows the grass;
Art might obey, but not surpass.
The passive Master lent his hand
To the vast soul that o'er him planned;

And the same power that reared the shrine,
Bestrode the tribes that knelt within.
Ever the fiery Pentecost
Girds with one flame the countless host,
Trances the heart through chanting choirs,
And through the priest the mind inspires.
The word unto the prophet spoken
Was writ on tables yet unbroken;
The word by seers or sibyls told,
In groves of oak, or fanes of gold,
Still floats upon the morning wind,
Still whispers to the willing mind.
One accent of the Holy Ghost
The heedless world hath never lost.
I know what say the fathers wise,—
The Book itself before me lies,
Old *Chrysostom*, best Augustine,
And he who blent both in his line,
The younger *Golden Lips* or mines,
Taylor, the Shakspeare of divines.
His words are music in my ear,
I see his cowled portrait dear;
And yet, for all his faith could see,
I would not the good bishop be.


## URIEL

It fell in the ancient periods,
    Which the brooding soul surveys,
Or ever the wild Time coined itself
    Into calendar months and days.

This was the lapse of Uriel,
Which in Paradise befell.
Once, among the Pleiads walking,
SAID overheard the young gods talking;
And the treason, too long pent,
To his ears was evident.

The young deities discussed
Laws of form, and metre just,
Orb, quintessence, and sunbeams,
What subsisteth, and what seems.
One, with low tones that decide,
And doubt and reverend use defied,
With a look that solved the sphere,
And stirred the devils everywhere,
Gave his sentiment divine
Against the being of a line.
"Line in nature is not found;
Unit and universe are round;
In vain produced, all rays return;
Evil will bless, and ice will burn."
As Uriel spoke with piercing eye,
A shudder ran around the sky;
The stern old war-gods shook their heads;
The seraphs frowned from myrtle-beds;
Seemed to the holy festival
The rash word boded ill to all;
The balance-beam of Fate was bent;
The bounds of good and ill were rent;
Strong Hades could not keep his own,
But all slid to confusion.

A sad self-knowledge, withering, fell
On the beauty of Uriel;
In heaven once eminent, the god
Withdrew, that hour, into his cloud;
Whether doomed to long gyration
In the sea of generation,
Or by knowledge grown too bright
To hit the nerve of feebler sight.
Straightway, a forgetting wind
Stole over the celestial kind,
And their lips the secret kept,
If in ashes the fire-seed slept.
But now and then, truth-speaking things
Shamed the angels' veiling wings;
And, shrilling from the solar course,

Or from fruit of chemic force,
Procession of a soul in matter,
Or the speeding change of water,
Or out of the good of evil born,
Came Uriel's voice of cherub scorn,
And a blush tinged the upper sky,
And the gods shook, they knew not why.


## THE RHODORA:
### ON BEING ASKED, WHENCE IS THE FLOWER?

In May, when sea-winds pierced our solitudes,
I found the fresh Rhodora in the woods,
Spreading its leafless blooms in a damp nook,
To please the desert and the sluggish brook.
The purple petals, fallen in the pool,
Made the black water with their beauty gay;
Here might the red-bird come his plumes to cool,
And court the flower that cheapens his array.
Rhodora! if the sages ask thee why
This charm is wasted on the earth and sky,
Tell them, dear, that if eyes were made for seeing,
Then Beauty is its own excuse for being:
Why thou wert there, O rival of the rose!
I never thought to ask, I never knew;
But, in my simple ignorance suppose
The self-same Power that brought me there brought you.


## HAMATREYA

Minott, Lee, Willard, Hosmer, Meriam, Flint
Possessed the land which rendered to their toil
Hay, corn, roots, hemp, flax, apples, wool, and wood.
Each of these landlords walked amidst his farm,
Saying, " 'Tis mine, my children's, and my name's:
How sweet the west wind sounds in my own trees!
How graceful climb those shadows on my hill!

I fancy these pure waters and the flags
Know me, as does my dog: we sympathize;
And, I affirm, my actions smack of the soil."
Where are these men? Asleep beneath their grounds;
And strangers, fond as they, their furrows plough.
Earth laughs in flowers, to see her boastful boys
Earth-proud, proud of the earth which is not theirs;
Who steer the plough, but cannot steer their feet
Clear of the grave.
They added ridge to valley, brook to pond,
And sighed for all that bounded their domain.
"This suits me for a pasture; that's my park;
We must have clay, lime, gravel, granite-ledge,
And misty lowland, where to go for peat.
The land is well,—lies fairly to the south.
'Tis good, when you have crossed the sea and back,
To find the sitfast acres where you left them."
Ah! the hot owner sees not Death, who adds
Him to his land, a lump of mould the more.
Hear what the Earth says:

### EARTH-SONG.

"Mine and yours;
  Mine, not yours.
  Earth endures;
  Stars abide—
  Shine down in the old sea;
  Old are the shores;
  But where are old men?
  I who have seen much,
  Such have I never seen.

"The lawyer's deed
  Ran sure,
  In tail,
  To them, and to their heirs
  Who shall succeed,
  Without fail,
  Forevermore.

"Here is the land,
  Shaggy with wood,
  With its old valley,
  Mound, and flood.
  But the heritors?
  Fled like the flood's foam,—
  The lawyer, and the laws,
  And the kingdom,
  Clean swept herefrom.

"They called me theirs,
  Who so controlled me;
  Yet every one
  Wished to stay, and is gone.
  How am I theirs,
  If they cannot hold me,
  But I hold them?"

When I heard the Earth-song,
I was no longer brave;
My avarice cooled
Like lust in the chill of the grave.


## THE SNOW-STORM

Announced by all the trumpets of the sky,
Arrives the snow, and, driving o'er the fields,
Seems nowhere to alight: the whited air
Hides hills and woods, the river, and the heaven,
And veils the farm-house at the garden's end.
The sled and traveller stopped, the courier's feet
Delayed, all friends shut out, the housemates sit
Around the radiant fireplace, enclosed
In a tumultuous privacy of storm.

Come see the north wind's masonry.
Out of an unseen quarry evermore

Furnished with tile, the fierce artificer
Curves his white bastions with projected roof
Round every windward stake, or tree, or door.
Speeding, the myriad-handed, his wild work
So fanciful, so savage, nought cares he
For number or proportion. Mockingly,
On coop or kennel he hangs Parian wreaths;
A swan-like form invests the hidden thorn;
Fills up the farmer's lane from wall to wall,
Maugre the farmer's sighs; and, at the gate,
A tapering turret overtops the work.
And when his hours are numbered, and the world
Is all his own, retiring, as he were not,
Leaves, when the sun appears, astonished Art
To mimic in slow structures, stone by stone,
Built in an age, the mad wind's night-work,
The frolic architecture of the snow.

## ODE,
### INSCRIBED TO W. H. CHANNING

Though loath to grieve
The evil time's sole patriot,
I cannot leave
My honied thought
For the priest's cant,
Or statesman's rant.

If I refuse
My study for their politique,
Which at the best is trick,
The angry Muse
Puts confusion in my brain.

But who is he that prates
Of the culture of mankind,
Of better arts and life?

Go, blindworm, go,
Behold the famous States
Harrying Mexico
With rifle and with knife!

Or who, with accent bolder,
Dare praise the freedom-loving mountaineer?
I found by thee, O rushing Contoocook!
And in thy valleys, Agiochook!
The jackals of the negro-holder.

The God who made New Hampshire
Taunted the lofty land
With little men;—
Small bat and wren
House in the oak:—
If earth-fire cleave
The upheaved land, and bury the folk,
The southern crocodile would grieve.

Virtue palters; Right is hence;
Freedom praised, but hid;
Funeral eloquence
Rattles the coffin-lid.

What boots thy zeal,
O glowing friend,
That would indignant rend
The northland from the south?
Wherefore? to what good end?
Boston Bay and Bunker Hill
Would serve things still;—
Things are of the snake.

The horseman serves the horse,
The neatherd serves the neat,
The merchant serves the purse,
The eater serves his meat;
'Tis the day of the chattel,

Web to weave, and corn to grind;
Things are in the saddle,
And ride mankind.

There are two laws discrete,
Not reconciled,—
Law for man, and law for thing;
The last builds town and fleet,
But it runs wild,
And doth the man unking.

'Tis fit the forest fall,
The steep be graded,
The mountain tunnelled,
The sand shaded,
The orchard planted,
The glebe tilled,
The prairie granted,
The steamer built.

Let man serve law for man;
Live for friendship, live for love,
For truth's and harmony's behoof;
The state may follow how it can,
As Olympus follows Jove.

   Yet do not I invite
The wrinkled shopman to my sounding woods,
Nor bid the unwilling senator
Ask votes of thrushes in the solitudes.
Every one to his chosen work;—
Foolish hands may mix and mar;
Wise and sure the issues are.
Round they roll till dark is light,
Sex to sex, and even to odd;—
The over-god
Who marries Right to Might,
Who peoples, unpeoples,—
He who exterminates
Races by stronger races,

Black by white faces,—
Knows to bring honey
Out of the lion;
Grafts gentlest scion
On pirate and Turk.

The Cossack eats Poland,
Like stolen fruit;
Her last noble is ruined,
Her last poet mute:
Straight, into double band
The victors divide;
Half for freedom strike and stand;—
The astonished Muse finds thousands at her side.


## BACCHUS

Bring me wine, but wine which never grew
In the belly of the grape,
Or grew on vine whose tap-roots, reaching through
Under the Andes to the Cape,
Suffered no savor of the earth to scape.

Let its grapes the morn salute
From a nocturnal root,
Which feels the acrid juice
Of Styx and Erebus;
And turns the woe of Night,
By its own craft, to a more rich delight.

We buy ashes for bread;
We buy diluted wine;
Give me of the true,—
Whose ample leaves and tendrils curled
Among the silver hills of heaven,
Draw everlasting dew;
Wine of wine,
Blood of the world,

Form of forms, and mould of statures,
That I intoxicated,
And by the draught assimilated,
May float at pleasure through all natures;
The bird-language rightly spell,
And that which roses say so well.

Wine that is shed
Like the torrents of the sun
Up the horizon walls,
Or like the Atlantic streams, which run
When the South Sea calls.

Water and bread,
Food which needs no transmuting,
Rainbow-flowering, wisdom-fruiting
Wine which is already man,
Food which teach and reason can.

Wine which Music is,—
Music and wine are one,—
That I, drinking this,
Shall hear far Chaos talk with me;
Kings unborn shall walk with me;
And the poor grass shall plot and plan
What it will do when it is man.
Quickened so, will I unlock
Every crypt of every rock.

I thank the joyful juice
For all I know;—
Winds of remembering
Of the ancient being blow,
And seeming-solid walls of use
Open and flow.

Pour, Bacchus! the remembering wine;
Retrieve the loss of me and mine!
Vine for vine be antidote,
And the grape requite the lote!

Haste to cure the old despair,—
Reason in Nature's lotus drenched,
The memory of ages quenched;
Give them again to shine;
Let wine repair what this undid;
And where the infection slid,
A dazzling memory revive;
Refresh the faded tints,
Recut the aged prints,
And write my old adventures with the pen
Which on the first day drew,
Upon the tablets blue,
The dancing Pleiads and eternal men.


HYMN:
SUNG AT THE COMPLETION OF THE
CONCORD MONUMENT, APRIL 19, 1836

By the rude bridge that arched the flood,
   Their flag to April's breeze unfurled,
Here once the embattled farmers stood,
   And fired the shot heard round the world.

The foe long since in silence slept;
   Alike the conqueror silent sleeps;
And Time the ruined bridge has swept
   Down the dark stream which seaward creeps.

On this green bank, by this soft stream,
   We set to-day a votive stone;
That memory may their deed redeem,
   When, like our sires, our sons are gone.

Spirit, that made those heroes dare
   To die, or leave their children free,
Bid Time and Nature gently spare
   The shaft we raise to them and thee.

## BRAHMA

If the red slayer think he slays,
　　Or if the slain think he is slain,
They know not well the subtle ways
　　I keep, and pass, and turn again.

Far or forgot to me is near;
　　Shadow and sunlight are the same;
The vanished gods to me appear;
　　And one to me are shame and fame.

They reckon ill who leave me out;
　　When me they fly, I am the wings;
I am the doubter and the doubt,
　　And I the hymn the Brahmin sings.

The strong gods pine for my abode,
　　And pine in vain the sacred Seven;
But thou, meek lover of the good!
　　Find me, and turn thy back on heaven.


## BOSTON HYMN
### READ IN MUSIC HALL, JANUARY 1, 1863

The word of the Lord by night
To the watching Pilgrims came,
As they sat by the seaside,
And filled their hearts with flame.

God said, I am tired of kings,
I suffer them no more;
Up to my ear the morning brings
The outrage of the poor.

Think ye I made this ball
A field of havoc and war,

Where tyrants great and tyrants small
Might harry the weak and poor?

My angel,—his name is Freedom,—
Choose him to be your king;
He shall cut pathways east and west,
And fend you with his wing.

Lo! I uncover the land
Which I hid of old time in the West,
As the sculptor uncovers the statue
When he has wrought his best;

I show Columbia, of the rocks
Which dip their foot in the seas,
And soar to the air-borne flocks
Of clouds, and the boreal fleece.

I will divide my goods;
Call in the wretch and slave:
None shall rule but the humble,
And none but Toil shall have.

I will have never a noble,
No lineage counted great;
Fishers and choppers and ploughmen
Shall constitute a state.

Go, cut down trees in the forest,
And trim the straightest boughs;
Cut down trees in the forest,
And build me a wooden house.

Call the people together,
The young men and the sires,
The digger in the harvest field,
Hireling, and him that hires;

And here in a pine state-house
They shall choose men to rule

In every needful faculty,
In church, and state, and school.

Lo, now! if these poor men
Can govern the land and sea,
And make just laws below the sun,
As planets faithful be.

And ye shall succor men;
'T is nobleness to serve;
Help them who cannot help again:
Beware from right to swerve.

I break your bonds and masterships,
And I unchain the slave:
Free be his heart and hand henceforth
As wind and wandering wave.

I cause from every creature
His proper good to flow:
As much as he is and doeth,
So much he shall bestow.

But, laying hands on another
To coin his labor and sweat,
He goes in pawn to his victim
For eternal years in debt.

To-day unbind the captive,
So only are ye unbound;
Lift up a people from the dust,
Trump of their rescue, sound!

Pay ransom to the owner,
And fill the bag to the brim.
Who is the owner? The slave is owner,
And ever was. Pay him.

O North! give him beauty for rags,
And honor, O South! for his shame;

Nevada! coin thy golden crags
With Freedom's image and name.

Up! and the dusky race
That sat in darkness long,—
Be swift their feet as antelopes,
And as behemoth strong.

Come, East and West and North,
By races, as snow-flakes,
And carry my purpose forth,
Which neither halts nor shakes.

My will fulfilled shall be,
For, in daylight or in dark,
My thunderbolt has eyes to see
His way home to the mark.

## DAYS

Daughters of Time, the hypocritic Days,
Muffled and dumb like barefoot dervishes,
And marching single in an endless file,
Bring diadems and fagots in their hands.
To each they offer gifts after his will,
Bread, kingdoms, stars, and sky that holds them all.
I, in my pleached garden, watched the pomp,
Forgot my morning wishes, hastily
Took a few herbs and apples, and the Day
Turned and departed silent. I, too late,
Under the solemn fillet saw the scorn.

# 4.

# Margaret Fuller

Fuller wrote verse sporadically, much of it in a vein of lofty diffuseness. But she was also capable of a compressed vatic intensity and soul-searching meditation, as these poems show. The third and most cryptic poem was inspired by a design of a statue of Orpheus by American sculptor Thomas Crawford (1813–57). Fuller here coordinates two interlocking myths. The first and more important is the story of Orpheus failing at the last minute to rescue his beloved Eurydice from the Underworld after his music charmed Hades into giving her up on condition that Orpheus not look back at her while returning to earth. The other myth is of Hades' kidnapped consort Persephone, who was fated to live six months of each year in his underground abode. "To a Friend" is one of the two introductory motto-poems to Fuller's travel book, *Summer on the Lakes.*

SOURCES: ("Meditations" and "My Seal-Ring") *Life Without and Life Within,* ed. Arthur Fuller. Boston: Taggard & Chase, 1860. ("[Each Orpheus]") "The Great Lawsuit," *The Dial,* 4 ( July 1843). ("To a Friend") *Summer on the Lakes, in 1843.* Boston: Little, Brown, 1844.

# MEDITATIONS.
## SUNDAY, MAY 12, 1833.

The clouds are marshalling across the sky,
Leaving their deepest tints upon yon range
Of soul-alluring hills.   The breeze comes softly,
Laden with tribute that a hundred orchards
Now in their fullest blossom send, in thanks
For this refreshing shower.   The birds pour forth
In heightened melody the notes of praise
They had suspended while God's voice was speaking,
And his eye flashing down upon his world.
I sigh, half-charmed, half-pained. My sense is living,
And, taking in this freshened beauty, tells
Its pleasure to the mind.   The mind replies,
And strives to wake the heart in turn, repeating
Poetic sentiments from many a record
Which other souls have left, when stirred and satisfied
By scenes as fair, as fragrant.   But the heart
Sends back a hollow echo to the call
Of outward things,—and its once bright companion,
Who erst would have been answered by a stream
Of life-fraught treasures, thankful to be summoned,—
Can now rouse nothing better than this echo;
Unmeaning voice, which mocks their softened accents.
Content thee, beautiful world! and hush, still busy mind!
My heart hath sealed its fountains.   To the things
Of Time they shall be oped no more.   Too long,
Too often were they poured forth: part have sunk
Into the desert; part profaned and swollen
By bitter waters, mixed by those who feigned
They asked them for refreshment, which, turned back,
Have broken and o'erflowed their former urns.
So when ye talk of *pleasure*, lonely world,
And busy mind, ye ne'er again shall move me
To answer ye, though still your calls have power
To jar me through, and cause dull aching *here*.

Not so the voice which hailed me from the depths
Of yon dark-bosomed cloud, now vanishing
Before the sun ye greet.   It touched my centre,
The voice of the Eternal, calling me
To feel his other worlds; to feel that if
I could deserve a home, I still might find it
In other spheres,—and bade me not despair,
Though "want of harmony" and "aching void"
Are terms invented by the men of this,
Which I may not forget.
                              In former times
I loved to see the lightnings flash athwart
The stooping heavens; I loved to hear the thunder
Call to the seas and mountains; for I thought
'Tis thus man's flashing fancy doth enkindle
The firmament of mind; 'tis thus his eloquence
Calls unto the soul's depths and heights; and still
I deified the creature, nor remembered
The Creator in his works.
                              Ah now how different!
The proud delight of that keen sympathy
Is gone; no longer riding on the wave,
But whelmed beneath it: my own plans and works,
Or, as the Scriptures phrase it, my *"inventions"*
No longer interpose 'twixt me and Heaven.

To-day, for the first time, I felt the Deity,
And uttered prayer on hearing thunder.   This
Must be thy will,—for finer, higher spirits
Have gone through this same process,—yet I think
There was religion in that strong delight,
Those sounds, those thoughts of power imparted.   True,
I did not say, "He is the Lord thy God,"
But I had feeling of his essence.   But
" 'Twas pride by which the angels fell."   So be it!
But O, might I but see a little onward!
Father, I cannot be a spirit of power;

May I be active as a spirit of love,
Since thou hast ta'en me from that path which Nature
Seemed to appoint, O, deign to ope another,
Where I may walk with thought and hope assured;
"Lord, I believe; help thou mine unbelief!"
Had I but faith like that which fired Novalis,
I too could bear that the heart "fall in ashes,"
While the freed spirit rises from beneath them,
With heavenward-look, and Phœnix-plumes upsoaring!

## MY SEAL·RING.

Mercury has cast aside
The signs of intellectual pride,
Freely offers thee the soul:
   Art thou noble to receive?
Canst thou give or take the whole,
   Nobly promise, and believe?
Then thou wholly human art,
A spotless, radiant, ruby heart,
And the golden chain of love
Has bound thee to the realm above.
If there be one small, mean doubt,
One serpent thought that fled not out,
Take instead the serpent-rod;
Thou art neither man nor God.
Guard thee from the powers of evil;
Who cannot trust, vows to the devil.
Walk thy slow and spell-bound way;
Keep on thy mask, or shun the day—
Let go my hand upon the way.

## [EACH ORPHEUS]

Each Orpheus must to the depth descend,
For only thus the poet can be wise
   Must make the sad Persephone his friend,
And buried love to second life arise;
   Again his love must lose through too much love,
Must lose his life by living life too true,
   For what he sought below is passed above,
Already done is all that he would do;
   Must tune all being with his single lyre,
Must melt all rocks free from their primal pain,
   Must search all nature with his one soul's fire,
Must bind anew all forms in heavenly chain.
   If he already sees what he must do,
Well may he shade his eyes from the far-shining view.

## TO A FRIEND

Some dried grass-tufts from the wide flowery plain,
A muscle shell from the lone fairy shore,
Some antlers from tall woods which never more
To the wild deer a safe retreat can yield,
An eagle's feather which adorned a Brave,
Well-nigh the last of his despairing band,
For such slight gifts wilt thou extend thy hand
When weary hours a brief refreshment crave?
I give you what I can, not what I would,
If my small drinking-cup would hold a flood,
As Scandinavia sung those must contain
With which the giants gods may entertain;
In our dwarf day we drain few drops, and soon must thirst again.

# 5.

# FREDERIC HENRY HEDGE

Hedge published many works of philosophical, theological, and literary criticism, as well as the English translation of Martin Luther's hymn "A Mighty Fortress Is Our God," which is sung in Protestant churches to this day. But he wrote only one memorable poem of his own. Composed "about 1834," he later recalled, it voices the intense epistemological questing of Transcendentalism's early years, complementing the "Idealism" chapter of Emerson's forthcoming *Nature*.

SOURCE: *The Dial*, 1 (January 1841).

## QUESTIONINGS

Hath this world, without me wrought,
Other substance than my thought?
Lives it by my sense alone,
Or by essence of its own?
Will its life, with mine begun,
Cease to be when that is done,
Or another consciousness
With the self-same forms impress?

Doth yon fireball, poised in air,
Hang by my permission there?
Are the clouds that wander by,
But the offspring of mine eye,
Born with every glance I cast,
Perishing when that is past?
And those thousand, thousand eyes,
Scattered through the twinkling skies,
Do they draw their life from mine,
Or, of their own beauty shine?

Now I close my eyes, my ears,
And creation disappears;
Yet if I but speak the word,
All creation is restored.
Or—more wonderful—within,
New creations do begin;
Hues more bright and forms more rare,
Than reality doth wear,
Flash across my inward sense,
Born of the mind's omnipotence.

Soul! that all informest, say!
Shall these glories pass away?
Will those planets cease to blaze,
When these eyes no longer gaze?
And the life of things be o'er,
When these pulses beat no more?

Thought! that in me works and lives,—
Life to all things living gives,—
Art thou not thyself, perchance,
But the universe in trance?
A reflection inly flung
By that world thou fanciedst sprung
From thyself;—thyself a dream;—
Of the world's thinking thou the theme.

Be it thus, or be thy birth
From a source above the earth.
Be thou matter, be thou mind,
In thee alone myself I find,
And through thee alone, for me,
Hath this world reality.
Therefore, in thee will I live,
To thee all myself will give,
Losing still, that I may find,
This bounded self in boundless Mind.

# 6.

# ELLEN STURGIS HOOPER

History has relegated Ellen Sturgis Hooper (1812–48) and her younger sister Caroline Sturgis Tappan (1818–88) to the status of "minor" Transcendentalists. Yet each was striking in her own way. Tappan was an intimate of Fuller's and Emerson's, with a charm, flair, and astuteness—both in person and as a letter writer—that attracted them both. In Emerson's case, at least, the attraction seems to have been at least partly erotic. With her husband, David, Tappan held court for a number of summers at their Tanglewood estate in the Berkshires, now the summer home of the Boston Symphony Orchestra, renting a cottage to the Hawthornes for a time. The quieter Hooper, also a participant in Margaret Fuller's Boston conversations, was by far the more talented poet, though she wrote less and died young. Hooper's poetry has a strong melancholy streak all the more provocative in light of the fact that her three children committed suicide in later life. (One was Henry Adams's wife, Marian.) Rarely does she make grand claims for the transforming power of the soul. Her respectful yet carefully qualified tribute to Emerson questions an ordinary soul's ability to inhabit such a rarefied atmosphere. A dying person's "caprices," the lure of the ultimate sin for one immured in respectability, the looks exchanged by newborn son and mother dying in childbirth—few but Emily Dickinson treated these moments with such compressed intensity as Hooper did.

SOURCE: *Poems,* ed. Edward William Hooper. Boston: privately printed, n.d. (ca. 1872).

## [I STOOD UPON THE SULLEN SHORE]

I stood upon the sullen shore,
    And marked the waves, with wild unrest,
And with a deep continuous roar
    Break onward to their mother's breast—

But no glad greeting waited there
    The sighing wanderers of the sea,
No grassy lawn or flow'rets fair,
    But sterile sands' dull vacancy—

Wailing, with upborne cry, they haste
    As if relief, redress, to find,
But on cold stones their passion waste,
    They back recoil—and die resigned—

## [OH MELANCHOLY LIBERTY]

Oh melancholy liberty,
Of one about to die—
When friends, with a sad smile,
And aching heart the while,
    Every caprice allow,
Nor deem it worthwhile now,
To check the restless will
Which death so soon shall still!

## [ONE LOOK THE MOTHER CAST UPON HER CHILD]

One look the mother cast upon her child,
As entered he one portal low of Time
While she the other past through—a first look
And last—never to greet him more
Till on Eternity's calm distant shore—

That look—and he was left this world within
A stranger here, and always closed those eyes
Which shed but one gleam o'er his earthly life—
Forever hushed that voice whose welcoming
Was the last note the unsphered soul did sing—

## [I SEE THEM . . . ]

I see them (men) wild with desire, cursing, fighting slaying—
some wandering far far away on a track where shines no light, some
denying a God who made them, some reckless throwing themselves
on destruction, others dooming to everlasting woe their fellows, but
not all—all held in the "hollow of his hand"—the while. It is like a
wild dream full of horrors, this strange life, from which one awakes to
find himself in his own home and in his very place in his home.

So methinks do the children of earth groan under the
experiences of a life or an age of evil and awake at last deep and safe
in the beginning and heart of all—

## [BETTER A SIN WHICH PURPOSED WRONG TO NONE]

Better a sin which purposed wrong to none
Than this still wintry coldness at the heart,
A penance might be borne for evil done
And tears of grief and love might ease the smart.
But this self-satisfied and cold respect
To virtue which must be its own reward,
Heaven keep us through this danger still alive,
Lead us not into greatness, heart-abhorred—

Oh God, who framed this stern New-England land,
Its clear cold waters, and its clear, cold soul,
Thou givest tropic climes and youthful hearts
Thou weighest spirits and dost all control—
Teach me to wait for all—to bear the fault

That most I hate because it is my own,
And if I fail through foul conceit of good,
Let me sin deep so I may cast no stone.


[TO EMERSON]

"Dry lighted soul,["] the ray that shines in thee,
  Shot without reflex from primeval sun—
We twine the laurel for the victories
  Which thou on Thought's broad, bloodless field hast won—

Thou art the mountain where we climb to see
  The land our feet have trod this many a year.
Thou art the deep and crystal winter sky,
  Where noiseless, one by one, bright stars appear.

It may be Bacchus, at thy birth, forgot
  That drop from out the purple grape to press
Which is his gift to man, and so thy blood
  Doth miss the heat which ofttimes breeds excess—

But, all more surely do we turn to thee
  When the day's heat and blinding dust are o'er,
And cool our souls in thy refreshing air,
  And find the peace which we had lost before—

    "Dry light makes the best souls."
       —R.W.E. [ESH NOTE]


[LO! CAST UPON THE SHOAL OF TIME]

  Lo! cast upon the shoal of time
    The helpless babe appears,
  In heav'n commended feebleness,
    Armed but with smiles and tears.

No ray lights up the way it came,
   It could not choose but be,
Within a life it did not claim
   It lies, unconsciously—

He grows, and finds the heavy trust
   Accepted by the need,
A loyalty beyond his ken
   Signs the primeval creed—

# 7.

# HENRY DAVID THOREAU

Thoreau may well have begun his writing life hoping to become a serious poet. As a young man, he studied the English poets, both major and minor, more systematically than did any other Transcendentalist. Thoreau was also an eager reader and translator of Greek and Roman poetry. Some of his own poems show this influence, particularly his apostrophes to "Haze" and "Smoke." Rather as Emerson liked to preface his essays with mottoes of his own composition, Thoreau liked to punctuate his prose with his own poems. After the 1840s, however, he largely forsook poetry for literary prose, at which he was more gifted. His first book, *A Week on the Concord and Merrimack Rivers* (1849), serves both as an anthology of Thoreau's poetry and also as a tomb in which to bury Thoreau the versifier and move toward perfecting his prose. But amid much doggerel, Thoreau also composed some short poetic gems.

SOURCE TEXTS: [Great God, I ask thee . . . ] *The Dial*, 3 ( July 1842). (Next four poems) *A Week on the Concord and Merrimack Rivers.* Boston: Ticknor & Fields, 1849. ("Smoke") *Walden.* Boston: Ticknor & Fields, 1854. Except for "The Inward Morning," the titles of the poems that have any titles at all are taken from earlier publications in *The Dial*, where "Haze" and "Smoke" appear as companion pieces under the general title "Orphics."

## [GREAT GOD, I ASK THEE . . .]

Great God, I ask thee for no meaner pelf
Than that I may not disappoint myself,
That in my action I may soar as high,
As I can now discern with this clear eye.

And next in value, which thy kindness lends,
That I may greatly disappoint my friends,
Howe'er they think or hope that it may be,
They may not dream how thou'st distinguished me.

That my weak hand may equal my firm faith,
And my life practice more than my tongue saith,
That my low conduct may not show,
Nor my relenting lines,
That I thy purpose did not know,
Or overrated thy designs.

## HAZE

Woof of the sun, ethereal gauze,
Woven of Nature's richest stuffs,
Visible heat, air-water, and dry sea,
Last conquest of the eye;
Toil of the day displayed, sun-dust,
Aerial surf upon the shores of earth,
Ethereal estuary, frith of light,
Breakers of air, billows of heat,
Fine summer spray on inland seas;
Bird of the sun, transparent-winged,
Owlet of noon, soft-pinioned,
From heath or stubble rising without song;
Establish thy serenity o'er the fields.

# [MY LOVE MUST BE AS FREE]

My love must be as free
    As is the eagle's wing,
Hovering o'er land and sea
    And every thing.

I must not dim my eye
    In thy saloon,
I must not leave my sky
    And nightly moon.

Be not the fowler's net
    Which stays my flight,
And craftily is set
    T' allure the sight.

But be the favoring gale
    That bears me on,
And still doth fill my sail
    When thou art gone.

I cannot leave my sky
    For thy caprice,
True love would soar as high
    As heaven is.

The eagle would not brook
    Her mate thus won,
Who trained his eye to look
    Beneath the sun.

## THE INWARD MORNING.

Packed in my mind lie all the clothes
    Which outward nature wears,
And in its fashion's hourly change
    It all things else repairs.

In vain I look for change abroad,
    And can no difference find,
Till some new ray of peace uncalled
    Illumes my inmost mind.

What is it gilds the trees and clouds,
    And paints the heavens so gay,
But yonder fast abiding light
    With its unchanging ray?

Lo, when the sun streams through the wood,
    Upon a winter's morn,
Where'er his silent beams intrude
    The murky night is gone.

How could the patient pine have known
    The morning breeze would come,
Or humble flowers anticipate
    The insect's noonday hum,—

Till the new light with morning cheer
    From far streamed through the aisles,
And nimbly told the forest trees
    For many stretching miles?

I've heard within my inmost soul
    Such cheerful morning news,
In the horizon of my mind
    Have seen such orient hues,

As in the twilight of the dawn,
    When the first birds awake,
Are heard within some silent wood,
    Where they the small twigs break,

Or in the eastern skies are seen,
    Before the sun appears,
The harbingers of summer heats
    Which from afar he bears.


## SIC VITA

I am a parcel of vain strivings tied
    By a chance bond together,
Dangling this way and that, their links
    Were made so loose and wide,
        Methinks,
      For milder weather.

A bunch of violets without their roots,
    And sorrel intermixed,
Encircled by a wisp of straw
    Once coiled about their shoots,
        The law
    By which I'm fixed.

A nosegay which Time clutched from out
    Those fair Elysian fields,
With weeds and broken stems, in haste,
    Doth make the rabble rout
        That waste
    The day he yields.

And here I bloom for a short hour unseen,
    Drinking my juices up,
With no root in the land

To keep my branches green,
But stand
In a bare cup.

Some tender buds were left upon my stem
In mimicry of life,
But ah! the children will not know,
Till time has withered them,
The woe
With which they're rife.


But now I see I was not plucked for naught,
And after in life's vase
Of glass set while I might survive,
But by a kind hand brought
Alive
To a strange place.

That stock thus thinned will soon redeem its hours,
And by another year,
Such as God knows, with freer air,
More fruits and fairer flowers
Will bear,
While I droop here.


SMOKE

Light-winged Smoke, Icarian bird,
Melting thy pinions in thy upward flight,
Lark without song, and messenger of dawn,
Circling above the hamlets as thy nest;
Or else, departing dream, and shadowy form
Of midnight vision, gathering up thy skirts;
By night star-veiling, and by day
Darkening the light and blotting out the sun;
Go thou my incense upward from this hearth,
And ask the gods to pardon this clear flame.

# JONES VERY

No Transcendentalist dramatizes more strikingly the link between Calvinist mysticism and Transcendentalist spirituality than Jones Very (1813–80). Very was at once the most pious and most blasphemous of all the Transcendentalists. Like Hawthorne, he was the son of a Salem shipmaster. He was a brilliant student at Harvard, where he became a Greek tutor and divinity student after his graduation in 1836, the year of Emerson's *Nature* and Transcendentalism's full emergence. His fellow Salemite Elizabeth Peabody called Emerson's attention to Very's poetry and his Harvard prizewinning essays on Shakespeare and epic poetry; and Emerson, impressed, took the trouble to edit a slim volume of Very's *Essays and Poems* (1839). Virtually all of his memorable poetry, however, including the eight selections here, was written over the course of a single year, 1838–39, when he was smitten by the conviction that he embodied the second coming of Christ. He was briefly incarcerated in Maclean Asylum in suburban Boston for alarmingly delusional behavior, including unwanted freelance evangelizing, though he was soon released as harmless. Meanwhile, sympathetic Transcendentalists expressed assurance that Very had not lost his reason, only his senses. Very's letters "To the Unborn" proclaim his apocalyptic mission, but his poems themselves make eloquently clear the author's sense of living in a state of intimate communion with God that sets him apart from mere mortals. The best are remarkable contributions to the literature of Christian spirituality. They are also remarkable for their poetic form. At first thought, it seems inexplicable that a visionary in a state of intense emotional agitation would have opted to express himself in the highly artificial medium of the Shakespearean sonnet. Neither Emerson nor Thoreau ever attempted a regular sonnet in his life. Obviously Very had internalized the form so that it was as much second nature for him as a champion gymnast's complex maneuvers. Unfortunately, for the last forty years of his life, he wrote virtually nothing of note, settling down as a part-time Unitarian minister in Salem.

SOURCES: (1) *Salem Observer:* "The New Birth" (October 27, 1838), "Thy Brother's Blood" (February 2, 1839), "Yourself" (November 22, 1839), "Thy Better Self" (November 23, 1839); (2) Jones Very papers, Houghton Library, Harvard University: "The Presence," "Nature," "The Barberry Bush," "The Garden." *Jones Very: The Complete Poems,* Helen R. Deese, ed. (Athens: University of Georgia Press, 1993), is indispensable for helping one choose among the many variant copies of individual Very poems, although I have not always followed its choices here.

## THE NEW BIRTH

'Tis a new life—thoughts move not as they did
With slow uncertain steps across my mind,
In thronging haste fast pressing on they bid
The portals open to the viewless wind;
That comes not save when in the dust is laid
The crown of pride that gilds each mortal brow;
And from before man's vision melting fade
The heavens and earth—their walls are falling now—
Fast crowding on each thought asks utterance strong,
Storm-lifted waves swift rushing to the shore
On from the sea they send their shouts along,
Back through the cave-worn rocks their thunders roar;
And I a child of God by Christ made free
Start from death's slumbers to Eternity.

## THE PRESENCE

I sit within my room and joy to find
That Thou who always loves art with me here,
That I am never left by Thee behind,
But by Thyself Thou keepst me ever near;
The fire burns brighter when with Thee I look,
And seems a kinder servant sent to me;
With gladder heart I read thy holy book,
Because Thou art the eyes by which I see;
This aged chair, that table, watch, and door
Around in ready service ever wait;
Nor can I ask of Thee a menial more
To fill the measure of my large estate,
For Thou Thyself, with all a Father's care,
Where'er I turn, art ever with me there.

## NATURE

The bubbling brook doth leap when I come by,
Because my feet find measure with its call;
The birds know when the friend they love is nigh,
For I am known to them both great and small;
The flower that on the lovely hill-side grows,
Expects me there when Spring its bloom has given;
And many a tree and bush my wanderings know,
And e'en the clouds and silent stars of heaven;
For he who with his Maker walks aright,
Shall be their lord, as Adam was before;
His ear shall catch each sound with new delight,
Each object wear the dress that then it wore;
And he, as when erect in soul he stood,
Hear from his Father's lips that all is good.

## THE BARBERRY BUSH

The bush which bears most briars, and bitter fruit,
Wait till the frost has turned its green leaves red,
Its sweetened berries will thy palate suit,
And thou may'st find, e'en there, a homely bread.
Upon the hills of Salem, scattered wide,
Their yellow blossoms gain the eye in Spring;
And straggling down upon the turnpike's side,
Their ripened bunches to your hand they bring.
I've plucked them oft in boyhood's early hour,
What then I gave such name, and thought it true;
But now I know, that other fruit, as sour,
Grows on what now thou callest *Me*, and *You*;
Yet, wilt thou wait the Autumn that I see,
'Twill sweeter taste than these red berries be.

## THE GARDEN

I saw the spot where our first parents dwelt;
And yet it wore to me no face of change,
For while amid its fields and groves I felt
As if I had not sinned, nor thought it strange;
My eye seemed but a part of every sight,
My ear heard music in each sound that rose,
Each sense forever found a new delight,
Such as the spirit's vision only knows;
Each act some new and ever-varying joy
Did by my Father's love for me prepare;
To dress the spot my ever fresh employ,
And in the glorious whole with Him to share;
No more without the flaming gate to stray,
No more for sin's dark stain the debt of death to pay.

## THY BROTHER'S BLOOD

I have no Brother—they who meet me now
Offer a hand with their own wills defiled,
And while they wear a smooth unwrinkled brow
Know not that Truth can never be beguiled;
Go wash the hand that still betrays thy guilt;
Before the spirit's gaze what stain can hide?
Abel's red blood upon the earth is spilt,
And by thy tongue it cannot be denied;
I hear not with the ear—the heart doth tell
Its secret deeds to me untold before;
Go, all its hidden plunder quickly sell,
Then shalt thou cleanse thee from thy brother's gore;
Then will I take thy gift—that bloody stain
Shall not be seen upon thy hand again.

## YOURSELF

'Tis to yourself I speak; you cannot know
Him whom I call in speaking such an one,
For thou beneath the earth liest buried low,
Which he alone as living walks upon;
Thou mayst at times have heard him speak to you,
And often wished perchance that you were he;
And I must ever wish that it were true,
For then thou couldst hold fellowship with me;
But now thou hearst us talk as strangers, met
Above the room wherein thou liest abed;
A word perhaps loud spoken thou mayst get,
Or hear our feet when heavily they tread;
But he who speaks, or him who's spoken to,
Must both remain as strangers still to you.

## THY BETTER SELF

I am thy other self; what thou wilt be
When thou art I, the one thou seest now;
In finding thy true self thou wilt find me,
The springing blade where now thou dost but plough;
I am thy neighbor, a new house I've built
Which thou as yet hast never entered in;
I come to call thee; come in when thou wilt,
The feast is always waiting to begin;
Thou should'st love me, as thou dost love thyself;
For I am but another self beside;
To show thee him thou lov'st in better health,
What thou wouldst be when thou to him have died;
Then visit me, I make thee many a call;
Nor live I near to thee alone but all.

# 9.

# WALT WHITMAN

We have already seen the similarity between Whitman's and Emerson's poetic theory and between their flowing, free-associative styles of writing (Section V-A). No less fundamental to Whitman's poetics, particularly in the formative stages of his career, was the creation of what might be called a post-Transcendentalist poetic voice that gives Emerson's idea of the god within a more intricate and also more "democratic" turn. In many poems of the 1850s, Whitman creates speakers that draw out the implications of the Emersonian paradox of the human self as both idiosyncratically personal and yet also potentially divine and universal. The speakers in such Whitman poems often shuttle back and forth between impersonating a mundane self and a godlike cosmic Self. This Self with a capital *S*, in turn, sometimes appears as a free-floating super-being and sometimes in the form of a life force or a personalized friend who inspires every individual to bring unity to all humankind. In the process, Whitman often intentionally blurs or breaks down the conventional boundaries between I, you, he, she, we, and they. His longest poem, the magnificent "Song of Myself" (1855), is his most ambitious effort of this kind. But the following poem, published the next year, is a fine short-form example of Whitman's experimental persona, inviting comparison with the last two poems of Jones Very in this collection as well as with Emerson's teasingly mysterious "Brahma."

SOURCE: *Leaves of Grass.* Philadelphia: David McKay, 1891–92.

## TO YOU

WHOEVER you are, I fear you are walking the walks of dreams,
I fear these supposed realities are to melt from under your feet and
    hands,
Even now your features, joys, speech, house, trade, manners, troubles,
    follies, costume, crimes, dissipate away from you,
Your true soul and body appear before me,
They stand forth out of affairs, out of commerce, shops, work, farms,
    clothes, the house, buying, selling, eating, drinking, suffering,
    dying.

Whoever you are, now I place my hand upon you, that you be my
    poem,
I whisper with my lips close to your ear,
I have loved many women and men, but I love none better than you.

O I have been dilatory and dumb,
I should have made my way straight to you long ago,
I should have blabb'd nothing but you, I should have chanted nothing
    but you.

I will leave all and come and make the hymns of you,
None has understood you, but I understand you,
None has done justice to you, you have not done justice to yourself,
None but has found you imperfect, I only find no imperfection
    in you,
None but would subordinate you, I only am he who will never
    consent to subordinate you,
I only am he who places over you no master, owner, better, God,
    beyond what waits intrinsically in yourself.

Painters have painted their swarming groups and the centre-figure of
    all,
From the head of the centre-figure spreading a nimbus of gold-color'd
    light,
But I paint myriads of heads, but paint no head without its nimbus of
    gold-color'd light,

From my hand from the brain of every man and woman it streams,
    effulgently flowing forever.

O I could sing such grandeurs and glories about you!
You have not known what you are, you have slumber'd upon yourself
    all your life,
Your eyelids have been the same as closed most of the time,
What you have done returns already in mockeries,
(Your thrift, knowledge, prayers, if they do not return in mockeries,
    what is their return?)

The mockeries are not you,
Underneath them and within them I see you lurk,
I pursue you where none else has pursued you,
Silence, the desk, the flippant expression, the night, the accustom'd
    routine, if these conceal you from others or from yourself, they do
    not conceal you from me,
The shaved face, the unsteady eye, the impure complexion, if these
    balk others they do not balk me,
The pert apparel, the deform'd attitude, drunkenness, greed,
    premature death, all these I part aside.

There is no endowment in man or woman that is not tallied in you,
There is no virtue, no beauty in man or woman, but as good is in you,
No pluck, no endurance in others, but as good is in you,
No pleasure wating for others, but an equal pleasure waits for you.

As for me, I give nothing to any one except I give the like carefully to
    you,
I sing the songs of the glory of none, not God, sooner than I sing the
    songs of the glory of you.

Whoever you are! claim your own at any hazard!
These shows of the East and West are tame compared to you,
These immense meadows, these interminable rivers, you are immense
    and interminable as they,
These furies, elements, storms, motions of Nature, throes of apparent
    dissolution, you are he or she who is master or mistress over them,
Master or mistress in your own right over Nature, elements, pain,
    passion, dissolution.

The hopples fall from your ankles, you find an unfailing sufficiency,
Old or young, male or female, rude, low, rejected by the rest, whatever
    you are promulges itself,
Through birth, life, death, burial, the means are provided, nothing is
    scanted,
Through angers, losses, ambition, ignorance, ennui, what you are
    picks its way.

# D.
## Narrative

# Margaret Fuller
## "Leila"
### (1841)

The number of Transcendentalist novels can be counted on the fingers of one hand, the most noteworthy perhaps being Louisa May Alcott's *Moods* (1865), a quasi-autobiographical novel in which the two chief male figures in the heroine's life are partly modeled on Emerson and Thoreau. But a number of Transcendentalists did try their hand at short-form narrative, both fictional and nonfictional. Fuller's tale is broadly typical of the Transcendentalist penchant for creating mythic masks to express thoughts that might be considered fanciful or extreme, to serve as idealized self-portraits. Emerson's "Orphic Poet" in the last chapter of *Nature* (sometimes alleged to be Bronson Alcott) is a distant cousin. Leila, too ("my wild-haired Genius"), seems to embody a prophetic vision toward which the author is striving—with the important difference that Fuller thinks of Leila as an ideal and a companion (a "fellow pilgrim") at the same time.

None of the Transcendentalist circle was more attracted to the creation of mythic self-images than Fuller, as her invention of "Miranda" in "The Great Lawsuit" shows (Section IV-C). "Leila" reveals Fuller at her most Poesque. In fact, the title, the opening sentence, and the dramatization of the intimate/ambiguous two-person relation may intentionally allude to Poe's "Ligeia" (1838) ("I cannot, for my soul, remember how, when, or even precisely where I first became acquainted with the lady Ligeia"). But if so, Fuller's design is certainly to swerve from Poe in order to represent a relationship of trust purged of fear.

SOURCE: "Leila," *The Dial*, 1 (April 1841).

## LEILA.
### "IN A DEEP VISION'S INTELLECTUAL SCENE."

I HAVE often but vainly attempted to record what I know of Leila. It is because she is a mystery, which can only be indicated by being reproduced. Had a Poet or Artist met her, each glance of her's would have suggested some form of beauty, for she is one of those rare beings who seem a key to all nature. Mostly those we know seem struggling for an individual existence. As the procession passes an observer like me, one seems a herald, another a basket-bearer, another swings a censer, and oft-times even priest and priestess suggest the ritual rather than the Divinity. Thinking of these men your mind dwells on the personalities at which they aim. But if you looked on Leila she was rather as the *fetiche* which to the mere eye almost featureless, to the thought of the pious wild man suggests all the elemental powers of nature, with their regulating powers of conscience and retribution. The eye resting on Leila's eye, felt that it never reached the heart. Not as with other men did you meet a look which you could define as one of displeasure, scrutiny, or tenderness. You could not turn away, carrying with you some distinct impression, but your glance became a gaze from a perception of a boundlessness, of depth below depth, which seemed to say "in this being (couldst thou but rightly apprehend it) is the clasp to the chain of nature." Most men, as they gazed on Leila were pained; they left her at last baffled and well-nigh angry. For most men are bound in sense, time, and thought. They shrink from the overflow of the infinite; they cannot a moment abide in the coldness of abstractions; the weight of an idea is too much for their lives. They cry, "O give me a form which I may clasp to the living breast, fuel for the altars of the heart, a weapon for the hand." And who can blame them; it is almost impossible for time to bear this sense of eternity. Only the Poet, who is so happily organized as continually to relieve himself by reproduction, can bear it without falling into a kind of madness. And men called Leila mad, because they felt she made them so. But I, Leila, could look on thee;—to my restless spirit thou didst bring a kind of peace, for thou wert a bridge between me and the infinite; thou didst arrest the step, and the eye as the veil hanging before the Isis. Thy nature seemed large enough for boundless suggestion. I did not love thee, Leila, but the desire for love was soothed in thy presence. I would fain have been nourished by some of thy love, but all of it I felt was only for the all.

We grew up together with name and home and parentage. Yet Leila ever seemed to me a spirit under a mask, which she might throw off at any instant. That she did not, never dimmed my perception of the unreality of her existence among us. She *knows* all, and *is* nothing. She stays here, I suppose, as a reminder to man of the temporary nature of his limitations. For she ever transcends sex, age, state, and all the barriers behind which man entrenches himself from the assaults of Spirit. You look on her, and she is the clear blue sky, cold and distant as the Pole-star; suddenly this sky opens and flows forth a mysterious wind that bears with it your last thought beyond the verge of all expectation, all association. Again, she is the mild sunset, and puts you to rest on a love-couch of rosy sadness, when on the horizon swells up a mighty sea and rushes over you till you plunge on its waves, affrighted, delighted, quite freed from earth.

When I cannot look upon her living form, I avail myself of the art magic. At the hour of high moon, in the cold silent night, I seek the centre of the park. My daring is my vow, my resolve my spell. I am a conjurer, for Leila is the vasty deep. In the centre of the park, perfectly framed in by solemn oaks and pines, lies a little lake, oval, deep, and still it looks up steadily as an eye of earth should to the ever promising heavens which are so bounteous, and love us so, yet never give themselves to us. As that lake looks at Heaven, so look I on Leila. At night I look into the lake for Leila.

If I gaze steadily and in the singleness of prayer, she rises and walks on its depths. Then know I each night a part of her life; I know where she passes the midnight hours.

In the days she lives among men; she observes their deeds, and gives them what they want of her, justice or love. She is unerring in speech or silence, for she is disinterested, a pure victim, bound to the altar's foot; God teaches her what to say.

In the night she wanders forth from her human investment, and travels amid those tribes, freer movers in the game of spirit and matter, to whom man is a supplement. I know not then whether she is what men call dreaming, but her life is true, full, and more single than by day.

I have seen her among the Sylphs' faint florescent forms that hang in the edges of life's rainbows. She is very fair, thus, Leila; and I catch, though edgewise, and sharp-gleaming as a sword, that bears down my sight, the peculiar light which she will be when she finds the haven of herself. But sudden is it, and whether king or queen, blue or yellow, I never can remember; for Leila is too deep a being to be known in smile or tear. Ever she passes sudden again from these hasty glories and ten-dernesses into the back-ground of being, and should she ever be detected it will be in the central secret of law. Breathless is my ecstasy as I pursue her in this region. I grasp to detain what I love, and swoon and wake and sigh again. On all such beauty transitoriness has set its seal. This sylph nature pierces through the smile of childhood. There is a moment of frail virginity on which it has set its seal, a silver star which may at any moment withdraw and leave a furrow on the brow it decked. Men watch these slender tapers which seem as if they would burn out next moment. They say that such purity is the seal of death. It is so; the condition of this ecstasy is, that it seems to die every moment, and even Leila has not force to die often; the electricity accumulates many days before the wild one comes, which leads to these sylph nights of tearful sweetness.

After one of these, I find her always to have retreated into the secret veins of earth. Then glows through her whole being the fire that so baffles men, as she walks on the surface of earth; the blood-red, heart's-blood-red of the carbuncle. She is, like it, her own light, and beats with the universal heart, with no care except to circulate as the vital fluid; it would seem waste then for her to rise to the surface. There in these secret veins of earth she thinks herself into fine gold, or aspires for her purest self, till she interlaces the soil with veins of silver. She disdains not to retire upon herself in the iron ore. She knows that fires are preparing on upper earth to temper this sternness of her silent self. I venerate her through all this in awed silence. I wait upon her steps through the mines. I light my little torch and follow her through the caves where despair clings by the roof, as she trusts herself to the cold rushing torrents, which never saw the sun nor heard of the ocean. I know if she pauses, it will be to diamond her nature, transcending gen-erations. Leila! thou hast never yet, I believe, penetrated to the central ices, nor felt the whole weight of earth. But thou searchest and search-est. Nothing is too cold, too heavy, nor too dark for the faith of the being whose love so late smiled and wept itself into the rainbow, and was the covenant of an only hope. Am I with thee on thy hours of deepest search? I think not, for still thou art an abyss to me, and the star which glitters at the bottom, often withdraws into newer dark-nesses. O draw me, Star, I fear not to follow; it is my eye and not my heart which is weak. Show thyself for longer spaces. Let me gaze myself into religion, then draw me down,—down.

As I have wished this, most suddenly Leila bursts up again in the fire. She greets the sweet moon with a smile so haughty, that the heavenly sky grows timid, and would draw back; but then remembering that the Earth also is planetary, and bound in one music with all its spheres, it leans down again and listens softly what this new, strange voice may mean. And it seems to mean wo, wo! for, as the deep thought bursts forth, it shakes the thoughts in which time was resting; the cities fall in ruins; the hills are rent asunder; and the fertile valleys ravaged with fire and water. Wo, wo! but the moon and stars smile denial, and the echo changes the sad, deep tone into divinest music. Wait thou, O Man, and walk over the hardened lava to fresh wonders. Let the chain be riven asunder; the gods will give a pearl to clasp it again.

Since these nights, Leila, Saint of Knowledge, I have been fearless, and utterly free. There are to me no requiems more, death is a name, and the darkest seeming hours sing Te Deum.

See with the word the form of earth transfused to stellar clearness, and the Angel Leila showers down on man balm and blessing. One downward glance from that God-filled eye, and violets clothe the most ungrateful soil, fruits smile healthful along the bituminous lake, and the thorn glows with a crown of amaranth. Descend, thou of the silver sandals, to thy weary son; turn hither that swan-guided car. Not mine but thine, Leila. The rivers of bliss flow forth at thy touch, and the shadow of sin falls separate from the form of light. Thou art now pure ministry, one arrow from the quiver of God; pierce to the centre of things, and slay Dagon for evermore. Then shall be no more sudden smiles, nor tears, nor searchings in secret caves, nor slow growths of centuries. But floating, hovering, brooding, strong-winged bliss shall fill eternity, roots shall not be clogged with earth, but God blossom into himself for evermore.

Straight at the wish the arrows divine of my Leila ceased to pierce. Love retired back into the bosom of chaos, and the Holy Ghost descended on the globes of matter. Leila, with wild hair scattered to the wind, bare and often bleeding feet, opiates and divining rods in each over-full hand, walked amid the habitations of mortals as a Genius, visited their consciences as a Demon.

At her touch all became fluid, and the prison walls grew into Edens. Each ray of particolored light grew populous with beings struggling into divinity. The redemption of matter was interwoven into the coronal of thought, and each serpent form soared into a Phenix.

Into my single life I stooped and plucked from the burning my divine children. And ever, as I bent more and more with an unwearied benignity, an elected pain, like that of her, my wild-haired Genius;

more beauteous forms, unknown before to me, nay, of which the highest God had not conscience as shapes, were born from that suddenly darting flame, which had threatened to cleave the very dome of my being. And Leila, she, the moving principle; O, who can speak of the immortal births of her unshrinking love. Each surge left Venus Urania at her feet; from each abjured blame, rose floods of solemn incense, that strove in vain to waft her to the sky. And I heard her voice, which ever sang, "I shrink not from the baptism, from slavery let freedom, from parricide piety, from death let birth be known."

Could I but write this into the words of earth, the secret of moral and mental alchymy would be discovered, and all Bibles have passed into one Apocalypse; but not till it has all been lived can it be written.

Meanwhile cease not to whisper of it, ye pines, plant here the hope from age to age; blue dome, wait as tenderly as now; cease not, winds, to bear the promise from zone to zone; and thou, my life, drop the prophetic treasure from the bud of each day,—Prophecy.

Of late Leila kneels in the dust, yea, with her brow in the dust. I know the thought that is working in her being. To be a child, yea, a human child, perhaps man, perhaps woman, to bear the full weight of accident and time, to descend as low as ever the divine did, she is preparing. I also kneel. I would not avail myself of all this sight. I cast aside my necromancy, and yield all other prowess for the talisman of humility. But Leila, wondrous circle, who hast taken into thyself all my thought, shall I not meet thee on the radius of human nature? I will be thy fellow pilgrim, and we will learn together the bliss of gratitude.

Should this ever be, I shall seek the lonely lake no more, for in the eye of Leila I shall find not only the call to search, but the object sought. Thou hast taught me to recognise all powers; now let us be impersonated, and traverse the region of forms together. *Together,* CAN that be, thinks Leila, can one be with any but God? Ah! it is so, but only those who have known the one can know the two. Let us pass out into nature, and she will give us back to God yet wiser, and worthier, than when clinging to his footstool as now. "Have I ever feared," said Leila. Never! but the hour is come for still deeper trust. Arise! let us go forth!

# 2.

# Henry David Thoreau

## from "Ktaadn"

## (1848)

From Thoreau's most famous works—"Civil Disobedience" and *Walden*—it is hard to appreciate how invested he really was in narrative during much of his career. The kind of contemporary writing Thoreau liked best was travel writing; and over the course of his own writing career, the form to which he most often turned was the excursion, a descriptive-reflective account of a trip taken somewhere. The three long pieces that make up the posthumously published *Maine Woods* all take this form: narratives of sorties into the New England back country. "Ktaadn" is the earliest of these, and also the most literary. It was published in magazine form while he was still at work on *Walden*. It is also a controversial work among Thoreauvians, who have quarreled about the image of nature that the author seems to be trying to present in this culminating section, where Thoreau recalls his attempt to reach the summit of New England's second-highest mountain. Some readers take it as evidence that Thoreau lost his nerve and became disoriented when he was plunked into "real" wilderness, whereas others argue that the "disorientation" here should be understood either as spontaneous excitement at confronting primordial reality, or as a conscious reprise of the experience of the Romantic sublime. But all agree that the latter pages of Thoreau's essay contain some of his most powerful writing.

SOURCE: *The Maine Woods.* Boston: Ticknor and Fields, 1864, slightly corrected in light of later editions.

In the morning, after whetting our appetite on some raw pork, a wafer of hard bread, and a dipper of condensed cloud or waterspout, we all together began to make our way up the falls, which I have described; this time choosing the right hand, or highest peak, which was not the one I had approached before. But soon my companions were lost to my sight behind the mountain ridge in my rear, which still seemed ever retreating before me, and I climbed alone over huge rocks, loosely poised, a mile or more, still edging toward the clouds; for though the day was clear elsewhere, the summit was concealed by mist. The mountain seemed a vast aggregation of loose rocks, as if some time it had rained rocks, and they lay as they fell on the mountain sides, nowhere fairly at rest, but leaning on each other, all rocking-stones, with cavities between, but scarcely any soil or smoother shelf. They were the raw materials of a planet dropped from an unseen quarry, which the vast chemistry of nature would anon work up, or work down, into the smiling and verdant plains and valleys of earth. This was an undone extremity of the globe; as in lignite, we see coal in the process of formation.

At length I entered within the skirts of the cloud which seemed forever drifting over the summit, and yet would never be gone, but was generated out of that pure air as fast as it flowed away; and when, a quarter of a mile farther, I reached the summit of the ridge, which those who have seen in clearer weather say is about five miles long, and contains a thousand acres of table-land, I was deep within the hostile ranks of clouds, and all objects were obscured by them. Now the wind would blow me out a yard of clear sunlight, wherein I stood; then a gray, dawning light was all it could accomplish, the cloud-line ever rising and falling with the wind's intensity. Sometimes it seemed as if the summit would be cleared in a few moments, and smile in sunshine; but what was gained on one side was lost on another. It was like sitting in a chimney and waiting for the smoke to blow away. It was, in fact, a cloud factory,—these were the cloud-works, and the wind turned them off done from the cool, bare rocks. Occasionally, when the windy columns broke in to me, I caught sight of a dark, damp crag to the right or left; the mist driving ceaselessly between it and me. It reminded me of the creations of the old epic and dramatic poets, of Atlas, Vulcan, the Cyclops, and Prometheus. Such was Caucasus and the rock where Prometheus was bound. Æschylus had no doubt visited such scenery as this. It was vast, Titanic, and such as man never inhabits. Some part of the beholder, even some vital part, seems to escape through the loose grating of his ribs as he ascends. He is more lone than you can imagine. There is less of substantial thought and fair understanding in him than in the plains where men inhabit. His reason is dispersed and shadowy, more thin and subtile, like the air. Vast, Titanic, inhuman Nature has got him at disadvantage, caught him alone, and pilfers him of some of his divine faculty. She does not smile on him as in the plains. She seems to say sternly, Why came ye here before your time? This ground is not prepared for you. Is it not enough that I smile in the valleys? I have never made this soil for thy feet, this air for thy breathing, these rocks for thy neighbors. I cannot pity nor fondle thee here, but forever relentlessly drive thee hence to where I *am* kind. Why seek me where I have not called thee, and then complain because you find me but a stepmother? Shouldst thou freeze or starve, or shudder thy life away, here is no shrine, nor altar, nor any access to my ear.

> "Chaos and ancient Night, I come no spy
> With purpose to explore or to disturb
> The secrets of your realm, but . . .
> .     .     .     .     .          as my way
> Lies through your spacious empire up to light."

The tops of mountains are among the unfinished parts of the globe, whither it is a slight insult to the gods to climb and pry into their secrets, and try their effect on our humanity. Only daring and insolent men, perchance, go there. Simple races, as savages, do not climb mountains,—their tops are sacred and mysterious tracts never visited by them. Pomola is always angry with those who climb to the summit of Ktaadn.

According to Jackson, who, in his capacity of geological surveyor of the State, has accurately measured it,—the altitude of Ktaadn is 5300 feet, or a little more than one mile above the level of the sea,—and he adds, "It is then evidently the highest point in the State of Maine, and is the most abrupt granite mountain in New England." The peculiarities of that spacious table-land on which I was standing, as well as the remarkable semi-circular precipice or basin on the eastern side, were all concealed by the mist. I had brought my whole pack to the top, not knowing but I should have to make my descent to the river, and possibly to the settled portion of the State alone, and by some other route, and wishing to have a complete outfit with me. But at length, fearing that my companions would be anxious to reach the river before night, and knowing that the clouds might rest on the mountain for days, I was compelled to descend. Occasionally, as I came down, the wind would blow me a vista open, through which I could see the country eastward, boundless forests, and lakes, and streams, gleaming in the sun, some of them emptying into the East Branch. There were also new mountains in sight in that direction. Now and then some small bird of the sparrow family would flit away before me, unable to command its course, like a fragment of the gray rock blown off by the wind. . . .

———

Perhaps I most fully realized that this was primeval, untamed, and forever untamable *Nature,* or whatever else men call it, while coming down this part of the mountain. We were passing over "Burnt Lands," burnt by lightning, perchance, though they showed no recent marks of fire, hardly so much as a charred stump, but looked rather like a natural pasture for the moose and deer, exceedingly wild and desolate, with occasional strips of timber crossing them, and low poplars springing up, and patches of blueberries here and there. I found myself traversing them familiarly, like some pasture run to waste, or partially reclaimed by man; but when I reflected what man, what brother or sister or kinsman of our race made it and claimed it, I expected the proprietor to rise up and dispute my passage. It is difficult to conceive of a region uninhabited by man. We habitually presume his presence and influence everywhere. And yet we have not seen pure Nature, unless we have seen her thus vast and drear and inhuman, though in the midst of cities. Nature was here something savage and awful, though beautiful. I looked with awe at the ground I trod on, to see what the Powers had made there, the form and fashion and material of their work. This was that Earth of which we have heard, made out of Chaos and Old Night. Here was no man's garden, but the unhandseled globe. It was not lawn, nor pasture, nor mead, nor woodland, nor lea, nor arable, nor waste land. It was the fresh and natural surface of the planet Earth, as it was made forever and ever,—to be the dwelling of man, we say,—so Nature made it, and man may use it if he can. Man was not to be associated with it. It was Matter, vast, terrific,—not his Mother Earth that we have heard of, not for him to tread on, or be buried in,—no, it were being too familiar even to let his bones lie there,—the home, this, of Necessity and Fate. There was clearly felt the presence of a force not bound to be kind to man. It was a place for heathenism and superstitious rites,—to be inhabited by men nearer of kin to the rocks and to wild animals than we. We walked over it with a certain awe, stopping from time to time to pick the blueberries which grew there, and had a smart and spicy taste. Perchance where *our* wild pines stand, and leaves lie on their forest floor, in Concord, there were once reapers, and husbandmen planted grain; but here not even the surface had been scarred by man, but it was a specimen of what God saw fit to make this world. What is it to be admitted to a museum, to see a myriad of particular things, compared with being shown some star's surface, some hard matter in its home! I stand in awe of my body, this matter to which I am bound has become so strange to me. I fear not spirits, ghosts, of which I am one,—*that* my body might,—but I fear bodies, I tremble to meet them. What is this Titan that has possession of me? Talk of mysteries! Think of our life in nature,—daily to be shown matter, to come in contact with it,—rocks, trees, wind on our cheeks! the *solid* earth! the *actual* world! the *common sense! Contact! Contact! Who* are we? *where* are we?

Erelong we recognized some rocks and other features in the landscape which we had purposely impressed on our memories, and, quickening our pace, by two o'clock we reached the batteau.[1] Here we had expected to dine on trout, but in this glaring sunlight they were slow to take the bait, so we were compelled to make the most of the crumbs of our hard bread and our pork, which were both nearly exhausted. Meanwhile we deliberated whether we should go up the river a mile farther, to Gibson's clearing, on the Sowadnehunk, where there was a deserted log-hut, in order to get a half-inch auger, to mend one of our spike-poles with. There were young spruce-trees enough around us, and we had a spare spike, but nothing to make a hole with. But as it was uncertain whether we should find any tools left there, we patched up the broken pole, as well as we could, for the downward voyage, in which there would be but little use for it. Moreover, we were unwilling to lose any time in this expedition, lest the wind should rise before we reached the larger lakes, and detain us; for a moderate wind produces quite a sea on these waters, in which a batteau will not live for a moment; and on one occasion McCauslin had been delayed a week at the head of the North Twin, which is only four miles across. We were nearly out of provisions, and ill prepared in this respect for what might possibly prove a week's journey round by the shore, fording innumerable streams, and threading a trackless forest, should any accident happen to our boat. . . .

---

1. The bears had not touched things on our possessions. They sometimes tear a batteau to pieces for the sake of the tar with which it is besmeared.

---

What is most striking in the Maine wilderness is the continuousess of the forest, with fewer open intervals or glades than you had imagined. Except the few burnt lands, the narrow intervals on the rivers, the bare tops of the high mountains, and the lakes and streams, the forest is uninterrupted. It is even more grim and wild than you had anticipated, a damp and intricate wilderness, in the spring everywhere wet and miry. The aspect of the country, indeed, is universally stern and savage, excepting the distant views of the forest from hills, and the lake prospects, which are mild and civilizing in a degree. The lakes are something which you are unprepared for; they lie up so high, exposed to the light, and the forest is diminished to a fine fringe on their edges, with here and there a blue mountain, like amethyst jewels set around some jewel of the first water,—so anterior, so superior, to all the changes that are to take place on their shores, even now civil and refined, and fair as they can ever be. These are not the artificial forests of an English king,—a royal preserve merely. Here prevail no forest laws but those of nature. The aborigines have never been dispossessed, nor nature disforested.

It is a country full of evergreen trees, of mossy silver birches and watery maples, the ground dotted with insipid, small, red berries, and strewn with damp and moss-grown rocks,—a country diversified with innumerable lakes and rapid streams, peopled with trout and various species of *leucisci,* with salmon, shad, and pickerel, and other fishes; the forest resounding at rare intervals with the note of the chickadee, the blue-jay, and the woodpecker, the scream of the fish-hawk and the eagle, the laugh of the loon, and the whistle of ducks along the solitary streams; at night, with the hooting of owls and howling of wolves; in summer, swarming with myriads of black flies and mosquitoes, more formidable than wolves to the white man. Such is the home of the moose, the bear, the caribou, the wolf, the beaver, and the Indian. Who shall describe the inexpressible tenderness and immortal life of the grim forest, where Nature, though it be mid-winter, is ever in her spring, where the moss-grown and decaying trees are not old, but seem to enjoy a perpetual youth; and blissful, innocent Nature, like a serene infant, is too happy to make a noise, except by a few tinkling, lisping birds and trickling rills?

What a place to live, what a place to die and be buried in! There certainly men would live forever, and laugh at death and the grave. There they could have no such thoughts as are associated with the village graveyard,—that make a grave out of one of those moist ever-green hummocks!

> Die and be buried who will,
> I mean to live here still;
> My nature grows ever more young
> The primitive pines among.

I am reminded by my journey how exceedingly new this country still is. You have only to travel for a few days into the interior and back parts even of many of the old States, to come to that very America which the Northmen, and Cabot, and Gosnold, and Smith, and Raleigh visited. If Columbus was the first to discover the islands, Americus Vespucius and Cabot, and the Puritans, and we their descendants, have discovered only the shores of America. While the republic has already acquired a history world-wide, America is still unsettled and unexplored. Like the English in New Holland, we live only on the shores of a continent even yet, and hardly know where the rivers come from which float our navy. The very timber and boards and shingles of which our houses are made grew but yesterday in a wilderness where the Indian still hunts and the moose runs wild. New York has her wilderness within her own borders; and though the sailors of Europe are familiar with the soundings of her Hudson, and Fulton long since invented the steamboat on its waters, an Indian is still necessary to guide her scientific men to its headwaters in the Adirondack country.

Have we even so much as discovered and settled the shores? Let a man travel on foot along the coast, from the Passamaquoddy to the Sabine, or to the Rio Bravo, or to wherever the end is now, if he is swift enough to overtake it, faithfully following the windings of every inlet and of every cape, and stepping to the music of the surf,—with a desolate fishing-town once a week, and a city's port once a month to cheer him, and putting up at the light-houses, when there are any,—and tell me if it looks like a discovered and settled country, and not rather, for the most part, like a desolate island, and No-Man's Land.

We have advanced by leaps to the Pacific, and left many a lesser Oregon and California unexplored behind us. Though the railroad and the telegraph have been established on the shores of Maine, the Indian still looks out from her interior mountains over all these to the sea. There stands the city of Bangor, fifty miles up the Penobscot, at the head of navigation for vessels of the largest class, the principal lumber depot on this continent, with a population of twelve thousand, like a star on the edge of night, still hewing at the forests of which it is built, already overflowing with the luxuries and refinement of Europe, and sending its vessels to Spain, to England, and to the West Indies for its groceries,—and yet only a few axe-men have gone "up river," into the howling wilderness which feeds it. The bear and deer are still found within its limits; and the moose, as he swims the Penobscot, is entangled amid its shipping, and taken by foreign sailors in its harbor. Twelve miles in the rear, twelve miles of railroad, are Orono and the Indian Island, the home of the Penobscot tribe, and then commence the batteau and the canoe, and the military road; and sixty miles above, the country is virtually unmapped and unexplored, and there still waves the virgin forest of the New World.

## 3.

# LOUISA MAY ALCOTT

## A TRANSCENDENTAL CHILDHOOD

### (1888)

Louisa May Alcott (1832–88) became a popular author more through necessity than desire. She always aspired to a literary career. But her specialization as a writer for children, on which her fame now rests, was an initially reluctant choice. She was motivated to publish in this area of fast-growing demand, which she herself helped create, by the need for a reliable breadwinner in a family whose patriarch was the most impractical of all the leading Transcendentalists. In *Little Women* (1868–69) and later novels, Alcott drew upon the memories of her girlhood in order to create a body of fiction suffused by a combination of drollery and nostalgia that paid a certain homage to Transcendentalism even as it reinforced mainstream impressions of it as a bygone moment of antebellum enthusiasm and whimsy. The following sketch, written for a leading children's magazine shortly before her death, is exemplary. Alcott weaves her early life into a kind of short story, with intriguing balancing acts along the way. She idealizes Emerson and claims him as her "Master," but in the same breath calls her crush on him a "girlish folly." She pays tribute to Bronson Alcott's mission as a progressive educator and social reformer, but the final and decisive lesson she extracts from this family history is that the Alcott women had to learn to be more practical. Here and elsewhere, Alcott drew on her Transcendentalist childhood to tell a story about its innocence as well as hers. The poetic quotation is from Alexander Pope's *Essay on Man.*

SOURCE: "Recollections of My Childhood," *Youth's Companion,* May 24, 1888.

One of my earliest memories is of playing with books in my father's study. Building towers and bridges of the big dictionaries, looking at pictures, pretending to read, and scribbling on blank pages whenever pen or pencil could be found. Many of these first attempts at authorship still exist, and I often wonder if these childish plays did not influence my after life, since books have been my greatest comfort, castle-building a never-failing delight, and scribbling a very profitable amusement.

Another very vivid recollection is of the day when running after my hoop I fell into the Frog Pond and was rescued by a black boy, becoming a friend to the colored race then and there, though my mother always declared that I was an abolitionist at the age of three.

During the Garrison riot in Boston the portrait of [British abolitionist] George Thompson was hidden under a bed in our house for safe-keeping, and I am told that I used to go and comfort "the good man who helped poor slaves" in his captivity. However that may be, the conversion was genuine, and my greatest pride is in the fact that I have lived to know the brave men and women who did so much for the cause, and that I had a very small share in the war which put an end to a great wrong.

Being born on the birthday of Columbus I seem to have something of my patron saint's spirit of adventure, and running away was one of the delights of my childhood. Many a social lunch have I shared with hospitable Irish beggar children, as we ate our crusts, cold potatoes and salt fish on voyages of discovery among the ash heaps of the waste [l]and that then lay where the Albany station now stands.

Many an impromptu picnic have I had on the dear old [Boston] Common, with strange boys, pretty babies and friendly dogs, who always seemed to feel that this reckless young person needed looking after.

On one occasion the town-crier found me fast asleep at nine o'clock at night, on a door-step in Bedford Street, with my head pillowed on the curly breast of a big Newfoundland, who was with difficulty persuaded to release the weary little wanderer who had sobbed herself to sleep there.

I often smile as I pass that door, and never forget to give a grateful pat to every big dog I meet, for never have I slept more soundly than on that dusty step, nor found a better friend than the noble animal who watched over the lost baby so faithfully.

My father's school was the only one I ever went to, and when this was broken up because he introduced methods now all the fashion, our lessons went on at home, for he was always sure of four little pupils who firmly believed in their teacher, though they have not done him all the credit he deserved.

I never liked arithmetic or grammar, and dodged these branches on all occasions; but reading, composition, history and geography I enjoyed, as well as the stories read to us with a skill which made the dullest charming and useful.

"Pilgrim's Progress," Krummacher's "Parables," Miss Edgeworth, and the best of the dear old fairy tales made that hour the pleasantest of our day. On Sundays we had a simple service of Bible stories, hymns, and conversation about the state of our little consciences and the conduct of our childish lives which never will be forgotten.

Walks each morning round the Common while in the city, and long tramps over hill and dale when our home was in the country, were a part of our education, as well as every sort of housework, for which I have always been very grateful, since such knowledge makes one independent in these days of domestic tribulation with the help who are too often only hindrances.

Needle-work began early, and at ten my skilful sister made a linen shirt beautifully, while at twelve I set up as a doll's dress-maker, with my sign out, and wonderful models in my window. All the children employed me, and my turbans were the rage at one time to the great dismay of the neighbors' hens, who were hotly hunted down, that I might tweak out their downiest feathers to adorn the dolls' head-gear.

Active exercise was my delight from the time when a child of six I drove my hoop round the Common without stopping, to the days when I did my twenty miles in five hours and went to a party in the evening.

I always thought I must have been a deer or a horse in some former state, because it was such a joy to run. No boy could be my friend till I had beaten him in a race, and no girl if she refused to climb trees, leap fences and be a tomboy.

My wise mother, anxious to give me a strong body to support a lively brain, turned me loose in the country and let me run wild, learning of nature what no books can teach, and being led, as those who truly love her seldom fail to be,

"Through nature up to nature's God."

I remember running over the hills just at dawn one summer morning, and pausing to rest in the silent woods saw, through an arch of trees, the sun rise over river, hill and wide green meadows as I never saw it before.

Something born of the lovely hour, a happy mood, and the unfolding aspirations of a child's soul seemed to bring me very near to God, and in the hush of that morning hour I always felt that I "got religion" as the phrase goes. A new and vital sense of His presence, tender and sustaining as a father's arms, came to me then, never to change through forty years of life's vicissitudes, but to grow stronger for the sharp discipline of poverty and pain, sorrow and success.

Those Concord days were the happiest of my life, for we had charming playmates in the little Emersons, Channings, Hawthornes and Goodwins, with the illustrious parents and their friends to enjoy our pranks and share our excursions.

Plays in the barn were a favorite amusement, and we dramatized the fairy tales in great style. Our giant came tumbling off a loft when Jack cut down the squash vine running up a ladder to represent the immortal bean. Cinderella rolled away in a vast pumpkin, and a long, black pudding was lowered by invisible hands to fasten itself on the nose of the woman who wasted her three wishes.

Little pilgrims journeyed over the hills with scrip and staff and cockle-shells in their hats; elves held their pretty revels among the pines, and "Peter Wilkins'" flying ladies came swinging down on the birch tree-tops. Lords and Ladies haunted the garden, and mermaids splashed in the bath-house of woven willows over the brook.

People wondered at our frolics, but enjoyed them, and droll stories are still told of the adventures of those days. Mr. Emerson and Margaret Fuller were visiting my parents one afternoon, and the conversation having turned to the ever interesting subject of education, Miss Fuller said:

"Well, Mr. Alcott, you have been able to carry out your methods in your own family, and I should like to see your model children."

She did in a few moments, for as the guests stood on the door steps, a wild uproar approached and round the corner of the house came a wheelbarrow holding baby May arrayed as a queen. I was the horse, bitted and bridled and driven by my elder sister Anna, while Lizzie played dog and barked as loud as her gentle voice permitted.

All were shouting and wild with fun which, however, came to a sudden end as we espied the stately group before us, for my foot tripped, and down we all went in a laughing heap, while my mother put a climax to the joke by saying with a dramatic wave of the hand:

"Here are the model children, Miss Fuller."

My sentimental period began at fifteen when I fell to writing romances, poems, a "heart journal," and dreaming dreams of a splendid future.

Browsing over Mr. Emerson's library, I found "Goethe's Correspondence with a Child," and was at once fired with the desire to be a second Bettine, making my father's friend my Goethe. So I wrote letters to him, but was wise enough never to send them, left wildflowers on the door-steps of my "Master," sung Mignon's song in very bad German under his window, and was fond of wandering by moonlight, or sitting in a cherry-tree at midnight till the owls scared me to bed.

The girlish folly did not last long, and the letters were burnt years ago, but Goethe is still my favorite author, and Emerson remained my beloved "Master" while he lived, doing more for me, as for many another young soul, than he ever knew, by the simple beauty of his life, the truth and wisdom of his books, the example of a good, great man untempted and unspoiled by the world which he made nobler while in it, and left the richer when he went.

The trials of life began about this time, and my happy childhood ended. Money is never plentiful in a philosopher's house, and even the maternal pelican could not supply all our wants on the small income which was freely shared with every needy soul who asked for help.

Fugitive slaves were sheltered under our roof, and my first pupil was a very black George Washington whom I taught to write on the hearth with charcoal, his big fingers finding pen and pencil unmanageable.

Motherless girls seeking protection were guarded among us; hungry travellers sent on to our door to be fed and warmed, and if the philosopher happened to own two coats the best went to a needy brother, for these were practical Christians who had the most perfect faith in Providence, and never found it betrayed.

In those days the prophets were not honored in their own land, and Concord had not yet discovered her great men. It was a sort of refuge for reformers of all sorts whom the good natives regarded as lunatics, harmless but amusing.

My father went away to hold his classes and conversations, and we women folk began to feel that we also might do something. So one gloomy November day we decided to move to Boston and try our fate again after some years in the wilderness.

My father's prospect was as promising as a philosopher's ever is in a money-making world, my mother's friends offered her a good salary as their missionary to the poor, and my sister and I hoped to teach. It was an anxious council, and always preferring action to discussion, I took a brisk run over the hill and then settled down for "a good think" in my favorite retreat.

It was an old cart-wheel, half hidden in grass under the locusts where I used to sit to wrestle with my sums, and usually forgot them scribbling verses or fairy tales on my slate instead. Perched on the hub I surveyed the prospect and found it rather gloomy, with leafless trees, sere grass, leaden sky and frosty air, but the hopeful heart of fifteen beat warmly under the old red shawl, visions of success gave the gray clouds a silver lining, and I said defiantly, as I shook my fist at fate embodied in a crow cawing dismally on the fence near by,—

"I *will* do something by-and-by. Don't care what, teach, sew, act, write, anything to help the family; and I'll be rich and famous and happy before I die, see if I won't!"

Startled by this audacious outburst the crow flew away, but the old wheel creaked as if it began to turn at that moment, stirred by the intense desire of an ambitious girl to work for those she loved and find some reward when the duty was done.

I did not mind the omen then, and returned to the house cold but resolute. I think I began to shoulder my burden then and there, for when the free country life ended the wild colt soon learned to tug in harness, only breaking loose now and then for a taste of beloved liberty.

My sisters and I had cherished fine dreams of a home in the city, but when we found ourselves in a small house at the South End with not a tree in sight, only a back yard to play in, and no money to buy any of the splendors before us, we all rebelled and longed for the country again.

Anna soon found little pupils, and trudged away each morning to her daily task, pausing at the corner to wave her hand to me in answer to my salute with the duster. My father went to his classes at his room down town, mother to her all-absorbing poor, the little girls to school, and I was left to keep house, feeling like a caged sea-gull as I washed dishes and cooked in the basement kitchen where my prospect was limited to a procession of muddy boots.

Good drill, but very hard, and my only consolation was the evening reunion when all met with such varied reports of the day's adventures, we could not fail to find both amusement and instruction.

Father brought news from the upper world, and the wise, good people who adorned it; mother, usually much dilapidated because she *would* give away her clothes, with sad tales of suffering and sin from the darker side of life; gentle Anna a modest account of her success as teacher, for even at seventeen her sweet nature won all who knew her, and her patience quelled the most rebellious pupil.

My reports were usually a mixture of the tragic and the comic, and the children poured their small joys and woes into the family bosom where comfort and sympathy were always to be found.

Then we youngsters adjourned to the kitchen for our fun, which usually consisted of writing, dressing and acting a series of remarkable plays. In one I remember I took five parts and Anna four, with lightning changes of costume, and characters varying from a Greek prince in silver armor to a murderer in chains.

It was good training for memory and fingers, for we recited pages without a fault, and made every sort of property from a harp to a fairy's spangled wings. Later we acted Shakespeare, and Hamlet was my favorite hero, played with a gloomy glare and a tragic stalk which I have never seen surpassed.

But we were now beginning to play our parts on a real stage, and to know something of the pathetic side of life with its hard facts, irksome duties, many temptations and the daily sacrifice of self. Fortunately we had the truest, tenderest of guides and guards, and so learned the sweet uses of adversity, the value of honest work, the beautiful law of compensation which gives more than it takes, and the real significance of life.

At sixteen I began to teach twenty pupils, and for ten years learned to know and love children. The story writing went on all the while with the usual trials of beginners. Fairy tales told the Emersons made the first printed book, and "Hospital Sketches" the first successful one.

Every experience went into the chauldron to come out as froth, or evaporate in smoke, till time and suffering strengthened and clarified the mixture of truth and fancy, and a wholesome draught for children began to flow pleasantly and profitably.

So the omen proved a true one, and the wheel of fortune turned slowly, till the girl of fifteen found herself a woman of fifty with her prophetic dream beautifully realized, her duty done, her reward far greater than she deserved.

VI

# REMEMBRANCES

# Nathaniel Hawthorne

## Glimpses of Transcendental Concord

### (1846)

Hawthorne liked to keep his distance from the Transcendentalists, although he was closer to them than he let on. Elizabeth Peabody, his wife's sister, was one of the inner circle. Hawthorne is less well known for being an early and moderately sympathetic Brook Farmer than for unsuccessfully suing the community for the return of his investment after he left it, and for satirizing it in his third major novel, *The Blithedale Romance.* But in 1842 it was Concord that Hawthorne and his bride, Sophia Peabody, chose as their first abode, and in a house where Emerson himself had once lived, a residence for ministers in his family for three generations. The Hawthornes owed the very roof over their heads to Emerson and their preplanted garden to Henry David Thoreau. They were not ideal tenants. They acted more like Transcendental hippies. They were late with their rent and scratched several windows of the house with memorable but defacing inscriptions like "Man's accidents are God's purposes." Nonetheless the local Transcendentalist coterie welcomed the Hawthornes back again in the 1850s to the house that proved Nathaniel's final residence, "the Wayside." When Hawthorne died in 1864, Emerson was one of the pallbearers at his funeral and also wrote a long-regretful note in his Journal that his hesitancy to encroach on Hawthorne's reticence had kept the two from closer acquaintance. The following selections suggest that Hawthorne may have wanted it that way. Though he exempts Emerson from the eccentricities of his admirers (and here Hawthorne was probably thinking of figures like Alcott, Fuller, and Thoreau, as well as casual Concord visitors), his portrait is a striking mixture of tribute, envy, and put-down. With the significant exception of Herman Melville, whose laudatory review of *Mosses from an Old Manse* touched off a brief but intense relationship, Hawthorne, eccentric as he himself was, in some ways, generally preferred companionship with solid, middle-of-the-road citizens to Transcendental intimacies.

SOURCE: *Mosses from an Old Manse.* New York: Wiley and Putnam, 1846.

Between two tall gate-posts of rough-hewn stone, (the gate itself having fallen from its hinges, at some unknown epoch,) we beheld the gray front of the old parsonage.... It was worthy to have been one of the time-honored parsonages of England, in which, through many generations, a succession of holy occupants pass from youth to age ...

Nor, in truth, had the old Manse ever been prophaned by a lay occupant, until that memorable summer-afternoon when I entered it as my home.... It was awful to reflect how many sermons must have been written there ... I took shame to myself for having been so long a writer of idle stories.... In the humblest event, I resolved at least to achieve a novel, that should evolve some deep lesson, and should possess physical substance enough to stand alone.

In furtherance of my design, and as if to leave me no pretext for not fulfilling it, there was, in the rear of the house, the most delightful little nook of a study that ever afforded its snug seclusion to a scholar. It was here that Emerson wrote "Nature"; for he was then an inhabitant of the Manse, and used to watch the Assyrian dawn and the Paphian sunset and moonrise, from the summit of our eastern hill. When I first saw the room, its walls were blackened with the smoke of unnumbered years, and made still blacker by the grim prints of Puritan ministers that hung around.... They had all vanished now.... In place of the grim prints, there was the sweet and lovely head of one of Raphael's Madonnas, and two pleasant little pictures of the Lake of Como. The only other decorations were a purple vase of flowers, always fresh, and a bronze one containing graceful ferns....

... There were circumstances around me, which made it difficult to view the world precisely as it exists; for, serene and sober as was the old Manse, it was necessary to go but a little way beyond its threshold, before meeting with stranger moral shapes of men than might have been encountered elsewhere, in a circuit of a thousand miles.

These hobgoblins of flesh and blood were attracted thither by the wide-spreading influence of a great original Thinker, who had his earthly abode at the opposite extremity of our village. His mind acted upon other minds, of a certain constitution, with wonderful magnetism, and drew many men upon long pilgrimages, to speak with him face to face.... People that had lighted on a new thought, or a thought that they fancied new, came to Emerson, as the finder of a glittering gem hastens to a lapidary, to ascertain its quality and value. Uncertain, troubled, earnest wanderers, through the midnight of the moral world, beheld his intellectual fire, as a beacon burning on a hill-top, and, climbing the difficult ascent, looked forth into the surrounding obscurity, more hopefully than hitherto. The light revealed objects unseen before—mountains, gleaming lakes, glimpses of a creation among the chaos—but also, as was unavoidable, it attracted bats and owls, and the whole host of night-birds, which flapped their dusky wings against the gazer's eyes, and sometimes were mistaken for fowls of angelic feather. Such delusions always hover nigh, whenever a beacon-fire of truth is kindled.

For myself, there had been epochs of my life, when I, too, might have asked of this prophet the master-word, that should solve me the riddle of the universe; but now, being happy, I felt as if there were no question to be put, and therefore admired Emerson as a poet of deep beauty and austere tenderness, but sought nothing from him as a philosopher. It was good, nevertheless, to meet him in the wood-paths, or sometimes in our avenue, with that pure, intellectual gleam diffused about his presence, like the garment of a shining-one; and he so quiet, so simply, so without pretension, encountering each man alive as if expecting to receive more than he could impart. And, in truth, the heart of many an ordinary man had, perchance, inscriptions which he could not read. But it was impossible to dwell in his vicinity, without inhaling, more or less, the mountain-atmosphere of his lofty thought, which, in the brains of some people, wrought a singular giddiness— new truth being as heady as new wine. Never was a poor little country village infested with such a variety of queer, strangely dressed, oddly behaved mortals, most of whom took upon themselves to be important agents of the world's destiny, yet were simply bores of a very intense water. Such, I imagine, is the invariable character of persons who crowd so closely about an original thinker, as to draw in his unuttered breath, and thus become imbued with a false originality. This triteness of novelty is enough to make any man, of common sense, blaspheme at all ideas of less than a century's standing...

# WILLIAM HENRY CHANNING

## RECOLLECTIONS OF A TRANSCENDENTALIST INSIDER

### (1852)

William Henry Channing (1810–84), nephew of William Ellery Channing, was one of Transcendentalism's most charismatic ministers. His combination of idealistic spiritual enthusiasm and social reform activism—on behalf of temperance, peace, women's rights, and abolition—drew Emerson's admiration but also put him on the defensive (see Emerson's "Ode" to Channing in Section V). During the 1830s and 1840s, Channing shuttled restlessly about the northeast and midwest, turning his hand to a number of clerical, reformist, and literary projects but sticking to none before committing himself to a monumental biography of his uncle in the late 1840s and, a decade later, settling in as successor to Britain's most eminent Unitarian minister, James Martineau, whose Liverpool pastorate Channing held for the rest of his life.

When his dear friend Margaret Fuller tragically died by shipwreck in 1850, Channing joined forces with Emerson and fellow minister and Fuller confidante James Freeman Clarke to assemble a two-volume memoir. In it, Channing composed the following affectionately comic requiem for a movement full of stir and excitement but too self-absorbed to have any lasting influence. In this respect, Channing's social radicalism and Hawthorne's conservatism converged. Both depict Transcendentalism as a dreamy, ephemeral moment. Yet for both, this depiction also reflects a sense of personal dissatisfaction with what they themselves had achieved in life thus far. As Channing's biographer politely put it, his thoughts, although "of great potency in their time, and admirable in expression, were addressed to the exigencies of the hour, and absorbed by them."

SOURCE: *The Memoirs of Margaret Fuller Ossoli,* ed. William Henry Channing, Ralph Waldo Emerson, and James Freeman Clarke. Boston: Phillips, Sampson, 1852.

The summer of 1839 saw the full dawn of the Transcendental movement in New England. The rise of this enthusiasm was as mysterious as that of any form of revival; and only they who were of the faith could comprehend how bright was this morning-time of a new hope. Transcendentalism was an assertion of the inalienable integrity of man, of the immanence of Divinity in instinct. In part, it was a reaction against Puritan Orthodoxy; in part, an effect of renewed study of the ancients, of Oriental Pantheists, of Plato and the Alexandrians, of Plutarch's Morals, Seneca and Epictetus; in part, the natural product of the culture of the place and time. On the somewhat stunted stock of Unitarianism,—whose characteristic dogma was trust in individual reason as correlative to Supreme Wisdom,—had been grafted German Idealism, as taught by masters of most various schools,—by Kant and Jacobi, Fichte and Novalis, Schelling and Hegel, Schleiermacher and De Wette, by Madame de Stael, Cousin, Coleridge, and Carlyle; and the result was a vague yet exalting conception of the godlike nature of the human spirit. Transcendentalism, as viewed by its disciples, was a pilgrimage from the idolatrous world of creeds and rituals to the temple of the Living God in the soul. It was a putting to silence of tradition and formulas, that the Sacred Oracle might be heard through intuitions of the single-eyed and pure-hearted. Amidst materialists, zealots, and sceptics, the Transcendentalist believed in perpetual inspiration, the miraculous power of will, and a birthright to universal good. He sought to hold communion face to face with the unnameable Spirit of his spirit, and gave himself up to the embrace of nature's beautiful joy, as a babe seeks the breast of a mother. To him the curse seemed past; and love was without fear. "All mine is thine" sounded forth to him in ceaseless benediction, from flowers and stars, through the poetry, art, heroism of all ages, in the aspirations of his own genius, and the budding promise of the time. His work was to be faithful, as all saints, sages, and lovers of man had been, to Truth, as the very Word of God. His maxims were,— "Trust, dare and be; infinite good is ready for your asking; seek and find. All that your fellows can claim or need is that you should become, in fact, your highest self; fulfil, then, your ideal." Hence, among the strong, withdrawal to private study and contemplation, that they might be "alone with the Alone;" solemn yet glad devotedness to the Divine leadings in the inmost will; calm concentration of thought to wait for and receive wisdom; dignified independence, stern yet sweet, of fashion and public opinion; honest originality of speech and conduct, exempt alike from apology or dictation, from servility or scorn. Hence, too, among the weak, whimsies, affectation, rude disregard of proprieties, slothful neglect of common duties, surrender to the claims of natural appetite, self-indulgence, self-absorption, and self-idolatry.

By their very posture of mind, as seekers of the new, the Transcendentalists were critics and "come-outers" from the old. Neither the church, the state, the college, society, nor even reform associations, had a hold upon their hearts. The past might be well enough for those who, without make-belief, could yet put faith in common dogmas and usages; but for them the matin-bells of a new day were chiming, and the herald-trump of freedom was heard upon the mountains. Hence, leaving ecclesiastical organizations, political parties, and familiar circles, which to them were brown with drought, they sought in covert nooks of friendship for running waters, and fruit from the tree of life. The journal, the letter, became a greater worth than the printed page; for they felt that systematic results were not yet to be looked for, and that in sallies of conjecture, glimpses and flights of ecstasy, the "Newness" lifted her veil to her votaries. Thus, by mere attraction of affinity, grew together the brotherhood of the "Like-minded," as they were pleasantly nicknamed by outsiders, and by themselves, on the ground that no two were of the same opinion. The only password of membership to this association, which had no compact, records, or officers, was a hopeful and liberal spirit; and its chance conventions were determined merely by the desire of the caller for a "talk," or by the arrival of some guest from a distance with a budget of presumptive novelties. Its "symposium" was a pic-nic, whereto each brought of his gains, as he felt prompted, a bunch of wild grapes from the woods, or bread-corn from his threshing-floor. The tone of the assemblies was cordial welcome for every one's peculiarity; and scholars, farmers, mechanics, merchants, married women, and maidens, met there on a level of courteous respect. The only guest not tolerated was intolerance; though strict justice might add, that these "Illuminati" were as unconscious of their special cant as smokers are of the perfume of their weed, and that a professed declaration of universal independence turned out in practice to be rather oligarchic.

# 3.

# CHARLOTTE FORTEN
## EMERSON OBSERVED
### (1855-63)

Charlotte Forten (1837–1914) was an aspiring writer from a prominent Philadelphia African-American abolitionist family. Her moral earnestness, intellectual seriousness, and literary gifts won her, even as a teenager, the attention of such leading New England abolitionists as orator Wendell Phillips and poet John Greenleaf Whittier. Forten was a talented essayist whose narrative of wartime experiences teaching southern freed men appeared in *The Atlantic Monthly,* then the leading literary magazine in the United States. After the Civil War, when mainstream media rebuffed black authors, her publications tailed off. Today she is best known as the author of the posthumously published *Journals of Charlotte Forten Grimké* (ed. Brenda Stevenson, Oxford University Press, 1988), from which the following excerpts are taken. Forten offers somewhat awestruck but by no means uncritical impressions of Emerson as a celebrity writer, lecturer, and public figure at the height of his fame. The intertwinement of her responses to Emerson's aesthetic sensitivity and his political commitment is especially striking. So too is her complex response to Emerson's lofty idealism, which both humbles and energizes her. Both patterns of response reveal much about Emerson's peculiar charisma. See Section V-C-3 for the poem Forten mentions in her last entry. In that same section, Emerson's "Days" is a more downbeat and compressed companion piece to the 1857 lecture that especially impressed Forten. Note also Forten's intensification of Hawthorne's focus on Emerson as the central Transcendentalist. Emerson is a personage of deepest interest to her; the movement associated with him does not interest her at all.

*Wednesday, March 14 [1855].* Heard Ralph Waldo Emerson lecture on France. The lecture was very interesting and entertaining though not particularly flattering does *his* estimate seem to be of the gay and fickle inhabitants of "la belle France." I had felt quite eager to hear the gifted man, who, Wendell Phillips says, is thought in England to stand at the head of American literature. He is a fine lecturer, and a very peculiar-looking man.

*Tuesday, September 30 [1856].* Just finished Emerson's "English Traits,"—which I like *very* much. The author's views of English character are far more liberal than those of American travellers generally. He evidently appreciates dear old England; and, loving her as I do, I like his book and thank him for it with all my heart.

*Wednesday, February 11 [1857].* Have just returned from hearing R. W. Emerson.—Subject "Works and Days" from Hesiod's poem—One of the most beautiful and eloquent lectures I ever heard. The lecturer spoke particularly of the preciousness of time, the too often unappreciated worth of a *day.* We *must live* in the *Present* rather than in the Past and Future, for the *present hour* alone is ours. *Now* we must *act*—*now* we must *enjoy.* Eternity is boundless,—yet the *present hour* is worth the whole of it . . . the impression made on my mind will be a lasting one. I have felt strengthened in all earnest and noble purposes since hearing that lecture. Never, never before have I so forcibly felt the *preciousness* of time. And oh, how deeply do the words and presence of such a man as Emerson, make us feel the utter insignificance, the great inferiority of *ourselves.* 'Tis a sad lesson, but a most *salutary* one, for who, while earnestly feeling that *he is* nothing, *knows* nothing, comparatively, will not strive with all his might to *know* and to be something? Poets and philosophers! the great, the gifted of the earth. I thank you for teaching me this lesson—so sad, so humbling, yet so truly useful and ennobling!

*Sunday, November 15 [1857].* [Read in *The Atlantic Monthly*] a poem "Brahma" by R. W. Emerson, remarkable only for its utter obscurity. Can't understand a word of it. Evidently poetry is not the philosopher's forte.

*Friday, Christmas Day [1857]* . . . went to the [antislavery fund-raising] Fair, and saw many beautiful articles. . . . Saw [Charles] Sumner, Emerson, Wendell Phillips, all in the Fair at once. It was *glorious* to see such a trio. I feasted my eyes.

*Thursday, January 20 [1858].* A lecture from Emerson—really on the true beauty of Nature, and the pleasure and benefit to be derived from walking amid this beauty. I have rarely enjoyed so rich a mental feast. I am really *grieved* that my mind is in such a stupid state, so "care-laden," that I cannot treasure up, as I once could, the golden words from the poet-philosopher's lips. A walk with Emerson would be intensely yet *silently* delightful. I cannot but believe that he is one of the truest of Nature's interpreters.

*Friday, February 19 [1858].* Finished the first volume of Emerson's "Essays." I cannot *quite* understand *everything* that he says; but I understand enough to admire and enjoy, and be benefitted by. He has taught me a good and noble lesson, for which I thank him with all my heart.

*Sunday, February 8 [1863].* [Dr. Seth Rogers, surgeon to the Massachusetts regiment of African-American soldiers commanded by T. W. Higginson] read me Emerson's noble "Hymn," written for the grand Jubilee Concert, on Emancipation Day in Boston. Dr. R. read it to the Regt. he told me, during the service, this morning. I am glad.

4.

# THEODORE PARKER

## A DYING TRANSCENDENTALIST LOOKS BACK

### (1859)

Prodigiously energetic, Parker eventually worked himself into the ground and succumbed to the tuberculosis that ran in his and many other New England families (the Emersons and the Thoreaus, among them), dying prematurely at the age of fifty. In the West Indies, on the first leg of an unsuccessful journey to recover his health, Parker wrote a long autobiography of his career as minister and reformer in the form of an open letter to his congregation. In it, he reflects back on a number of the key episodes of the Transcendentalist movement. Like William Henry Channing, Parker viewed the heyday of Transcendental ferment as a season of youth. But in sharp contrast to Channing, he did not see it as a sealed episode of little long-term consequence but as a crucial preparation for his work over the past dozen years or more as a reformist pastor that he hoped he might be able to continue.

SOURCE: *Theodore Parker's Experiences as a Minister*. Boston: Leighton, 1859.

In due time I entered the Theological School at Cambridge, then under the charge of the Unitarians, or "Liberal Christians." I found excellent opportunities for study: there were able and earnest professors, who laid no yoke on any neck, but left each man free to think for himself, and come to such conclusions as he must. . . . They were honest guides, with no more sophistry than is perhaps almost universal in that calling, and did not pretend to be masters. There, too, was a large library containing much valuable ancient lore, though, alas! almost none of the new theologic thought of the German masters. Besides, there was leisure, and unbounded freedom of research; and I could work as many hours in the study as a mechanic in his shop, or a farmer in his field. The pulpits of Boston were within an easy walk, and Dr. Channing drew near the zenith of his power.

I soon found that the Bible is a collection of quite heterogeneous books, most of them anonymous, or bearing names of doubtful authors, collected none knows how, or when, or by whom; united more by caprice than any philosophic or historic method, so that it is not easy to see why one ancient book is kept in the canon and another kept out. . . . I found each writer [in the New Testament] had his own individuality, which appears not only in the style, the form of thought, but quite as much in the doctrines, the substance of thought, where no two are well agreed. . . .

I believed in the Immanence of God in man, as well as matter, his activity in both; hence, that all men are inspired in proportion to their actual powers and their normal use thereof; that Truth is the test of intellectual inspiration, Justice of moral, and so on. I did not find the Bible inspired, except in this general way, and in proportion to the Truth and Justice therein. It seemed to me that no part of the Old Testament or New could be called the "Word of God," save in the sense that all Truth is God's word.

. . . As I found the Bible was the work of men, so I also found that the Christian Church was no more divine than the British State, a Dutchman's shop, or an Austrian's farm. . . .

I studied the historical development of Religion and Theology amongst the nations not Jewish or Christian, and attended as well as I then could to the four other great religious sects—the Brahmanic, the Buddhistic, the Classic, and the Mohammedan. As far as possible at that time, I studied the Sacred Books of mankind in their original tongues, and with the help of the most faithful interpreters. Here the Greek and Roman poets and philosophers came in for their place, there being no Sacred Books of the Classic nations. I attended pretty carefully to the religion of Savages and Barbarians, and was thereby helped to the solution of many a difficult problem. I found no tribe of men destitute of religion who has attained power of articulate speech.

I studied assiduously the Metaphysics and Psychology of Religion. . . . I found most help in the works of Immanuel Kant, one of the profoundest thinkers in the world, though one of the worst writers, even of Germany; if he did not always furnish conclusions I could rest in, he yet gave me the true method, and put me on the right road.

I found certain great primal intuitions of human nature, which depend on no logical process of demonstration, but are rather facts of consciousness given by the instinctive action of human nature itself. I will mention only the three most important which pertain to religion.

1. The Instinctive Intuition of the Divine, the consciousness that there is a God.

2. The Instinctive Intuition of the Just and Right, a consciousness that there is a Moral Law, independent of our will, which we ought to keep.

3. The Instinctive Intuition of the Immortal, a consciousness that the Essential Element of man, the principle of Individuality, never dies.

. . . I preached Natural Laws [in his first post, the small Unitarian congregation in West Roxbury, 1837–45,] nothing on the authority of any church, any tradition, any sect. . . . The simple life of the farmers, mechanics, and milk-men, about me, of its own accord, turned into a sort of poetry, and re-appeared in the sermons, as the green woods, not far off, looked in at the windows of the Meeting-House. I think I preached only what I had experienced in my own inward conscious-ness, which widened and grew richer as I came into practical contact with living men, turned time into life, and mere thought became char-acter. . . .

. . . The years of my preliminary theological study, and of my early ministry, fell in the most interesting period of New England's spiritual history, when a great revolution went on—so silent that few men knew it was taking place, and none then understood its whither or its whence.

———

Mr. Garrison, with his friends, inheriting what was best in the Puritan founders of New England, . . . was beginning his noble work. . . . Dr. Channing was in the full maturity of his powers, and, after long preaching the Dignity of Man as an abstraction, and Piety as a purely inward life, with rare and winsome eloquence, and ever progressive humanity, began to apply his sublime doctrines to actual life in the Individual, the State, and the Church. In the name of Christianity, the great American Unitarian called for the reform of the drunkard, the elevation of the poor, the instruction of the ignorant, and, above all, for the liberation of the American slave. . . . The brilliant genius of

Emerson rose in the winter nights, and hung over Boston, drawing the eyes of ingenuous young people to look up to that great, new star, a beauty and a mystery, which charmed for the moment, while it gave also perennial inspiration, as it led them forward along new paths, and toward new hopes. America had seen no such sight before; it is not less a blessed wonder now.

... The writings of Wordsworth were becoming familiar to the thoughtful lovers of nature and of man, and drawing men to natural piety. Carlyle's works got reprinted at Boston, diffusing a strong, and then, also, a healthy influence on old and young. The writings of Coleridge were reprinted in America, all of them "Aids to Reflection," and brilliant with the scattered sparks of genius. ...

The Rights of Labor were discussed with deep philanthropic feeling, and sometimes with profound thought, metaphysic and economic both. The works of Charles Fourier—a strange, fantastic, visionary man, no doubt, but gifted also with amazing insight of the truths of social science—shed some light in these dark places of speculation. Mr. Ripley, a born Democrat, in the high sense of that abused word, and one of the best cultured and most enlightened men in America, made an attempt at Brook-farm in West Roxbury, so as to organize society that the results of labor should remain in the workman's hand, and not slip thence to the trader's till; that there should be "no exploitation of man by men," but Toil and Thought, hard work and high culture, should be united in the same person.

The natural Rights of Woman began to be inquired into, and publicly discussed; while in private, great pains were taken in the chief towns of New England, to furnish a thorough and comprehensive education to such young maidens as were born with two talents, mind and money.

Of course, a strong reaction followed. ... Mr. Norton—then a great name at Cambridge, a scholar of rare but contracted merit, ... opened his mouth and spoke: the mass of men must accept the doctrines of religion solely on the authority of the learned ...; the new philosophic attempts to explain the facts of religious consciousness were "the Latest Form of infidelity"; the great philosophical and theological thinkers of Germany were "all Atheists." ...

Of course, this reaction was supported by the Ministers in the great Churches of Commerce, and by the old literary periodicals ... the Unitarian journals gradually went over to the opponents of freedom and progress. ... Prominent Anti-Slavery men were dropped out of all wealthy society in Boston, their former friends not knowing them in the street. . . .

The movement party established a new quarterly, the *Dial,* wherein their wisdom and their folly rode together on the same saddle, to the amazement of lookers-on. The short-lived journal had a narrow circulation, but its most significant papers were scattered wide by newspapers which copied them. A *Quarterly Review* was also established by Mr. Brownson, then a Unitarian Minister . . . but now a Catholic. . . . In [the *Boston Quarterly Review,* 1837–41], he diffused important philosophic ideas, displayed and disciplined his own extraordinary talents for philosophic thought and popular writings, and directed them toward Democracy, Transcendentalism, "New Views," and the "Progress of the Species."

I count it as a piece of good fortune that I was a young man when these things were taking place, when great questions were discussed, and the public had not yet taken sides. . . .

[Beginning his present Boston ministry in 1845,] I knew well what we had to expect at first; for we were committing the sin which all the great world-sects have held unpardonable—attempting to correct the Errors of Theory and the Vices of Practice in the church. No offense could ecclesiastically be greater; the Inquisition was built to punish such. . . . I knew that I had thoroughly broken with the ecclesiastic authority of Christendom; its God was not my God, nor its Scriptures my Word of God, nor its Christ my Saviour; for I preferred the Jesus of historic fact to the Christ of theologic fancy. Its narrow, partial and unnatural heaven I did not wish to enter on the terms proposed, nor did I fear, since earliest youth, its mythic, roomy hell. . . .

Preaching such doctrines [Note: Parker refers here to his social as well as his religious radicalism.] in a place so public, and applying them to life, I am not surprised at the hostility I have met with from the various sects. . . .

. . . [Yet] all I asked was a hearing; that has been abundantly granted. YOU opened wide the doors, my opponents rang the bell all Saturday night, and Sunday morning the audience was there. I think no other country would allow me such liberty of speech. . . .

To me, Human Life in all its forms, individual and aggregate, is a perpetual wonder. . . .

In your busy, bustling town, with its queerly mingled, heterogeneous population, and its great diversity of work, I soon learned to see the Unity of Human Life under all this variety of circumstances and outward condition.... The cunning Lawyer, selling his legal knowledge and forensic skill to promote a client's gainful wickedness; the tricksy Harlot, letting out her person to a stranger's unholy lust; the deceitful Minister, prostituting his voice and ecclesiastical position to make some popular sin appear decent and Christian, "accordant with the revealed word of God"—all stand in the same column of my religious notation. In the street I see them all pass by, each walking in a vain show, in different directions, but all consilient to the same end....

In my preaching I have used plain, simple words, sometimes making what I could not find ready, and counted nothing unclean, because merely common.... I have always preferred to use, when fit, the every-day words in which men think and talk, scold, make love, and pray, so that generous-hearted Philosophy, clad in a common dress, might more easily become familiar to plain-clad men. It is with customary tools that we work easiest and best, especially when use has made the handles smooth.

Illustrations I have drawn from most familiar things which are before all men's eyes, in the fields, the streets, the shop, the kitchen, parlor, nursery or school; and from the literature best known to all,— the Bible, the newspapers, the transient speech of eminent men, the talk of common people in the streets, from popular stories, school-books, and nursery rhymes ... for this I must not only plead the necessity of my nature, delighting in common things, trees, grass, oxen, and stars, moonlight on the water, the falling rain, the ducks and hens at this moment noisy under my window, the gambols and prattle of children, and the common work of blacksmiths, carpenters, wheelwrights, painters, hucksters and traders of all sorts; but I have also on my side the example of all the great masters of speech ... of poets like Homer, Dante, Shakespeare ...

———

Let no fondness for me, now heightened by my illness, and my absence too, blind your eyes to errors which may be in my doctrine, which must be in my life; I am content to serve by warning, where I cannot guide by example. Mortal, or entered on Immortal Life, still let me be your Minister, to serve, never your Master, to hinder and command. Do not stop where I could go no further, for, after so long teaching, I feel that I have just begun to learn, begun my work....

# RALPH WALDO EMERSON

## FROM "HISTORIC NOTES OF LIFE AND LETTERS IN MASSACHUSETTS"

### (1867)

The tone of Emerson's reminiscence strongly contrasts with Parker's. Emerson, too, writes at the end of his active career, though this piece was not published until shortly after his death fifteen years later. Parker sees the Transcendentalist ferment of the 1830s and 1840s as having put intellectual and social forces in motion that are still very much alive, even though he himself will not live to see the upshot. For Emerson, Transcendentalism belongs to a past far more distant than even Channing saw it as being. Part of the difference between the two retrospects has to do with the occasion. Emerson's "Notes" are designed as an entertaining lecture, not as the summation of his life work. Part of the difference was temperamental: Parker's passionate intensity versus the wry irony that marks many of Emerson's later essays on the state of nineteenth-century American culture, beginning with "The Transcendentalist" (1841). No less important, however, is the difference in historical moment. Parker writes on the eve of the Civil War, whereas for Emerson that paroxysm has thrust the prewar era back into the recesses of history, proved the country's mettle through the triumphs of antislavery and Unionism, and brought the nation to a new level of mature consolidation whose future downside—Reconstruction's failure and Gilded Age materialism—Emerson is not in a position to foresee. Where Parker and Emerson agree is that modern thought has confirmed the existence of a bedrock human spiritual and moral nature, indwelling in the individual person.

SOURCE: "Historic Notes of Life and Letters in Massachusetts," *The Atlantic Monthly,* 52 (October 1883).

There are always two parties, the party of the Past and the party of the Future, the Establishment and the Movement. At times, the resistance is reanimated; the schism runs under the world, and appears in Literature, Philosophy, Church, State, and social customs. It is not easy to date these eras of activity with any precision, but in this region one made itself remarked, say, in 1820 and the twenty years following.

... The key to the period appeared to be that the mind had become aware of itself. Men grew reflective and intellectual. There was a new consciousness. The former generations acted under the belief that a shining social prosperity was the beatitude of man, and sacrificed uniformly the citizen to the State. The modern mind believed that the nation existed for the individual, for the guardianship and education of every man. This idea, roughly written in revolutions and national movements, in the mind of the philosopher had far more precision: the individual is the world.

———

... Instead of the social existence which all shared, was now separation. Every one for himself; driven to find all his resources, hopes, rewards, society and deity within himself.

The young men were born with knives in their brain, a tendency to introversion, self-dissection, anatomizing of motives. The popular religion of our fathers had received many severe shocks from the new times.... [Emerson proceeds to describe some of the Anglo-European influences and early-nineteenth-century New England intermediaries.]

... But I think the paramount source of the religious revolution was Modern Science; beginning with Copernicus, who destroyed the pagan fictions of the Church, by showing mankind that the earth on which we live was not the centre of the universe.... But we presently saw also that the religious nature in man was not affected by these errors in his understanding. The religious sentiment made nothing of bulk or size, or far or near; triumphed over time as well as space; and every lesson of humility, or justice, or charity, which the old ignorant saints had taught him, was still forever true.

———

... Margaret Fuller, George Ripley, Dr. Convers Francis, Theodore Parker, Dr. Hedge, Mr. Brownson, James Freeman Clarke, William H.

Channing, and many others gradually drew together, and from time to time spent an afternoon at each other's houses in a serious conversation. With them was always one well-known form [Bronson Alcott], a pure idealist, not at all a man of letters, nor of any practical talent, nor a writer of books; a man quite too cold and contemplative for the alliances of friendship, with rare simplicity and grandeur of perception, who read Plato as an equal, and inspired his companions only in proportion as they were intellectual,—whilst the men of talent complained of the want of point and precision in this abstract and religious thinker. These fine conversations, of course, were incomprehensible to some in the company, and they had their revenge in their little joke. One declared that "it seemed to him like going to Heaven in a swing"; another reported that, at a knotty point in the discourse, a sympathizing Englishman with a squeaking voice interrupted with the question, "Mr. Alcott, a lady near me desires to inquire whether omnipotence abnegates attribute?"

I think there prevailed at that time a general belief in Boston that there was some concert of *doctrinaires* to establish certain opinions and inaugurate some movement in literature, philosophy and religion, of which design the supposed conspirators were quite innocent; for there was no concert, and only here and there two or three men or women who read and wrote, each alone, with unusual vivacity. Perhaps they only agreed in having fallen upon Coleridge and Wordsworth and Goethe, then on Carlyle, with pleasure and sympathy. Otherwise, their education and reading were not marked, but had the American superficialness, and their studies were solitary. I suppose all of them were surprised at this rumor of a school or sect, and certainly at the name of Transcendentalism, given nobody knows by whom, or when it was first applied . . .

. . . Nothing could be less formal, yet the intelligence and character and varied ability of the company gave it some notoriety, and perhaps wakened curiosity as to its aims and results.

Nothing more serious came of it than the modest quarterly journal called The Dial, which, under the editorship of Margaret Fuller, and later of some other [i.e., Emerson himself], enjoyed its obscurity for four years. All its papers were unpaid contributions, and it was rather a work of friendship among the narrow circle of students than the organ of any party. Perhaps its writers were its chief readers; yet it contained some noble papers by Margaret Fuller, and some numbers had an instant exhausting sale, because of papers by Theodore Parker.

# 6.

# OCTAVIUS BROOKS FROTHINGHAM

## FROM *TRANSCENDENTALISM IN NEW ENGLAND*

## (1876)

O. B. Frothingham (1822–95) was the son of a Unitarian minister of William Ellery Channing's generation. He himself became a minister of more radical stamp, with close ties to the Transcendentalists. He also became the movement's first true historian, and one of the best. Before writing *Transcendentalism in New England,* a chapter from which is excerpted below, Frothingham had written a biography of Theodore Parker, and he was to go on to write memoirs of George Ripley and his own father, Nathaniel Frothingham, who stood out from most other moderately conservative Unitarians in maintaining cordial relations with figures like Emerson and even Parker. *Transcendentalism in New England* casts a far wider net than any other history of the movement written for more than a century afterward in its panoramic account of the movement's European backgrounds in German, French, and British thought (the first five chapters) and—despite the book's emphasis on the movement's spiritual and philosophical aspects—its insistence that Transcendentalism had a permanent impress on many facets of American life. In the book's title chapter, from which these selections come, Frothingham stakes a stronger claim for the movement's significance than the movement's leaders themselves did. His explanation of why it made historical sense for Transcendentalism to root itself more deeply in New England than elsewhere is especially shrewd.

SOURCE: *Transcendentalism in New England: A History.* New York: Putnam, 1876.

Theodore Parker was our Savanarola, an excellent scholar, in frank and affectionate communication with the best minds of his day, yet the tribune of the people, and the stout Reformer to urge and defend every cause of humanity with and for the humblest of mankind. . . .

The vulgar politician disposed of this circle cheaply as "the sentimental class." State Street had an instinct that they invalidated contracts, and threatened the stability of stocks. . . .

[After this comes a long, gently but persistently satiric critique of the utopian socialist movement, particularly Fourier's theory and Brook Farm.]

I recall these few selected facts, none of them of much independent interest, but symptomatic of the times and country. I please myself with the thought that our American mind is not now eccentric or rude in its strength, but is beginning to show a quiet power, drawn from wide and abundant sources, proper to a continent and to an educated people. If I have owed much to the special influences I have indicated, I am not less aware of that excellent and increasing circle of masters in arts and in song and in science, who cheer the intellect of our cities and this country to-day,—whose genius is not a lucky accident, but normal, and with broad foundation of culture, and so inspires the hope of steady strength advancing on itself, and a day without night.

The title of this Chapter is in a sense misleading. For with some truth it may be said that there never was such a thing as Transcendentalism out of New England. In Germany and France there was a transcendental philosophy ... but it never affected society in its organized institutions or practical interests. In old England, this philosophy influenced poetry and art, but left the daily existence of men and women untouched. But in New England, the ideas entertained by the foreign thinkers took root in the native soil and blossomed out in every form of social life. The philosophy assumed full proportions, produced fruit according to its kind, created a new social order for itself, or rather showed what sort of social order it would create under favoring conditions....

New England furnished the only plot of ground on the planet where the transcendental philosophy had a chance to show what it was and what it proposed. The forms of life there were, in a measure, plastic. There were no immovable prejudices, no fixed and unalterable traditions. Laws and usages were fluent, malleable at all events. The sentiment of individual freedom was active.... No orders of men, no aristocracies of intellect, no privileged classes of thought were established. The old world supplied such literature as there was, in science, law, philosophy, ethics, theology; but an astonishing intellectual activity seized upon it, dealt with it in genuine democratic fashion, classified it, accepted it, dismissed it, paying no undue regard to its foreign reputation.... A feeling was abroad that all things must be new in the new world. There was call for immediate application of ideas to life.... In the new world, the thinker was called upon to justify himself on the spot by building an engine, and setting something in motion. The test of a truth was its availability. The popular faith in the capacities of men to make states, laws, religions for themselves, supplied a ground for the new philosophy....

The religion of New England was Protestant and of the most intellectual type.... The Congregational system favored individuality of thought and action.... This theology too had its purely spiritual side—nay, it was essentially spiritual. Its root ran back into Platonism, and its flower was a mysticism which, on the intellectual side, bordered closely on Transcendentalism.

———

... The Unitarians of New England, good scholars, careful reasoners, clear and exact thinkers, accomplished men of letters, humane in sentiment, sincere in moral intention, belonged, of course with individual exceptions, to the class which looked without for knowledge, rather than within for inspiration. The Unitarian in religion was a whig in politics, a conservative in literature, art and social ethics.... The Unitarian leaders were distinguished by practical wisdom, sober judgment, and balanced thoughtfulness, that weighed opinions in the scale of evidence and argument. Even Dr. Channing clung to the philosophical traditions that were his inheritance from England....

[On the other hand,] they were open inquirers, who asked questions and waited for rational answers, having no definite apprehension of the issue to which their investigations tended, but with room enough within the accepted theology to satisfy them, and work enough on the prevailing doctrines to keep them employed. Under these circumstances, they honestly but incautiously professed a principle broader than they were able to stand by, and avowed the absolute freedom of the human mind as their characteristic faith.... The intellectual among them were at liberty to entertain views which an orthodox believer would not have touched with the ends of his fingers.... This profession of free inquiry, and the practice of it within the extensive area of Protestant theology, opened the door to the new speculation which carried unlooked-for heresies in its bosom; and before the gates could be closed the insidious enemy had penetrated to the citadel.

There was idealism in New England prior to the introduction of Transcendentalism. Idealism is of no clime or age.... [But Emerson] alone was competent to form a school, and as soon as he rose, the scholars trooped about him. By sheer force of genius Emerson anticipated the results of the transcendental philosophy, defined its axioms and ran out their inferences to the end....

From what has been said it may be inferred that Transcendentalism in New England was a movement within the limits of "liberal" Christianity or Unitarianism as it was called, and had none but a religious aspect. Such an inference would be narrow....

... Transcendentalism was a distinct philosophical system. Practically it was an assertion of the inalienable worth of man; theoretically it was an assertion of the immanence of divinity in instinct, the transference of supernatural attributes to the natural constitution of mankind.

Such a faith would necessarily be protean in its aspects. Philosopher, Critic, Moralist, Poet, would give it voice according to cast of genius....

—

... The Transcendentalists of New England were the most strenuous workers of their day, and at the problems which the day flung down before them. The most strenuous, and the most successful workers too. They achieved a more practical benefit for society, in proportion to their numbers and the duration of their existence, than any body of Baconians [e.g., rational empiricists] of whom we have ever heard. Men and women are healthier in their bodies, happier in their domestic and social relations, more contented in their estate, more ambitious to enlarge their opportunities, more eager to acquire knowledge, more kind and humane in their sympathies, more reasonable in their expectations, than they would have been if Margaret Fuller and Ralph Waldo Emerson and Theodore Parker and George Ripley and Bronson Alcott, and the rest of their fellow believers and fellow workers had not lived. It is the fashion of our generation to hold that progress is, and must of necessity be, exceedingly gradual; and that no safe advance is ever made except at snail's pace. But ever and anon the mind of man refutes the notion by starting under the influence of a thought, and leaping over long reaches of space at a bound. Transcendentalism gave one of these demonstrations, sufficient to refute the vulgar prejudice.

# 7.

# Caroline Wells Healey Dall
## Transcendentalism as Feminist Heresy
### (1895)

The well-educated daughter of a wealthy Bostonian who later went bankrupt, Caroline Dall (1822–1912) was the most prolific and long-lived women's rights advocate among the Transcendentalist circle. She greatly admired Margaret Fuller. Dall published a report of Fuller's 1841 series of public "conversations" on "The Mythology of the Greeks and Its Expression in Art" as *Margaret and Her Friends* (1895). Dall's much later lecture-essay printed here is unique among Transcendentalist memoirs in the strong case it makes for Frederic Henry Hedge and especially Margaret Fuller as more significant shapers and definers of Transcendentalism than Emerson was. Dall traces Fuller's intellectual ancestry back to the first great New England heretic of Puritan times, Anne Hutchinson, the center of the "antinomian" controversy of the 1630s, who held that the highest spiritual authority must be the dictates of the Holy Spirit to the individual soul. In a few confident brushstrokes, Dall draws a line between seventeenth- and nineteenth-century New England that modern scholars have laboriously tried to reconstruct. Dall cribs some of her account from Emerson's "Historic Notes" and other sources, but her perspective is distinctively her own. Unlike Hedge and Emerson, Dall remained to the end an outspoken advocate of what she took to be Transcendentalism's core values. She herself was an embodiment of Transcendentalism's ability to outlive the epoch that ended with Fuller's death in 1850.

SOURCE: *Transcendentalism in New England: A Lecture.* Boston: Roberts Brothers, 1897.

I am asked to speak to you of Transcendentalism in New England. The phrase is a misnomer; out of New England, Transcendentalism had no practical existence. In Germany it belonged to the scholars, and never affected popular life. It began to do this in New England a hundred years before "The Critique of Pure Reason" was printed, and independently of the causes which brought that philosophical classic into existence.

The idea of One originating cause lay at the basis of every system of Puritanism; but the limitations of the sixteenth century prevented its theologians from recognizing that the revelations of the Creative Cause are perpetual. When the religious instruction of Helen Keller became a necessity, it was intrusted to the Rev. Phillips Brooks, with the distinct understanding that he should not convey to her any sectarian limitations. When, on the first day, the bishop undertook to define for her the nature and being of God, the child of eleven interrupted him with this pathetic outburst: "I have always known him; but I did not know his name!"

More pathetic still is the fact that the earliest settlers of New England, who had always known the name of God, who were more than ready, even eager, to lay down their lives in what they believed to be his service, were nevertheless ignorant of his nature. This led to many painful episodes in the development of New England life, the first of which was the persecution of Anne Hutchinson. You will be surprised when you hear me say that the history of the Transcendental movement stretched along two hundred years, beginning with a woman's life and work in 1637, and ending with a woman's work and death in 1850. The arc, which we call transcendental, was subtended by a chord, held at first by Anne Hutchinson, and lost in the Atlantic waves with Margaret Fuller....

———

In tracing the Transcendental movement to Anne Hutchinson, I had always supposed myself to be doing something original; but in looking up material for this paper I found the following sentence in Emerson:—

"In action the Transcendentalist might be counted an *Antinomian,* because he asserts that he who has the Lawgiver may not only neglect but contravene every written command!"

Emerson overlooked Anne Hutchinson, which he would not have done ten years later; but he recognized the ripple left by her movement. This showed itself above the surface, here and there, all through the century and a half that led to the advent of William Ellery Channing; and this spiritual impulse saved the Unitarianism of New England from becoming the dead, materialistic thing which Priestley made of it in the old country.

Locke insisted that all knowledge came from experience; Berkeley, that the outward world had no existence whatever as a substance. The two schools annihilated each other, and resulted in the scepticism of Hume. Stimulated by this, and moved also—there is little doubt—by the impetus given by the studies of others, Kant published in 1781 "The Critique of Pure Reason." In this remarkable and now classic book Kant asserted the veracity of consciousness, and demanded an absolute acknowledgment of that veracity. The fidelity of the mind to itself constituted his first principle. *He* first used the term "transcendental" when he asserted that there was a very imperative class of ideas which transcend experience, but are the means by which experience is to be tested. Then followed throughout Europe a general illumination of philosophic thought, which came in time to pervade the theology of New England, although at first indirectly.

We had no German students then, but one of Channing's earliest utterances was this: "A spiritual light brighter than that of noon pervades our daily life. The cause of our not seeing lies in ourselves."

From 1830 to 1840 was a period of intense mental activity in New England. "It produced some confusion when Leibnitz, Spinoza, Kant, Goethe, Herder, Schleiermacher, and Jean Paul came sailing all at once into Boston harbor and discharged their freight." The wharves were littered with the spoils of a century. Idealism, which had originated with Anne Hutchinson, was "now imported in foreign packages from France and Germany." It is only fair to say that the commander of this fleet was Frederick Henry Hedge, a man whom no historian has ever mentioned in connection with it. He was, as Chadwick says, "one of the principal leaders in the great drama of progressive thought." An intimate friendship of more than fifty years' duration allows me to say that he was more than this: he was one of the noblest of men. . . . He was the most completely qualified German scholar in the Transcendental movement. His enthusiasm was contagious, and passed from him to Margaret Fuller, George Ripley, and James Freeman Clarke. As early as 1835 he was desirous of establishing a periodical, but going to Bangor in that year delayed the undertaking, and it was not until 1840 that "The Dial" was started.

I must not be betrayed into a biography of Dr. Hedge. It is probably known to you that he held the German chair in Harvard College, and was for twenty-one years Professor of Ecclesiastical History in its Divinity School. When, in 1877, Frothingham published his "History of Transcendentalism in New England," the survivors of the movement made in 1840 were both amused and amazed at the omission of the master's name from the story. It was the play of "Hamlet" with the part of Hamlet left out! . . .

———

Emerson, of course, put in an irregular appearance all along the line. In 1836 the first edition of "Nature" was printed. Then came the wonderful address before the Divinity School, "Idealism in Full Blaze." In 1840 Theodore Parker threw his massive understanding into the arena. He was our Savonarola, an excellent scholar in affectionate communication with the best minds of his day, the tribune of the people, a stout reformer to urge and defend every cause of humanity in behalf of the humblest. Some passages of his prose glow with inspired beauty. . . .

———

The Transcendentalist made an extravagant demand on human nature,—that of lofty living. He quarrelled with every man he met. There was not enough of him! "So many promising youths," said Emerson, "and never a finished man!"

The anthropologists may find in this movement the origin of nearly every one of their multiform lines of inquiry. "It is a misfortune," said one, "to have been born when children were nothing, and to have lived until men have become nothing!" New voices began to be heard in the air. Channing had prepared the way by his magnificent vindication of the dignity of human nature. New principles in philosophy, new methods of criticism, began to stir. The origin and contents of the Scriptures were carefully scrutinized. The mind of New England was leavened by the thought of Emerson and the scholarship of Hedge. The "Transient and Permanent" were examined and contrasted by a fearless iconoclast. The title "humanitarian" began to be applied to theologians. God is not outside the world, a mere lawgiver: he is in the world; he is the world; man's relation to him is immediate. God is the Over Soul; above all, through all, *under* all, as well. The spirit must speak to spirit. Jesus was but a man, therefore a child of God who had attained to his proper heritage. He was the ideal man, type of mankind, become so through entering into perfect harmony with the Divine. If he wrought miracles, they must have been manifestations of normal law not yet perceived by undeveloped souls. Conceptions like these inspired the best spiritual life of the time, and modified the sentiments of many who were still unwilling to break the bonds of their training.

The characteristics of the Transcendental movement were shown in the temper of its agitation for the rights of woman and the enlargement of her duties. Like Dryden, every Transcendentalist was ready, and indeed had good reason, to assert that there was "no sex in souls." The editors of "The Dial," which was first issued in July, 1840, and lasted hardly four years, were Margaret Fuller and Ralph Waldo Emerson. In this, besides exquisite poems which, dropped from their original setting, have since travelled all over the world, the "Great Lawsuit" of Margaret Fuller, seven wonderful chapters on the "Ethnical Scriptures," a remarkable paper of Theodore Parker's, and the absurd "Orphic Sayings" of Alcott were first given to the world.

Transcendentalism had now come to be a distinct system, and, practically, to be the assertion of the inalienable worth of man, and of the immanence of the Divine in the Human. Its votaries were now the most strenuous workers of their day—not only that, but the most successful. Men and women are healthier in their bodies, happier in their domestic and social relations, more ambitious to enlarge their opportunities, more kind and humane in sympathy, as well as more reasonable in expectation, than they would have been if Margaret and Emerson had never lived. Under the influence of transcendental thought and hope, the mind of universal man leaped forward with a bound. The Transcendentalist of that day was always on the wing. A new hymn-book, issued by Samuel Johnson and Samuel Longfellow,—for which reason it was called by Theodore Parker the "Sam Book,"—was not only one of the manifestations of clerical sympathy, but had much to do with securing popular attention to the new ideas.

The Transcendentalists did not write about immortality. Theodore Parker called it a fact of consciousness, and in all their conferences faith in it was assumed. No belief was more characteristic of them than this. Emerson's life and walk and literary utterance were full of this faith. His power lay in his pure idealism, his absolute faith in thought, his supreme confidence in spiritual law. He lived in the region of serene ideas: "he did not visit the mount now and then, but set up his tabernacle and passed the night among the stars, ready for the eternal sunrise." He was the descendant of eight generations of Puritan clergymen,—some of whom had persecuted, some of whom had cherished, the "exaltation" of Anne Hutchinson. He inherited their thoughtfulness and their spirit of inward communion. The dogmatism fell away, the peaceful fruits of discipline remained. He bore with him the atmosphere of eternal youth. For what he says or what he does he makes no apology. He never explains. He trusts to affirmation pure and simple. I appealed to him once, when a wholly unnecessary misunderstanding had put me in a painful position: "What should I do?" "Do?" he answered, with the look of a bewildered child; "if understanding were possible, misunderstanding would not have occurred!" I have never tried to explain myself since; but many a time has that serene dogma comforted my soul.

———

For myself, I am a Transcendentalist of the old New England sort. I believe myself to be a child of God; and if a child, then an heir,—a very condensed way of saying that the spirit within me is the breath of the creative spirit, and therefore infinite in its reach, in its possibilities, and its final destiny. The Over Soul is the Under Soul as well. Matter is immortal. No agency, human or divine, has so far been able to destroy one particle of it; and yet, the world over, we see matter not only plastic in the grasp of mind, but subordinate to the uses of the race or the individual solely through the spirit's power. Is the spirit less, then, than the flesh which it masters? If matter cannot be destroyed, it can be transformed. So can spirit. I remember to have heard James Freeman Clarke say of another whose virtue was in question: "Do not dwell on his transgressions. *His face is set the right way.* He keeps his heel firmly on every tempting thought. If it slip now and then, what matter? The purpose is the thing!" This, I suppose, is rank antinomianism, capable of great abuse; but is it not the doctrine we all accept to-day? Life is a glorious thing, whether it is the life that now is or the life that is to come. To be born immortal; to pass through life in the consciousness of an immortal destiny; to try steadfastly to be worthy of this,—what grander atmosphere could encompass a man? There is only one thing sweeter and more desirable,—to trust one's self wholly to the love of the informing Spirit. There is only one clew which it is safe to hold as we pass through the mysteries of this life to the confines of the next. It is a *Surrendered Will.*

The body, to be healthy, must be constructed and sustained in harmony with psychical and physiological law. No less must the soul be held to the conditions of that spiritual law which underlies both....

You will ask me now for some word concerning the permanent results of this movement of souls. Did you not see them in 1860, when Colonel Shaw and Colonel Higginson rushed to the head of the black regiments? It was the Transcendentalists and the children of Transcendentalists who responded promptly to the varied calls of John A. Andrew, who filled the ranks of the Seventh Regiment in New York. It was the Transcendentalists who organized the Sanitary Commission, and who became those chaplains of the regiments who scattered the "White Tracts."...

—

I began this paper with one woman's name; I must close it with another's.

It is hopeless to convey to those who never saw her any idea of Margaret Fuller, to give to those who never lived in the circle that she inspired any impression of her being and influence. She was not beautiful, people said; but she was more than beautiful. A sort of glow surrounded her, and warmed those who listened. It was dimmed sometimes when she yielded to the temperament she inherited; but it burned afresh in the instant impulse of her better self. She was thought to dress magnificently. It was this glow that touched and colored her garments, for poverty compelled her to great simplicity. It was true of her, as of Richelieu, that her death left a vacancy greater than any space she had filled. Many of the young women who grew up with her have since become distinguished. Those who have not, have not failed to introduce into sacred homes the high ideal that she imparted. I consider it the greatest blessing of my life that I was admitted almost as a child to the circle that surrounded her, and felt from my first conscious moments the noble atmosphere that she diffused. Among the girls of that circle one saw no low, ignoble motives, no vanity, no poor ambitions, no coquetries, no looking to marriage as an end, no proneness to idle gossip. Margaret's life began in the constant sacrifice of personal aims to the material wants of her family. It continued, like Anne Hutchinson's, attracting larger and larger crowds of women as long as she had strength to speak, until the men who knew her begged admittance to her audience. This granted, she was no longer her best self. It was only with women that she became both priestess and oracle....

Margaret left America in 1846, but the impulse she had given was not lost. In Italy she became the intimate friend of Mazzini, and during the rise and fall of the Republic wrote a careful history of all that occurred,—a history that perished with her. Here, again, her life presents a parallel to that of Anne Hutchinson; for she had not been more celebrated in New England for her intellectual sway than she became in Italy as the superintendent of the hospital "Fate Bene Fratelli."

"Why this waste of magnificence?" wrote Alpine Conway, standing before the golden throne of the Himalayas, twenty-three thousand feet above the sea, in a solitude no human voice had ever broken. The clouds for answer shut the sunset glory from his view. While we waited with heartfelt longing for Margaret, the savage waves tore her away and hid in their hollows all that she had loved. Is it not good that there should be bounty beyond our conceiving? The sunset was not wasted that only Conway saw. The tragedy of 1850 swallowed carelessly much that we held precious; but it promised more, and the glory of Margaret's life did not perish.

NOTE.—I do not forget that Emerson survived Margaret Fuller thirty years; that Henry Hedge survived her forty; while Dr. Bartol is still living, with his eyes uplifted. But Emerson belonged to the whole world; Henry Hedge, to the scholarly ranks of Harvard men; and Dr. Bartol, if no other, was born a Transcendentalist. Prophet and seer he walks among men; and organizations, whether of New England or Old England, are powerless to hold him. I do not think I am mistaken in saying that what is meant by New England Transcendentalism perished with Margaret Fuller.

# HENRY JAMES

## A CONCORD PILGRIMAGE

### (1907)

As part of an extensive tour of the United States in 1904, the aging expatriate novelist Henry James (1843–1916) undertook a sentimental jaunt to Concord. This little suburban town had long since become a magnet for the tourists, as the site where the American Revolution began (see Emerson's "Concord Hymn" in Section V-C-3) and for its fame as the Transcendentalist epicenter. But James viewed Concord with more than a purely historical interest. His father, Henry James Sr. (1811–82), had been Emerson's friend (and also critic). Emerson sometimes stayed with the Jameses during New York lecture tours; the Jameses sometimes visited the Emersons in Concord; and the James boys were almost exact contemporaries and friendly acquaintances from childhood with Emerson's children. Henry Jr., the novelist, was a satirist of the Transcendentalist ferment rather than a sympathizer, most notoriously so in his novel *The Bostonians* (1886), whose lovable but dotty Miss Birdseye is thought to have been based on the aging Elizabeth Peabody. But he genuinely respected Emerson, with qualifications; and he was drawn by Concord's still-bucolic charm and the sense of its historical significance, out of all proportion to its size and surface appearance. In James's memory, revolutionary and transcendental Concord fuse into one composite image and so too do all the Concord literati. The urbane charm of James's sketch rounds us back to this section's first selection by Hawthorne, James's personal favorite, who would have squirmed at being lumped together with Emerson and Thoreau. But after all, Hawthorne had been the only one of the Concordians to invest in Brook Farm.

SOURCE: *The American Scene.* New York: Harper, 1907.

I FELT myself on the spot, cast about a little for the right expression of it, and then lost any hesitation to say that, putting the three or four biggest cities aside, Concord, Massachusetts, had an identity more palpable to the mind, had nestled in other words more successfully beneath her narrow fold of the mantle of history, than any other American town. "Compare me with places of my size, you know," one seemed to hear her plead, with the modesty that, under the mild autumn sun, so well became her russet beauty; and this exactly it was that prompted the emphasis of one's reply, or, as it may even be called, of one's declaration.

"Ah, my dear, it isn't a question of places of your 'size,' since among places of your size you're too obviously and easily first: it's a question of places, so many of them, of fifty times your size, and which yet don't begin to have a fraction of your weight, or your character, or your intensity of presence and sweetness of tone, or your moral charm, or your pleasant appreciability, or, in short, of anything that is yours. Your 'size'? Why, you're the biggest little place in America—with only New York and Boston and Chicago, by what I make out, to surpass you; and the country is lucky indeed to have you, in your sole and single felicity, for if it hadn't, where in the world should we go, inane and unappeased, for the particular communication of which you have the secret? The country is colossal, and you but a microscopic speck on the hem of its garment; yet there's nothing else like you, take you all round, for we *see* you complacently, with the naked eye, whereas there are vast sprawling, bristling areas, great gray 'centres of population' that spread, on the map, like irremediable grease-spots, which fail utterly of any appeal to our vision or any control of it, leaving it to pass them by as if they were not. If you are so thoroughly the opposite of one of these I don't say it's all your superlative merit; it's rather, as I have put it, your felicity, your good fortune, the result of the half-dozen happy turns of the wheel in your favor. Half a dozen such turns, you see, are, for any mortal career, a handsome allowance; and your merit is that, recognizing this, you have not fallen below your estate. But it's your fortune, above all, that's your charm. One doesn't want to be patronizing, but you didn't, thank goodness, make yours. That's what the other places, the big ones that are as nothing to you, are trying to do, the country over—to make theirs; and, from the point of view of these remarks, all in vain. Your luck is that you didn't have to; yours had been, just as it shows in you to-day, made *for* you, and you at the most but gratefully submitted to it. It must be said for you, however, that you keep it; and it isn't every place that would have been capable——! You keep the look, you keep the feeling, you keep the air. Your great trees arch over these possessions more protectingly, covering them in as a cherished presence; and you have settled to your tone and your type as to treasures that can now never be taken. Show me the other places in America (of the few that have *had* anything) from which the best hasn't mainly been taken, or isn't in imminent danger of being. There is old Salem, there is old Newport, which I am on my way to see again, and which, if you will, are, by what I hear, still comparatively intact; but their having was never a having like yours, and they adorn, precisely, my little tale of your supremacy. No, I don't want to be patronizing, but your only fault is your tendency to improve— I mean just by your duration as you *are;* which indeed is the only sort of improvement that is not questionable."

Such was the drift of the warm flood of appreciation, of reflection, that Concord revisited could set rolling over the field of a prepared sensibility; and I feel as if I had quite made my point, such as it is, in asking what other American village could have done anything of the sort. I should have been at fault perhaps only in speaking of the interest in question as visible, on that large scale, to the "naked eye"; the truth being perhaps that one wouldn't have been so met half-way by one's impression unless one had rather particularly *known,* and that knowledge, in such a case, amounts to a pair of magnifying spectacles. I remember indeed putting it to myself on the November Sunday morning, tepid and bright and perfect for its use, through which I walked from the station under the constant archway of the elms, as yet but indulgently thinned: would one know, for one's self, what had formerly been the matter here, if one hadn't happened to be able to get round behind, in the past, as it were, and more or less understand? Would the operative elements of the past—little old Concord Fight, essentially, and Emerson and Hawthorne and Thoreau, with the rest of the historic animation and the rest of the figured and shifting "transcendental" company, to its last and loosest ramifications—would even these handsome quantities have so lingered to one's intelligent after-sense, if one had not brought with one some sign by which they too would know; dim, shy spectralities as, for themselves, they must, at the best, have become? Idle, however, such questions when, by the chance of the admirable day, everything, in its own way and order, unmistakably came *out*—every string sounded as if, for all the world, the loose New England town (and I apply the expression but to the relations of objects and places) were a lyre swept by the hand of Apollo. Apollo was the spirit of antique piety, looking about, pausing, remembering, as he moved to his music; and there were glimpses and reminders that of course kept him much longer than others.

Seated there at its ease, as if placidly familiar with pilgrims and quite taking their homage for granted, the place had the very aspect of some grave, refined New England matron of the "old school," the widow of a high celebrity, living on and on in possession of all his relics and properties, and, though not personally addicted to gossip or to journalism, having become, where the great company kept by her in the past is concerned, quite cheerful and modern and responsive. From her position, her high-backed chair by the window that commands most of the coming and going, she looks up intelligently, over her knitting, with no vision of any limit on her part as yet, to this attitude, and with nothing indeed to suggest the possibility of a limit save a hint of that loss of temporal perspective in which we recognize the mental effect of a great weight of years. I had formerly the acquaintance of a very interesting lady, of extreme age, whose early friends, in "literary circles," are now regarded as classics, and who, toward the end of her life, always said, "You know Charles Lamb has produced a play at Drury Lane," or "You know William Hazlitt has fallen in love with such a very odd woman." Her facts were perfectly correct; only death had beautifully passed out of her world—since I don't remember her mentioning to me the demise, which she might have made so contemporary, either of Byron or of Scott. When people were ill she admirably forebore to ask about them—she disapproved wholly of such conditions; and there were interesting invalids round about her, near to her, whose existence she for long years consummately ignored. It is some such quiet backward stride as those of my friend that I seem to hear the voice of old Concord take in reference to her annals, and it is not too much to say that where her soil is most sacred, I fairly caught, on the breeze, the mitigated perfect tense. "You know there has been a fight between our men and the King's"—one wouldn't have been surprised, that crystalline Sunday noon, where so little had changed, where the stream and the bridge, and all nature, and the *feeling,* above all, still so directly testify, at any fresh-sounding form of such an announcement.

I had forgotten, in all the years, with what thrilling clearness that supreme site speaks—though anciently, while so much of the course of the century was still to run, the distinctness might have seemed even greater. But to stand there again was to take home this foreshortened view, the gained nearness, to one's sensibility; to look straight over the heads of the "American Weimar" company at the inestimable hour that had so handsomely set up for them their background. The Fight had been the hinge—so one saw it—on which the large revolving future was to turn; or it had been better, perhaps, the large firm nail, ringingly driven in, from which the beautiful portrait-group, as we see it to-day, was to hang. Beautiful exceedingly the local Emerson and Thoreau and Hawthorne and (in a fainter way) *tutti quanti;* but beautiful largely because the fine old incident down in the valley had so seriously prepared their effect. That seriousness gave once for all the pitch, and it was verily as if, under such a value, even with the seed of a "literary circle" so freely scattered by an intervening hand, the vulgar note would in that air never be possible. As I had inevitably, in long absence, let the value, for immediate perception, rather waste itself, so, on the spot, it came back most instantly with the extraordinary sweetness of the river, which, under the autumn sun, like all the American rivers one had seen or was to see, straightway took the whole case straightway into its hands. "Oh, you shall tell me of your impression when you have felt what *I* can do for it: so hang over me well!"—that's what they all seem to say.

I hung over Concord River then as long as I could, and recalled how Thoreau, Hawthorne, Emerson himself, have expressed with due sympathy the sense of this full, slow, sleepy, meadowy flood, which sets its pace and takes its twists like some large obese benevolent person, scarce so frankly unsociable as to pass you at all. It had watched the Fight, it even now confesses, without a quickening of its current, and it draws along the woods and the orchards and the fields with the purr of a mild domesticated cat who rubs against the family and the furniture. Not to be recorded, at best, however, I think, never to emerge from the state of the inexpressible, in respect to the spot, by the bridge, where one most lingers, is the sharpest suggestion of the whole scene—the power diffused in it which makes it, after all these years, or perhaps indeed by reason of their number, so irresistibly touching. All the commemorative objects, the stone marking the burial-place of the three English soldiers, the animated image of the young belted American yeoman by Mr. Daniel French, the intimately associated element in the presence, not far off, of the old manse, interesting theme of Hawthorne's pen, speak to the spirit, no doubt, in one of the subtlest tones of which official history is capable, and yet somehow leave the exquisite melancholy of everything unuttered. It lies too deep, as it always so lies where the ground has borne the weight of the short, simple act, intense and unconscious, that was to determine the event, determine the future in the way we call immortally. For we read into the scene too little of what we may, unless this muffled touch in it somehow reaches us so that we feel the pity and the irony of the *precluded* relation on the part of the fallen defenders. The sense that was theirs and that moved them we know, but we seem to know better still the sense that wasn't and that couldn't, and that forms our luxurious heritage as our eyes, across the gulf, seek to meet their eyes; so that we are almost ashamed of taking so much, such colossal quantity and value, as the equivalent of their dimly-seeing offer. The huge bargain they made for us, in a word, made by the gift of the little all they had— to the modesty of which amount the homely rural facts grouped there together have appeared to go on testifying—this brilliant advantage strikes the imagination that yearns over them as unfairly enjoyed at their cost. Was it delicate, was it decent—that is *would* it have been—to ask the embattled farmers, simple-minded, unwitting folk, to make us so inordinate a present with so little of the conscious credit of it? Which all comes indeed, perhaps, simply to the most poignant of all those effects of disinterested sacrifice that the toil and trouble of our forefathers produce for us. The minute-men at the bridge were of course interested intensely, as they believed—but such, too, was the artful manner in which we see *our* latent, lurking, waiting interest like, a Jew in a dusky back-shop, providentially bait the trap.

Beyond even such broodings as these, and to another purpose, moreover, the communicated spell falls, in its degree, into that pathetic oddity of the small aspect, and the rude and the lowly, the reduced and humiliated above all, that sits on so many nooks and corners, objects and appurtenances, old contemporary things—contemporary with the doings of our race; simplifying our antecedents, our annals, to within an inch of their life, making us ask, in presence of the rude relics even of greatness, mean retreats and receptacles, constructionally so poor, from what barbarians or from what pigmies we have sprung. There are certain rough black mementos of the early monarchy, in England and Scotland, there are glimpses of the original humble homes of other greatness as well, that strike in perfection this grim little note; which has the interest of our being free to take it, for curiosity, for luxury of thought, as that of the real or that of the romantic, and with which, again, the deep Concord rusticity, momentary medium of our national drama, essentially consorts. We remember the small hard facts of the Shakespeare house at Stratford; we remember the rude closet, in Edinburgh Castle, in which James VI of Scotland was born, or the other little black hole, at Holyrood, in which Mary Stuart "sat" and in which Rizzio was murdered. These, I confess, are odd memories at Concord; although the manse, near the spot where we last paused, and against the edge of whose acre or two the loitering river seeks friction in the manner I have mentioned, would now seem to have shaken itself a trifle disconcertingly free of the ornamental mosses scattered by Hawthorne's light hand; it stands there, beyond its gate, with every due similitude to the shrunken historic site in general. To which I must hasten to add, however, that I was much more struck with the way these particular places of visitation resist their pressure of reference than with their affecting us as below their fortune. Intrinsically they are as naught—deeply depressing, in fact, to any impulse to reconstitute, the house in which Hawthorne spent what remained to him of life after his return from the Italy of his Donatello and his Miriam. Yet, in common with everything else, this mild monument benefits by that something in the air which makes us tender, keeps us respectful; meets, in the general interest, waving it vaguely away, any closer assault of criticism.

It is odd, and it is also exquisite, that these witnessing ways should be the last ground on which we feel moved to ponderation of the "Concord school"—to use, I admit, a futile expression; or rather, I should doubtless say, it *would* be odd if there were not inevitably something absolute in the fact of Emerson's all but lifelong connection with them. We may smile a little as we "drag in" Weimar, but I confess myself, for my part, much more satisfied than not by our happy equivalent, "in American money," for Goethe and Schiller. The money is a potful in the second case as in the first, and if Goethe, in the one, represents the gold and Schiller the silver, I find (and quite putting aside any bimetallic prejudice) the same good relation in the other between Emerson and Thoreau. I open Emerson for the same benefit for which I open Goethe, the sense of moving in large intellectual space, and that of the gush, here and there, out of the rock, of the crystalline cupful, in wisdom and poetry, in Wahrheit and Dichtung; and whatever I open Thoreau for (I needn't take space here for the good reasons) I open him oftener than I open Schiller. Which comes back to our feeling that the rarity of Emerson's genius, which has made him so, for the attentive peoples, the first, and the one really rare, American spirit in letters, couldn't have spent his career in a charming woody, watery place, for so long socially and typically and, above all, interestingly homogeneous, without an effect as of the communication to it of something ineffaceable. It was during his long span his immediate concrete, sufficient world; it gave him nearest vision of life, and he drew half his images, we recognize, from the revolution of its seasons and the play of its manners. I don't speak of the other half, which he drew from elsewhere. It is admirably, to-day, as if we were still seeing these things *in* those images, which stir the air like birds, dim in the eventide, coming home to nest. If one had reached a "time of life" one had thereby at least heard him lecture; and not a russet leaf fell for me, while I was there, but fell with an Emersonian drop.

# FOR FURTHER READING

1. OTHER COLLECTIONS LIKE THIS ONE

The best previous collections are *The Transcendentalists: An Anthology,* ed. Perry Miller (Cambridge, MA: Harvard University Press, 1950), and *Transcendentalism: A Reader,* ed. Joel Myerson (New York: Oxford University Press, 2000). Both contain some readings not printed here, as well as vice versa. Miller's anthology is especially strong on the subject of religious controversy during the movement's early years, Myerson's on Transcendentalism's feminist aspect.

2. HISTORY AND CRITICAL ANALYSIS OF THE
  TRANSCENDENTALIST MOVEMENT

For a wide-ranging anecdotal history, with vivid sketches of all major players and many of the minor ones, O. B. Frothingham's *Transcendentalism in America: A History* (New York: Putnam, 1876) still makes an accessible entry point. But by far the best general history of the movement, erudite and complexly woven yet also very readable, is Barbara Packer, "The Transcendentalists," *The Cambridge History of American Literature,* ed. Sacvan Bercovitch (Cambridge, Eng.: Cambridge University Press, 1995), 2: 329–604.

*Transient and Permanent: The Transcendentalist Movement and Its Contexts,* ed. Charles Capper and Conrad Edick Wright (Boston: Northeastern University Press, 1999), is a solid assemblage of scholarly essays with up-to-date accounts of most aspects of the movement. For more on its religious dimensions, see William R. Hutchison, *The Transcendentalist Ministers* (New Haven, CT: Yale University Press, 1959), and Arthur Versluis, *American Transcendentalism and Asian Religions* (Oxford University Press, 1993). A logical entry point for the less-studied subject of Transcendentalism's place in the history of American philosophy is Elizabeth Flower and Murray G. Murphey, "Transcendentalism," *A History of Philosophy in America* (New York: Putnam, 1977), 1: 397–445. For more on the movement's literary facets, see Lawrence Buell, *Literary Transcendentalism: Style and Vision in the American Renaissance* (Ithaca: Cornell University Press, 1973). Sterling Delano, *Brook Farm: The Dark Side of Utopia* (Harvard University Press, 2004), is an able, up-to-date history of Transcendentalism's leading commune.

For further information about participants, trends, and events, two useful reference works are the *Biographical Dictionary of Transcendentalism* and the *Encyclopedia of Transcendentalism,* both edited by Wesley T. Mott (Westport, CT: Greenwood, both 1996). Joel Myerson, *The New England Transcendentalists and the* Dial: *A History of the Magazine and Its Contributors* (Rutherford, NJ: Fairleigh Dickinson University Press, 1980), also provides a wealth of biographical and historical facts and insights.

### 3. INDIVIDUAL AUTHORS: WRITINGS, BIOGRAPHY, CRITICISM

The works of a number of the leading Transcendentalists have been collected, and book-length memoirs or biographies (of varying quality) are available for almost all.

For RALPH WALDO EMERSON, a generously full collection, including the majority of his major books of essays and virtually all his poems, is *Ralph Waldo Emerson: Essays and Poems,* ed. Joel Porte (the prose) and Harold Bloom and Paul Kane (the poetry) (New York: Library of America, 1996). An exceptionally fine shorter collection, still in print after half a century, is Stephen E. Whicher, ed., *Selections from Ralph Waldo Emerson: An Organic Anthology* (Boston: Houghton-Mifflin, 1957), which includes many luminous passages from Emerson's Journal as well as essays and poems.

The twelve-volume *Complete Works of Ralph Waldo Emerson,* ed. Edward Waldo Emerson (Houghton-Mifflin, 1903–4), is the most comprehensive edition of Emerson's published writings to date, though it is in the process of being superseded by more scholarly, accurate editions, the most important of which is the Harvard University Press edition of his *Collected Works,* ed. Alfred R. Ferguson et al. (six volumes to date). *Emerson's Antislavery Writings* has been edited by Len Gougeon and Joel Myerson (Yale University Press, 1995).

Emerson's letters and journals are illuminating and at best highly readable. Two good one-volume editions are *Emerson in His Journals,* ed. Joel Porte (Harvard University Press, 1982), and *The Selected Letters of Ralph Waldo Emerson,* ed. Joel Myerson (New York: Columbia University Press, 1997). The correspondence between Emerson and Thomas Carlyle, originally published in the nineteenth century, is fascinating in its entirety. The first edition became a late-Victorian-era classic. An excellent modern edition is *The Correspondence of Emerson and Carlyle,* ed. Joseph Slater (Columbia University Press, 1964). For a truly comprehensive edition of Emerson's journals, see *Journals and Miscellaneous Notebooks,* sixteen vols., ed. William Gilman, Ralph Orth, et al. (Harvard University Press, 1960–82), and *The Topical Notebooks,* three vols., ed. Ralph H. Orth et al. (Columbia: University of Missouri Press, 1990–94). For Emerson's complete letters, see *The Letters of Ralph Waldo Emerson,* ten vols., ed. Ralph Leslie Rusk and Eleanor Tilton (Columbia University Press, 1939, 1990–95), as well as Slater's edition of the Emerson-Carlyle letters.

Emerson's *Complete Sermons* in four volumes, ed. Albert J. von Frank et al., have been published by the University of Missouri Press, 1989–92. The texts of his public lectures that survive in manuscript have been published in five volumes by two different presses: *The Early Lectures of Ralph Waldo Emerson* (1833–42) in three volumes, ed. Robert E. Spiller et al. (Harvard University Press, 1966–72); *The Later Lectures of Ralph Waldo Emerson* (1843–71) in two volumes, ed. Ronald Bosco and Joel Myerson (Athens: University of Georgia Press, 2001).

Several excellent Emerson biographies exist. The best single gateway to his life and thought is Robert D. Richardson, Jr., *Emerson: The Mind on Fire* (Berkeley: University of California Press, 1995). It is deeply learned yet eminently readable. The best detailed factual biography, albeit dated in a number of respects, is still Ralph Leslie Rusk, *The Life of Ralph Waldo Emerson* (New York: Scribner's, 1949). Albert J. von Frank, *An Emerson Chronology* (New York: G. K. Hall, 1994), is a valuable guide to Emerson's life record in detail. Stephen E. Whicher, *Freedom and Fate: An Inner Life of Ralph Waldo Emerson* (Philadelphia: University of Pennsylvania Press, 1953), provides a concise, probing, sententious interpretation of his mental trajectory. Despite its discounting of Emerson's later "pragmatic" phase, now rightly disputed by Robert Richardson and others, *Freedom* had greater influence on Emerson scholars of the last half of the twentieth century than any other single book. Phyllis Cole, *Mary Moody Emerson and the Origins of Transcendentalism: A Family History* (Oxford University Press, 1998), is an extensively researched, searching interpretation of the significance of the aunt-nephew relationship that takes in more than a century of New England cultural history.

Of the hundreds of critical books on Emerson's thought and writing, three accessible works of broad scope are Jonathan Bishop, *Emerson on the Soul* (Harvard University Press, 1964); Barbara Packer, *Emerson's Fall: A New Interpretation of the Major Essays* (New York: Continuum, 1982); and Lawrence Buell, *Emerson* (Harvard University Press, 2003). Milton Konvitz and Stephen E.

Whicher, eds., *Emerson: A Collection of Critical Essays* (Englewood Cliffs, NJ: Prentice-Hall, 1962), is an excellent collection of "classic" essays on Emerson.

For HENRY DAVID THOREAU, the most comprehensive, readily available one-volume selection of his longer work is still *Walden and Other Writings*, ed. Brooks Atkinson (New York: Modern Library, 1937). For his shorter work, see *Henry David Thoreau: Collected Essays and Poems*, ed. Elizabeth Hall Witherell (Library of America, 2001). For an excellent annotated edition of Thoreau's two best-known and most influential texts, see *Walden and Resistance to Civil Government*, second edition, ed. William Rossi (New York: Norton, 1992). *A Week on the Concord and Merrimack Rivers*, Thoreau's first and most Transcendental book, has been ably edited by H. Daniel Peck (New York: Penguin, 1998).

For many years the standard edition of Thoreau's "complete" works was *The Writings of Henry David Thoreau*, ed. Bradford Torrey and Francis Allen (Houghton-Mifflin, 1906), including six books and fourteen volumes of journals. This edition is now being superseded by Princeton University Press's scholarly edition, ed. Elizabeth Hall Witherell et al. (fourteen volumes to date). For now, the best edition of Thoreau's letters is still *The Correspondence of Henry David Thoreau*, ed. Walter Harding and Carl Bode (New York: New York University Press, 1958).

For Thoreau's life, as for Emerson's, the best place to start is the biography by Robert D. Richardson, Jr.; *Henry Thoreau: A Life of the Mind* (University of California Press, 1986). More compendiously factual is Walter Harding's *The Days of Henry David Thoreau* (New York: Knopf, 1965). For still greater detail, see Raymond R. Borst, *The Thoreau Log: A Documentary Life of Henry David Thoreau 1817–1862* (G. K. Hall, 1992).

For a comprehensive critical analysis of Thoreau's writing that moves discerningly through all the phases of his career, David Robinson's *Natural Life: Thoreau's Worldly Transcendentalism* (Cornell University Press, 2004) is one of the best and most recent. Robert Milder, *Reimagining Thoreau* (Cambridge University Press, 1995), more exclusively targeted to a scholarly audience, is also excellent. An older, somewhat diffuse and dated but still luminous study of the evolution of Thoreau's thought and writing is Sherman Paul, *The Shores of America: Thoreau's Inward Explorations* (Urbana: University of Illinois Press, 1958). Stanley Cavell, *The Senses of Walden*, revised edition (New York: Viking, 1972), is a wonderfully discerning philosophical essay on Thoreau's masterpiece, hard going at times but well worth the effort.

For MARGARET FULLER's writing, many one-volume collections exist. One of the best is *The Essential Margaret Fuller*, ed. Jeffrey Steele (New Brunswick, NJ: Rutgers University Press, 1992), which includes the two most ambitious books she published during her lifetime, *Summer on the Lakes* and *Woman in the Nineteenth Century.* Bell Gale Chevigny, ed., *The Woman and the Myth: Margaret Fuller's Life and Writings* (Old Westbury, NY: Feminist Press, 1976), provides a judicious arrangement of short selections of her work that follow the different phases of her life together with thoughtful interpretative commentary.

No comprehensive edition of Fuller's writing is in print or in the works. But *The Letters of Margaret Fuller* have been beautifully edited by Robert Hudspeth in six volumes (Cornell University Press, 1983–94), as have her journalistic letters from abroad, under the title *"These Sad But Glorious Days": Dispatches from Europe, 1846–1850,* ed. Larry J. Reynolds and Susan Belasco Smith (Yale University Press, 1991). The Norton Critical Edition series includes a fine annotated edition of Fuller's *Woman in the Nineteenth Century,* ed. Larry J. Reynolds (1998).

For Fuller's biography, the two-volume *Memoirs of Margaret Fuller Ossoli,* assembled by her friends William Henry Channing, James Freeman Clarke, and Ralph Waldo Emerson (Boston: Phillips, Sampson, 1852), is flawed but also fascinating and indispensable. Madeline B. Stern, *The Life of Margaret Fuller* (New York: Dutton, 1942), is so far the best modern narrative biography that takes in the whole sweep of her career. But see also Chevigny (above) and especially Charles Capper's two-volume in-progress scholarly biography, which will supersede Stern's as the authoritative source. Volume 1 has been published as *Margaret Fuller: An American Romantic Life: The Private Years* (Oxford University Press, 1992).

Fuller criticism is less extensive and more spotty than Emerson or Thoreau criticism. For a study of broad scope, Margaret Vanderhaar Allen, *The Achievement of Margaret Fuller* (University Park: Pennsylvania State University Press, 1979), is a place to start. The best Fuller criticism typically focuses on specific portions of her work rather than the whole sweep of her career. Jeffrey Steele's "Margaret Fuller's Rhetoric of Transformation" (written for the Norton Critical Edition of *Woman in the Nineteenth Century:* see above) is a thoughtful essay on a centrally significant pattern in Fuller's prose. Two scholarly monographs that range astutely through Fuller's thought and writing to place them in (different) nineteenth-century contexts are Christina Zwarg's Transcendentalism-focused *Feminist Conversations: Fuller, Emerson, and the Play of Reading* (Cornell University Press, 1995), and Julie Ellison's *Delicate Subjects: Romanticism, Gender, and the Ethics of Understanding* (Cornell University Press, 1990), a comparative study of Fuller in relation to a tradition of sympathetic reciprocity within international Romanticism exemplified previously by Samuel Taylor Coleridge and German theologian Friedrich Schleiermacher.

For BRONSON ALCOTT's writings, see especially the selected *Journals of Bronson Alcott,* ed. Odell Shepard (Boston: Little, Brown, 1938), and the selected *Letters of A. Bronson Alcott*, ed. Richard L. Herrnstadt (Ames: Iowa State University Press, 1969). Odell Shepard, *Pedlar's Progress: The Life of Bronson Alcott* (Little, Brown, 1937), is still the best biography. Charles Strickland, "A Transcendental Father: The Child Rearing Practices of Bronson Alcott," *Perspectives in American History,* 3 (1969): 5–73, gives a fascinating account of Alcott's implementation of his pedagogical theories within his family circle.

For a fuller sense of the range of LOUISA MAY ALCOTT's work, see *Alternative Alcott,* ed. Elaine Showalter (Rutgers University Press, 1988), and *Louisa May Alcott: Selected Fiction,* ed. Daniel Shealy, Madeline B. Stern, and Joel Myerson (University of Georgia Press, 1990). For biography, see Madeline B. Stern, *Louisa May Alcott,* revised edition (Northeastern University Press, 1999), and Martha Saxton, *Louisa May: A Modern Biography of Louisa May Alcott* (Houghton-Mifflin, 1977). As in the case of Margaret Fuller, the best Alcott criticism consists of essays and book chapters focused on particular aspects of her work and career. For a broad-based critical study, see Elizabeth Keyser, *Whispers in the Dark: The Fiction of Louisa May Alcott* (Knoxville: University of Tennessee Press, 1993).

For ORESTES BROWNSON, there is no modern successor to *The Works of Orestes Brownson,* edited by his son H. F. Brownson, twenty volumes (Detroit: Thorndike, Nourse, 1882–87). The best biographical study of Brownson's Transcendentalist years is still Arthur M. Schlesinger, Jr., *Orestes A. Brownson: A Pilgrim's Progress* (Little, Brown, 1939).

ELLERY CHANNING's sizable but very uneven poetic output has been gathered in *The Collected Poems of William Ellery Channing the Younger, 1817–1901,* ed. Walter Harding (Gainesville, FL: Scholars' Facsimiles & Reprints, 1967). Frederick T. McGill, Jr., *Channing of Concord: A Life of William Ellery Channing II* (Rutgers University Press, 1967), is the biography of first resort.

The scattered writings of WILLIAM HENRY CHANNING have never been collected. The one biography is O. B. Frothingham, *Memoir of William Henry Channing* (Houghton-Mifflin, 1886).

For CHRISTOPHER CRANCH, see the *Collected Poems of Christopher Pearse Cranch,* ed. Joseph M. De Falco (Scholars' Facsimiles & Reprints, 1967). Leonora Cranch Scott, *The Life and Letters of Christopher Pearse Cranch* (Houghton-Mifflin, 1917), is a Victorian-style memoir. A more scholarly though more selective treatment is F. DeWolfe Miller, *Christopher Pearse Cranch and His Caricatures of New England Transcendentalism* (Harvard University Press, 1951).

JOHN SULLIVAN DWIGHT's work has not been collected. The one biography is George Willis Cooke, *John Sullivan Dwight: Brook-Farmer, Editor, and Critic of Music* (Boston: Small, Maynard, 1898).

FREDERIC HENRY HEDGE's work has not been collected, either. The best biographical recourse is Bryan F. Le Beau, *Frederic Henry Hedge: Nineteenth-Century American Transcendentalist* (Allison Park, PA: Pickwick, 1985).

ELLEN STURGIS HOOPER has been virtually untouched by biographers and critics. Her one published volume of poems was privately printed by her son (probably in Boston, about 1872) long after her death.

THEODORE PARKER'S work has been collected in two turn-of-the-twentieth-century editions, the more compendious and accessible being the fifteen-volume *Centenary Edition of the Works of Theodore Parker* (Boston: American Unitarian Association, 1907–12). The best extant narrative biography covering Parker's entire life is Henry Steele Commager, *Theodore Parker* (Little, Brown, 1936). It is now being superseded by Dean Grodzins's two-volume scholarly biography. Volume 1 has been published as *American Heretic: Theodore Parker and Transcendentalism* (Chapel Hill: University of North Carolina Press, 2002).

A small but valuable fraction of ELIZABETH PEABODY's writing is collected in *The Letters of Elizabeth Palmer Peabody, American Renaissance Woman*, ed. Bruce A. Ronda (Middletown, CT: Wesleyan University Press, 1984). Two fine biographical accounts are Ronda's *Elizabeth Palmer Peabody: A Reformer on Her Own Terms* (Harvard University Press, 1999), and Megan Marshall's *The Peabody Sisters: Three Women Who Ignited American Transcendentalism* (Houghton-Mifflin, 2005).

GEORGE RIPLEY's writing has never been collected. A reliable biography is Charles Crowe, *George Ripley: Transcendentalist and Utopian Socialist* (University of Georgia Press, 1967).

For JONES VERY's poetry, a comprehensive scholarly edition is *Jones Very: The Complete Poems*, ed. Helen R. Deese (University of Georgia Press, 1993). Edwin Gittleman's *Jones Very: The Effective Years* (Columbia University Press, 1967), is the best book for biographical and critical insight into the work of Very's most productive period.

# Acknowledgments

To several generations of Transcendentalism scholars, starting with my teachers Stephen E. Whicher and Jonathan Bishop, I owe debts too numerous to count. For Joel Myerson's encouragement and counsel at various stages of this project, I am especially grateful. For crucial research assistance, my sincere thanks to Emma Beavers, Gretchen Hults, Jared Hickman, and Tony Domestico.

———

Selections from the letters of Mary Moody Emerson (Section I-1) are by permission of the Ralph Waldo Emerson Memorial Association. The original manuscripts, in Harvard University's Houghton Library, are bMS Am1280.226 (815, 817, 820, 828, 830, 836, 850, 853, 857, 864, 888, 898, 940).

The selection from Ralph Waldo Emerson's Sermon CLXII (Section I-5) (Houghton Library bMS Am 1280.215 [162A]) is also quoted by permission of the Ralph Waldo Emerson Memorial Association.

Lidian Emerson's "Transcendental Bible" (Section III-8) (Houghton Library bMS Am1280.220 [134]), published in *Studies in the American Renaissance 1980* (© Joel Myerson), is quoted by permission of the Ralph Waldo Emerson Memorial Association and of Joel Myerson.

The record of Margaret Fuller's conversation on gender (Section IV-C-1), from *Studies in the American Renaissance 1994* (© Joel Myerson), is quoted by permission of Joel Myerson.

Selections from R. W. Emerson's "Seventh of March Speech on the Fugitive Slave Law" (Section IV-E-4), from *Emerson's Antislavery Writings,* ed. Len Gougeon and Joel Myerson (© 1995 Yale University Press), based on

Houghton Library bMS Am 1280.201 (20), is quoted by permission of the Ralph Waldo Emerson Memorial Association and of Yale University Press.

The selection from Hawthorne's *The American Notebooks* (Section V-B-4), ed. Claude M. Simpson, appears by permission of its publisher, Ohio State University Press (© 1972 Ohio State University Press).

The selection from Henry David Thoreau's *Journal* (Section V-B-5), volume 2, ed. Robert Sattlemeyer (© 1984 Princeton University Press), is reprinted by permission of Princeton University Press.

The following poems of Jones Very (Section V-C-8), based on Houghton Library MS Am 1405, are quoted by permission of the Houghton Library, Harvard University: "The New Birth," "The Presence," "Nature," "The Barberry Bush," "The Garden," "Thy Brother's Blood," "Yourself," and "Thy Better Self."

## ABOUT THE EDITOR

LAWRENCE BUELL is one of the world's foremost authorities on the American Transcendentalist movement. His books include *Literary Transcendentalism* (1973), *New England Literary Culture* (1986), and *Emerson* (2003), all nominated for the Pulitzer Prize. *Emerson* won the 2004 Christian Gauss Award for excellence in literary criticism. For the last thirty-five years he has taught the work of Ralph Waldo Emerson, Henry David Thoreau, Margaret Fuller, and the other Transcendentalists, first at Oberlin College and then at Harvard, where he is Powell M. Cabot Professor of American Literature.

## A Note on the Type

The principal text of this Modern Library edition
was set in a digitized version of Janson, a typeface that
dates from about 1690 and was cut by Nicholas Kis,
a Hungarian working in Amsterdam. The original matrices have
survived and are held by the Stempel foundry in Germany.
Hermann Zapf redesigned some of the weights and sizes for
Stempel, basing his revisions on the original design.

# MODERN LIBRARY AT
## WWW.MODERNLIBRARY.COM

MODERN LIBRARY ONLINE IS YOUR GUIDE
TO CLASSIC LITERATURE ON THE WEB

## THE MODERN LIBRARY E-NEWSLETTER

Our free e-mail newsletter is sent to subscribers, and features sample
chapters, interviews with and essays by our authors, upcoming books,
special promotions, announcements, and news. To subscribe to the Modern
Library e-newsletter, visit **www.modernlibrary.com**

## THE MODERN LIBRARY WEBSITE

• The Mo

• A list of

• Reading

• Special

   other p

• Excerpts from new releases and other titles

• A list of our e-books and information on where to buy them

• The Modern Library Editorial Board's 100 Best Novels and

   100 Best Nonfiction Books of the Twentieth Century written in

   the English language

• News and announcements

Questions? E-mail us at **modernlibrary@randomhouse.com**.
For questions about examination or desk copies, please visit
the Random House Academic Resources site at
**www.randomhouse.com/academic**